A DECENT MAN

Thoma ally, Booker prize-winning author of Schindler's List:
'Wri h directness and pace, promises fulfilling reading'

Majo l Bryan Colley CB CBE:
ading command of language an exciting and
l story of suffering and bravery in World War II'

Sir C er Leaver GBE, Past Lord Mayor of London:
'I'v waiting for this first novel. I was not disappointed'

Chec
to ren
www.b
www.bi

Bir

A DECENT MAN

From gulag to gold – a wartime odyssey

Clive Birch

Medavia

First published in 2006
by Boltneck Publications

ISBN 0 9546399 6 0
ISBN 97809546399 6 9

Published by Medavia Publishing in 2006
ISBN 0 9546399 2 8
ISBN 97809546399 2 1

Typeset in $9\frac{1}{2}$ on $10\frac{1}{2}$ Palatino and Arial
by Academic & Technical Typesetting, Bristol
and printed in England by
Bath Press

A CIP catalogue of this book is available from the British Library

A DECENT MAN is a work of fiction,
based on, and inspired by, true events

Books by Clive Birch include

NON-FICTION

Carr and Carman – London's transport
The Freedom – the City of London (with V.Hope etc)
The Book of Chesham
Royal College of Art 2006 vehicle design (ed)

Cover design by Mark Ralph of ATT and Clive Birch
from photographs by the author – sunset and Dakota – and in 1910 by
Sergei Mikhailovich Prokudin-Gorskii: Simskaia Station on the
Samara-Zlatoust Railway, Russia

CONTENTS

1 Cjortkow	5 Tara	2 Moskva	8 Kermene
2 Moskva	4 Omsk	3 Kujbysev	9 Tehran
3 Kujbysev	3 Kujbysev	6 Tashkent	10 Khanaqir
4 Omsk	2 Moskva	7 Samarkand	11 Rechovor
5 Tara		8 Kermener	12 Capmati

12 Capmatifu   17 Vimoutiers   18 Bitola   19 Liverpool   24 Cracow
13 Sicily   20 Naples
14 Glasgow   21 Ostuni
15 Ashford   22 Rome
16 Audley End   23 Cotto

For Lisa, Paul and Alicia

There shall be
In that rich earth a richer dust concealed

Rupert Brooke, *The Soldier*

For nought did I in hate, but all in honour.
Speak of me as I am; nothing extenuate

Shakespeare, *Othello*

PROLOGUE – *At a Stroke*

In the silence of the skull there is no peace. I suppose that, after seven decades, there are miracles, but not to be able to speak of them – that is a silence of anguish, of the unredeemed. I sit here smiling; I know, yet I cannot say. She is over there, her softly roseate skin aglow with a young mother's caring, her sounds also silenced – for me.

The 'phone rings. You see, I can hear, I can mouth the simple words. 'Hello?' 'Fine, thanks you.' 'Good, would be good. Yes, come. Ol' frien'.' 'Thanks, yes, somester repstun comat slurpstin...' You see, I can speak a little, but the strokes have limited me, sent me back to prison, back to the gulag, back to the forest, the hemming trees, the damp huts of my seething discontent. I can say 'Hello' and I can shit and pee and fuck, and there's the baby to prove that.

Mind you, the wedding was a miracle, if not a bloody farce. They asked me if I would, and I said 'Yes', but when they asked me to repeat 'I, Eduard Cjaikowski', I was buggered if I could get more out than 'I, Svesjaw Sharlstri...' but Peter promised them it was Polish and the stolid, sensible registrar biddy believed him – or was that just being kind?

And she was, is, so incredibly young, and she has silenced her talent, her searing, soaring, piercing, sweetling notes for me, her old, ancient, second cousin how ever many times removed. And I have certainly been removed, you could say, including being removed from some exceedingly strange places. Why her, when I have always had the pick, any woman, any place, any time – a blessing, or perhaps not. More like, why me?

Ah well, here in the closed-in head, I can wonder about that as long as I last, as long as the pills keep me going, as long as I don't get another of these bloody strokes. And when I do, she can go back to Polska, back to the orchestra, back to her music, to her first love, while little Anna will always remind her of me, of her second love, of the old goat who was tamed, first by a plump, ordinary, extraordinarily sweet, tumbling, fumbling relative, echo from the past, from Grandpa Luke, and little Bruno, and father Jozef, gracious Rosalia, my small mother, and then by the great catching up in one second of massive leaching away of energy, of will, of word and deed and sense of place, of strength, of strong right arm, of moving leg, of arching back in orgasm of nothingness – a stroke. God help us.

So I sit and watch my Anna and my latecome wondrous life-suspended wifelet, and have nothing else to do but smile, and say 'hello' or 'yes' or 'thank you' or try to 'love you' and wait for night-time when I can be my small, hard self again, and tup her triple lips, and live a little bit of light-time, and remember. Because only I know what happened, where the gold went and the first time I met Kolanski.

1

No-one could hear me, and if they could, they wouldn't believe me, so I'll pretend I'm making it up, and describe it as if I am not really me, as if Eduard Cjaikowski is another man, from another time, a boy even, in 1939. In Poland. In Cjortkow. By the river Seret, in the long grass... before the gulag, Fort Kermener, and before Normandy and Greece, and long before the gold, and Whitehall, Anthony Eden, and dinner for four. Eden, our Polish Prime Minister in exile, the Holy Catholic Father, Primate of all Poland – and me. And that was after we had fought, and killed, and nearly died...

WAR I: 1939–1941

ENEMIES OF THE STATE

Eduard swung through the ragged grass that grew to the river's edge as he pushed on, south of the town, away from home, imagining the deeds of valour that a fourteen-year-old may dream, late on an autumn afternoon.

Unaccountably, he paused and glanced back at the farmhouse, standing half a mile from any other, within its own orchard – what was left of grandpa Luke's farm. The old man didn't know it, but he was a lucky old man; he died that month an octogenarian, with his memories of old Vienna intact, the birth of holocaust beyond his time – others' memories to come.

The farm was a century old, two-storeyed, with stables, a half-timbered structure with hard grey stone, limestone from the mountain quarries. It stood, with its barns and buildings, in six acres of orchard – apples, pears and plums, ripe for the vats and the pressing.

As the late sun glanced off the zinc-squared roof, Eduard squinted at the old house, conjuring up the depths of the cellars with last year's harvest in the great vats, ready to be thieved each year by one young Cjaikowski or another, teenage-tempted, more mature than the wine in its youth, a little too wise, a touch too clever, especially with a game gun under his arm. Eduard laughed, turned away and started running along the track as he had run so many times that year, away from home, from authority.

He made for the quarries, towards the mountain screes, where the oakwoods grew and *kuwaptwa* flew, the Polish grouse shot on the wing and stewed in the wine. Once he had stolen away one night, eased into the stables behind the house, softly treading on the tongued and grooved floor, to slip out with the fastest, fleetest, fairytale horse, a lad's knight's charger, the best of the Arabs his mother had once raised and raced.

That was in 1934, when the Reich was a world away and life was growing, going well, and getting licked for it – if you were caught, which wasn't often – like that time the horse threw him in the river and he walked home so wet Rosalia pretended he had slipped in the pond helping her. An exceptional day.

Usually nothing much happened at the aptly named 2 Border Street in the suburbs of Cjortkow, 40,000 people living 32 miles inside Poland on the eastern flank, 3,000 feet of snow-brushed mountains ten miles distant, shedding rocks down their rolling screes towards the river Seret.

The older river wound through the old town, with its suspension bridge, cathedralous church, gaunt castle and military barracks, and

3

the railway station and goods yard complex lay behind. Zeromski School was past the bridge, where children took their entry exams to college, there to learn German, Russian and – the language of the old emperors – Latin. Eduard learnt fast and left first on autumn afternoons, to head for the moorland heather below the white rocks.

The house itself stood to one side of the old Crusader town, a town which had withstood the might of Ghengis Kahn, repulsed by the even mightier Polish warrior, Charteriski. Shoes and engineering slippered and strutted the local economy but it was the rail junction that put gold in the bank – north, south and west lay Russia, Rumania and Hungary.

The house gathered round the long room with the oak table and 20 chairs – the core of the Cjaikowskis. Everything happened around this table, or was discussed at it, dissected, picked over, gathered up, cleared up, closed down. Here in this great room, with its ceramic stove in the deep fireplace, and the wooden shutters which came off in the summer, children drank milk, adults took wine, and the business of life focussed on lunchtime; everyday life every day; matters of family fortune and national concern on special days, when the serviettes came out, to keep a clean mouth and clear thoughts.

As he glanced back at the house, Eduard paused, troubled by something he could not quite pin down. Perhaps it was the sun slanting across the roof, or the flash of light off a trotting horse's mane or the glint from a tram in the distant town.

Perhaps it was that sense of the past because, if you are Polish, you are born with a certain national consciousness, a sense of history and, some would say, of impending doom. Poland, forever partitioned and stitched up together again against the next time, gives to her heirs a permanent nostalgia, ready for that next time, and the inevitable days of renewed loss. Eduard felt a passing sadness, without recognition.

His slight figure dwindled into the distance alongside the plastic waters of the sombre Seret, in that softly lit, almost Mediterranean valley, with its walnuts and its vines, on that golden autumn afternoon in 1939.

Jozef locked his Stationmaster's office and walked slowly to the tram stop. He unfolded the newspaper again. It was just as he had feared, so many weeks ago, the day Eduard had stripped his favourite watch, jamming it back together again, with no regard to its proper function. He had leathered the boy, perhaps unfairly, because of his fear and sense of doom.

Hitler was threatening the western borders. Perhaps France and England would stand by their word and declare war. But would they act? Jozef had been Chief of Police in Cracow in 1919, and had seen rather more of official papers than he was perhaps permitted. He had developed a distrust of any piece of paper that committed men to actions they could not fulfil. They would see, they would see. Perhaps the French would march. They were the old friends, the ones who lent inspiration and ideas to Poland. Now perhaps *la belle France* would set forth against the enemies of her friends.

Meanwhile, what of Bruno? Eighteen and stationed at Tarnopol. Ah, little Bruno, the second son. Rosalia was always accusing him of indulging Bruno – something he never extended to Frank, six years older, or the rascally Eduard. Bruno, lithe and upright, always a little gay, a flier, a pilot, an officer in the Air Force. Thank God he was here in the east. For in the east was Russia, the great ally.

Jozef reached home late after stopping off for a quick slivovitz with Frank, tired after a gruelling day in the great goods yard north of the town. They met often, after work, at a small café near the tram terminal. Nothing was said of war. They talked instead of Frank's job as chief maintenance engineer and Jozef secretly thanked God once more for giving him the foresight to put Frank in an essential occupation.

As he stamped through the door, brushed back his steel-grey hair, grunted at his wife and nodded to housekeeper Maria, there was little doubt in his mind that a week or more would see Russia, the ancient sworn enemy of the Hun, force a pause on Hitler. Then perhaps France and possibly England would steal up on the Nazi, on his western flank, and Poland would be relieved. But the radio that night told a different tale.

There was nothing but condemnation from Moskva. No action, then or foreseeable. France and England had done nothing. And when Eduard came home long after dark, he found his father too tired and too anxious to notice him, so he slipped the gun upstairs and himself into bed.

In August the Russians signed a pact with Nazi Germany. On September the first the Reich invaded. On September the third England declared war. And the Russians invaded in the east fourteen days later.

The garrison town of Cjortkow was taken without a struggle. The only blood spilt was that of a single guard who thought, quite rightly, that the Ukrainian militiaman had no business in the castle, armed and in broad daylight. The Ukrainian shot and then mutilated him.

The next day Jozef never reached home. The militia stopped him as he left his office; he was taken to the central prison, where he found himself in good company. All senior-ranking civil servants were under arrest. Jozef was 52.

Within days Bruno was also arrested, while on duty at Tarnopol, and accused of subversion against the Soviet Union. He was imprisoned against trial. Eduard and Rosalia were sent for and, in November, heard him accused, tried, found guilty, and sentenced to death – in ten minutes. His crime was to fight against the invader; the

Russians had offered surrender terms, which Poland refused. Those who fought were 'traitors'.

On the evening of his trial Rosalia was forced to watch him die. He was executed by firing squad. The Russian officer in charge echoed Beria's casual comment: 'What's the difference, one Pole?' Eduard felt the difference. One day he would speak of his family's destruction – 'I was annihilated by circumstance.'

Not long afterwards, in February 1940, Jozef died. His police past kept him in prison; he was tortured for seven days, sent home, and contracted pneumonia. From that moment, Eduard knew hatred – 'I am not important; I am not important, not any more.'

That hatred was to keep him alive. Hatred for Russians, for Jews, for Ukrainians, and for Germans, for all those he held responsible for his family's fate. Poland now faced the first stirrings of its unfolding holocaust.

The first police force after occupation wore suits and red armbands, taking over from the Russians. The new militia was part Jewish, mainly Ukrainian. Many Jews were inclined to the Left. When Hitler evicted them in 1936, Poland took them in. That was their destiny for, when the Germans took Poland, they caught up with them, using Poles to find their Jews, and then send them in their turn to their destruction.

One week after Jozef's death, a few minutes past midnight, the uneasy quiet of 2 Border Street was shattered. The door shook under the repeated hammerings of rifle butts. Maria reached the door first, Rosalia hastily gathering a robe round herself at the head of the stairs. Eduard opened his bedroom door, standing in his pyjamas.

Over the threshold tramped two Russian soldiers, a Ukrainian militiaman and a 'suit', a civilian, a collaborator. When he spoke, there was something 'Russian' about his voice.

The family reluctantly stepped into the hall.

The civilian produced a sheet of paper and read: 'Eduard Cjaikowski, the Soviet Government on the command of Kamerad Stalin sentences you to twenty years' hard labour in a Siberian labour unit.'

The fourteen-year-old looked confused. The man repeated the sentence.

'Why? What have I done?' asked Eduard.

'You have endangered the people's state. Just as your father did. You were both subversive elements within the state.'

The man in the suit paused, then thrust the paper forward.

'Sign this.'

Eduard stepped back and lied.

'I cannot read Russian. What does it say?'

The civilian appeared bewildered, then irritable, and repeated his demand. Eduard refused. An argument erupted. Rosalia and Maria kept quiet. The militiaman waved his rifle about and threatened to beat him up, to shoot him. The soldiers leant against the wall, disinterested. 'What's the difference, one Pole?' Finally one turned to the 'suit' and said, 'You sign it for him.'

He looked quickly at Eduard, reached inside his coat, found a pen, and scribbled a scarcely legible line across the page. As he turned, it slipped, and fluttered to the floor. Eduard bent to collect it, was shoved aside by a rifle, and barely had time to read a word. Yet, as the 'suit' retrieved the paper, he saw what had been so hastily scrawled – one name: Kolanski.

Kolanski turned to Rosalia.

'Rosalia Cjaikowska, the Soviet Government, on the command...'

Eduard could hardly hear the words as he clattered through the same formula. '...twenty years' hard labour.'

'No!' he shouted and reached out for his mother's hand.

Then it was Maria's turn. In vain did mother and son explain that she was not Maria Cjaikowska but merely a servant. Maria solved the crisis by fainting. The militiaman tried to drag her upright, but she was too heavy, so he left her. Unconscious on the cold flagstones.

'You have fifteen minutes, all of you.'

In his room, Eduard looked at the gun, his trophies, the little crucifix he had hardly bothered with for years now, even though the family was Catholic and devout. He dressed in his toughest clothes, with extra socks, heavy boots, and hesitated over the gun, but what was the point? It would be discovered, and he would only get shot.

He ran downstairs, made a bundle of food and found a bottle of pear spirit, then knocked on his mother's door. She was sitting on her bed, until so recently shared, weeping without a tear to show for her sorrow. Briefly Eduard sat with her, and offered her the food. She shook her head. The door slammed open. Kolanski.

'Goodbye mother.'

Eduard paused on the stairs. Maria had gone. He never saw her again. His mother's silhouette was still visible through her bedroom door as the militiaman started up the stairs. She turned, with a desperate smile of encouragement – the last he was to see of her, perhaps forever.

Outside, a lorry waited, its engine idly rumbling, the two Russian soldiers leaning against the cab, smoking. As he walked towards them, he heard the 'suit' say, 'Get rid of him – and don't waste too much time either.'

The truck thundered through Cjortkow to the station – his father's station. Eduard and its other occupants were hauled and shoved outside into the empty yard. The Russians watched them lurch out, then one beckoned to Eduard.

He pushed him away from the truck, prodding him with his rifle, until they were out of sight, alone. Then he raised the gun, pressed the muzzle against Eduard's chest. He smiled and Eduard tried to swallow, but could not, his mouth dry, his heart stilled, his hands rigid, cold; he closed his eyes, waited. The hard metal snout stirred, then stilled, pressed against him.

The Russian laughed, bent over him: 'Behave yourself, and you might survive.' He laughed again and added, 'But you don't know what I'm saying do you? Because you don't understand Russian.' And he poked his rifle into Eduard's chest even harder, and pushed him down the path and into the station and then, abruptly, turned, and was gone.

In the station, the Ukrainians were everywhere, all dressed in the familiar grey-green uniform. Many of them were from nearby villages, and Eduard even recognised one. They were the spearhead of the Russian advance, and of the occupation.

At first Eduard had not believed the tales he was told. How the militia drove the priests from the cathedral, into the fields to the north, and had then taken them singly, or in pairs, into the woods, to slaughter them by bullet or by bayonet. Some had even been clubbed to death, or so it was said.

The older monks, unable to walk that far, were simply shot on the spot, in church. The same went for all the clerics in all the town's churches.

The Ukrainians were settling old scores, within 24 hours of reaching the rich hinterland around Cjortkow. Eduard found it was true as he spoke to first one, then another old farmer, for some tilled land near 2 Border Street, and he knew them well.

They told him that, after the 1918 war, many western Polish soldiers of farming stock had found themselves landless. Under government act, they had been granted land in the east, within the 'new' borders, mere smallholdings, with a modest grant. These 'colonists' were murdered on that first day of occupation, their wives ravished and mutilated, their children killed. The Ukrainians took over their homes and their holdings.

Obstinate colonists were cut to pieces. During the occupation of eastern Poland, the Russians deported countless Poles, some said 2.5 million, that the Ukrainians murdered almost as many. Then the Germans destroyed three million Polish Jews – later.

His lorry had gone. Eduard was herded along with a small, but increasing crowd of men from a convoy of lorries piling up alongside the station. Inside, the trains were waiting, with their curious dual gauge bogies, designed to take the change to Russian tracks. Eduard's train was like all the others – an unending line of cattle trucks, closed, windowless, unfurnished save for some shelving at one end. The sliding door was hauled open, the human contents spilling and bulging out until roughly pushed back inside, and Eduard was forced in, to join sixty or seventy others. And there they waited for two long hours.

Just as dawn was breaking, the train shuddered and started to pull out of Cjortkow. His journey had begun. The journey to Tara.

I can say this without a word of a lie – and that's not bad for a naturalised Anglo-Saxon who never quite got the hang of the language, though I can speak several, or should I say think several now I can't say any. Oh yes, I did have some Russian that day they took us all away. And I knew German. And later I found it expedient to learn a little Eyetie, for the *dolce vita*, as it were. And the French? No problem at all.

Especially the girls. I remember one... well, perhaps another time... and I can say this – I was certainly no soldier the day we went to Tara, and I was damned sure I was going one way only. I had heard about the gulag. You got there, but you didn't go anywhere else, you didn't get 'out' in the old sense of 'out'. Once I was on that truck, I could think of nothing else but getting out. First of all, the floorboards – we could rip them up and drop out. Unfortunately there were too many bodies between me and the floor, except where I was standing, leaning, because we were all leaning on one another; in fact, had the side dropped off, we would all have dropped off.

THREE DAYS TO MOSKVA

The wagon was full. Eduard contracted inside his overcoat, tried to make himself small, insignificant, unnoticeable. Of average height for his age, he could see little beyond the bodies pressed against his. He could hear everything – the exhalations, sighs, muttered imprecations, occasional choked-back cries, uneasy stomachs and unrepressed backsides; it was more comfortable to close his ears and his eyes, and to consider himself – and his companions.

Companions. Comrades? Not really, not when you're fourteen and everyone else is a hundred and ten, or smelt like it – his companions were varied in age, temperament and background.

There was the Colonel, who tried to keep some semblance of system in the standing-room only which they called home, for four days' virtually non-stop travel. There was a pickpocket who had lost a hand in the fighting and constantly whined about his lack of a living, until the Colonel pointed out that he would be fortunate to live, let alone earn one.

Before they started, there was a collective sigh further down the truck – heads turned, like dominoes, one after another. There were the women. Eduard had wondered why there were none with his truckload. Straining to look downline, he could just discern a melting, shifting grey mass; the sigh must have been the susurration of their coats and skirts and dresses as they adjusted to the commands of the guards.

They heard the staccato shouts, the irritability rasping on the air, and the occasional involuntary groan. Was Mamita there? Was she among that ceaseless throng, crushed, pushed, hushed and curdled with the fear of the weak, meek and vulnerable? He prayed inside his head for her safety.

Inside their wagon they were like women themselves, cowed and cowards – flinching every time the guards stamped past, turning away if they glanced up at them, diminishing themselves physically as well as mentally, wishing themselves into smaller spaces, contracting muscles, shortening and shallowing their breathing, willing their hearts to be silent.

Gradually, Eduard eased and slithered and crept and shuffled towards the far corner, beside the Colonel, away from the cold doorway, no longer the entrance, but the eventual exit to a black, bleak, bled-dry future.

They waited. There was little movement. Earlier attempts to keep warm by stamping feet, clip-clapping arms this way and that, hugging and rubbing one's body, slowed and sluggishly stopped. The only way to combat the seeping, creeping cold was to stand absolutely still and detach mind and effort from each finger, hand, arm, foot, leg, ear and eyelid, until the cold was something outside self, on the surface of their tenuous existence, a separate matter to be considered, if at all, at arm's length. It was better to think of others.

Those close by were too immediate for study; the eye and the mind moved to those one or two removed. It was not difficult, for most had their eyes closed, empty, or wrapt inwardly, downcast, dropped into the lowest curve of their bones.

Before, people had been uncles, cousins, classmates, friends, brothers, father, mother; trader, horseman, cleaner, butcher, cooper, fisherman, farmer, furrier, farrier. They were known for what or who they were. Eduard could not remember the colour of his mother's eyes. Here they would have to be given names and, because words were scarce, and by age or stature or innocence denied him, those names would have to come from their appearance.

There was therefore Small Beard. In truth his beard covered most of his face, and it was the face, or the head, that was small, so the beard seemed so; the eyes were closed, the head cropped, the ears close-set with elfin peaks and lobeless; the mouth hidden behind the small mat of hair. Contracted, like so many, he stooped; nearer Eduard's height than the Colonel's, he was a small man. His hands were drawn inside his pockets, and no more could be seen of him, so close were they stacked.

As Eduard was moving past him in his stationary identification parade, he suddenly looked up, opened his eyes, and stared straight at the young Pole. They were an opaque grey, the lashes thick and tangled, and his beard seemed immediately more imperial, darker, defined, as his mind reached momentarily for Eduard's. Big Beard then.

Next to him there loomed an attenuated lean fellow, with a sharp chin and a high, gleaming forehead: the Brain. His hair was white, tinged with a tinselly gold, and fell past his collar. His eyes spoke all the time – to himself – as they probed, picked and pattered everywhere he could not step.

Eduard imagined that mind collecting scraps of the past from every scan as it seamed the minerality of its' fellows' fears and forgetting. His lips spoke as in silent films; their captions might have told of betrayals and temptations, of all the tumbling todays that had slipped into the past tense for all of them. Bird Brain.

Eduard turned to look at the man next to the Colonel.

Startled, he turned away. He was regarding Eduard steadily, with malice – a clearly telegraphed desire to have none of him lighting his eyes; his mouth a down-turned snub, one hand stroking a ruddy earlobe, the other clasped round his neck. He wore an emerald tie, loosely knotted, which lay just below his hand. Green Man. No, Enemy.

Beyond him there was a curiously turned and half-hunched figure, with a white face in sloping profile, dirty sideburns straggling down to

11

pockets of white hair in the hollows of the cheeks. Hedgehog. His nose snouted and truffled the air, his fingers scratched his lapel. The hair on his head stood, wired for sound. His ears seemed to seek long signals.

There was a lurch, then a clatter. The truck had moved, jerked against the couplings, and Enemy's knife dropped out of his hand. 'I'll take that,' said the Colonel as Enemy bent down. Hedgehog retrieved the long, slanting blade, and handed it, haft first, to the Colonel, who slid it inside his voluminous greatcoat. He glanced at Eduard and, without moving mouth or muscles, he smiled – with his clear-cutting eyes. When he was not the Colonel, he was Friend.

There was another lurch, a grating, scraping, girding, grinding, snapping and straining and the train started to move. Suddenly, guards' faces appeared alongside, hands on hasps as they rammed the doors closed, and snapped the locks shut. They were on their way.

How many were they? He could not tell, or perhaps he did not want to, perhaps... what's the difference? They were too many. The weak slid to the floor, passed in and out of life until they finally stayed away in that escapologist's nightmare, the place of no return, the dream world of the defeated.

The strong stood, leant tensely against one another, hands sometimes crossed, shoulders aching, backs rigid. Sometimes someone would jerk with muscle spasms, urge the body upright, shift against the next one, whose face betrayed irritation in those first few hours, then passivity, then nothing.

Individuals became ciphers, intertwined, and the cold seeped beneath the skin, through the flesh, into the bones, until the very structure of body dissolved, and then a neighbour's involuntary movement nudged nerves in dull recognition of place and time and person. The strongest stood on the weak, to breathe less breath, to see what there was to see, a swamp of heads, some matted, some brisk, some with the dim patina of dried-out skulls, bald.

Minds slept. Eyes closed. Ears shut. Hands still, save when an intolerable itch jangled the nerves, dragged a loose hand up through the mass of pressed men to reach the taut, dry skin. Most were clearly unprepared for the journey.

Eduard was lucky. He had his coat. He held his warmth a little longer, beneath the skin. The Colonel had his coat too – a great trench coat – but his body denied its warmth, for he was old, where the boy was young. He had fought his war; Eduard's was yet to come.

By now everyone stank, which was hardly surprising, since death was among them. They stopped briefly each day for water, and to pour out the pee from the communal buckets – and the rest of their outpourings. They had so far been given little food, and most of that had initially gone to the toughest.

Eduard shared his bread with the Colonel and he kept the others off his protégé. When they stopped, they gave them fish, two buckets of it

– *chotka*, small fish like whitebait or sprats, pickled, salty and gone in a flash. Then they were thirsty. And they had thrown out the pee. What foresight.

People started having bad dreams, hallucinating. There would have been fights, but there was not the room. Then the Colonel died. Eduard tried to hold him up, but he slid from his grasp. It was hard holding anything, because of the cold.

When they stopped again, Eduard banged on the door. Someone said that that was not a good idea. They would shoot them. The door slid open. The half-light turned searing white, and they cried out with the pain of seeing. The guards were Russians.

'You make a noise and we shoot you. Any disturbance from now on and we shoot, no warning. OK?'

Well, hardly anyone knew what they were saying, but they all understood. A rifle is persuasive when it's waving about in front of a lot of uninteresting people – especially when the person holding it is the one who is uninterested.

'We've got a dead man here.'

'So what?'

'Well, take him away. He's dead.'

'No.'

'Why not?'

Eduard couldn't believe he was doing all the talking. The others shrank back, insofar as anyone could shrink anywhere or any more.

'Why not?'

'Can't.'

'Why?'

This was becoming ridiculous. One scared teenager arguing the toss with two armed bastards with not the slightest interest in the human refuse which had them travelling on a filthy, cold and seemingly endless train to nowhere. Ridiculous. Nonetheless...

'Why?'

'The numbers.'

'What numbers?'

'It wouldn't correspond with the numbers.'

'Eh?'

'The numbers' – they must have thought he was exceptionally stupid – 'we must have the same numbers at the end which we had at the beginning.'

'Even if they're dead numbers?'

'Even if they're dead,' and they suddenly realised he was talking their language.

Eduard looked at these two unspeakable morons. They looked at him. And they all simultaneously realised the futility of further discussion. They slid the door shut, and as they did so shouted, 'You'll have to keep him.'

So they put the Colonel in a corner, somehow, and they kept him – and themselves – sane by turning away from him. Because within a few hours he began to smell; that is, they noticed his smell more than all their own other smells, even the shit and the pee. It was unbearable, but when you are on a train to Tara, you bear the unbearable, because you have no choice, nowhere else to go.

There were some intelligent people in that truck – scholars. As they crossed the border into Russia near Lvov, someone said, 'Now I'm a prisoner, a slave,' and another asked, 'What's going to happen next? What's going to happen to us?' The rhetoric was fairly obvious until someone else quietly answered, 'Providence – wait and see.'

The endless, clattering train took three days to reach the outskirts of Moskva, leaving Kjiev the first day, and lurching interminably north-east towards Zelebogorsk and Tula. Outside Moskva, the train lay silent, until the guards rasped the doors back, and dumped two bucketloads of *chotka* on the boards.

Dazed by the daylight, fearful of the guards, those nearest the door remained still until the twilight of the closed truck returned, then scrabbled on the floor, scooping up the salty, dried-out, flaking pieces, passing them onto the next one, for to exhibit greed would be to invite conflict. By now the surviving occupants of the truck had realised that their continuing survival depended upon co-operation and a certain grudging consideration. Any expectation of privilege had been legislated away by the equality of despair.

Eduard slid to the floor, chewing his *chotka* ration, and closed his eyes, the better to savour the sensation of eating. He imagined the *chotka* was one of Mamita's succulent salmon, afterwards drifting into half-sleep. The door grated open again. This time the guards brought water.

THE ORIENT EXPRESS

The first time they tried it, they failed. For some time, five of the academics had huddled together, murmuring among themselves. No-one else showed any interest. After all, these were the scholars, the slick, quick-thinking, pontificating, well-read purveyors of scientific logic, philosophical verities and long knowledge. They could contribute little to the business of survival.

Better to let them get on with it, probably consoling themselves with their superior intellects – which had not saved them from this journey and its manifold discomforts, fears and deprivations.

As the train lumbered on its endless haul, nothing mattered beyond the daily ration of *chotka,* the water hour, and the business of combating the cold. Once they had left Moskva, the guards allowed them to move out in small groups of perhaps five or six, for supervised relief – the accumulated excrement of the first three days shovelled to one side, with the bodies, for now two more had died.

Near Penza, the train clanked to a halt, and once more the guards pulled back the door, and beckoned the nearest five. The three academics hung back. The sun was low in the folds of land to the west, and the shadows thrown by the trucks were deep and undifferentiated. After twenty minutes or so, the guards were leaning against the truck, occasionally shoving a slow prisoner into line, to stumble down the slight embankment as they laughed, smoking and joking about the 'stupid Polskas'.

One of the teachers fell out of the truck, and a guard leant down and manhandled him down the slope. Another academic slipped off the truck edge, and rolled underneath, as a third fell against the second guard, and the third guard bent to help his comrade, just as a fourth and fifth academic slid down, under and froze.

The guards cursed, shouted at the prisoners to hurry back, and told the rest to get out now, or they would have to wait until the next stop, tomorrow morning. Within ten minutes, everyone who had the strength and inclination had stepped down to the open drain below the embankment, and back again. The guards slammed the door shut, the clanging slap of door to jamb echoing down the train, as each contingent cloistered its charges for the next stage of the endless odyssey.

The train lurched and spat, and hissed and stuttered, and ground its irons to the brittle track, and the two remaining academics huddled in a corner, silent but complacent – they had outwitted the morons.

Then, above the clatter and clang of the wheels, the forward churning of the engine and the creaking, grinding, scraping timbers of the truck, they heard it. A single shot, then another, then two more. Then silence. Eduard tensed.

Surely the train would stop, the guards would tear them all out, line them up, interrogate them, and then make an example. Nothing. One mile, two, ten, twenty. Nothing.

Enemy smiled at him.

'The train, it's guarded too – at the back. They are dead. Serve them right.' Eduard shook his head.

'Surely they will come to check the truck, to punish?'

'Certainly not.' They had no means of knowing who they were, which truck they were from, unless they counted everyone in every truck, 'and that they will not do until we reach our destination, if then.'

'But they left the dead to keep the numbers straight.'

Enemy shrugged.

'Perhaps they did, perhaps that was a joke, perhaps it was just to avoid the labour of handling the bodies.'

So now the academics were dead too.

'Three less to share the *chotka*.'

Again Eduard shook his head, unconvinced, and started to contemplate escape. Perhaps there was another way, alone, without trusting anyone else, reducing the danger. He was smaller, slimmer, quicker, quieter. He started to consider the options.

Days followed nights followed days; *chotka*, water, relief – and death. In the second week, yet two more died. Death came silently, sidling up to the old, the weak, the defeated, without announcement – no sudden pain, no alarm, no irrational nightmare. Just oblivion. When those nearest noticed, and they often did not notice for some time, sometimes hours, if it was night-time and they were fitfully asleep, they simply sighed, caught sufficient eyes, then cranked themselves down to half-lift, half-drag, half-slide the body to the end of the truck.

Eduard was ignored, not because he was the youngest, or the late Colonel's protégé, but because everyone was more or less ignored. There were no easy friendships on this Orient express, just occasional alliances over food or water, brief lapses into abbreviated talk, about their destination, the time, the distance, the time to the next stop, the next food, the next water hour.

Eduard was tacitly allowed his share of food and drink and relief, without rancour, perhaps because it was clear he posed no threat, and perhaps because his very youth reminded most of their families, their own youth, their fading hopes and dreams and desires.

Enemy was the exception. He took an interest. He rarely spoke; he kept to his station hard by the door, to be the first out, the first fed, the first watered. Eduard knew he had the knife, because he had seen the man slip it into a back pocket, when they moved the Colonel to his corner of the cattle car. Eduard also knew that Enemy was watching, waiting, but for what, he had no conception.

Escape. It was now clear the train was moving north-east, towards the *tayga,* the wet, sub-arctic forest beyond Omsk. This was clear because Eduard overheard two guards talking about 'home' in Omsk, and their relief that 'the Polska scum' would be off their hands once they arrived. They were destined for 'camp' further north.

That must mean the feared labour camps of the Soviet system, random terror tales of which had filtered south, even into Poland. Timber was a staple Russian product, cheap and plentiful – plentiful because of the extensive forests of the southern steppes, cheap because it was culled and cut and carried by the infinitely available enemies of the state, hitherto largely from within, but now, fortuitously from without.

Escape was essential, if he was to avoid the camps. Escape was becoming a life motif in his mind. It is not easy to reconcile oneself to captivity after the freedom of the Cjortkow fields, the dancing waters of the Seret, the comfortable constraints of home. The older men perhaps accepted what they were beginning to perceive as inevitable – a time of trial and limitation until the war turned, or an uneasy fate intervened in their favour. But for youth, confinement was not inevitable.

There was the hope born of inexperience, incapacity to accept the unacceptable, and innate self-belief. He had a choice – to wait until this journey was over, to look for an opportunity now, or to take a chance when something happened which was unexpected.

It was the same at home. Sometimes he waited until the day had turned, and another day opened new doors; sometimes he just took a chance; sometimes he deliberately sat it out until something happened – someone was sick, father had to visit family in Cracow, Bruno was home, Mamita wanted a little extra from him. Always there was a chance.

On this train, there was a deadening certainty about the routine – stop for water, start again, stop for *chotka,* start again, stop for relief, start again. Always the same doors, guards, controls – and risks.

The journey was inevitable. Omsk, if it was Omsk that beckoned, might be different. Omsk would be different. Omsk would be a testing ground, a potential series of opportunities, and after Omsk? There must be another journey, and it was predictable that would be as deadening and intractable as this. So it was after the journey after Omsk perhaps.

It is difficult to be patient when you are young, easier when you have lived a life or two – or a thousand. Eduard was learning – learning to hone his patience against the stone of suffering because, even if you are young, you can with clarity see the suffering of others, without the clutter of experience, as a vision of fear and fearful foreboding. Eduard saw the suffering, and sharpened his patience against it. He would wait. He would see. He would act.

He was not to know that there would be no escape at Omsk, but that escape would become a habit, an addiction in so many different ways and guises, so many places, and with so many others, that a time would come when he had no further need for it.

He was asleep. He dreamed of high clouds, sparse sunshine, an attic room and the girl who wished to make him a man, and she reached out to touch him, and he found in himself a response which was like a sheathed knife, withdrawing softly from its scabbard within her gentle grasp. But this time, she held him, stroked him, and his eyes were on her eyes, holding him, stroking his gaze.

He felt the mounting urgency, the need for her stroke to become a strike, and the moment before the spasm – so he reached out for her, to touch her shadowed skin, to share, return, give back some of the swelling sensation she was gifting him. His hand touched her, and she was rough, and scabbed, and he could smell her sweat and old urine, and he opened his eyes.

He was lying against the truckside, and Enemy was crouched over him, Enemy's hand on his privacy, Enemy stealing his essence as he slept. Enemy grinned and Eduard still reached out, stroked Enemy. Enemy seemed surprised by this wakening response, this tying of the tryst, as Eduard groped, and found what he sought.

He curled his own hand round Enemy's weapon, pulled back fast and hard, then leant forward, thrusting the knife into the stubbled neck that only a moment before he had caressed. Blood seeped round the shaft, Enemy's hand joined his other hand at his throat, Eduard slowly slid the knife out of its seeping sheath, and the blood followed, gouting as Enemy tried to speak, failed, faltered, and fell forward, across Eduard's lap.

There were those nearby who had dimly perceived this transaction; they showed no surprise. Two shuffled forward and dragged Enemy off Eduard's thighs, ignoring the catflap to his privacy. Enemy was consigned to the sodden pyre of the dead – now both quick and dead.

I had killed. I had killed another man. I have often wondered why this did not matter, did not seem to matter, then, when I did it. I did not scream, or faint, or even shudder, or worry, or ask for God's forgiveness, or my own, or ask myself how I could come to do such a thing. I did not throw the knife down or away, or even clean its blade. I did not do or think anything. At least I cannot remember, even now, in this kind darkness, thinking anything in particular, except that I was glad I had stopped Enemy, quickly and efficiently – and finally.

I had killed. He was dead. That was that.

I have killed again since, and again, and again. Yet I am no killer born to knife or bullet, ligature or hell-honed hand. I killed only in war, and only Enemy and enemies. There was no passion in it, no desire, no lust – indeed, no liking. And there was no regret. What was necessary was done.

18

I think now, perhaps when the fires burn low, and my evening shadows shallow lie upon my inner eye, that it was that first act of death that slipped past my nature and my beliefs, that entrained in me a journeyman's acceptance of the craft of death – a necessitous act, a necessary end, and a needless concern.

Perhaps I was fortunate. I have met many men who still suffer for their deeds of valour and obedience in the theatre that is war, convincing themselves it was all an act, a performance for which they had rehearsed, for an audience that expects a man to do his duty, dealing death to those who would otherwise deal it to him, or to those he loved.

I have talked, when I could, to those who regretted the meridians of their soldiering, and wished they had avoided the necessities of conflict, found another way for King and country. And I have heard the sorrowful sighs of those who truly believed in their cause and their God, and killed in His name for their purpose, and still suffered the haunting eyes of their close victims and the winking fires of their distant targets.

I have also met those who did not care, whose hearts were still, minds focussed, acts automated by the exigencies of war, and who have neither thought nor regret for what they did. Some even boast of their unconcern. I am not like them. I make no case for killing, yet cannot suffer for my actions. I killed only when I must, and then I did so without hesitation. It was always the act of that younger me, of necessity, in need.

I still wonder why that did not matter, but it stops with wonder, and it ends. For it really does not matter, not now, and did not matter then.

TIME TO GO

The train sliced through Syrzan, crossing the Volga, and rattling towards the riverside city itself. Eduard slept as it drew into the marshalling yards, unaware that he would one day return to Kujbysev to start another journey – on the golden road to Samarkand.

It was dawn when the doors were hauled back. They were let out only two at a time, in the dank, mist-wrapped outer edge of the yards, flanked by shuttered shale wagons, and a long, silent train of flat trucks loaded with timber from the *tayga*. The ground fell away slightly towards a drainage ditch, where they relieved themselves, steam rising from their pooled piss.

The doors were left open, with a single guard. Eduard peered out, and round the truck doorway, left, then right. The same scenario unfolded: open doors, guards accompanying pairs of prisoners, and a single guard on each door. Not much chance there. He leant over and glanced under the truck. The guard jerked him back.

There was an indistinct rumble, and the adjacent truck started moving, from side to side, swaying slightly, then gathering force, as the rumble rose to a roar, punctuated by thuds and shouts, screams and curses and, for the first time, Eduard acknowledged to himself that there were indeed countless other communities of captives, up and down the train, each with their own problems, personalities, leaders and led, each perhaps containing someone else, like him, calculating when and how and whether to escape.

The riot in the next truck suddenly spewed onto the grit and weeds between the tracks, the guard thrown to the ground. Eduard's guard ran across, just as two more, hustling their prisoners along, half running, appeared from the ditch. Almost immediately, other pairs of guards and prisoners surfaced, while thirty or forty captives spilt out of the neighbouring truck, most fighting, or seeming to fight, some elbowing guards away, and one or two simply slipping under the trucks.

As other guards converged, roughly shoving captives into Eduard's truck, a sharp crack erupted right by Eduard's head, and he realised he too had slipped out of the truck. It was his guard, firing over the heads of the indiscriminate rabble yards away.

The riot froze for an instant, and then redoubled; the guard lowered his rifle and pumped two rounds into the roiling mess. One body fell and then another was detached from the churning crowd, and pitched to its knees. It was the neighbouring truck guard. He looked up at his comrade, appalled. The guilty guard dropped his rifle and ran forward. By then others had encircled the prisoners as Eduard's dragged his comrade through the grit.

Eduard started to run. He had no idea what was on the other side of the trucks, but he could see the guards were all to his left, containing the riot. He could also see other prisoners cautiously peering out of the trucks on his right, and isolated figures dropping down to the ground, crouching, then running towards the ditch. It was a small chance of freedom. Then something made him turn.

His guard was looking at him, as he dragged the wounded man, and then away towards the ditch. Eduard slowed, then stopped. He turned, and walked back to the two men, and reached out to take the wounded guard's arm, helping to lift him against a baulk of timber lying yards from the truck.

Without warning, his guard swung round, slicing him across the temple, dazing him, and he slumped to the ground, his eyes faltering. When he opened them, he was staring into the guard's eyes, inches away. The ground erupted. There was an acrid smell as the guns stuttered, and they both turned. The armoured carrier had risen beyond the ditch bank, its machine gun raking the ground within two or three yards of the line of trucks.

The escapers had no right of appeal. They died as they ran, as they stood, as they turned, as they sought by their actions to demonstrate they were not really serious, they were not really running, they were not escaping. They were not. They were dead. Ten, twelve, thirteen prisoners died that misty morning in the old freight yards of what was once the merchant town of Samara, victims of their own desire to escape the Soviet system.

It did not end there. The riot had stopped, but the guards knew several men had escaped, under the trucks. The armoured carrier was not alone. A file of riflemen emerged, and followed the vehicle across the lines, towards the timber trucks, and beyond. The mist was lifting, and it became clear that the yard was bounded on that side by a high brick wall. Some reached it. None left it. They were filleted as they stood or stumbled, by the deathly laughter of the carrier's automatic weapon.

Even that was not enough. The carrier swung round, and returned to the scene of the riot. The door opened, and an officer stepped down. He beckoned two guards, instructed them and waved them back. They climbed into the next-door truck. There was a momentary pause, then two, three figures fell out, thrown to the ground.

The officer strode the length of the train, issuing orders, beckoning, gesturing. Two more prisoners from several trucks away were slung to the ground. Finally, ten men were herded together, then marched to the wall, deliberately forced to step across some of the dead or dying would-be escapers.

They knew what was coming. Everyone knew. Nothing was said. The trucks were all emptied. Everyone was ranked along the train's length, several deep. The carrier steadied, took aim, then fired – single shots, at several-second intervals, to ram home the officer's lesson.

It does not pay. Don't ever try it again. No-one spoke. No-one complained. There was nothing to say. No point. The lesson was learnt. But Eduard learnt another lesson that dank, chill morning in the Kujbysev freight lines. Escape is an absolute; only the time, the place and the means must be learnt with extreme caution.

The guards beckoned Eduard, and looked inside the truck. They manhandled two of the fitter captives, and pointed at the wall. Their meaning was clear – it was time to clear up their mess. Two more jumped down – Big Beard and Hedgehog. Big Beard turned to Eduard. 'We'll do it; you just help.'

The post-mortem party marched across the yard. Bodies lay tangled together where they fell. Scattered along the wall's length were other bodies – those who had tried to escape. Escapers and executed were only differentiated by their wounds – single shots for the punished innocents; multiple wounds for those who dared to flee. Same difference.

They were all dead – except one. Lying still, his baldness a clean obscenity among the welter of bloodied limbs and faces and torsos, Bird Brain opened his eyes, and looked at Eduard.

The guards were impatient: they shouted, shoved, kicked at the bodies, threatened with raised rifle butts. Hedgehog stepped between Eduard and Bird Brain. Softly he murmured to the others. 'Shield me. Lift another one. Stand in the way.'

The other three captives separated one of the victims, pulling a leg or an arm, dragging him off the pile, away from the wall. The guards turned to supervise, and Hedgehog bent down, as Eduard lifted another victim by an arm, and dragged him the other way. For a moment, four men and two bodies screened Hedgehog from the guards. He hoisted Bird Brain to his feet.

'How bad is it?' The old man grunted.

'It hit my flask. Just a bruise.' Hedgehog grimaced.

'Not going to be easy. Help me with that one there.' He pointed at another body. Together they bent, straightened, dragged the body clear. Hedgehog spoke softly.

'Quick, all of you. Pull them quickly, towards the track. Confuse them. They won't count us if we move fast.'

The six stumbled, half dragging, half carrying the three bodies, when one guard suddenly shouted 'Stop!' He waved the other guards back to the train, and walked over to Hedgehog and Bird Brain. He looked hard; he was counting.

'How many does it take to carry two men? There are SIX of you. Two to a man. Find another.' And he turned away.

It took an hour for the pressed gangs to shift the free men. Altogether there were seventeen who would not suffer the gulag. They were allocated between Eduard's and the neighbouring trucks, slotted in under the shelves, next to the already dead. The stench was sweet, sickening, yet by now familiar.

Twenty minutes later, the train gathered itself, couplings colliding and clattering, as puffballs of dirty steam chased across the truck rooves; the wheels screeched, rustily grinding the tracks, and the train started the journey from Kujbysev to Omsk.

Inside the truck, Eduard had retreated to his corner. Hedgehog and Big Beard had followed, to take up station alongside. Bird Brain leant against the door, breathing shallow and fast, holding his rifle-racked ribcage. Hedgehog looked at Eduard.

'You are young. What happened?'

Eduard looked at him. What difference could it make to this roughly spoken townie – for his accent marked his provenance – to know why and how he was here? He shrugged.

'They came for me. My brother was shot – a pilot. I was a traitor. Or so they said.'

Big Beard hawked, and wiped phlegm on his sleeve, glissaded with dried snot.

'We are all their traitors, for they are children of their system, and we betray their cause with our freedom'.

Bird Brain laughed, choking into a coughing spasm, his eyes sparking involuntary tears.

'Freedom is in the mind, my friend.'

'Exactly. That's my point. We are still free. They are prisoners of their system. They know that. We know that. So they hate us.'

The three men looked at Eduard.

'Do you understand what we're saying? Freedom,' said Bird Brain, 'is absolute.'

'Like escape,' said Eduard.

The men smiled.

Bird Brain held out his hand.

'I'm Mazloff.'

Hedgehog: 'Wolski.'

Big Beard: 'Vatek.'

Eduard took their hands.

'I'm Eduard.'

'Do you have another name?'

Eduard shook his head.

'I am too young. Perhaps one day...'

'You mean you won't tell us. And you're right. You keep what you can and give what you may.' Mazloff paused. 'That's freedom, young man.'

It was night-time, and they slept. Except Eduard, who woke some time in the grey morning hours, and stopped to look through a gap in the wooden wall; there was nothing to see, but grey wastes of wheatfields and the distant black forestline.

The greyness lightened as he fell asleep again, until the train began to slow, and slither to a standstill. Apart from the hiss of steam from

23

the engine, and an indistinct rumble of waking movement and desultory talk truck by truck, silence. Nothing happened. No guards. No water. No *chotka*.

Vatek squinted through the slats.

'I can't see anything. Why the hell have we stopped?'

Wolski shrugged.

'Perhaps they are taking on water for the boiler.'

'Who knows?'

The train stood for ten, twenty, thirty, fifty minutes, an hour, two. Nothing happened. The captives had mostly returned to an uneasy sleep, some shifting irritably as the sun rose, and the stench grew.

Eduard was daydreaming. Back by the Seret, walking, stalking, when he fell. The truck had lurched violently back – and again.

'What the hell's going on?'

Vatek tried to scrape a space at the corner of the slats, screwing up his eyes to peer down the length of the train.

'We are on a curve. Must be points.'

There was another jolt, then a series of juddering, grinding, gut-leeching jerks. Then silence.

'I think they've detached some trucks.'

The doors slammed open, the sun streamed into the foetid, slightly steaming air, dust motes sparkling across the shafts, as two guards ordered them off the truck.

Vatek: 'I don't like the smell of this.'

They stood apart from the truck. They could see the length of the train. It was on a slight curve, and Vatek was right – there were points, and they were just outside a town – Ufa. The train was now divided, and stood, its two parts separate, as guards hustled inmates into the sunlight. Water was produced, then *chotka*, and unusually, small chunks of black bread. Then the guards started counting.

When they totalled the standing captives, they clambered into the trucks, retching, and totted up the dead. Papers were signed, as an officer came striding down the train, collecting each 'manifest'. As he returned, his accompanying aides issued instructions.

'They're shifting the dead. Those three trucks at the back – that's where they're going.'

And it was true. The prisoners were detailed off in small parties, and told to heft the bodies out of the trucks, and carry them down to the three detached wagons at the rear of the train.

Vatek: 'I think they think not many more will die, so it's time to have a clearout. They want us to live.'

'Freedom!' murmured Mazloff.

'You can call it that. Those poor buggers are freer than we are.'

'Not so, my friend. They have no hope now. Only heaven, or hell, or more likely, nothing.'

'You're no believer, then?'

Mazloff smiled.

'Oh yes. I believe. In me.' He paused. 'That's freedom.'

As they brought out the last body, which was the Colonel, Eduard crossed himself.

'By the grace of God, Eduard?'

Eduard turned and, he knew not why, swept a guilty tear from his eye. He had not cried before. He should not cry now. Yet somehow, this man had been his father, brother, mother for a few days, a few critical days, and with his final departure, even as a putrefying body, came the real aloneness that he had ignored ever since he had left 2 Border Street. He turned back to Mazloff.

'Perhaps. I don't know. That's what I was taught. I don't think about it much.'

'Time to think now, eh?'

Eduard nodded, as they lifted the Colonel onto the hand cart and wheeled him away.

Within an hour, the trucks were cleared of corpses. A bowser appeared, and a perfunctory hosing cleared the worst of the mess and stink. Ten minutes after that, they were ordered back on board, and the train slowly stuttered into movement, and started again on its long haul to Omsk.

Without the scholars, the truck was quieter. Mazloff showed no signs of grief for his lost colleagues – he and Wolski huddled together with Vatek and Eduard by the shelves, as Eduard carefully whittled away at the slit Vatek had found between the slats. Other groups might have formed, but the constant twilight and the number of travellers made it impossible to assess.

Certainly, the attempted escape and the subsequent execution had drawn like to like, and generated some sense of entity within the truck. Eduard supposed it was much the same throughout the train. By now, the numbness of loss, deprivation, fear and an uncertain destiny had worn off, and inevitably some sense of community, if only for mutual support and a solidarity against the faceless foe, was emerging.

The routine monotony of stop – relief, food, water – go; stop again – relief, food, water – go again inhibited effort, and conversation was infrequent, and often desultory.

'Where d'you live?'

'Cjortkow.'

'Whereabouts in Cjortkow?'

'Border Street.'

'Border Street – don't know that.'

'It's outside, near the mountains.'

'Oh.'

There would be a silence, while Eduard scraped again at the slit that had become a slot.

'What do you do?'

'Do?'

'Yes – work. You know, to live.'

'I was at school.'

Wolski laughed sharp and short.

'Rich kid, eh?'

'Not really.'

Wolski suddenly looked bleak and sodden with his own anxieties.

'No, I suppose not.' He paused. Lifting his eyes to the slot, he gently pushed Eduard to one side.

'Bad enough for the workers. Must be bloody awful for someone like you. Life unlived. No idea of death, or love, or hunger. Now all this.'

He looked back at Eduard, a certain sympathy etched in his eyes.

'Poor little bugger, you.'

Eduard smiled uneasily, then shrugged, pocketing the knife, warming his red-sore hands inside his coat.

'I think perhaps it is not so bad. I am learning. I am not afraid. It must be worse for you – you have a wife, children?'

Wolski seemed to slip from strength to fragility instantaneously. He looked at Eduard, tears seeping, mouth tight.

Eduard tentatively reached out. They grasped hands. Wolski smiled uncertainly. Eduard shook his head. He was too young for this, for sympathy and understanding and caring, yet somehow he sensed that in Wolski's need was his own strength. That you can offer better that which you need than find it within yourself. Briefly he thought about Mamita, and about Frank, and then he glanced again at Wolski.

They would survive. They were strong, experienced. Had they not always looked after him? They knew about life and living, loss and giving. Wolski knew too, but had slipped from his own grasp of his own life. There was always someone to respond, if you cared to look, and he, Eduard, could share the power of his ignorance, his youth and his inexperience with this older man, and give him back his hope, and with it, his self-respect. Wolski released his hand, grunted, and turned again to the slot.

'It's getting darker.'

Vatek leant over as Wolski straightened up. He looked through their miniature window onto the wilderness.

'I wonder where the hell we are.'

Mazloff opened his eyes. The others thought he had been sleeping.

'I estimate we should reach Celjabinsk by morning.'

'How can you possibly know that?'

Vatek laughed.

'Are you a gypsy, with the power?'

Mazloff shook his head and suddenly the other three were back at school with the Professor silently suffering the God-given ignorance of his young pupils. Back at school, where the teacher always knew every damned thing, and you knew nothing, and felt so bloody stupid.

'I am a mathematician. The speed is obvious. I have kept a mental note of the stops, and I—'

'Even when you were "dead"?' jeered Vatek.

'Yes, even when I was "dead", as you so sweetly put it.'

They all looked at him, then laughed again.

'So where exactly are we?' asked Wolski.

'Probably passing Salka – can you see any lights?'

Vatek peered through the slot.

'Not much – ah, yes. We're going through some sort of freight yard again. There's a lamp there – and another.'

He stepped back from the wall.

'Perhaps you're right – not that it makes much difference, since we are all going north, whether we like it or not.'

'North-east, actually, then finally north, after we leave Omsk.'

Wolski coughed, wiping the phlegm on his sleeve.

'After we leave Omsk. Why Omsk?'

'Because that's where the railway stops, and the river begins.'

'Oh.'

There did not seem much more to be said, so the four companions sat and, one by one, slipped off to an ungentle sleep.

Sitting here now, in the comfort of my comfortable mind, moving quietly against the memorial background noise of those darkening, difficult days, I wonder how I kept my sanity.

Perhaps it was a certain lack of imagination, that prevented me from realising an image of captivity, for this was an interim arrangement, this journey to Omsk, an insubstantial fragment of my time, neither here, then, there or tomorrow.

Perhaps it was simple weariness, after the melodrama of my arrest, the physicality of the soldiers, the sharp finity of death never met before, the virginity of execution – perhaps my child's mind was too tight and trim and uncomprehending, so that it lacked the suppleness of adulthood, and was uncorrupted by the devastation of those other lives.

I scull around in my little mental skiff, and it all seems far removed from the short, simple sanities of my everyday long-lived life, here with my little girl and my warming wifelet.

Of one thing I can be sure – I stopped growing up on that train, and leapt into life, beyond ignorance, through others' pains, onto a carousel of deaths and dares, escapes and torments, excitement and endurance, the like of which I can never live again, for I am almost alone within myself, without fear, or ambition, hope or care, except to live a little longer, just to see my Anna safe beyond the same years, into a sane and normal life, an ordinary life, a life without the ligaments of war. Is that possible? Or is every life its own conflict incarnate? Who knows... I know I don't. And who cares – not me, not any more.

FIRE FIGHT

It was late the next morning when the train pulled into Celjabinsk, hesitantly lurching to a slow halt. This time the guards were at the doors, crashing back the bolts, rousting the captives, forming them up into more or less orderly groups, then marching them across the untidy yard to a low, concrete shed. To their surprise, there they found tables and benches, and a row of latrines.

Some groups were marched off to queue in front of the latter, others told to sit at the tables, but Eduard's group was marched through to a wide door at the other end of the shed, through it down a twilit passageway, into an identical structure, where they were allocated small platform trolleys, one to four. Then they were shown sacks of salted meat, hard black bread and dried olives from Georgia, which they hefted onto the trucks.

Two pushed, two pulled. The sacks were allocated, one of each to each table, and the rest trundled back to the train, and loaded onto the rearmost truck.

'Food at last – proper food,' muttered Wolski.

'You call this food?'

Vatek shrugged.

'I suppose it is compared to the shit we've had so far, but what I wouldn't give...'

'Enough!' Wolski raised his hand. 'It's food. We'll survive. Be thankful.'

They joined the others at the table, as the guards slashed the sacks open, and doled out rations of loaves, olives, meat. There were no platters, and certainly no knives, and Eduard was careful not to use his. They pulled the loaves apart, tore strips of meat off with their teeth, and grabbed handfuls of olives. Two guards came over.

'You. You. You.' Pointing at Eduard, Vatek and Mazloff. 'Get the water.'

They were given tin pots, and marched to the latrines, where there was a single standpipe. The water ran fast but ochrous. The stained stream looked muddy, but tasted clean, with a sharp, slightly brackish taint.

'Iron,' said Mazloff. 'Good for you,' and smiled as he tipped his head back. The blow sent him staggering to one side, and he dropped the pot. The guard hit him again.

'Wait your turn.'

Mazloff retrieved the pot, and refilled it. The pots were set on the tables, two to each one. They sat. Eduard offered Mazloff a pot. He shook his head. Rubbing his cheek, he smiled.

'I've had my share.'

Within an hour they were back on board, and the train was creaking and clattering with refreshed and energised inmates, the engine breathing hard, as it hissed and frothed in readiness.

'This'll be the last leg,' said Mazloff. 'The final journey. Not far now.'

'How far?' asked Vatek.

'About the same time it took to get from Kujbysev – three, four days.'

'Then Omsk.'

Mazloff nodded.

'Yes. Then Omsk, the river...' He paused, then added, 'and the wilderness.'

They were thrown against each other as the train suddenly lurched into life and, gathering speed, rumbled and tumbled out of the freight yard, through the city and out again into the steppelands.

Eduard settled down to his task, and recommenced whittling. He had a definite peephole now, enough for one eye. He wanted to widen it for two, but not so as to make it obvious to casual inspection.

Vatek slept, while Wolski stared at the wall, and Mazloff appeared to be making calculations behind his veiled eyes, sometimes mouthing silent equations. The rest of the truckload shifted and grumbled, small conversations sputtering into life, then as quickly dying out. Others slept. Some watched them. Some stood, leant or squatted in trance, or boredom, or both.

Routines developed. Stop, relief, food, drink, go – twice a day. The trip, for by now the journey had lost its drama, and was simply an enforced excursion, took on a meaningless monotony. Escape was clearly not an option, the destination was accepted, death had visited, and departed again – *pro tem* – so that most of the captives simply endured the smells, stifling daytime atmosphere and the seeping cold of night, suspended between their memories and their fears, waiting.

Somewhere between Mamjlutka and Petropavlovsk trouble erupted. Whether it was boredom, frustration, renewed hope after more and better food, or just another escape attempt, one of the truckloads near the back, perhaps the last one, managed to destroy the truck doors.

It was during yet another stop, this time in a narrow gap between the marching lines of forest trees, far from any settlement. Here in the vast Russo-Siberian Forest, something stirred.

The guards had just succeeded in herding the captives back into their trucks, when the trouble began. Most of the guards had returned to their own wagons, in the centre of the train, at the front, and at the very back, behind the commissariat trucks, and beyond the flatbeds and tankers that had been bolted on at Celjabinsk.

Eduard's guard was just about to ram home the hasps, when there was a cracking, splintering, crashing crescendo, followed by a hollow thud and, as Eduard peered out of the now slithering door, one guard was running down the line, and others were pouring out of the guard trucks.

Seven, eight wagons back, the prisoners were boiling out of the shattered truck. As Eduard's guard reached them, they engulfed him. There was a sharp crack, then a howling, vulpine cheer, prolonged and searing. The guard's body was hurled up into the air, and fell back, to be thrown high again, then higher, and then spun away, to slam into the nearest pines.

Before the guards could react, the molten mass of men had turned towards the rear of the trucks, and met the emerging rearmost guards chest to chest, thigh to thigh, hand to clutching, vengeful hand.

It was too late for the other guards to fire, without risking their fellows. Instead they encircled the writhing mess of flesh, and hesitated, waiting for an order, an initiative, a command – for someone to take a decision.

Another soldier was ejected from the dense thicket of limbs and heads, lying limp on the frosted ground. Then a smaller object spun up out of the crowd, arcing up and away over the line of trucks, to fall on one of the flatbeds. There was a white flash, then a thud and an echoing crack, as the grenade exploded, and bales of fur and crude cloth disintegrated in a choking cloud of hair and skin and fibre.

The guards had scattered, but now they realised that action was needed, with or without orders. They moved back into an untidy semi-circle, and advanced slowly, inexorably, towards the struggling mass. Then they stopped. The chaotic crowd was no longer moving without reason. There was a shape and a purpose, a menace where before there was madness. The outer ring was entirely composed of guards – without weapons. They faced their comrades, speechless, stark, terrified, pallid beyond the pallor of the winter frost. Behind them, the prisoners were ranked in rows, and the foremost held their rifles.

Now, thought Eduard – now we will escape. He turned to Wolski, who shook his head.

'If you're thinking what I think you're thinking, don't think it.'

Eduard waved his hand up the line.

'But look what's happening. This is our chance.'

'Never,' said Wolski. He pulled Eduard down, to crouch in the lee of their truck, Vatek on the other side.

'Look,' he said, pointing back up towards the engine. 'Do you see anyone else?'

'Of course not; their trucks are still locked.'

'Exactly. This is one truck, and they will lose. But that's not the point.'

Eduard shrugged irritably.

'Well, what is the bloody point?'

Wolski sighed. God, what it was to be young.

'The point, my dear young friend, is that we are in the middle of a godawful wilderness, without food, without water, without weapons. We are a million miles from nowhere, when even somewhere isn't much in this godforsaken wasteland.'

'He's right, you know.'

They turned towards Mazloff, standing in the truck's opening. He smiled.

'Think about it – less than a quarter of a person to every square mile. The whole damned Socialist Soviet Republic of Yarkutsk – which is where we are, bang in the middle of it – contains 400,000 people, and probably twice as many bears, and millions of pines and spruce, and larch and alder and birch, and bogs and peats, and little tiny towns of 1,500 if you're lucky. As the people hereabouts would say, "You're a *lapotnik*" if you try – a clodhopper. Yarkutsk itself is only 15,000 souls. You don't stand a chance. So don't even think about it, Eduard. You'd be dead within a week.'

They looked up the track again. The two groups were still, except for a slight movement to the rear of the rebels. A voice rang out.

'Give us the train.'

There was a moment's silence. Then an answering voice rasped low and glottal, but cutting clearly through the winter wisps' breath as an officer appeared at the forest's edge.

'No.'

Vatek turned to Mazloff.

'Where in the name of Christ did he come from?'

Mazloff shook his head.

The officer's pistol was holstered. He was smoking. He was still.

'Give us the train, or they die.'

'Kill them then.'

'If you don't give us the train, we will destroy it.'

'Then you will all die – from cold, starvation and thirst.'

The officer paused, and tapped the ash from his cigarette against his boot.

'The locomotive and the first truck can easily be detached – the rest of you will perish.'

The stand-off was complete.

It was clear that to shoot the officer was to achieve nothing. To kill the guards was counter-productive, because then there would be no hostages, and the remaining guards would execute the rebels. The officer slowly detached himself from the trees, and walked away towards the engine. Then he stopped, bent forward slightly, expelled a stream of smoke, dropped his cigarette, ground it into the earth, and turned slowly.

'Why don't you just let them go, get back in the truck, and we can all get on with it?'

But they all knew they could not do that either, because then they would certainly be dead – executed without compunction. One man stepped slightly out of the circle, with a guard half shielding him, roughly pushed in front.

'Alright then, we'll negotiate.'

'With what?' asked the officer.

'With these,' and the spokesman rolled another grenade towards the guards, who turned and scattered, and then threw themselves on the ground.

The officer stood, immobile.

A second passed, and another.

'It's alright. I haven't pulled the pin,' adding, 'this time.'

Vatek looked grim.

'Bloody hell. What do they think they're doing? They'll get us all killed.'

Wolski pointed.

'Something's up.'

The officer had been joined by several guards, who seemed different from the others.

'Those are specials; they look as if they're regulars,' said Vatek.

'Yes, well they're certainly not militia, and they're not run-of-the-mill like the rest of that mob.'

Wolski jerked his head towards the re-formed outer ring of guards, their weapons drooping a little now, except when one man would jolt himself, and pull his rifle up again.

The officer stood slightly apart from the soldiers, who glanced from time to time back at the train, shifting their stances, moving about in the way men do when they are deep in discussion, the tension of debate growing into decision. Then they broke away. The officer remained standing, and lit another cigarette. Two soldiers strode back to towards the front of the train, two moved between the trucks, to the other side, and two walked slowly but steadily past the stand-off, towards the rear.

The spokesman stepped forward again, this time shielded on both sides by a guard, held close to his body, two rifle muzzles showing behind them from the outer edge of the rebels.

'Well? Do we talk?'

The officer cupped his cigarette and drew in, dropped his hand, then slowly expelled smoke. There was a sharp crack, and the spokesman fell to the ground. The soldier dropped back from above the truck, where he had quietly climbed, while everyone's eyes were on the officer.

There was a howl from the rebels, then one, three, five cracks, and the bodies of five guards were kicked out of the circle.

The officer drew another lungful of smoke, apparently unmoved. The rebels started moving, pushing and pulling the remaining guards with them, until they were at the front of 'their' truck. Then first two, then six, then more disappeared between the trucks.

There were more sharp cracks, and a strangulated cry, then silence.

'Bad move,' said Vatek.

As if to echo his thought, the officer abruptly threw his cigarette into the forest, and strode down towards the engine. He turned, then dropped his arm suddenly.

The ring of guards turned, uncertain, as the two soldiers at the rear appeared round the end of the train, and started firing at the rebels, clearly under orders to shoot, whether they killed guards or not.

'They don't give a damn about those conscripts,' muttered Vatek. 'This is it.'

The rebels shot back, then two stepped forward, raking the ring of guards with repeated fire. At last the guards reacted, firing back.

Eduard looked away from the indiscriminate death-dealing, and caught the eye of the officer, by now walking quietly up the side of the train, and nearing their truck. He was smiling.

Shots came from overhead and, as Eduard glanced up, he saw the shadows of the two soldiers from the front, who had clearly run down the rooves of the trucks.

'They're trapped,' he gasped.

'Without question,' agreed Mazloff.

Now the soldiers had the rebels boxed. Two were firing from the truck behind Eduard's, one from the rebels' truck roof, and two from the rear. The rebels had killed their hostages, and were divided, either side of the train. It was a matter of minutes.

There was another white flash, thud, crack, and then the entire forest melted as Eduard instinctively closed his eyes. The grenade was the rebels' last throw – literally. It was also the first in a series of blistering flashes, as the rearmost tanker disintegrated, blasted out of the train, toppling the flatbed behind, and setting light to the timbers as they rolled and flew into the pines. The forest ignited.

Eduard, Vatek, Wolski and Mazloff hurled themselves back into the truck. Now they shielded their eyes against the flaring forest.

The officer was beside them.

'Out. Out. Out,' he shouted. 'Follow me.'

They did as he bid, running towards the back of the train. Beyond the gap where the tanker and the flatbed had been, there was a single cattle truck, then the final flatbed and the guards' van. The flames at the front of that truck had already gripped the slats, and were reaching round the sides, towards the doors.

'If you want to save them, open the doors,' yelled the officer as he shot the hasps clear. The bolts were already buckling, and the timbers were alight. Inside the captives were screaming or coughing or moaning, as heat and smoke gathered and intensified.

Eduard and Wolski heaved at one door, Vatek and Mazloff the other. Within seconds they fell back, scorched. Then they threw themselves at the truck again, but Vatek screamed as his sleeve caught fire, and rolled away in agony, Mazloff hurling himself on him to smother the flames.

Wolski and Eduard kicked at the door, unable to touch it and then, slowly, somehow seeming to shrink away from them, it slid open, and grimed, bloated figures fell and tumbled out.

Mazloff reached out and dragged one clear, then another, and Eduard pulled a third while Wolski hauled two, one in each hand, away to the dead ground between track and forest. The pines crackled as the flames scooted up their trunks, crisping the branches, silhouetting them as if they were veins in an arm. The truck was now awash with fire, and thirty or more men lay groaning and cursing on the ground.

'That's it,' gasped Vatek. 'We can't do any more.'

'But they'll die!' screamed Eduard, wildly gesticulating towards the truck. Mazloff turned him away.

'They're dead already.'

The officer reappeared.

'Another lesson learnt,' as he grimly surveyed the fallen men.

The remaining guards and the soldiers stood aside as he gestured towards the train.

'Let them take their own. Open the doors. Five to a truck.'

Eduard looked back at the forest. It seemed to be shrinking. The line of trees was like a rainbow, the colours strongest in the middle, fading at the ends. Mazloff took his arm.

'It's going out. The trees are too damp at this time of the year. They only burnt with the fuel.'

He helped Eduard back onto the truck.

'Well, we'll get there sooner now.'

Eduard looked up at him, blankly.

'Less trucks, less weight, fewer people, less feeding, more time, greater speed. It's the law of increasing returns.'

'But the officer?'

'Odd, isn't it? He kills without compunction, no hesitation at all. He sacrifices his own, yet he spares ours.' Mazloff sucked his pipe.

'Perhaps he has a different set of values – you fight, you die; you don't, you live.' He paused. 'Who knows?' and he looked out at the embered trees.

Who knows indeed. She is sitting over there, cradling little Anna, smiling down at her, and the coffee steam curls away from the open cups on the low table between us, in our quiet room, in this simple house, at the end of the lane, in our English village, with its waving grasses and shuffling trees, enclosed in the enfolding hills, which so reminds me of Cjortkow, by its very differences, yet stubbornly reflects the same peace, the endless days of young content for my little girl, who cannot perceive of any other life than this, with her sibilant, monosyllabic dad, more often silent than speaking, and her soft-toned, warm-fleshed, embracing, always-mother.

What were my values? What are they now? Or do I simply waive them, in acceptance of my captivated comfort? I believed then, in one God, the holy Catholic Church, in Jesus Christ my saviour and the life everlasting.

At least that is what I said I believed each Sunday in church, and what I had been taught to believe each week in school, and what my father told me to believe, at prayers at home. And in our time, those times, our land, that land, we did believe – without question.

That is exactly what we believed – a faith without question. So when it came to values on a train to Omsk, with an officer who executed with one hand, and strove to save with the other, I doubt I questioned faith – his or mine. I doubt I even thought about it – faith, that is. I certainly do not remember calling upon my God for help, or food, or water, or to deal with that particular representative of those who had put me on that train.

Yet, if I am honest – and there is no gain in dishonesty when my only listener is myself, in this small space I call my mind – if I am honest, I did believe, ultimately, in God, in the ultimate goodness, in my redeemer, or rather, in my own eventual redemption. Perhaps that is why I did not concern myself with values, or prayers or utterances of faith. I just believed. It would end.

There would be justice. We would survive. And if we did not, I suppose, if I had thought about it, I would have brushed it away as 'God's will', without asking myself who the hell was it who had the right, God-given, God-originated, or from God knows what other source, to will my journey or my journey's end. Faith is bountiful, boundless, without reason, beyond question.

It is also pretty stupid. So when you are fourteen, you don't think about it. You just let it be there, part of you, without admitting, examining or justifying it. God is. I am. Let's get on with it.

STEPPE BY STEPPE

The door stayed open, but no-one was inclined to venture out. From time to time a lone guard walked past, glancing up indifferently. Once the officer strode past, hands clasped behind his back, cap pulled down hard over his prominent nose, pistol holstered but unflapped for instant use.

They stayed there for several hours, as the sun hovered above the darkening treeline, melted into the evening mists, and scuttled out of sight, quickly followed by the dusky gloom, then the grey darkness of the Siberian night.

The train was still.

By then, they were hungry and cold, thirsty and needing relief. After an hour or so, Eduard sat on the edge of the truck. The doors were still open. No-one seemed concerned. Mazloff leant out, pulling Vatek to the door, who swung down from the truck, warily peered up and down the track, then beckoned Wolski. Two others jumped down after them. The guard appeared, standing, rifle cocked, but sloping to the ground. He jerked his head towards the trees, as if to say, 'Go on, it's OK, I won't do anything'.

They walked slowly, as openly as they could, then stopped. Within minutes the truck emptied, and the men shuffled about, uneasy, cold, stamping and cuddling themselves. Wolski glanced up and down the line, as the officer strode past again, ignoring them.

Wolski beckoned, and Vatek joined him. Together they made their way to the forest edge; others joined them, then Mazloff, and Eduard, until all the captives were strung out. Then, as if orchestrated by a mistress of the ballet, they all peed.

When they were finished, they gathered round the doors, outside the truck, stamping their feet, threshing their arms. The guard stood off to the side, watching, but without much interest. The officer came back, passing them without a glance, mouthing a short command at the guard, who moved to the next truck, slid back the hasps, then the doors, and beckoned the inmates out.

Down the line, an occasional guard followed suit. Within minutes, the train was like an escalator in a department store, men going up and down, in and out. Within minutes, the entire trainload was congregated in groups, outside the trucks, moving around cautiously, with the few guards evenly spaced, watching, but uncaring.

Gradually, as all the trucks emptied, the inmates made their way to the trees, until a cloud of urinous steam hung over all their heads.

The officer was standing by their truck as they straggled back. He was motionless, except for the thin stream of smoke from his narrowed lips. They stood slightly apart, as he smoked, watching the treeline.

They heard the lorries before they arrived, their upright exhausts rasping and cursing as they bucked and bounced over the uneven ground towards the train. Minutes later they had halted in an uneven line, alongside the tracks.

The officer opened his mouth, dropped his cigarette, heeled it, looked up and pointed at Eduard, Vatek, two others, younger and fitter than most.

'Follow me.'

The same was happening on either side. Twelve captives were loosely formed up and the little squad, led, flanked and followed by the soldiers, marched to the back of the train. The lorries were there already, and the officer was supervising their unloading.

The rear of the train was unscathed, the flatbed twisted and leaning over the track, which was apparently undamaged. The more or less orderly squad marched loosely towards the lorries. There they halted, and the officer dispersed them, Eduard and Vatek to a small winch, the rest to the flatbed truck, straddling the line, its remaining bogie sunk between the rails. From another lorry they had grabbed two small jacks and some chains.

The chains were attached to the winch, and the jacks eased under the bogie. After several attempts, some repositioning and a great deal of under-breath swearing, the truck was eased over the tracks, and dragged clear.

The guards' van was re-coupled to the flatbed behind the now rearmost truck, the soldiers disposed the squad alongside the remaining van – and slowly it was pushed down the rails, to join the surviving flatbed behind the last truck. The rails had escaped the fireball.

'Blast,' said Vatek, 'is whimsical. Lifts and waves all over the place, but not in any pattern.' He pointed at the tracks. 'Obviously missed the rails, hit the truck and shifted everything over there,' pointing to the forest, 'a circle of rails.'

Eduard's memory was sharp, sweet and yet painful. Frank had brought back the model one day. A visiting inspector had left it. A clockwork engine, two crudely painted wagons, and a circle of rails, with a little trip you could set to catch the train, so it stopped right beside the small tin hut, bright green, that sat beside the track. Thinking about it, his eyes closed. It was a long time ago, or so it seemed.

As he daydreamed of the fussy little engine, chattering around the track, their train lurched back a yard, paused, then lurched again, and all the couplings closed with a stammering cascade. They started to walk back to their truck when the soldiers pointed at another lorry. It carried two upright canisters, with stopcocks at their base. Vatek pulled his sleeve.

'More work.' The squad formed up again, and marched over to the lorries. The officer was standing by the two upright canisters, with their rusty stopcocks. He handed Eduard a mug.

'Drink.' Another to Vatek. 'Drink.'

'Thank God. Water,' said Vatek. The officer held out his hand, took Eduard's mug, filled it, then drank himself, handed it back, and gestured to the squad.

'Serve them all.'

Vatek and Eduard drew water, passed it out, withdrew the mugs, filled them, handed them out again, and again, as the prisoners queued patiently. They kept the line going, filling the mugs, passing them out, retrieving them, until the canisters ran dry. There was a second supply.

When all the prisoners had drunk, the soldiers waved them back to the trucks. Eduard and Vatek had a final, slow and satisfying drink, then returned to their own mobile home. The officer was standing there, legs apart.

'Time to go.'

Eduard looked at him. 'What about food?'

'Food? What food?'

The officer flicked ash from his tunic.

'There is no food.' He paused. 'Not even for me.'

He looked away at the forest, then back at the train, then straight at Eduard.

'There'll be no food, until Omsk.'

Vatek stepped forward.

'What about the next place?'

'What next place?'

Mazloff intervened.

'Petrapovlovsk.'

The officer laughed.

'That little place? Full of miners and underground crap.'

He started to walk away, then paused, turned, and added, 'Right little shithole – no food, not until Omsk.'

Minutes later, the guards walked down the train, pointing at the trucks, and the captives slowly hauled themselves on board. The doors were closed, but Eduard noticed the hasps were not secured, at least not on theirs.

Within an hour they were in Petrapovlovsk, and the officer was right. The train paused for a few moments in a filthy freight yard, where sullen workers stood in lumpen clumps, glowering at them. No-one felt like leaving the truck. The train moved out.

Around mid-morning, the sun glittered through the dissipating mists, as they rode round a long, wandering bend. The train hesitated, then slowed, then stopped. The forest was some way off, and on the stubbled ground of the wheatfield the moujiks sat astride their small, sturdy horses, shrouded in coarse cloth, with cloth wound round their dishevelled heads, creased leather boots down the horses' flanks, their hands resting on their manes, tattered bags hanging down. Separately, one man sat astride a much finer horse, still despite its restlessness.

Mazloff jumped down as Eduard sat on the truck edge, and Vatek leant out.

'It's an Orlov Rostropshin.'

Eduard gulped, and then the fit hit him. He could not control himself. He was engulfed in laughter, choking, coughing and exploding with paroxysms of mirth. Vatek was infected and started shaking too, then Wolski, and without warning, the entire truckload was spilling out, staggering about, one or two rolling on the ground, all caught up in this magical moment of hysterics.

Eduard blinked, looked at Mazloff.

'Orlov Ros-strop-shvic – what?' and then he was off again, out of control. He had not laughed for days, but this amazingly grand pronouncement had set him off, until the tears were streaming down his face. They were all in an uproar of laughter, coughing and spluttering, gripping their sides, and one another, as the moujiks looked down at them, uncomprehending.

Mazloff looked slightly irritable, as if he could not see the joke, and tried to explain.

'Orlov Rostropshin – it's an Anglo-Arab from the Don Valley crossed with an Orlov trotter.'

That simply set them all off again.

Vatek: 'An Orlov trotter – you mean,' and he gasped as he tried to catch his breath, 'you mean an Arabian, a bloody Muslim horse crossed with a, a pig?' and his eyes streamed as he fell back against the truck, shaking.

Mazloff took out his pipe.

'Barbarian.' He sucked the empty stem. Then he drew Eduard towards the peasant elder.

'This horse is an Anglo-Arab saddle horse – a crossbreed. From the Orlov trotter and the Anglo-Arabs of the Don Valley. A wonderful beast. Fast and strong. Ideal for the steppes.'

He pointed the pipe at the horse.

'It's an Arabian racehorse crossed with a light vanner. They make the fastest cross-country carriers in the world, and this chap has got a splendid example. He's the village elder,' he added.

Then he turned to Eduard.

'You are an ignorant lot of townies – and you, Eduard, should know better. Your mother raised horses, didn't she?' and the instant he spoke, he regretted it. Eduard's joy went out as fast as the memories came in. Mamita. Where was she? Was she alive? Was she ill? Where was she? And the tears came fast unbidden, as fast as the laughter, and as uncontrolled.

'I'm sorry, son.'

Mazloff touched his arm, and Eduard swept the tears away with his sleeve.

'Not your fault. And it is a bloody silly name for a horse.'

The chief of the moujiks dismounted, which was the signal for the rest to follow suit. They swung the bags free of the horses, and gathered round him. He squatted in front of Mazloff, and extracted a fresh loaf of rye bread. He looked up, reached out and offered it to Mazloff.

The prisoners encircled the moujiks, silenced by the sight of the food, and the unexpectedness of the gift. Then the moujiks split, spreading out down the track, handing out bread and dried fruit to all the prisoners.

They sat on the hard ground, or leant against the trucks, eating without haste after the first flustered mouthfuls, as a seemingly endless supply of bread and fruit was pressed upon them.

Vatek noticed him first. The officer was standing near the engine, his soldiers beside him, not moving. Vatek tapped the nearest moujik on the arm, pointed at the officer, and held out both hands. The moujik handed him his bag, and Vatek walked down the trackside, until he reached the officer. He put the bag on the ground, looked up briefly, then turned and walked back.

Wolski: 'Why'd you do that? The man's a bastard.'

'He gave us drink. He has to eat too. We're supposed to be better than them.'

He looked up briefly.

'Anyway, my mother always told me to turn the other cheek, and to share my good fortune with those less fortunate than me,' and he laughed.

As the train gathered speed, the moujiks rode alongside, inscrutable, then they wheeled away, stopped and, as the long line of trucks pulled out of sight, their leader turned back towards the tracks, raised his hand in salute, and they were gone.

There were no more stops, as they steamed across the steppes towards Omsk.

I never had friends like that at home. There was Jerzy, who lent me things, and Janusz, who tried to steal them, and then made me laugh, so I didn't care. There was Andrzej, whose maid 'liked' me, and there was Wieslaw, who came to tea sometimes. But there was never any spontaneous group generosity that I can recall.

Here, on the steppes, for no clear reason, a group of men who lived hard, made a hard living, shared their bread with strangers. It made a lasting impression on me. Of course, I found that same 'team spirit' in the Army, and in the SFA, but that is not quite the same thing. This was not only collective, generous and spontaneous, it was pointless. There was no bond to be made or secured, to be maintained or reconnected. This was giving for

40

the sake of giving. No-one would praise them, as today we praise the charitable acts of the self-sacrificing Westerner, giving up job, or time, or promotion or hard-earned cash, to help others less fortunate than oneself. Here there could be no self-congratulation, no mental MBE, no sage nodding of the spectating colleagues, friends and family for one's 'innate goodness'. They gave for giving's sake, for the sake of those who had not what they had to give. They gave me something else too.

They gave me my first conscious understanding of hope.

I had travelled thus far without thinking much about the future, not dwelling on the maybes or what-ifs, and so not wanting the let's-hope or the if-we're-lucky. These hard-eyed, horsed riders of the harsh steppe told me that there were men who obeyed orders, and men who were not constrained by state so much as by weather and terrain and opportunity, and by training and forbearance and trust, and stripped-down effort to live that day with one's fellows, unquestioning. They were there. We were there. They knew our need because it was their everyday experience. They had. They gave.

I learnt that day the reality of innate goodness – it is unconscious, does not advertise, because it has nothing to sell and no perceived market. It is not of God, nor needs God to justify itself. But like God, it is.

It was the first time for me, but not the last. I see it in Anna – every day. And she does not even know it is there.

41

ONE CATHOLIC CHURCH

Within seconds of pulling in to Omsk, they opened the doors, and thousands poured into the station, onto the platform, were marshalled under guard, and taken, in that understated way fate has, after faith has been tested almost beyond endurance, to a church. A disused church, true, empty for twenty years, since the glorious revolution, but a church nonetheless – sanctuary.

It was barbed with wire, and well guarded. Then began the process of processing them. They were all duly listed. Were there any wounded? No? Only dead? Good.

There was a blank block of stone where the altar once stood, and no-one seemed anxious to be seen there. Behind it Eduard found an old storeroom, more of a cupboard really, but unoccupied. He occupied it – as he thought, appropriately since they were all in fact 'occupied' in one sense, while pretty well unoccupied in another. Between two and three thousand went to church that day. A collective act of unintentional worship.

The doctors and the lawyers and other officers in the other trucks were split up and reassembled with others from yet more trucks, but there were no old friends for a 14-year-old in that seething church. Of Wolski and Vatek and Mazloff there was no sign. Nor was there the same comprehension as he listened to the variations played on the eternal theme.

'What chance have we got? Will we survive? Where are we going?'

For Eduard there were no friends: he had found his old ones among the carpenters and market traders, the cottagers in the valley and his family, his new ones in the transient adversity of a train journey – but all train journeys come to an end, when the passengers disembark and disperse.

'You can all lie down' was a concession, rather than a prelude to massacre. There was no other evidence of organisation, except the food and drink: some hours after their arrival there came gruel, bread, some soup, and water.

Once more, the prisoners were bleakly cheered – they meant them to live, otherwise why squander precious resource? The bread was black, wet and tasted unlike bread. The gruel was grey, thin and tasteless, with soggy lumps of unabsorbed flour. The soup was tepid, with globules of grease and occasional fishbones, and the water was stale.

They sat, or stood, or lay about the church, listless, simply surviving.

Eduard crept out of the storeroom, to see if there was any more food. There had been none for most of the second day – except for the guards. These were not the same conscripts from the train, but militiamen, clearly uninterested in the prisoners or their wellbeing.

There were many strangers in the Church of St Nicholas – not only Poles, but Rumanians, Bessarabians, Czechs and Hungarians. By the end of the first day a routine had evolved. The guards – there were only a dozen or so – ignored the prisoners, and the captives ignored the guards. There was absolutely no communication between them, so the captives organised their own food and sanitation.

Local people visited the church unchallenged and unregarded. They brought some food and they provided makeshift latrines with buckets, spades and disinfectant. They were allowed through the barbed wire two or three at a time, noted by a private, and sometimes a corporal – there were no officers – and then counted back out again, nothing more.

Their concern was masked, whether for their church, the captives, for humanity's sake, or out of an inherent dislike for authority was not clear. They rarely smiled, seldom spoke, simply came, gave, and went.

Nobody died, nobody cried. The different nationalities tended to group together, the older people kept themselves apart and the scholars, for there were academics in every national group, argued deep into the nights, about the war, the politics and the politicians, but ultimately and always returning to themselves, their fate, their likely destinations, for everyone was acutely aware that the church was but a way station to more deprivation and loss – loss of hope, of values, of self-regard, perhaps even of sanity.

There had been tales of forced labour in the cold north of the Russian sub-continent for years, and none were so well-informed as the men of learning, whose Russian colleagues had disappeared year by year, class by class. Learning knows no frontiers, and makes few friends, but always learns the lesson of experience. Gradually the dense congregation thinned out, the pews cleared, the food improved as it became more plentiful and the sanitation flowed less.

Some went to Uzbekistan, some to Kazakhstan, and some to God knew where. And Eduard went to Tara.

The corporal pushed through the small crowd of Czechs and pointed at the Hungarian contingent. They gathered themselves together, picked up the few portables they had fought to keep on the train, and followed the soldier towards the west door. Then he pointed at a group of Rumanian 'travellers', perhaps the most adaptable of St Nicholas's temporary children, and they fell in behind; as they shuffled down the aisle, the residue of the original 3,000 watched in muttering apathy and indifference. The corporal waved them all on and stepped aside, striding back to the small group of Czechs.

'You too,' he barked. Eduard watched, almost wishing he was leaving too. The kick was not hard, but the shock sent a stabbing sickness from his leg to his stomach as the corporal shouted, 'I said "you too".'

The evening's selection was marched in some disorder through the town to the riverside and into the small 'harbour', for the river Irtys was a wide thoroughfare and boasted jetties and warehouses, docks and slipways. Tied up at one jetty was a paddle steamer – a side-paddler modelled on the *Mississippi Queen*, with a tall, black smokestack, log fired, and two open decks. With black and white trim, she was obviously new, designed for pleasure, and not for prisoners in bulk. The bottom deck was already full, so Eduard's group was hustled onto the top deck. Eduard asked for water and the guard spat, as he turned away and clattered down the gangwalk to the jetty. Eduard backed out of his little group and pushed through the increasingly congested throng to find another guard. This time it was a private.

'We need water,' he said. The guard looked at him and shrugged. Eduard touched his arm and he snatched it away, as if he might be contaminated, and snarled 'No', pushing his rifle into Eduard's chest. He started marching, his finger twitching round the trigger guard.

Eduard stumbled back, the gun pressing harder, now in his stomach as the guard screamed 'Niet! Niet! Niet!' and again 'Niet!' as he stepped back, and spat straight at Eduard, who lost his balance and collapsed onto the decking.

The loose knot of Czechs parted as two men shouldered past them. Wolski and Vatek bent towards Eduard, helped him, dragging him behind a group of older men, Rumanians, as the guard abruptly turned, and marched back to the gangplank.

Within minutes the slender stack was belching black smoke and the great white wheels started churning the scummed waters by the jetty. Yellow froth flew like spittle as the boat started turning in her own length to start the long haul upriver – and Eduard found his friends again.

The pain was inside, not in the muscle stabbed by the soldier's kick, not in the scraped elbow, dragged along the decking, and not in the head, where it glissaded off an inconvenient boot on the way down, but within. Wolski bent down, and the pain seared to the surface, breaking like a coruscation of bursting blisters, all the anger and hurt and self-pity flooding out in crystalline liquefaction.

I remember a dream I had many times as a child, when my back erupted with a three-inch-wide raised rack of blackcurrant spots, crisp and shiny until I scratched them and the bloody juice spurted out. It was the same as I cursed him, my mother, brother, family, hometown, birth, very existence, which had led me to this finity of waste.

Yet there was no hostility, in the sense of personal animosity, just indifference, and casual cruelty if you got in their way. There was no time to think then, to arrange thoughts, or indeed actions. You lived, or you died. You went, or you suffered. You gave way because you could not get your way. This was Russia and this was indeed hell. If you can describe hell, then call it Russia.

44

I remember one other thing about that church. I found my father's watch. I had forgotten when I took it apart and he beat me for not putting it back together again that, after he mended it, I pinched it and hid it in my best coat – which, being the thickest one I possessed, was the one I grabbed before I left 2 Border Street all those light years before.

And it worked. I knew the time. I had the time. I could count the hours to Tara, for I certainly had the time through those endless hours and days, though I did not then know that Tara was my destination, and my introduction to real life – and to love.

Not that I knew much about that then either – about love. My first 'experience' was when Andrzej's maid one day said 'I like Eduard' and smiled in a peculiar, secret sort of way, which I really did not understand.

We were playing games of 'jump the canoe' in the back yard of his house in Cjortkow, his parents were out and, when the time came to go home, the maid – she was old, 17 or 18 or so – came to chuck me out before they returned, for they did not approve of this son of an ex-policeman, and she simply said 'I like Eduard' and smiled at my friend as she took my hand and led me away.

Once outside the salon, she put her other hand to her mouth, smiled again, shook her head, and motioned me to keep ever so quiet. We stood there for several seconds, while she cocked her head to listen for my friend, but he stayed behind, so she led me up the stairs to her small bedroom.

She pushed me through the door, closed it slowly, holding the handle to stop it clicking shut, then pointed at the bed. I sat on the coarse blanket, wondering 'what next?' and she stood over me, unfastening the buttons on her blouse. She was bare beneath, and I looked at her chest, and she slipped a hand inside, and stroked herself.

Then she sat beside me, and put my hand inside too. It was warm there, and soft and yielding. Then she put her hand on me.

There was a distant sound of doors shutting, and steps – my friend's parents had arrived and it was too late.

I crept back down the stairs, confused, crying, unclear, half virgin, half man, sticky in mind and body and wondering what it was that a woman could do or be that could diffuse my mind and heat my body without resolution or release. Her name was Anna.

Vatek was sitting by the stern rail, Wolski beside him, while Mazloff was slowly pacing back and forth.

'You know where we're going?' he asked Eduard.

'No.'

'Tara.'

Mazloff leant on the rail, gazing across the river, and the snow-dusted trees.

'The river is still sluggish, even though the ice has gone.'

He glanced back at the others.

'Only days, and we'll be there.'

Vatek looked up.

'You make it sound as if we're on holiday.'

Mazloff sucked his pipe, said nothing.

Wolski grumbled, 'Some holiday. Easter in Siberia. Huh!'

Other prisoners lay sprawled on the deck, or leaning against the rails. There was an air of subdued relief. They were in the open, they could watch the admittedly monotonous banks slide by, follow the flight paths of the birds of the river. And from time to time, they were fed. Water was plentiful.

When the boat started turning in towards the bank, everyone turned to look for the quayside and township, but there was nothing – just a landing stage jettied out into the slow currents of the river bend. A squad of soldiers stood, watching impassively.

The great paddles churned in opposition as the riverboat sidled up to the jetty, its stack belching great gouts of greasy, sooty smoke, in the effort to control thrust and steerage. She bumped once, then twice, then settled against the stage. Crewmen lowered a gangplank, and the soldiers waited.

The guards marshalled them in groups, and they started stumbling down the seamed and shiny planks, slipping and sliding, and jostled together. Once on land, they were ordered into rows, as pairs of soldiers detached themselves from the shore squad and started knocking them into line. They were not gentle.

Within half an hour, the riverboat was gone, and the captives were told to 'start walking'.

IS THIS TARA?

The snow lay, dense, sticky, compressing slowly beneath each footfall. It was winter in Tara.

Slowly the silent column of captives trudged through the snowscape, minds bent to blankness, each step automatic, their awareness limited to the stiff feathers of breath lingering between them, the occasional mechanical grunts of their Asiatic guards and the crackling progress of the heavy, long-sided carts, four-wheeled, flat, thickly packed with unknown intangibles and certainly nothing of interest to the prisoners. There was no road, simply a clear way between the dank, stiff, snow-burdened trees, a presumed trackway beneath the dirty white, unwashed lunar landscape, endlessly perpetuating itself before their neutered eyes.

Imperceptibly, the way widened, broadened, flattened, the trees receding to a misty perimeter, and there was a small, low cabin, thatched with snow, barbed with icicles, rimed with fretted windows, frost-patterned, the doorway dark and drab, save for a red and white notice, indecipherable to the now stationary cavalcade. The guards clustered, exchanging brief grunts without laughter. The captives stood, listless.

Beyond, a single, broad-beamed hut, with a steeply pitched roof, snowscaped, regular gaps where windows might have been, and one central, squat smokestack, stood centrally itself within the clearing. There was no visible fence; there were no gun towers, no armed militia, no fierce dogs – just the hut, the cabin, and white, solid space.

This was the camp; this was Tara. This was Tara? Eduard turned to Wolski. 'Is this Tara?'

His companion shrugged.

'I thought Tara was a town, a village.'

'Perhaps it is. Perhaps it's the landing stage. Perhaps it's somewhere else altogether.'

Mazloff interrupted: 'Tara's a small settlement, the landing stage its link to the world. This is just a camp.'

'Clever dick,' muttered Vatek.

Eduard smiled.

'Well, at least we know where we are.'

'For what that's worth.'

'Which is not a helluva lot,' added Wolski.

The guards had vanished, and the captives were left beside the carts. No-one moved more than a few paces away; some huddled near the horses to share their warmth. Most just stood, and shuffled about, and tried to distance themselves from the biting cold, for the day was waning, and the dank birch and aspen forest hemmed them in.

One of the guards emerged from the cabin, hands cupping a mug, steam curling slowly away, dissolving above his head. A wisp of smoke eddied from the stump of a chimney above the log cabin. They could hear the murmur of voices, and an occasional shout, then silence, then voices again. After a few moments, the guard turned and disappeared.

The steaming mug had made the captives restless; there had been no food or drink since they left the boat, and that was several hours before they reached camp. As if on cue, the guards streamed out of the cabin, and prodded them into line again, pointing at the hut, then leading the way inside.

As they entered, they were split into four files. One file was pushed to the left, another to the right, and two down the centre. There were four rows of bunks, two flanking the walls, two more forming a passageway on either side. The centre was clear and wide enough for a man to lie full length, head to one row, feet to another. In the centre was a large cast-iron stove, cold and empty. The bunks were in two tiers, and not so much bunks as shelves, supported by rough-hewn posts and cross-members. There were no mattresses, just boards. They were divided by crude rails at body-width intervals.

On either side of the stove, a metal door hung open, and there was a pile of what looked like dry earth. 'It's shit,' said Vatek, unbelieving, as he scraped a section away with his foot, and it was – cow dung. A rusty pipe stretched from the stove to the roof ridge and beyond.

The guards pushed them against the bunks, and then indicated they should, could rest. Wearily some climbed up to the top row, others heaved themselves onto the bottom boards, and the rest simply leant against the posts, unbelieving. One guard beckoned Vatek and Wolski and, in heavily accented Russian, commanded them, 'Follow me.' Another pulled Mazloff and Eduard forward and gestured that they should follow too.

Vatek: 'What accent's that?'

'I'm not sure,' said Mazloff. 'They're Asiatic, I think, possibly Voguls or Ostyaks from the *tayga*, certainly not European Russians, and not locals either.'

Wolski grunted. 'What difference does it make anyway? They look pretty wild to me.'

If the guards understood the exchange, they gave no sign, but simply prodded the four Poles along the path to behind the cabin. There they found a smaller hut, almost a shed, and a water tank. Inside the shed were shelves, with tin mugs, plates, boxes of spoons, and pitchers. They were told to take the pitchers and some mugs, fill them from the tank, and return to the hut with them – one mug of water to each prisoner. There was no food.

'What about food?' asked Mazloff, in Russian.

'No food today,' rasped the first guard. 'Food tomorrow. Plenty of food,' and he laughed, but there was no mirth in his laughter.

Vatek was about to protest when Mazloff caught his arm.

'He means no food for anyone – including them.'

'Bloody hell. I'm starving.'

The others looked at him, hard.

'Okay, okay, I know, so's everyone else. Pity we didn't escape from the boat while we had the chance.'

Wolski exploded.

'What bloody chance, you idiot? Across a river that wide? Are you mad?'

The guards were watching, without amusement, and without comment. Mazloff spoke softly, urgently.

'Calm down. We don't want any disturbance here. Let's just wait and see. In the morning, we'll get some food, and after a few days we can decide what to do.'

He turned and smiled apologetically to the guards.

'My friend is tired, like you, and, like you, he's a little hungry but, like you, he'll wait until tomorrow.'

The guards nodded, and waved at the hut. One of them added, 'We always wait until tomorrow.' And then they turned too, and walked back to the cabin, leaving the four friends to tap the tank, and take the water back to the hut. A roster soon established itself, with the last man to drink nominated to return to the water butt for more; Eduard volunteered to show them the way.

By nightfall, everyone had drunk as much water as he needed – for the first time since the cattle trucks left Cjortkow with lorryloads from so many places, all bound for now cosmopolitan Camp Tara.

As Eduard tried to find a comfortable way to get some sleep on his bed board, he reflected that they were certainly an international fellowship. Yet it was strange that there were so few of his countrymen among 300-plus, condemned to hard labour, in this Godforsaken outpost of empire.

It was morning. A pale sun lit the clearing, casting soft shadows on the snow. The trees were silent. There was no breeze. The camp was quiet. Eduard swung down onto the hut floor, and walked quietly outside. There was no sign of a guard; smoke still lifted from the cabin chimney, and the carts had gone, but there were two newly arrived long-wheelbase flatbed lorries parked by the forest edge. He looked round the clearing, and noticed a pathway behind the log cabin. Glancing round the clearing to ensure he was unseen, he walked slowly towards the shed, as if he was going for some water, then cut off behind it, along the treeline to the pathway.

It curved between the trees, and then widened into another clearing. There there were three more buildings. One was concrete, somehow tauter, cleaner cut, more businesslike, than any in the first clearing; it also had modern windows, and a lean-to from which the low hum of a generator could be heard. Most surprising of all, the gleam of electric light flashed through the windows.

To its right there was a small, wooden, two-storey building, with a gantry and granary door. To its left there was an open-fronted shed, with three hand-carts and what looked like a workbench and a set of logging tools – axes, hooks, saws, and some heavy, two-tined forks. This was obviously the work yard; theirs the domestic site. Eduard realised that Tara was a logging camp. They were here to cut wood.

Twenty years of cutting wood for their Russian masters! Eduard looked at the axes and the hooks, and started to think again about escape.

He heard the footsteps and the breathing before he turned, and flinched in anticipation. The guard came right up to him, then pointed at the shed and walked on. Eduard followed. The guard reached up, and pulled down a long, single-handed saw. He pointed at a stack of timber which Eduard had not noticed before, stacked at the back and one end.

'Firewood – for us,' and the guard grinned, his mouth bare of teeth. 'Twenty minutes – bring it,' and he strode off, leaving Eduard to contemplate the spindly trunks, the rusty saw, and his own folly for inviting an extra chore before the others were even awake.

Half an hour later, he staggered across the clearing, down the path and dumped the logs beside the cabin. It took six journeys to clear the entire pile, by which time two of the guards were lounging against the cabin doorposts, watching him, exchanging the odd comment, and clearly enjoying his discomfort.

When he had finished, one beckoned him.

'You get the others,' he said. 'All of them.'

Eduard returned to the hut. Mazloff was already up, standing in the doorway, contemplating the clearing, his pipe stub in his mouth. Eduard peered inside. Most of them were asleep, including Vatek. Wolski was leaning on his elbow, half awake.

'Been busy?' asked Mazloff.

'Chopping wood.'

'I didn't see you.'

'There's another clearing, buildings, workshed, tools. I think this is a logging camp.'

'Makes sense – we're in the forest tundra, where the birch trees grow. They've mechanised with sawmills down in the *tayga* pine forests. Here that doesn't make sense, so they would use forced labour.'

Mazloff sucked reflectively at his pipe.

'It's going to be hard work.'

'Well, it starts now – they want us all out, over there.'

Eduard pointed to the cabin, where the two guards still leant against the doorposts.

Gradually, the inmates roused themselves, grumbling and shivering and trying to stamp some life into their cramped limbs. Eventually, they formed up in a vague semi-circle before the log cabin. The guards nodded, then disappeared inside.

A moment later a stocky, black-bearded figure appeared, a military cap on his head, a long greatcoat failing to conceal his exceptional strength as he hefted a substantial log from beside the entrance.

'This is a birch log.'

He paused.

'Those of you who understand, tell the others.'

There was a confused shuffle and a series of muttered comments as the Russian speakers identified themselves and gathered others around them.

'What we want are cut logs. Two kinds.'

He lifted the log to chest height.

'Large ones like this,' he dropped the log, thrust a hand in his greatcoat and brandished a small cutting, 'and small ones like this. You will be divided into two teams.'

He stepped forward, until he was close to Eduard.

'You will cut the small logs' – pause – 'because you are smaller.'

Then he wheeled sharply, and strode down the line, until he came to a group of Bessarabians.

'You can cut the big ones, because you are bigger.'

He looked enquiringly at the men, as if waiting for someone to share his little joke. No-one did. He returned to the cabin, and stood, hands sunk deep in the folds of the greatcoat.

'If you want to, you can change places between the teams, but I want exactly the same number in each team, every day.'

He glanced at the guards.

'There are six men here; they are special conscripts in the Army. They don't like being here, so don't tempt them. They will be watching you. Every day. All day. All the time.'

He inhaled deeply, and sighed.

'I am your boss. I am in charge. If you want anything, you ask me. If you take my advice, you won't want anything.'

He turned round, stepped into the entrance, and then slowly wheeled round again.

'Just one thing. Food.'

The prisoners stopped shuffling and stood in still anticipation.

'You will be fed once a day – good soup, nice bread, sometimes other things, and you can drink as much water as you have time for.'

He smiled, a synthetic, warmthless smile.

'If you work extra hard, you get extra soup.'

He stood for a moment, then explained.

'I expect four cubic feet per person a day. If you cut more, you eat more.'

And with that he was gone.

The guards advanced, and shepherded the two teams along the path to the shed. Tools were issued, but the guards made it clear these were not the means to escape, as they cocked their rifles. One guard adjusted the belt round his tunic, just to make sure they could see the knife too.

Then they started out, into the forest, each guard peeling off with his own squad, down the narrow paths across the mossy, swampy ground, into the depths of the woodland belt.

I suppose, in a circular sort of way, that year and the next were a bit like now. It was the same then – routine, repetition, 'round and round, like a bloody great wheel'. Oh yes, I learnt all the naughty rhymes from my English friends, when I found them, after the war. In and out of the forest, the hut, the forest again, and again, and again; in and out we went 'like the prick of steel'. Funny how words do that to you, when you have the time to think about them, and especially when you can't get your bloody great tongue round them, or make your stupid hand write them down. They form patterns, conjure associations, and lead you all over the place, rather like dreams.

I had one the other night. It took me right back to the hut. We were lying there, dozing, the heat from the stove making popping sounds, the odd grub dropping fatly on the fabric of shirt or trousers, to be mindlessly squashed, another stain, another death, when the lorry caught fire, and my best friend Wieslaw jumped onto it, shouting, 'Come and join me – she really likes you!' Then the lorry was gone, Wieslaw ran away and the whole hut ran after him, that is to say, all of us in the hut – except me. I watched them run until they had all disappeared, then I took out my watch, father's watch, and hurled it after them, yelling, 'I haven't got the time, I haven't got the time.' And I started laughing. 'Haven't got the time' – what a dreadful pun. And 'watching them' – another one. Words, associations.

In fact, I hardly ever dreamt during those days. I was too damned tired. But I remembered that dream for days, for when the axe fell, and all that followed, I was often to ask myself if there was something in the old belief that dreams were a window of sorts on the future, often a warning. Of course, I don't believe it now, and I don't think I really believed it then, but I did wonder the other day, when I had that dream, because it was the same one I had had that day in the hut, the day before the accident. The day before the escape.

Perhaps there will be an accident one day soon, and I will escape. Perhaps my mind will go up in flames and I will walk out, talk out, throw the time away and – then again, perhaps it would be better if there was no accident, and no escape.

Day followed day; week, week. The routine was invariable. They got up, relieved themselves in the communal ditch they themselves had to dig, washed and watered themselves at the butt, which was always full, and then marched off into the forest to cut logs. There they stayed until midday, when they marched back for food, more water and relief, then marched back again, until the sun slithered out of sight, and they returned to the hut, to talk, or sleep, or amuse themselves as best they could.

The only variation came after one week. The pile of small logs had grown, and was stacked up beside the shed. The larger logs were carted back to the clearing, loaded onto the flatbeds, and hauled off to some unknown destination. When the small logs reached the eaves of the shed, the squads were all assigned to logging proper, and only Eduard was ordered to maintain the supply of *curku*, or firewood – not for the cabin, for that was cut by the guards themselves, but for the generators.

Apart from the office generator, which powered the only electricity in the camp, there was a container, or box, on the side of each lorry. Once the engine had been started, the exhaust was routed through this box, into which the 4 × 5″ *curku* was fed. Once ignited, the *curku* fumes were recycled back to the generator, which pumped gas to the engine. For the rest of the day, until they returned overnight, the lorries ran on *curku* gas.

When Eduard's firewood supply outstripped the demand, he asked a guard for some for the stove in the hut. The guard shrugged and walked away but, that evening, the bearded charge-hand waylaid him as he stacked the last *curku*.

'You can take some for the hut – as long as there's enough for the generators but only to start. After that, use shit.'

'Where do we get that?' asked Eduard.

'From the farms – there's a supply due any day now.'

And he was right. Several days later two cartloads arrived, horse-drawn, led by two boys, who remained silent throughout their visit.

They lit the stove that night, and the fumes hung heavy under the roof, sending several prisoners into the night, hawking and coughing and holding their chests. The mosquitoes left, but the bugs came out with the warmth, and climbed up the posts, and bit them. The charge-hand had given Eduard a small jug of paraffin to help the kindling, so he fetched several plates, poured paraffin in them, and put them under the beds.

Mazloff laughed.

'It won't work, you know.'

'Yes it will.'

'Never.'

That night the bugs bit less, but the next night, they had crawled up the posts to the ceiling and, as the hut warmed up, they dropped on the men – and they still bit them.

Winter faded into spring, then summer, and the snows slowly melted; the woods remained dank and inhospitable, and soon the prisoners were visited with coughs and colds and sundry minor infections. One or two asthmatics were relegated to the hut, when the guards realised they were slowing production. The rest were told to 'get on with it'.

By mid-summer, the need for *curku* was less, and Eduard was reassigned to logging proper, except for one day each week. Often their squad was unguarded, and after three days working unsupervised, Wolski drew Eduard to one side.

'It's about time we do something.'

'Do something? Do what?'

'Escape.'

'How?'

Wolski dropped his axe, waited until they were unseen, and led the way into the wood. Turning abruptly off the narrow path, he plunged through some thin undergrowth, then stopped and pointed. Eduard saw a neat pile of timber.

'What's that for?'

'A raft.'

'A what?'

'A raft. Let's build a raft.'

'Have you told the others?'

'Not yet, but Mazloff's probably guessed. He knows I slide off every day.'

There was a rustle behind them, and they froze.

'Quite right. I've followed you once or twice anyway.'

'Why the hell didn't you say?'

'Didn't want to spoil your little surprise.'

Behind Mazloff, Vatek stood, grinning.

'You've been pretty obvious, you know.'

'I'll be buggered.'

Wolski patted the timbers.

'Well? What do you think?'

Mazloff pondered.

'How do we get it to the river?'

Wolski rubbed his sleeve across the timber.

'We can make a sled, and drag it there.'

'Hmmm.'

Eduard turned.

'We don't know how to make a raft.'

Wolski laughed.

'Of course we do. I'm a builder, aren't I? I started as a carpenter, and I've not forgotten my trade. No problem.'

So they started on the great project, an hour a day, two at a time, only when the guards were absent, and without telling any of the others.

The first escape was in hand.

54

Mazloff suggested they move the timbers – nearer the camp.

'But the guards will find it,' protested Wolski.

Mazloff tried to insist and, for the first time since they had joined forces, he and the other three Poles fell out. He stumped off, back to the work squad, while Wolski, Vatek and Eduard sat around on the timbers, worrying.

'He's mad,' said Vatek. 'If we move the wood, they'll not only find it, we'll never get away to build the bloody thing.'

Eduard kept quiet; let the older pair fight it out. Eventually Wolski got up.

'I'm going to find him. He's got to realise this time he is wrong.'

Vatek: 'Good luck, but Mazloff is never wrong.'

'I know...'

They sat, waiting. After an hour, Vatek was restless. He started pacing round the timber.

'Where the hell is he?'

Then he picked up his axe and threw it at a tree. He missed.

'Sod it!'

Eduard said nothing, just sat, whittling at a *curku*.

After another ten minutes, Vatek slung the axe over his shoulder.

'I'm going back. Coming?'

Eduard shook his head.

'Up to you, then. I'm going.'

Vatek disappeared through the trees and Eduard was left alone with the timber, the genesis of an escape. As he sat, he imagined the raft, the cross-bound timbers, roughly shaped planks lashed across them, the four of them balanced on each side, paddling against the current, and suddenly he realised the difficulties they faced. Apart from leaving the working party together or separately, they had to find the tools and materials to more than cut wood – to lash and nail and caulk and fasten and weight and on top of that, they would need food, drink, warm clothing, and how far were they to go before they were free?

The whole enterprise was adrift with uncertainties. If they went north, with the current, they would risk freezing to death as they travelled through the tundra to the Arctic. Eduard stood and kicked at the leaves. This was ridiculous. They could not possibly float north. They would have to go south – and that was the way they had come. And that way were boats, and soldiers, and towns, and capture.

It was then that Eduard realised the raft was a dream, a mental escape, but not a reality. They would make the raft, because it would give them a purpose; they would even perhaps drag it to the river. They might even launch it but they would never actually use it, they would never go anywhere on it, they would not escape – not that way.

That was when he realised why Mazloff wanted to shift the timbers nearer the camp – so they could slip out in the evenings, and sit by the raft, and dream – of an escape that could never be.

Eduard collected his axe and set off for the work squad. There he found Vatek and Wolski piling logs on the cart, and no Mazloff. In answer to his unasked question, Wolski muttered, 'He's gone off in a sulk. Won't speak to us.'

Later, when they had returned to camp, and eaten, Eduard sought out Mazloff.

'I know what you're going to say – so don't trouble yourself.'

Eduard waited, saying nothing. Mazloff sucked his pipe.

'Come with me.'

They walked off, beyond the hut, past the cabin, down the path to the shed. Mazloff walked straight past the shed, the office and the log pile. Eduard followed him through the woods, until they came to a small clearing. Mazloff pointed.

There was a makeshift shelter – some logs laid at an angle to a tree, nailed roughly together to form a triangular wall. Underneath this was some brushwood, and Mazloff stooped below the shelter and scuffed about in the brush, straightening up with a pitcher in one hand and two knives in the other.

'Where—'

Mazloff shook his head.

'Don't ask. Just say I found them, liberated them.'

'Is this where you want the raft built?'

Mazloff sat down, and indicated the log beside him. Eduard perched on it.

'Young Eduard – though you are not so young now, are you? – you know just as well as I do that the silly raft will never be built or,' and he smiled as he saw Eduard shake his head, 'it may be built,' and the emphasis was on 'built' as he added, 'but it will never be launched, or go anywhere, because there's nowhere for it to go.'

He looked away, and then sharply returned his gaze to his companion.

'There's no escape.' He paused. 'Not that way, anyway.'

'I know,' Eduard answered softly.

Mazloff smiled again, and leant over, patting Eduard on the knee.

'I know you know.'

He added, 'Because you are a thinking young man, aren't you? There really isn't any escaping, when you consider the options – only in the mind.'

Eduard looked at him, and weighed up the options.

'The river is not necessarily the answer.'

'Aha! Now you are a thinking young man.' Mazloff took his pipe out of his mouth and waved it all around them.

'The lorries? Never get them away without waking the guards. The river's useless, because it's too cold, too open, and runs the wrong way. Which leaves the railway.' He looked at Eduard. 'But first you have to reach the railway.'

Eduard looked blankly at him. Mazloff shrugged.

'No, I don't know either – yet – but I do know one thing; we can't all escape together. It's impractical. And I'm too old to start running. Your best bet is yourself. Vatek and Wolski are strong, and probably brave enough. But not necessarily supple enough – in the mind. You need to be flexible, to avoid preconceptions, to adapt, exploit, improvise.'

He leant forward and put his hand gently on Eduard's.

'You can make it – on your own.'

He straightened up.

'I don't know how, or when, but you can.'

He gestured towards the pitcher, knives, the shelter.

'If we make the raft here, you will have somewhere to come, without raising suspicions with the others, somewhere where there will be those things you might need.'

He stood up and turned again to Eduard.

'And meanwhile, we can all dream, and build our lovely raft, and thus escape from the realities of this place, if not the place itself.'

And he walked off.

Over the next few weeks, they moved the timbers to the new site, and set to work building their raft, whenever two or three of them could drift away from the work squad without attracting attention. When they had to work, they made sure they produced more than their fair share of logs, so that no-one could complain they were not doing their share of the work, and the guards, on the rare occasions when they joined the squad, would not suspect.

As the summer waned, the squad was split again. One morning, the charge-hand called twelve of them together.

'There is a new consignment.'

They looked at him, uncomprehending.

'Consignment. People. More mouths to feed, bodies to house.'

So what? More people, more captives? What difference did that make?

'We shall need another hut. You will build it.'

And that is what they did for the rest of that month, before the snows came and the new captives. Then they were set to work, to build huts for the next 'consignment', and the routine reverted to logging, and building the raft, talking plans, planning escape, all the time Mazloff contributing his share of the physical labour, but nothing to the increasingly imaginative scenario, which saw them all paddling down the river to freedom.

Sometimes, some of the others would sense there was a scheme afoot, and they would question Eduard. Never Vatek, because he was too brusque, or Wolski, because he was feared, but Eduard, because he was the young one. Eduard said little, and certainly nothing to fatten their suspicions. Instead, he told them their fortunes.

GAMES OF CHANCE

It was the Rumanians who started it. One of them came over to Eduard and showed him a photo of his wife and children. The cracked and creased image was quite clear, where the corner had not been torn off, and the crease had not cracked the glaze. A smiling woman with her arms akimbo, two small boys, flat-faced, unsmiling, one with his face slightly turned away, as if he feared the flash bulb. There was an ornate chair in the background, and all three subjects were dressed in some style. Clearly this was a family of some means.

Eduard pointed at the chair and asked, though it must have sounded as if he was making a statement: 'Your father's chair.'

The Rumanian snatched back the picture, and stuffed it inside his tunic, backing away, then stumbling back to his bunk. Three or four of his compatriots gathered round, and they all started talking at once. As suddenly, they fell silent, and turned to look at Eduard. The photo-father hesitated, then walked slowly back.

'You have the gift?' Eduard must have looked puzzled, for he added, 'The gift of second sight.'

Wolski snorted and muttered, 'Agree with him; they're a difficult bunch. Best not to disagree. Might lead to trouble.'

'Yes, of course,' agreed Eduard.

The Rumanian shuffled forward, and offered him the picture again. Eduard took it.

'Well?' asked the man.

'Well, what?' asked Eduard.

'What can you see?'

He pointed at the photo.

'In the picture. What can you see? The future – what does it say?'

Wolski: 'He thinks you can see his fortune in the picture. Come on, let's have some fun. Make something up.'

'You just told me to agree, not lie – you said they're difficult. This could mean trouble.'

'Don't be bloody stupid. It'll mean trouble anyway, if you don't do something. Say something. Anything. Tell him he's going home – one day. Anything. But be quick about it. He's beginning to look anxious.'

It was true. The Rumanian was jabbing the picture in Eduard's hand.

'What does it say?'

Eduard thought: what's the harm? Let's try to make him happy. He looked hard at the photo, sitting down slowly on the nearest bunk.

'Watch it,' said its occupant as he shifted across to make some room.

'Sorry,' muttered Eduard.

'Sorry? What for? What is wrong? Is there going to be a death?'

The Rumanian was now on his knees, clutching Eduard's hands.

'Tell me. What is the worst thing you see?'

Eduard put the picture on the bunk, crossed his hands, almost in an attitude of prayer.

'We-ell, I can see a long journey, and one of the boys—'

'Yes?'

'One of the boys is out in the town, speaking.'

'Ah, that's Balint. He'll always speak to anyone.'

'Yes, well. Balint, he is speaking to a crowd. He is telling them the war is over. He is telling them his father will return. Yes, he is definitely telling them his father will be back. One day. A long time away, but one day.'

'Oh God bless you, for this is God's will. Thank you.'

The Rumanian took the picture, then put his hand on Eduard's.

'You have the gift. You are a giving person. Thank you.'

The Rumanian returned to his bunk, foraged for a moment, then came back to Eduard, and pressed some bread into his hands.

'For you. For the future.'

And so it was that Eduard rapidly became the hut's crystal ball – for the Rumanians and the Hungarians, if no-one else. He would look at family photos, pictures of loved ones, of sweethearts, sons, mistresses even, and prognosticate, not to say pontificate, usually in the vaguest possible terms, and certainly on a long time scale, about their future good fortune, except where he saw an ageing face, or an ancient stick, or a diseased limb, when he would adopt a mournful expression, a properly saddened, not to say contrite face, as if it were somehow his fault and responsibility, and then he would forecast comparative calamity.

In time, he essayed death for the most obviously decrepit relatives, though he was careful to confine himself to generalities, and non-specific causes, while studiously refusing to put a date on the day of disaster, explaining that that was to risk a pre-emptive strike by the Almighty, whose prerogative it was to determine the diary of death's visitations.

When one day faced with a picture of his supplicant, he refused point blank to forecast the man's destiny, on the grounds that he would run the risk of sharing his death by association, and that in any case, he preferred not to even guess at the future of any of his friends, lest the burden of what he might discover be too much for his own sensibilities. The Rumanians, far from seeing this for the painfully obvious excuse that it was, praised him for his sensitivity.

Every day Eduard sat down to his fortune-telling, and every day he was 200 grammes richer in bread, for that became the staple fee for his time and his gifts.

Every day the log piles grew. Each pile was four cubic metres. Each pile was stamped with the day date, with a special hammer on the final log. The security guards stamped them and one day Eduard walked down the ranks of log piles, until he came to another path. It ran for about 30 metres, and then opened out to another clearing, larger than the working site, larger than the storage area he had just left.

Here were endless piles of logs, all date stamped, many of the logs rotting. He walked for over a hundred metres, until the piles were crumbling, and stooped down, and looked at the remnants of a log where the date stamp was particularly deeply indented, and had survived the rot. The date was initially indecipherable. Eduard pulled out his knife, and gently cleared the damp fragments away. As the date emerged, he looked at it more closely, unbelieving. The year was 1916 – in the Czar's time. The camp had been in existence for over twenty years.

Back at the worksite, he told Mazloff what he had found.

'Doesn't surprise me at all,' was his gruff response. 'This is not a productive place. It is designed to destroy us. This is simply hard labour, bad food, and death. You'll see.'

The first deaths came after the first month.

One of the Hungarians was found in the morning, stiff with *rigor mortis*. Four of his fellows were detailed to take him into the woods and bury him. No formality, no records, no ceremony.

'Just bury him.'

Within weeks, this became the norm. Death, burial party, bushes, unmarked grave. Some of the prisoners started fashioning crosses, so that there could be an impromptu 'service' and a cross planted at the head of each burial mound. The guards showed no interest. One more death meant one less problem. What the prisoners did about it was not their concern.

They were presiding over slow genocide, of Rumanians and Hungarians, and Poles. Eduard wondered what had happened to those other nationalities who were on the train to Omsk. Mazloff enlightened him.

'They have a fast way with the Belorussians and Bulgarians. They just kill 'em. With us it's different. They are afraid of the Poles. They are afraid of our superior civilisation. After all, we had the first university in Europe after the Czechs. Us they kill slowly.'

Eduard called it 'the lingering way', as more and more fell victim to malnutrition, to scurvy and dysentery, when the camp supply ran out and they forgot to boil the marsh water.

Death accelerated when prisoners were punished. Punishment was simple. Anyone failing to produce his quota of logs was denied food. Without food, strength sapped, a prisoner could not produce enough wood. So he went without food again.

Once the carted cow dung was exhausted, there was nothing left to burn. First one, then another, then several of the fitter prisoners developed colds. The workforce diminished until it became obvious the work rate was well below par. The guards became short-tempered, and there were sporadic outbursts of mumbled anger from the remaining captives.

The charge-hand appeared at the worksite.

'Not enough logs. Food will be less. Work harder.'

As he spoke, one of the older academics suddenly slipped to his knees, swayed for a moment, then collapsed.

'What the hell's wrong with him?'

A guard roughly grabbed the man's arm, and tried to haul him upright. When he let go, the man fell back, unconscious. Eduard was on the reduced roster, in an attempt to restore production. He stepped forward, pulled the man into a sitting position, and dragged him to a tree, propping him against the trunk.

The charge-hand walked over.

'What's wrong with him?'

'He's old and he's weak, because he hasn't been sleeping, because it's too cold, and the fires have gone out.'

'So? Why don't you keep them going?'

'Because there's no fuel. We've run out of cow shit.'

The charge-hand nodded slowly, prodded the academic with his boot, then turned, shouting at the guards.

'Take him back to camp. Use *curku*. Feed their stove.'

Turning to Eduard: 'We'll get some cattle and make our own bloody shit.'

And so it was. Within days, cows were safely grazing on the swampy grass beyond the camp. A detail was ordered to collect dung and pile it under the lean-to by the toolshed, turning it daily to ensure it dried quickly, and then barrowing it to the hut.

The incident brought other benefits. The work squad was ordered to split logs, and ram the half logs into the hut floor, providing a ready-made dry surface. They gathered moss, dried it, and spread it on the floor – a natural carpet. One guard showed the inmates how to exploit birch bark for lighting – using the resinous tar in small enamelled containers, crude pots from the eastern settlements whence the guards came. When water was short, marsh water was collected in buckets, then boiled. Best of all, the supplies from Tara increased, horsed carts hauling supplies of bread, though little else. As one guard said, 'There's plenty to eat – bread and bread.'

To compensate, sugar was extracted by boiling aspen bark, and Vatek scrounged some wire, when Wolski reported a rabbit run near the raft hide. Within days, there were rabbits to bake on the stove – wisely, Mazloff took the first two to the charge-hand, to share with the guards.

In the forest, they found fungi and berries, but no-one knew which were safe and which fatal, until a guard offered Eduard a handful of 'black berries' – a grape-like fungus, which grew six inches in height from the leafmould.

61

'Good with bear steak,' he laughed.

The guards shared little else, least of all the product of their hunting forays. Armed with simple shotguns, fashioned from piping, and primed with pellets made by shaving and chipping the lead from Army-issue bullets, they hunted the brown bear. Sometimes, they took favoured prisoners to beat the underbrush and drive the beasts towards the guns.

Eduard was asked to beat, and told, 'If you hear one, stand still. They won't attack if you don't move.' Only once did he see one; it came close, crashing and smashing its way through the scrub and grasses beneath the trees, blundering its way past, and away from the guns.

Bear hunters came to the camp, Tatars, from the northern steppes, compact, broad, olive-skinned men with folded almond eyes, weathered, with quilted coats and thonged leggings, furred hoods and mittens, and a knowledge of bears. For them, there were no guns, and no need for guns. They hunted their quarry with ball and chain.

The chain was rust-brown, nearly three feet long, a ring at one end, a steel ball at the other, short harpoons embedded in its entrails. They tracked the bear by night and, as the slow sun slanted through the trees, stalked him to a clearing, flanking him left and right. As the bear lunged towards the hunter, he threw the ball, the bear grabbed it, impaled himself, and could not release it. Within minutes the animal slowed, staggered, and sank to the ground. The Tatars would encircle him, wait until his strength was sufficiently sapped, then move in with knives, the long knife for the *coup de grâce*, the short to slit the animal's belly, from genital to throat.

Eduard was bored. The endless vista of woods and swamp and grass depressed him. The dreary routine sapped his mind. He looked for other work. Wolski had been sent to the river to float great rafts of logs downstream, hard and soft wood together, criss-crossed on top of one another, and had returned, even more enthusiastic for their raft, their escape. The months passed as gradually it took shape.

He was tidying the *curku* one morning when a Russian appeared.

'Who can sharpen the saws?'

Each team was equipped every day with axes and saws, and inevitably, the teeth became blurred, the edges blunted, the blades unseated. Eduard volunteered.

'I can.'

He was taken to the clearing, and into the concrete cabin, a workshop. There was a workbench, a cylinder attached to a crude set of pulleys, and several whetstones.

'Set them for seven o'clock.' It was five in the morning.

By eight two Russian guards were back.

'What the bloody hell're you doing?'

The saws would not work for they were incorrectly set. One guard left and the other ripped a blade from Eduard.

'Look at this – useless!'

Eduard: 'Sorry. I know nothing about it. I just wanted to try something different.'

The guard looked at him, then laughed.

'Fool! I show you how to do it.'

He was good at it, and Eduard learnt fast. Each day after that for the rest of that week he sharpened saws. Often it only took an hour and a half, so he took the rest of the day off. He gained little privileges. One was a coat like those the guards wore – a cast-off, but still a coat.

It was 'special issue for Siberia' – a duffle coat made of inch-wide quilted segments, machined like sausages half an inch apart. Weeks later he acquired a muff cap of the same material. Then he obtained leggings made of half-inch compressed felt, in the shape of knee-length boots, without soles, but with winding wrappers, in lieu of socks.

The nights were now shorter – an hour and a half – and sleep was hard to find. When the saws were all sharpened, Eduard found himself back on the logging roster. The work was unremitting. As one guard said, 'You will keep living, but you won't want to fuck.' And he was right.

When the women came to the camp, and another hut was built, Eduard visited them. Some had daughters. When whole families came, they were all shifted round, to allow the families to live together. One mother and daughter, Bessarabians, befriended Eduard, and together they played cards, flirted a little, but it went no further.

'You will keep living, but you will not want to fuck.' He was right. In two whole years, there were no babies born in Camp Tara.

Mind you, you can tell people anything, and they will believe it, if they want to, and if the evidence seems incontrovertible, whether it is to their advantage or otherwise. You can tell them with an implicit threat, daring them to think or wish otherwise, or you can tell them with a smile, and a card in your hand.

You can tell people anything, and then correct it by extracting the other side from their reactions, so that it corresponds to their beliefs and expectations. Now that I cannot tell anyone anything, I remember how I romanced those Rumanians for 200 grammes of bread. Children are good at invention – they have less inhibition, their imaginations less fettered, and they instinctively know just how far to go.

I was no different. I had always been adept at persuading my little mother of my innocence and, so long as I was not angling for advantage over others, which was anathema to our family anyway, I could get away with all sorts of nonsense, from riding her horses to eating her plums, wearing her scarves or 'telling' the tarot.

It was the tarot which taught me the lessons of card conviction. The Death card was the ace. You could always tell when adults were worried, when Death turned up – if their eyes fluttered, their hands trembled, however slightly, and they shifted about, crossing their legs, or tapping their feet, or suggesting it was all a lot of nonsense anyway.

The moment Death appeared, you looked for the vulnerable one, and concentrated on him or her and, depending upon whether or not you liked your 'victim', you could unseat their anxieties even further and corrode their confidence, or mend their mental fences for them and throw veils of illusion across their worried minds.

Children are the very devil when it comes to adult anxiety. They feed off it, turn it to comfortable convenience, rattle it about, open it up, slide along its paths until they are insinuate within the very core of their subject's concerns. Then they can make everything alright by a sweet word, a soft look or a simple touch.

Of course, Rosalia knew perfectly well what I was about even as I went about it, whereas my ponderous papa was unreached by any tricks of mine and simply ignored my games of chance until and unless I overstepped the mark, and upset somebody, but I rarely made that mistake, because in truth I did not enjoy causing real distress, just a frisson of fear.

In all of this I was no different from most of my friends, for we all tested one another with simple synapses of terror – the shadows between the trees, the rustles in the grasses, the moon on the scree, all these were turned to good effect by any one of us to extend the imaginative corners of our friends' minds, so they came face to face with their own tiny tremors of delightful fright.

I was as often the victim as the perpetrator so that, when I was at home, the family round the table, and perhaps a cousin or two with aunt and uncle, friends of my father, or even a visiting railwayman come to talk of tomorrow's trains, I would let someone else suggest the tarot, and then portentously examine my fate.

What they never realised was that I knew the tarot was card-thick – or thin – that there was nothing on the other side except the printed pattern, no surprises in the card turn, no glimpse into past or future, no magical mysteries in the conjunction of card and player. It was just a game.

They, on the other hand, cluttered with their lived lives, memories and beliefs, failures and fears, losses and limitations, half believed, and only needed a small shove to send them spinning into the tarot's fantasy of predestination and absolutes. You only had to say something vaguely sinister and sufficiently general for the subject to murmur, 'Oh yes, yes, I knew that would happen,' or pronounce a fairly obvious fact for someone else to compound the séance of superstition with, 'Ah this is true, so true.'

It was such fun pulling the adults' legs, when they were looking to be pulled. The trick was not to pull too far, not to cause too much foreboding, because that could turn to real fear, revulsion and reaction, and that would be when papa would start fingering his belt.

So I learnt the balance of probability in prediction, by the balance between acceptance and disbelief on people's faces. The real gift is to read your subject's eyes, hands, bodies. That is what tells you the proper facts, and their probable destinies. You are helped rather than guided by the ephemera of their lives.

Families are easy – you know all about them, except perhaps those darker secrets of the past, which are not the business of the fortune-teller except insofar as they may be extracted by diligent and seemingly innocuous questioning, and then resurfaced and offered anew as fresh facts, newly discovered, to entrench your subject's belief in all your powers – something that pre-exists by very definition as soon as someone asks someone else to tell the tarot.

That is why I would not now attempt the cards, even by myself. I know they will only tell me what I know to fear, or fear to know – they are a self-fulfilling means to punishment, extracting existing sadness and eliminating enlightenment.

It is just a game, like the one I play inside my murdered mind – one day my mouth will open and words will out. I do not need a Death card to tell me that is just an illusion. And I do not need any card to talk to me of love, for that I have in abundance.

A BLOODY BUSINESS

In the woods behind the clearing, the raft grew. After five months it was complete. There began the endless discussions about how to get it to the river, and then, how to make best use of it. As Mazloff explained, 'It will only go at three or four miles an hour, and it's 400 miles to Omsk – upriver. You'll never make it.'

Wolski disagreed.

'Of course we will. And anyway, what do you mean "You'll never make it"? I thought we were all four going together?'

Mazloff looked at him.

'You know my views. You've always known my views. I'm too old.'

And with that, he stumped off.

'Silly old fool,' grumbled Wolski.

'No, he's right.'

Vatek leant against the nearest tree.

'He is too old and he's being very good to say so.'

Wolski was unconvinced.

'We need him. He knows the way, and besides, he's full of ideas. He could be the saving of us if we run into any trouble.'

Vatek cleared his throat, hawked, and spat into the undergrowth.

'Well, he's not coming, so we'll just have to manage.'

And it was the same the next time they met. And the next. The discussion would circle the route, the means, the problem with Mazloff, and the seemingly insurmountable difficulties of paddling the raft 400 miles without being seen.

The raft itself was made of softwood, the ends notched to interleave in the form of an X, just as the walls of the huts they had built for the newcomers. Made in sections, it comprised two main structures – the timber floor and the cross-members, strutted apart to form pontoons. It was of a size that would fit on a cart, always assuming they could purloin a cart.

The problem was not the raft, or even the transport. It was the ride upriver in what would have to be dressed up to look 'normal', a floating accompaniment to the logjams moving to the mills. Otherwise they would face the daunting task of drifting the raft downriver, to the open sea – and that meant the summer, but the summer only lasted a mere three months, and three months would not be long enough. So upriver it had to be.

They discussed every aspect of the journey. Food – trapping game in the forest, catching fish in the river, but lifting provisions before their departure; drink – boiling river water; security – travelling overnight, without compass or maps, avoiding lights, whether of other vessels or settlements; the journey from camp to river, with raft and cart, risking discovery in their absence before they could make waterfall – waiting till guards were cabined and captives asleep, but not so long as to waste those precious hours of night.

Eduard remembered his father's stories of the first world war, when he too was a prisoner of war. He had escaped – he and one other, in rags. They had walked across marshes, the turf frozen, water trapped beneath. Jozef knew something about soil, water and chemical reactions. When he and his companion first stepped off the frozen turf onto clear, frozen water, it was only the shimmer of ice that warned him. He stopped, but his companion did not.

The ice cracked behind him, he tried to retreat, and it gave way. Jozef watched him slip slowly through the fractured surface, into the warmer water below. He could do nothing. The other man sank in silence, more surprised than fearful, and Jozef stood still, made the sign of the cross, prayed silently, then moved on, treading softly across the solid sheet of water waste back onto frozen turf again. He survived, returned to the Army, and served throughout the last few months of war in 1918.

Eduard remembered and he knew that he too could escape – if his father could do it, so could he – yet he had little faith in the raft. It was as if they were like his father's companion – stepping on uncertain waters – and Eduard reminded himself of one other fact: his father was older, wiser and altogether more experienced. They would make the raft, but not the attempt.

It was during one of these interminable discussions, early one morning, that second summer, when Mazloff suddenly appeared, showing signs of uncharacteristic agitation.

'You'd better come back to the hut, now.'

'What's the problem?'

'AKWD.'

Vatek stiffened, and Wolski got up off his knees.

'AKWD? Here?'

'Yes. AKWD. Here.'

They abandoned the raft and walked swiftly back to the hut. The Rumanians were sitting silently, the Hungarians huddled at one end, talking softly, everyone clearly concerned. Eduard was resting, recovering, just back from Tara. The charge-hand appeared at the door...

The wound was an accident, a pure accident. Eduard was still cutting *curku*, chopping the already sized segments of log to the required four inches, when the axe slipped. One minute he was raising the axe, sweeping it down, kicking the severed section away, raising it yet again, and swinging it down, a rhythmic pattern he had perfected over the weeks. The next, hesitating for a second, as his foot snagged on the log, the axe came down and slid into his foot, deep, crushing bone, a five-inch gash. It was his right foot, just at that moment when it was ahead of him as he kicked to the left and away, to shunt the section forward, before he stepped sideways for the next slice. He had raised the axe on its next swing before he realised what had happened. Then he felt the throb, the precursor to pain, glanced down, and saw the blood trickle from the side of his makeshift boot onto the still frost-glazed leaves.

He dropped the axe, and knelt, pressing the boot. That was when the pain came. He let out an involuntary cry, then tightened his muscles, clamped shut his mouth, and sat down, slowly, carefully, drawing his knee up, and clutching his wounded foot.

He was at least two miles from the camp. There was no-one working with him. He was alone, isolated, without help, and with no means to staunch the blood. He thought of removing the boot, then realised this would only open the wound. Instead, he tore at the rags wound round his neck for warmth, twisting them together, and then winding them round his calf as a temporary tourniquet. It was only a foot wound he reasoned, but common sense told him it was also only a matter of time before it would be infected. It was also a matter of time before the tourniquet would so reduce the blood flow that he might not be able to walk. Two miles.

He had to move, and move as quickly as he could, notwithstanding the pain, and the bleeding. He started off, then stopped. The axe. The shaft would act as a prop, a crude crutch. As so often happens in crisis, he found the strength to smash the axe head off the shaft with one massive swipe of the flat side of the tool against the nearest tree trunk. The wood splintered and the metal blade sagged. Two more swings, and it fell to the ground. Eduard started walking, limping, staggering, down the path, towards the camp.

The first hundred yards were enough. He slipped to a halt, leant against the nearest tree, and then slid to the ground, the axe shaft beside him. His eyes blurred, he felt drowsy, they closed, he slept. Minutes passed.

Vaguely he heard it. A sibilant rustle, then silence, then another, and another. The third roused him, his eyes open, still blurred, watering. He felt beside him, fingers fumbling in the leaves, his thumb blunt against the hard wood, then his hand curled round the shaft, as he shook his head, wiped the tears away with his free hand, and peered ahead.

Nothing. Then the rustle again, like a stealthy whisper of leaves and twigs and fronds and grasses – and the familiar sucking sound of feet pulling free of the swampy undergrowth, suctioning out of the boggy ground. He pulled himself up the tree, standing awkwardly, his right foot limp, the blood, as he moved, welling through the boot again.

Then he heard it. The breathing. Not breathing – sniffing, snuffling, tasting the air, his blood's fumes carried delicately on the cold, silent atmosphere to whatever it was that paused and waited out of sight, in the muddle of saplings, grasses, thorny shrubs before him, beside and behind him.

The rustle became a rattle, the sniffing louder, the succulent slopping of paws and claws closer. Eduard held his body together in taut expectation, and shouted, 'Raus!' Why German and not Polish, or even Russian, he could not have explained, yet somehow, this was the word that rose out of his fears into his mind and onto his lips. 'Raus!'

The rustle slapped to a stop. The squelch subsided. The breathing faltered. Whatever it was had stopped, was stilled, considering the options. Eduard breathed quietly, deeply, then, with the strength that fear brings as adrenalin storms to the body's defence, he smashed the axe shaft against the tree, again and again, bawling, 'Raus! Raus! Raus!' and with a final, operatic Gotterdamerung 'RAUS!', launched himself onto the path, hopping, skipping, limping and jumping along, thudding the shaft to the ground, then slapping it against each tree as he developed a rhythm of sound and movement, as if he was cutting *curku* simply and solely to save his life – which he was.

Foot throbbing, blood seeping, shaft battered, lungs seething, eyes dry, hot and fierce, he surged into the camp, to the charge-hand's hut, through the door, and fell, heart pumping, against the table, the axe shaft clattering to the floor beside him.

'What the hell?'

'It was a bear, I know it, was, a bear. . .' Eduard sagged.

The charge-hand jumped up, leapt round the table, looked at Eduard, then down at his foot.

'Jesus Christ.'

He knelt, and took the makeshift boot in both hands, and pulled.

'Christ. We'll have to bandage that.'

Eduard nodded, and slid down onto the floor, his back against the table leg, his eyes closed, and his face pallid and streaked with sweat.

'Looks more like an axe wound to me.'

Swiftly the charge-hand unlaced his own jackboots, and heaved them off. Underneath he wore no socks, but wrappers, like puttees, wound round and round his stocky legs. Cursing and sweating and snorting, he rapidly unwound first right, then left leg, the wrappers curling across each other as he discarded them, piece by piece.

Weakly, Eduard tried to explain.

'A bear, the blood, cut it. . .' but it was too much effort, so he stopped.

The charge-hand gathered up the coarse cloth, and squatted between Eduard's legs, tightly winding piece by piece under and over, across, round the ankle, and under and over again, encasing the wounded foot in a dark brown shroud.

There was no disinfectant, no ointment, no medication of any kind, but the bleeding was stifled, and Eduard opened his eyes. His breathing had steadied, but he looked down and noticed his right hand was shaking. He scrabbled about on the floor until he found the axe shaft, and gripped it. The tremor slowed its beat, shuddered, and stopped.

The charge-hand sat back on his heels, and contemplated his handiwork.

'No way you can work.'

He added, 'And next time you go down to the woods, remember the bears,' or that's what Eduard thought he said.

He straightened, heaving himself up onto the bench, then the table, and sat there, his legs crossed at the ankles, grimed with dirt, and gently swinging back and forth. After a moment, he smiled.

'No. You certainly cannot work, so it's good you have cut enough *curku*.'

He reached down, hefted his boots, and pulled them on, then slid off the table and stood over Eduard, looking down at him with an almost fond, conspiratorial grimace.

'Tomorrow morning. That's when.'

He walked towards the door.

'Go now. Take the handle. Eat. Sleep.'

As Eduard hobbled through the door, leaning heavily on the axe shaft, the charge-hand put his hand on his shoulder. Eduard looked at him, their eyes holding.

'I shall take you to Tara, to a nurse, and have you attended.'

He pushed Eduard out, gently, and closed the door.

Eduard stayed in the hut with the sick and dying when the work squads formed up the next morning. He felt sick himself, and slightly faint. The bleeding had clearly ceased, for there were no stains on the cloth wrapping, but his foot throbbed and, when he tentatively slid off his bunk, pain seared his tendons, and clawed up his calf muscle, so that he sat back down again, quickly and heavily.

The axe shaft lay beside him and, after a few moments of sweating, breathing hard, and steeling himself to combat the pain, it seemed to reduce to a series of throbs and smaller slivers of agony each time he moved. He reached down for the makeshift crutch, and tried again. As he leant against the bunks, and took a first, hesitant step, the doorway darkened.

'I see you are ready then.'

The charge-hand stepped inside, and gestured.

'Come then. We must go to Tara. Now.'

Eduard shuffled across the hut floor. The charge-hand stood aside as he reached the doorway. Clearly his humanitarian instincts had stopped Eduard's bleeding, and perhaps saved his life, but his status precluded any helping hand for the halt and maimed. Aid he would give, but not support. You might be saved, but you made your own way after that.

Eduard followed him to the cart. It was two-wheeled, open, and drawn by a single horse. He hauled himself onto the open back, and slithered to the front, leaning against the backboard, above which the charge-hand now sat. He looked down at Eduard, nodded, turned, then flicked the reins, and they set off.

There was no discernible track; only the rough, meandering clearway through the woods. From time to time they stopped, as the charge-hand clipped open a hand-held compass, consulted it, and adjusted their direction. After a mile or so, Eduard fell fitfully asleep, the throbbing settling into a percussive resonance with the horse's hooves.

Morning gave way to noon and, halfway through the afternoon, the woods thinned, the trees gave way to scrub and grasses, and then open space. Scattered across the corrugated ground were shacks and hovels, wooden, some with tin rooves, an occasional chimney seeping smoke.

They stopped outside a small cabin, tidier than the rest, and the charge-hand jumped down. As he approached the cabin, the door opened, and a large woman, with a white apron, a pinafore over a dark green cloth dress, with heavy boots and her granite hair tied back in a bun, stood, hands tucked into the apron, her broad face shining with a cleanliness Eduard had not seen since he left Cjortkow.

'What's wrong with him?'

'He hurt his leg.'

The charge-hand beckoned. Eduard slid along the cart and swung his legs over the back, then hesitated.

'Come on. It won't kill you.'

Still he hesitated. The charge-hand strode across and grabbed his arm.

'Right. Jump! I'll catch you.'

Eduard half jumped, half fell off the cart and staggered as his wounded foot hit the ground. The other man held him up, and gripped him under the arm.

'Now walk. You're lucky to be alive. Show some gratitude.'

And to himself: 'Bloody Poles.'

The woman had disappeared inside the cabin as Eduard limped up the steps, still supported by the other man. He steadied himself against the doorjamb and the charge-hand released him.

'Right. That's that then. You're alright now.'

Eduard turned to go inside, and then turned back.

'I need – I think I need a doctor,' and he slipped down onto the step, his face a sodden yellow, sweat beading his upper lip and temples.

'Doctor? Doctor? You are a comedian, yes? There's no doctor here. She's our nurse and our doctor and our surgeon. This is our hospital.'

He looked down at Eduard, before stamping down the steps.

'You're lucky to be here at all. Others would have suffered, died, there, in the camp, in the hut. I don't know why the hell I brought you. You're lucky, so make the most of it.'

He climbed up on the cart, flicked the reins and, without another glance at Eduard, started back to camp.

Eduard sat there, foot beating louder than his heart in his imagining, his mind struggling with the implications. He was alone, away from the camp – no guards, no bonds, no reason to stay here an instant longer than necessary. But then, it was necessary to stay here, to get help, to recover. But afterwards? Well, he would wait and see. Afterwards, perhaps escape – and freedom.

He pulled himself up by scrabbling up the doorjamb, and forced himself inside the cabin. The woman was standing beside a dull fire, damp wood spitting and glowing on a bed of ruddy ash, a table between her and him, and on the table a bowl of water, steam wisping off it in the still air.

Beside the bowl was a pile of clean, white cloth and sundry bottles, dark brown, crazed blue and milky white. Beside the table was a single chair, rough-hewn and high-seated.

She pointed at the chair.

'Sit.'

Eduard sank onto the waxed surface, and leant against the solid, diamond-shaped back.

'Give me your leg.'

He put both hands beneath his thigh and calf and lifted his leg up, as she took the bowl, and slowly lowered it to the floor. Then she pushed her sleeves back, and grasped his ankle. Eduard cried out. She looked at him without expression, and then began to unwind the wrappings.

One by one, the pieces of sodden cloth fell to the floor. The last piece was cemented to his foot by scabbed, congealed blood. The woman picked at the end of the grey, crystallised puttee. Each time she pulled, Eduard bit the inside of his mouth, determined not to cry out again. The bandage would not budge. She bent down and reached inside her boot. As she straightened, Eduard caught the gleam of the fire on a dull, flat tongue of metal. She placed the knife carefully on the table, its rusty brown bone handle towards him.

Then she picked a cloth off the pile by two corners, rotated it between her hands, loosely rolling it into a thick strand, and dunked it in the water. Then she slapped the rolled cloth across his foot, letting the ends dangle. She picked another cloth, rolled it, dunked it, slapped it on his foot. And another, rolled, dunked, slapped. The heavy cloths dripped on the floor.

The woman reached over and pulled the knife towards her, then dipped that in the bowl, shaking it clear of water as she lifted it, adjusted her hold, then, with her other hand, peeled away the sodden cloths, before prodding the swollen puttee with the tip of the blade. Eduard tensed. She glanced up at him, unsmiling.

'This will hurt,' she said, as she slid the blade beneath the blood-blotched mess, sharply twisting it and then heaving it towards her. Eduard felt his gorge rise, fought the rising nausea, failed, then held his breath, swallowed his bile, bit his tongue, and screamed despite

72

himself as the back of the blade bit into his flesh, into the wound, and the puttee fell away, severed neatly along its length.

She kicked the foul cloth to one side, and reached over for another piece of clean fabric, wiping the blade on her apron, and dropping the knife on the table with a quiet clatter. Gently, she pressed the cloth to the wound, and blood and lymphatic fluid seeped into and through it. That, too, dropped to the floor, as she leant back and inspected the wound.

'That's quite clean. The bone will heal. You are lucky.'

Eduard nodded, grunted, clenched his hands, the nails scoring furrows into his palms. He could taste the salty blood inside his mouth, where he had bitten through the linings of his cheeks.

They both regarded his foot for a while, as the blood oozed up, and then slowed, and settled into a sorbet over the clear-cut gash. The woman sucked her lip, then nodded to herself in decision, as she selected one of the bottles – dark brown, glittering darkly. It was then that Eduard began to realise what was different about this room and its occupant.

Everything was clean. The floor was speckless, the fireplace tidy, the table scrubbed pale cream and bleached white in the grain, the cloths stark white, the bottles glistening; the woman herself was spotless in her white apron and green dress, apart from pale rust patches on the well-worn fabric, her coarse, streaked grey hair drawn sharply back from her forehead, and clasped with a metal pinion, her hands ruddy with frequent washing. There was no disinfectant, no sterile instrument, but this was the cleanest place he had seen since he had left the house in Cjortkow – and possibly even cleaner than that.

He smiled at her, a careful, half-hearted, anxious smile. She did not smile back, but nodded quickly and put the bottle to her mouth. There was a soft plop as the cork pulled free, and she threw it in the still-steaming water.

'This will really hurt,' she warned, as she lifted another cloth onto the wound, pressed it down slowly, then peeled it back. Eduard felt little, thinking how needless was her warning, until the pain seared into his foot, leapt up through his leg and smashed into his chest, as he fought to regain his breath.

'Iodine.'

'Oh my God,' under his breath, as the pain ebbed, and his heart banged and thumped and reverberated in his ears. The red stain sank into the skin around the wound, and disappeared into the bloodwell.

'Again.'

She poured more of the red liquid into the wound, and it splashed onto the table.

'Ugh!' The woman reached into her apron and extracted another cloth, striding over to the sink, where she collected a slab of yellow grease. Pushing Eduard's foot to one side, she smeared the grease into

73

the table, and rammed the cloth onto the surface, raking it back and forth, lifting and turning it to examine the results, until the stain was excoriated from her tabletop. Then she threw the cloth onto the pile of discarded puttees and soiled swabs, and pulled his leg towards herself again. One by one she wound fresh cloths around his foot, until it was swathed and cocooned in white.

'Hold that,' she commanded him, pulling his hand across the table and putting it over his foot. Then she took the knife, plunged it into the water, wiped it again on her apron, and fumbled in the stitched pocket than ran across its front.

Out of this personal armoury came a length of twine, whiskery and waxed. Swiftly she turned this round the foot, pulling it tight as Eduard winced, then knotting it and severing the frayed ends.

'Right. You'll do.'

Eduard looked up at her, his mind disconnected. He wanted to say 'thank you' but something warned him this would be meaningless, so he simply nodded, gestured to his foot and wagged his head from side to side, as if to say 'Well, that was pretty stupid of me', heaving himself off the chair, and looking around him for the axe shaft.

'Here.' She shoved the shaped wood at him, and he shifted his weight onto his left foot, adjusting the shaft, as he started to hobble towards the doorway. He turned once to say something, but her back was turned, as she bustled about the table, clearing her equipment away, and tossing the soiled accumulation onto the fire.

Outside, the steps were a small hazard, and the roadway a greater obstacle course of loose scree, smooth-rimed ruts and occasionally embedded tussocks of straw and twig. He moved down them and along it slowly.

When the first stroke struck, there was a great deal of movement. Family and friends moved things, moved me and moved about, making connections, commendations and comment. Medical men and nice nurses bustled. There was much consultation and concurrence. Tablets and tapes, wires and widgets, swabs and swipes. In all of this I was frozen, a small justification for others' momentous movements. Not like Tara.

Speech was splattered, and hand closed; one leg lifeless and evacuation embarrassing. I decided, once I realised what had happened to me, that the best course was masterly inactivity while everyone else exhausted the possibilities of redemption on my behalf. I started to recover as soon as they deemed it probable that I would recover. I co-operated in their reasonable hopes and in their realistic prognostications. Their caring optimism was emotionally binding – one simply had to make their dreams come true. Once past that point, it was not difficult to become convinced that this was also enlightened self-interest.

Patients are best behaved when they are slightly behind the administering trend. It leaves room for improving thoughts and conspicuous care, especially for the properly concerned amateurs whose care is simply an extension of what they never knew they felt. Calamity personal equals opportunity public.

So I slowly got better, exactly as everyone wished. Wonderful! The difficulties came when I had the second stroke. That was a real disappointment to everyone, cause for some adjustment of prognosis, and the commencement of cautious pessimism. Everyone likes the cards stacked in the direction of likelihood, which means expecting less and competing in dire prediction. A bit like the tarot.

I suppose I first learnt the lessons of acceptance in Tara. I also learnt that there are natural carers, whose mission is the welfare of others but who are rarely self-consciously caring. They do what has to be done, treat of it as a necessary satisfaction of need. My clean lady of Tara was no angel of mercy, ministering to the poor Pole. She was a practical exponent of simple skills, providing a local service. Hers was a niche market in basic medicare.

Yet to accomplish a successful conclusion for fishermen's frostbite or woodman's wound, such a person must be possessed of that emotional flair for quiet compassion, a certain empathy, however well hidden or understated. At Tara, a young man understood what it is to be of service, to help when help is needed, and especially when it is perhaps unexpected, or even undeserved, without expectation of reward, whether by thanks or cash or kind. My good lady of Tara showed me the chalice of charity.

PASSPORT TO FREEDOM

Eduard stood silently, and glanced up and down the cleared path and across towards the river. The water was flat, hard and seemingly still, with small rushes of ripples towards the centre. The far bank merged with misted outlines of forest trees, the water beneath it black and lifeless. He limped towards the edge, and looked down at the slippery planks that bounded the Tara waterfront, the water slinking up to the unsighted piles, whispering gutturally as it slid round each timber.

Eduard shuddered. And that was the route to freedom. He turned back, and she was standing on the step, watching him. He stared back. Then she smiled. It was not a friendly smile, or a secret smile, but a smile of genuine humour. She was simply amused.

'So where do you think you're going?'

It was not a threatening question; there was no hidden meaning, simply the question. Eduard shrugged and limped back towards her, then paused.

'You'd better go to Viktor. He's expecting you.'

As Eduard thought carefully how to ask, she anticipated him. 'Third hut down there,' and she pointed towards the waterfront, past the landing stage, where a straggling outline of low buildings with steeply sloping rooves clustered together, backs turned away from the water. Eduard shuffled along, dragging his bad foot, trying to avoid scuffling it across the ground.

The huts were simple structures, with sturdy uprights, heavy halved logs across their bases, and rough-hewn lapped planks across their walls. They wore high hats, steeply eaved, and the landward walls were pierced with simple openings – shuttered windows and heavy planked doors. The rooves hung, deeply browed over the ends, and falling beneath the front and back walls by generous margins. They were simple homes, harshly built but strongly, to withstand the rigours of long winters.

Eduard lurched along to the third hovel, turned to check the woman's watching eyes, but she was gone. He turned back, and jumped, startled by the silent proximity of the fisherman. The man had stepped quietly down his steps, and stood within a yard of Eduard, contemplating him from within a forest of fibres. For a moment, Eduard's vision was of a tree come to life, until his eyes cleared, and he found himself looking straight into the cold, hard eyes of a man used to constantly scanning below the surface of the water.

The eyes were set between a thicket of whiskers. The loose, cold grey beard spread across the fisherman's chest, its tendrils climbing over his face, shrubbing his cheeks, the dense moustache hiding his mouth, only the mottled lavender nose visible below those shallow eyes. Viktor's hair was, by contrast, sparse, his pallid scalp streaking between faded old twigs of head hair, carefully oiled and set onto the skin. Viktor was old, squat, tough and dirty. His trousers were dankly colourless, a woollen shift hanging loosely over his midriff, its rolling collar high under his beard, the sleeves torn and stranded with loose threads round his thick, blunt-boned wrists.

He beckoned Eduard, and marched back into the hut. Inside Viktor sat down at the central table, a curtain off to one side, the essential log burning sullenly on its bed of glowing ash. His woman stood to one side, thin, old papery skin yellowed under a dull white headcap, her apron dusty with grime, her hands folded out of sight.

She nodded slightly as Eduard followed Viktor into their home. The fisherman pointed at the stool to his right. Eduard sat. There was a slight movement to his left. He glanced across, and saw the curtain tremble. As his hearing adjusted, he could make out a quiet busyness behind the curtain and a moment after, a younger woman appeared. She did not look directly at Eduard, but carried a bowl round the table, putting it before him.

'Eat!' commanded Viktor.

Eduard looked down. He had eaten nothing since the previous day's soup. He was suddenly aware of his hunger as he reached towards the plate. There before him, piled higher than he had ever seen them, was the most unwelcome and least likely food he could have imagined – a plate of *chotka*. With the river not more than six strides away, and a host who made his living from river fish, here he was, faced with the dried denizens of the oceans – the poor man's whiting. Nonetheless, hunger ruled. He set to, and did not pause until he had finished every morsel.

The girl appeared again, and took his plate, returning with a length of unleavened bread, fresh from the baking. Eduard fantasised about home – first salmon, then fresh cake – as he chewed his way through this unexpected gift.

At that point, Viktor reached into the pouch tied to his belt, and lifted a cloudy, pale green bottle to the juncture of beard and moustache and poured the contents down his gullet, his Adam's apple still, a small pulse alone signalling the continuous stream of liquid until, satisfied, he swallowed once, lowered the bottle, wiped his whiskers with his sleeve and proffered it to Eduard.

Eduard took the bottle, and tipped it to his lips. The scalding firewater burnt the bleeding, rawcut interior of his mouth as it coursed across his tongue, and into his throat, paralysing his muscles, anaesthetising his nerve-ends, and making him heave and heave and clutch for air, as he fell back and nearly off the stool. The bottle slipped from one hand as both reflexed to his neck, and he tried to find his breath.

The old man's hand darted forth and caught the bottle before it toppled over, as he laughed, and tipped it to his lips again. Throughout, the woman stood impassively, hands folded out of sight, eyes weakly averted, and the girl remained out of sight, behind the curtain.

When Eduard found his breath, and cautiously drew it down, past the scorched ravine that was his throat, he muttered his thanks. Viktor grunted, then waved vaguely overhead.

'You want to sleep?'

Eduard nodded.

'Follow me.'

The fisherman rose, and together they walked outside again, and round the side where, under the eaves, was a square opening reached by a rudimentary ladder made of lashed poles and branches. Eduard contemplated this further test of his reduced agility and was wondering how the hell he was going to get up it, when Viktor grabbed his arm, and pushed him towards it. He grasped the furthest rung he could reach and hauled himself up with his good leg balanced halfway and the damaged one hanging uselessly. By a series of jerks and lifts, he finally scrabbled across the threshold of the loft, and dragged himself inside.

It was surprisingly warm. As he adjusted his sight to the gloomy interior, he realised that a chimney broached the inner wall across most of its width. To one side was a heap of clean, new straw.

The air was quite still inside; there was the merest murmur from the chimney as the fire drew up within it, sucked into the cool air above. Eduard shuffled the straw around him, and pulled the shapeless smock over his head, rolled it up for a pillow, and relaxed. No work tomorrow, no roll call, no rota, no regimenting, no requirement to cut *curku*. Nothing.

No doubt the charge-hand would return, and he would be returned to camp. But now, nothing. Eduard turned onto his side to ease the throbbing in his foot, and wondered – how long? How long until his foot was healed, or healed enough to walk however many miles were necessary to vanquish camp, charge-hand, *curku* and captivity. Escape.

It was a possibility. He slept.

He dreamt of the river, and the raft, Vatek and Wolski swimming alongside, Mazloff running along the shore, waving, the fisherman forcing vodka down his throat as he sank lower and lower, through the logs, down into the water, Mazloff still laughing, his face distorted by the currents, and Vatek and Wolski swimming down beside him. Suddenly they surfaced, and the river was molten – a slithering mess of crumbling mud, slick and viscous, brown with red flecks of blood streaking the surface, exposed at the edges with mossy tendrils floating in depthless waters, and he was sliding and slipping into the mud, his mouth choking, his nose constricted, when a hand grasped his and pulled him towards the bank. He opened his eyes, and her face filled the door, her eyes inches away, fathomless, blank; flat, pale blue. She released his hand.

'Do you want to eat?'

Eduard felt his watch in his inside pocket, but decided to leave it there. She would steal it.

'What time is it?'

'Morning.'

He looked past her; she was sitting back on her heels, gazing at him. The sky was clear, the shadows soft and long on the yard. He guessed it was about six, the sun behind the hovel, on the river side of the track.

'Yes. I'll come down.'

She shook her head, as she knelt forward, and touched his cheek. He looked down at her hand, rough, raw, cold and hard. She smiled, dropped it and stood up, her hair falling over her face as she bent towards him. He lay there, as she looked at him.

'I'll bring you some food. Soon. Wait here.'

She put her hands on her waist, arched her back, shook her head, the strands of dark hair flung back either side, then turned, and stepped out onto the makeshift ladder, looking down as she sought her footing.

For an instant she paused, looked up, straight at him, and opened her mouth. Her tongue curved across the underside of her top lip, then withdrew as she pulled her lip back with her teeth, and disappeared. Eduard pulled his watch out; it said six o'clock.

He grabbed a handful of straw and rubbed it across his face, then scraped it between his hands, dusting the residue away with his smock before flailing that against a rafter. Then he sat against the chimney-breast and waited, contemplating the sky and the treeline and what he could see of the yard.

Ten minutes had passed, when he heard her shuffle in the yard, then on the ladder, and a moment later, her head appeared against the sky, then her hand, clutching a bowl.

'I'll take that,' as he knelt down, and she passed him the bowl, climbing into the loft, then pulling a cloth out of her belt, and a tin mug from her pocket. In the bowl was a pancake, soft and white and cold, fat with fish flakes and a mess of paste and pepper. Eduard ate without pause or ceremony, the cloth spread on his lap, the mug beside him.

She left him for a moment, then returned with a can, slopping with water, and a bottle, produced with a flourish from the folds of her dress. Eduard poured some water into the mug, but shook his head when she proffered the bottle.

She shrugged, pulled the stopper, and tipped it to her lips, pouring the contents down her throat like her fisherman father. She held it away for a moment, sucked in a deep breath, blew it out and drank again, then stoppered the bottle and laid it to one side. As Eduard ate and drank, she sat before him, watching. Eduard said nothing. He had nothing to say.

She was not much younger than him, probably about 14. Her dress fell in soft folds about her hips, the hem just above her ankles, the skirt a dirty white, the bodice patterned vertically in dark colours – reds and purples and greens. The sleeves were loose and long, the neck high and ragged. Her hair was oily, but her skin was clear. He put the bowl down, the mug inside it, and sat back against the chimney.

'That was good. Thank you.'

She smiled and nodded, and reached forward towards the bowl, her hand brushing his bad leg. Eduard winced.

'I'm sorry.'

He smiled ruefully, and she gently lifted the leg, and pulled his trouser back. The bandages were soiled, but there was no blood. She lowered his leg to the floor, then leant forward and touched his cheek again.

Eduard's hand closed on hers, and she reached for his other hand. He pulled her towards him, and she fell clumsily against him, her face turned up towards his. His hands locked behind her back, he leant forward and their mouths met, hard and harshly. Hers opened, and she forced her tongue between his teeth, as they rolled over onto the straw, side by side. Eduard felt her hand on him as he hardened, and gathered folds of her dress, yanking it up towards him.

He could not see what he was doing, and suddenly she put her hands between them, pushed him away and, as she did so, he thought of her father, and their hospitality and her age, and his inexperience, and his urgency faltered. But she knelt before him, and gathered her dress in both hands, lifting it clear of her waist.

She wore nothing beneath it, and her skin was pallid, and her hair was black, and her scent was pungent, and her hands were on his belt, unravelling him, and he sprang out of his clothes, rank and rearing, her hands around him, then pulling him into her as she sank down and towards him. There were no words.

She wanted him, he needed her, it was primitive, and honest and fast and pure as he roiled to an explosive climax, subsiding slowly to find her shuddering, eyes clamped closed, her hands on her hips as she rode him hard, and came herself, with a contained grunt and a series of gasps, falling against him, her dress settling in dusty folds around them.

They lay there for minutes, then she felt for him, found him, and rubbed him with a deft simplicity that aroused him swiftly, turned on her back, pulling her dress up and gazing up at him, willing him to take her up on her offer of a reprise. This time he found a certain rhythm, and enjoyed the means rather than invoking the urgent end, while she stroked his cheek with one hand, supporting the small of her back with the other as they rose and fell together, in a sweet, unsophisticated harmony. Then they slept, until a series of shouts roused them, and she crawled to the opening and looked down.

'My father.'

And she was gone. Her name was Ara.

Eduard crawled to the opening and looked out. There was no-one in sight. He sat on the edge of the loft floor, his legs swinging, and contemplated the yard below, the treeline, and the slip-slap water quietly licking the jetty, that he could hear behind him, behind the fisherman's hut, inviting him to taste its freedoms, moving past Tara to the sea.

There was no-one to stop him. His leg was stiff, his foot still sore, but he could feel the healing that had begun in his bone and blood; it was time too to heal the scabbed scars of loss and longing, to find a way back, if not to home and family, to the freedom of growing up, the learning of life's liberties, the right to be a manchild, make mistakes, to stumble without being pushed and find a way forward, to fight back, to combat those who had torn his home from his heart, his family from his future, and his country from its soil.

Eduard slid down the ladder, and tested his foot. It felt no worse for his weight, as he stepped forth on the first step to freedom.

'There you are!'

The charge-hand stood by the corner of the hut, hands muffed and arms folded across his deep chest, greatcoat draped to the ground, military cap flapped down his cheeks, his beard glistening with rimed sweat. He posed no threat, offered no rebuke, but smiled, revealed a hairy hand, and waved Eduard over.

'Let's have a look at you.'

Eduard limped across and the charge-hand looked down at his foot. 'Looks better. Is it?'

'Yes, it is. Very good.' And he paused before adding, 'Thank you.'

'Come along then – they're waiting for you back at the camp.'

At the front of the hut, the fisherman sat on his step, smoking a short, tarred clay pipe.

'Well Viktor – we're on our way. Any fish for me today?'

The fisherman reached down beside himself, and hefted a greasy cloth bundle, lifting it to head height. The charge-hand took it in both hands, peeling back the cloth to reveal a gleaming perch.

'Excellent. Excellent. I shall bring you a bottle – on my next visit.'

Viktor nodded, grunted and removed the pipe, jetting smoke, but saying nothing. Of Ara there was no sign.

They climbed onto the cart, and started back from Tara. Nothing was said for the first few miles until the charge-hand turned to Eduard.

'Vassil.'

Eduard looked at him, eyes wide, questioning.

'Vassil. It's my name.'

'Oh.'

'You can call me Vassil.'

'Thank you.'

'No "thank you". Just Vassil.' He looked away. 'That's me,' and after a few moments, added, 'Remember, when you think of Tara – Vassil, he saved your life.'

'I will – when I leave Tara.'

Vassil started swaying back and forth, raising the reins and cracking them expertly, and began to laugh. It began as a grumbling, grinding murmur, grew to a series of explosive, coughing exclamations, and crescendoed with a great snorting, hacking, gasping torrent of merriment. Just like a grubby Saint Nicholas, thought Eduard.

'What you say?'

'Nothing.'

'Thought you said something about the old devil.'

And he started laughing again.

'The old devil. Vassil, the old devil. Old devil Vassil. That's me.'

A few more miles passed in silence.

'Eduard – that's your name, isn't it?'

'Yes, Eduard is my name.'

'Well, don't forget. Remember Vassil, when you think of Tara.'

And he nodded sagely to himself, adding softly, under his breath, 'They will always remember Tara, but none will remember Vassil.'

Aloud: 'You see, you are my immortal soul, young Eduard. You are my memory, my only fame. When you leave Tara.'

And nothing more until they reached camp.

It was clear. There was an atmosphere of unrest, of movement, of change. Eduard sensed it the moment he dropped down from the cart, wincing as his foot hit the ground. It must be getting better; he had forgotten the wound until his foot touched earth.

......Vassil stood at the door.

'Come with me.' He pointed at Eduard, Vatek, Wolski and Mazloff. Turning, he led them to the cabin. Inside there were two Asiatics in uniform – AKWD uniform. These were officers from the secret police, the later NKVD, then KGB. One was clearly of senior rank, a captain.

'You Eduard Cjaikowski?'

'Yes.'

'Jozef Wolski?'

'Yes.'

'Mariusz Mazloff and Adam Vatek?'

'Indeed,' and, 'Yes.'

'Good. Sit.'

The four Poles sat on the bench beside the table, while the officers sat opposite them on chairs, and Vassil stood by the stove, his hands muffed, his face impassive.

'Kamerads!'

They looked at each other. Kamerads? Friends? What was going on? Was it a trick, a ruse, some sort of a trap, a trapdoor, to yawn beneath them before the rope tautened and they died, kicking away the little lives of Russian internees?

'Kamerads, cigarette?'

The junior officer extended a gunmetal case, snapping it open, offering a row of flat, slightly crushed and highly aromatic gaspers.

Eduard shook his head, Mazloff brought out his empty pipe, but Vatek extracted two cigarettes, handing one to Wolski, and leant forward as the Captain flipped over the lid of a cheap lighter, and thumbed the wheel. A small spark sparkled briefly, then sighed and died; another, and a sluggish flame climbed up the wick. Vatek inhaled, coughed gutturally, then swallowed, and tried again. He offered the glowing tip to Wolski, who cupped it and drew in slowly and carefully, held his breath, then expelled a stream of acrid smoke.

'Thanks.'

The Captain reached over the table and took Eduard's hand, shaking it vigorously.

'I have news for you. We have instructions from London City, from your government there, your ministers in exile. General Sikorski has made a pact with Kamerad Stalin. Young Polish people are free. They are to be released from their temporary homes – camps such as this, to join Mother Russia's forces, to fight the Nazi Germans, and defeat them!'

He paused, while they absorbed the news, the implications, the assumed generosity, and the threat.

'Of course, you will fight. You're not compelled to. But you will.'

He looked at each of them, smiling with complete conviction.

'From now on, you are a completely free citizen!'

He beamed at Eduard and pumped his hand several times, before turning to Vatek and grabbing his, shaking it as vigorously, while the other officer turned to Mazloff and shook his hand. Anxious to be part of the party, Vassil strode across and grasped Wolski's hand, and pulled him to his chest, hugging him briefly before wiping his beard and reaching for his pocket, brandishing a bottle, pulling the cork with his teeth, upending it, and drinking deeply before waving it about and crying out, 'Glorious Oktober! Down with the hordes. Well done!'

The Captain continued to smile, adding, 'From now on you can walk anywhere in Russia and here is a certificate – *undastawarenie* – your passport. Signed by the Commandant!'

He flourished four papers, before slapping them down hard on the table.

'You are free to go – anywhere you want!'

Then he held out his hand to his junior.

'The purse?'

The other officer stooped, then straightened, holding a leather satchel. He placed it on the table, unbuckled two straps, and reached inside. Out came a bundle of dirty bank notes, of low denomination. The captain counted out four piles.

'There you are – fifty roubles each.'

The two officers rose, shook hands with each new citizen of Mother Russia, and walked to the door.

'The truck?' asked the Captain.

'Behind the workhut, sir.'

Vassil eased himself past them, and led them off to their transport, leaving the four Poles sitting, smoke hanging sulkily between them.

Mazloff was the first to speak.

'Well, I suppose we had better say our goodbyes. If we start now, there's just about time to reach Tara.'

The others nodded, thoughts so confused, there was nothing to say. Together, they walked out of the cabin towards their hut, to take leave of their companions of nearly two years.

An hour later, they started walking to Tara, the river, a boat, any boat, and freedom. They had escaped.

I was going home. There was time to think.

Odd, now that I have all the time in the world to think that, during nearly two years of physical immolation, with the companionship of three men, two old enough to be my father, and one my grandfather, with no common interest, only common cause, I had had no real freedom of thought.

Only with physical freedom came the freedom to think. It was perhaps partly to do with age. I was fourteen when my life was abruptly arrested, my brother shot, my father tormented to death, my mother torn from me. I was fourteen when I confronted not cruelty so much as callous indifference, dogma and that which we now call racism – the hatred of that which one does not understand in others' difference, of skin, or creed, or behaviour, but most of all, of culture.

Now, somehow, the moment of escape, of freedom, of time for pause, brought thought: torrents of half-formed fancies, fantasies of the future, fortune cookies of freedom.

Of course I remembered Ara. My first.

I have often thought again of that quick connection, and wondered if somehow my ways were set that morning in Viktor's loft, learning light years fast of unlove, for I had no feelings for her save gratitude in memory of her gift.

Was that all there was, I also wondered? If that fast fuck was the be-all and end-all of consenting congress, then the sweet mystery I had half guessed when I was with strange girls, saw strange men kiss soft women, heard the muffled mating of my parents, was no more than the grandstanding studship of our horses at Cjortkow, or the makeshift mounting of the farmers' pigs and goats and sheep.

Yet, the thought persisted, that strange morning of my first freedom of two years, that perhaps there was something missing, something more to be discovered, some secret denied Ara and, by extension, my incoherent self.

As Ara receded, my thoughts raced on, like bolting horses, undirected, wheeling, braking, streaming across the landscape of my little life, and I tried to brake them, slow them down, so that I could separate the kaleidoscope of fragments into some coherence, make sense of my day-dream drama.

School was over, with lessons yet to be learnt – how would I recover the lost academic ground, and did it matter anyway? What of home? My eyes were sticky with the pain of past happiness, and the probability that those days were freeze-framed in pictures of the past brought a sullen pain to my guts. Home was then, I told myself. Home was once and for ever, and not henceforth. Home was a single image multiplied by all the small events of yesterday.

With the resilience that only youth can lean into, I told myself not to be silly, to think clearly, to consider the days ahead, tomorrow, the next day and the one after. Plans? You do not plan inside the head of a teenager. You lurch from sick sorrows of momentary deprivation to bright peaks of expectation.

I concentrated on the peaks. Tara, not Ara. The river. Work, food, rest, and above all, travelling away from camp and captivity, from the tyranny of constraint, into increasing release, the edges of hope, towards a renewed youngness, and perhaps, revenge.

If home itself was a shimmering mirage in the memory, in every other sense I was going home, one way, from east to west, but first, by river north to south. Eduard Cjaikowski was going west, to civilisation, to war, to fight, to combat the cause of my confusions and my losses, in order to set to rights my addled brain.

Today, as I beat yesterday's drums against the hollows of my headbones, I remember that extraordinary day, the day I began to grow up and become a man.

And I remember the day we collected the gold.

ANGEL OF OMSK

Twilight lingered, leaning towards the short nightfall, as they entered Tara. There were no lights visible, though thin trails of smoke stood upright in the even thinner air. The ruts in the road were ridged with old frost, and they could hear the river mutter in its sleep as it licked the landing stage. Wolski was in favour of knocking someone up, to find somewhere to rest for the night. Mazloff, shivering, disagreed.

'Nobody's interested. We will only be turned away. Better to find somewhere ourselves,' and he started off down the rough track between the hovels, looking for an outhouse, a shed or a shelter – anywhere enclosed, where a wall might insulate them from the night air.

Vatek and Eduard walked the other way, to the river's edge, and then along the bank, where Vatek reasoned there must be a boat tied up somewhere and, where there was a boat, there might be shelter, somewhere to store tools and tackle.

The boats were moored alongside the jetty. There were no stores or sheds so, after standing listlessly looking out over the river, peering through the threads of mist woven across the water, they walked back to the line of huts and cabins. Wolski was sitting, his back to a hut, muttering to himself.

'What's wrong with you?' asked Vatek.

'Wrong? What's bloody right? This is a dump, and I thought we were free men: nowhere to sleep, nothing to eat, nowhere to go. I almost wish we were back at the camp.'

Vatek looked at Eduard, rolled his eyes, and turned away, peering into the gloom for sight of Mazloff. Wolski pulled out his roubles.

'We've got money. Surely we can buy shelter, or at least something to eat?' He waved the money under Eduard's nose.

'Come on – you've got the same. Let's find somewhere.'

Eduard: 'There isn't anywhere. There's no tavern, just a run-down old café and a co-operative shop, and I don't know where that is – never saw it when I was here.'

'What about your friends? The woman who treated you? The place you stayed? Surely one of them will help.'

'I doubt it. I was a guest because Vassil brought me. Now I'm nobody. You are nobody too, as far as they're concerned.'

'Worse.' They turned as Mazloff loomed up, sucking his empty pipe. 'Much worse. We're less than nobody – we're Poles. They don't like us, and they won't want us.' He took his pipe out and examined it critically. 'However' – he put it back in his mouth and sucked reflectively – 'I have found an empty cabin. We can stay there until morning.'

He noticed Wolski's handful of notes.

'You can put that away. It's worth less than you think, and you'll need it when we get to Omsk.'

Eduard and Vatek together: 'Omsk? Who said anything about Omsk?'

'Omsk. We have to go back whence we came. So it's the next boat to Omsk, and then the train.'

'Oh my God,' moaned Wolski, 'not that bloody train again.'

'Not that train, but a train nonetheless. How else do you suppose you'll get to civilisation?' He started walking down the track. 'Come on, if you want to rest.'

The sun strained through the wet air without warmth – morning in Tara. In the damp, grey light, they examined their sleeping quarters – the remnant of a respectable chalet, clearly once the home of an official, but now three walls, half a roof and a pile of rotten timbers, open to the weather and any curious passer-by. Two children stood watching them as they shook sleep off, and stamped the circulation back. When Wolski walked out towards them, they looked gravely at him, then turned round and walked away.

'Silly little buggers. What are they afraid of?'

'They're not afraid of you – just curious.'

Mazloff had already been out to survey the settlement.

'There's a small eating place at the jetty, closed. Otherwise, just huts, cabins and an occasional chalet like this one – all this side of the landing stage. The other side is wooded. Eduard's right. There is a shop, a sort of co-operative, I imagine. Closed like the café. Probably neither opens unless there's a boat due.'

He pulled his pipe out.

'When that happens, we should be able to buy tobacco, perhaps fish. We'll get some water from the villagers before then.'

He looked at the other three.

'The boats are our only chance.'

Eduard said nothing. Wolski grumbled softly under his breath. Vatek smiled and said, 'If the café's closed, I wonder where the rubbish is kept. There must be something there. I'm going to see,' and he strode off towards the jetty.

Wolski: 'Well, if there's nothing here, I'm staying until the bloody boat arrives.'

Mazloff: 'I'll stay with you until Vatek returns.'

When Vatek returned, he was followed by four children, at a distance.

'Right, gentlemen. Where there's fish there's food. Where there's food, there's waste, and where there's waste is where we're going.'

He led them back to the landing stage, and the long, low, windowless shed beside it. Mazloff nodded.

'The shop, the café.'

'Exactly,' exclaimed Vatek. 'Follow me.'

Between the shed and the jetty was a narrow stretch of uneven ground, punctuated with mounds of discarded metal, old wheels, broken spars and all the detritus of a riverside workshop. Half hidden behind the shoreward jetty piles were three bins. Vatek lifted the lid from the first, pushed his hand down and pulled it out, brandishing a handful of fishbones.

'See? Rubbish to fishermen and riverfolk, but worth something to us.'

He looked at Eduard.

'Did you bring matches?'

'Yes I did.'

'Good – then we'll get some water, and boil some broth.'

He dipped into the magic box again, and withdrew a congealed mess.

'Onions!' and with the third handful, 'Potato peelings!'

Mazloff tapped Eduard on the arm.

'Why don't you go and ask that nice young girl for some water?'

Eduard shook his head.

'I'm sorry, but no. I'm not going back there. Not ever.'

He looked down and added, 'That's past, when I wasn't free.'

Then: 'But I will go and ask the nurse. She might give us some.'

Back at their makeshift home, Wolski broke up some wood and, at the third attempt, Eduard managed to light a small, smoking fire. Mazloff picked through the peelings and fishbones, selecting the cleanest, and discarding the mildewed, while Vatek stirred the battered tin they had rescued from the dump, brimming with the water Eduard had obtained from the nurse.

For three days they scavenged, once eating bread brought to them by one of the children – in silence, with her mother hovering a few yards behind. Most of the day they sat on the rough wooden benches on the jetty, scanning the river for the boat from Omsk.

Mazloff had tried to find out how often the boats called, but no-one could – or would – tell him. It seemed the boats came when there was a reason, not to any timetable. They talked about what they were going to do.

Mazloff intended to find a way home, back to Poland. Vatek said he would go with him. Wolski hesitated, for he was afraid of what he might find when he got there. Eduard knew. Home was at best empty, at worst, gone. It would wait. He was going to fight. He was going to war . They were all going to Omsk, that much was certain.

On the fourth day, the settlement stirred. The co-operative opened, as villagers brought goods to barter with those on the boats, and in exchange for government clothing – a consignment due with the next boat, they said. The café prepared for the visiting trade – sailors, conscripts, traders. Eduard saw Viktor, working in his boat, but Viktor either did not see him, did not recognise him, or did not want to.

Then they heard it – the distant thud-thud of the engines, and soon the flushing flutter of the great water wheels. The paddler was just like the one that had brought them to Tara two years before, possibly even the very same boat. It churned and turned, easing itself against the current, as it moved past the half-moon jetty, so as to harness the river's will and haul into the arms of the haven. As the steamer bulked through the morning mists, its wheels in opposition, the fishermen ranked themselves alongside, waiting to catch the ropes, loop them over the bollards, and take the strain as the high hull backed towards the uneven rows of old tyres that lined the pier.

The stern touched first, slewed away, then touched again, and they hauled the ropes taut. Slowly the bow rode in, hesitated, then slowed and dipped, as the ropes snaked round the forward post and were made fast, the great wheel secure in the crook of the stage, neatly housed. There was a shout from above, the gangplank was slid out, protruded several feet, then dropped slowly, to bounce off the planking, and settle.

The café-restaurant was unshuttered, and the adjacent 'cohors' co-operative shop abustle with local fishermen, woodcutters, dairy smallholders and their wives and children. Tara was suddenly alive and open for business.

At Mazloff's suggestion, they split up, Vatek staying by the cohors, Wolski and Eduard waiting to board the boat, and Mazloff himself, spending precious roubles, sitting in the café, sipping a brackish tea from the great, hammered metal samovar which dominated the counter. Armed with their 'little passports', they were prepared to take on any job they could get, to earn the money to leave Tara. They agreed to meet an hour later, back at the cabin.

Eduard and Wolski watched as crewmen filed off the boat, making straight for the cohors or the café. They were followed by a stream of conscripts, young Mongols, destined for the western front, cannon fodder for the German advance, for the Reich had turned on Mother Russia, and had embarked on its Napoleonic adventure. They were closely chaperoned by watchful corporals, who shepherded them into the café for food and tea.

A small detachment wheeled past the café and halted hard by Wolski .

'You. Fall in.'

'Me? What for?'

'Don't argue. Fall in!'

The NCO unslung his rifle, and prodded Wolski. Eduard tapped him on the arm and he swung round.

'What do you want?' seeing a mere youngster.

'He's a Pole.'

'What?'

'He's a Pole. He's got his orders. To report to Omsk. Look. He's got papers.'

Wolski smiled and nodded eagerly, pulling his *undastawarenie* from his vest, and waving it about in front of the soldier. The NCO scowled, looked at the little passport without comprehension, then nodded.

'Alright then. You go to Omsk. We need good soldiers. Bloody Poles. No good at all.' And off they marched.

Wolski put his passport back.

'He didn't look at it.'

'Of course not; he can't read.'

'How'd you know that?'

'I didn't. Just a guess.'

'Bloody hell.'

'Lets go on board. The others will talk to the sailors. I want to find the Captain.'

Together they made their way up the unguarded gangplank, and onto the deck. Two sailors sitting, smoking, glanced up, then back to their card game.

'How long're you here for?' asked Eduard.

'Twelve hours.'

'Where's the Captain?'

'Why? What do you want?'

'I have a message for him.'

'A message for Ilya? That'll be a surprise.' And they both laughed. 'He's usually up there,' and he waved in the direction of the bridge.

Wolski and Eduard picked their way over the detritus on the deck – haversacks, bedrolls, lashed crates and boxes – and found a deck door. Inside, a narrow corridor led fore and aft, with a steep stairway at the for'ard end. They clambered up to the bridge. It was deserted.

'What now?' asked Wolski.

'We wait. He's bound to turn up sooner or later.'

They looked around. The bridge was simply equipped, with engine-room speaking tubes, a shelf fixed to the aft wall, charts and basic instruments, the wheel, and a squat radio set. Eduard looked at the radio, and hesitated. Then he reached up and fiddled with the dial. There was nothing but static. He looked at each side, and peered underneath, but there was only a single connection, presumably to the engine-room power supply, and a speaker grille. It was a basic shortwave radio.

'Nothing much here, then.'

'No. It must be just for local contact – other boats, landing places and so on.'

Wolski looked amused.

'Why? Did you think you could raise Warsaw, then?'

'And did you think you could use it without my permission?'

They both instinctively fell back against the bulkhead as first the red-pom-pommed cap, then the dark-veined, dirty swart hands, followed by brief, thick arms in black wool, a dark-browed, sallow, long, tracklined face, rollneck, bulky chest, sagging belly, short-booted legs rose up through the hatch and came to rest a yard away.

'Well? What the hell're you doing on my boat, on my bridge, in my office, with my radio?'

'Looking for you, sir.'

'Well, you've found me. So what do you want?'

'Work. A job. Two jobs. Actually, four, if you've got them.'

'Jobs? What jobs? I haven't got any jobs. Go on. Clear off. Get out. There's no jobs here.'

And he rummaged about in a drawer below the navigation shelf, pulled out a pipe, some tobacco and matches, and started to ream it, knocking dottle and cinders out on his boot.

'Alright. Then will you take us all to Omsk?'

'Omsk? That's weeks away. We've goods to collect, soldiers to find, jobs to do.' He paused. 'And anyway we've no room on board.'

He filled his pipe, tamped it down, and struck a match.

'Go on, get off.'

Eduard shrugged, and Wolski started down the ladder.

'Wait a minute.'

They stopped and looked up at him.

'Got any money?'

Eduard balanced on the top rung, and reached into his belt.

'Five roubles.'

'Five roubles? That won't get you tea in Tara.'

He lit the pipe and puffed vigorously.

'Nothing doing. I've already got a boatful. Five roubles. Mary Magdalena!'

As he spoke, he shifted the pipe back and forth, smoke dribbling between his clenched teeth.

'Anyway, what do you do?'

Wolski looked at Eduard and Eduard raised his eyebrows, climbed back onto the bridge, leant against the bulkhead, tucking his hands into his waistband.

'Engines. I do engines.'

'Engines? I've got an engineer. I don't need anyone to do engines.'

He relit his pipe.

'What's he do?' gesturing at Wolski, now hovering halfway out of the hatch.

'Engines. We both do engines.'

'Waste of time engines. Don't need anyone to do engines.'

He looked at Eduard, leant forward and poked his chest.

'You're too thin. You couldn't do a bloody thing.'

'I can do anything. I can do any chores you name. Try me. So can he.'

'Well, he looks a bit tougher than you, but you're both half-starved. Go on. Get off and don't come back,' and he turned back to his charts. Eduard shook his head, and waved Wolski down the gangway.

'We'd better go.'

Once off the boat, they made their disconsolate way to the café. Mazloff was still there, still sipping tea. Vatek sat motionless before him.

'How'd you get on?'

Mazloff: 'I've arranged to stay here – for a short while.'

He glanced at Vatek.

'He's staying too. We have found some work. I have agreed to teach the local children in return for lodgings and food for us both. It's too cold to travel. We'll wait for better weather, then we'll leave. Vatek will find work too – probably with the fishermen.'

Vatek nodded. 'We'll be alright. What about you?'

'Nothing – not yet, anyway. We tried the boat. No luck.'

The door swung back against the wall in a gout of smoke. Captain Ilya waddled in, and made straight for the samovar, holding a curious vessel, which he filled with boiling water.

'What the hell's that?' asked Vatek.

'It's a *kipyatok*, a sort of hot water bottle. Very common, universal in fact.' Mazloff called to the Captain.

'Good morning, Captain. I hear you have a full engine-room.'

Ilya turned round and appraised them, pulled his pipe out and stuck it in his mouth unlit, walked across and sat heavily at the table.

'You have some tea?'

'Just finished.'

'Your friends have tea?'

'No I don't think they have.'

'Well, there'll be tea on the Angel.'

He looked at each of them in turn, then took out his pipe, tapped it on the table and rose.

'*The Angel of Omsk*, my little Angel. You two, come with me. You can do the fire. You and your friend. That is, if you still want to sail to Omsk.'

Balancing his *kipyatok* carefully with one hand, pipe back in teeth, he yanked the door back, and strode out. The four Poles rose and silently Vatek walked round the table, and put his arms round Eduard.

'God bless you.'

He thumped Wolski across the shoulder.

'You too, old fool. Never thought your bloody raft would swim. But you will now. One day...' He brushed his eye quickly. 'Now bugger off.'

Wolski raised his hand, then dropped it. Mazloff looked at Eduard.

'I shall miss you, young Eduard. I shall miss teaching you. Instead I shall teach little Russians. But one day we shall meet – that I promise you.'

He looked at him, eyes dry but soft with affection, then as suddenly, bright with assurance.

'And as you know, I am never wrong.'

The four of them laughed, then cried, and wrung each others' hands, walking as one to the quayside. There they stood apart, hands touching, until Eduard and Wolski climbed up the gangplank and Eduard turned as Wolski waved, shouting back at the two older men: 'Thank you both. Thank you. Thank you. Thank you.'

Once again they climbed the companionway to the bridge, where Captain Ilya sat on a venerable leather swivel chair, a metal beaker cupped within his dark-veined hands. He was still, his eyes fixed somewhere beyond the smeared for'ard screen. Without moving, he spoke quietly, reflectively.

'The river, she is a great beast, smooth and silky one day, tormented the next, sometimes indifferent, sometimes friendly, sometimes cold-tempered and unhelpful. My Angel knows her mind and her moods and she respects that.' He turned to them.

'You have no idea what I'm talking about, have you, my scrawny little engineers?'

He leant forward, gesturing with his hands still round the beaker, towards the navigation table.

'Tea. Help yourselves.'

There were two more beakers, and the *kipyatok*, steam tendrils escaping from its lid, and there was a rough cloth bag and a bent tin spoon. Eduard dug into the bag with the spoon and ladled tea into the beakers, then swore as he tried to remove the scalding hot lid.

'Ha! Keeps the heat in, my little one, doesn't it? Use the bag.'

The tea was strong, black and hot. Wolski sipped it slowly, while Eduard blew on his; both cupped their hands like Ilya, and felt the warmth percolate their bones and sinews. The great comforter.

'When we've finished, I take you to the engine-room. Pride and joy. Wonderful miracle of modern science. You'll see.'

Five minutes later they were standing on the narrow platform alongside the great boiler, marvelling at the brass, the black and red and green paintwork, the shafts and cylinders, shanks and pistons and all the paraphernalia of the engine-room, 'the heart of my Angel' as Ilya had it, patting the shining brightwork. The contrast with the deck, bridge and general appearance of the boat was uncompromising.

Captain Ilya clearly had priorities and a pristine engine-room was foremost. As he put it, 'This is what makes her move, what we hear as we move, what echoes in our own hearts. This is the powerhouse.' He looked at them. 'And I am trusting you to keep it going.'

With that, he jumped down, they followed, and he strode briskly over to the business end of the boiler.

'This is the heart of the heart.' And he swung the crosspiece on the boiler door, pulled it towards him, and the door swung back, to reveal the flickering flames of the furnace, tamped down for the standover. Ilya carefully closed the door, and spun the handle back again.

'There's your fuel,' pointing to the cages on either side, neatly stacked with cut logs which reminded Eduard of the campsite.

'Every hundred miles, we stop and take on more. Once we start, you feed my Angel all the time. Understand?'

They nodded.

'You can stay down here if you like. There's a space at the end, a mattress, some cushions.'

When they looked surprised, he added, 'My engineer, he and I share the work. One rests, one works. He is sick. You share the work, you rest too.'

Ilya patted the boiler.

'Look after her. We start in two hours. I come down then, and show you how.'

Two hours later, Eduard was asleep, Wolski resting, his feet up on a cross-member, when Captain Ilya slid down the companionway.

'Right, my friends. Time to begin.'

He unhasped one of the cages, and lifted three logs down, piling them beside the furnace door. Wolski did the same with the other cage. When Ilya opened the door, Wolski heaved the first logs in, and the Captain adjusted the valves, the flames climbing, slowly first, then higher and faster, until the heat blasted out at them. They developed a rhythm, with Wolski supplying the logs, and Eduard feeding the furnace, as Ilya stood back; then, satisfied, he climbed up out of sight, to take the wheel. They felt the shudder as the great wheels started to turn, and the force as the boat turned into the current, and started slipping upstream.

Within minutes, Captain Ilya was back.

'Crew's on station; wheel's secured. Just come to see how you are.'

Eduard was flagging. His back ached, his foot hurt, his arms felt flaccid and rigid with disuse. As he shoved yet another log towards the flames, he slipped, and seemed unable to release it, sliding towards the door.

Ilya pushed him aside, wrested the log from him and threw it into the furnace, then another. Wolski continued to pile them on the floor.

'You nearly went with the log, my little engineer.'

Glancing at the dials, the Captain grunted, brushed the sweat away, and pushed the door closed, flicking the lever across.

'That'll do for five minutes. We've settled down now.'

He looked at Eduard.

'You have a rest,' and he was gone.

Within minutes he was back, balancing a wooden platter on one hand, as he slid down the companionway.

'Here.' He pushed the platter into Eduard's hands. It was fresh boiled fish.

Eduard sat up on the mattress and pulled a lump off. It was sweet and tender. Ilya smiled.

'Fresh river carp. The best.'

He watched as Eduard finished the fish, then took the platter and called Wolski.

'Off you go; there's more in my cabin – behind the bridge. Help yourself. I'll watch the boiler. Ten minutes. Alright?'

When Wolski had gone, he sat beside Eduard.

'You're not Russian. Are you?'

Eduard shook his head.

'You speak too well, better than me.' He laughed. 'So who are you, my little engineer, my skinny boilerman?'

So Eduard told him – everything, about Cjortkow, Rosalia, the man Kolanski, Tara and the camp, the axe wound; but he left out Ara. That was nobody's business but his and hers.

The Captain silently nodded, then asked, 'Where are you really going, then?'

Eduard shrugged.

'Omsk, then – well, I don't really know.'

The Captain stood and looked down at him.

'Well, you can work when you can. Your friend is strong. He can manage most of the time. I'll help when I can. Together we'll get to Omsk. Then I return to Tara and beyond, so then – well you must go wherever God takes you,' and he touched Eduard's shoulder briefly. 'You are so young; you remind me of my son...'

The journey took over three weeks, as the *Angel* stopped, took on logs, conscripts and put down goods and occasional passengers, running against the current instead of with it. But eventually, the boat came to rest against the same pier Wolski and Eduard had left nearly two years earlier and, when the conscripts had marched off, and the crewmen taken leave, they sat with Captain Ilya in the Captain's tiny cabin, sipping strong black tea, the great boiler dormant, the wheels still, the river anxiously slithering past the black hull beneath them.

'Well, my little engineer – and my big boilerman – it is time to go. I have enjoyed having you on board.'

He slapped each of them playfully on their knees.

'And pleased to help you just a little, but mainly, just a bit happier for helping to put things a little bit back.'

They looked at him, uncertainly.

'You see' – and he glanced around as if to check there were no eager ears about – 'You see, I'm not a very good Captain. I don't like the kamerads. I don't like what they do, especially to other peoples. Like you. It's why I help you – because I can, and because it...'

He closed his fist, and banged the edge of the bunk.

'Because it is a balance to the bad things they do for the state, for what they call the cause, which doesn't help people like me or you.'

He sat back against the bulkhead, slightly flushed, his arms hanging loose, then suddenly clapped his hands.

'To hell with Soviets. I love my Angel, and I believe in God. You go, and you remember, Ilya is not a kamerad, but he is your friend.'

Eduard and Wolski rose, each shook the Captain's hand, and then they left him sitting there, gazing at the door long after they had gone. When they reached the river bank, Wolski turned to Eduard.

'Now what?'

You remember people when you get older – people from the long past. You rely on remembering them, when you are caught up inside your own mind, to people the distant days again, to replace the dusty present.

They may be dead, no longer part of their context, senile, or still what they were, but you remember them as they were, then, and what they were, then, to you, and it is that same self that occupies your memory, somewhat like a fragment of rewound videotape of a film, an old favourite, for they will all be old favourites, whether friend or villain, in the remembering, or they are not worth the memory. You associate those old friends with the moment they occupy in that memory, with the faded but nonetheless real image of that moment.

I remember Ilya and his tea. What Ilya was rests in that tea. The taste and smell of it. I can still taste it, smell it in the cavities of my mind. Tea and sympathy? Nothing so obvious, for Ilya was a chimera, a monster of a shadow across my future, yet a chimera, a sleeveless episcopal gown around my life. Unpredictable, opportunist, obstructive yet helpful, heartening and ultimately emotional – a lonely man with his own memories and a man embalmed within a vessel moving back and forth along the same flat waters week after week, like an ambrous fly in a swinging pendant on a short chain around the same neck.

He was what I have become – a prisoner of limited circumstance. And whatever happened to him, whether or not he moved on to other boats, other rivers, or retired to a sedentary life ashore, or lived with his son, if indeed his son still lived, he remains preserved in the fissures of my memory – Ilya and his tea.

When I poke about in my cranial crannies, I have only the vaguest recollection of Ilya's boat, but I can always call up his tea – strong, black, hot and steaming, in that battered tin beaker. It is as if the tea was the man, and today, when I nod and smile and mouth a mucous 'thank you' for the cup that cheers, as the old women say, in the place to which I am repaired when my lady has to go away for a day, when I lift the thick-lipped pretend china mug to my lips, I sometimes suddenly taste that tea, and the mug is a tin beaker, and there Ilya sits before me, the icon of escape.

That is what Ilya means – escape. The tea means freedom. It was with Ilya and his tea that first I knew I was myself – not a child any more, not a subordinate family person, not a son, a brother, a dependant, and no longer a captive, a Polish non-person, not a man on the look-out for the exit, no more a sparrow battering against the window, but a free man.

Sitting with Ilya, sipping tea with Ilya, that instant before we walked away, off the boat, from the river, into Omsk, I knew I could go anywhere, do anything, be someone. The tea was the key. He came to find us, offering tea. He let us go, sipping tea.

With Ilya teatime was free time. I flew from the past on Ilya's wings, for Ilya was the Angel of Omsk.

FALSE START

As they walked away from the river, Eduard and Wolski kept close company, afraid to speak lest they be identified as aliens, yet it soon became clear their fears were unfounded. They were no better or worse clothed than those around them, in the general bustle of the day's commerce. Then Eduard detected a German voice; he was so startled he bumped into Wolski, jarring the older man.

'Watch where you're going.'

'Sorry. But I heard a German.'

Then he heard another, and another. He whispered to Wolski.

'They're Germans. I don't understand. If they've invaded, they should either be at the front, or interned, like us.'

He stopped and scanned the crowds and the streetscape. Then he stepped off the road, into an untidy bakery, while Wolski loitered outside. Rummaging in his waist for the makeshift pouch, he pulled out several five rouble notes, and asked for bread. The woman who served him was small, pale, nondescript and taciturn but, as he selected a loaf from the pile on the wooden counter, a florid, flour-bedecked figure emerged from a doorway to one side.

'Good day stranger, and where d'you hail from?'

'From Tara, master baker.'

'From Tara!'

The baker was obviously intrigued and walked round the table which doubled as counter, wiping his hands on his apron.

'From Tara you say. Well there's not much at Tara – fish, fishermen, mostly Asiatics, and a few Ukrainians. That's one place the Ruskies haven't taken over – yet.'

He leant companionably against the counter, his hand gripping its edge, as he shuffled his backside into a comfortable stance. He nodded towards Eduard's purchase.

'Good bread. Best you'll get in Omsk. We know how to make bread in the *tayga*.'

Eduard raised his eyebrows, smiled and asked, 'You're from the *tayga*, then?'

The baker laughed, looked down at his boots, scuffing the dirty grey flour on the floor.

'Indeed I am. My family are Yakut – we are the true people of the place. All these Ruskies and Pruskies are foreigners, yer know. Still, their money's good, and that's why we're here, to feed their faces, God help us, and fill our pockets.'

'Pruskies?'

'Why not? Pruskies – probably more of them than us now. Hundred thousand or more of those Germans in Chkalov, Celyabinsk, the

Kulunda and round here. Progress, my son – Soviet progress. It's called the Sovietisation of the steppes.' And he roared with laughter at his own good humour, hastily adding, 'Of course, I approve, kamerad, as I'm sure you do too.'

Glancing around to ensure there were no eavesdroppers from the AKWD, he added.

'But you're not really from Tara, are you?'

Eduard simply smiled, said 'Thank you' for the bread and started towards the door. The baker pushed himself upright.

'You're right. Best to say nothing. That way you stay free. Tara? Hmm. I heard there was a camp at Tara. D'you ever see that?'

Eduard shook his head.

'No. Just on our way through. Thanks again.' And he left, grabbing Wolski's arm, and hurrying him down the street.

'What the hell was all that about?'

'The baker – told me about the Germans. There's thousands of them – must have come here in the twenties, after the Revolution. I wonder if they'll fight their Nazi cousins.'

'Well, there's one way to find out – ask one.'

Eduard glanced at Wolski.

'That is a joke, presumably. No, we'll keep well away from them, but they may come in handy, if we're stuck.'

He stared straight ahead, the muscles in his face tight with anger.

'I hate the bastards.'

'What for? They weren't the ones who sent you packing, or took your mother, and they certainly had nothing to do with Tara.'

'No, but they started it all, and it was the bloody Germans that my father fought. I will fight them too.'

Wolski put up his hands in mock-defence.

'OK, OK, I've got the picture. You don't like the Krauts. Now let's talk about something else, such as, where's the station?'

After a brisk walk, they found it, awash with conscripts, noisy and crowded, filthy and hot. They had eaten the bread on their way there, and now they were thirsty. Eduard gripped Wolski's sleeve.

'See those girls over there?'

'Where?'

'Over there, by the cart stand. Come on, let's see if we can get some help, water perhaps, and some idea of how to get out of this place.'

Wolski breathed deeply, then expelled a great sigh.

'I wondered when we were going to get to that bit.'

'What bit?'

'The "how are we going to get out of there" – that bit. We haven't enough cash for tickets, that's certain.'

'True, but those girls have, and I bet they've never seen two handsome Poles like us before.'

'So what? And anyway, who said you're handsome?'

'It's you who's the handsome one; I'm just young. And that might be exactly what we need, or rather, what they want. Come on.'

They walked across to the little group of three girls and Eduard suddenly put his hand to his head, groaned, and buckled, slipping slowly to the floor of the concourse. The girls watched him with indifference. Wolski bent over him, shook him, and asked, 'What're you playing at? Can't you see these girls are frightened? Just get up, and stop messing about,' and he tugged at Eduard's hand.

Eduard groaned again, and clutched his face.

One of the girls sauntered across. 'What's his trouble?'

'I don't know. He was alright a minute ago. It's probably the lack of water. He hasn't had a drink for a day.'

'Why not?'

'Because he's just been released from prison, and he hasn't anything left in the world.'

Wolski extemporised as he sensed her quickening interest.

'Poor fellow. His mother's gone, his father's dead, his brother shopped him, and he's been inside for nothing. Never did a thing. Now he's been let out, pardoned, clean record. But he's very shaky, very young and very thirsty. You haven't any water by any chance?'

By now Eduard was half sitting, slouched against a cartwheel, still moaning, and holding his face. The girl had by now been joined by one of her companions.

'What's wrong with him?'

'He's faint. Needs some water.'

'Well, we've got no water.'

'No, but we have got...' And she whispered to the other girl, who giggled and felt about in her dark woollen bag.

'Here. Try some of this,' and they both spluttered with laughter.

Wolski took the bottle, unscrewed the lid and sniffed.

'Phoar – that smells a bit rough. What the hell is it?'

'Fruit juice,' said the first girl.

'Fermented,' added the second.

'From our fields,' offered the first.

'Brewed by us,' explained the second.

'Here Eduard, try this.' Wolski bent down and put the bottle to Eduard's mouth. He sipped, then drank, then took the bottle, tipped it back, and let the liquid swirl down his throat.

'Hey, that's enough,' cried the first girl, adding, 'Leave some for your friend,' and she wrested the bottle from Eduard, by now sitting much more comfortably, handing it to Wolski, as she slid down beside Eduard, taking his hands away from his face, and looking more closely at him.

'You've lovely eyes,' she observed.

'So have you,' he replied, stroking her hands.

101

Wolski swallowed a slow, deep draught, and handed the bottle back to the second girl, looking around for the third one, but she had disappeared. Between them, they emptied the bottle, and a second one which Irma produced. She told them that she and her sister Olga were on their way home, through Celjabinsk, to Plast, a small town nearby.

'Have you got tickets?'

'Of course we've got tickets. You can't go anywhere without tickets.' Eduard smiled at her, as he handed the second bottle back.

'We haven't got tickets. They don't give you tickets when they let you go, you know. Only papers. We've got to find our own way back.'

'Back where?'

'Well, Celjabinsk would be a start, wouldn't it, Wolski?'

Wolski nodded.

Irma looked at his thin face, his brown hands and his deep, brown, Polish eyes, and cocked her head to one side.

'You'd like to come with us, wouldn't you?'

'Yes, we would.'

'Wait here a minute.' And she rose, paused, looked down at him, then clasped Olga's hand, and the two women walked a few yards away, in consultation. They stood, talking and glancing every so often at the two men, then separated, and Olga came back.

'Irma and me, we'll help you. On one condition.'

'What's that?' asked Wolski, sourly.

'No nonsense. No funny stuff. No messing about. Just because we're women who help men like you doesn't mean we are whores.'

Eduard rose stiffly, catching hold of the cartwheel.

'We are not thieves and robbers. We don't attack ladies. We will never do anything we would regret.'

He straightened his back, folded his arms, looked straight at Irma and added, rather pompously, Wolski thought, 'We may look scruffy, but at home we are regarded as gentlemen.'

Wolski resisted the temptation to clap this performance, and gazed absently towards the furthest platform. A train had drawn in, steam curling from the sweating engine, and skeins of workers seeping through the crowded conscripts who stood in clumps, waiting to be entrained.

Irma joined them, and the two girls each linked arms with the men.

'Now do exactly as we say, and say nothing yourselves.'

They marched down the platform, scything through the crowds, the conscripts making way, some whistling quietly, with an occasional 'Lovely legs' or 'Look at that, then' as they forced a path to the rear of the train. There the crowds had departed, there were no conscripts, and two officials stood, uniformed, talking quietly, occasionally glancing at the departing passengers.

Irma pulled a door open, and pushed Eduard in; Olga signalled to Wolski to follow, then waved at the officials, who waved back. They sat along the wooden bench seat, and then Irma pushed the door, and walked down the platform to the railwaymen. She showed them her papers, then the two tickets, and they nodded, glancing perfunctorily at them, and handed them back before conducting what to Wolski, who was watching carefully, seemed to be a brief but animated conversation. Then Irma returned, handed the tickets to Olga, who in turn walked towards the two officials, smiling, and waving her papers. They pushed them aside, glanced at the two tickets, smiled, and repeated the Irma performance. After a few moments Olga returned.

'That's that then.'

'What was that all about?' asked Wolski.

'Nothing. I showed them our tickets – yours and mine – just as Irma showed them your tickets, hers and your friend's.'

She laughed as he frowned.

'No need to look so bewildered. They've seen four tickets. They've seen four people. They know now that two couples – husband and wife, that's you and me, and a sister and her young, sick brother, that's Eduard and Irma – are travelling together to Celjabinsk. So that's that. And now we can have a restful journey.'

'Just like that?'

'Just like that.'

Twenty minutes later, there was a series of jolts, the officials appeared briefly at the window, and waved at Irma and Olga, glancing indifferently at the two men, and the train moved out. Irma and Olga sat together, whispering to one another, sharing the bottle of 'fruit juice', and occasionally offering it to Eduard. Wolski slept.

No-one disturbed them; nobody questioned them. Soon Olga drifted off, and Irma slumped down, her eyes closed.

Eduard looked out at the ghostly landscape sliding past. Then he looked briefly at Irma, and their eyes met. He smiled, about to speak when Irma raised her right hand, her eyes turning to Olga and back to his. He sat back, hands in his lap, watching her. She eased herself onto the edge of the wooden slats, and stood, grabbing the rail over the window to steady herself, before swaying cautiously across to slip down beside Eduard. She turned, took his hand, and raised it to her face, all the while her eyes on his. His hand traced her cheek, her brow, her ear, the nape of her neck, reaching up into the folds of hair, and gently stroking the sensitive skin beneath. She leant towards him.

Their lips brushed. Eduard felt a moment of delicate desire, suspended, and knew this was not the same as Ara. They both leant back, linked hands, and sat looking at one another. Eduard was confused. He sensed some enlightenment denied him. He wondered if this was the beginning of what it felt like to love a woman, when there was a sudden judder, and the train convulsed, as it came to a shrieking, scraping halt. Olga and Wolski were instantly awake.

'What the hell was that?'

Irma joined her sister, and shrugged.

'They often stop without reason.'

Wolski turned to Eduard.

'Do you think they're after us?'

'Course not. We're going home. We're free. Probably a false alarm.'

Then they heard the banging, doors opening and slamming shut, shouting. Nearer came the noise. Their door was suddenly pulled open, two soldiers peered in, looked at them, the girls shook their heads and shoved the door shut.

A moment later they heard voices raised, then shouting, and two shots. Then silence. The door to the next compartment closed with a quiet thud. The soldiers walked past and within minutes, the train eased on its way. Eduard looked through the window, glimpsing two bodies crumpled by the track.

He looked at Wolski.

'This time it wasn't us they wanted.'

Night and half the next day passed, until the train drew into Celjabinsk. They jumped down onto the platform, and walked slowly to the barrier, where the officials nodded at the girls and waved them all through.

On the draughty concourse, Irma took his hands.

'We have to go now.'

Olga stood beside her, impassive. Wolski stamped his feet, his hands thrust inside his quilted jacket.

'Eduard...'

He drew her towards him, enfolded her, whispering into her ear, 'I think I love you – just a little, Irma.'

'I know.'

She pushed him gently, then put her hands on his arms, and looked again at this strange young man she had known for so short a time.

'We will keep these moments all our lives.'

Then the four of them were hugging and laughing and shouting and slapping each other, as they said their small goodbyes. A moment later, the girls were gone. Eduard tapped Wolski's arm.

'Come on. We need somewhere to sleep before we decide what to do next.'

'I'm not sure I know what I want to do next.'

'What do you mean?'

Wolski was troubled.

'We are supposed to be free. But where's my daughter?'

'Where's your daughter? What do you mean where's your daughter?'

'She was taken too. No good going to Moskva. She's not there, is she? She's still somewhere in the east. I must find her, take her home.'

'Don't be daft. My mother's somewhere in the east too, but there are

104

dozens of camps. I haven't the faintest idea where she is, which camp. I wouldn't begin to know, and I don't suppose I could find the camps, let alone her.'

'Makes no difference. I have to go. I have to find my Maria.'

While they were talking, they walked. Within minutes they had circled the station, and found their way to the marshalling yard. They could see lines of trucks parked behind the barbed wire. Eduard tested the fence. It was old, rusty and sagging with neglect. He took out his knife, and started to saw at a thin, flaking strand. It parted immediately. It took several minutes to work a hole large enough for a man to clamber through. He and Wolski crouched inside the fence.

'That way,' pointed Eduard, towards a long line of indistinct, bulky cattle trucks. 'There should be animals, and straw, which means they'll be warm.'

Wolski held his arm.

'You go.'

'What?'

'You go. I'm not coming with you.'

'Don't be ridiculous. We've got this far. You can't give up. Not now.'

'I'm not giving up.' He looked at Eduard, his eyes moist. 'I'm going back. I'm going to find Maria.'

He pulled Eduard towards him, and clasped him.

'Eduard. You are young. You must go, fight for Poland. I must return, fight for Maria. If I find her, I'll follow you.'

Eduard sat abruptly on the hard ground, his head in his hands. Then he looked up at Wolski.

'But you're my friend. We were going to do this together.'

'I am still your friend, and you are like a son. But I have a daughter and she is a real daughter. I have to find her. If I do, I'll see you in London, with Mr Churchill, when we win this stupid war.'

And he laughed, holding out his hand. Eduard stood, unbelieving.

Wolski: 'You see, she was with child. When they came, she was carrying my grandchild. They took my daughter and my family and my future.'

He looked at his friend, pain in his eyes.

'There are many camps, and they're not near Moskva. They're in the east. Somewhere there's a camp and there is my Maria, and her young one. They need me and I need them. You understand?'

They stood there, immobilised by the pain of parting, then Eduard sighed.

'I suppose you're right. I know I cannot come back with you.'

He looked away, then back at his friend, searching his eyes for other answers.

'I will see you some day, when it's all over, perhaps before that. Goodbye.'

What is a friend? Do we choose our friends or do they choose us?

I don't think a fourteen-year-old consciously chooses a friend, and I doubt that a man like Wolski would give a youngster like me a second glance in the usual way of things. But these were not the usual ways and Wolski and I had one thing in common – our country, or was it something more than that? Was it deeper, more racial than patriotic?

If I could turn back the silent clock that deafens my brain, I would hit the stopwatch button again and again, until I found the moment when Wolski stood with his daughter Maria and answered the priest,'It is I who gives this woman away' – but I do not know if he ever found his Maria, or if she was wed, and if she was, if he was still there to give away that which was his most precious, his blood, his very soul. And what happened to his grandchild? I am never to know, for Wolski will now be long gone, and I cannot call out to him. I mourn our friendship.

For there is, in that constant calculation, that measuring of one's life, one's actions, one's failures, the demon of regret that always hangs over friends past and no longer present. When Wolski left me in that freight yard, I knew it was temporary, a parting like the mill leet that separates from the mainstream, then rejoins it after the millrace, sluice and calm waters of the millpond. And so it was. How then could our later lives drain away down ditches of discontent, contact diminishing from our two times together in close comradeship to occasional letters, then cards at Christmas, then silences by default. Now the permanent silence which is mine precludes a resurrection.

Was Wolski really my friend, or an enforced comrade in captivity? Was I, Eduard, simply his partner in escapology? When Wolski left me in that railway wilderness, I was bereft of feeling, numbed, affection cauterised by the catastrophe of my loneliness. When later I cried for my loss, I cried for him too, for his quest and his uncertainties, and for my imperfect understanding of his fatherhood, for I had no criteria by which to judge his need and his decision.

Wolski was my friend – he had offered me his skills and strength, shared his thoughts and fears, journeyed with me, but therein lay not his friendship. He was my friend, for he honoured me with his paternity – 'You are like a son', and he treated me as his own. But was I his friend?

I think I was too confused to know what friendship demands, took what happened as it came, accepted what was offered, grew into the acts of friendship as most must do, without conscious intent. The day Wolski left I became his friend, for it was then that I knew that I cared – and there is one regret I do not suffer, for I did tell him, when we met again, despite the loss of innocence between the distant then and the later then. I met him and shook his hand, and looked at him, and laughed, and said to him, 'I love you, Wolski.' And he just smiled, nodded, and answered, 'I know.'

BLOOD BROTHERS

After Wolski had gone, Eduard stood uncertainly by the fence, then made up his mind. It was time to take the next step, to find a train to Moskva. He strode towards the looming line of trucks.

As he neared the first train, he saw the low platform, deserted. He climbed onto the crumbling surface – roughly tarred planks, stacked with crates, some on low, four-wheeled trolleys. As he clambered over the freightage, he noticed labels. Each crate was designated for a specific place, with its contents and place of origin clearly defined.

It did not take long to work out that the crates were a sure guide to destination. Eduard reached the end of the platform, which was clear and glanced up at the goods wagons. Similar labels were slapped on their sides, 'Omsk' and 'Kujbysev' among them, but Eduard sought the labels that declared themselves for Moskva, without success.

He jumped down beside the slumbering length of unengined train, and slipped between two trucks. There was a great claw, its fingers curled and clutching the shank of the truck ahead, its wrist broad and flat. Eduard pulled himself up onto the claw, and found a handhold on the chains hanging either side of the small peephole which permitted a check of contents at the end of the wagon. He lowered himself to the other side, and scanned the freight yard. There were oil tankers ahead of him and beyond them, a line of flat, long timber wagons.

To the right were two engines, cold and silent; to the left another line of closed wagons, with a squat, shunting engine spitting and fussing, as it stood waiting to marshal its charges onto the main line. Eduard reasoned this must go to Omsk or Moskva, for it comprised a substantial length of trucks, clearly destined for a long journey.

He eased his way along the line within a few yards of the waiting train, then crouched and scampered across the uneven ground until he was beside the engine. As he paused, gathering his breath and his courage to sidle past to the line of wagons, he heard a shout, saw the slight movement as a hand, then an arm reached out, a greasy hand clasping the dirty rail, and the driver's body swung down, its back to him. He ducked under the engine as it started to move.

He dropped to the ground between the tracks, compressing himself as close to the ground as he could, and the engine slowly slipped over him. In a moment, he would be exposed, and the driver would be standing there, and turning, would instantly see him. He reached over his head to the sleeper and hauled himself forward, matching his movements to that of the engine, then quickening, grasped another sleeper, and another, and another, hauling himself more and more rapidly forward, until he doubled the speed of the labouring shunter, reaching the tender, then the first truck, when the engine hissed and belched and stopped. Eduard slowly turned his head. Two feet away were two boots. The driver was beside him. He froze.

'Baz? You there Baz?'

Eduard closed his eyes.

'Course I'm here. When're you taking this bloody lump of shit?'

'Soon as you get down here and sort out this couplin'.'

'Mother of God; fireman, spare driver, now I'm a sodding mechanic as well.'

Another pair of boots appeared.

The two pairs mumbled and argued and Eduard waited, wondering when they would come round to 'sorting out the couplin'' and discover him lying full length within a few inches of it.

'Baz?'

'Now what?'

'The couplin'.'

'Yer. OK. I'll deal with the little bugger now.'

Eduard clenched hands and buttocks, wishing he had his knife other than unreachably in his waist pouch, which he was lying on. One boot disappeared, then another. The driver had remounted his iron horse. Another boot tentatively raised itself, then rubbed itself contemplatively up and down the leggings stuffed into the other boot.

Eduard decided hesitation was the thief of decision, grabbed the sleeper ahead and pulled himself forward. The stones beneath him rasped against each other, and he froze again. The noise was enough to bring all the railway boots in Russia down on his head. Nothing happened. The engine was still spurting and spittling, and he reasoned that Baz was either deaf, or nearer the valves than he was.

Eduard rapidly hauled himself forward, under the coupling, and past it, not stopping until he was under the far end of the next truck. He rolled over and looked back. Baz's boots were wider apart and relocated – in the centre of the track, as he presumably wrestled with the 'little bugger' itself. Eduard moved along the track one, two, four, six wagons, then lay just short of the coupling.

As he waited, it came to him that he had not the slightest notion of the train's destination. He watched Baz's boots shift and shuffle as the man worked the recalcitrant claw and shank. Then they turned, and departed. Eduard waited another two minutes, then slid between the wheels, and peered back along the line of wagons. Baz was standing within four feet of him, glaring at another coupling. Eduard rolled back under the truck, and across to the other side.

There was no sign of the driver or the little tank engine. Instead there was a great brute of a long-distance steamer sweating and straining, steam thrusting out from its skirts, smoke belching into the night sky, acrid and sulphurous.

Eduard pulled himself up alongside the wagon, and worked his way along until he found the label. 'Cloths. Omsk–Moskva'. He sidled along the wagon until he reached the coupling, slipped between the two trucks, and pulled himself up onto the great claw. As he reached for the metal chains his foot slipped, his arm was wrenched and he flailed in a half turn, the wagon crashing against his side. The train had started its journey. He fumbled for a sound footing, steadied himself again, and clasped the loops with both hands. He hoped he was on his way to Moskva.

It was cold. Eduard was cold. He grew cold by degrees, quickly. His hands were welded to the loops, his eyes clamped shut against the wind, his bones rattling inside his taut skin, his quilted clothing rammed against his suffering body. He could not feel his feet, but his ears scorched with the fiery gale that tore between the trucks. Eduard wondered with his entirely detached mind how long he would last. Then the train slowed, perhaps twenty miles after the journey began, and came to a lurching, cantankerous halt in an anonymous siding. Eduard realised he could not survive another twenty miles on the claw.

As the blood seeped back to the surface of his concrete hands, he released them from the chains, and tentatively raised one foot, then the other, banging them down again and again on the claw, until gradually the circulation returned, and he could move. He moved cautiously, until he could glance round the edge of the wagon. There was no-one in sight.

He dropped clumsily to the trackside, away from the halt, and stood momentarily, weighing up the options. Ahead was the engine and between him and it were perhaps five wagons. Extending into the distance in the other direction were many more. Realising that he should be further away from the engine, he sidled down the line of wagons, until he reached the twelfth one. The sliding door was ajar.

He reached up and pulled. It would not move. He steadied himself with one hand on the door and jumped, falling back and grazing his head as it slipped against a protruding bolt. He sat on the trackside for a few seconds, until a wave of unaccustomed anger swept through his usually calm mind. The bloody train would not defeat him.

He had come a long way. He had a long way to go. This was a small matter. He would not allow it to beat him. Again he reached up, grasping the door edge with one hand and the grazing bolt with the other, and jumped. He lodged a foot in the gap, balanced the other against the truckside, and hauled hard against the door. It gave with a grating rush, and he fell into the wagon, tumbling over a flat case of cloth onto a pile of bales. Recovering quickly, he kneeled, reached over the case, and pulled the door shut. The bolt was now outside, so he was unable to secure it.

Eduard dragged the case to the opening, and wedged it against the flange of the door, slumped down onto it, and pushed himself against it too, one hand forcing the door shut. It would require some force for anyone to open it until he was ready for them. As the train started moving, he reached inside his pouch, drew out the little knife, and prepared to meet whatever the journey might bring.

Eduard slept, unaware that Christmas approached. The train laboured into Ufa, as he stirred. His legs were numb, his knife long since dropped in his lap, his eyes itched and he was hungry. He stretched and his elbow struck the case. Irritably, he kicked out at it and it inched away, almost as if it wanted to escape his ill temper. He kicked it again, with both feet, and it slid against the door. It occurred to him that, if he pushed hard enough, he could jam the door closed with the case, and be free to find a more congenial resting place.

After twenty minutes of pushing and pulling and manoeuvring the case, he succeeded in barricading the door, and turned his attention to the disposition of bales. After another fifteen minutes he had hauled two to the end of the truck, and set a third at right angles, to form a draught-screen and upright 'pillow'. Checking his knife, he settled in for the rest of the day, reasoning that he could survive until the next stop before seeking food and water.

As he crawled inside his makeshift bailiwick, a sliver of light fell across his feet, and the door on the other side of the truck slowly rolled open. In his anxiety to secure himself, he had failed to realise the truck could be loaded from either side. He burrowed into the bale, pulling his feet quietly out of the light and out of sight. He heard voices – in German.

'This'll do. Give me a hand.'

'Are you sure?'

'Ja. Ja.'

'Here's your food, and some vodka. Sorry it's not schnapps, but it'll have to do.'

The first voice was that of a young man, the second older, a woman's.

'Hans?'

'Ja, mutter?'

'Be careful...' and she started weeping, slowly, quietly, drawing great shuddering breaths between each sob.

'Must you really go?'

'You know I must.' There was a pause. 'It's a matter of honour.'

At that the woman started crying again, and there was an indistinct muttering and murmuring, then silence, then, 'Auf weidersehn, mein mutter. Auf weidersehn.'

The woman started to wail, then stopped abruptly, as the door rolled shut, and Eduard heard Hans shuffle towards the other end of the truck. Here was an unexpected crisis – yet not so surprising, for here was another escaper, following the same route, the same reasoning, and thereby using the same train, and perhaps by happenstance, perhaps through fate, the very same truck. And perhaps here was Eduard's first opportunity to strike a blow against the hated Boche.

Hans was undoubtedly a first-generation Sovietised Prusskie, who had heard of the German invasion and felt drawn to the master-race and its Napoleonic offensive, enthusiastic for honourable bloodshed, in the name of the Fatherland. Well, Hans was in for a little surprise, as Eduard stealthily drew out his small, sharp, lethal and proven knife, and started to edge his way through the untidily stacked bales. It was a mistake.

Without any warning, a bale leaning precariously on edge against a horizontally stacked pile of other bales, tottered towards him as he brushed past. At the same time, the train lurched, and Eduard just had time to realise the trucks were being shunted into an overnight siding, when he fell against something soft, lost his footing, and found himself lying between two bales, with an astonished, young, blond, fur-clad boy lying on top of him. In the confusion, he had lost his knife. They stared at each other in the half light, then Eduard raised both his hands, palm upwards. He was in no position to fight, for young Hans was a heavyweight, and Eduard's legs were pinioned. The German was the first to speak.

'Who are you?'

Eduard grunted, and not for the first time breathed silent thanks for his facility with language.

'Franz, Franz Stockhauer. And you?'

'Hans Biedermaier. You are from where? Not Ufa surely? It is far from our home town.'

'Nein, nein. I am from Petropavlovsk, but my family is from Koln.'

'You don't sound German...'

'I was born in this country. Weren't you?'

'Ja, ja.'

'Well then,' Eduard coughed, his chest compressed by the other's weight. 'D'you mind getting off me? Please?'

'Of course, of course. I'm so sorry, but I did not expect to find anyone else here, that is...' he tailed off, as he pushed himself off Eduard and stood, as Eduard staggered to his feet. They peered at each other. The train lurched again, and they were both thrown against the bales, Hans reaching out to steady Eduard, as he lost his footing.

'Thanks. I think we had better sit down.'

Hans nodded, and they slid down opposite one another.

'Would you like some food?' asked Hans, and Eduard simply held out a hand. The German reached down to a rucksack and unhooked the straps, plunging his free hand inside. Out came a long, fat parcel, wrapped in crackly greased paper.

'Mein mutter makes ein good bratwurst.'

He passed the parcel to Eduard, diving once more into the bag.

'Here is bread too – proper bread. Not that rubbish the Russians eat.'

He pulled out a short, sheathed knife, and Eduard stiffened, feeling naked without his own. Hans peeled back the cloth wound round the loaf, and hacked off a neat slice, proffering it to Eduard on the point of the knife.

'It is like a field ration, no?' he laughed.

'You want some schnapps – no, sorry, it's not schnapps, it's vodka. Would you like some?'

Eduard could hardly speak, his mouth stuffed with sausage and bread, so he simply held out his hand again, and grasped the heavy bottle. As he chased the lively loaf down with the next best thing to slivovitz, he considered the youngster opposite.

He was perhaps the same age if not older than Eduard, yet he was a child. By the look of him, a well-fed, well-cared for, wealthy child at that. He was hardly the harsh Hun Eduard yearned to meet and fight and kill. Even when – if – he found his knife, it would not be Hans who would meet his end along its supple blade.

Eduard made a decision. He would try to make this impractical patriot see that his future lay not in the ranks of the Wermacht, but back home, helping his 'mutter'. Meanwhile the German was a Godsend, solving the problems of food and drink, providing companionship, and possibly a means to bypassing Moskva and all its vague pitfalls. If he could somehow turn the German connection to account, he could get through the German lines and, at the same time, send Hans home to 'mutter'.

When they had eaten, Hans asked how long it would take to reach the German lines. He had learnt that by December 1941 the German Army Groups had reached Leningrad in the north, and almost encircled Moskva, driving through Kalinin north of the capital, and Tula to the south. The Southern Army had pushed through the Ukraine and threatened Rostov; Hitler was poised to strike at Stalingrad. Hans wanted to find his way out of Moskva to join those armies of the Reich. Eduard wanted to find his way past them.

'A week, perhaps two. It depends on the trains.'

Hans passed the bottle and Eduard sipped more cautiously. He looked carefully at the young German, and it crossed his mind that this young boy was almost certainly older than he was, yet so much younger in heart and behaviour. One thing they clearly shared was a certain idealism, and Eduard now knew beyond doubt that his fiercely forged will to fight was no excuse for indiscriminate violence.

The Germans were the collective enemy, but not every German was a natural foe. As he slowly sipped, he reflected that if he was to be true to his beliefs, he should bring this blond believer to understand that, beyond the symbolic swastika and its forbear, the double-headed eagle, lay a corrupt system, an evil regime, and almost certain death for a young, headstrong and willing recruit.

Yet he also realised that he could not change Hans's mind any more than Hans might change his. They were both victims of their circumstance. Eduard made up his mind. He would carry on as if nothing had happened, making his way past the German lines. He would do nothing to hinder Hans, but he would not help him to a certain death and he would divert him, if the opportunity arose. He would do this as much to salve his own conscience as to help the boy and, he realised, to rob the Reich of at least one willing martyr to the wrong cause. Satisfied with his homespun philosophising, Eduard handed back the bottle.

'We will soon be in Kujbysev – we must make sure we are not found.'

Hans nodded, and put the bottle away with a certain economy; Eduard saw that the boy had wrapped the sausage and stowed that away as well, and the bread was also carefully fitted into a side pocket of his rucksack. The orderliness of it both amused and scared him. This was a disciplined youth. If he inadvertently made a stupid move, said something silly, Hans might react with impetuosity, but he might also act swiftly, with an economy of movement and the cutting edge of his doubtless well-honed knife.

'Will you fight when we get to Moskva?'

Eduard shrugged.

'I don't know. I have no training. I will try to go home, to train perhaps.'

'I can fight. I was in the Corps.'

'The Corps?'

'The Corps at Omsk – I was in the school Corps. We did rifle drill, with wooden guns, and once a week we shot at the firing range. Blanks.'

'I think it is a little different at the front.'

Hans pulled his lower lip back and raked it with his teeth.

'I suppose it is.' He looked up at Eduard. 'But we can learn, can't we?'

'Yes, we can learn.' Eduard shifted against the bale, and felt it warn against his leg. He put his hand down, and brought it back up to his face. He was bleeding. The knife had stuck in the bale, and he had impaled himself. He rolled over and pulled the cloth open – it was a shallow wound, a mere scratch. He glanced at Hans, but the boy was preoccupied with rearranging his rucksack. Eduard pulled the cloth round his leg again – the wound would soon dry out. His tucked the knife in his waistband.

'Hans?'

'Yes?'

'Can I see your knife?'

The German dipped into the bag and pulled out the knife, tossing it in the air and catching it haft first, then proffering it to Eduard. Eduard took it, gently, turned it, and stroked the blade against his thumb. It was paper-thin and extremely sharp.

'Nice. Better than mine.' And he produced his own weapon.

Hans leaned over and reached for the two knives. Eduard smiled, leaning back and closing his hands over them.

'First lesson. Never give your weapon to a stranger.'

'But you're not a stranger.'

'Oh yes I am. You only met me a little while ago. You have only my word for what or who I am, and I yours.'

Hans looked puzzled.

'I was always taught to trust people,' he said, his face furrowed.

'Well, there's a war on, Hans, and you cannot trust everyone, so it's best to trust no-one. Here.'

He handed Hans's knife back.

Hans laughed.

'There you are. You trust me, or you wouldn't give me my knife back.'

'That's true, but you have proved yourself trustworthy. You have shared bread and meat and that revolting drink with me. But I have done nothing to earn your trust.'

Hans smiled, and leant over Eduard, putting a tentative hand on his shoulder.

'You gave me back my knife. If you weren't my friend, you would have kept it, or used it.'

Eduard considered the lad, then made a decision.

'My name's not Franz, I'm not German, and I don't come from Koln.'

Hans stiffened, then relaxed again, laughing.

'You are telling me stories?'

'Not any more.'

'Then who are you?'

Eduard stood up, and shuffled between the bales, so that he was out of the other's reach.

'My name is Eduard, I am Polish, I have been in prison for two years, and I am returning to my country to fight your soldiers.'

Hans jumped to his feet, dropped his knife, then sagged against the bales, his hands to his face.

'Then you will kill me.'

Eduard shook his head.

'I will not kill you, Hans. You are not a soldier, you are not that kind of a German either. You are a good boy, a kind person, and I like you too.'

He moved towards the boy.

'Besides, you gave me food, and you offered me friendship. And I really do like you.'

He put both hands on Hans's arms, gripping him.

'I think you should go home, and leave the Nazis to do their own fighting.'

'Never!'

'Hans, Hans. This is not your fight. Your mutter needs you at home. You will die. It will be for nothing. One day it will be over. Then you can fight for your country. Let me tell you a little about this war, and what it is really about.'

They sat side by side, the bottle between them, occasionally passing it back and forth, as Eduard, hesitantly at first, then faster and more fluently as he found the words, tried to explain what he knew, what Mazloff had told and taught him, what he could recall of his father's tales and young Bruno's sharp knowledge of war and its bureaucracies, and gradually, he convinced the innocent young German until, after a lengthy pause, as they drained the bottle, Hans turned to him and said, 'Eduard, you are the first person I have ever met who told me his own truth, without trying to persuade me. I believe you.' He paused. 'But I am still German, and my country is at war. I must do something.'

'Then help me, because I am going to war to win, to help finish this fight, so that we can live in peace, with our families, and the horses can roam again and I can stalk the wild birds above the Seret – and you can come and visit me and we will remember this journey, and we will tell our children, and they will be amazed – and I will come to your home, where the real Germans love their country and work for a future without wars.'

Eduard stopped abruptly, aware that he sounded simplistic, at least to himself, and that he had lurched enthusiastically somewhat out of his political and philosophical depth. Then he did something that echoed the rituals of childhood. He clasped Hans's right hand, and drew his blade down the wrist until bright beads of blood started up through the surprised skin.

'Do the same to me,' as he stretched his own arm out, wrist uppermost. Hans obeyed. Eduard then put his hand over the other's, and rubbed their blood together.

'Now we are true friends, brothers in the blood, not Pole, not German, but men.' And he drew the blond boy to him, and embraced him.

As they stood, two boys but one man and a child, the floor beneath them shifted, as the train braked, and drew slowly into Kujbysev. They were more than halfway to Moskva, on their way to war, or home, or both.

Hans and Irma, Irma and Hans. Brief shadows. I remember Irma sometimes, especially when I look at my sweetling. I think that, had I stayed, had I not sped so eagerly on my warlike way, I could have loved Irma, for she was truly the first to stir my heart more than my loins. In her there was that sparkle, like a shimmering sheen on the surface of feeling which tells you something inexplicable is happening in your darkness, that part of you which will not respond to rational thought, which is outside your control yet which you can kill with a wordless thought – I shall not. And it is gone, that kindling, as if the damp timbre of your heart has snuffed out the opportunistic spark. Irma was my introduction to that love which needs no reason, has no purpose, just is.

Of course, I did not realise it then, and I daresay I have, perhaps deliberately, ignored it time and again since then, for I have ever been the lover of instant contact, urgently forgotten in the hope of continuing novelties. Perhaps that is the price we pay for hearts damaged by hate.

Hans, on the other hand, was a beginning. I knew him for but a few days, yet here was someone who actually needed me, even if he did not know it and I only half guessed it. I suppose that, in our skin-deep culture, to instantly and truly love another human being for himself, and to act accordingly, is so foreign that we cannot comprehend its value, much less equate it with old rules of faith and hope and charity. We are the poorer for that, and I often wonder what happened to Hans, and where he went and whether or not he brought joy to his 'mutter'. I suspect that, in our brief encounter, we both grew up a little, and that I profited more than he in understanding then how little I knew of myself.

I suppose that Irma, and Hans, brought me from action and reaction to the beginning of a process of self-enlightenment, beyond simple gratification of needs and desires. Hans was my philosopher's stone. I had yet to discover alchemy – how to transmute such a sense of others' need to control one's own. Now that I have, I can do nothing about it, for I am silenced, forever.

What happened with both Hans and Irma that far transcended the emotions of the moment was trust. Trust was implicit in our transactions but trust was also, for the first time, visible to me. I understood the commitment. It had no need of a future to justify itself – no action to spawn reaction to ensure result to fettle the future in my favour – or theirs. In our worlds of policies and premia, trust is conditional on signature and contained in the courtrooms of contingency and circumstance. It shifts and shatters.

In my world of memory, trust was absolute.

A CROOKED MILE

Eduard cautiously slid the door open, a sparse two inches, Hans behind him, knife ready. He could see the same drainage ditch he remembered from two years before. It was, if anything, closer to their train. Eduard inched the door further open, and risked a quick glance up the train, then down. Nothing. Nobody. The light was fading, and the train was silent. He turned back to Hans.

'I think we're safe. I'm going over there.'

He gestured towards the ditch.

'You stay here.'

'Will you be long?'

'Only long enough to have a quick pee, and see what's happening. Then you can go.'

'What about food? We haven't much left.'

'I know. Let's think about it. We don't want to miss the train, do we?' and he laughed, and Hans joined in, and soon they were coughing and spluttering, and clapping one another on the shoulders, overcome by the simple humour of it all, when Eduard stiffened. He put his forefinger to his lips.

'Shhh.'

Hans whispered, 'What is it?'

'I don't know. But I heard something.'

They stood, either side of the partly opened door, waiting.

Five minutes passed, then six, seven, and Hans, impatient, moved. Eduard reached out to stop him, but he was too late. The German had stuck his head out, and then he was gone, hauled out by some invisible force. Eduard flattened himself against the truckside, his breath shallow, his knife held out. Nothing.

He waited, then moved, cautiously, inch by inch, towards the other side of the truck, and slipped behind the bales. Minutes passed. Then he heard it again, the soft crunch of footsteps, one after the other, poised on the balls of invisible feet, as whoever it was approached the truck. Then silence. Still Eduard waited. Still there was silence.

Then he heard the door creak slightly, as if a hand gripped it, and he felt the slight tremor of the truck as a weight swung up onto it. Someone was inside, somewhere on the other side of the bales. Eduard slowly reached down for Hans's rucksack, and felt for the strap. His fingers curled round it, and he lifted it gently, ducking his head through the strap, then softly fumbling inside for the bottle. As his fingers found it, he heard the faint footfalls as the intruder approached.

With the bottle held aloft, and the knife in front, he poised, waiting.

It happened quickly, so fast that Eduard had no time to think, simply to act. The bales toppled and fell towards him, he sidestepped,

117

reflexively backwards and sideways, away from the thrust and, as he did so, a bulky figure materialised. He brought the bottle down where he judged the man's face to be, and thrust the knife forward at chest height. Then he pulled the knife back, dropped the bottle, and scuttled round the fallen bales, towards the now half-open door. His assailant was out of sight as he sprang out of the truck, falling onto the sharp chippings, and rolled automatically beneath it, glimpsing, as he went, a still figure below the doorway. He froze midway.

There was a shuffling, then a hard thud, and he looked swiftly left, then right. He found himself staring directly into a pair of glittering black eyes. The assailant threw himself onto his back, then rolled under the truck, towards Eduard, who hauled himself across the sleepers, to the gap between the trucks, and leapt to his feet, reaching up for the claw, and hauling himself up – just in time as the other man followed him.

Eduard grabbed the chains, and crabbed up the end of the wagon, until he was doubled up, hanging above his adversary. As the man straightened, cracked his head on the claw, staggered, and looked up, Eduard dropped, kicking his face as he fell, slashing at it with the knife as he passed, rolling over and over on the sharp chippings, away from the truck, onto his feet, racing for the ditch. He half fell, half jumped into the stagnant, foetid water, and crouched for a moment, before lifting himself up over the edge and, seeing nothing, scrabbled up the opposite bank.

Again he ran, until he was nearing a line of corrugated sheds. Once there, he paused, and looked back, but there was no sign of pursuit.

As his breath eased, he glanced down at the knife, which was rusty with blood; he wiped it on his sleeve, adjusted the rucksack, which had slipped round to his chest, and considered the options.

Hans was probably dead. That much was clear. The intruder, whoever he was, was almost certainly alone, and equally certainly, a fugitive like themselves, for otherwise he would have brought help, or called for it. Eduard reasoned that the loner, if that was what he was, might have supplies, which would turn a threat to an advantage. He resolved to return to the truck, if nothing happened after a further five minutes.

He waited. Nothing happened.

This time Eduard utilised the advantage of open terrain, and quietly walked to the other end of the shed, before risking a glance towards the ditch and the track. There was nothing to be seen, except the train, still and waiting. He drew back, and gave it another minute or so. He cautiously moved round the shed, and took a step into the open, then he ran to the ditch, half crouching, and slid down the bank into the muddy water.

After a moment's pause for reaction, he raised his head above the bank, and immediately saw an indistinct figure bent over something on the ground. He swore to himself. Now he could risk neither going back, nor making a dash for the train. While he was wondering what to do next, he heard a soft call.

'Franz,' and again, 'Franz.'

What the hell? Who on earth was Franz? Then he remembered. Franz was his pseudonym when he was attempting to persuade Hans that he, too, was a second generation Russo-German. It must be Hans calling. His eyes strained as he peered through the gloom towards the train.

'Franz?'

There it was again. The figure seemed to be standing, then it was walking towards the ditch, dragging something. Eduard ducked down and, with infinite caution, avoiding any more than a minimal disturbance of the water, waded away a yard, two, five, ten, then stopped. There was a sucking, slithering sound, a subdued splash, the water rippling, and then the figure was striding rapidly towards him.

There was no option. He crouched, ready to spring, knife in hand, as it approached.

'Franz?'

He looked up. It was impossible to see who it was. The figure stood, motionless. Eduard put his hands over his head, the knife concealed, and waded to the bank, to find himself face to face with a stranger.

'Alright, come straight out, and drop the knife.'

Eduard threw the knife onto the bank, and the stranger stooped and retrieved it, as he clambered onto firm ground.

'You had better come back to the train.'

The stranger prodded Eduard with what looked like a rifle, and together they walked back to the truck.

'Up. Get up in the truck.'

He prodded Eduard again, and Eduard reached up, grasped the door hasp and swung himself onto the truck. He glanced back, but the stranger was standing well clear, far too far away for Eduard to make any move.

'Move inside,' ordered the other.

Eduard complied and the stranger leapt up and into the truck.

'Sit.'

Eduard sat on the case, and the stranger sat opposite him. He put the rifle down behind him, regarded Eduard with half a smile, then leant forward. Eduard flinched. The stranger slowly extended his hand.

'Neumann.'

Eduard glared at him.

'I'm Neumann.'

Eduard made no move, and the stranger shifted on the bale, and grasped his hand, shaking it vigorously.

'Neumann, from Abatski, at your service.'

119

The stranger turned.

'Hans. You can come out now.'

Hans loomed out of the darkness, threw himself at Eduard and hugged him to his chest.

'I thought we were both going to die.'

Eduard held him and murmured, 'So did I, so did I.'

They disengaged, and Hans sat beside Neumann and the three of them laughed. Hans pointed at Neumann.

'I thought we would die, and then Neumann here killed him.'

'Killed who?'

'Killed the bloody Russkie who guards this part of the yard,' said Neumann. 'I've been watching him for hours, wondering how to get rid of him, and how to get on this train.'

He waved a hand at Hans.

'Then this young man suddenly appears, our Russkie friend hauls him out of the van, and jumps inside. There is a struggle, and then he appears, looking somewhat the worse for wear. So I take care of him with this bit of timber I happen to have handy, and then I bundle Hans inside the truck, take the body for disposal, and before I go searching for this other unknown who I saw running to the ditch.'

'Me,' said Eduard.

'Yes, you, my friend.'

Neumann put his hand in his pocket.

'Here's your knife. I don't really need it now I have his rifle.'

He offered the blade to Eduard, holding it vertically between thumb and forefinger. Eduard took it, noticing the other man's pale, smooth skin.

Neumann was long in the body, but short in the leg, with a smooth, seamless face, a slick little moustache, combed away from the centre, and flat, silky, short dark hair combed forward, small ears, narrow black eyes, and even teeth. There was a noticeable neatness to his appearance, even to the way he held himself, poised, legs tidily crossed, hands resting lightly on his knees. Eduard decided he did not much care for this latest companion.

'So... you are going to Moskva?'

Eduard nodded.

'Hans told me.'

Then why ask, said Eduard to himself.

'So am I. We can travel together.'

He must have noticed the flicker of doubt across Eduard's face.

'Three is better than two and besides, Hans and I have something in common,' establishing his right to comradeship at the same time as isolating Eduard, however slightly.

'We come from the same background.' He paused. 'I gather you are Polish?'

Again Eduard nodded.

120

'Well, that's the next best thing, isn't it?'

Neumann added, 'I spent some time in Cracow, before the war,' as if this gave him credibility and proprietorial rights over Eduard's country.

'Now, let us see. This train is travelling to Moskva, where we must decide what to do next.'

Eduard muttered under his breath.

'I didn't quite catch that,' observed Neumann.

'I didn't say anything, really,' lied Eduard, 'but we have already decided, Hans and me.'

Neumann regarded him impassively, then raised one eyebrow slightly, saying, 'I gather you are going to fight – but against whom? Hans wants to fight, but he tells me you are not in favour, that you think he should return to his mother, after he has helped you find a way to the war. Is that right?'

Eduard was beginning to realise that Neumann was a far bigger threat than the shadowy figure he had first identified as hostile, at the ditch's edge. Neumann was manipulating them.

'Yes, I am going to fight, but I am not sure where, not yet anyway.'

'You will fight the Russians?'

'No.'

'Then who will you fight?'

'I will join my countrymen, and someone else will decide,' lied Eduard.

Neumann leant forward and tapped him on the knee, to emphasise each word.

'We' – he gestured towards Hans with the other hand – 'we are going to fight for our people, against the tyrants.'

His eyes gleamed, and Eduard began to sense a certain zeal, an enthusiasm beyond the norm, an incipient madness. Neumann was indeed a dangerous companion.

'We are going to fight for a cause,' and he turned to Hans, 'aren't we, my fine friend?'

Hans nodded uncertainly.

'And you, Mister Polish prisoner, you must come with us and fight with us, for the cause, mustn't you?'

Eduard stood abruptly.

'I will fight when I have found my own people. I will help you find your fight, I promise.'

'Ah, that is good, very good. Thank you.'

For the time being, Neumann seemed satisfied, as if he had scored a notable victory, and now held the future of both boys in his hands. He rummaged about on the floor between them, until he found Hans's rucksack.

'Time to eat, I think,' pulling out sausage, 'and for a little drink,' removing the top from the bottle and taking a long swig. He glanced at Hans and then Eduard.

'You want some?' as if it was his to deliver, holding out the bottle, and carefully scribing a slice of sausage, piercing it dead centre with his own knife, and proffering both, one to Hans, the other to Eduard. Eduard handed the bottle to Hans, and held his hand out for the sausage.

'Not much left, eh?' Neumann handed him the snub-nosed remnant.

When they had finished, Neumann secured the rucksack, and deposited it at his own feet.

'The train may go any time now. We wait for the next stop, then we forage for food and water.'

With that, he leant back against the bales, and closed his eyes. Eduard waited a few moments, then gestured to Hans to join him, as he moved to the end of the truck. Neumann's eyes opened at his first step.

'Going somewhere?'

Eduard shook his head, sighed, and sank down, his back to the case. Hans stayed behind Neumann, and they dozed. Less than twenty minutes later, they heard the first hiss of steam, the grumbling of axles slowly turning, the complaint of jostled couplings, a shudder running down the length of the train as it began to move out of Kujbysev.

'On our way, then,' murmured Neumann, his eyes still closed, his hand on the rifle.

Dawn filtered through the cracks as the train slowed down. Eduard was instantly awake, to find Neumann's eyes already upon him. Hans slept on, untidily sprawled across a broken bale. Eduard shuffled across, stepping over Neumann's legs, and shook him. The boy started, dragged his arm across his eyes, and sat up.

'Where are we?'

'No idea, but we're stopping.'

'Time to get some food,' added Neumann.

He pulled the bottle out of the rucksack and thrust it at Eduard.

'You get the water,' and, turning to Hans, 'you see if you can find some food,' handing him the rucksack.

He leant back against the case. 'I'll stay here and keep guard.'

His hand was still on the rifle.

Eduard pulled the door ajar and squinted out. They were drawn up against a black, brick wall. He pulled the door open and looked up, then down. Nobody.

'It's clear.'

He jumped down, and Hans joined him. Neumann slid the door to behind them.

'This way,' and Eduard moved down the trackside towards an opening in the wall. Once there, they could see stacks of bales in ordered ranks, long shadows cast from the overhead light through the transparent roof.

122

'It's a warehouse,' said Hans.

Once inside, they paused, but there was no sound or sign of activity, except a distant swishing.

'That's running water,' whispered Eduard. 'I'm going to find it.'

He started down the aisles, following the sound as it magnified in volume until it sounded like a waterfall, and they emerged into a clear space, with an internal lean-to, its door open, and a shimmer of water on the floor.

'This is it.' Eduard motioned Hans to wait by the door, and peered inside. 'It's clear. I'll fill the bottle. You keep a watch, and whistle of there's anyone coming.'

Inside, a tap was gushing water into a wide gulley, the water slopping onto the floor, and rippling across the concrete. Eduard pushed the bottle under the flow, and tried to direct the water with his thumb. Within seconds, it was full, and he started to cap the bottle when he heard voices.

'Have you got it, then?'

'Been long enough.'

Hans: 'It was too heavy.'

'Mother of God. Alright then, we'll get a trolley, Wait here.' And the voices receded, as Hans appeared, white with terror.

'What was all that about?'

'I don't know.'

'What was too heavy?'

'I don't know. It's the first thing that came into my head.'

'It seems to have worked. Come on, let's get out of here.'

'We can't.'

Hans pointed. There was a group of smoking, chattering workers, standing at the end of the aisle, back the way they had come. Eduard pushed Hans.

'Go down the next aisle, and behind them, back to the truck. I'll deal with this,' and he started walking towards the group.

'Hello. Late again?'

'No, no, just had to try to turn the water off.'

'Waste of time. It always does that when they throw the valves. It'll sort itself out soon.'

The speaker detached himself slightly from the group, and looked more closely at Eduard.

'Have I seen you before?'

Eduard patted his pockets, then reached into one, then the other.

'Damn, damn, damn. Left them behind.'

Diverted, the man asked, 'Left your smokes behind then?'

'Yeah.'

'Well, it'll cost you, but have a drag of this,' and he pulled the bedraggled roll-up out of his mouth and offered the wet, stained end. Eduard took a shallow pull, and then coughed the acrid smoke out.

'Thanks,' he rasped, and handed the cigarette back.

'Left your lunch behind too?'

Eduard felt his pockets again.

'Oh God. Yes.'

'Along with your cock, eh?' and the man laughed, inviting the group to join him in mutual discomfiture of this young latecomer.

'You'd better go home and fetch it, then,' and they all roared with laughter at such a preposterous proposal.

'I'd better do that, hadn't I?' smiled Eduard, and that set them off all over again, until the speaker raised his hand.

'OK comrades, time to laugh, time to work. Let's get on with it.'

At that exact moment, Eduard heard it. The train was hissing and spluttering, and making ready to depart. The majority of the group was walking past him, into the depths of the warehouse. The remainder was separating and going down different aisles. He was left standing, when he saw the trolleymen swing round the corner, and make towards the lean-to.

'Hey!' he shouted, and they glanced back, slowing, the trolley pulling them forward with its own momentum.

'Hey! Where the hell are you going?'

'To the water shed.'

Eduard stood as tall as he could project himself, assumed an imaginary mantle of authority and, without moving, lowered his voice and slowly enunciating every single word, commanded, 'Bring it here – now!'

The two looked at one another, shrugged, then wheeled, and brought the trolley to him. They looked at him questioningly. When he judged he had their complete attention, he wagged a finger at them in admonition.

'You have no orders to take this anywhere. Have you?' He spat this last straight at them, leaning forward slightly as he did so. Clearly alarmed, the older of the two wiped a hand against his leg and waved vaguely towards the lean-to.

'He said it was too heavy, so we thought—'

'Thought? Thought? You thought? You are not paid to think. That is the privilege of the Party. And you are not the Party. You are the servants of the Party. Leave it here, and get on with your work – now!'

Dismayed, the trolley pair slouched down the aisle the way they had come, leaving Eduard trembling with elation and trepidation, and with the trolley. Having resolved the dilemma of the not-needed trolley and the absent Hans, Eduard now realised he had at best a few seconds to reach the train. He rammed the trolley brake forward and leant against it, pushing with all his strength. Gradually it moved, and he was striding steadily towards the doorway, when he saw a figure silhouetted against the trucks.

124

Nearing the opening, Eduard saw it was the speaker from the group, and he was looking directly at Eduard as he raised both hands.

'I don't know who you are, but I do know you aren't who you said you were. STOP!'

In that nanosecond, Eduard took his decision and, summoning every muscle and sinew, shoved the trolley hard, straight at the man.

Astonished, his hands still aloft, the speaker shouted again 'STOP!' and held his ground. Eduard gathered speed, and gave the trolley a final massive shove, head down, legs ramming into the concrete. The trolley slammed into the man's thighs, and he toppled, falling sideways and underneath, his cap flying one way, his rucksack ricocheting from his shoulder into Eduard's face. Eduard clutched at it, threw it forward and away, as the man disappeared.

The left-hand wheels both lurched over his chest, and he screamed as his ribs collapsed, and punctured his lung. The train was moving as the door slid open, Hans gripping the door edge, Neumann's eyes glittering from its depths, and Eduard jumped, missed his footing, slammed against the truck, stumbled, started running, reached up, as Hans reached down, clasped his hand, and felt his arm wrenching away as he swung up and in. Falling against Neumann's feet, he registered a final image of the warehouseman's mouth gouting blood.

They slammed the door closed as the train gathered speed, and Eduard lay gasping on the floor, Hans bending over him.

'Are you alright?'

Eduard kept on swallowing, licking his lips, wiping his hand across his mouth, unable to answer.

'Of course he's alright.' Then, 'Give him some water. After all, he did fill the bottle.'

'Oh God. The bottle. Where is it?' Silently, Hans handed it to him.

'You gave it to me.'

As his breath slowed, and his heart stopped trying to break out of his chest, Eduard remembered.

'We forgot the food.'

Hans smiled.

'No we didn't. Look!' and he tipped the rucksack upside down. Out poured bread, sausage and several apples.

'Where on earth did that come from?'

'You got it.'

'I got it?'

'Yes. You got it when you threw that man's rucksack away. Straight into the truck!'

Neumann chipped in with, 'That was lucky, wasn't it?'

Eduard ignored him, reached for one of the apples, and took a deep bite.

'I think we've earned these,' as he offered another to Hans.

The train thundered on through the afternoon, into the night, throughout the night, and well into the next day. From time to time, Neumann would essay a brief conversation, Hans responding, and Eduard contributing without enthusiasm. Towards the evening, Neumann lifted the rifle and worked the bolt mechanism. He glanced up at Eduard, who was standing, leaning.

'We may need this soon.'

'Why?'

'I think we are near our journey's end.'

Eduard pulled the door ajar, wincing as the cold air rushed in. The fields fled by, featureless, and he closed the door.

'I can see nothing but open country.'

'Nonetheless, we are nearing the outskirts.' Neumann smiled. 'Moskva next stop, eh?'

Around midnight the train slowed and stopped. Again Eduard pulled the door ajar, and looked out. There were no lights, no voices, nothing to indicate where they might be. Then he heard it. A dull crump. Then another.

The sky flared briefly, twice. Then again, as if a distant storm was playing out its passing drama. Thud followed thud, flash, flash. It was all a long way away, but it was clearly no storm. It was war.

As Eduard pushed the door closed, Neumann spoke softly.

'It will be soon. We will soon be fighting. We should sleep.'

This time there was no menace or inflexion in his voice.

They did sleep, not all at the same time, nor deeply, but they slept, enough to refresh themselves for whatever might be to come. Not long after, the sun came up, and a weak light glimmered between the timbers, the train edged forward, and slowly steamed towards the battlefields.

The thud of artillery was louder, though the flash of fire was weaker in the morning sun, as they all stood in the doorway, their faces turned towards Moskva.

As the train slid into a small station, Eduard pushed the door to, leaving a sliver of space through which to maintain a watch. Scanning the sight slot, he caught the name of the place – Chapievski. He told the others and Neumann swore.

'Gotterdamerung! Chapievski. That's thirty miles from Moskva. They must be close.'

As he spoke, leatherclad hands grasped the door, and shoved it open. They looked down, and there were two greatcoated, capped and holstered officials, without insignia but with the indelible stamp of authority. They said nothing, but one beckoned the trio. They jumped onto the crude platform.

'Follow us.'

The platform was awash with soldiers, officials, militiamen, in a maelstrom of motion. Neumann shouldered past Eduard and caught up with the officials. As they made their way down the platform, sidestepping here, standing aside there, Neumann's head was close to that of one of the officials, who was nodding vigorously. Halfway down the platform, they turned into a long, low room, with several internal doors. The leading official pushed one of these open, and strode inside, throwing his cap down on a table, and peeling his gloves off. The other stood to one side with Neumann, talking quietly as the first man shuffled some papers on another table, and then looked up at Eduard and Hans.

'Well then. How far have you come?'

Hans looked at Eduard and Eduard looked at the official.

'From Omsk.'

'You came in a truck, without tickets.'

It was a statement. Eduard saw no point in lying.

'Yes. We had no money. We wanted to get to Moskva. So we found a truck. And here we are.'

'Sit.'

The official remained standing.

'You are Polish?'

'Yes.'

'They are not Polish.'

'No.'

'They are Russian.'

Eduard said nothing.

'They wish to go to the front.'

Eduard still said nothing.

'You wish to go to the front?'

'I want to go home.'

'Home?'

'Poland.'

'Ah yes. Poland. Yes.'

The official sat, drew some papers towards him, and started writing. He beckoned the other man, and handed him the papers.

'Find them somewhere.'

Dismissed, the junior official adjusted his cap, and gestured to Hans and Neumann. Hans started towards Eduard, only to be restrained by the first official.

'You can say goodbye from there.'

'But—'

'No buts. Just say goodbye.'

Tears smeared Hans's eyes as he held out his hands towards Eduard.

'I don't understand,' he said.

'You will.'

Eduard raised his hand in farewell, adding, 'Good luck, Hans. And thank you.'

And they were gone.

'Well, the question is, what are we going to do with you?'

Eduard shrugged.

'I think the best thing we can do is keep you here a while, and then we can find some answers.'

Eduard said nothing.

'You are not stupid, that much is clear. But then, you wouldn't have got this far if you were, would you?'

The official pondered again.

'You see, I have a problem. I know you were at the warehouse in Kazan, but I don't know if your prisoners are right about what happened there.'

'My prisoners?'

'Yes, those two hybrids that you held with your rifle.'

'Rifle? My rifle? That was Neumann's rifle.'

'No, it was not Neumann's rifle. It was standard issue militia rifle, one of hundreds of thousands, so we have no idea where you got it, but it was certainly not Neumann's rifle. The question is why did you terrorise them with it and who did what at the warehouse?'

'Warehouse?'

'Come now. You know perfectly well what warehouse. I am just interested to know if Neumann was lying, and you are as calculating as he says you are, or if you are simply the innocent young Polish lad that you are trying to fool me you are.' He smiled at Eduard. 'Or something in between.'

He pushed the papers on his table together, dropped them into a folder, collected his gloves, and rose.

'Hand me my hat.'

Eduard glanced around and saw the cap on the other table. He reached for it, and turned to hand it to the official. The man had disappeared. Eduard looked round the room. There was no other door. The way in was open, and it was also the way out. Cautiously he edged towards it, and looked out into the anteroom. People were coming and going, and no-one gave him a second glance. Of the official there was no sign. Eduard walked slowly across the room to the door opposite the platform. He opened it. Outside was a similar bustle of people, and a few vehicles.

He was looking at the town of Chapievski.

Within minutes he was walking through the town centre, and down a side street. Several doors down, he saw two shops. One was a butcher's. He looked inside. There were several women, queuing, and one harassed man, apron bloodied, cutting and wrapping, taking roubles and trying to keep up with the custom. There was little on display on the crude shelf behind, and nothing hanging from the meathooks above.

The butcher appeared to be cutting horseflesh and counting sausages. Ignoring protests, Eduard shoved his way to the front, round the counter.

'Hey. Where do you think you're going?' shouted the shopkeeper.

'To help you,' answered Eduard, as he lifted a sausage, fumbled under the counter and found a knife and asked the woman before him, 'How much?'

The morning rush soon subsided and, as he wiped his hands, the butcher looked at Eduard with some curiosity.

'So, you did well, but who are you, and what made you think you could help me?'

'I'm looking for work.'

'That's obvious. Why?'

'My family is joining me here, but I have no food, and no money, and the war is close, and I am going to fight, as soon as they are settled. I need work – please.'

'Where have you come from?'

'Behind the Urals.'

'I don't need a butcher. I am a butcher. This morning – well that often happens, because we have so little, and they all want something. I have no work.'

'I will do anything. I will wash floors. I will carry things. I will run errands. Anything. Please give me some work. Just enough to feed my family when they arrive.'

The butcher looked at Eduard and shook his head sadly.

'You young people. OK.'

Eduard smiled and stuck out his hand; the butcher took it in his and then as quickly dropped it.

'Mind you, I have no room. You can't stay here. Come back tomorrow. I give you work then.'

Eduard thanked him, several times, and emerged into the morning's weak sunlight. The problem now was to find somewhere to stay. Behind him he felt a short, sharp tug on his sleeve. He turned back. The butcher was standing behind him, holding out a small package.

'Here. An advance payment. Mind you turn up tomorrow.'

Eduard took the proffered package, and unwrapped it. Sausage, and a thick slice of new bread.

'Thank you so much.'

The butcher waved dismissively.

'Tomorrow, then.'

'Tomorrow.'

Several yards away, Eduard found a narrow street which led to a small square, where there were benches, and he sat there watching the people go about their business, punctuated by the constant battery of distant noise from the other side of Moskva. He noticed the lack of fear in people's faces, the apparent acceptance of Hitler's threat within a day's march of their homes and livelihoods. Not for the first time, he marvelled at the phlegmatic, almost fatalistic attitude of the Russians.

129

After an hour, he ate some lunch, then wandered across the square to a small café, where he bought a strong, dark, sugarless coffee with some of his remaining roubles. He checked his knife and the small rucksack which still contained two apples and walked away from the square. He traversed small spaces, mean streets, wider thoroughfares and found himself on the town's edge, before he retraced his steps as night fell, and the distant artillery threw brief fans of instant light against the cycloramic twilight. There were no obvious places to sleep, so he decided to risk the station. There must be a waiting room, and it was clear the officials had no real interest in detaining him. Nonetheless, there seemed little point in courting danger, so he avoided their building and mounted the latticed bridge across the track. There was a waiting room on the other side.

Inside there were about a hundred people, some sitting on benches, many slouched or lying on the concrete floor. He was not alone in seeking the comparative comfort and convenience of a roof for the night. Espying a small space in one corner, furthest from the door, he picked his way across, and slipped down beside a small woman in layers of clothing, with a large bag of vegetables on her lap, and a thin, elderly man with a mongrel dog beside him, his battered fur hat pulled down over his eyes. He offered the woman an apple, but she shook her head.

Two hours later he was sound asleep when he was shaken violently.

'Wake up! You! Wake up!'

He opened his eyes. The old man was still shaking him, but stopped when he saw he had roused him.

'NKVD,' he hissed.

Eduard looked across the rows of the sleeping and the restless. There were two bulky individuals in dusky grey uniforms, with green armbands and red caps. These were the footsoldiers of the NKVD.

'Papers!' First one, then another sleeper was roused, rummaged for the requisite identification, passed them up, had them scrutinised, and received them back, to revert to some sort of rest. It was Eduard's turn. He handed the man his passport, his *undastawarenie*. The man turned it over, frowning. Then his face cleared. Eduard sighed inwardly with relief.

'Aha! You come from Tara, yes?'

'Yes, I have been released.'

'Congratulations. Very nice. Where are you going?'

'Nowhere. I've got a job.'

'Job? Where?'

'Here. Butcher's shop. Assistant. Starting tomorrow.'

'Afraid not,' said the NKVD man, folding the paper, and letting it flutter back down onto Eduard's lap. The old man had tipped his hat

130

up and was listening keenly to this exchange, and the old woman was surreptitiously feeling for Eduard's apples.

Eduard started to remonstrate, but the NKVD man cut him short.

'This is a forbidden zone. No newcomers. You've already come too far.'

'I will go back then.'

'No. We'll take you back.'

'Where?'

Eduard waited, and thought he detected an unholy gleam in the NKVD man's eye as he glanced at his kamerad and back to Eduard.

'Back to Siberia.'

Before Eduard could protest, he added, 'We've got a train waiting for evacuees from Moskva, and you're booked into this compartment,' and he pulled out a paper, signed it with a flourish and handed it to Eduard. Then he bent down and showed him another paper, which he carefully unfolded.

'Here is the list. Here are the compartments. And here's yours!'

As he straightened, he added, 'The guards will count you all, and look after you – all the way to Omsk. They will allocate you a camp after that.'

Mischievously he concluded, 'It might even be Tara! Home from home, eh?'

He reached down, gripped Eduard's hand, and hauled him up, not unkindly, but with determination.

'Now we go to your train.'

Outside the waiting room, a train stood, breathing hard. The NKVD man soon found Eduard's compartment and ushered him in with a mock bow. Then he surprised him by reaching into his knapsack and pulling out a loaf, a water bottle and a slab of sweet pudding.

'War is bloody, my friend, and we're not all bastards. At least you're not going to that,' and he jerked his thumb over his shoulder at the cracks and crumps and flashes and flares of the distant battlefield.

As Eduard sank back on the bench beside another 'evacuee', he also knew beyond all reasonable doubt: he was not going back to Omsk.

The worst kind of betrayal is that where you let yourself down, and the worst let-down is the one when you are impotent to prevent it. If I had lived differently, if I had listened when they said 'see a doctor', if I had taken more exercise, if I had eaten more sensibly, drunk less, smoked not at all – if, if, if – then perhaps I would not be caged up like this, abbreviated by my inability to communicate. Thus my betrayal of myself. Yet, if I had done all those things I was told to do, and none of those I did do, would it have made any difference? I shall never know.

And that is the real betrayal: the ignorance beyond the impotence. Like Neumann. With Hans I found trust; with Neumann, betrayal.

Neumann was my introduction to malevolent manipulation, and the simplicity of betrayal. From the moment he 'saved' us, he used us, and as quickly abused us, discarding me once my usefulness was at an end, and doubtless Hans, once he had reached his destination.

Betrayal is not the same as deception, for had I not deceived those trolleymen, and indeed the warehouseman? Yet I had not betrayed them. I was about the business of our survival, Hans's and mine. They were obstacles. To deceive them was to survive. Yet with Neumann the deception was deliberate and despicable, as much as it was also gratuitous. He posed as our saviour, deployed us for his own ends, then discarded us as he transferred his deceptions to the newly useful.

Betrayal is almost always with prior intent, and not a reactive process. There must be trust for betrayal to function and, even if I had my doubts, Hans trusted Neumann implicitly and Neumann set about generating grounds for my trust, in order to betray me.

The Judas within us is bred of self-interest, and thrives where the trust of others feeds it. In Neumann's case, and I must be charitable when I can, there was some element of madness, an insanity of purpose if not of person and, given that, I can forgive him, while not condoning what he did. The real betrayal was not at Chapievski, but in the warehouse, where Neumann projected poor ignorant, innocent Hans as well as me, and stood aside until our mission was over. I shall never know if the result would have been the same, had Neumann been other than he was, had he shared our risk, participated in our skirmish, stood beside us as we brought bread and water.

Yet perhaps something of his shiftless stance, the quicksand of his acquaintance, seeped into me, so that in future I would hesitate to trust, lest I be betrayed again. Thus does others' treachery reduce one's own purity of spirit. After Neumann, I became more cautious, less spontaneous in my affections, more calculating, careful and so less condign of others' trust.

I trust the doctors – up to a point, for I am betrayed by their impotence to release me; yet I fear the real betrayal is within myself, for it is I who cannot break out. Once the indomitable Eduard could escape, again and again. Now the same Eduard is imprisoned – through the betrayal of his own body.

THE GARDEN OF EDEN

There were no other Poles in the compartment – only Russians. Eduard kept himself to himself, nodding or grunting when spoken to, and holding his rucksack close to his chest, his knife in his right hand and that hand in his coat pocket.

The compartment was simple, with a bench either side, wooden floor, narrow shelves overhead, stacked with evacuees' packages, and a door at each end, with a narrow, sliding window above each one. Eduard was next to the door and he studied the window. It was a simple device, locked into place by a small handle; a quick turn and the window would drop down. It was not so much a question of whether as when he would execute that simple manoeuvre and jump out. The train would have to slow down, especially when it was negotiating the mountains.

Eduard ate the last apple, and sipped water from the almost full bottle, then dozed until the train made the first of its twice-daily halts. Each wagon was guarded at intervals, and only one compartment released at any one time, for personal relief, and to fill water containers at a single oxidised tap.

By the second day, the Russians had forged uneasy alliances, sharing food and fears. Discouraged by Eduard's apparent indifference, they made no effort to include him, for which he was grateful. The time passed uneventfully, with stops as before, and the train moved through Kujbysev, towards Ufa and the Urals.

On the third day, they approached the foothills and, after two brief stops, the train made moderate speed until, as night fell, it started the long climb. Eduard readied himself.

One by one those of his fellow passengers who were not already sleeping dozed off, until they were all asleep. Once he was satisfied he would not be stopped, Eduard cautiously eased himself away from his neighbour's lolling head, tightened the strap securing the rucksack to his chest, pushed the knife deep in his pocket, and stood, swaying with the train's motion, hard against the door. He knew that, once he opened the window, the draught might arouse someone, and that anyone could raise the alarm, but he reasoned that, in the confusion, he would be long gone. After all, there were no guards in the compartment – though there might well be 'plants', common enough in this system of Soviets.

The train was labouring and Eduard prayed silently that it would shortly reach a curve as well as the steepening gradient. Five, then ten minutes passed, and still the train struggled upwards, too fast to leave without risk of injury. Then he heard a change of note in the previously rhythmic clatter and a thud, a pause almost, and the train began to slow, until it was barely moving, as it curled around the flank of the mountain.

Eduard steadied himself, one hand on the window-bolt, then pulled, and a cool draught fanned his face. The man next to his seat half coughed, swallowed, and squinted at the window, then closed his eyes, and started snoring. Eduard reached up to the shelf, raised his left foot on the bench, and pushed his head through the window. It was cold, and the night air slapped his face, his eyes watered, and he could just discern the slope below the train. If he climbed out now, he could drop a very long way.

He ducked back inside, and pushed the window up.

He glanced round the compartment. Everyone appeared to be asleep. He pulled the coat up over his mouth, and his hat hard down over his eyes, and once more, this time more cautiously, he released the window, and looked out and down. The slope was still there, but the surface was uneven, and seemed further away, until he realised he was looking at scrub and bushes and shrubs.

Without hesitation, he grabbed the shelf, hoisted one leg on the seat, pushed through the opening, and then reached up to the carriage guttering, pulling himself out with a final spasm of effort, for a split second hanging onto the roof, then barrelling off the wagon and falling, into the bushes, rolling, sliding, slipping, turning, as he fell through scrub and sandy soil, dry grasses and occasional saplings, coming to rest against a more substantial bush. He looked up and saw the tail light of the train disappearing what seemed a mile away, the groaning of the locomotive lingering in his ears long after it had gone.

Eduard felt his legs, arms, face, and found only a few scratches, and a single tear in his leggings. The rucksack was round his neck, but his knife was still in his pocket. He undid the pack and reached for the water bottle. Undamaged, it was still almost full, and he drank long and deeply. Then he looked around, but there was no moon, and the vegetation was dense. He pulled his coat around him, and settled for the night.

Eduard awoke to the sound of dislodged stones, movement through the scrub and something he could not identify until he saw them: there were goats munching their way across the slope. There was no sign of a goatherd, but he took no chances, first kneeling, then standing half upright until he could see up to the track, and both ahead and behind.

The goats were spread across the slope, some of them on the track itself, and that was where the goatherd was. Some of the goats were making their way down, and Eduard kept them company, moving quietly away from their keeper. As he walked, he pulled out his father's watch, and realised he had slept through the best part of the day.

The tug on his quilted coat was annoying. He turned to release it from whatever branch or spike on which it had snagged. Two narrow eyes regarded him without fear or threat, and the hand pulling his coat let go. The boy was half his height, probably eight or nine years old, and mute, for he pointed to Eduard, placed his hands together in an attitude of prayer, closed his eyes, and smiled. 'You were asleep' he seemed to say. Eduard smiled back, and nodded his head in agreement. The boy pointed to his mouth, then rubbed his stomach. 'Are you hungry?' Eduard nodded his head vigorously. The boy held out his hand, but Eduard shook his head.

The boy regarded him for a moment without moving, pointed down the slope, away from the goatherd, again rubbing his stomach, then began to pick his way deftly across the stone-scattered ground, zig-zagging between the stunted trees wind-drawn one way, the thorny undergrowth and sparse grass. Eduard followed him, glancing back from time to time towards the track and the goatherd, who appeared oblivious of the interloper.

After half an hour of quick but careful descent, they emerged from the stony hillside onto relatively level ground, and Eduard gasped. He had been concentrating on guiding his feet and following the boy; he had not consciously scanned the horizon. Now, as far as he could see, a misty sea of rippling light blue fabric lay folded across the earth, supple and yielding as it responded to the pale breezes changing its contours, folding and refolding, stirring then settling, mantling the open lands to the horizon.

He stood still, the boy a few yards before him on the edge of this ocean, then walked slowly forward, and bent down to take the pellucid petals and rub them in his palm. On the edge of his vision, he registered a slight movement, and instinctively lowered himself to a crouch. The horse and crude cart laboured around the indented edge of the fields of flax towards an indistinct huddle of smudged shapes and Eduard glanced back at the boy, who was jumping up and down and waving at the carter, trying to attract his attention.

As the cart almost reversed in its tortuous progress round the fields' edge, the man saw the boy and waved back, hauling on the reins, slowing, then stopping. The boy smiled, nodded, returned to Eduard, plucking his sleeve, and making a sign, an imperative; 'He will take us.' Eduard hesitated, then smiled his agreement, and they started walking towards the cart.

As they drew near, the carter jumped down, leaving the reins slack, and opened his arms. 'Come my Molochka, come,' and he gathered the little boy to himself and swept him off his feet and up into the air, holding him aloft and smiling up at him. As he lowered the child and released him, he looked at Eduard. 'You left the train then.' It was not a question. Eduard inclined his head in tacit consent, and the man offered his hand. 'Razin.'

'Cjaikowski,' responded Eduard. Razin made a little gesture, as if a miniature bow and instrument had magically appeared in both his hands, tucked his chin into his shoulder and danced around, mimicking a polka.

As suddenly as he had begun, he dropped the mime, and clapped Eduard across the back, lifted Molochka onto the cart and swung himself up, glancing back to ensure that Eduard was aboard before clicking his tongue, flicking the reins, and guiding horse and cart towards the smudges a mile or more away.

His accent was harsh, the language direct, not so much dialectic as disurban, the language of the countryside, of the pervasive Great Russian peasantry, and Eduard found it oddly comforting, with its absence of urban colloquialism.

'You decided to walk then. Train not going where you want?'

'That's right.'

'There are many thousands bound for the camps.'

'I believe there are.'

'Don't want to be one of them, then.'

'No.'

'Neither would I.'

Razin kept his eyes on the track, never once looking back as he spoke, but now he turned, his face lifted in a half-smile.

'Nichevo, my friend, nichevo.'

Eduard automatically responded to the old rural lay, repeating it softly: 'Nichevo – it doesn't matter; no, it really doesn't.'

With that they rumbled down the track in companionable silence, Eduard content that he had stumbled on the right man at the right time in the wrong place. As if reading his thoughts, Razin broke in on them with, 'No commissars at Sulacinsk; we are too small, too poor, too far away, too much trouble. No collectives, no co-ops, no commissars. Just as we like it, huh?' and he laughed a low, burbling, bubbling laugh deep in the belly, a man at ease, comfortable in his beliefs and his simplicities.

As the rhythm of the ride combined with a rising sense of relief, Eduard found himself relaxing, Molochka's sleepy head resting against him, his eyes slowly closing as he watched the smudges take on size and shape and specificity, the closer they came, and the flaxen fields lose their infinity as the shadows shrank them, and their piercing blue faded to lavender, mauve, purple, until night's blue-black curtains closed them out, and waxen flames darted up in window after window, as each lamp was lit against the homecomings. For theirs was not the only cart, and Razin not the only wanderer returned, as men and women converged from the fields onto their homes. For Eduard too, after train and camp, it was a homecoming of a sort, to a place entirely unlike Cjortkow in size or shape or situation, yet somehow redolent of that distant memory of home.

There was no street as such, but a single, straggling track between a double row of *izba*, each one low-logged on a solid limestone base, deep-eaved, and hugging the ground, its thatch straggling as unkempt hair on a thickset child. The sturdy, rough-trimmed and mud-filled walls were broken only once on each squared-off, corner-tied side with a flat, hooded window whence the lamplight shone. In all there were perhaps thirty houses, separated by yards and backed by ill-defined 'gardens', crudely fenced off to protect the beet and maize and sunflowers from the rooting animals which squelched and snorted and shuffled alongside each home. A belt of stunted trees signalled the boundary on the windward slope that fell away from the village, while a limestone outcrop protected its other flank.

The boy ran into one of the first houses, disappearing down the central passageway, as Eduard followed, sallow light spilling into the passage from the living room, warm with low-burning moss-crusted wood, and warm with the welcome of a kerchiefed, slight figure that embraced her Razin, then held out her hands to Molochka and gathered him to her, smiling over his head at Eduard, saying 'Welcome stranger, welcome friend'. Eduard felt the tears spring unwanted into his eyes, and turned away momentarily, lest they think him weak or sick or—

'Be not afraid. Here you are safe, and here you can cry without fear. We know what it is like...' and Razin grabbed his hand and thrust a coarse pot into it: 'Drink, my friend, drink!' and he raised his own pot, dashed it against Eduard's and downed it in one smooth swallow. Eduard, weaned on Polish vodka, was unprepared for the raw spirit, and felt his throat grow numb until, almost paralysed, he could hardly breathe, swallow, and certainly not speak. Razin thumped him on the back.

'Go on, get it down. The first time is always the worst,' and, rumbling with laughter, he busied himself at the crude table, ladling thick, creamy potato soup into wooden bowls, pushing them across.

'Eat. Eat until you can eat no more. Here we have food, drink and shelter – and freedom. What more can you want?'

The meal was a blur of simple delights – broth, vodka, bread and fruit in such quantities and of such freshness and fullness that Eduard could not recall since Cjortkow. He thought perhaps he was not in Sulacinsk but a surrogate heaven, where he had chanced, after perhaps striking his head on the leap from the train. When Molochka gravely inclined his head in 'Goodnight', climbing onto the great stove, banked down for the night, in its crudely decorated brick inglenook, Eduard was already half asleep, and Razin pushed him bodily in his chair against the wall, throwing a loosely woven rug across him, and turning to his wife with, 'He'll sleep the sleep of angels, and tomorrow we shall see what we can do with him.'

He looked down at the slight, boyish figure with its drawn face, faintly lined beyond its years, and slowly shook his head from side to side.

'What do they want with these youngsters? Why do they do this to them?'

Then he put his arm about his wife, and led her out of the room into the small, curtained cubicle with the iron bedstead and its quilts, pulled off his ragged coat and laid down to rest, as his wife joined him, pulling the soft blanket of goat's hair over them both. She had said nothing until now, but spoke softly into the night: 'It's God's will, Oskar, God's will.'

He sighed. 'So it is, my dove, so it is,' and they slept.

The dawn silvered the fields, animals squealed to be fed and wheels creaked as carts prepared for the working day. Eduard awoke to see Molochka sitting on the bench, leaning on the table, munching an apple.

He groped in his pocket to find his watch. Six o'clock.

The boy grinned at him and picked over the fruit in the bowl, selecting another, polishing it on his sleeve, then hurling it across the room. Eduard fumbled and dropped it, and it rolled under his chair. As he scrabbled about, Molochka pushed him aside and snatched it back, regarded it for a moment, then stuffed it into his pocket, reaching up to the table to find another, which he duly polished, and gravely handed to his guest. Pointing to the watch, Molochka beckoned Eduard, then described the rolling motion of the wheels, mouthing 'We go' and leading the way outside.

There Razin was manhandling a protesting pig, hamstrung hock to hock.

'Hallo friend. Help me with this animal'.

Between them they hoisted the hog on board, where Molochka nimbly looped a ribbon of rags through the hind legs and secured the animal to the cart rail.

'Come. We go to sell the pig. Then we buy some things. We decide what to do with you, and you decide what you want to do.' Seeing Eduard's hesitancy he added, 'You can stay as long as you want, as long as you work,' and he laughed his rumbling laugh, waving to his wife, standing outside the *izba*, arms folded, awaiting their departure. 'Nuta agrees.' Slapping the billboard, and pulling Molochka close: 'Ride up here with us.'

The journey was slow and uncomfortable, for there was no more road the other side of Sulacinsk than on the mountainside. After an hour or more, they smelt smoke, and within minutes rounded a low belt of trees to enter the outskirts of a small town, with typically wide, dusty streets, similar wooden houses, some of them larger than in Sulacinsk, and a few two-storeyed. As they approached the central square, with its neglected stone church, many houses boasted tin rooves, some of them once painted, but curling with rust. In the square there were shops, and outside one such shop Razin halted the cart, and disappeared.

Within minutes he emerged with a leather-aproned companion.

'This is Hercules. He has bought our pig.'

Hercules was well-named; taller than most, he was compact, short-necked, broad in the back and deep in the chest, with curling simian arms which reached up and slid under the hog's hindquarters, hauling the beast out and holding it aloft as he strode back into the shop.

Razin returned, counting notes in a thick wad of roubles.

'Now you have a quick drink and a hot coffee and I go to buy some things. Molochka will show you.'

Razin slung the reins over the horse, lifted a roughcut stone from the cart and kicked it into place behind the wheel, then strode off down a side street. Molochka clasped Eduard's hand and led him across the square. Almost directly opposite the butcher's shop there was an open-fronted house with benches and a long table. Deserted except for one solitary drinker, it was nonetheless stifling inside, with a massive central stove, glowing red-hot, on which a black pot hissed and steamed. Molochka went through a curtain at the back of the room clutching some of his father's roubles, and returned minutes later with a tin mug of black coffee, a chipped and cloudy glass of vodka, and another glass, of milk. He placed the coffee and vodka in front of Eduard.

Eduard was halfway through his coffee when Razin returned, slapped him on the back, and himself disappeared through the curtain, whence issued his familiar rumble before he returned, clasping another glass.

'Well. There is a cattle train tomorrow. It stops at Kujbysev. There you can go south.' He looked hard at Eduard and added, 'If you want.'

He tossed back his vodka, sat back, hands thrust in his pockets, and glanced back and forth between Molochka and Eduard as they drank milk and sipped coffee.

'I think I should take the train,' mumbled Eduard, but he was unsure.

He sensed Molochka beside him, and he sensed the boy's simple affection. He could stay. Razin had said he could stay. Nuta would let him stay. He could stay a little while, and then leave. After all, he had wasted nearly two years in Tara. Another week or so would make little difference. Yet he knew that, if he delayed, he might never leave. He cleared his throat and looked into Molochka's eyes as he repeated, 'I should take the train.'

The boy turned to his father, who ran a protective hand through his son's hair. 'You are right. It would be good to stay, but it would be better to leave – for you, that is.'

Razin reached across the table, his hand over Eduard's.

'You are a good boy. I don't need weeks to know that.' He stood. 'I will take you to Hercules. I have already asked him. He will look after you until tomorrow.'

As they walked across the square, Eduard felt in his pocket. The knife was there, and so was the watch. They reached the cart, where Razin retrieved Eduard's rucksack. It was bulging. He handed it to Eduard.

'Nuta thought you might need some food. Bread, apples. Your bottle is full. And there is a little vodka – for the cold nights.'

The butcher emerged, and Razin spoke softly to him. Hercules nodded, turning to Eduard.

'You are welcome. Razin's friends are always welcome,' and gesturing to him to follow him inside, he left them outside, a sudden family as suddenly divided.

'God be with you, friend,' and Razin hugged him to his chest, then released him as Molochka, tears in his eyes, touched Eduard's hand and mouthed 'Goodbye'.

Razin lifted his son onto the cart and swung himself up, flicking the reins when Eduard shouted, 'Stop! There's just one thing more.'

He pulled out the watch, his father's watch, the watch that took him back in time to Cjortkow, and he thrust it into Molochka's hand. To Razin: 'Tell him I will always have time for him, wherever I am,' and to Molochka he mouthed 'Thank you' and then they were gone.

The next day the cattle train was waiting and that night Eduard climbed on board, refreshed and rejoicing.

I have been asleep but now I lie awake, my wifelet still beside me, and little Anna not so little now, a young girl, restless as I can hear, in the other room, and we have all we need of food and drink and shelter, and they have freedom and I have loving kindness, and I am free of hate.

I hated all Russians before Sulacinsk. There I was freed from that universal hatred by Russians and thereafter my hatred descended by degrees.

There I was bound by freedom, granted by a small deaf-and-dumb boy.

It was in Sulacinsk that I first considered freedom as an obligation, where before it had been merely the antithesis of captivity. Perhaps we need simple times and uncluttered circumstance to understand that truth. Few of us stop to consider the nature of freedom until it is lost. Now that I have lost it again, I cannot even rail against that loss.

I have lost my freedom of movement and of speech, so that I am as detained as once I was long ago. Yet my freedom is guaranteed while I can still think without constraint, and articulate my own truths without fear or coercion. All those freedoms are mine and always were – I found that out in Sulacinsk.

IVAN THE TERRIBLE

The cattle truck was unguarded, and Hercules led Eduard down the blind side of the station. 'This looks as good as any.' He pointed at the slatted wagon, from which emanated sundry grunts and shuffles.

'Pigs! Like the one you brought yesterday. Off to Kujbysev.'

Eduard screwed his face up in disgust and Hercules laughed.

'Better the pigs than the guards. You go in there, they won't know the difference...' He must have noticed the irritation on Eduard's face as he hastily added, 'Noises, I mean, not smells. In there they'll only hear pigs, so you'll be safe until Kujbysev,' and he helped Eduard slide back the door, bent down, encircled him with his great arms, and heaved him up into the truck.

For a moment they both stood there, then Hercules raised his hand in farewell and salutation, turned briskly and walked away. Eduard contemplated his carriage. The pigs were snuffling in the straw, and had backed away from him to the far side of the wagon. The door was still open. He pulled it closed, scuffed some straw into a pile in the corner, sank down into it, using his rucksack as a pillow, and closed his eyes, composing himself for the night's journey.

Within minutes the train started; Eduard dozed on and off, snatches of old dreams alternating with a semi-wakeful torpor, punctuated by the restless pigs, snorting and scuffling. The train moved slowly, drawing its cumbersome load of livestock, timber and coals, and Eduard closed his eyes, ranging back over the tranquil option he had jettisoned, and the uncertain future, and how long it would take to reach Kujbysev, sliding down into the straw, trying to find a more comfortable niche, gradually fading into forgetfulness as sleep came at last.

The pain was acute.

He could not focus. His head was afire. He could see nothing, but he could feel the wetness dribbling down his face. He wiped it away, and tasted blood as he licked the back of his hand. 'What the...'

He could hear the pigs and, as his eyes cleared, he could see they were still at the other end of the wagon, strangely silent, poised, their small eyes glittering. He rolled over and felt the foot in his side. One of the pigs must have lashed out, fallen and dazed itself. 'I'll have him,' he murmured to himself, grabbing the leg – but cloth shifted in his hands. There was no time to find his knife; he twisted, and there was a cry. He saw the other knife as it flashed towards him, and twisted again.

As he did so, his hand slipped down to a boot. This was definitely not a pig's leg. He kept twisting.

'Let me go!' he said in Russian.

'I'll let you go if you drop the knife.'

'OK, OK,' and the knife clattered onto the floor; Eduard swept it away with his own foot, pulled the leg towards him, and grabbed the hair of the young boy he had discovered.

'What are you doing here?'

'Same as you – escaping.'

'Where are you going?'

'Don't know.'

'What's your name?'

'Ivan.'

'Well, Ivan, if I let go of you, will you behave?'

'Yes, yes, I promise I will.'

'Right,' and Eduard cautiously released his captive. The boy shuffled away, his back to the truckside, and rubbed his ankle with one hand, pushing his hair back off his forehead with the other.

'So where are you from?' asked Eduard.

'Prison.'

He did not look as if he had come from prison. By contrast to Eduard's thin, lean frame, the boy was stocky, gleaming with good health, clearly well-fed, his features glowing with a ruddy tan, his dark hair thick and curly, springing round his face like that of a Renaissance drawing of a frisky faun. His clothes were new, clean and almost elegant in their simplicity – a buttoned tunic, belted in leather, with soft, baggy trousers and leather boots. His hands were restless, Eduard noticed, the short, square fingers twisting and turning as he spoke.

Ivan talked, as if he was anxious to unburden himself of his past.

He was sixteen, and had been in prison on and off since he was twelve. His profession was robbery, with or without violence. He had escaped from Moskva and from Orlofsk and now he was running away again, living off the land and whatever he could steal. He had stolen food and drink in Ufa, and Oktjabr'ski, in Bugul'ma and Abdulino, and was looking for a larger town where he could ply his trade and 'settle down' to a steady life of crime, 'earning' good money to pay for clothes and vodka and perhaps a little jewellery.

'And you? What yer running from? Yer not a robber, are yer?'

Eduard shook his head, and edited his biography.

'I was in Tara, in a camp. I am on my way to Kujbysev.'

Ivan smiled a cheerful smile, a smile of innocence, a careless smile, and reached behind him. Eduard jumped up, pulled his knife from his pocket and stepped back.

'Don't worry. It's me little box, that's all,' and Ivan threw a leather case, with straps, in front of him.

'Go on, open it; 'sonly food.'

'You open it – there, where I can see you.'

'OK.'

Ivan was still smiling, as he slipped the straps through their buckles, and snapped the case open.

'There!' He pulled out half a side of smoked bacon and flourished it at Eduard. 'Want some?' and he laughed as he added, 'If you do, you'll have ter cut it off yerself, 'cause I don't know where me knife's gone.'

Eduard kicked the knife across. Ivan skilfully pared slice after slice, offering several to Eduard.

'Come on. Eat, my friend.'

Eduard took the proffered ham.

'What was it like in prison?'

'Terrible. Most of them were older, and some of them "wanted" me. But I always had a knife, somethin' sharp, so they didn' get me.'

'How did you escape?'

Ivan speared an apple, and bit deeply into it, between mouthfuls adding: 'We had one guard, he was a prisoner really, but they made him a guard. Hadn't had much school, but clever, he was.'

He finished the apple, and took a draught of water, passing the bottle to Eduard.

'One day he charged me with his head, in the chest, to get me on the floor. Then he kicked me. He had these jackboots they'd given him. Hurt a lot. I stuck him with me knife, between the legs. Didn' like that much!'

Ivan rummaged around in his case, and found a lump of hardened goat's cheese, and chewed a lump off it, offering it to Eduard, who shook his head.

'And?'

'Oh yeah. Well, he was 'owlin', and another man who liked me 'it 'im, lifted 'im up and split 'is 'ead on the stone arch.'

Ivan smiled secretly to himself as the memory ran across his mind.

'It killed him and there was a lot of trouble, and while all that was goin' on, I sorter slipped away.' He smiled at Eduard. 'And here I am.'

Ivan rummaged in the case and extracted another bottle, unwound the fastener, pulled the cork and handed that to Eduard.

'Vodka! Only the best for Ivan the Terrible.'

Eduard ate and began to relax, keeping his knife beside him, listening as Ivan told him about his childhood in the Moskva *slobody* where the houses were damp and small, food scarce and crime rampant, where whole families were rounded up to be deposited in new concrete barracks, and recalcitrant workers consigned to Siberia. His mother had died during the birth of his sixth sister, his father deported for daring to demand a doctor, and he had made a new life for himself, living off his wits with his friends until he was caught.

As Ivan spoke, he drank, long, deep slugs of vodka, without discernible effect. When he had finished telling his tale, he flicked his knife onto the ground between them. 'Just in case you was worried,' and Eduard realised he had little to fear from this urban urchin except the danger he might court, and so he began to unfold his own past.

When he in his turn had finished, Ivan's eyes were glinting with glee and fellow-feeling.

'From now on, yer wanter survive, do what I do, and yer'll be alright.'

'What exactly do you do – apart from robbing and stealing, I mean. How do you do it?'

'Wait till we get to Kujbysev. Then I show yer. Perhaps Kamerad Stalin will give me a job when I get there! After all, I come from Georgia too – where me family started, and I can ride a horse like a Cossack.'

He laughed.

'But then perhaps 'e won't, 'cause we were *raskolniki*.'

'What on earth's *raskolniki*?'

'Ain't yer heard of the *raskolniki*? They're the Old Believers, the ones who stuck ter the old ways, the old church and all that. Not popular.'

He squinted at Eduard, and retrieved his knife, stowing it away in his belt.

'If yer don't do what I do, I'll be gone,' and he hitched his tunic over his trousers as he added, 'And yer'll be gone too, definitely.'

'So? What must I do, then?'

'Rob people, not ordinary people. Officers, their wives, people who've run away from the front to Mister Stalin's headquarters in Kujbysev.'

'So that's where you were going all along. You knew perfectly well.'

'Clever. You're clever, Eduard. Quite right. Live dangerous. Live well. That's me. In Kujbysev. And you can too.'

'So you know the place?'

'Know it? Never been there in me life.'

The railway station at Kujbysev, when you approached it properly, was partly underground. Eduard and Ivan left the truck as soon as the train paused in the marshalling yard, and doubled round the tracks until they found a broken fence, scrambling through, and dropping down a short bank into an unlit alley, before making their way towards the town, and the front of the station. They joined the shifting crowds in the domed concourse, and strolled nonchalantly down a platform, noting the military presence, and the considerable chaos.

'Plenty of people here,' observed Ivan, 'so we got to rob 'em.'

He pushed his way through the crowds without apology, Eduard finding it difficult to keep pace without giving offence. At one point he accidentally knocked a woman's bag, and she cursed him as he passed. She was gone by the time he had muttered 'Sorry', rushing to catch up with the insouciant Ivan, who laughed and said, 'I'll show yer'ow ter do it, and after a bit, yer'll be OK.'

They had reached the end of the platform. Ivan leant against a trolley, pulled Eduard close and murmured, pointing, 'Over there – an officer.' Eduard looked down the platform, then realised the object of Ivan's attention was nearby, only a few yards away, standing irresolute on the platform's edge.

'Wife, two kiddies, and their luggage. They've got ter go somewhere, hotel, or camp, and ter do that, they need a taxi.'

He had stopped leaning, and was tensed, almost vibrating, as he added, 'Yer go over to them and say yer'll help. Yer'll carry their cases. Yer a porter. There are taxis at the front – outside. Tell 'em.'

Eduard hesitated. Ivan held him, gripping his arm.

'There are corridors; saw them on the way in. They'll tell yer ter walk in front, if yer've got their cases. Take yer time.'

He pulled Eduard closer, whispering out of the side of his mouth, while apparently gazing anywhere but at the officer.

'When it gets crowded, and yer reach the turnings, speed up. Turn right and then duck down and cross over, and go left.'

He released Eduard.

'Then run like hell, before they see yer. And when yer get outside, cut round the back of the station, to those huts we saw. I'll meet yer there.'

'What are you going to do?'

Ivan punched him sharply but lightly in the arm.

'I'm going ter do that lot over there,' and he inclined his head slightly towards another group, this time two officers, standing further down the platform.

'Now GO!'

Eduard walked slowly towards the first officer.

'Good evening, sir. Take your cases?'

'What?' The officer wheeled and looked at him. 'No.'

'Taxi, sir?'

The woman intervened.

'Igor?'

'Oh, I suppose so, yes. Alright you. Find us a taxi. And be quick about it.'

'Yes, sir.' And Eduard lifted the cases and stood, waiting.

'Alright. Off you go then. Presumably you know the way.'

Spurred by the man's sarcasm, Eduard set off, determined to execute Ivan's plan, where a moment before he was half inclined to take the cases, find a taxi, grovel for a tip and depart.

They followed him through the shifting crowd, and several times the woman's voice trailed him with 'There he is; we'll lose him Igor' and 'Come ON, you two' to the slightly surly children, one in each hand. 'You will lose him,' muttered Eduard to himself, 'if I have anything to do with it,' and he quickened his pace, until he was almost trotting down the platform, weaving his way between the passengers.

'Oi, you!' He heard the shout behind him, and paused, glancing back, smiling, then setting off again, as the passage entrances appeared some twenty yards ahead.

'Igor!'

'Oh for God's sake, woman, do keep up.'

Then he was ducking, scrabbling forward at an uncomfortable crouch, when he nearly lost his footing, cannonading off a burly back, as two officers stepped back to avoid a small child.

'Look where you're going, you idiot.'

This officer was clearly of senior rank and Eduard dropped his head, muttered 'Sorry, sir' and scurried away, 'his' officer drawing closer by the second.

'Wait!' he heard, and paused, glancing back, half-lifting one case-hung arm, then making for the right-hand entrance. The officer and his wife had stopped beside their superior, desperately waving at Eduard to stop too, when he tacked to the left and started running down the passage.

Overhead the concrete arching walls met in a latticework of opaque glazing, and dim lanterns were strung along its centre. As dusk approached, they flickered on, barely illuminating the dank corridor. At the end, he found himself in a smaller concourse, and realised he had emerged at the side of the station – the wrong side.

He dropped the cases, and moved rapidly to the nearest door, shoved it open and glanced out, into a busy street. Collecting the luggage, he backed out through the door, and walked briskly down the street to the corner, pausing and looking warily across the forecourt. There were trams, taxis, trucks and a shifting mass of people, officers among them.

It was a simple lottery. Either go back the way he had come, and risk confrontation with Igor, or cross the station forecourt – and risk confrontation with Igor. What the hell, he thought, it's all the same, and strode out into the crowd, setting an oblique course, so that, the further he walked, the more distance there was between him and the entrance. Once he was halfway across, he set course for the far corner, nearing the station as he passed it on his right.

'You there! Wait!'

In the deepening dusk he could not see who called; perhaps it was Igor, perhaps not – no point in waiting to find out, so he ran, until he was past the corner, and doubling down the side street towards the alleyway and the embankment and safety.

Once through the fence, he dropped the cases, sat on one of them, and breathed deeply, before reaching inside his rucksack for the water bottle. As he wiped his mouth, he heard the footsteps, measured and deliberate. 'Oh Christ,' he thought, 'who the hell is this?' heaved the cases up, and started a broken, half-hearted scramble along the fence-side towards the scrub beyond the yard.

'Wait fer me!'

Through the gap in the fence appeared one, then two cases, followed by a smiling Ivan.

'Got 'ere alright, then?' and he indicated Eduard's cases. 'Let's see what we've got, when we've found somewhere to sleep,' and he led the way down the yard, through the scrub, and across a broken wasteland, sloping downhill, alongside an embankment, pierced with low arches where the railway crossed over.

'This'll do.' Ivan stopped outside the second arch, half concealed by bushes. 'Stick 'em be'ind there and we'll sort 'em out in the morning. Time ter eat, and get some sleep.'

Although it was summer, the night air was dank and chill; the vodka substituted for a fire, and they huddled together against the cold stones, sharing bacon and apples, until Ivan rolled himself up and within seconds was asleep. Eduard sat for some time, his thoughts ranging across the evening's events, finding himself unsurprised by the criminal turn his life had taken.

For Igor he had nothing but contempt. How could the man let a stranger rob him with such ease, and in any case, who cares? He was a bloody Russian and this was one way of starting his personal war.

'I'll bet he's cross without his night gear and his razor and all his precious papers,' said Eduard, poking Ivan with his foot, but Ivan simply stirred slightly, grunted and turned over, saying nothing.

In the morning, they opened the cases. Ivan jettisoned anything unsaleable – papers, a book, some medicine, an old wooden toy and a threadbare doll, jars and a tin of stale bread. He kept the clothes, except a spare tunic with epaulettes, and produced two sacks with a flourish.

'Where'd you find those?'

Ivan smiled knowingly.

'Trade secret. 'ere – stuff 'em in there.'

They filled both sacks, then pushed three of the cases with their rejected contents deep into the bushes, and Ivan stretched, yawning and shaking his head violently from side to side, then threw one sack over his shoulder and swung the most nondescript of the cases with his left hand, his own 'box' strapped to his back.

'Right. Into action.'

In every Russian town there is a marketplace, a square where rubbish is exchanged for roubles, for one person's rubbish is someone else's riches. So it was in Kujbysev. Second-hand clothes predominated.

'Teach me,' said Eduard, and Ivan taught him, setting up stall behind the case, opened, upended and serving as a convenient triangulated table, with his box across its edges. The sacks sat between the case's jaws, and Ivan tastefully displayed selected wares, lifting this, then that item, and softly speaking to passers-by.

'Lovely stuff, warm in winter, cool in summer, and I've got lots more like that.'

Within half an hour, it had all gone. Officers' clothes were of a quality beyond the norm, and customers milled round Ivan and his tyro assistant until the last vest went, and they closed the case, stuffing the sacks in Eduard's bag and their pockets full of roubles.

'Now fer some food,' and Ivan led the way across the square to another 'stall' where black bread, fresh baked, was stacked.

'Coupons, kamerad?' sniffed the stallholder, eyeing Ivan cautiously.

'Nar. Got no coupons.'

'No coupons, no bread then.'

'No bread then? No bread, no roubles,' shot back Ivan.

The stallholder balanced a loaf in his rough, wrinkled hands.

'Roubles? Cost a lot of roubles without coupons.'

Ivan turned to Eduard.

'They're all the same – it's like a dance. Yer got ter go this way first, then that, and finally, yer get ter do the polka,' and he swung his case around his head, slammed it down in front of the bread-man, stuck his hand in his pocket, and brought it out, bristling with notes.

'Aaaaaah, roubles. How many loaves, young sir?'

Each with a loaf under arm, they strolled through the motley, found a salami seller, repeated the process, and then purchased some fire-water from a wizened wisp of a woman with a sharp tongue and a selection of bottles, guarded by two silent, sullen youths. At the side of the square there were rows of wooden benches, and there they sat and took lunch together.

'This's the life, eh?' quoth Ivan and Eduard perforce agreed. It was as if Kujbysev was the end of an arduous road, and here all things were possible. As the spirit soaked into his brain, he began to dream of a life on the lam in Kujbysev as a possible scenario for days, or even weeks to come. Why move on when the pickings were so good?

For fourteen days they stole in the evenings, sold in the mornings, and disported themselves in the afternoons in park and boulevard, street and alley, ogling stray girls, avoiding the military and occasionally joining casual groups for a few drinks, a hand of cards and some spurious exchanges, always avoiding politics, war and religion.

'Don't do to talk serious – that way leads to trouble,' confided Ivan, and Eduard sagely nodded, as the vodka seeped into his veins.

They slept under bridges, in the waiting room on the day they stole nothing, even under the steps in front of the larger stone-built houses of the citizenry. Within two weeks, they became fixtures, notable if not notorious and Ivan, if not the less thrusting Eduard, was acquaintance to a score of the town's petty criminals. By then it was clear to some stallholders where the clothes were coming from, and Eduard reasoned it was only a matter of time before they were caught.

'We should move on,' he murmured to Ivan one afternoon, when they had made a substantial killing with an officer's leather greatcoat.

'Soon, soon,' Ivan vaguely replied.

That evening, they were strolling down a side street when they saw the police, an instant before the police saw them. They backed swiftly away, and then ran, fast. That night Eduard raised the question again.

'We really must go, Ivan. That was too close.'

Ivan nodded. 'Yer right. One more go termorrow, then that's it.'

'OK.'

The next day they moved into what was by now a smooth routine. Ivan stood mid-platform and surveyed the prospective victims. Eduard took the first, always a small family group, essentially with a woman and child – that slowed pursuit. Ivan selected single officers of higher rank, for richer pickings, and the thrill of what often became a noisy chase.

Eduard emerged as usual into the side street, and paused to catch his breath, when he heard a considerable commotion in the corridor he had just vacated. This was unusual, for they never used the same passage together. Ivan shot out of the tunnel, racing across to the door, panting and yelling, 'Quick, out, now.'

Eduard pushed the door open, and saw two military police walking swiftly towards him.

'Police! Outside. The station!' and he started running across to the concourse. Ivan wheeled and followed him, just as two more police span out of the passageway, looking right and left for their quarry.

'Over there,' shouted one, and the four MPs raced across as Eduard and Ivan broke into the crowd.

'Drop the bloody cases,' spat Ivan, but Eduard already had; as they ran he shot back, 'Separate – two's harder to catch than a pair.'

'OK. See yer at the arches.'

Ivan doubled back, passed the MPs, one catching sight of him and breaking off to shove and shoulder his way towards the exit, where Ivan was fleetingly outlined, before disappearing beyond the taxis. Eduard, yards ahead of the other three, ducked, and ran at a crouch, weaving left and right, and then doubling into the very passage he had vacated only moments before. Buffeted against the stream of emergent passengers, he forced his way through, and then ran back down the next corridor, into the concourse. The MPs had vanished, caught up in his deception. Slowly he edged out of the station, round to the right, and down to the alley, back through the fence, across the tracks, until he reached the wasteland, and slid down the embankment to the arches.

Inside, Ivan was already there, slowly masticating bread and sausage, and sipping water.

'No vodka tonight, eh? Just in case those bastards come lookin' for us.'

As he spoke, a light swept across the archway.

'Bugger! They've found us,' and he was off down the tunnel, Eduard on his heels. At the other end, the night was impenetrable, and they felt their way along until they came to the bank.

'Up here,' whispered Eduard, scrabbling up, and leaning down to pull Ivan up behind him. Bent low, they ran up the single track, back into the goods yard, leaping across rails, between trains, sprinting alongside tracks, trying to identify which train was going where. Across the yard they could see the fence, and the bouncing lamps of a police van as it probed the wasteland. A great swathe of light cut through the night, scything across trains, tracks and catching their figures momentarily, before they fell to the ground and rolled beneath a stationary shunter.

'This is gettin' too close,' gasped Ivan.

Eduard pointed.

'Look. Over there. That train. It's got long-range tanks. It must be going south.'

Ivan turned and patted Eduard's hand.

'So now yer in charge. Very good. Lead the way.'

They waited until the searchlight had crossed again, and then raced across two sets of tracks until they reached the goods train. It was taking on water. There was a flush of covered wagons between lowloaders and bowsers and cattle trucks. They made for the central one.

Eduard pulled the door open, and peered inside. It was filled with rakes and shovels and forks and long-tined hoes.

'Here. This'll do.'

They climbed inside and pulled the door closed. As they did so, there were two short whistles, and they were off.

'Are yer sure yer know where it's goin'?' asked Ivan.

'No, I'm not, but it's too late anyway,' and he settled into the corner, adding, 'You'll just have to wait and see,' and they both laughed quietly.

'At least we've plenty of clothes.'

'And roubles,' chuckled Ivan.

As the adrenalin drained away, they slept. The next morning they awoke to sunlight streaming into the wagon and, as Eduard pulled the door open, they looked out onto yellow snow – sand as far as their eyes could see.

That was the life: a life of self-indulgence, living on the edge, caring for nothing but the opportunity taken, the spoils of our own particular war – Ivan's against 'them', mine against representative Russians – and the exhilaration of winning, gaining, selling, spending, and then doing it all over again. I was seduced by the immediacy, morally blinded by my self-styled warrior status, justified when I thought about it, which was not often, by the evils perpetrated against my family and myself by 'the system', which I was ridiculing with my successful personal piracy.

Whether I was also seduced by the novelty of Ivan's solution to my previously intrusive needs for food, rest and shelter, by the vicarious thrill of outwitting the enemy's officer class, or the sense of power, I know not, but I no longer cared. As we left the real Russia and embarked on our voyage across the seas of sand, I was detached from my recent past and distanced from my determinations, content to wallow in the warmth of the desert sun, Ivan's approbation and my new status as the outlaw Eduard.

It was not dissimilar to my reaction half a century later to the burst of activity surrounding my stroke, when all was solicitude, creature comforts and the luxury of not having to take my own decisions, the more so when my faculties recovered sufficiently for me to interfere in others' care, and force small changes of direction, while never essaying decisive action *per se*. Perhaps this was, is, a flaw, a fissure in personality, yielding a fissiparous duality – two Eduards, one core id able to survive through purity of word and action, another superficial persona flitting through events with deceit and pretence, for profit at others' expense.

One advantage of prison is the reduction to essentials, first of body, then in mind. It is as true of mental as of physical prison. The only victim of my deceits today is me. The release from prison then released me from the restriction to essentials; my adventures with Ivan were perhaps my long-deferred youth compressed into a few weeks of frenetic, frenzied fantasy made real by opportunity and circumstance. If so, that egotheist rampage incidentally taught me lessons in the science of survival, how to exploit the element of surprise, the need to think reflexively, with no conscious recourse to 'rules', philosophical or otherwise.

My desert days were days of delight and danger, and they were a necessary nexus between those years when I was but a child learning manhood and the time when I came of age.

I would give a great deal to go back to Kazakhstan. Just for a day!

THE ROAD TO SAMARKAND

They had travelled for ten hours, though they did not know it then, from Kujbysev to Orenburg, from Orenburg to Orsk, and from Orsk to Karabutak and beyond, moving all the time south-east, across the immense plain of the Aralo-Caspian deserts on the Trans-Aralian Railway to Aral'sk, on the tip of the Aral Sea.

It was flat, dusty and monotonous, and water was scarce, in *chors* – salt marshes, *takyrs* – clay-lined ponds dry in summer, brackish, ten-foot-deep water-wells or salt-crusted, sand-strewn lakelets. At Orsk the engine paused to take on water, and again at Karabutak. On the 100-plus miles to Aral'sk, it slowed again, as it approached a deserted well. The engine driver and fireman jumped down and dropped a hose into the well, hand pumping water to the tank.

Ivan slid back the door, and watched, then jumped out. Eduard watched him as he walked towards the trainmen. They looked briefly up as he approached, turning back to their task without acknowledgement or challenge. Eduard dropped onto the sand and caught up with Ivan.

'They don't seem to care.'

'Not much point if they do – we're miles from anywhere.'

They stood a few feet away from the well, and Eduard shouted, 'Thirsty work.'

The fireman looked up, nodded and then said something to the driver. The driver laughed, but continued without even a glance in their direction. Eduard moved closer.

'Need any help?'

The driver grunted, then pulled the hose clear, wiped his sleeve across his brow and replied, 'Not unless you can stop the sun.'

'We've hitched a lift.'

'Obviously.'

Ivan interjected, ''ope yer don't mind?' and the driver shrugged.

'Wouldn't make any odds if we did.'

He leant against the well, appraising them.

'In fact, you can go as far as we go, if you want.'

Eduard: 'Where are you going?'

'Tashkent.'

'Then Samarkand,' added the fireman.

'Thanks.' On an impulse, he pulled out a wad of roubles, and handed half the notes to the driver, who took them slowly, counted them, then tapped them together.

'Take you to Teheran for that,' stuffing them into his pocket, 'if we were going to Teheran.'

With that he swung himself up on the footplate, and the fireman walked round the engine, checking the steam condenser that recycled scarce water, and joined him on the other side. Ivan and Eduard barely had time to reach their wagon before the train pulled out.

Inside, the truck was airless, its timbers crackling as the sun dried the resin, and dust eddied through the cracks. Eduard tore two strips of cloth off a shirt they had salvaged from their final foray, poured water sparingly over both, and tied one behind Ivan's head, securing it across his nose and mouth, before masking his own face.

It was too hot to talk, or sleep, or even eat; they sat listlessly, their backs to the front of the wagon, where the dust was minimised, until once more the train slowed to a halt.

Outside the sun was low, simmering above the layered horizon, which shifted and shimmied as the day's heat rose to meet the cold air of the coming night. The train was drawn up between three pools of salt-crusted water, one of them larger than the others, with clear water glistening in the centre, where the salt had yet to meet, or had perhaps been broken. Between the pool and the track was a water-tower, metal stilts topped by a cloth-wrapped tank.

The driver and fireman stood by the tower, talking as Ivan and Eduard joined them. The driver waved as they neared him.

'We'll leave at dawn, stop here the night. We've watered the beast. There's a place there,' and he pointed to a low, flat-roofed house of loess, standing apart from the hamlet proper, its ochrous walls cracked and fissured by the heat.

Inside, the floor was hardened mud, with skeins of sand woven across, and the furniture restricted to a splintered plank thrown across two torn, galvanised cans, a broken bench and a wooden shelf laid over an uneven bank of loess. There was a single square hole in one wall, opposite the doorway, which lacked a door.

'I'll sleep here,' said the driver, perching on the shelf, and the fireman pushed the 'table' against a wall, commenting, 'This'll do me.'

Ivan looked at Eduard and Eduard smiled.

'We'll sleep in the truck.'

'Suit yourselves.'

The sun had set, and the sudden desert night cooled damp skin; Eduard shivered as Ivan pointed across to the settlement, still distinct in the day's afterglow, squat silhouettes. There were three houses, flat-roofed like the way-station, of identical size, with square window holes and each walled around to deter the sand in a storm, the walls rough-gated, and otherwise pierced only by culverts to channel water from the pools to the lush gardens within, and drainage holes to take waste away.

Inside the nearest enclosure, vines hung from lashed poles of wormwood, and the goosefoot grass and fescue of the surrounding land had been eradicated in favour of melons. The former were ripening, but the latter were, as Ivan put it, 'in need of harvesting'.

They scouted round the wall, until Ivan pointed to a culvert, wide enough to accommodate a nimble intruder.

'You go first, yer thinner. I'll follow.' Ivan held out his hand for Eduard's rucksack, and wiped his knife against his trousers. Cautiously, Eduard eased himself into the semi-circular gap at the foot of the wall, and manoeuvred himself along its length. The wall was six feet thick, and the culvert protruded another two. Inside it was streaked with caked mud, which crumbled in his hair as he scraped his way along.

Eduard could hear Ivan close behind, breathing shallowly as he pushed his more thickset frame through. The culvert ended with a crude grid on the inner side. Eduard forced it loose, then carefully eased it away, and propped it against the wall. He wriggled out, and knelt beside the hole, until Ivan's head appeared.

'I'm stuck,' he gasped. 'Give me a pull.'

Eduard hauled his hands, then gripped his arms and pulled hard. Ivan suddenly shot out of the culvert and fell in an untidy heap on the dry grass, which crackled noisily. They froze, staring across the cultivated ground to the low, mud house, unlit, silent. After a few moments, Ivan pushed himself up on all fours, and scuffled sideways, until he was at the end of a row of melons. Crouching, he moved slowly and methodically along the row, feeling, sniffing, then selecting the fruit, and bagging them in Eduard's rucksack.

Eduard moved soundlessly along the wall, until he reached the vines, then reached over his head, squeezing and nipping the fruit until he found a bunch ripe for the picking, slicing the neck with his knife, and secreting it in the old clothes sack. When he had half a dozen bunches, he returned to the culvert. Ivan was at the far end of the row of melons.

There was a sudden, sharp snap. Eduard pushed himself flat against the wall; Ivan had dropped to the ground, still. A light flickered in the house, then wavered towards the doorway, where it flared, silhouetting a long, robed figure. 'Ayha! Who's there?'

The garden was still. The figure stirred slightly, and Eduard could discern the cloth headdress and what appeared to be a long, but ragged beard. The Tatar held a lamp in one hand and a long stick in the other. He took a step into the garden, and swung the lantern one way, and then the other, then turned, and disappeared, the lamp flickering briefly until it, too, disappeared.

Eduard slid into the culvert, pushing the sack before him, and slithered through as quietly, yet quickly, as possible, dropping the sack over the lip, then reaching down and pushing it to one side before slipping out himself. He could hear Ivan behind him. The rucksack appeared first, and he pulled it clear, then he saw Ivan's hands scuffling in the mud.

'Pull me out fer God's sake,' he spluttered, and Eduard grasped his hands and heaved. At that point, war broke out in Kazakhstan.

The explosion was ear-splitting, and reverberated inside the compound, followed within 30 seconds by another. The flash behind the wall momentarily lit the night sky like a firecracker at a firework display. The silence that followed was deafening. Ivan screamed, Eduard pulled, and the boy's body came plunging out of the culvert.

'Me arse, me arse,' he screeched, 'me arse is on fire.'

'Never mid your arse. Bloody run like hell,' yelled Eduard. 'Make for the train and I'll get the driver.'

As he raced towards the restroom, he saw the driver and the fireman tumble outside.

'What the hell. . .?'

Eduard pivoted, and started back towards the train, shouting as he ran.

'Come on. It's Ghengis Khan. He's coming to get us.'

Eduard could see Ivan limping up the low embankment to the train and, glancing back, saw the door in the wall swing open. The Tatar leapt through, then dropped to one knee, placed his lamp on the ground, and brought his 'stick' to his shoulder. There was another massive 'crack' and a hail of old nails and shards of metal flew past Eduard's head, missing him by less than a foot. By now, all four of them were hurtling towards the train, when the Tatar let fly with another volley of projectiles.

'Holy mother of God, what the hell's going on?'

The driver was standing, one foot on the footplate, as Eduard paused alongside, and the fireman stoked the embers.

'Later, later. Go, go, go.'

The driver pulled himself up, and released the valve, as the Tatar appeared at the foot of the embankment.

'Come on, come on Vanya, get that fire going. The bugger's got a cannon and it's pointing at us.'

The Tatar was stuffing ammunition down the long barrel of his gun as Eduard joined Ivan, pulled the door to, and Vanya nodded his readiness, piling more timber into the furnace. The engine shivered for a moment as the valves were opened, then the brake was off, and the great line of trucks started moving.

The train slowly gathered momentum and the Tatar raised his rifle. There were two short, piercing blasts from the whistle as the engine passed him, he started back, the rifle slewed, and a stream of metal spouted vertically into the air as he lost his footing, fell backwards, and tumbled down the bank.

Eduard was watching through the remaining narrow gap between door and doorway, and could not resist a valedictory wave as they passed the fallen Tatar, his turban awry, his whiskers in one hand, and his other shaking in malediction. Ivan was groaning in the corner of the wagon. Eduard knelt, and gently turned him over.

'You'd better drop your pants.'

His buttocks were pocked with pieces of lead and rusty iron, welted with bloody sores, and rapidly purpling with bruises.

'This is going to hurt,' and Eduard applied his knife to the nearest and first of many fragments, as he excavated his companion's backside. When he had finished, he cleaned his hands on the rest of the torn shirt, and turned to the rucksack, extracting a melon. Slicing it open, he regarded the supine Ivan and, smiling, added, 'This is the first summer fruit I've tasted in two years.' There was no reply.

There were other stops, and other oases. The train crew shared the fruit, and Ivan's backside recovered. There were other Tatars too, but no more fruit-picking. The train collected mail as it trundled through small stations, catching the packages in a trap from a ring, or simply from a well-aimed cast by the stationmaster. After a long, hot, dusty journey, they pulled into Tashkent, Eduard and Ivan bade farewell to their train crew, and went in search of 'work' and food and rest.

Outside the station, the city unfolded in wide, tree-lined boulevards, spacious squares, colourful gardens and monumental Russian buildings. Eduard and Ivan found themselves outside the theatre, with its soaring façade, triple-arched and dramatically offset by the 40-foot central fountain. The square was lined with concrete benches. They sat and considered their options.

'Got any money left?' Ivan spread his hands wide. ''cause I ain't.'

'About twenty roubles.' Eduard counted the thin, worn, crumpled notes for the third time. 'Enough for some bread.'

They contemplated the slowly moving crowds, spread out across the square.

'Not much pickin's 'ere,' observed Ivan. 'Better off in the oasis,' rubbing his backside, and grinning at Eduard. 'Let's walk a little further; see what we can see.'

They strolled down the avenue, with its graceful acacias and tall poplars, keeping to the shade as the midday heat struck the paving, passing stolid stone buildings as they traversed streets and squares, past museums, libraries, schools and occasional large stores.

Imperceptibly, the grandeur diminished, the streets narrowed, and the buildings became more business-like, before abruptly giving way to a different town – the native quarter, with narrow paths and alleyways, puffing dust and dirt with every footfall, blank, windowless walls turning their backs onto the streets, gulleys and gutters trickling scummed and oil-filmed water, their merry notes belying the odoriferous content.

From every alley and passageway their nostrils were beguiled with conflicting scents and smells of gentle flowers and pungent herbs, slithering skins and mildewed cloth, sharp sweat and acrid fumes, until they emerged without warning onto an irregular space, bounded on one side by the brutal blocks of revolutionary Russia, where the new town began to encroach on the old, bordered on another by a tapestry of fruit gardens, reaching fingers of green and gold between the mazy network of puddled clay homes. Beside them, on the third quadrant, stretched the bazaar, tent and shack, labyrinthine and cacophonous.

'Ah! This is more like it,' exulted Ivan as he plunged into the jostling, bustling crowds that streamed in and out of every entrance. Eduard hesitated, and lost sight of him, before thrusting himself into the motley.

Inside the bazaar Uzbeks proffered wares, balancing melons and cotton cloths, silks and walnuts, hard baked cakes and dripping sweetmeats, cackling cajolery or muttering money, while Kazaks and Russians, Sarts and Kirghiz, Kalmuks and even Chinese elbowed their way past, pausing to taste or finger, pinch and weigh, before making their offers or shaking them off. The thrust and parry of exchange and commerce rose and fell, ebbed and flowed, and Eduard strove through the press, glimpsing Ivan, then losing him again as they penetrated deeper and further into the web of stalls.

Ahead there was a sharpening of the bustle, a shrilling of the salesmen, a vortex in the eddies of vendors and purchasers. Eduard perforce stopped, and peered past a portly Chinese in voluminous cottons.

Ivan was standing in the still centre of a tight triangle of traders, a melon tucked under one arm, his box on his chest, and his knife in his hand.

'Course I bought it. What d'yer think I did?' He glanced round, his face betraying no sign of danger perceived, and glimpsed Eduard.

'There! See? We paid for it – ask 'im. Ask 'im if 'e's got the roubles.'

Ivan lowered his knife hand, and inclined his head towards Eduard, who stepped into the loosening space, as vendors and spectators alike began to lose interest. The aggrieved stallholder pointed at the pile of fruit.

'Where's the top one, then?' One of the bystanders laughed, and tapped his head as if to say 'Lost your memory then?' and another muttered, 'All the same, these bloody Uzbeks. Try to pound you for an extra rouble every bloody time,' and the jostle recommenced, as they went on their ways, leaving Ivan and Eduard with the stallholder, whose trade had so suddenly evaporated.

'Tell yer what,' said Ivan, 'my friend 'ere'll buy another one, just to show there's no bad blood,' and he held out his hand. Eduard stuffed their remaining roubles into it, and Ivan put down the melon, carefully gripping it between his feet, selected another, tossed it to Eduard, and peeled off two roubles.

'There you are. Now we're even.' He picked up his melon, and wheeled away. 'Come on, mate. Let's see what else we can find,' with the emphasis on the 'find' as he sauntered off.

Next time, Ivan instructed Eduard to distract each vendor as he quietly hefted first a salami, then some bread; a sausage, apples, and a cheese. Eduard eschewed thieving to act as distractor or rearguard for his companion, until he smelt the fish. He nudged Ivan. 'Wait for me,' and he eased his way through the throng, sniffing this way and that, until he knew he was right. Visions of Cjortkow flooded through his mind as he paused behind a semi-circle of officers and bureaucrats, gathered before the fish slab, two of them methodically turning over the glistening corpses in their mortuary straw.

'That one, that one and' – the officer paused, casting his eyes across the array of river fish – 'and that one,' with satisfaction, turning to smile at his aides. An official busily counted out roubles, while the stallholder carefully wrapped the fish and, as he ceremoniously handed them over to yet another aide to the officers' right, Eduard cautiously reached out and filleted a small, gleaming salmon from the surrounding straw, and surreptitiously slid it into his rucksack, backing slowly away from the slab as the claque of warriors and their minions marched off in the opposite direction, the fish merchant's eyes resting fondly upon his important customers until they had all departed. Ivan mock-saluted the retreating squad, and winked at Eduard as they too moved off at a tangent. 'Nar yer 'ooked.'

Outside the bazaar, the sun still stood high and the heat delved deep into their blood and bones. Throughout their foray they had eaten nothing, drunk little, for their water reserves were low, and the vodka had long gone. Now they had food aplenty, and Ivan flourished a long green bottle of clear liquid, but of water they still had none. In the old town water flowed freely down the gutters and along the *aryks*, the irrigation ditches in every orchard. Ivan was in favour of invading the first garden they found, but Eduard objected.

'If there's water for plants, there's water for people,' and, as they crossed the first street, he pointed to the tap in a stone set into the wall of an obviously public building.

'*Kipyatok* – boiled water. I knew it,' and he pulled his water bottle free, filling it until it was brimming over, and knelt, letting the water spill into his mouth, down his chin, and onto his clothes.

The old town pulsated with heat, the dust acrid and irritating. The Russian city offered some shade but little respite from the afternoon temperature. They nibbled some bread, sipped more water, and rested on a bench beneath the acacias, watching the populace about its business, until the sun's trajectory presaged dusk. Without discussion, they headed back towards the station.

'Samarkand?' asked Eduard.
'Definitely,' responded Ivan.

'He's an idle burgher' was one of those senseless, not especially amusing plays on words that abounded in the post-war years, when all things German were contemptible, and spivery was endemic in our pre-Utopian island of socialist experiment. I applied for naturalisation and got my papers – after all, I had fought for my country and for theirs, spoke the language, which is more than can be said by them of mine, and was totalitarianaly *persona non grata* in my own fair land. I worked in electronics, which is to say I repaired the new domestic wonders of the age – radios, record players and that rarity, a television set, resplendent in its bakelite reticule, its small eye on the monochromous world of rations and coupons and shortages.

In Tashkent, Ivan and I were idle, spoke the language and were immigrants. Today too I am idle, because I cannot speak any language, and no-one will give me asylum, though they might well shove me in one, if my sweetling was not there to guard me.

Today my world is polychromatic and plentiful and you might think that would be some compensation for being struck dumb.

Who needs colour on a screen, when life is so many shades of grey? Who wants a life *in camera* – and God knows mine is about as *in camera* as you can get – when the camera probes every nook and prods every cranny?

In Tashkent we were idle, yet effective. We were in the public eye, yet of no common interest. We sought no attention, nor were we conscious of ourselves, yet we hid from no man. We stayed but 24 hours in that university town, yet you could argue that Tashkent was our rite of passage, our *alma mater*, our single simple stage between one life and another, when we learnt without payment, lived without commitment, loved one another, all for the one purpose of moving onto the next stage. Tashkent was our university.

Ah yes, I hear you say, but you were only there one day, so how can you make so much of one place? It is not the place, so much as the pause: there is always a moment between one thing and another, like that when I was moved from elegant maturity to ugly old age by a single act of physiological interruption.

We were idling in Tashkent, and we idled faster thereafter and it is to that place that I attribute my propensity for short cuts and simple solutions, where we bought our souls in the bazaar and came out into the midday sun, Ivan none the wiser, and I, in some wise, otherwise. The melons were ripe, the water plentiful and the salmon wild and we were idle burghers.

PICK A PECK OF PEPPER

Seasoned travellers, Ivan and Eduard swung down from the cattle train as it trundled into Samarkand, clutching rucksack and leather case, and carrying their quilted coats. Eduard had stuffed his leggings inside the coat, and his feet chafed against the shapeless shoes, while Ivan sweated inside his leather boots. It was hot and it was humid.

Watered by the Zeravshan river, Turkistan's ancient capital was embedded in its valley oasis before the otherwise arid plain in a fold of the Alayski mountains, the old town comfortably wed to its young Russian partner.

Near the railway station they found a park, embellished with banks of shrubbery, and broken by undulating mounds; Ivan ran up and down them like a schoolboy on half-holiday, while Eduard scouted the bushes to find somewhere to rest.

Climbing a low rise topped by graceful tamarisks, Eduard spotted a semi-circle of shrubs, denser than most, with a hollow, a grassy dell, tucked into the elbow formed by two *boyalych* bushes, and overshadowed by acacia. A small dun-coloured *suslik*, a ground squirrel, hopped past him and disappeared beneath the bushes. 'Ideal,' he breathed to himself, and turning to Ivan said, 'Here – this'll do. Plenty of shade too,' as he spread the quilted coat out, and collapsed onto it, legs spreadeagled.

Ivan was whooping up and down the rises, and came tearing down into their sheltered vale, flinging his case, coat and boots this way and that and tumbling down beside Eduard, impulsively flinging his arms round his friend with, 'Lovely Eduard – I could 'ave yer if yer was a woman,' and as rapidly rose and, stretching, hauled his tunic over his head before dropping back onto the grass, arms outstretched, eyes closed, a vacuous grin across his face.

'What we going ter do now, then?'

Eduard propped himself on his elbow and considered his companion.

'Well, for a start, you could do with a wash.'

'Wash? What fer? Who we goin' to dinner with?' and he laughed.

Eduard lay back again.

'Dinner. That's the next problem.'

'Nar. No problem. Bound to be somethin' somewhere.'

'Not now the markets are closed.'

Ivan sat up, his arms encircling himself, scratching his sides.

'Right. Let's find the best end of town, and see what the rich don't want.'

'I don't think that's a very good idea.'

'What?'

'Breaking into people's homes.'

'Who said anything about breakin' in? We'll just be good little jackals, and scavenge fer our supper, eh?' saying which he picked up his tunic and wriggling back into it, kicked his case under the bushes, pulled on his boots and started back up the slope. Eduard followed.

The grasses in the gardens were seeded with speedwell, poppies and stars of Bethlehem, and geraniums rioted along the borders, punctuated by pipits and starlings, as they foraged and chattered. Wooden houses mingled with stone residences, intersected by broad streets leading inexorably to public places, then back to shaded avenues. Most houses had a back yard or garden, and in most yards and gardens there was a shelter of some sort, where domestic detritus was stored, alongside the rubbish box.

At the first house they considered, Ivan was halfway across the garden when the dog saw him. It was a large, lumbering cross between a German shepherd and an Afghan, with spindly legs, shaggy coat and sleepy eyes, but it was not asleep when Ivan reached the lean-to. It growled, tossed its head, and charged.

'Look out! Dog!' yelled Eduard as Ivan plunged his arm into the bin. The dog leapt at him and he stumbled, pulling rags and waste out of the canister, and hurling it straight at the dog's muzzle. Then he ran, chasing Eduard down the avenue, across a square, into another street, until they found themselves in another quarter, where some houses were lower, windowless and climbed on one another's backs, others made of clean white stone, some cylindrical, some square, the older ones with overhanging first storeys. The round houses wore their turreted hats with old tiles pulled low over their long, narrow windowed faces. Here and there were new buildings, of concrete, and between them tall, spindly minarets, God's sentinels, overlooked the narrow, cobbled streets.

This was the old town. The dog had disappeared, and they slowed down. The marketplace was deserted, dusty rubbish listlessly drifting across their feet. Beyond there were old factories – wine presses, distilleries, cotton gins. They turned about and made their way back towards the modern city, passing ancient buildings until Eduard suddenly stopped.

'Look at that. Isn't that wonderful?'

Before them, beyond the nodding fronds of acacia, and past the gnarled walnut trunks, bounded by a simple pathway, broad, shallow steps beckoned travellers to a wide, round, soaring pillar of decorated stone, surmounted by a multi-ridged dome set down upon a double row of brick teeth, the whole seated upon a sculpted sequence of rectilinear spaces. This was Tamerlane's tomb.

Ivan stared at the mighty edifice, then at Eduard, then back again, then sighed, shrugged and set off towards the Russian quarter.

'Don't see what's so wonderful about that,' he said in a subdued mutter, while Eduard stood for another moment, marvelling, when he too sighed, and made his way back to reality.

Within an hour they had filled the rucksack with provisions purloined from other people's leavings and Eduard once more found the ubiquitous *kipyatock*. Hard by the water tap was a small fountain.

'That's wonderful anyway,' observed Eduard, leaning towards the water and dousing his hair, running his hands through his greasy locks, and splashing his legs and feet. Ivan stood and watched indifferently, peeled off his tunic and walked through the fountain, back and forth, washing the filthy garment separately, grimacing and spluttering.

'Satisfied?' and Eduard nodded.

As they returned to the park, the sun was lowering and the temperature dropped; they sat, wrapped in their quilted coats, picking over the food. A soggy bag of parboiled rice, half a pepper and some dried bacon made a sufficient supper, washed down with lukewarm water.

'We'll have ter do better than this,' grumbled Ivan, as he rolled himself into a ball and closed his eyes.

Early the next morning, they stowed the case and rucksack under the shrubs, and made their way back towards the station.

'Maybe there'll be officers there, like in Tashkent,' opined Ivan, but there were none. What there were were Poles – scores of them, camped out in clusters in the open parkland hard by the railway. Ivan avoided them, and made off into the cavernous depths of the station, while Eduard lingered on the outskirts of one group, until he could insinuate himself into their conversations.

Like him, they had come from Siberia, from the many camps and, like him, they had been released in the general amnesty and found their ways south, some directly, others by more circuitous routes, though none, it seemed, like Eduard, *via* Moskva.

He trawled the travellers for news, for scraps of information, about the war, about their country, and about the other camps, wondering rather than hoping whether or not he might glean some hint of Rosalia's survival. Of women's camps he learnt, and of women in other camps, but nothing which indicated his mother's whereabouts.

When Ivan rejoined him, the group he had joined drew back. They seemed to sense the outlaw in Ivan and, when he opened his mouth, they walked away. Like Eduard, they hated the Russians , and Ivan was patently Russian.

'What's a matter with that lot, then?'

'They're Poles. You're Russian. It's what's the matter with you, not them.'

'Well, sod 'em then. You're Polish and you're OK.'

'Yes, but I'm your friend, your mate, because I know you. They don't and you aren't their mate. They'd kill you if they thought they could get away with it.'

'Better leave then, han't we?' And they skirted the clumps of Eduard's countrymen as they set off again.

'Station no good then?' asked Eduard.

'Nar. Not an officer in sight. Nobody much really. Did get this though,' and Ivan brandished a leather purse with a drawstring.

'Where?'

'Off a feller 'oo 'appened to be passin'.'

'What do you mean, "happened to be passing"?'

'Well' – and Ivan grinned the grin that told Eduard he had once again been acting out his favourite fantasy of crisis management: create a crisis, then manage it – 'bumped against this bloke, and there was this lump – in 'is pocket – so I made 'im more comfortable,' and he tossed the purse at Eduard. 'Look inside.'

Eduard eased the strings apart and delved into the little sack, drawing out some worthless coins, a bundle of notes and a short length of gold chain, attached to a string of beads.

'Don't know what that's for,' observed Ivan, running his finger over the beads, 'but the gold'll sell for something, and the money's for food.'

'It's a rosary, I think, though I don't know, could be worry beads.'

'Don't matter. The gold's what matters.'

Ivan held out his hand and Eduard returned the trophies.

'Let's get some food.'

They walked quickly through the waking city to the old town and the market, where business had already begun. There were fish, fruit, fine cottons, supple silks, Kharakal sheepskins, close-patterned carpets, skins of *jeiran* antelope, Astrakhan furs, polished tortoise shells, slick snakeskins, lazy lizards in damp jars, dusky grapes, dried apricots, sacks and bowls of maize and rice, dried peas, wrinkled beans and blowsy melons, red-cheeked pomegranates and plump pears, mauve mulberries, woven scarves, embroidered caps, beaten copper cans and pots and pans, graceful ewers and chunky platters, tumbling beads and gossamer chains spread on dusty cloths and old carpets, stacked against walls, cascading down planks, piled in boxes and jars and baskets.

Stallholders stood or sat, singly and in groups, some robed, others in tunics and trousers, many well-whiskered, and some turbaned, a medley of hardy Kazaks and lean Black Kirghiz, stocky Kara Kalpaks and long-faced Turkomen, upright Uzbeks, bearded Tatars and sleek Tadzhiks, nomadic Yomuds and earnest Goklens, black-eyed Sartes, and handsome Bukharan Jews.

The cacophony of language bewildered Eduard, unaccustomed to the Tatar *Jagatai*. Around the edge of the marketplace, the old houses leaned, brick and wood and puddle clay and, clustered to one side, the harbour for all these transients, billowing brown and ochre, tan and yellow sere sails of the yurt, the Asian nomads' tents.

Ivan was indifferent to the mass and colour of the marketplace. He was watching the patterns of commerce, the eddies and flows, where the business moved, and where it paused, the nature and bearing and focus of the buyers as they stitched their ways through the asymmetrical weave of stand and stall. As business increased, Ivan tensed; as the crowds became denser, he became tenser. Once the marketplace was filled, and it became almost impossible to distinguish this buyer from that, Ivan moved. He slid into the most congested corners, where there was some stillness born of attention to vendors, multiplicity of choice, questions of price and value, and inserted himself between those persons most attentive to the purchase in mind or hand, and then slithered out again.

Eduard watched his first reconnaissance, then lost sight of him, and contented himself with wandering with the crowd's currents, making an occasional purchase with the purse of roubles which Ivan had handed him with the words, 'Need all the pockets I got fer this caper.'

Ivan was cunning. He watched the pick-pockets until he identified the lone wolf, the most polished practitioner. He became part of the pick-purse's progress, always following two or three people behind.

In the midst of the marketplace, Ivan struck. As the other thief coiled himself into that instant of stillness, only his hand, subtle and smooth, snaking between folds of clothing and retracting in one fluid, silent ripple, Ivan grafted his body to the thief's and relieved him of his previous profits. By the time the pick-pocket had palmed his trophy, Ivan had gone, was six, ten, twenty people away. In the course of three hours, Ivan worked three single pick-purses until his own pockets were full, and the small, narrow-mouthed sack tied between his legs was replete with roubles.

Eduard circled the marketplace twice, without sighting Ivan, and settled on a stone bench, sipping the vodka he had bought and nibbling a sweet cake. When he had finished, he examined his other purchases, running the cool cotton robe through his fingers, twisting the silken cords that would fasten it, and every so often, curling his toes inside the supple calfskin slippers he had slipped on as soon as he had paid for them.

'There you are,' and Ivan slumped down beside him, his tunic streaked with brown dust, folded over his pockets, the secret sack invisible.

'Let's 'ave some of that,' and he grabbed the bottle. 'I've earnt it.'

Eduard offered him a cake, which he took and bit and swallowed without pause, washing it down with another copious slug of spirit.

'Like yer shoes then.'

Eduard showed him the other clothes too.

'Proper little Ay-rab with that lot, en't yer?'

Before them the market ebbed and flowed as the crowds thickened, many workers and officials from the offices and factories putting their lunch break to good use.

'Time ter go, before one of those buggers realises,' and Ivan stood, wiped his hands down his tunic, and waddled off. Once clear of the market, he took Eduard's arm and pulled him down a side street.

"ere, take this; it's killin' me,' and he tugged the slim sack from between his legs, as he unknotted the cord that secured it to his belt.

'Pockets full too, but I can 'andle 'em, if yer carry this.'

'What? So I get caught with the goods?'

Ivan stopped, stepped back and gazed at Eduard.

'Yer really think I'd do that to yer? Bloody 'ell,' and he walked off, shaking his head from side to side, raising his right hand twice, and letting it fall to his side despondently. 'Bloody 'ell.'

Eduard trotted after him, catching him up, and put his hand on Ivan's sleeve. The other made no attempt to shake him off, but walked on, staring straight ahead.

'For God's sake, Ivan. I was joking.'

'Not very funny.'

'Alright, alright. I'm sorry.'

'Yer'd be sorry if there en't any food, wouldn't yer?'

Eduard said nothing.

Back in the park, they skirted the Poles, and made for their bushes by a circuitous route. Ivan retrieved his case, then emptied the sack. The principal cache was of cash, but there were also several trinkets, a leather wallet with some identification papers and a small, torn, fuzzy photograph of a young girl, plus some keys. Ivan scraped a hole in the soil and buried the keys and the papers, and stuffed roubles into the wallet, handing it to Eduard.

'Now yer got somewhere to keep yer money.' He held up the picture and added, 'I'll keep this. Ain't got anyone, so may as well 'ave 'er.'

He tucked the trinkets in the case – 'In case we run out a cash' – and replaced it under the bushes, then reached over to Eduard's rucksack, and examined the food he had bought: smoked bacon, maize bread, a melon and more of the sweet cakes, some cooked rice, and two gaudy peppers.

'Why yer pick them?'

'Makes the rice taste better.'

'Pickled peppers is best.'

'Alright. Next time I'll buy some pickled peppers.'

'Then you'll need some of these,' and Ivan poured a pile of copper coins onto his sack.

'Pick a pile of copecks for packs of pickled peppers,' tumbled out of Eduard's lips before he could stop himself, and he said it in English, an involuntary reflex born of an instant image of schooldays in Cjortkow, and a riddle-me-ree he barely remembered.

'What?' asked Ivan.

'Oh nothing – just an old joke in another language. Nothing important.'

But it had set Eduard's train of thought into a new pattern, away from the idle, catch-as-catch-can nature of his days with this irresponsible Ivan.

He found himself yearning for home, returning slowly but inexorably to his original plan – to escape, to run, not to stop until he was back, and then to fight for that larger freedom. Eduard shook his head, and opened his eyes. Ivan was gazing at him somewhat quizzically.

"'ad a brainstorm, then?'

'No, not really. Just dreaming,' and Eduard smiled, handing Ivan the vodka with, 'Have another drink, and just forget it.'

They idled another hour away, until they had eaten and drunk their fills, when Ivan jumped up and announced, 'Time fer some fun, then.'

'Fun?'

'Yeah. Fun. There's a bit of bettin' goin' on in the old town tonight. We should try our luck.' He looked down at Eduard. 'Yer any good at cards?'

Eduard smiled back up at him.

'As a matter of fact I am.'

'Good. Then yer can play your game, and I'll play mine. Come on.'

Eduard, robed and corded, and Ivan in his freshly laundered tunic, leather belt and boots, cut a singular dash when they returned to the marketplace, once again deserted, empty of stalls, though stacks of planks were haphazardly stored to one side, and many of the yurts glowed softly from the oil lamps within them, carts standing alongside, piled high with baskets and boxes.

Ivan led the way down a narrow defile between the houses, until they reached an open-fronted *khata*, on the Ukrainian model, with smooth clay walls, whitewashed, overhanging thatch and beamed ceiling, with a bench on either side of the deep verandah.

A dozen or more traders sat sipping black tea from deep saucers, steam drifting across the café, mingled with acrid smoke. Eduard sniffed and detected a pungent odour, and guessed that not all that was smoked was tobacco. The buzz of conversation sharpened slightly when they entered, then resumed its lilting rhythms as they took their seats. Ivan placed several notes on the table, two saucers appeared without comment, and the notes swiftly disappeared. The man next to Eduard shifted closer. In the half light, shadows played across his gaunt cheeks, and his hand rasped across his stubble.

'You are new here.'

It was not a question. Eduard nodded.

'You are Russian?'

Eduard shook his head.

The man contemplated him, grunted, then rose to his feet, planting his hands squarely on Eduard's shoulders.

'If you are not Russian, and you are not local, what are you?'

Before Eduard could answer him, Ivan spoke up.

'I'm Russian. He's my friend.'

'Ah. Well, that's alright then.'

He looked down at Eduard again.

'We'll say you're a poor Russian then, after all.'

He turned to Ivan.

'You play?'

Ivan smiled, pulled out a bunch of roubles, waved them about, replaced them and then clapped his hands together, so that the sudden snap stopped all conversation dead. The other patrons all looked at him.

Ivan stood slowly, his hands still clasped together, then he revolved twice, opened his hands, and there was an ace in each, a spade in his left and a heart in his right. He offered them to Eduard's interlocutor, who hesitated, delicately removed them between finger and thumb, as Ivan reached out to Eduard, and plucked a card from his astonished mouth – ace of diamonds. Then Ivan tapped his own head, pointed at the long pipe held in mid-air by the nearest drinker, reached across, cupped the bowl, then slowly unfolded his hand to reveal – the ace of clubs.

There was desultory applause, with a cynical note about it, as the other man returned the first two cards and Ivan asked, 'Where's the club, then?'

'Downstairs,' was the answer.

They followed their host into the back of the *khata*, to a black, planked door, with no handle. He knocked sharply, and it swung back, revealing a flight of stone steps, lit by oil lamps. Down they went, and turned into a large, clay-lined cellar, whitewashed like the *khata* above, and lit with kerosene lamps in pot-bellied glass containers, their smoke hanging under the ceiling, like a matt cobweb.

In the centre of the room was a thick-planked table, and seated at it were four players, each robed, bearded and turbaned. In the flickering light, Eduard could discern little difference between them, except the greyness of one beard and the intense black of the other three. The greybeard slapped the seat beside him, and motioned to Ivan to sit, pointing across the table to another vacant place, and jutting his beard at Eduard. They sat.

In front of each player was a knife, its point buried in the wood. Eduard shuddered, and realised he had his knife hidden beneath his new robe, in his belt. He decided to keep it there, reasoning to himself that if he had no knife, no-one would challenge him with theirs, and his life would be that much more secure, insofar as any life might be secure in this gaming house. Ivan produced his with a flourish, and stuck it, quivering, in the table, glancing at the empty places.

Their host bent and muttered something in the greybeard's ear and he turned to Ivan, holding out a sinewy, tanned and hairless hand. Ivan grinned, and put his pack of cards in the other's palm.

Behind them more players were descending, until all twelve places were filled. Small glasses appeared before each man, and two flagons were placed in the centre of the table. The greybeard produced three packs of cards, and chairs scraped as the players settled more closely together into three schools. Eduard and Ivan found themselves in different ones. The greybeard dealt Eduard his first hand.

Eduard was a sound player, without being spectacular, and his skills at tarot had taught him how to dissemble. He lost a little, won a little, and by the time the greybeard called a pause, was up 50 roubles – enough to gain respect but not so much as to engender envy or manufacture malice. He decided to lose a little, before making a final claim to some spoils, so that he might leave the table with respect.

From the tension evident in straightened backs and silent chairs, Ivan's school was more serious, and it soon became clear that Ivan was in the ascendant, and his competitors were displeased. Suddenly one of the players shoved his chair back, threw down his cards, plucked his knife out of the table, and left, without a word. The other two sat back and looked impassively at Ivan as he gathered his winnings into his little sack and swivelled round.

'My cards please.'

The greybeard felt under his robe, and produced the pack, handing it over without comment, and Ivan stood.

'Thanks. Good game.' Turning to Eduard, he asked 'Ready to go?' and they left.

A pattern developed – rise, eat, fountain and wash, market to buy food, and in Ivan's case, relieve thieves of their thefts, 'home' to eat, rest, then back to market for tea, then vodka and cards. Each night Eduard won a little, and each night Ivan won a great deal.

It was clear to Eduard that he was cheating, though they had not discussed it. It was in his bearing, the way he bet, the way he dealt, the way he sat, head cocked to one side, eyes unblinking, a slow smile, then a swift move. And it was in his winnings, which were disproportionate, to age, to the school, and in the experience of the gamblers. Eduard became more and more uneasy, and tried to tackle Ivan.

'We should give it a miss – the gambling. We have enough cash. And I don't think they're happy. There'll be trouble one of these days.'

'Nar. It's good money and they're just rustics. They don't know our city ways. They think we're big players.'

'I don't think they do,' said Eduard softly. 'I think they think we're cheating.'

'Cheating? Nobody's cheating,' and Ivan punched him in the chest. 'Yer not cheating are yer?'

'Of course not.'

'Well then.'

That afternoon they were walking back from the market when Ivan nudged Eduard. 'Keep walkin',' he hissed, adding, 'this way,' and steering Eduard down a side street. There was only one other pedestrian, a bulky Persian in a voluminous robe, wrinkled leather boots, a crimson sash and a purple turban. The Persian paused, and dipped into his robe, hauling out a fat gold watch on a heavy chain, which he snapped open, and peered at short-sightedly, then returned to its hiding place.

'Look at that Ay-rab; he's got a big, gold watch and I'm going to have it.'

'Not a good idea,' but Eduard was too late.

As Ivan walked away: 'You can't.'

'Yer bet me?'

'Ten roubles?'

'Done. Wait 'ere,' and Ivan was gone, as the Persian rounded a corner and disappeared. Eduard waited and, within minutes, Ivan returned, swinging the gold watch on its chain, smirking and, as he approached Eduard, dancing a little jig, bending his knees more and more, until he was kicking his legs out Cossack-style, twirling the clock around his head, and clicking the fingers of his other hand, yipping and yaying as he went.

'For God's sake, stop! Someone'll see you.'

Ivan slowed his dance, and sat softly on the dusty street, still twirling the watch, more and more slowly, until it hung from his fingers, gently swinging to and fro.

'What d'yer think of that, then?'

'What have you done? Have you done him in?'

'Course not,' and he snapped the watch open, glanced at its face, snapped it shut, and stowed it away in his purse.

Eduard heard the Persian before he saw him. The man rounded the corner, peering in the gutter, this way, then that, until he was almost on top of them. Startled, he looked up, smiled uncertainly and asked, 'Have you seen a watch? A gold watch?' He hesitated and added, 'I'll reward you.'

Ivan looked at him, bold, smirking, exulting almost.

'Nar, no watches 'ere, mate,' and turning to Eduard, 'Yer seen any watches?'

Eduard said nothing, and the Persian continued up the street, searching the gulleys for his misplaced timepiece.

169

'There y'are. Easy, en't it?' and Ivan skipped off up the street, dancing from side to side as he went.

That night Eduard lost a little at the table, and Ivan, as usual, came away with several hundred roubles. He had bought two bottles of vodka and, by the time they reached the park, he was singing in his cups. Eduard tried to sleep, but Ivan was determined to drink both bottles, and the more he drank, the more he sang until, in an alcoholic stupor, he finally fell over, hiccoughed twice, and was asleep.

The next day was Friday, and Ivan was nowhere to be found. Eduard ate a little, then secreted his rucksack, noting Ivan's case was still under the bush, and made his way to the water tap and the fountain. After he had washed, he walked through the city to the marketplace, and started buying food. He was standing by a fruit stall when someone pulled his sleeve. His hand fell to the concealed knife, and he half-turned.

The man from the café was holding his arm.

'Are you coming tonight?'

Eduard considered, and was about to shake his head and make an excuse, when the man said, 'I wouldn't if I were you,' and was gone.

Relieved, Eduard bit into the cheese he had just bought, and wandered through the marketplace, wondering what had happened to Ivan. Then he saw him, working his way through the throng, some ten stalls away. Eduard saw him stop behind a small, tight group being harangued by a silk salesman, and he watched as Ivan positioned himself behind a short, ragged youngster, who was clearly dipping the pockets of those around him. He saw Ivan's hand snake out. Then the boy pivoted, and slashed him across the cheek with a curved blade. Ivan fell back, his hand to his face, and started to weave and dodge, duck and turn, as he extricated himself. Eduard caught up with him sitting in the fountain, bathing his cut cheek.

'Where the hell have you been?'

'I went out early, ter clear the 'ead.'

'Well, you seem a little bit cut up.'

'Nar, s'nothing,' and in truth the cut was superficial and had already stopped bleeding. Yet, to Eduard, taken together with the landlord's injunction, it was an omen.

'I'm not going to the cellar tonight, and if I were you, I wouldn't either.'

Ivan grinned, a mad gleam in his eye, the same gleam Eduard had noticed every time his companion went into action on a light-fingered spree, in the station at Kujbysev, the market at Tashkent, and here in Samarkand. He had a genius for crime but, like so many geniuses, he was also a little mad, and that Friday the madness was in control.

Eduard stayed in the park that night, and cast his mind back over the nights of gambling, remembering the previous night, when the greybeard solemnly informed him he was the Mayor of Samarkand, and told him, 'I know you're a Pole. I have met many Poles. Your country was once under the yoke of the mighty Ghengis Kahn,' and his eyes had glittered with the historic joy of it.

'Poland was Lechastan in those days, gambled her freedom – and lost,' and the Khan of Samarkand gripped Eduard's arm so tightly he nearly cried out as he softly added, 'You are a Pole, and you are gambling with your freedom too,' and as quickly released him, and dealt the cards. And Eduard knew then that he was right not to return to the cellar.

Eduard slept for an hour and awoke suddenly, looking across the hollow towards Ivan's place, but of Ivan there was no sign. He woke several times during that night, wishing Ivan back, but the young Muscovite did not return. In the streaks of dawn, Eduard sat up and uncharacteristically reached for the vodka. He rinsed his mouth out with water and tidied himself, pulling the rucksack out from under the bushes, and slinging it around his neck. Ivan's case was there too, and he retrieved that as well, and opened it. It was empty – no trinkets, no watch, no clothes, no boots, nothing. He pushed it back under the shrubs, and sat watching the *suslik* cautiously venture out, scavenging the crumbs before it sat regarding him, then scampered off.

That day Eduard scoured Samarkand for Ivan again, without success. He washed, bought food and fetched water, and finally walked down the side street to the tea café. The host brought him a saucer, and he slowly sipped the black tea.

'Have you seen Ivan?' he asked, but the host shook his head. One by one the gamblers appeared, passed through the shop and vanished down the stairs. When the Khan paused by Eduard's bench, he looked up, about to ask, when the greybeard said, 'I'm afraid we haven't seen your friend,' and he too disappeared down the stairs.

Each day Eduard followed the same routine, and each day the answers were the same. One week after Ivan had disappeared, the Khan invited him down to the cellar. The room was empty but in the middle of the table, there was a single knife, its blade quivering, the point buried deeply in the log. It was rusty with dried blood. It was Ivan's knife.

'You should take it, my son,' and the Khan pulled the knife out, and proffered it to Eduard, haft first.

By the end of the next week, the money had gone, and he started scavenging again. After ten days, he joined the Poles outside the railway station, and the next morning he was woken abruptly by a considerable commotion. The sky was still dark; the sun was struggling below the horizon. It was three o'clock. The Poles were shifting in groups, moving back and forth.

'What's going on?'

'Nobody knows. The NKVD are here.'

The sombre uniforms materialised out of the morning mist. They were surrounded.

'Everyone over here!'

They shuffled towards the gates, and there were the lorries. The NKVD ushered them onto the trucks, armed militiamen ranged along the railings, in case anyone thought to escape.

'Where are we going?'

'Obruchev.'

'Where the hell's that?'

'North. Two hundred miles.'

'Why?'

'To work – you are going to build a railway for Russia.'

I kept Ivan's knife for many years, as a reminder. A reminder of his friendship, but also of his amorality. I regretted his death, for I was certain he had died, knifed by one of those gamblers who had been cheated once too often, and I regretted his life, which was designed by circumstance. Most of all I regretted the manner of my fall from grace through his criminality. Ivan and I were displaced persons, but we were worse than that, we were aliens, mutations, carnivorous plants that grew out of the soil of discontent and greed and idleness.

He was a superior crook, and a brilliant analyst of situation and circumstance. In another life, he might have been a millionaire, an entrepreneur, a leader of men, for he was certainly a leader of one man – me. I absolved myself of blame through Ivan, admired his slick talk and slicker actions. I abdicated my responsibility for myself because Ivan held all the cards, including the ace of hearts, which he could whip from my head or my chest with that simple smirk, as he fooled me and, of course, himself.

Ivan was my other, my dark soul, my pied piper and I was the sink of his iniquity. I shudder in my quiet mind when I remember his 'Cheating? Who's cheating? You're not cheating are you?' and my answer. Because I was cheating – even if I played a straight hand at cards. I was cheating my self. I was not being Eduard. Freedom comes from self-knowledge, and today I cannot cheat if I want to, for there is no-one left to cheat except me, and I have to face myself every waking minute, so what's the point?

Ivan's death saved me. If he had not died, I would not have been with the other Poles, and if I had not been with them, I would not have been recaptured and, though at the time it seemed as if my world was once more one of captivity and coercion, I was at least free – free of my own demons.

I feel in my pocket for the one remaining copeck that I have kept all these years: pick a pile of copecks for packs of pickled peppers...

THE RED DEATH

'You and you!'

The selection was fast and indiscriminate, despite the personalised commands. Obruchev was a desolate settlement in the desert, and the railway had spurred fifteen miles off the heel of the main line when Eduard reached its frontier. At this nameless outpost, a siding had been constructed and on the siding were six carriages, five equipped with double bunks, the sixth with a galley, storage and generator. In that wagon worked seven galley-slaves, who cooked, and cleaned and served the food for some 400 men.

The food was simple but plentiful – soup, bread, tea or water, and dried fruit. There were two guards to each carriage, and the engineers in charge of construction lived with the conscripts. There were rudimentary showers – a string and a bucket, replenished from a water tank, which was filled twice a week by the shuttle from Obruchev.

Each morning, at five, the guards roused the workforce, and each wagonload used the showers once weekly in rotation – the engineers and cooks had them to themselves every sixth day. After food and drink, the teams were manually propelled along the track to the end of the line on flatbeds, taking turns to work the lever.

The Poles were divided into teams of three. The first dug, the second wheeled, the third spread the earth. Each barrowload was pushed up an eight-inch steel plank to the top of the embankment, to extend the structure, or across its width, so that the bank grew both in width and extent, before the engineering team laid the next set of five foot rails. These were the special gauge the Tsarist government decreed before Red Oktober, to maintain Russia's isolation, an isolation favoured even more by the Central Committee.

The flat terrain encouraged the engineers, but the erratic supply of ballast infuriated them, and often enough the embankment stretched a mile or more ahead of the rails, for the want of road-metal. When the ballast did arrive, it was spread thinly, so that the task of laying sleepers was made more difficult.

Eduard was one of those who had to lay the timber baulks, first levelling the earth, then spreading the intermittent layer of ballast where the sleepers must lie, and precisely positioning the unwieldy length of wood. The teams were supervised by the few Polish officers, standing at intervals along the embankment. Soup was distributed per team, according to work rate: the more they laid, the more they got. Those teams which exceeded the 'norm' received double rations. Eduard's team set the pace, with Wladek shovelling, and Jacek spreading the soil.

Wladek was one of those people others hardly ever notice – self-effacing, soft of voice, small of stature, regular in feature, unremarkable in every way. He seemed neither to suffer unduly nor to rejoice at all; if he had opinions he did not share them, and even his eyes were light grey, reflecting his personality, his skin pale, his stubble light and his hair light brown. Jacek was a man of some melancholy, with sombre dark brown eyes set between continuous eyebrows and mauve smudges beneath; his cheekbones were sharp, his face drawn, his chin blue with badly shaven beard; he was tall, bent, almost cadaverous, yet moved with a controlled ferocity, a barely concealed power, his hands capable, his limbs long. Jacek was Jewish, Eduard discovered.

One night as he walked near the siding, he heard a soft chant, and strained to see whence it came. It seemed to come from beyond the huts, somewhere in the wasteland. He trod quietly until he discerned a shadow darker than the rest, and stopped, listening again. The chant was merely murmured, and he did not recognise the sounds.

It stopped suddenly, and the shadow was no longer there. He waited for it to recommence, but there was no tremor in the still night air except the soft fall of anxious footsteps, moving away from him.

When he returned to the siding, Jacek was apparently asleep in the bunk above his. The following night, Eduard left early for his evening walk, moving in the same direction as that of the previous evening, and waited, sitting with his head down, and his arms clutching his knees. He heard someone approach, then pass him a few yards away, then stop, and once more, the chanting. When it stopped, he waited until the quiet footsteps were within reach, and quietly rose, then followed close behind. As he passed the first carriage, a hand brushed his arm. Automatically, he felt for his knife.

'You won't need that.'

'Who's there?'

'It's me, Jacek, but you knew that anyway.'

'Was that you out there?'

'Yes, it was.'

'What were you doing?'

'You know what I was doing.'

'You were chanting?'

'I was reciting the Kaddisch.'

'What's the Kaddisch?'

'It's the prayer for the dead.'

'Why would you pray for the dead, here, at night, now?'

'I pray for my family, who are dead.'

'Your family? Dead?'

'Yes. They are all dead. I am the only one left.'

'How do you know?'

'Because I watched them die.'

'Where?'

'In Warsaw.'

Eduard said nothing and the silence stretched, its membrane taut and menacing. Jacek severed it.

'You want to know how?'

'I suppose so. Yes.'

'The Germans. The Nazis. They cut them down because they were Jews.'

The silence gathered itself again between them. It was Eduard who cut it down this time.

'Because they were Jews? That is not a reason to kill people. Were they fighting, shooting the Germans?'

'No. They were living their lives, at home. They were dragged out. They were frightened. They were shot. They were Jews.'

Eduard: 'All your family?'

'All my family. My mother, my father, my brothers, my baby sister, and my aunt, who lived with us.'

Eduard felt an overpowering need to speak to Rosalia, to touch Bruno, to argue with his father, as he considered the stark facts of Jacek's loss, and remembered his own. The bond was immediate, the comparison odious, the need comparable, and he enfolded the younger man, and together they cried dry tears that night.

After six weeks, at a mile a day, the railway stretched over 40 miles across the uncertain sands, and equipment arrived to bore a well. A new siding was built, utilising the rails from the old one. Sick or not, the workforce was given no respite, and one day Eduard felt the onset of fever. At the workface, he stumbled, the barrow halfway up the plank. As he faltered, the wheel slipped and dropped over the edge, the barrow jarred to a halt, and slowly tipped sideways, depositing the earth onto the desert floor. Eduard yanked the barrow back, called his team-mate, and they refilled it, before he reversed and tried again.

Once more he stumbled. The heat was intense, he was runelled with sweat; his head boiled, and his pulse was shallow and fast. He set the barrow down, holding it steady, pausing for a moment before trying again, but it slipped, and the contents cascaded onto the sand. As he tried to wipe the salt water out of his eyes, his other hand, slick with sweat, lost its grip and the barrow slid out of his grasp, cartwheeling over and over and off the plank, crashing into the side of the bank, where the rusty fork disintegrated with the force of the impact, the wheel careening over the silicate surface until it settled slowly on its stub, and was still. Eduard sat.

The officer clambered up the plank and raised his hand, cuffing Eduard across the head, first left, then right, twice, three, four times.

'You stupid fucking slob – you've broken the bloody thing. Get up!' and he lunged at Eduard again, grasping his sleeve, and swinging him onto his knees. Eduard fell sideways, the officer lost his grip, and Eduard tumbled off the plank, and struck his head on the barrow handle.

By now the nearest teams had gathered round the scene, and another officer had joined them.

'What's the trouble?'

'This stupid Polack has broken the stupid barrow.'

The second officer took his sleeve, and gently pulled him away.

'We're all stupid Polacks here, or we wouldn't be building this damned railway, would we?'

He released his colleague, and returned to Eduard.

'What's the problem?'

Eduard was slumped against the barrow, rubbing his head. All he said was, 'Have my soup.'

The first officer returned.

'What?'

'You can have my soup,' repeated Eduard and the officer raised his hand again, slamming Eduard against the barrow.

'Bloody man.'

Eduard pushed himself up onto his knees and shuffled forward towards his team-mates. One was leaning on the shovel. Eduard punched both hands forward, tore the shovel away and, in the same swinging movement as the officer leant over him, brought it sideways across his face, welting him with the flat blade. The officer fell, pole-axed. The small crowd of workers divided as a Russian guard pushed his way between them.

'What's going on up here?'

'I feel queer. I must have hit him.'

The guard bent down, and felt the officer's pulse. As he did so, the man stirred, rolled over, and pushed himself onto his knees and hands, shook his head, and stood unsteadily.

'You alright?'

'Bloody man – he hit me.'

'Are you alright?'

'Yes, I suppose so.'

'Good. Well, he's not,' and turning to the others, the guard added, 'Two of you help him back to the track; take him as far as the siding, then bring the trolley back here. OK?'

His team took an arm each, and led the faltering, swaying Eduard up the plank, and along the embankment to the line of trolleys. The guard walked beside them. As the nausea advanced and receded, Eduard tried to focus on his face, the face of a Kazak, not a Mongol or a Russian; this was a 'local'. At the trolley he took Eduard's pulse observing, 'Your heart's going 140 – not good.'

He looked down kindly at the young Pole, eyes blurred, breath shallow, skin sallow and sheened, his eastern eyes appraising him.

'You're no good to us here – why don't you clear off to Obruchev?'

They helped him onto the last trolley, then started the haul back to the carriages. Once there, they heaved him into the carriage and, while one sat with him, the other went to fetch water and bread.

It was still early, the sun was mounting the sky, outlining the derrick, and the noise of the drill, grinding into the substrata, echoed across the sands.

'You OK now, Eduard?'

Summoning a wispy smile, he nodded slowly.

'I'm fine. Fine. Thanks. You go. I'll be fine.'

'No. We'll stay with you.'

'No. Waste of time. I'm going to Obruchev.'

'Don't be so bloody stupid.'

Eduard rolled over and closed his eyes. Minutes later he heard them leave. He sat up, digging his heels in the palliasse, pushing his back hard against the wagon wall, and reached below the bed. His rucksack was still there, with his knife and a few scraps of clothing. He steadied himself with one hand, then swung his legs onto the floor. A wave of dizziness swept across him, his eyes glazed, and he shook his head violently. The nausea passed, and he stood slowly and cautiously.

Outside, the heat was rising off the desert strand, the air was still, and only by the derrick was there any movement. Eduard stumbled erratically down the line of wagons to the galley, climbed step by step to the open access, and looked about him. There was one cook washing pots. He turned. 'Yes?'

'I've got to get to Obruchev. Can I have some water, and some fruit – please?'

'Why not?'

The cook put down the pan, wiped his hands with the cloth, threw it aside, and reached up for a mug.

'No. In here, if you don't mind,' and Eduard held out his water bottle.

The cook filled it, and felt underneath the galley shelf.

'Here's some melon, and a few dried plums.' He bent again. 'And some pork fat – gives you energy, makes you sweat.' He looked at the sick young face before him and added, 'If you're sure you're going.'

'I'm sure.'

'Right. Then don't tell anyone about the fat. OK?'

'OK.'

The cook turned his back, and picked up the pan. Without looking, he added, 'Good fortune, and I hope you make it – it's a long way, fifteen miles at least. Keep walking by the line; you can't go wrong. It goes all the way!' and he laughed at the simplicity of his joke.

Eduard walked, and the sun mounted ever higher, until it was overhead. His head throbbed, his heart pounded, his legs ached, the rucksack grew heavier and the water more appealing, as he walked, sipping a bare mouthful at increasing intervals. He did not pause, for he knew that if once he did so, he would find it difficult to start again and, after a second or perhaps a third stop, he might never start again.

He walked through his agony until his mind wandered, his eyes blurred and his mouth thickened; he walked past the pain into an automaton's world of hard heat, detached motion, unthought and clamped systems, where it was enough to push out one foot, then the other, to focus only on the straight line of track, and to pretend that this was a journey into infinity, where there was no end, so there was no reason to stop, only an imperative to continue, for ever. He marched through the midday solstice, into the searing afterday, and through the hours of concentric heat until he stumbled at last to the junction, and fell against the wall of the mud house at Obruchev.

That is where they found him, at eleven that evening, dry as dust, his sweat crusted upon his skin, his lips blistered, eyes closed, feet scabbed and bleeding, and the palm of his right hand bloody, where the nails had scored the flesh in his determination to reach sanctuary.

It was Voztas the priest who found him, Komowski, the one-time chief of Danzig police, who revived him, and Vitalis, the Italian count, who once monopolised the bakery business in Poland, and predictably finished up with his customers, who helped to carry him inside, and produced medication and liniments to ease his wracked body and soothe his tortured skin. It was one-legged Stoklosa who asked him, 'What have you come back for?'

Komowski felt his pulse.

'It is good you are back – I had heard your name and searched for many days, but could not find you. You are Jozef's son, are you not?'

Eduard nodded.

'Jozef Cjaikowski?'

He nodded again.

'Of Cracow police, then Cjortkow?'

'Yes,' whispered Eduard.

'I thought so. I am sorry they took you to the railway. I could have stopped them. You look rough, and by the feel of you, you are very sick. Show me your chest.'

He peeled away the rags that were once Eduard's clean new cotton robe and took one glance.

'You've got red typhus. You'd better rest.'

They laid him on a straw bed and Stoklosa whispered into his ear, the last thing he heard for fifteen days.

'We'll try to look after you.'

There was little medicine, and no expertise, except one Polish doctor, who served the elite committee of senior officers who controlled their countrymen. Komowski enjoined him to attend Eduard and the doctor somehow found some camphor oil, which he administered sparingly, to stimulate his weakened heart. In the second week he extracted some morphine from the Russians, and injected his patient, to relieve his symptoms, and to deaden the pain.

Eduard was not alone. Of over 200 at the base camp, half contracted the disease. Eduard was young, privileged, treated – and survived. The camp was isolated, but the Russians eventually provided a limited number of nurses to attend the Poles. It was too late. One hundred and three 'free' patriots, released over so many months, only to be restrained again, died. The survivors were packed onto lorries, and transported away from the plain, into the foothills, to a mountain valley, and to a 'hospital', where they were housed in a temporary sickroom in the cellar. It was 3 am when they arrived.

Eduard was recovering; Stoklosa was fading.

'I shall not survive tonight.'

'Of course you will. You cared for me – I will care for you. We will go home, and this will all be forgotten.'

They slept. The next morning Eduard awoke and turned to his crippled companion. His eyes were closed. He was still and, when Eduard reached out to touch him, he was cold. He would never go back to Poland.

At eight that morning the door slammed back. Eduard looked up. The gap was filled by the largest woman he had ever seen – a 16-stone corpulent colossus in white cap and strained apron, pillared legs widespread in white stockings, bulbous hands clutching shears and bucket. She advanced, a malevolent galleon in full spite and sail, followed by her twin, their colourless hair bunched beneath their caps, a stool in each protuberant claw.

'Everyone, get into line. We cut the hair,' and the second woman planted the stools side by side and gestured to Eduard and Komowski to step forward, while the other retracted one bucket from within another, clanged them down by each stool, handed a pair of shears to her partner, and flexed her hand as she scissored the air. She pointed at Stoklosa. Eduard explained.

'He's dead.'

'Next then.'

One by one their heads were shorn. Then the first woman announced, 'Trousers down.'

Komowski protested. For a moment the stocky, grey-haired, short-necked, deep-chested ex-policeman stood his ground, and the tension spread insidiously through the room; for a moment, the Pole held his ground, and the fat lady hesitated, but the moment passed.

The woman advanced, brandishing the shears.

'You take the trousers down, or I cut them off, along with your cock.'

Reluctantly Komowski dropped his pants, and stood before her, as she settled her haunches, wriggling the fat into comfortable folds, then grasped his member, and sliced away his pubic hair, none too gently.

As the women handled the last pricks and pubes, two orderlies arrived with a pair of galvanised bath tubs and a hose, with which they filled them with surprisingly hot water.

'Now all off. Everything off,' commanded the massive matrons, and each pair of men was subjected to a thorough scrubbing. As they emerged, the orderlies handed them clean linen shirts, cotton pantaloons and cloth shoes. Those who could, walked. The weaker ones were stretchered out, and they all found themselves in the hospital, in several neat, clean wards. Voztas looked at Eduard, his eyebrows disappearing into his hairline.

'It's like being born again.'

'A resurrection?'

'Don't be blasphemous,' but he smiled as he said it.

The priest hid his godliness beneath a mantle of faint amusement, as if the ways of men were a constant source of slight merriment, and he the sanctifier of human error, his slender, fluttering hands the only overt signification of his deeper concerns. They were ever on the move, twitching the once long strands of lank, black hair over his left ear, adjusting his coarse robe, tugging the cord that bound it. He was, in one respect, a true man of God. He frequently refused food, passing it onto others, seeming to feed off an inner nourishment, a certainty that he could only share at one remove.

The patients were recovering; twenty to a ward, they were treated for their dysentery, for several were passing blood. They were fed burnt bread – charcoal loaves – and injected with anti-bacterial drugs, clearly variable, according to their differing shapes and labels.

Yet still they died, albeit fewer, and less frequently. In the evening, they would gather together, sipping black tea. In the morning, one, perhaps two, would not rise. Their companions called them. No reply. Then someone would reach to touch a face, cold and lifeless.

Eduard recovered and helped the burial detail. He and Voztas said a few words over the makeshift graves. The last to go was a captain of artillery. They buried him in his greatcoat, with his jacket shrouding his face, so that no part of him was exposed to the unforgiving soil and no dog could scratch a living from his flesh.

Within fourteen days, the deaths subsided and the majority of the survivors were transferred to a cluster of wooden huts, and the day after that, all except Eduard and his immediate companions were shipped out. No-one knew where they were going, but Komowski surmised it was back to the railway gangs. The committee of officers went with them.

The first day after that they were given water, but no food. Voztas complained. The guards, who came and went, apparently indifferent to the possibilities for escape, shrugged.

'Ask your officers.'

Voztas: 'What are we going to do? If we don't eat, we starve.'

The guards ignored him.

The following morning, they were given bread, and some water. The same rations were issued that evening.

'We won't survive long on this,' observed Komowski.

There, in the mountains near the Afghan border, there were sheep, and watching the sheep were hillsmen, shepherds. The shepherds had dogs and the dogs came sniffing round the huts, scavenging for non-existent scraps. Eduard dragged Voztas outside.

'Look. Dogs.'

'What of it?'

'They're looking for food too.'

'So?'

'Well, that means there isn't any – except them.'

'Eat dog? Ugh.'

'Eat or starve.'

'But "thou shalt not kill".'

'I'm not suggesting you kill. I'll kill. You skin it.'

'I'd rather you killed a sheep.'

'I'd rather I didn't. The shepherds would not be pleased, and anyway, we can't leave the camp to find sheep. And the sheep won't come to find us.' He paused, then added, 'But the dogs will.'

Eduard sat outside the hut, and waited for the light to fade, for that was when the sheepdogs came down the mountainside, across the screes, and into the camp, sniffing around the base of the huts, treading gracefully across the new-dug graves, pausing to snuffle the freshly turned earth, then lifting their heads, growling softly, their ears pricked, noses twitching, still in the twilight.

One dog paused hesitantly, a paw raised, dangling, eyes unblinking, ears tuning into the slight sounds from the huts, nose dilated to catch the hint of supper. Eduard threw a lump of bread. The dog lowered its head and regarded him, then cautiously edged forward, until it was near the morsel. It stopped short, gazed at Eduard, and turned away, circling, then stopping back where it started, a foot or more from the bread.

Eduard did not move. The dog lay down, its head slowly lowered onto its extended paws. They stayed thus for a full minute. The dog shuffled forward six inches, then stopped. Eduard remained still. The dog moved forward another few inches, until the bread was almost between its paws. Eduard was motionless. The dog brushed the floor with its tail, from side to side, as it continued to watch Eduard. Then it rose slowly, stepped daintily forward a single step, dipped its muzzle, and snapped the bread between its jaws. Eduard broke another piece of bread, and placed it below the hut step.

He moved to one side, and sat on the ground. The dog looked back at the mountains, then towards Eduard. It drifted back to the graves, sniffed around, then looked back at Eduard briefly, before continuing its investigation. It trotted back towards the hut, and lay down again in the same place, its head on its paws, watchful. Eduard remained where he was. The dog sat up on its haunches, threw up its muzzle and addressed the faint moon that rose behind the buildings. As the last howl faded, it jumped up, and trotted confidently towards the hut, lifting the bread as it passed the step, circling back to the graves, where it stood, once more watching.

Eduard rose quietly, and cautiously, paused in front of the hut, and with an exaggerated gesture, threw a piece of bread into it. The dog laid its head on one side, one ear dangling, the other cocked. It sidled towards the hut, then backed away, and lay down a few feet from the step. When nothing further happened, it cautiously approached, and put a tentative paw upon the step. It retracted the paw, and sniffed around it, underneath, and across the front of the hut, returning to the step for a final reconnaissance before deliberately climbing up, over the threshold, and into the interior.

Voztas slammed the door shut. Eduard brought down the axe – and missed, as the dog bounded the full length of the empty chamber, snaffled the piece of bread and turned, momentarily pausing. Eduard was halfway down the room, raised the axe and brought it down, intending to split the animal's skull. The dog jinxed, and the axe severed an ear. Blood gouted and the dog went wild. It leapt straight at Eduard as he reversed the blade and sliced it across, severing the jaw and half the head as it passed, its momentum and fear carrying it almost to the door, before it collapsed in a flailing bundle of legs and slithered against the wall. It was dead. Eduard wrapped the body in a torn blanket, and opened the door.

'Voztas? Are you there?'

The priest appeared, frowning.

'Have you done it?'

'Of course I have,' and Eduard thrust the sodden lump in his arms.

'Now it's your turn – and don't give it the last rites. It tried to eat me.'

Voztas glared at Eduard.

'I don't know how you could do it.'

'I'm hungry. That's how I could do it. And so are you, so let's get on with it.'

Outside, the priest had built a fire, well away from the huts, and now he set to work with Eduard's knife. When the animal was skinned, he rodded it with a long, thin pole, waited until the flames died down, then thrust it into the fierce embers. As he turned the improvised spit, Komowski joined them, then Vitalis, and eventually the remainder of the survivors.

'What is it, then? One of those sheep?'

'That's right.'

Voztas looked sharply at Eduard and Eduard stared back at him without expression.

The meat was sweet and rangey, the bones succulent, and the grease from the remnants enhanced the evening's bread. They slept well that night and, as so often happens in times of war, were greeted the very next day with a consignment of newly baked bread, dried apricots and jars of dark, pitted olives in impenetrable oil, laced with pungent peppers.

Eduard muttered to Voztas, 'Dog brought us luck then,' and Voztas replied, 'A hound of heaven, you might say.'

A week later they told Komowski, who looked at them as if they were insane, then grinned and turned to Vitalis and told him. The Italian raised his eyebrows and smiled.

'I knew it was not Mussolini.'

Over the succeeding days, they were joined by several new intakes, reduced by several more deaths. Komowski persuaded the guards to let them retain their hut and, in general, remain segregated from the others, where typhus raged, until a new batch of barbered, cottoned and clean Poles was transferred to their quarters.

As the days passed, Eduard regained his vigour, and his anxiety to remove himself from this stultifying existence. Voztas was sympathetic, but not sanguine.

'How can we escape? Where can we go?'

Komowski was cautious and disinclined to risk lives.

'If you go, you might endanger others. It is a risk. Are you prepared to take it?'

Vitalis was simply indifferent.

'I was there. I am here. Tomorrow, who knows? *Che sera*.'

There were others who shared Eduard's goals, and there were those who arrived with rumours of Polish forces massing in the south, under British command. Still contingents were assigned to the railway, yet Eduard was not required to return, though sick workers appeared, released from the gangs, who died or survived, to be barbered and reclothed, then consigned to the huts, until they too were sent elsewhere. One day, Eduard was idly watching the latest batch, when he saw a familiar face.

'Jacek!'

'Eduard – you disappeared. They said you had walked into the desert and died.'

Eduard held his friend at arms' length, gravely asking, 'Did you say Kaddisch for me?'

Jacek smiled and shook his head.

'No. I knew you were not dead.'

The camp housed some 150, when the morning's routine was shattered by hurried commands to assemble before the huts. Komowski was worried.

'I don't like the look of this.'

The guards ranged them into some semblance of military order. A Russian officer appeared.

'We need more for the railway.'

There was a murmur through the ranks. No-one wanted to go to the railway, especially those who had left through fever, and had had the time to remember the tough regimen.

'We also need volunteers.'

Eduard looked round and caught Komowski's eye.

'Volunteers?' he whispered.

'Bad principle. Don't ever volunteer,' the other rejoined.

'Anyone here worked with animals? Any farmers?'

One or two put up their hands, the officer indicated them, and the guards hustled them to one side.

'What about vets? Any vets here?'

Vitalis muttered, 'What does he mean? We're all veterans.'

'Vets. Animal doctors. Anyone worked with animal medicine?'

Eduard looked round. Everyone looked blank. Some shook their heads.

'I have.'

The officer was delighted.

'Good, good, good. Come over here, please.'

'Please?' Komowski hissed at Eduard, 'Fool – you're in serious trouble now.'

'Well, I know where the head is, and I know where the tail is. Can't be that difficult.'

Eduard advanced until he was standing in front of the Russian.

'What is your experience?'

'My friend at school, his father was a vet. We all helped out. I used to work with him a lot.'

'Can you use a needle?'

'Of course.'

'Excellent, excellent. Come with me.'

The officer took his arm, and marched him off, past the hospital to a half-track. 'Get in, get in. Not far away.' And he signalled to the driver to get on with it. They drove out of Obruchev, and turned to face the mountains, bouncing down the track away from the camp. As they emerged from a belt of trees, Eduard saw them – thousands upon thousands of sheep, milling about in a series of wired enclosures, guarded not by shepherds or sheepdogs, but by armed Russian guards.

The half-track slid to a halt, and the officer jumped out.

'Come along then.'

The driver followed, carrying a large, white, rectangular carton. They stopped outside the nearest enclosure, and the Russian turned to Eduard.

184

'Put this on.'

The driver had placed the carton on the ground, and folded back the lid. Inside was a neatly folded white coat, which he held up, shaking it out, and holding it so that Eduard could slip his arms into the sleeves. Beneath that was a tray of syringes, and row upon row of phials of serum.

The officer beamed at Eduard.

'We catch them, you inject them. It is good you know this. We have found nobody among our people who can. Excellent, excellent.'

Eduard was motionless, the white coat hanging off his frame. The officer, who was unusually tall, bent down with some solicitude.

'You can do it?' he asked anxiously.

Eduard breathed in, blew the air out, buttoned the coat, held out his hand, took the syringe, then a phial, broke the end, inserted the needle, spurted an experimental spurt, having never in his life done any such thing, and grinned.

'Bring them to me.'

'Wonderful! Wonderful!' cried the officer, unbuttoning his greatcoat and leaning back against the half-track.

'Guards! Bring them on, one at a time, slowly, carefully, and keep them STILL!'

The sheep were *karakal*, originally an Australian breed. Their tails were plump and that is where Eduard injected them. Two guards herded the sheep towards the wire, where there was a slip gate, pushed one through, then released them into the adjoining enclosure, when they had been treated. Another guard held the animal steady for the instant it took for Eduard to jab the needle home, depress the plunger, and then retract it. After the first dozen, he developed a rhythm, and extracted the syringe with an increasing flourish, while the officer leant back and from time to time exclaimed, 'Marvellous! Excellent! Wonderful!'

It took the entire day, with occasional rests, and a break for food – the best food Eduard had tasted since Samarkand, with the best Russian vodka, courtesy of his new-found protector, the Russian officer.

That evening, the half-track took them back to the camp, and the officer shook Eduard's hand, vigorously pumping it up and down, as Eduard smiled weakly, exhausted by the day's exertions.

'Four thousand sheep. Four thousand jabs. Wonderful!'

The Russian let him go, saying, 'Wait here a minute,' and vanished inside a stone building hard by the hospital. When he reappeared he was clutching a bottle and a box.

'Here. Have some vodka, and some chocolates – they're Hershey bars, American. Wonderful!' and he clapped Eduard across the back, and once more vanished inside the house.

Back in the hut, the others crowded round him, wondering at the gifts.

'How many sheep?'

'Four thousand – or that's what he said. I lost count after the first fifty.'

Eduard handed the chocolate bars out, and they passed the vodka round.

'I never want to see a bloody sheep again as long as I live.'

Komowski: 'Serves you right for volunteering,' and they all started laughing. 'Serves you right,' repeated Jacek, and again, 'Serves ewe right,' which set them all off, until they were gasping, hysterical with relief, and the sheer enormity of it all.

Afterwards, as Jacek and Eduard sat alone outside the hut, and passed the bottle for the last time, Eduard made up his mind.

'We're all like bloody sheep here. It's time to go.'

'Go where?'

'Go to find the Army, and join up, and fight.'

Jacek put the bottle down and turned to Eduard.

'Are you serious?'

'Of course I'm serious.'

'Then let's go tomorrow.'

The next day Eduard and Jacek approached Komowski.

'We're leaving.'

'What for? Where are you going?'

'To find the Army.'

Komowski sighed.

'You'll have a long walk. They're in Samarkand.'

Eduard smiled.

'I know. And I know Samarkand. We'll find them.'

He held out his hand and Komowski took it in both of his. Nothing more was said except, 'Say goodbye to Vitalis for me.'

It was a long walk to the railway, but this time they were equipped with food and water, and each other. The 'station' was a wayside halt apart from the junction with the unfinished spur, and trains merely slowed down to 'catch' the mail as they went through.

They watched the first train pass, and mentally measured its speed as it slowed, and the optimum jumping-on point. When the next train came, they were ready, but it was a passenger train, and it was moving much faster than its predecessor. As it 'caught' the mailbag, it accelerated, and Eduard, running alongside ahead of Jacek, reached up and grabbed the brass rail on the second carriage. Jacek jumped, grasped the rail, his hand slipped, and he fell, his legs disappearing under the train.

He screamed as the wheels amputated them. Eduard was swinging wildly, banging against the carriage, his body flying behind him, almost horizontal. He was holding the rail, but his grip was gradually weakening. He started to pray, for survival, that he would not go under the wheels, that he would die instantly. He shouted to himself inside his mind 'Hold on! Hold on!' when a hand dug into his neck, and another tugged his collar, and he was hauled up, winched into the corridor of the train by a burly Russian soldier. As he lay gasping on the floor, he was surrounded by soldiers, all Russians. One of them pulled him upright, dusted him down, and offered him something. It was a slab of pork fat.

'Are you going to Samarkand?' he asked and Eduard replied, 'Yes, I'm going to Samarkand.'

Funny thing, religion. I was brought up to believe. Transubstantiation. Original sin. Life everlasting. It all gets a little less literal in life itself. But the beliefs remain, and with them the arrogance of the only way, your way, the way you were taught and accepted, and believe. When other ways bring pain, like the fatwa and freedom of expression; Khali and the burning of temples; Temple Mount and displaced Palestinians, one wonders. Yet, there was the Inquisition, the extinction of the Incas, the Salem trials, Mr Jones and his poisoned hosannas.

God's in his heaven and all's wrong with the world as we worship His lamb and follow like sheep.

What is it about belief that spawns prejudice that leads to bigotry? Is it fear, otherness or simple lack of conformity? Man eats dog when there's nothing else, so what price prejudice born of conformity?

Jacek survived – so I heard years later – though he lost his legs. I can empathise with that loss, now that I am at a loss, so to speak.

Jacek was a Jew. I do not know if, in his survival, he was embittered, or if he made something of his life despite his double disadvantage – his lack of limbs and his burden of Semitism. Did he believe to the exclusion of all others? What were his tolerances? What else did he lose? And what did he gain through knowing me as I gained from knowing him?

I was taught to distrust Jews. Jews taught me to hate Jews. Then I met Jacek, and heard his lament for the lost tribe, his lost tribe. You cannot truly hate one who prays thus. To be honest, I never even contemplated hatred for him, before I knew he was Jewish, nor could I after I discovered he was. It was simple prejudice born of the original sin of my Catholicism and the transubstantiated blood shed by Jews which became the blood of inferred guilt. The body of Christ sanctified through the martyrdom of his kind.

Is the agent of death the angel of the Lord, the devil incarnate or just the lost soul collectivised in the surge of history as it is made?

Jacek was an ordinary man whose instrument of grief in loss was his belief, just as for others their instrument of joy in achievement was their belief – same creed, different prayer.

I believed then. I believe now. My belief is not exclusive, as it was when I first learnt it. It is inclusive, as I later earnt it. It includes Jacek. It includes Jews.

I wish I could tell them now.

SWEET SEVENTEEN

Samarkand was seething with Poles, at the station, in the park, crowding the squares in the Russian quarter, swelling the crowds in the marketplace. There were Poles everywhere. At the station Eduard realised he had left his rucksack behind – he had no water, and no equipment except his knife. The Russians had gone, leaving him some bread. Eduard stood uncertainly in the concourse when he heard his name. 'Eduard!' He looked about him, and could see nobody he knew in the press of ragged bodies. The crowd parted before him, and there was Wladek, from the railway gang.

'Eduard! Thank God I found you. I thought you were lost. Did you see what happened to Jacek? Terrible, terrible, I could do nothing, it was so fast. Then we were on the train. . .'

Eduard interrupted. 'Hang on, you're going too fast. You were on the train? The same train?'

'Yes. I followed you there, and when you jumped, I jumped – further along.'

'I didn't see you.'

Wladek looked confused, and Eduard was about to speak when a Polish Captain pushed between them.

'You. Take this bag, and follow me.'

Wladek bent to pick up the portmanteau, but Eduard restrained him.

'You don't have to do that.'

The Captain's eyes glittered. His mouth compressed, he spat out, 'If I say so, you certainly have to.'

Eduard: 'Not any more. This is Russia, I'm not your servant. And neither is he.'

The officer opened his mouth but Eduard forestalled him.

'You are a prisoner, just like us. In this war we are all equal.'

The Captain glared at him, retrieved his bag and stormed into the crowd.

Wladek and Eduard pushed their way to the edge of the concourse.

'That was dangerous,' commented Wladek.

'Rubbish. Before the war they behaved like that, the cavalry officers, like him. They were "them" and we were "us". I'm no communist, but it doesn't work like that any more. Not for me anyway. Not after what I've done and where I've been.'

They made their way to the park, and mingled with their fellows. Wladek had a can and they cadged some soup. As they sat on the concrete bench, stretching their meagre meal, a man in uniform approached them. The uniform was neither Russian nor Polish; plain khaki cloth, the bulky blouse was fastened at the waist and covered with a dull matt belt, while the trousers terminated in strange gaiters, which gathered them above the boots. A plain forage cap sat uncomfortably at an angle on the man's head and, as he neared them, they scanned the insignia on his shoulders.

He stood before them, looking down, and Eduard read the single word on his epaulettes: 'Poland', in English. The man pulled the shiny leatherbound swagger stick from under his arm and tapped it on his hand as he spoke.

'When did you get here?'

'Today.'

'Where from?'

'Obruchev.'

'And before that?'

'Tashkent, Kujbysev, Moskva, Omsk and Tara.'

'So you were sent to Siberia?'

Eduard nodded.

'And where do you come from?'

'Cjortkow.'

The officer sat beside them, and looked at Wladek.

'And you?'

'Warsaw.'

'Before that?'

'Obruchev.' He hesitated, then went on. 'And the same – a camp, up north.'

'Good.'

The officer tapped his stick thoughtfully, contemplating its shiny surface for a moment before making up his mind.

'Right. I'm recruiting ex-Russian prisoners for the Army. Interested?'

Eduard folded his arms, and sucked his lip. What Army? If he said 'yes' would he find himself fighting with the Russians? That would never do.

'What Army?'

'The British Army – Polish forces are working under British command.'

Wladek said nothing and Eduard hesitated.

'I'm seventeen.'

'Ah.' The officer rolled the stick in his fingers. 'What languages do you speak?'

'Russian, German, a bit of English, some French and I know Latin too.'

'And you're seventeen.'

'Yes.'

'Which makes you the youngest volunteer officially recruited.'

He turned to Wladek.

'You're older.'

'I'm twenty.'

'You'd better both come with me, then.'

The officer led the way to the station, outside which there were numerous lorries, one of them filled with a motley group of relatively young Poles. The engine was running.

'Right. Up you go. Report to Captain Grela when you get to Loerki.'

He saw the question in Eduard's eyes.

'Village near here – transit camp. Lots of tents. Off you go.'

They climbed on board and the lorry lurched into movement, gears grating, the complement of recruits swaying on its ageing springs as it ground its way out of the town and along the valley road. Within a mile it veered sharply onto a track, and slowly climbed to a low plateau, the track winding between the wheat and cotton fields, until it reached a straggling, ill-kempt settlement, with an open ditch running the length of the main street, sluggish with oily water, sludge and sundry rubbish. Beyond Loerki the track petered out between the first of countless rows of small canvas pyramids.

The lorry stopped and Eduard jumped out, reaching up to help Wladek; together they waited for the remainder to disembark, when the lorry reversed and started back to Samarkand. The recruits stood in a loose group, some muttering to one another when someone said, more loudly than the rest, 'What a dump. Where are we supposed to go?'

Eduard looked round, and saw a hut halfway down the first row of tents. He took Wladek's arm.

'Let's go and find out,' and to the others, 'Stay here. We'll come back when we've found out what's what.'

Together they strode off, with more bravado than either of them felt. At the hut, Eduard paused, then knocked on the doorpost.

'Come!'

Inside they found several soldiers at tables, with ancient typewriters and boxes of papers – a makeshift office. The voice spoke again. 'Over here,' and for the first time, Eduard noticed a young man with officer's insignia seated behind a table like the others, but with no papers or typewriter, except a single pad. He was slight of build, his hair stiff and dull like tallow, and soft-skinned, yet something about the parallel lines that framed his thin, wide mouth suggested caution – this was no desk soldier. The officer was sucking a pencil. He took it out of his mouth, briefly examining it, then smiled.

'Over here,' he repeated, and they walked across, standing in front of the table.

'Right. Names?'

'Cjaikowski, Eduard.'

'Wladek, Tomasz.'

'Age?'

'Seventeen.'

'Twenty.'

'Seventeen? You must be the language boy.'

He stood, extending his right hand.

'I'm Captain Grela. I'm glad you're here.'

Shouting at a soldier 'Bring chairs' then pointing at them with 'Sit', he rubbed the pencil dry against his tunic and started writing, asking questions as he wrote.

'Right. You go to the next hut, behind this one. You've got to have a medical. Then you can get rid of those filthy rags when you collect your uniforms. Here's your pay book. Don't lose it.'

Reaching beneath the desk he brandished two small red stapled booklets, before entering details and stamping them.

By evening, they had stripped, showered, had their balls lifted, backsides scrutinised, chests sounded, said 'Aaargh', eyelids peeled and knees bounced. They were given shirt and tunic, pants and trousers, boots and gaiters, belt and cap and, with that extraordinarily unnecessary efficiency for which the British are bureaucratically renowned, a tie – as Eduard remarked, the least useful piece of equipment for a budding soldier he could conceive.

The one piece of useful equipment Eduard did possess, he kept – his knife. They were directed to a tent, and shown where the canteen was, where meal times were posted, and told they would be roused by Reveille at 6 am the next day. 'Report to the Square', which was a wide open space in the centre of the rows of several hundred tents. Behind the tents were open trenches – latrines, the stench overpowering, until they got used to it.

The tents themselves were small, designed for fifteen; they housed 50-plus and, when Eduard and Wladek reached theirs, they found most occupants lying with their legs and bodies outside, only head and shoulders within. There was a swell of grumbling round the tent as they arrived, until one skeletal youth showed surprising strength, pushed his neighbour, and there was space for them both.

As Eduard discovered, Loerki was home to over 10,000 for several months, as the hard-pressed and inadequately small number of officers strove to absorb, record, equip and prepare the embryonic Anglo-Polish forces for the next stage in their march to war.

The open sewer in the village and the trenches in the camp bred disease. Many of the recruits came carrying their own. Deaths were commonplace. Typhus and dysentery were rife. A small cadre of medical officers, despite a reasonable supply of medicines, was unable to stem the tide of death. The overall command, a handful of British officers, had no conception of the concentration camps, the forced labour, the hardships their young allies had faced. They had made insufficient allowance, and their absent landlords in Britain were far too preoccupied with the North African campaign, accommodating the GI invasion of England and supporting Stalin in his defence against Barbarossa to worry about the details of Polish ex-prisoners' welfare.

'Volunteers needed.'

Captain Grela had detained Eduard's squad on the square.

'Burial detail. Double rations.'

Rations were Russian; the cookhouse was manned by Russians and the food was simple if nourishing, but it was not enough.

Eduard stuck his hand up, and Wladek followed suit. They were the only ones.

'Follow me.'

Grela dismissed the rest and led the two volunteers back to his hut. There they were issued with shovels, and given instructions. The bodies were laid out behind the medical shed, in the open air, uncovered. There had been no time to bury them since the camp opened.

That was three weeks before. There was a backlog of corpses, sprayed daily with disinfectant. The powerful ammoniac aroma made their eyes water. Eduard tied a cloth across his nose and mouth, and did the same for Wladek. They surveyed the ragged ranks, and then cast about them for a suitable burial site.

'Over there, beyond the trenches,' suggested Wladek and Eduard followed him to a spot some ten yards away. They started digging. The ground was hard and unyielding at first, then crumbled as they struck softer sand and grit.

'If we're going to shift that lot, we'll be here forever,' observed Wladek, then swore as his shovel hit rock, some three feet down. 'No wonder the latrines are so shallow – you can't get any deeper,' and he wiped the running sweat away from his eyes.

Within an hour they had contrived a shallow trench, several yards long, and they rested on their shovels. Eduard looked back at the bodies.

'Better get the first ones in then.'

They started at one end, and lifted the first cadaver by the arms and legs, and swung him between them as they walked unsteadily to the trench and dropped him in. The second was easier, the third simple and they found themselves grimly lifting, carrying, heaving and dropping one after another without comment, and breathing as little as possible.

Then Eduard bent to lift the next one. The arm came away in his hand and he dropped it, crying out in disgust. The flesh was rotten. Choking as the bile leapt into his throat, Eduard half-ran away from the graveyard and stood near a stunted tree, gasping to catch his breath. Wladek joined him. When they had recovered, they tried the next one, Eduard mumbling, 'You first.' Wladek grasped the man's leg, and his hand slithered down, as the flesh came away, exposing the bone.

'Jesus Christ. I can't do this,' and he staggered away again.

Eduard had composed himself. He surveyed the remaining rows.

'We haven't much choice. We volunteered.' He smiled wanly at Wladek as he added, 'Whoever would bury foul bodies for two bowls of soup?' and answered himself simultaneously with Wladek as they both said, 'We would,' laughed, and walked down the rows, looking for a body entire. Once the first trench was finished, they went back to the hut, and sought out Captain Grela.

'Is there a problem?' he asked.

'No problem,' responded Eduard, 'just that we need some help.'

'Nobody else volunteered,' pointed out their Captain.

'Not that sort of help. We need something to put them on,' and he explained the near-impossibility of lifting diseased and decomposing corpses between two men.

Captain Grela was a man with a creative bent. He thought a moment, then clapped his hands.

'I've got it – tables.'

'Tables?'

'Yes, tables. Trestle tables. The ones we eat off.'

Eduard winced and Wladek's face paled.

'Commandeer two tables – the smaller ones, the ones the officers use; then you can roll 'em onto a table, and carry that, tip 'em off, and get another one. When one table's too slippery with muck and gore, use the other. OK?'

By the end of the day, they had disposed of half the corpses. They had extracted some cloths from the medical officer, and these they placed over the dead men's faces. Then they shovelled the sandy soil back over the trench. On the second day they completed the task; henceforth death would descend to the grave as it happened, by Grela's decree. He knew he would find no more volunteers for the detail of the dead.

By the third week, Eduard and Wladek had been pronounced fit, but not fit enough for Eduard's request to be granted. He had asked for an Air Force posting, without success. They gave him signals, and his final days at Loerki were spent in the stifling air of a closed hut, where he sat exams in Morse, simple electronics, and above all, languages.

The results came through within hours: pass, pass – just, and distinctions. Postings followed. Eduard was ordered to Kermener, a fully fledged private in the Anglo-Polish Army.

Wladyslaw Sikorski and Soviet Ambassador Maisky had struck a deal. The Pole wanted recognition that Poland's partition was null and void, and all Polish prisoners released. The Russian was obdurate about the former and ambiguous about the latter. Under British pressure, they compromised: the Nazi pact's frontiers, it was agreed, 'have lost their validity' and a Polish Army would be raised in Russia. This suited Roosevelt, newly committed to a European war; it pleased the Soviet, because it meant cannon fodder for the hard-pressed front; it satisfied Sikorski, because he had conned the Russians. They envisaged men for the Red Army; he meant men for the British – and Sikorski had an ace: Stalin was dependent upon American supplies and the British ships that carried them.

In the end, Sikorski won: 'Liberate my people and we fight with the English.' Stalin had no choice. Polish HQ estimated ten divisions, the 5th, 3rd, 7th, 8th and 10th were formed but officers were in short supply; General Anders and other senior officers were duly released, some 400 in all, but of 8,000 officers there was no sign. The Russians blamed the Germans, but 14,500 Polish officers died in the forests round Katyn, near three originally Russian internment camps. Sikorski was in no doubt – they were victims of Soviet slaughter but, as Churchill told him: 'Nothing you can do will bring them back.' At Nuremberg, Katyn was never probed.

Kermener was a walled fort, an ancient place, with solid mud walls, a massive, meandering sixteenth-century fortified enclosure as large as a race course, set in the glowering mountains of Ghengistahn, east of Tashkent. Ten thousand lived in huts and tents, drilled, shot, fixed bayonets into sagging sacks, and learnt how to look after rifles, ammunition and themselves.

Eduard was assigned to an NCO course. The major in command of his battalion was an impatient man. There were thousands of recruits, but the Army needed trained men. There were too few officers, and hardly any NCOs. Somehow, with no time and little equipment, he had to convert a sloppy sponge into a hard pumice stone, and for that he needed help. On his rounds, he peered into one particular tent, and noticed a young man honing a knife.

'What's that?'

'Knife, sir.'

'I can see that. How d'you get it in here?'

'It's mine, sir.'

'Obviously.'

'I mean, it was mine before – you know...'

'You had it in Poland? Before the war?'

'Yes, sir.'

'I'll be... OK. You're young enough. Let's see what you can do. Report to Hut C 10 in the morning.'

'Sir!'

And so it was that Eduard embarked on an NCO's course.

Some equipment was British, but it was not new, and it was not modern. Kit included a billycan which was an improvement, in Eduard's view, on a rusty can or an old rucksack. Cutlery was a luxury and a blanket was bliss. Rifles were Russian, and fired five rounds, single shot, breech loading. They frequently broke down, and required constant maintenance. Eduard's first course was basic – rifle drill, dismantling and assembling a Bren gun, Morse, radio and signals were simple.

Bayonet practice was not difficult. He was spared drill on the square, which was for 'squaddies' who needs must learn to conform. Major Ptak was not interested in conformists – he wanted individuals who could be taught the finer arts of killing. He found Eduard an apt pupil. On his recommendation, Eduard would be made up to Corporal.

Then his real training began. The instructor was half Russian and he was called Baccovitch. He was small, compact, bald, snub-nosed, clean-shaven, short-legged, and acted with sharp, swift movements and everybody called him Bacco.

The assault course was in the mountains, and the obstacles were real, with equipment which was adequate but not excessive – ropes, picks, packs and rifles, stick grenades, clumsy transmitters, water bottles.

Bacco led the way along the stony track, across streams, splashing and stumbling through shallow, stagnant pools, small *bliuda*, or saucers in the grey-brown, limey loess, onto the lower screes of the striated mountainside, then through brittle thistles, dry, tough, tearing thorns, onto the slopes, all at two paces – brisk, and double march.

'One-two, one-two; one-two, one-two; come on, pick those feet up, and one-two, one-two, keep up Wladek, one-two, one-two; faster, faster – you're not trying Mister Ed; quick-quick, quick-quick, one-two, one-two, that's better, now we go fast – and run, one-two-three-four, one-two-three-four, one-two-three-four. You think fast, you move fast, the Germans do; one-two-three-four; try harder, you can do more; one-two-three-four, one-two-three-four – and HALT!'

The slope ended abruptly at a cliff face, and Bacco surveyed his breathless group.

'Right. At ease – and, easy. You can rest – five minutes. Then we climb a mountain.'

They collapsed onto the broken ground, and Eduard examined the rock face. Behind it soared the fearsome Alayski – at 26,400 feet an awe-inspiring sight, its peaks diffused by cloud. The north face was concave, and ended abruptly some thousand feet up, where there appeared to be a horizontal cut back into the mountain. Bacco followed Eduard's gaze.

'You look at the mountain. You are afraid?'

'Not afraid. Curious.'

'Curious,' Bacco mused. 'What is it that makes you curious?'

'That ledge, or whatever it is,' and he pointed at the lip that seemed to overhang the cliff.

'You mean the *syrt*.' Bacco spread his arms to embrace the majestic eruption of static stone. 'That is where we go. That is the seat of the lesser gods, which God himself carved out of the mountainside, so that they might realise his strength – and their smallness.'

The instructor stood motionless, his arms outstretched, a small Christ against a gargantuan Calvary. Then he abruptly dropped them, and busied himself with his kit, clearly embarrassed.

The closer they came to the slope, the more it revealed its secrets. The sheer face sharpened as they approached, its lines and crevasses growing deeper and better defined, like the face of a handsome woman in her middle years. Eduard detected folds and cracks, hollows and outcrops, smooth, glaciated planes, suddenly terminated by carbuncular excretions. The rock face was a tapestry of wildly varied texture and opportunity.

Baccovitch supervised the rope-line, splitting the group into small teams of four, three climbers and a baseline anchorman, and designated the leaders. Eduard found Wladek in his team and was told to take their lead. Bacco led the assault with a team of the toughest men.

'Remember. The rock is your friend. The enemy is yourself. Take your time, secure your lines, help one another. You are a team. You climb or fall as a team. Watch me, and follow where I go.'

With that he reached up and dug his fingers into the rock face, into a small fissure, and swung off the ground. Hand over hand, line slack, then taut; foot, hand, hand, foot; hand, pick, hand, foot.

Eduard was exhilarated. He looked out over the narrow plain, down the disappearing valley towards Kermener. The gritty wind blew fitfully across his face, an inconvenience, but not a nuisance; the air was sharp and rare; the quiet was enlarged by the wind's occasional whisper, and underscored by his companion's whipped-away words, which he could not hear and did not miss. There was a skein of tension between rock and man, an elastic togetherness that was strange yet stimulating, snapped when he turned to reach up for the next handhold, and relinked the moment he turned his back, and looked out with the mountain at its domain. The line pulled, slackened, then tautened twice; he looked down, to see Wladek looking up, grinning. It was the first time he saw absolute joy and serenity in the other's face. He swung back to the stone, scribbled in the wind, and hauled himself up and up and up.

The *syrt* was a wide expanse of smooth, wind-polished rock, as if the mountain had slid its lower lip out, frozen in a fossilised pout. Eduard was reminded of the theories of continental drift, where tectonic plates slid against one another over aeons. The mountain's plates had slipped gracefully apart to give them this small gods' seat.

Within ten minutes, all the teams broke over the lip and gathered together, smug with accomplishment, and relieved to be off the face, with a short tenancy on level ground. No-one thought about the return, until Bacco stood and indicated the mountain behind.

'We go over there, and you will see how we descend.'

Old-fashioned word, descend, thought Eduard. They walked across the ledge, close to the mountain's cheek, until they stood on the edge, where it had curved round into the mountainside.

The whaleback ridge curled away, rising, then falling back towards the valley, serrated, ugly, and sheer on either side, with glacial excrement rubbling its feet. If the rock face had seemed like a bad but acceptable dream, the ridge was the dark side of their worst nightmares.

Baccovitch roped them in line as a single team.

'Follow me.'

Eduard was the middle-man, instructed to keep his eyes on the ground, behind and in front.

'You are my second-in-command.'

Slowly they traversed the angular blades of the crossover from *syrt* to ridge. Wladek was the backstop. As Bacco stopped and looked back, Wladek slipped, crying out as he fell. Eduard watched, his breath caught fast, as the far, small figure slid, staggered, paused, slid again, then somersaulted before hanging at the end of the rope, caught in a cleft, his body inside a V-shaped funnel of rock. Baccovitch pulled a monocular out of a pouch on his tunic and put it to his eye. He turned, and climbed back a few feet, gesturing to the team to fall back, slowly.

The man before Wladek eased back, looping the rope over his shoulder as he approached the cleft where it was caught. Baccovitch halted, and the team slowed, then stopped. They all watched the man bend cautiously over, then he straightened and put his hands up, signalling, 'No good, it's stuck.'

Baccovitch was still, and Eduard sensed his will across the void, and bent his to the same task. Wladek stirred, looked across, and Eduard thought he discerned a smile, though the distance was too great to be sure. Wladek seemed to hover, then merge with the stone, and the stone shifted, its tone and colour changing as it rippled upwards. Wladek's head appeared outside the cleft, and his arms, his body, and he was patting the other man's back, as they checked the line. Baccovitch had already started forward.

It took twice as long to climb down as to reach up. At the foot of the ridge, they assembled, silent, each with his own thoughts apart, a natural communion, not with each other, but with each man's vision of his descent, and his version of the mountain. Bacco stood, relaxed.

'Right. You have met the mountain. You have met and joined hands with something elemental, but it is not evil. In war you will meet men, and in those men will be evil. Today is a small lesson. If you did not trust my mountain, you trusted yourselves and each other. You survived.' And he roared with laughter. 'You see, it is only a mountain.'

Then it was time to go.

'Right. Fall in. Ten-SHUN. By the right, quick march! Ep-die, ep-die, ep-die, and now, double march: one-two-three-four, one-two-three-four. You are *not* tired Wladek, just because, one-two-three-four, you nearly fell off a mountain, one-two-three-four, so pick those feet UP, one-two-three-four.'

The days passed in practical lessons – throwing grenades, defusing shells, first aid, improvisation, signals; rifle practice, bayonet practice, Bren gun practice, and signals. Eduard learnt fast. So did Wladek and half a dozen others. Some were slower, and some were hopeless. Gradually men became soldiers, and some soldiers became good ones.

Came the day when Major Ptak called Eduard and Wladek to the battalion hut.

'At ease.'

He walked round the table and lifted the flap of the pocket of Wladek's tunic and let it drop, continued behind him, and poked Eduard's knife pocket with his swagger stick, then rounded them again, and stood for a moment, contemplating them both.

'Well. You two have done moderately well. I'm going to promote you. Corporal Wladek. Corporal Cjaikowski. Congratulations.'

He extended his hand and shook each of theirs in turn.

'At this rate you'll be off my hands soon, but I want you to repay my little investment. I'm making you instructors. Knock a little sense – gently – into your less capable colleagues, because very shortly we need some of them as a sop to Stalin. A little contingent to keep him sweet, if anything keeps that bastard sweet.'

Eduard's frown was involuntary.

'Don't worry, Cjaikowski. They're only going to help sort out the chaos at Samarkand, working with Russkies. They are not going to the front. They are, after all, in the British command, are they not? Right. Report to Sergeant Major Grybos. He's the drill sergeant. Diiiis-MISS.'

Grybos was as tall as Bacco was small, as lean as he was broad, and as dour as he was twinkling. Grybos had the thankless task of drilling the raw and the reject recruits on the square, day in, day out.

'Ip-die,ip-die,ip-die, ab-OUT-tun and ip-die,ip-die,ip-die, wait for it, you nasty little man, don't you know yer left from yer right? God help us, ip-die,ip-die, and about – not yet, Szozynski – a-bout... TUN and HALT!'

He turned to the two corporals.

'Come to assist me? Help me out? Make my life easy? Would that you could. But my life is conditioned by these... Bracek, keep your eyes FRONT!... unfortunate young men. However, I shall gladly hand them over to you now for a little re-lax-ayshun. You can teach them what you know about first aid. Kit's in the long hut. Tomorrow, report to me at o six thirty hours and we'll see what can be done about a little programme. Now you horrible little persons; ten-SHUN. Qui-ick MARCH. Ip-die, ip-die.'

The squad was marched to the hut, and their new instructors started their joint and several learning curves.

Grybos and Wladek never made friends, but Eduard instantly recognised another Ivan in the apparently strict DI. As a drill instructor he was sharp and sarcastic, long-suffering and yet infinitely patient. It soon became clear that he liked his work, not for its sadistic stance, but because he genuinely sought standards. He knew his charges would leave to fight, to inflict injury, be hurt and in some cases to die, and he wanted to give them a temporary toughness, discipline and interdependence. He succeeded and he was good enough at his job to know that, yet he was dissatisfied. He craved excitement, and it was this which sent him to Tashkent whenever he could slip past the Military Police. It did not take Eduard long to discover what took Grybos there.

He was smuggling. Kermener had a canteen, and in the canteen were supplies of canned food, packs of sugar, fat, flour. Grybos stole provisions, which he traded in Tashkent for tobacco. It was a slight trade, but it satisfied his need for excitement. He called it 'contraband'.

When Grybos was caught, his crime was not 'contraband' but being AWOL – absent without leave – a court martial offence in wartime, for Kermener was on a war footing. He was caught, tried, convicted and summarily sentenced. There was no time for niceties, and no opportunity to appeal. The sentence was inevitable in time of war – death.

Pending execution, Grybos was imprisoned in the only totally secure building – the lock-up in Loerki, in the centre of the village, a stone building with tiny windows and only one door, hard against the cemetery.

Wladek had evinced a singular aptitude for instruction. Eduard had no liking for the repetitive tasks, the rebarbative business of wrapping phoney wounds for pseudo-medicos to tend. He yearned for combat, for the real war, and he cajoled Ptak into permitting him additional sessions with grenades and rifle, and even some pistol practice – a rare privilege, since only officers were assigned hand-guns.

It was a simple matter for Eduard to seek and secure guard duty between sessions, to look after Grybos, so that the two spent many hours in close company, becoming if not friends, companions in recollection, for Grybos could match Eduard's escapades with Ivan with tales of his own, on the run from the Russians. They grew closer, and as they did so Grybos seemed to become dependent upon Eduard, for news, for small pleasures – fruit, extra soup, even cigarettes, and his pace-stick, which had been integral to his command as a DI. Eduard would hand the tapered, split, wooden 'dividers' to him each time he mounted guard, and retrieve it at the end of his duty. Within a week, Ptak put Eduard in command of the guard detail so that he controlled Grybos's life in every detail, and for every day.

Once each day Grybos exercised. He was unpenned from the stone building, and encouraged to walk round the compound that enclosed it, a stone-walled yard with one exit only, which was guarded at all times, day or night. A routine developed. Eduard would bring lunch, relieve the prison guard, and sit with Grybos, then take him out for exercise, while a single guard remained outside the compound wall.

On the seventh day, Eduard saluted the guard, who locked the gate behind him, walked across to the building, unlocked the door, and entered. Grybos greeted him cheerfully.

'Seven days, and I see lunch is the same.'

Eduard smiled.

'I've brought you some fruit, and a sweet cake. Wladek asked me to give it to you. He wasn't feeling so hungry.'

'Tell him thank you for me.'

Grybos ate his food slowly and carefully, masticating each mouthful with a meticulous, mechanical motion, then washing it down from the water bottle Eduard had provided.

'Special treat today.'

'Oh. What's that?' and Eduard sensed the fear in the prisoner.

'Vodka. It's not for any reason. I was given some – by Ptak in fact, so I saved some for you. Here.' And he shoved the glass bottle across. Grybos picked it up, sniffed it, and drank.

'Not bad. For a condemned man, eh?' then laughed nervously. 'Time for a walk?'

Eduard got up, and unlocked the door, standing aside for the drill sergeant to get through the narrow aperture. His pace-stick under his arm, Grybos walked straight outside and across towards the wall, as Eduard fiddled with the lock. He had been ordered, 'Always lock the door.' 'Even when he's outside?' 'Even when he's outside. Regulations.'

As he straightened and turned, he noticed Grybos was standing near the wall. Grybos winked, put his pace-stick on the compound dustbin and, using it as a lever, vaulted over the wall. Eduard sprinted after him, and looked over the rough stones. Grybos had landed on all fours alongside one of the granite slabs which marked the graves. He glanced back, winked again, and started running.

'Come back, you fool,' shouted Eduard but Grybos either did not hear him or did not want to, for he continued to run, jinxing between the gravestones. By that time, the guard outside the gate had rushed round into the cemetery, yelling as he went, 'The Major's here, Corp'ral. At the gate. I've unlocked it.'

As Eduard looked back, Ptak stormed into the compound.

'Where is he?'

'In the graveyard, sir.'

'Did you see him jump?'

'No, sir.'

The guard was by then shooting indiscriminately.

'Why not?'

'I didn't see him.'

'Here, give me that bloody gun.'

The guard handed the rifle over the wall, and Ptak steadied himself, his elbow on the stone coping; he fired, once, twice, three times and, as he did so, the distant figure wove from side to side, presenting an impossible and receding target. Ptak swore, and shot again. He missed, threw the rifle at the guard, screaming, 'Shoot him, shoot him!' and vaulted the wall, interposing himself between marksman and target. The guard lowered his rifle.

'Can't bloody shoot him now, can I?'

As Ptak raced after Grybos, Eduard heard a faint cry. He heaved himself over the wall, and ran after the officer. He found him at the far side of the cemetery, standing over Grybos. The drill instructor had evaded all the bullets, only to trip on a projecting granite slab. He had fallen, twisted his ankle, and caught his leg against the slab as he fell. His ankle bones had snapped – a double fracture. Ptak supervised his return, Eduard and the guard each taking an arm across their shoulders, as he limped, one-legged, back to camp, to the makeshift hospital. His leg was set and placed in plaster, and he was confined for three weeks, shackled to the bed.

On the third of May, the anniversary of the abolition of feudal slavery in Poland, his plaster was removed, he was handed a stick – his pace-stick had been confiscated – and put in a lorry alongside a crude coffin, opposite six young, armed soldiers. The lorry was new, an American Studebaker, and a ride in it much prized. Grybos was impassive.

Eduard was in charge of the detail – he had pleaded with Ptak to 'have the honour to accompany Grybos' to his execution. The lorry moved smoothly through the camp, out of the village, along the valley, to a dried riverbed, a tributary deprived of the waters of the mountains in the summer months. 'The valley of the shadow of death,' said Grybos when he dismounted. The soldiers carried a wooden post down into the silt, and hammered it home. A jeep followed the truck, and Ptak marched across to the chosen ground, flanked by a Russian, the Khan of Loerki, and a priest.

'Tie his eyes,' ordered Ptak.

'No!' countermanded Grybos.

'As you wish,' the officer conceded.

The priest stood by Grybos. They spoke softly, alone, with God.

The priest rejoined Ptak.

Eduard had spoken to each soldier that morning, individually.

'You must make peace with your soul, and tell God. Then you must fire once, accurately. You will not help him if you miss, or if you wound him. Shoot to kill.'

That is what they did. Grybos died without pain and without fear and, as Ptak gave the final order, he looked at Eduard, and winked.

It was not the last execution, as the weeks wore on and the nascent army grew restless. Men stole cheeses, thieved fruit, were caught, and died. Ptak explained.

'We must be disciplined. There can be no exceptions. It is the only way,' and one day he said to Eduard, 'I hate the waste – after all they have been through, to come to this. I hate it. But it has to be done.' And Eduard agreed.

Eventually, the officers realised there was a problem, and they contrived short passes for half a day, utilising the growing fleet of trucks to convoy troops to neighbouring villages for fruit and freedom.

Eduard and Wladek preferred the countryside, where there were lush orchards along the well of the valley, with scattered settlements, homesteads and farms in unexpected folds of the otherwise flat landscape. Eduard especially coveted the *arak*, a small, sweet fruit somewhat smaller but like a peach, and they would climb the trees to filch it, stuffing themselves as they went. Sitting in a tree one day, they heard voices, women's voices, one Polish-accented, and peered, astounded, at the two girls who had sat beneath their tree.

Eduard mischievously dropped a skin, and it plopped onto one girl's lap. She brushed it away and continued talking. He dropped another, and she picked it off, and flung it from her irritably. When he dropped a third, she looked up, and gasped.

'Who's that?'

'Eduard Cjaikowski and Tomasz Wladek, from Cjortkow and Warsaw.'

There was a moment of silence, then a voice: 'Men from heaven. How wonderful. Come down, come down.'

They climbed down, and sat beside the girls. One was Russian, and plain. The other was Polish, and pretty. She had escaped, befriended Ludmilla and lived with her family while she decided what next to do. Sara was seventeen too. Her father had had a clothing factory in Vilnlo; he had been deported, like her. They were a family divided, like Eduard and Rosalia.

The soldiers escorted the girls back to Ludmilla's homestead – a compact single-storey *manzanka*, constructed of dried loess under a turf roof, and surrounded by similar outbuildings within a fenced enclosure. Inside, the space was divided into three rooms – a living area, a small bedroom and a storeroom. Ludmilla and Sara slept in the living room, which boasted an uneven floor of baked clay tiles and the customary hearth and stove. The windows were shuttered and the house was cool.

Ludmilla's parents were harvesting in the orchards when they arrived; she offered them sour milk and fresh fruit, and they sat at the solid, planked table, delicately exploring their separate existences, probing occasionally into the wartime past, then falling back onto matters farm and camp whenever the recollection touched a nerve.

Ludmilla busied herself making her guests comfortable and Wladek was amused by this ungainly, straight-haired birch-pole girl, with her prominent chin, thin-lipped mouth, aquiline nose, continuous eyebrows and lean cheeks. He watched her hands fly as she cleaned their pots, and wondered about the fire that might lie beneath the cool embers of her workaday life. Her one remarkable feature was her eyes – violet, and with a soft, lustrous depth.

Eduard found Sara irresistible. Her movements were liquid, her green eyes flecked with hazel, set wide above high cheekbones, sharp against the soft fall of her undisciplined chestnut hair. Her mouth was never still, and he yearned to feel its soft pressure on his own. When she made a point, slender fingers gesticulated, and once her hand rested briefly on his.

'We have to go,' he observed. 'Our pass is only for four hours.'

As they stood outside the *manzanka*, Ludmilla spoke awkwardly, holding herself a little apart.

'Perhaps we see you again?'

Wladek answered 'Of course you will. The day after tomorrow. Shall I come here?'

Ludmilla lowered her head and muttered, 'Please. Yes, that would be nice.'

'Come on Eduard.'

As they tied the gate to the post, Eduard leant over it and held out his hand. Sara took it, and they shook hands gravely, with a certain deliberation.

'Will you come too?'

'Next week. I have guard duty till then.'

She nodded. 'I understand,' and held onto his hand, drawing him gently towards her. He looked at Ludmilla, but she was already walking back to the house, and Wladek had started towards the camp.

Their faces were inches apart. He lifted his other hand, and touched her cheek. He felt her fingertip on his hand. He leant over and their lips brushed as they released one another. She whispered something.

'I'm sorry – what did you say?'

Without smiling, she raised her hand in farewell.

'I said, "men from heaven", that's all,' and turning, she was gone.

I thought a lot about Grybos and the manner of his dying. Today, as the silent hours shrink, he often returns to my thoughts, with that final wink, so like Ivan. It was a harsh sentence for something less than a modern misdemeanour. At the time, it seemed like the loss of Ivan and the arbitrary end of the train rebels – all of them killed, not because they broke ranks and rules, but because an implacable, irreversible authority vested accidentally, it seemed, in men of lesser worth was challenged, and had to be seen to be absolute.

There was, in truth, more to it than that. Ivan died because he challenged men who had survived longer with similar skills, on their own ground. His was a territorial death: he was the alien destroyed for the threat he posed to a complex web of relationships and to the acceptable limits of trickery, beyond which he constantly stepped. He was effectively executed, not for cheating *per se*, but for outwitting his hosts on their own ground. He was the eternal outsider, who must be assimilated or rejected and, since he was transient and incapable of absorption, he was disposable, and deposed. Yet they might have let him live, and encouraged him to leave. They failed in that through the weakness which was their fear of the foreigner, the unknown. They did not know what he might do next and they were afraid to be discoverers. Their very insularity sealed his sentence. They were not bad men; they were simply intelligent fools.

The train rebels were the victims of their affront to the officer in charge; they had dared to challenge his outright authority, yet he could have as well disciplined them with deprivations and chastisement. He did not have to kill. His was the corruption of absolute power. He was a man in whom evil had come to pass, and stayed.

Grybos died for an entirely different reason. Whether from madness, boredom, mischievousness or a simple death wish, he broke the rules. Worse, he was charged with maintaining the rules. Grybos flouted the rule of law, and in that enclosed, ragged, half-formed, learning rag-tag-and-bobtail that constituted the embryonic Anglo-Polish Army, the only barrier between the despair and deprivation of two years and the hope and promises for the future was the rule of law.

Harsh as it may seem, and I only fully realised this in my own response to the life-sustaining rule of medication rigorously applied, which held my life in its hands, Ptak was not only within his rights to sentence Grybos; he had no choice if he was to sustain his role in that rule.

He served the Army. He followed orders. The orders were absolute, and they made absolute sense. Grybos was a good man who sinned. Ptak was a better man who forgave him through his obliteration. Grybos, in that final moment, faced his death with a gesture, not of carelessness, but of complicity. He winked to clear me of guilt.

I should have learnt the lesson then, but I was only seventeen.

WOMEN AT WAR

There were no women at Kermener – except ministering angels of mercy. The Red Cross was active. Largely British, partly Polish and with a scattering of Swiss officials, it strove to supplement the health care of the over-stretched medicos, organised, received, warehoused and distributed a generally useful, occasionally useless and sometimes unnecessary but welcome range of otherwise unobtainable items – knitwear which would have been treasured in Tara but was surplus in Kermener; chocolate, much-prized for barter; books, spurned by most but seized by others; and a wide range of foodstuffs, canned, packaged and bottled, which went a long way towards slowing disease, generating pleasure but mostly, relieving boredom, by contrast to the monotony of Russian rations. Above all, it supplied and serviced a network of information, striving to put families back together again.

The canteen noticeboard carried bulletins, updated daily, on quests and discoveries. Names were posted of those who sought relatives, and of those listed, but still held, in faraway camps. Most of those were women, equally eligible for release, but with nowhere to go, since the deal with Stalin did not envisage Polish women in the front line.

Every day Eduard scanned the board for a reference to Rosalia. Every day he turned away disappointed. After several weeks he missed a day, then hurried to the canteen after Reveille, spurred on by a sense of guilt, but there was nothing there for him. After that he looked perhaps once or twice a week, until the habit fell away as he sank ever more deeply into the vortex of training, perfecting his skills at arms, polishing his knowledge and use of language, and mastering intricacies of signals.

Between whiles, he relaxed with Sara.

In the beginning, Wladek and he visited Ludmilla's farm to share their hours off duty with the two girls, on their third visit meeting Ludmilla's mother, Tanya, an older version of her daughter, weathered by the valley winds, finer boned and easily mistaken for a sister rather than a mother.

Wladek was drawn to her quiet confidence, as he had been drawn to the contrast between Ludmilla's ungainly appearance and her fleet domestic finesse. Mother and daughter shared the same violet eyes. Of the father they saw nothing, for their visits were perforce daytime visits, within camp regulations, while Piotr worked from dawn to daylight's end.

As Eduard sat at the table, listening to Sara, Wladek restlessly prowled about the *manzanka*, in and out of the living room, as Ludmilla prepared food, and her mother cleaned.

'Let's go for a walk,' he suddenly suggested, standing close by Ludmilla.

Sara looked up and smiled, and Eduard experienced a sharp surge of lust, as soon replaced with an emotional urgency which vacuumed his gut.

'Good idea.' He jumped up, and held out a hand. Sara took it, and they both waved at Tanya, standing in the bedroom doorway. 'Won't be long.'

Wladek ushered Ludmilla after them, his hand hovering inches behind her back. He glanced at Tanya as he passed her, his eyes held briefly by hers in what he took then to be a slight approval of this strange Polish boy, who seemed so interested in her hitherto unromantic and unromanced daughter. Of course, nothing would come of it, for these young men were transients, aliens, intensely patriotic and, for all she knew, at best indifferent, at worst antipathetic towards their unchosen Russian hosts.

Yet in this outstation of war, in the backlands of Great Russia, where the shadows of a mighty past were reflected in the very name Ghengistahn, Tanya sensed an opportunity for Ludmilla to momentarily escape the changeless rote of bare country life, to learn beyond her experience, and perhaps to love a little.

Tanya turned back into the bedroom and went to the small cupboard on the wall beyond the bed, opened the door, and ran her fingers lightly across the worn books, salvaged from that faraway time of study, in Tashkent, before Piotr claimed her from his cousin's homestead, before she succumbed to tradition's whipping-in to the larger pack, the family of farmers who needed wives to bear sons and daughters to work the immemorial land of their forefathers. She took down Tolstoy and sank onto the bed to read.

Eduard led them down the track, then into the fields, across to the orchards where the *arak* grew. They found a tree, much like that which had brought them together, and he climbed up into its branches to select some fruit. Ludmilla and Wladek wandered down the rows of trees as Sara leant against the trunk beneath Eduard. He dropped down, brushing leaves and twigs away, and offered her a selection. She pointed at one, and he carefully placed the others on the ground, then pulled out his knife, and peeled the skin away, to reveal the soft flesh.

He looked at the succulent fruit, and then at her; she was not looking at it; she was gazing at him, and yet her hand unerringly found the fruit, detached it and raised it to her lips, as she held his gaze, moving closer, reaching for his hand. He dropped the knife and it clattered onto the roots, as he felt their fingers intertwine. She had bitten into the fruit, and was slowly savouring it, her lips not yet closed over it, as Eduard gently pulled her into his embrace.

Their lips touched, her eyes closed, he could not see her clearly as he pressed into her, tasted the fruit, and then clasped her tight, as she ran her hand up and down his back.

It was more than a kiss. It was for Eduard the first rites of passion, wherein combined the desperate desire of flesh deprived and an entirely unfocused yearning to share and be shared. Eduard was learning the lesson of young love. So was Sara. Afterwards, they stood loosely together, falling side by side against the tree, and reflectively munching fruit as they began to talk, Eduard of Cjortkow and Rosalia, field and creature, Frank and Bruno, always avoiding all mention of war and camp and the odyssey of his captive days; Sara principally of Chopin, Polish literature and Shakespeare, of other music, writers and again, of Shakespeare.

She constantly quoted from play and sonnet to drive the debates with herself on life and love, faith and calamity, man's monstrosity and his acts of achievement. Eduard listened to the stream of ideas and conjectures, proofs and posits from this formidable woman who was both bemusing by body and mighty of mind.

They heard Wladek and Ludmilla before they appeared, arms entwined, talking softly the words of love. Eduard looked down at Sara and observed, 'It seems we are not the only ones,' and she laughed.

'Isn't that wonderful?'

At Kermener, Eduard returned to the canteen for an early supper, while Wladek stayed in their tent.

'Not hungry,' he offered, in short response.

'You mean you're in love,' riposted Eduard.

'Maybe.'

After despatching a platter of slightly acid soup, two pieces of black bread and a chipped glass of black tea, he rose and sauntered to the bulletin board, scanning it rapidly and without bothering to read the detail. His eyes flitted across the rows of names until he reached the Notice of Refugees – Women, and slowed down, pursuing the list, but there was nothing under C, and he idly stepped back, casting a final eye down the lists more for the sake of it than in any hope of discovery.

His eye passed over the Rs, Ss and Ts onto the Us and Vs and Ws and he was about to summarily dismiss the small remainder of this alphabetical array when his mind hesitated, and something suggested he take one more, second glance. He could not understand the impulse – it was not reasonable, since he had no personal interest, only curiosity. Perhaps something spurred him to seek out a Wladek, for his friend's sake. Then his eyes froze, his mind stuttered, and he found himself spelling out loud, 'T-c-h-a-i-k-o-v-s-k-y.' Tchaikovsky, spelt the Russian way the English used.

Of course, the Red Cross would use that form, would they not? The initial was R. So there it was. R. Tchaikovsky. Was it Rosalia? His finger traced the column back, and again down to the foot and up again, and again, faster and faster, until he returned to the legend Refugees – Women. He ran out of the canteen, and down the camp road, across the square, past the first huts, until he found the Red Cross office. Breathless, he stamped both hands down onto the table in front of a startled woman.

'Refugees – Women. Tchaikovsky, R – records. Who is she? Where is she? Is R for Rosalia? Please, help me.' And he straightened up as he realised how startled she was.

'I'm sorry. It's just... I was not expecting... I saw her name, the name, on the board, the canteen. Is it my mother? Oh please.' And he started to cry.

'Sit down. I understand. Just sit down, and I'll check. Was it in today's notice?'

Eduard brushed his eyes, muttering 'sorry, sorry' and ran his tongue over his suddenly parched lips.

'I-I don't know. You see, I haven't been looking, that is I last looked, oh I can't remember. Anyway it's up there now.'

'It must be today's, or yesterday's, then. We take them down every other day and post a revised one. You wait here and I'll have a look.'

She stood, smoothing her jacket, and Eduard realised that she had been speaking in English. She smiled comfortably, patting his shoulder as she passed him, a ministering angel with a British air of assured authority, her dark hair bobbed, her uniform sharply pressed, her sensible shoes and silken stockings at odds with each other and her gentle, small-town face.

'Won't be long.'

He waited, hands held tight and tense, watching for her return.

'Are you alright?'

He glanced up at the question, in English again.

'Yes, thank you.'

'I see that Audrey's looking after you.'

'Yes, that's right.'

'Good. She's one of our best operators.'

'Operators?'

'Yes, radio operators. She talks to the Russians in their own language, in every sense. Got a knack with them. Digs all sorts of information out we can't get. Lovely girl.'

He was left wondering about Audrey – where she came from, who she was before she found herself in an ancient fort in the backlands of Russia helping lost Poles – until his reverie was broken by the lady's return.

'I've got it here. It's spelt the Russian way, but that's someone's transcription. The original signal's quite clear. C-j-a-i-k-o-w-s-k-a.'

Eduard was shaking, his hands cold and damp, his chest thundering.

'And the other name? The R?'

She leant over, extricating one hand, and held it calmly between her own.

'You mustn't be disappointed if it's not who you think.'

'No, no. I know. But what's the name – please?'

His anguish was clear and she pressed his hands firmly as she replied, 'Rosalia.'

Eduard's control of face, body and mind disintegrated. He sobbed and gasped and cried out and shook and shuddered, and Audrey came round to his side of her table and knelt beside him, holding him, stroking him.

'There. Cry. It'll do you good. Isn't it wonderful?'

When he had composed himself, she released him and took her seat.

'Now we have to begin the process of extracting her.'

'Can I go and get her?'

'When we have their permission, the Russians.'

'How long will that take?'

'It varies. Anyway you will have to ask your CO for leave.'

Eduard found Ptak in his quarters.

'Sir. Sorry to trouble you, but I've found my mother. I need leave.'

Ptak studied his young protégé.

'Calm down, man. I can't give you leave. You are due to be posted. Any day. See me in the morning.' And he turned away, adding, 'You'd better go. Dismiss.'

' "The crown o' the earth doth melt. My Lord! O, wither'd is the garland of the war." That's from *Anthony and Cleopatra*, and it goes on, "The soldier's pole is fall'n; young boys and girls Are level now with men; the odds is gone," and then it finishes off with, "And there is nothing left remarkable Beneath the visiting moon." '

Sara sat, clasping her long, dull tan, heavy cotton skirt over her knees, her laced boots shapeless and clumsy on such a light framework. The pale blue cotton blouse fluttered in the faint breeze – a welcome cool wind off the mountain. Her hair was slightly ruffled in the restless air, and by Eduard's solicitous hand.

'There, you see; Shakespeare proves that, in the end, war is not glorious, it makes no distinctions, and leaves nothing but death. We may love our country, but to die for it is not necessarily worthwhile.'

'So what do you suggest? That I desert? Run away with you? Let the war take its course, never mind what, let the bloody Germans and the Russians trample all over us? That's not right.'

'No, no, no, of course not. What I'm saying is that patriotism is all very well, but war destroys everything, and you can't ultimately win; victory is meaningless to the dead.'

'You're far too clever for me. I know I have to fight. And in any case, I haven't any choice. I'm in the Army.'

He was used to these debates. Every time they went walking, Sara would recite Shakespeare, once she knew he understood English. She would use the poet to prove her points, and endlessly rehearse her mantra – leave the camp, escape, build a new life, forget the war. She had for so long devoted her thoughts to a future unbound to family or war, she needed but one component to make it come to pass – a partner. When Eduard had descended from the *arak* tree, he was indeed a man from heaven.

'You have been waiting for someone for months. I came along, so you shut your eyes and said "This is the one" without thinking. Ever since you have been trying to prove it. The question is, who are you trying to convince? Me or yourself?'

'Now you're the clever one, Eduard. And that's not fair.'

She took his hand and twined her hair about his fingers, leant forward quickly, and kissed him briefly, then jumped up.

'Time to go home.'

It was the same whenever they were alone – passionate kisses, yards of Shakespeare, a flash of emotion, then nothing. Eduard's loins ached, his heart clattered and his hands sweated. He wanted her, and he knew his emotions were embroiled. He feared that with each meeting he fell deeper into thrall and that, one day, he would become her lover, through a compliance entire. He resisted his feelings, cleansed his mind of her extraordinary skills of intellectual attraction, and tried to concentrate on what should have been the simple task of seduction.

They sauntered back; the gate was open, the sun was still seething, and there was no sign or sound of Wladek as they approached the house. As they crossed the threshold, Sara put her fingers to her lips; Ludmilla was lying on her mattress, asleep. Her skirt was tumbled, her legs apart, and one arm hung down over the iron-frame bedside, the sleeve loose; her shirt-tunic was unbuttoned, and her tiny breasts exposed. She wore nothing under those dishevelled outergarments.

When Eduard softly tip-toed across, Sara was standing, looking down at her friend, a puzzled frown disturbing her face. Eduard stood beside her, considering the half-naked Ludmilla, surely left thus by Wladek, and the lust rose within him without remorse. He put his arms about Sara, lifting her blouse, and ran them up under the dry fabric until his hands found the warmth of her breasts. He felt her body stiffen against his, as the blood engorged her nipples, and they hardened in his fingers.

Her hands reached behind her and found him, and she gently rubbed him through the cloth. He slowly pulled her round, untying the blouse, and letting it drop round her wrists. With mounting urgency, she pulled the buttons open, and his risen cock free. He lifted her skirts, backing her into the alcove, where the stove stood, banked down, but warm, and lifted her bodily onto it, spreading her legs, hooking his fingers in her knickers and flipping them off one foot. She slid forward towards him, leaning back, her eyes closed, her mouth open and whispered 'Yes' as he slipped inside her, pulled her towards him, sought her mouth with his tongue and found the beat and rhythm of their need.

The first time is so often the wrong time and does not work, but for those who have waited, and yearned, and found the moment, it can also be the right time, the more so if the physical fit knows perfection, and the journey towards the point has been mutual and convergent. They came together, and the climax was absolute, admitting no other thought or feeling, or care or concern, or voice or presence.

Wladek had heard them, and crept into the room; when he saw them, he was nonplussed, and retreated. When Eduard detached himself, and helped Sara onto her feet, he was unaware of the silent interruption.

Ludmilla remained asleep. Sara shakily tied her blouse, then impulsively grabbed Eduard and started kissing him, between kisses repeating, 'Oh God I love you,' and, 'I love you so much,' and, 'I don't care if you fight if you want to,' and, 'I'll wait for you for ever.'

They sank onto the old Turkistan carpet and lay together, loosely entwined, as Eduard matched her protestations, hardly crediting his own incautious words: 'I love you, Sara,' and, 'I'll never let you go,' and, 'We'll go anywhere,' and, 'I've never felt like this before,' which last was at least entirely true, and the one declaration not to be regretted.

After a while they fell silent. Sara sat up, and looked embarrassed.

'I have to wash. I'll be back in a moment,' and she disappeared into the tiny bedroom where Tanya kept a wash-stand and a basin. Seconds later she came running out, and fell to her knees by Ludmilla, her head on the bed, her hands running through her hair. Eduard joined her.

'What's the matter?'

She shook her head violently, and pulled away. Eduard looked round. Wladek stood in the doorway, naked.

'What the hell...?'

Wladek gestured behind him. Eduard walked past; Tanya lay on her husband's bed, dry-eyed, staring back at him, a torn blanket across her legs, her arms crossed over her chest.

'I thought it was Ludmilla?'

'It was.'

'But Tanya...'

'Tanya too.'

'Both of them?'

'Both of them.'

Eduard looked hard at his friend, at the torment in his eyes.

'You'd better get dressed. Then we can talk – if you want to, of course.'

211

Wladek nodded, and bent down to retrieve his uniform. Tanya lay still, impassive.

Sara was kneeling beside the bed, looking past Eduard at Wladek through the bedroom door.

'Did he force her?'

'I don't know.'

'Let's go outside.'

They sat together on the low wall, yet apart, saying nothing. Wladek emerged, dressed and clearly disturbed.

'Well? What happened?'

He sat beside them, not looking at either of them.

'We came back and Ludmilla asked me if I wanted to and I said "yes" and she said she'd wanted to since that first day, so why didn't we? And I said "good idea" and we got on the bed, and we did it.'

'And?'

'What do you mean "and"?'

'Was it alright? Did she mind? Were you both happy?'

'It was OK. I mean, it wasn't anything special, like that, but it made us both happy. I think it was what we both wanted.'

'Yes?'

'Well, she went to sleep, and I was tired, so I decided to lie down. Her bed's too small; I mean, it was OK when we were doing it, but side by side, well, you know...'

Eduard nodded.

'Anyway, I saw Tanya's bed, and thought that would be a good place for a rest, and lay down – I hadn't dressed or anything, just took the stuff with me and dropped it on the floor.'

Sara's hand touched Eduard's and he clasped her reassuringly. Wladek stared at the fields.

'Well? What happened then?'

'Well, I was asleep when I felt something.'

He looked at Eduard and then at Sara.

'I was half asleep, really.'

'Go on.'

'It was Tanya. She'd obviously come back, seen Ludmilla asleep, like, well you know what she looked like, and came in here and then saw me, and I suppose, well I don't know; we'd both had a sort of feeling about each other; I mean, oh God. I wanted her, really wanted her. Ludmilla was my friend, and it was bound to happen, but Tanya's who I wanted. And there she was. And she took hold of me, and that was that.'

'So it was all Tanya's fault,' said Eduard with heavy sarcasm.

'Yes, it was all Tanya's fault,' said Tanya, who had approached them as they all stared out across the fields, unawares. She sat beside them.

'But perhaps not all Tanya's fault, since Tommy wanted it too,' and she put her arm round the distinctly uncomfortable young soldier.

The four sat in silence, until Eduard broke in with the obvious question: 'So what happens now?'

'I think that's up to Tommy.'

Wladek tensed and Eduard spoke in his stead.

'Why up to Tommy?'

'Well, Tommy wants me, I want Tommy, Ludmilla likes Tommy and Tommy likes Ludmilla. I would think it was obvious.'

'You mean...'

'Oh for God's sake, Wladek, she means you sleep with her because that's what you both want, and you sleep with Ludmilla because that pleases her, and doesn't displease you.'

Tanya nodded.

'Exactly.'

'And what about Piotr?' asked Sara, who had been silent throughout revelation, justification and resolution.

'What about Piotr?' asked Tanya.

'Doesn't he care?'

'Piotr long since lost interest in me, and anyway he's hardly here during the daytime, which is the only time you're here.'

Tanya paused, then went on.

'If you're worried about vows, forget it – Piotr married me for the land. And if you're worried about romantic notions of right and wrong, well that's the difference between stoic Tajiks and romantic Poles,' and she jumped off the wall and went back into the house, shouting back as she went, 'Mother and daughter – we make a good combination, don't you think?' and she laughed, her laughter lying on the evening air, mocking them all.

Eduard looked at Wladek and commented, 'Looks as if you're stuck with them both. Serve you right for being so bloody greedy.'

He slipped off the wall, took Sara's hands in his, kissed her lightly and added, 'Never mind them. We're different. I'm different and I love you.'

Ptak was pacing up and down, clearly irritated.

'I've told you once, and I tell you again, you simply cannot have any leave.'

Eduard stood rigidly in front of the officer's table.

'Sir. I've found my mother. She is in a prison camp. I want her out. I need leave.'

Ptak stopped and spun on his heel, came over to Eduard and tapped him repeatedly on his chest.

'I can't give you bloody leave, man.'

He added, 'Anyway, you need permission from the Russians.'

'How do I get that?'

'Apply.'

Ptak returned behind the table.

'Alright. Supposing you get it, and I do give you some leave, you'll need British permission too.'

'Thank you, sir.'

Eduard found Audrey in the Red Cross office, sorting papers. He explained the problem, and she waved him to a seat.

'It'll take a while, but we can organise something. Leave it to me. Oh, and come back the day after tomorrow.'

But the day after tomorrow Audrey was troubled.

'They are being awkward. The Russians.'

'Why? What about the Brit – your people?'

'Oh, they're OK. It's just the Russians – there's a problem, someone interfering, a liaison officer. He's being difficult. A man called Kolanski.'

Eduard froze. It was how he imagined it would feel when a bullet hit you – a cold, hard pain, then a flash of searing heat, and a complete loss of control. His hands shook, his eyes would not focus and his mind staggered. That name. With an effort, he controlled the shaking, and looked at her. She had not noticed anything.

'Look, why don't you get on with things, and I'll send someone for you when it comes through? OK?' She put her pen down and took his hands in hers. 'I know it's difficult, and I know you love your mother very much. It'll be alright. I promise.'

It took five weeks. During that time, Eduard saw Sara several times each week, and each time they met they made love, and every time they made love it was like the first time, and Eduard was enmeshed in feelings of which he had never dreamt. Each time Sara sharpened her blueprint.

'India is the other side of the mountains. It is a vast country. They speak English in the cities. We could live there,' and Eduard found himself moving inexorably towards a scenario of escape from war where, as Sara said, they could prepare themselves for a return to Poland 'when all this is over'.

Then she added:

' "Who doth ambition shun
And loves to live i' the sun,
Seeking the food he eats,
And pleas'd with what he gets."

You see? Shakespeare's always right – a simple life.'

Eduard and Wladek had themselves come to a simple agreement: they made their visits to Tanya's house separately and, when he was there, Eduard noted Tanya was absent or, if he arrived unexpectedly, she made some excuse and herself scarce. Ludmilla appeared indifferent to Sara's obsession with Eduard and, content with her shared lot, only once referring to the events of that afternoon with, 'Tommy's alright, and it's nice to have a boyfriend and anyway, mother makes sure he's happy. Suits me.'

Audrey was obviously excited. She fidgeted as she stood in Ptak's office, waiting for his return. When he strode in, she smiled sweetly at him.

'Good afternoon,' she said in Polish.

'Madam. Please be seated. What can I do for the Red Cross?'

'Cjaikowski.'

Ptak grimaced. 'Yes. Cjaikowski. I suppose he's been harping on about leave.'

'I have his tickets.'

'Tickets?'

'Ticket to Aksu, and two back, with his mother.'

'When?'

'As soon as you release him. I have the authority from the British.'

'And the Russians?'

'That too.'

'Very well, I'll see him and I'll see about leave.'

Nobody said anything about a man called Kolanski.

The next day Eduard, fitted out with a new British uniform, left for Aksu, 1,200 miles to the north. The route lay from Tashkent to Frunze, and from Frunze to Karaganda, and thence to Celinograd and Kokcetay, between which he would leave the train and find other means to Aksu. Armed with pass, tickets, papers and permissions, he travelled light. At each stop, he found the Russian Army canteen, showed his pass, and was fed at no charge, his uniform raising no comment but frequent twitches until, on the fifth day, in a carriage reserved for officers, he was accosted by one.

'Who are you?'

'A soldier.'

'I can see that, but what soldier?'

'A Polish soldier.'

The officer studied him for a moment.

'Your uniform?'

'British.'

The other man crossed his legs and folded his arms, relaxed against the worn upholstery. His companions were smiling in anticipation.

'Where are you going?'

'Same as you.'

'What's that mean?'

'To fight the Germans.'

The officer unclasped his arms, leant forward and poked Eduard in the chest. Eduard kept his right hand in his pocket, clasping his knife. The other, junior officers leant forward in unison, all three of them. Four against one, thought Eduard; bad odds.

'Fight the Germans? You couldn't fight the Germans. You're full of wind. You're nothing.'

He stayed in the same position, his hand lightly on Eduard's chest, looked round to ensure his audience, and observed, 'Look here, I'll fight – you.'

All five men remained motionless. Then the Russian clapped both hands round Eduard's shoulders, pulled him half out of his seat, hugged him, kissed both his cheeks, let him go, banged his hands down on the knees of the officer each side of him and laughed.

'Fight the Germans,' and he paused to catch his breath, 'I'm sure you will,' and stuck his hand out.

Eduard nervously withdrew his from his pocket and took the other's, and they solemnly sealed their newfound friendship. For the next and final 300 miles, they were inseparable; Eduard was regaled with copious drafts of vodka and even the occasional dollop of caviar.

When the train ground to a jolting halt at the wayside station at Aleksejevka, the Russian jumped down with him.

'Let's see what we can do,' he said, and marched off to find an official. He returned with a sleepy bureaucrat in tow.

'This is Shubyelev and he has a room in the station you can use. Tomorrow he will provide a cart.'

The Russian embraced Eduard.

'Good luck my friend. And I'll see you at the front. We'll kill those Germans together. You'll see.' And he roared with laughter, his merriment rolling on the cold air as he clambered back on board, and the train pulled slowly away.

The following morning, Eduard was woken by Shubyelev, who grudgingly supplied him with a rudimentary breakfast of broth and bread, washed down with somewhat stale water. He was taken into a small lean-to beside the station, and confronted with a decrepit two-wheeled cart, a high-sided contraption with one loose shaft. In an adjoining stable stood an ancient nag, grey, rackety, thin and completely indifferent to commands. With difficulty the horse was harnessed, the doors opened, and Eduard left Aleksejevka for Aksu.

The first few miles passed slowly; then the horse stopped, whinnied, and gradually subsided, awkwardly suspended between the shafts. Eduard swore, dismounted, and walked round to the tired animal. It cost him half an hour of effort to unravel the harness, and release the horse, which promptly staggered to its feet and stumbled to the side of the track, where it started to nose about in the harsh stubble.

Eduard realised that the day was halfway done, and his hopes of reaching Aksu before nightfall slight. With a sigh, he pushed and heaved the cart to the side, and contemplated the way ahead. As he was wondering what to do, he heard the clip-clop of hooves, and a rumble of wheels as a smart equipage, four-wheeled and two-horsed, drew alongside.

A fur-hatted and astrakhan-collared, bulky figure accosted him.

'Stopped to admire the view?'

Eduard said nothing. The stranger scratched his nose.

'If you want a ride to the next village, jump up.'

Eduard joined him on the jump seat and they set off. The stranger said no more until they reached a small settlement.

'This is as far as I go.'

Eduard clambered down, and the carriage rumbled off. He looked about him. He was in a small square, surrounded by *izby*, and one stone building. He went up to the door, and knocked. Nothing happened, so he knocked again. The door rattled, and opened an inch or so.

'Yes?'

'I'm on my way to Aksu. Is there anywhere I can eat?'

The door opened further, and he saw a child of ten or eleven years. The child beckoned him inside, and he entered. The door closed behind him. He followed the child down a long passage into a shadowy room, lit by candles. The child vanished, and he peered into the gloom.

A faded, broken voice startled him, and he followed the sound to an indistinct chair outlined against candlelight off to the left.

'Over here,' the faint voice suggested.

He walked cautiously across, and stood by the chair. It rocked slightly, and quivered as the voice continued.

'Sit. There. In front of me, where I can see you.'

Eduard felt behind him, and his hands encountered the soft edge of an upholstered upright carver.

'There.' There was a pause. 'You're a stranger.'

'Yes I am. I was looking for some food.'

'Nobody's here nowadays. Only Mushkin. Mushkin's the one you want if you want food.'

Eduard was beginning to regret his choice. The stone house clearly housed a recluse, if not a madman.

'Is that the child?'

The disembodied voice cackled slightly, then coughed. When the coughs subsided, there was brief silence, and then, 'The child? Oh yes, the child. Never mind the child. You need Mushkin.'

'How do I find him?'

'Mushkin? Find him?' There was another bout of cackling, and coughing and silence.

'You'll not find Mushkin, but Mushkin'll find you. Oh yes.'

Eduard decided. Waiting for Mushkin was not an attractive option. He stood, stepped across to the candle, lifted it, walked back to the chair, and held it close to the source of the voice.

217

Expecting an old man, he found it difficult to comprehend what he saw, revealed in the flickering glow. Before him sat a once powerful man, his legs concealed beneath a blanket, one hand gripping the arm of the rocker. Of the other arm there was no sign, for the empty sleeve was pinned back across a massive chest. The man's face was shadowed by a wide-brimmed hat, but the mouth was blisteringly cankered, and the granules piled up on one another down his chin and across what could be seen of his neck. As Eduard stepped back, the man in the chair rasped out faintly.

'Now you have seen me, you know why I sit here, in the dark. Nobody comes. They are fearful. They fear my past, for I was strong, and they fear my presence, for I am ill. And you, young man, you fear me too?'

Eduard sat down, carefully placing the candle on the floor.

'No, I don't think so. I am sorry you are ill. Are there no doctors?'

'Too late for that. I am left alone to die.'

This time there was no cackle, just a continuous, straining, sad cough. Eduard started as another voice intervened.

'Konrad, you know that's not true.'

Eduard stumbled to his feet, as the woman brushed by, bent over the man, and kissed him lightly on the cankered mouth. She turned to Eduard.

'I'm sorry I was not here to greet you. I am Mushkin.'

Eduard inclined his head, unsure if she could see him. She read his thoughts.

'I can see you. I am used to the dark. Konrad's eyes, they cannot take the light,' and she picked up the candle and replaced it in its original holder.

'Now then. You are hungry, and little Kyril has gone to get some eggs. We will eat soon. You will stay, perhaps?'

'I shouldn't stay really. I am trying to get to Aksu.'

'The camp?'

'That's right. My mother's there.'

'Then you are the Polish who Shubyelev sent?'

'Yes. I had to leave his horse. It was lame.'

'It was found. Come.' She held out a hand, and he took it. 'Konrad, I'm taking our visitor to wash. He has had a hard journey.'

The light was fading when Mushkin, Konrad, little Kyril and Eduard sat to a table, drawn up by the man's chair, and ate a simple meal of eggs, beaten and spiced, spread on thin slices of a dark, malt bread and accompanied by vodka. A small fire flickered in the basket grate at the far end of the room. Konrad said little and dozed off after the meal and little Kyril was taken to bed. When Mushkin returned, she drew her chair close to the fire, indicating to Eduard to do the same.

'Tell me about yourself. We see so few people these days.'

Eduard began to explain, haltingly at first, more fluently as his story gained momentum, encouraged by the close attention this shadowy lady paid him. He found himself studying her as he spoke and, when he reached a recollection of Irma and Olga, broke off, and asked her, 'What about you? What happened to Konrad?'

She sighed, and picked at her skirt.

'It is a long story, like yours, but I prefer not to talk about it. Let us leave it as a little mystery. We are married, Kyril is ours, and Konrad was once an important man, a giant among men. Then someone died, he was accused, there was a trial, he was acquitted, but the town found him guilty nonetheless and one night, he fell ill. You have seen how he looks. He had treatment, but it just got worse. He lost an arm. His voice changed. And...'

She stifled a cry, and was silent. Eduard reached over and touched her arm. She put her hand over his, then sat back and closed her eyes.

'Konrad was a doctor. He has what his victim had. Now nobody will treat him, and he is dying.'

She opened her eyes again.

'Life is like that, Eduard. It creeps up on you when you least expect it. Don't let that happen to you. Find your mother, and go home to Poland.'

She stood up.

'Now I must get some rest. I will show you to your room.'

Eduard stood too, for a moment restraining her.

'Thank you. No. I won't stay. Just show me the way to Aksu. I have to go.'

Mushkin nodded, and they left the room, Konrad still, and the house around them silent. At the door, Mushkin pointed to the east.

'Strike across the steppe; it is sandy soil, but dry. If you follow the stars you cannot go wrong. Goodbye,' and she closed the door softly.

Eduard walked past the stone house, down a straggling street, which soon petered out, and struck off across the grit-strewn ground. The moon was full and bright, the stars filled the night sky, and he settled into a steady rhythm as he navigated his way the remaining six miles to Aksu.

The camp was quiet, when he arrived. There was no fence. All he could discern were rows upon rows of wooden huts, candlelight flickering at their windows. There were no guards. He approached the first hut, and pushed at the door. It swung open, and he was confronted by two ranks of metal beds, with groups of women huddled here and there, an occasional sleeping figure, and one or two sitting, reading. The low murmur of conversation stopped the moment he opened the door.

Someone said, 'A man!' and someone else laughed. Then there was silence. Eduard approached the first group.

'I'm looking for my mother.'

Within minutes the word had spread. A man for Rosalia Cjaikowska; her son.

He was sitting on a bed, between two younger women and a girl, when someone came into the hut.

'Are you Eduard?'

One of the women said, 'Stupid question. How many men are there here?'

'Yes, I am.'

'Then here is your mother.'

He rose from the bed, and stepped forward, his legs shaking. She came towards him, her arms outstretched. They met. She put her arms about her son, and he wept.

The hut was in turmoil. Someone had produced a balalaika, and there was music, low and plangent. Eduard had offered his vodka, which lasted a few seconds. In the midst of it all sat Rosalia, hand in hand with her son, the tears now dry upon his cheeks.

'I knew you would come one day,' and he started crying all over again.

When he had recovered his composure, he held out the tickets.

'I have a ticket for you. To go south, to Kermener.'

Someone snatched the tickets, and there was pandemonium for a moment before the hut leader shouted, banging a metal bed with a spoon.

'Enough. Stop it. Give those tickets back.'

Eduard put the tickets in his pocket. The leader explained.

'Everyone wants to go. Have you any other tickets?'

'No.'

'Well then, could you take the daughter of a friend of Rosalia?'

'I only have tickets for us.'

The women fell back, disconsolate, and dispersed to their beds.

'It is agony for them,' said the leader. 'They have sons, husbands, brothers, and they don't hear from them, they don't know where they are, if they are even alive.'

Eduard spread his hands.

'I can do nothing. Until recently I was a prisoner too.'

'I know, I know. Get some sleep.'

They slept fitfully that night, Rosalia in the next bed, her hand constantly reaching out to Eduard to ensure he was truly there. The next day they left at dawn, to walk across the steppe. Eduard feared for his mother's strength, but forgot her will. By the time they approached the little town, she was ahead of him. Passing Mushkin's house, they stopped a carter on his way to market in Aleksejevka, and hitched a lift. There they waited for a train, and six days later, Eduard brought Rosalia to Kermener.

Audrey had arranged a room with carpet and bed in an Uzbek house, and Eduard reported to Ptak. He said nothing about Kolanski, for nobody had said any more about the 'difficulties' and Eduard decided it was just a coincidence, a twist of fate, and best set aside, even if it was impossible to forget.

'You found your mother.'

'Yes, sir. Thank you, sir.'

'Good. Now what are we going to do with her?'

'She is renting a room.'

'Good. Good. Well, I have made some enquiries. We can post her to Bombay.'

'India!' and Eduard thought suddenly of Sara and her dreams of escape.

'Yes. India. It is the only place the British can arrange outside Russia.'

He smiled at Eduard.

'Don't worry. From there she can go to Tangyanika, then South Africa, and on to England, where you can perhaps join her – after the war.'

Eduard saluted and turned to go.

'I haven't dismissed you yet.'

'Sorry, sir.'

'I've been worrying about you while you were away. I've decided. You have languages. You could be useful. You're posted. To Persia. Say goodbye to your mother this week. Next week you're off – to Krasnavosk.'

Sara. All that night Eduard lay awake. Rosalia was safe. At last he was off to war. But there was Sara. He loved her, of that he was in no doubt. She would go wherever he went; he had only to ask. But she could not go to war. The choice was simple – Sara or Krasnavosk; love or war.

He thought of all the days they had shared, and he remembered her words, Shakespeare's words – 'ambition shun'. He remembered too, the words of another woman, Mushkin: 'Don't let life creep up on you.'

Wladek was philosophical about the posting.

'We've had some good times. I'll be there one day soon. We'll meet again.'

Sara was not told. They met as usual, twice in that same last week when once more he would say goodbye to Rosalia. He told her about the journey, about Konrad and Mushkin, though not what Mushkin said. They made love. It was as fresh and wondrous as ever. On the second day he lingered before leaving, until Tanya returned. As mother and daughter cleared the meal away, he took Sara outside.

He touched her cheek, held her close, and spoke into her hair.

'I will always love you, Sara.'

She pulled away instinctively.

'What's that mean?'

'Nothing. Just that I really love you.'

'For a moment I thought – oh never mind.'

They wandered back inside the *manzanka* and Eduard waved at Ludmilla.

'I must go back to camp. I'll give your love to Wladek.'

'Thanks. 'Bye Eduard.'

Sara smiled and said, 'I have something for you,' and disappeared into Tanya's room.

Tanya spoke softly.

'You're not coming back, are you?'

Eduard looked down, shaking his head.

'She senses it, but she doesn't know. Say nothing. It's better that way.'

'I know.'

At that moment, Sara returned, holding something in her hand. She held it out to Eduard. It was a piece of soft leather, embossed with a simple figure S with a cross in each curl.

'For your knife,' and she kissed it, handed it to him, and he kissed her.

Two days later, Eduard joined the small contingent bound for Krasnavosk, led by Baccovitch. Major Ptak saw them off. Equipped with knapsacks, rifles, Sam Brownes and gaiters, they formed up. Ptak spoke briefly of the dangers and their duties, then saluted as Bacco gave the order

'By the left, qui-ick MARCH. Ip-die, ip-die, ip-die,' and his voice faded as they swung away from Kermener on their way to the Caspian Sea.

I have the sheath as well as the knife. I still love Sara. That kind of love never dies. But Mushkin was right and Sara was wrong. It was my war and I had to fight it. Love comes second in the affairs of men. At least, it does when the men are Polish, young, and without a country.

I feel differently today, but then I would, wouldn't I, locked as I am in age, incapacity and another love – and with a whole country to call my own?

A STICK HAS TWO ENDS

Trucked to Tashkent, the last contingent in the new Polish Army boarded one train to Bukhara, then another across the desert to Aschabad, on past Nebit Dag to Krasnavosk. There they disembarked, and marched along the Caspian coast to the peninsula port – not much more than a jetty, some warehouses and a breakwater. They left behind half a million Poles to fight with the Russians on their western front – right up to Berlin, under General Lubelsk. The remnants of the 7th Polish Division took ship for Persia.

Eduard contemplated their vessel, the ss *Srat* – a small, scabbed, rusty oil- tanker, hastily converted for passengers, which is to say that the pungent holds were sealed, and the superstructure modified to accommodate as many as possible topsides. The metal railings had been strengthened round the ship's perimeter, hatches battened, and a complex and somewhat ramshackle set of pipes and valves connected to a rudimentary desalination plant. The troops were tired, some had dysentery, and the sun beat down on the buckled, oxidised plates.

Shade was at a premium, and tarpaulins fought over for makeshift tents. Only the water was fresh, if still a little salty. The tired steamer bucked and gasped and clanked its way on its asthmatic three-day voyage south towards Babol, as man after man sat on the rails and voided his aching bowels into the waters of the Caspian. When it hove to off the Persian coast, landing craft chugged out and were warped to the starboard beam.

Eighty per cent of the men were jaundiced. There were no buoyant farewells to the surly Russian crew as the troops filed across the deck, slid and lurched down the ladders and dropped into the boats. As they pulled away, the tired tanker belched black gobs of smoke, and listlessly turned.

'Bloody well named, that boat.'

'What, *Srat*?'

'Yeah, Russian for "shit".'

Lorries waited in line along the coastal track. At Pahlevi the Persians mobbed the soldiers as they poured off the trucks. They were deluged with chocolates, sweetmeats, soft bread, lemon juice, sprayed with water to lay the dust, and everywhere saluted, embraced and made welcome. The transit camp was on the outskirts of Tehran – tents and huts, shower sheds, shielded latrines, canteen and even a temporary shop. Gradually they were all processed – their uniforms handed in, their bodies cleansed, their heads deloused and, freshly clothed, they ate their first European meal, in some cases, for nearly three years.

Then they boiled out onto Tehran's crowded streets, and everywhere they went, they were hailed as if they had already won a war. The only lingering memory of their years in Russia was the one luxury they could not find in Persia – vodka.

Eduard walked the streets in a daze, automatically smiling when greeted, giving thanks when given fruits, and returning the innumerable 'Inshallahs' with suitable humility and finger-tipping hands. It lasted for a week. Then the orders came through to embark for Iraq. Tents were struck, huts stripped, and the camp closed down to tick-over status, before they climbed on board for the cross-mountain journey to Khanaqin, 100 miles north-west of Baghdad.

Eduard said his farewells to those of his hosts he could find; some handed him fruit for the journey and one, a goatskin of water. A wise mullah held his hands in his and, wiping them, first on his robe, then on Eduard's tunic, softly declared in English: 'A stick has two ends' – an ancient Persian proverb, offering hope without assurance – things might go well, they might not: 'A stick has two ends'. They talked of the journey ahead, and Eduard commented, 'It's not just a truck ride; it's the road to war,' and the mullah's eyes pierced his own, and seemed to reach into his mind as he added, 'The holy book says this, my son: "travel through the earth and observe the fate of those before you".' The old mullah let go. He laid one hand on Eduard's head: 'Goodbye fine friend. Inshallah.'

The trucks climbed slowly 3,500 feet to Hamadan, and then laboured across Kermanshahan, the sun striking through worn covers stretched over metal frames, and searing the skin until it blistered, then peeled. There was no escape as they traversed one of the hottest, driest regions on earth, silent, thirsty, eyes itching, heads throbbing, minds numbed.

The earth bore no sign of life, arid, desolate, scorched, and torn by dust, seared by wind. The rock reflected the unheeding heat, shadows stark, stones sightless, sand sullen. Not a lizard, bird or dry grass could be seen as the convoy ground up each gradient, round each indifferent shoulder and down again, until they grated into each virgin valley, and thundered through their own dust storm to scratch and score the further flanks. Eduard lost track of time until, several hours after they had left Tehran, they saw the sun blink on the waters of the Naft, and dropped down through the foothills above the rich Tigris plain, into Khanaqin.

Divisional Headquarters housed many of the 60,000 men in a modern, hutted base, with barracks blocks, officers' mess, and civilian staff. Others lived in tents, staked to the hard ground. Khanaqin also hosted the British No. 2 Hospital, a clean, clockwork facility.

Two days after Eduard arrived, Wladek appeared.

'I told you we'd meet again!'

They did not speak of Sara or Ludmilla, for if they had, then Tanya would have come between them. Instead they sought release in the bustling township, and there they met Abdullah.

Eduard was strolling past a concrete store, when Wladek called him across the street.

'Look at this – shoes, modern shoes, European shoes, in wartime, here, in Khanaqin!'

The shop was bright and clean, and advertised 'Bata'.

'Let's go in – see what they cost.'

'What on earth do you want shoes for? You're in the Army.'

'I don't want any; I'm just amazed they're here. I want to look at them, feel them. Come on, then,' and he led the way.

Inside, the store was cool, a sluggish fan stirring the air, and blinds drawn against the windowed sun. A slender, cream-suited Arab approached, thick black hair creamed back over his ears, a polished light teak pate beaming between the gunwales, brows raised over two laughing black eyes, and a sensuous mouth carved into a vendor's smile.

'Gentlemen, welcome to my humble emporium. Be seated. Have some tea.'

Wladek looked at Eduard and Eduard shrugged: 'Why not?'

'Tea before feet, gentlemen. It puts the mind in mind of nimbleness, and tickles the toes, don't you think?'

Wladek looked at Eduard again and Eduard laughed.

'Tea to tickle the toes – what a good idea.'

The Arab bowed slightly, smoothed his impeccable suit, and moved silently but swiftly to the rear of the premises, where he raised an imperious hand and spoke softly to an unseen assistant, his words inaudible, and his assistant invisible. He returned as quickly as he had gone.

'There. That is arranged. Gentlemen. . .' and he composed himself before them, his hands clasped below his buttons, his lightly pocked and olive skin equally composed in a warm, yet not too intimate smile. Thus they sat and stood, a tableau in suspension, awaiting tea.

Moments later, a rustle of silks preceded a veiled and enfolded figure, concealed from head to heel, with exquisitely boned ankles slipping in and out of view, as she glided towards them, balancing a circular copper tray, her slight slippers slithering across the marble floor.

As she bent, Eduard glimpsed khol-heightened eyes set either side of a high-bridged nose – then she was gone, leaving three translucent bowls and a tall, tapering jug, steam wisping out of its modest mouth.

'Tea,' announced their host, 'English style, with the teapot and the cups.' He poured the aromatic brew, adding, 'Of course, the tea is not

English, that is to say it is neither the India nor the China tea. It is our tea, mint tea – most fragrant, and refreshing.'

He slid their 'cups' towards them, and lifted his own, sniffing appreciatively, then gesturing to each of them, 'cup' in hand, before sipping with exaggerated gentility – 'To tickling the toes.'

'Toes,' murmured Eduard, and 'Yes' uncertainly from Wladek, whose grasp of English was uncertain.

'Now, gentlemen, I am Abdullah, and you...?'

'Eduard'

'Excellent,' and he leant forward, his hand extended.

'Tomasz.' Wladek stuck his hand out and the Arab took it in both of his.

'You are most welcome to my humble emporium.' He paused, then added, 'which you have entered because you are curious, not because you wish to buy my shoes, yes?'

Wladek buried his nose in his tea, so that it was left to Eduard to respond.

'Well, in fact my friend was so surprised to see European shoes, that he came in before we had had time to think about it and, well, here we are.'

'Here you are and am I not glad that you are here?'

He rose, gathering himself, placing one elegantly shod foot slightly before the other, clasping his hands and cocking his head to one side.

'As you know, I am Abdullah, and this is my little emporium. I have many other interests and if I can be of service, please do not hesitate to ask.' He paused. 'You have drink at the camp?'

Eduard looked quickly at Wladek – this was a Moslem country. The Prophet forbade alcohol.

'It is not allowed on the camp.'

'Aha! We can perhaps be of service then,' and he sat down again, poured more tea, and sipped reflectively, considering them blandly over his raised 'cup'.

'Please advise me where you live in the camp.'

Eduard explained that they were housed in a hut, close to the main barracks block, where they each had a small room.

'It has a number – H12.'

'The twelfth hour! Most appropriate,' and Abdullah laughed, a soft, receding gurgle in the back of his throat which died almost as soon as it started.

'I shall call upon you this evening – a little before six. Yes?' and he ushered them out of the shop, standing in the doorway until they lost sight of him through the afternoon crowds.

'What d'you make of him?' asked Wladek.

'Courteous, slightly amusing, and obviously after something.'

'What I thought too. Odd sort of bloke.' Wladek hesitated, then added, 'And the girl – did you see her eyes?'

226

'Yes I did. Haven't you had enough of that?'

'Never have enough,' and Wladek smirked to himself.

Eduard ignored him as they entered the camp. When they reached the hut, there was a jeep idling outside, and the driver jumped down.

'Corp'ral Cjaikowski?'

'That's me.'

'Major Ptak wants to see you.'

Eduard glanced at Wladek, who snorted as he pushed the door into his room.

'Thought we'd left him behind to fight with the Russians.'

'Apparently not.'

The driver was impatiently waiting, revving the engine as Eduard slid into the passenger seat.

'Where's the Major?'

'Admin, Corp'ral – suh.'

Eduard nodded, clutching the folded-down windscreen pillar as they spurted dust from tyre-spin, cornering round the barracks. 'Admin' was at the other end of the multi-acre site.

The jeep skidded to a halt outside a shining white hut with blinds and post-and-chain borders. The driver gave an insolent salute as Eduard jumped out, and let in the clutch so violently that small stones spat against his legs. He dusted his hands down his tunic, straightened his back and marched into the hut. An orderly barred his way.

'Corporal?'

'Cjaikowski, to see Major Ptak.'

The orderly nodded, and pushed open the door on his left. Eduard went in. Ptak was pacing back and forth and in the chair behind the desk was another officer – Grela.

'You know each other,' observed Ptak.

'Sir!'

'At ease. The Captain'll explain.'

Grela was twirling his customary pencil, his mouth compressed, unsmiling.

'So – you left Kermener then.'

Eduard said nothing. Grela sucked his pencil, extruded it slowly, and studied it, then wiped it on his sleeve, and put it down, pedantically, in the exact centre of the pile of papers neatly laid on his desk, beside his usual pad.

'So did we, so did we, didn't we Ptak?'

Ptak nodded, and stopped pacing, leaning against the window, looking down at his boots.

'You weren't happy about Grybos, were you?'

'It happened – sir.'

'Yes, it happened.' Ptak looked at him pensively, pulling the right side of his lip with his teeth. 'You'd better tell him, Grela.'

Grela picked up the pencil again, and tapped it against his nail.

'We have a little problem.'

'Sir?'

'Oh, for goodness' sake, Corporal. Sit down, relax.'

Eduard sat.

'And you too, Ptak.'

Ptak pulled up a chair, spun it round, and sat astride it, his arms on the back. Not for the first time, Eduard wondered how it was that Ptak, the senior officer, seemed to defer to Grela. Then it came to him – Ptak had never seen combat. So Grela held the advantage.

'You see, the 7th Division is going to Palestine. Sixty thousand men, off to the British protectorate.'

Ptak added, cynically, 'To the land of Jesus – before they face the devil.'

Eduard wondered where all this was leading, but still kept his counsel. Grela twirled his pencil, leant forward, and tapped the papers.

'We have to abandon camp, this camp. Close it down. Strike tents. Dismantle huts. Store things.'

Eduard contained his bewilderment. What it had to do with him, he could not imagine, since he was part of the 7th Division, and was presumably slated to go to Palestine too. Grela's next words changed all that.

'We have to go. You don't. We need someone here – to sort it all out. You did well at Kermener. You and that other fellow, what's his name?'

'Wladek?'

'Yes, Wladek, that's it.'

Grela looked at Ptak and Ptak looked away.

'You will get to fight, Cjaikowski, I promise you, but frankly, we need someone we can trust and we can't spare an officer.'

'What's involved, sir?'

'You have got to get some help, and close the camp – everything except the barracks and the hospital block – and they've got to be mothballed. Think you can cope?'

Eduard did not hesitate.

'Of course, sir. When do we start?'

Over the next few days the Division pulled out, until there were only Wladek, Eduard and one other, a taciturn ex-teacher called Kania. On the last day, Grela handed Eduard a packet.

'These are your orders. They include an authority to draw the necessary funds to pay the workmen. You must find your own labour, and remember, you'll be held to account if anything goes wrong.'

He took Eduard's hand and shook it.

'I'll see you in Palestine.'

Eduard saluted as Grela swung into the jeep. Ptak nodded and the driver pulled away. Wladek and Kania watched from the hut.

As he walked back towards them, Eduard voiced their unspoken thought.

'We're going to need Abdullah.'

Abdullah had called on them, just as he promised that very first day. He was carrying a parcel. He stayed but three minutes, clasping his hands, then made an excuse – 'Business, you understand' – and left.

In the parcel was a bottle of whisky – Johnny Walker Black Label – and a note: 'If I can be of service – Abdullah'. On the back was an address in the old quarter, at the edge of the modern town.

'We have to clear all the tents, and fill the holes. The latrines must be disinfected and filled in. The small huts must be dismantled. Everything has to be stored, and that means we need storage.'

Eduard spread his hands.

'We are going to need transport, warehousing, and labour.'

Abdullah inclined his head, and unclasped his hands. They were sitting in a spartan office in a single-storey concrete building incongruously built behind a series of white-painted baked-clay houses on the edge of the old quarter. The usual noise and bustle of the narrow streets was absent in the midday sun, and their voices echoed in the harsh interior. Abdullah stood, for he had insisted that Eduard and Wladek and Kania took the only chairs.

'You will also need permissions, and inspections and papers.'

Eduard waved the orders he had been given by Grela.

'I have them here.'

Abdullah smiled, his head cocked to one side.

'Assuredly. But those are British papers. You will need other papers, for the British are no longer here. The camp is on Iraqui property, no?'

Eduard agreed.

'So. I will get them.'

Abdullah spread his hands wide.

'I shall get you papers, permissions, and people.' He paused. 'All you need to get is some money. These things cost money, you know.'

'I know. That can be arranged.'

'Good. Then I shall see you tomorrow – at the camp, and I shall bring my brothers. Now – you will take some tea?'

They heard her before she entered – the same rustle preceded the same robed wraith, her ankles bewitching, her eyes averted. Eduard sipped the mentholated confection, its aromatic steam cleansing his mind.

'Brothers? You have brothers?'

Abdullah lifted his cup, inclining it slightly towards Eduard.

'Akbar is Khanaqin's larder – he grows everything, especially fruit, and particularly *arak*, from which is made the most delicious beverage. You must try some. More tea?'

Abdullah served them, then clasped his hands again.

'Ali-Said is Khanaqin's protector – he is a colonel in our service.'

But Abdullah did not clarify whether by that he meant armed, or family, and they had to be content with that.

The following day Eduard was awoken by a continuous grumbling roar. He stumbled to the hut door, and shut it as quickly as he had opened it, for roils of dust billowed in and the noise was implacable. The camp had been invaded by a fleet of lorries of many different makes and power. Five minutes later, there was a discreet tap on the door. It was Abdullah.

'I trust we are not too early? The sun is not yet high.'

As he explained it, there were 40 trucks and 800 workmen, four suitable warehouses, and plenteous permissions, courtesy of Ali-Said. The men would be fed by Akbar, there was plenty of water onsite, and the job would take three weeks.

'It will cost £1,000 each week – in dinars, of course, to cover men, trucks, food, papers – and us.'

Abdullah half turned, and two other men stepped forward. One wore a jellabah, sandals and headdress, the other was in shorts and short-sleeved shirt, neat knee-length socks, leather belt and smart brogues. It occurred to Eduard he was wearing the uniform of an English officer, save for his Arab insignia.

'Akbar,' and the corpulent, white-robed, bald and bearded figure rolled forward, hands closed in greeting before him, 'and Ali-Said,' at which the tall, scimitar-nosed soldier gave a short neck-bow, his hands behind his back.

'They will take care of everything, while you and I supervise. We will pay the men their share each week. You sign the draft, I will get the cash, and we will bring the dinars here by van.'

The work proceeded every morning; it ceased at midday. At the end of the first week, the tents had gone, their holes filled. The latrines had been filled in, and work had started on the huts. One squad was ordered to clear the barracks, and Abdullah's most trusted men were deputed to seal the windows and bar the doors. The hospital remained and, by agreement with the British doctor in charge, continued to function until the last sick Pole was able to leave, its future expressly excluded from Eduard's orders. A skeleton Red Cross presence there served their other needs.

'You found your mother?'

Eduard was standing in the sparse reception room, waiting for the nurses to come off duty; Abdullah had suggested a party in town. The voice was familiar. He turned.

'Audrey!'

She walked over to him and took his hands, as she had done the day she found Rosalia on the refugee list.

'She is safe?'

'Yes. She is safe – in Tangyanika.'

'I'm so glad. And you? I thought everyone had gone. I came to close the mission down.'

'Everyone has gone, except us – three of us; we're closing the camp.'

She released his hands, and he thought again how clean and straightforward and terribly English she was, with her bobbed hair and sensible shoes, yet with a hint of something more glimpsed in her eyes – and in the sheer stockings.

'We're having a party,' and at that point four nurses tumbled through the door, laughing and smoking, and jostling and surrounding them both.

'Come on Eduard, who's she?' and 'Your girlfriend, Eduard – thought I was alright this afternoon' and 'Hey, who's your ladyfriend?' all amid gusts of good-natured laughter.

He was saved by a cloud of dust and two Cadillacs, fat, sleek, shiny, beige with cream-walled tyres and curvaceous lines, and Abdullah and Ali-Said at the wheels.

'Will you join us?'

'Another time.'

Audrey touched his hand lightly, then walked back into the hospital.

'Come on Eddie, let's go.'

Kathleen was the senior nurse, and their natural leader; auburn, sleek, tunicked and trousered, her pale skin shadowed under a wide-brimmed straw hat. She bundled the other three into the first Cadillac with Kania, and stood back to let Eduard take her arm and help her into the second car. Wladek was already sitting in the front, well away from Abdullah on the bench seat. He twisted round, his arm resting casually on the leather backrest.

'Are you ready?'

Eduard smiled his agreement, Abdullah depressed the horn ring twice, and Ali-Said gunned the lead car, Abdullah hard on his tail, as they slewed round in the dust and headed off for the desert. The two cars sped between the remaining huts, weaving past stationary lorries, horns blazing at workers too slow to make way.

Eduard reached down and extracted three bottles of pils from a crate, unscrewed the stoppers and handed one each to Kathleen and Wladek.

'Have you got the food?'

The Arab glanced up at his reflection in the driving mirror and smiled.

'In the back, with the scotch. Ali's got the rest. We're going to have a party!'

'Where are we going?' asked Kathleen, leaning against Eduard.

Abdullah glanced up again, one eyebrow curled as he caught Eduard's eye.

'A small oasis in the desert. Akbar is already there, preparing.'

They drove for half an hour, Kathleen's hand resting lightly on Eduard's thigh, as they steadily consumed their second and third bottles of the cool, fresh lager. Wladek was singing softly to himself as they approached a clump of low, white clay houses among a scattering of pear and plum trees.

'Is this Akbar's farm?' asked Eduard and Abdullah laughed.

'No sir. This is a cousin's humble holding. We have borrowed it for the afternoon.' He winked at Eduard in the mirror as they slowed. 'There's nobody here except us.'

The other Cadillac was stationary outside the largest of the houses, a long, low, whitewashed structure with an overhanging roof, and blue painted posts slotted between the dusty timbers of the verandah. They could hear the other girls laughing. Eduard pulled the crate of pils out of the car as Kathleen sauntered into the house. Abdullah waved his hand.

'Leave it there – my women will bring everything.'

Inside, the house was shuttered, cool and dusky dark. The floor was laid with close-woven, throbbing-red carpets, and there were more hanging on the walls. There was a low table in the centre of the room, already laden with dishes of sweetmeats. Akbar sat cross-legged, facing the entrance, a nurse on each side. He fed each one alternately with morsels from the table, delicately placing each piece between their lips, fastidiously rinsing his fingers in a bowl, and wiping them clean on a damask cloth before repeating the process. Two veiled women moved quietly, fetching platters, and arranging cushions.

When Ali-Said entered with the third nurse on his arm, Akbar rose, bowed, then sank back again. Ali-Said sat by the girl on his left, and commenced feeding her.

Eduard and Wladek took their seats opposite the Arabs, Kathleen between them, and Eduard pushed a pilsner across. Akbar waved it away.

'It is not Allah's will.' And he turned to beckon one of the Arab women. 'Wine for our guests; goat's milk for me.'

Pale, opaque, tall fluted glasses were placed before them, and the women poured liquids from pitchers, and removed the half empty pils bottles. As they drank, Abdullah appeared, and bent down towards Kathleen, murmuring in her ear. She looked questioningly at Eduard, who shook his head as if to say 'You do what you want'.

Kathleen pushed herself up, and moved round the table, following Abdullah. He sat next to the nurse on Akbar's right and she sank down onto the cushions beside him. The Arab women glided back and forth, removing the sweetmeats and serving small dishes of rice and herbs, filleted raw fish and sauces, and constantly replenishing the glasses.

Eduard noticed that none of the Arabs touched the girls, though their gestures and courtesies wove an invisible network of intimacy about them. As the meal progressed, the two women stood to each side, impassive, invisible, unmoving and silent.

Akbar clapped his hands with a small, pliant movement of the fingers of the right in the palm of the left, and the women reached up and lifted their veils. Then they unwound them, until their eyes, their flared nostrils, and finally their wide mouths were revealed, smiling and sensuous.

Wladek whispered to Eduard: 'I thought they were his wives,' indicating Akbar, and Eduard muttered, 'Maybe they are, maybe they are.'

The two women moved gracefully, sinuously, lithe and supple, their bodies passing, merging and separating in something less than a dance and more than a tableau, as they gravely moved about the room, leaning forward here and back there, languorous and yet powerful and, as they did so, Eduard began to appreciate that this was not a suggestive sideshow as at first he had imagined, but a small *coup de theatre*, an evocation of the spirit bound into the flesh – sensuous but not sexual.

The nurses saw it differently.

Little Rachel, the girl on Akbar's left, was already light-headed, and slopping scotch from the bottle into her glass. A short, slightly thickset girl with close-cropped blonde hair which belied her thick dark eyebrows, she had one of those slightly bulbous noses that made merry with her pale blue eyes, to project mischief and mayhem. In contrast, Sylvia, on his right, was thin, angular, her planed bones prominent in cheek and on wrist, dark brown eyes somnolent below her side-swept dark brown hair. She was drunk already, but in a closed-in, internalised, sombre manner, her fluted glass regularly lifted to wide wet lips. The third girl was equally sober, sipping goat's milk, her fair-fuzzed arms reflected in sandy lashes, virtually no eyebrows at all, and curly white-blonde hair. She wore a shirtwaister, split between her breasts, and falling off her thigh. As Eduard appraised them, and surprised himself in realising he was so doing, he knew that Ann was the dangerous one.

He glanced at Kathleen, and looked away immediately, for she in turn was clearly appraising him, her eyes glinting, her hand steady, as she drained another bottle of pils, without any obvious effect. The two women moved away from each other, as Rachel started fondling Akbar, and Sylvia snuggled up to Ali-Said. Neither man reacted.

Eduard looked again at their hosts: Akbar the courteous, Ali the contained and Abdullah the bonhomous master of them all, and he began to understand that this was a trial run, a test to see what was possible and what was not. At that point Abdullah threw him two keys.

'Take them for a drive – the desert is a free road.'

'What will you do?'

'Me? Us? We shall wait for you here. Go. Take the girls. Enjoy yourselves.'

The two women were now still, their veils back in place. Eduard spoke quietly to Kania and he got up and walked round to Rachel, disentangling her from Akbar, his arm around her waist as he steered her outside; Wladek moved behind Sylvia and helped her up. Ann was already halfway to the door, and Kathleen took Eduard's arm, as if to protect him.

The Cadillacs were hot, despite the netting that had been thrown over them, and the fact they were now parked beneath trees. Rachel and Sylvia climbed in with Kania between them, and Wladek took the wheel. Eduard helped Kathleen into the other car, and Ann pulled open the front door and slid along the bench seat, to make way for Eduard.

The two cars stood side by side, and perhaps more by accident than by design, they started simultaneously and moved off side by side, accelerating as they bit into the desert sand.

Once clear of the settlement, Eduard pulled the wheel over, to steer away from Wladek, but Wladek pulled his too, so that the cars described a joint curve. Eduard gunned the V8 and so did Wladek. Sand spurted, and as one, they started an automotive dance, imitating that of the two Arab dancers. The cars cavorted, and suddenly Eduard threw the wheel left then right, executing a zig and then a zag. Wladek crossed his path in a similar manoeuvre, and the drive developed into a competition to outspin and swerve and stream each other.

Kathleen lay across the rear seat, eyes closed, her feet and hands braced against the doors, quietly in control, and regularly emitting small, staccato comments: 'faster', 'tighter', 'closer', as Ann slid down the seat onto the floor, and reached up into Eduard's lap, and started to undo his trouser buttons. Eduard had his hands occupied with the wheel and an occasional gear change with the wheel-mounted stick; he felt utterly detached from this other game that was purposefully developing out of sight. 'Faster' and Ann moved with more urgency, both her hands fully occupied. 'Tighter' and Ann squeezed as she moved. 'Closer' and he felt her mouth close over him.

Wladek's car was describing wider and wider circles, pulling further and further away, as Eduard pushed his car onto a full lock, and glanced down. As he did so, Kathleen's arms came from behind and enfolded his head, and he could see nothing. She bit his ear and he cried out. Ann slid down into the footwell as he braked. The car slithered to a standstill, Kathleen toppled over the seat onto him, and Ann reached up again, but it was all too late. Their three faces collided, and they broke away, giggling.

234

There was a tap on the window, and Wladek was yanking open the door.

'We've got some netting. Let's catch some girls!' and he brandished a roll of mosquito netting, and pointed behind him, to where Rachel and Sylvia were loping off over the sand.

'Tally ho!' shouted Kania as he chased them with netting flaring out behind him.

'You've got ten seconds' start,' shouted Wladek, and he pushed Ann, who stumbled off, her words slurred as she yelled back, 'Spoilt a beautiful moment...'

Kathleen stood, leaning against the car.

'You go ahead. I'll wait here.'

Eduard was about to remonstrate, when he saw the compressed mouth and the knowing eyes.

'OK. I'll catch her, and then I'll be back,' holding his pants with one hand.

Wladek was gaining on Kania as Kania projected himself in a flying tackle, and smothered Sylvia with netting. They rolled together in a grey film and a cream cloud as Wladek caught Rachel.

Ann sat down suddenly, and Eduard fell over her with the momentum of his pursuit. He gently enfolded her in the netting, and bent down to kiss her. The response was smudged and less than satisfactory, so he sat up, pulled his trousers together, and refastened them. They sat, still and disconnected as Wladek rolled across the ground, his catch perforce rolling with him, and Kania's beside him, their shrieks and cries drifting into silence quickly in the desert air.

The sun was low, and the heat of the afternoon was evaporating as Eduard helped Ann back to the cars. Kathleen was behind the wheel. She moved over as they approached, and beckoned Ann beside her. They waited for the others, then slowly, sedately, retraced their tracks and pulled up outside the house. Abdullah was standing in the doorway as they left the cars, dusty and dishevelled.

'Some *arak* perhaps, to conclude a pleasant afternoon?'

Inside the women had laid out new platters, with soft cakes and plump fruit. Small glasses glistened, each filled with a satin draught.

As Abdullah bade them farewell outside the hut, the nurses once more safely ensconced in their hospital rooms, Eduard held out his hand.

'Thank you for your hospitality – and a happy afternoon.'

The Arab took his hand and pressed it lightly.

'Our homes are yours. Soon we finish the work and you will go. Then we will have a real party – in my home.' And he bowed slightly, turned, and climbed into the remaining Cadillac.

The window wound down, and he leant out towards Eduard.

'You have a war to attend but, before that, we will tickle the toes, no?' and with a laugh he was gone.

Strange interludes. Two years of captive tension and the boiling desire to escape, then freedom; captivity again, then a different freedom – or was the army simply another captivity? Yet, as soon as I left Russia, escape no longer the imperative, and preparation for war all around me, I found a different escape, in pleasures uninvited, unexpected and unlike anything in my life before then.

Today we would say it was hormones, that I was naturally inclined towards women, that I was bound to experience my first infatuation, even possibly love affair, and that a little lust hurt no man in the course of his development. But today we would also view my captivity with great seriousness and counsel, counselling for post-traumatic stress disorder – poor chap; he was torn from home, saw the most frightful things, you couldn't imagine – murder, and mayhem and horrors such as we cannot experience, sated as we are by tabloid exaggerati, televisual instamotics and cinematic phantasmagoria.

Fact was, I was but one of many, growing up the hard way, harder and faster, moving into and beyond adulthood in the helter-skelter of hands-on human conflict and all its accessories after the fact of war – brutality, displacement, separation, execution, transience and above all, violent changes of direction and truncations of time that allowed few moments for reflection, regeneration or regret. My 'disorder' was born of those times – a concentration of acts and images that would sate ambition and diminish expectation, pitching me into the pleasures of the moment.

Fact was, I was drawn to Sara by an aching need for affection, and she to me and that, plus propinquity and the opportunity it offered and our physical attraction, combined to produce a wholly natural love and liaison.

Fact was, I was drawn to Audrey by something more distant and appealing, a ragged glimpse, a vestige of normality that would somehow return me to life and life to me, but that is another story for another day.

Fact was, I was drawn to Ann by sex, Kathleen by ambiguity and the veiled ladies of the oasis by mystery.

Fact is, only now do I have the time for reflection, it is too late for regeneration and my condition precludes regret, for that would destroy what is left within me – hope.

Strange interludes indeed. And that is all they were at the time – interludes between the train to Tara, the boat from Omsk, the journey to Samarkand and the trauma of Tashkent, and what was to follow.

I was an ordinary man stepping insignificantly across the stages of a drama which swept millions back and forth, when the grand vizier suddenly appeared and rubbed his magic lamp and showed me a world of wizardry to prepare me for the trials of tomorrow.

At the end of the second week, the van arrived, laden with dinars, and the workmen shuffled along to collect their dues, Abdullah their paymaster, Ali-Said his protector. When the last man wheeled away, Abdullah closed his ledger, folded the canvas carry-alls, and rose from the pay-bench. Eduard and Wladek pushed it against the hut wall.

As Ali-Said fetched the Cadillac, Abdullah approached them both.

'I wish you to see my finest shop, and then we go to Akbar.'

The car appeared round the corner, and whispered to a halt; Eduard noticed that it was once more gleaming, dustless, and immaculate.

'What about Kania?'

Abdullah grimaced.

'Your friend, he is perhaps singular; he prefers his own company. I lent him my car. He has gone to the river.'

Eduard and Wladek exchanged sighs of exasperation. In two short weeks they had indeed discovered Kania's propensity for 'singularity' – he was a lonely man who made clear his desire to remain alone. As much as they endeavoured to probe his persona, they could discover little, beyond his home town of Gdansk, his vocation and training as a teacher and his subject – mathematics. He was unremarkable of visage, stature or presentation. Indeed, he was one of those whose features cannot be recalled, whose expression is negative, and whose very voice lacks colour. Whenever Eduard thought about him he was at a loss to conjure more than a dark shadow of the man. Perhaps it was because there were no 'connections' – no family, no wife or son or daughter to discuss.

Kania was like a piece of dirty paper, tossed about by the circumstance of war, with nothing written on his presence. Thus, they left him alone, except when he chose to join them. Sometimes Eduard felt an urge, whether of guilt or curiosity he could not tell, to press the man, to demand something of him, even to pressure him to admit to pain, or hunger or agonies of mind, anything, to explain his separateness and detachment. But he always drew back when it came to the point, out of another guilt – that of interference with another's mental freedom.

They climbed into the car and moved smoothly away from the camp, towards Khanaqin. The shop was on the other side of town, this time no concrete single-storey structure thrown up in haste for speedy profit. They drew alongside a continuous wall, which stretched for 100 feet between ancient tiled houses. Behind the wall was a paved courtyard before an arcaded walk, slender pillars beneath rich rusty tiles. Behind the arcade were dark archways, sunlight angled across their thresholds, striking sparks of colour from the rugs of Turkistan. White-robed servants swept the walkway, and sprinkled water on the rugs. Inside, pillars supported the dark, longitudinal beams, and censers swayed beneath them, drifts of aromatic smoke suspended below the ceiling.

Wisps of woodwind music strayed across the chambers of silk and coloured cottons, handmade shirts and handsome boots; cascades of silver bracelets tangled with spun copper bangles; gold ewers stood sentinel among pale porcelain dishes. Attendants stood, arms folded, or sensuously stroking a fabric, dangling a bangle or draping soft satin about the shoulders of a quiet customer. Eduard was astounded by the contrast with the souk of Samarkand, by the absence of persuasion and the presence of price without need. Wladek was riveted by the sheer splendour of it all, and could not resist darting from one display to another, feeling, fondling, fantasising.

'How much is that?' he asked, pointing at a slim gold band. The assistant lifted it gently, and immediately the band broke into a filigree of fragmented links, as he wound it onto Wladek's wrist. Abdullah had silently arrived beside the awe-struck Pole.

'You like the bracelet?'

Wladek touched it on his wrist.

'It's beautiful.'

'It's yours.'

Wladek had no words; he simply reached out and took the Arab's hand, and the Arab smiled, patted him, and turned to Eduard.

'And what do you see, my friend?'

Eduard spread his arms wide, and pirouetted. His arms dropped to his sides, and he smiled at Abdullah.

'I see an Aladdin's cave – it is enough to admire; I have no need of gold or silk where I'm going.'

Abdullah examined him, placed his hands on his shoulders and said, 'You are an honest young man and I shall give you something too.'

He turned, and walked slowly between his displays, lifting this, touching that, discarding all, until he came at last to a small table. In the centre was a sundial, and to left and right small, exquisitely traced clock faces made up of fine gold filigree on porcelain, with jewelled hands, all within a gold orb. He lifted one, and showed it to Eduard.

'Is that not beautiful? Is not the time worthy of the craftsman?'

Eduard nodded, and thought of his father's watch. Abdullah looked closely at him for a moment, his eyes opaque, then sighed, replaced the clock, and reached out behind it. His hand closed on a small leather purse, with tasselled drawstring.

He held it in the palm of one hand and regarded Eduard.

'I think this is what you want.'

He pulled the drawstrings apart, spread the purse, and delved inside. As his fingers emerged, Eduard saw they were holding a slim, silver disc. Abdullah inserted a fingernail into the rim of the orb and it split. He held it out on his hand, a silver watch, 'For the pocket of a Pole.'

The tears slowly fell down Eduard's cheeks as he took the gift. Abdullah put his arm about him.

'There is no need for words. I trust you. I am not a man who trusts his fellows, but I trust you. May the watch always tell your time.'

He moved away, and out of the shop, and they followed.

'Let us go now to Akbar.'

Akbar's farm was near the river. It was not so much a farm as a continuous orchard – groves of fruit trees set in grassland, alongside the river. The road skirted the orchards for two miles, and Eduard counted fifteen sandalled workers, their keffiyeh corded on their heads, kaftans loose and billowing in the light breeze. Only Akbar wore a sash around his waist and he appeared grave as they pulled up.

After customary greetings, he led them to his storage compound and into a tall, dark building, where crates and boxes lined the walls, and more men toiled at packing fruits. At the end of the shed, there was a partition, and behind the partition, a simple office. Before the table that served as a desk, there was a makeshift trestle, and on the trestle, a bundle of stained white rags.

Akbar whispered to his brother and, their hands in prayer, they approached Eduard. Abdullah spoke first.

'A dreadful accident. I am so sorry.' He indicated the rags, and Akbar gently rolled them down, to reveal the face of Kania, eyes closed, bloodless, leached and grey.

Eduard asked, 'What happened?'

'He was swimming; the currents are dangerous; one minute safe, and then, well, who knows.'

Abdullah spread his hands, palms uppermost. 'It is the will of Allah.'

'The will of Allah,' murmured Akbar, and both men stood, heads bowed.

Wladek and Eduard carried the dead man out to the car, and laid him across the back seat. Akbar held the door open as they climbed into the front beside Abdullah.

'I offer my regrets that my land brings you sorrow,' and he bowed deeply as they pulled away.

Kania's death subdued the two soldiers as they went about the business of the final week. Neither Eduard nor Wladek was personally touched by his death, for he had made no contract of comradeship with either of them but, as they sat together in the cool of the evening, they talked about his loss as another price of war, another countryman gone, another Polish family somewhere at a further loss. As mourning becomes those most affected and does not befit the casual comrade, so Eduard and Wladek sloughed off their depression day by day, until Kania became a small memory, and their spirits lifted as the day of departure approached.

Two days before that, Abdullah rolled up to the hut to arrange the final pay-out, and to issue his promised invitation.

'My brothers and I would be honoured if you would come to our home.' He paused and added, 'Alone – just you and your friend Mister Wladek.'

There was a specificity to the invitation that Eduard could not for a moment fathom. Then he realised – no women; there were to be no women, at least none of the nurses. Perhaps this meant there would be hourglass houris dancing the dances of the seven veils for their delectation, and then again, perhaps not. The invitation was strangely formal, almost a deckle-edged, embossed invitation, until Abdullah suddenly smiled and said, 'We shall tickle the toes, no?'

He declined Eduard's offer of refreshment, even though they had been careful to stock cans of American cola and fresh goat's milk in their thrumming refrigerator.

'No, but I thank you both. Tonight at seven?'

They dressed with some care, for Wladek had been unable to resist Abdullah's splendid emporium, and had invested his wages in a short silk shirt, incongruous over his Army trousers, Italian shoes, and a voluptuous belt, in which were embedded nuggets of silver. Eduard had acquired a cotton kaftan, which he wore over shirt and shorts, and supple leather sandals. He kept the watch in one pocket, and his knife in the other.

Just before seven, a vehicle drew up outside, as they splashed Abdullah's lotions on their newly shaved cheeks. Eduard glanced up as he fastened his sandals, to see, not the Cadillacs, but a long-wheelbase jeep, with a covered-wagon top in camouflage rig. Ali-Said was at the wheel.

They clambered on board, to find the compartment behind the driver laid with rugs and hung with silks, two veiled women cross-legged with shallow trays before them containing the ubiquitous sweetmeats. They sat with their backs to the vehicle's flanks, as the journey began, and every so often one of the women would lean forward and proffer a tray, or pour a long, cool drink of crushed fruits into hollowed gourds.

Ali-Said accelerated as they settled back, and announced over his shoulder that, 'Our home is in the desert, at the oasis of Hab'id Said,' and added, 'about fifteen miles.' They could see nothing of his face, for he was wearing a keffiyeh checked black and white as the bedou do, and his arms were swathed in the folds of a dark blue jellabah.

After some twenty minutes, he slowed, and announced, 'We are nearly there,' and shut off the engine. 'It is better to walk the last few yards.'

They jumped out, and the women glided away. Ali-Said pointed and Eduard gasped.

Before them, framed between palms from a picture book, stood the brothers' home. The gateway was carved out of a high cream-washed wall, punctuated at intervals with slender pinnacles, each topped by a clove of stone. The gateway itself was curved as the blades of two scimitars, the heavy oaken gates swung wide, the shadows of wall, masts and arch thrown in elongated relief onto the desert floor by the flaring lights from a score of fires on poles behind.

As they moved under the soaring arch, they were confronted with the sloping walls of a small citadel, a soaring block of brick and clay pierced by myriad pencilled slits of light, where lanterns glowed through their embrasures. An identical archway beckoned them into a courtyard, round which the building lay, arcaded with slender pillars surmounted by delicate capitals, the cloister patterned with curving rays of mosaic, which reached across the courtyard itself to form a swirling sun of ochre against a ground of peacock blues, azures and cobalts, torn across with flaring orange flames in tesserae, centred on a shallow bowl of water, with a central fountain, the water slipping up and down, two quiet columns effervescing as they alternated, refracting the light from lanterns suspended from wires, beneath elegant turrets.

Beyond the courtyard was a third and identical archway, beyond which they found themselves in a half-moon terrace, with a central obelisk of wrought iron tracery, through which climbed and intertwined exotic flowers – and simple, creamy roses.

Curving round the terrace was a continuous stone bench, with carved rosewood arms at intervals, between which were scattered cushions – round, square, oblong and diamond in shape, in creamy silks and flaming satins.

Abdullah and Akbar came forward as Ali-Said removed his keffiyeh, slinging it to one side, and led Eduard and Wladek forward. They were all dressed identically, in loose jellabah and sandals, each with a sea-blue sash around his waist.

'Welcome to our humble home.'

'Welcome.'

'Welcome.'

Abdullah guided them to the bench and the brothers joined them, one on either side, Abdullah in the middle. As if at a signal, through the archway poured two, four, six, ten women, unveiled, their bellies bare, wisps of cloth trailing as they danced, and as they did so, the women from the jeep served glasses of *arak*. The men sipped their *arak* and the ladies of the night danced, for Eduard was sure these were not ladies of virtue.

The women swayed and gyrated, dipped and rose, touched and parted, until they formed two groups of four, languidly circling on either side of the obelisk, as the remaining two joined hands, then mouths, and moved in unison, their hands tracing patterns on each other's backs, plucking the flimsy fabric, until each unwound the other, and they turned and turned, revealing first a small, taut breast, then another, and another and another.

They circled, and the other women sank to the floor, resting in artless pose, caressing one another as the two principals slowly pulled the tassels on their hips, and revolved, the gossamers of their privacies slowly unwound until they were fused as one, unadorned save for the glass jewels in their hair. Legs intertwined, they stood, swaying, each undoing the other's headdress, the glass baubles dropping to the tiled floor, one splintering, another splashed into a thousand fragments, until their massed, black tresses engulfed them, and they were, once more, masked and hidden.

Abdullah clapped once, and the women left, gliding across the terrace without a glance at the brothers or their guests.

'French,' said Abdullah.

'French?' asked Eduard.

'Yes, French – all of them. We have local girls, but they are, er – unclean. I would be ashamed for you to see them thus. These are French ladies who entertain our society – from Baghdad. They are ladies who are quite careful where they go, who they see, and what they do, if you understand,' and he smiled conspiratorially.

Eduard took another sip of *arak*.

'You would like to meet one, some?'

Eduard shook his head.

'No, no thanks. They were terrific. Let's leave it at that.'

Abdullah laughed.

'Do they not tickle your toes then?'

He clapped again, and the veiled women brought fresh cloths and glass bowls of limpid water, with petals floating on the surface. They washed. Then the food appeared – heaped platters of rice and saffron, dishes of steaming lamb in a rich ragout, fat round goat's cheeses and flat, dry breads, piled-high olives of every hue from black satin through dusky purple to soft green, mixed with wrinkled red peppers and sprinkled with cardamom seeds. Cold pils in frosted glasses, short fat tumblers with scotch incognito, and pitchers of viscous yellow fruit juice encouraged appetite and cleansed the palate. Sweet cakes and tumbling fruits accompanied more *arak*, until Eduard felt light-headed and detached from all his realities. Wladek leant across Ali-Said and tapped Abdullah.

'I'd like a Frenchie.'

'You shall, you shall,' beamed their host and clapped again. One of the women approached and Abdullah pointed at Wladek, made a simple sign with finger and circled thumb, and nodded. The woman helped Wladek to his feet, and guided him towards a door set in the terrace wall, gently pushed him through, and closed it quietly, returning to serve the brothers and their remaining guest.

'Music!' cried Abdullah, and Akbar rose. Ali-Said followed him out of the terrace and minutes later they returned, one pushing, the other pulling a cream and black bakelite cabinet on castors, with a rounded lid, gold dial and numerous knobs protruding from its convex belly.

'My radiogram,' explained their host, as he twiddled with the knobs. A blast of static cut the air, then a drone, a buzz, and suddenly Astaire's 'Night and Day' rent the terrace, followed by the Inkspots harmonising 'I'd climb the highest mountain'. When Jeannette MacDonald started to croon 'Dream Lover' Abdullah jigged towards Eduard and bowed low.

'May I have this dance?' he asked, giggled, grabbed Eduard's waist and started to waltz around the terrace.

Eduard was drunk. His head ached slightly, his eyes were moving in and out of focus, his heart was pounding and he was sweating. Now he found himself in the arms of a sex-crazed Ay-rab, and he started to struggle.

'No! No!' cried Abdullah, 'I don't want you – I have four wives,' spinning Eduard round twice, 'and anyway, I never did like little boys,' giving him a smart shove that sent him reeling, then catching his hand and hauling him in like a fish on a fly-rod. 'I love to do the dancing – it's what tickles *my* toes!' and he span Eduard round thrice, let him go and, as Eduard staggered against the cushions tumbling onto the floor, Abdullah caught him up again, hugged him, and then gently set him down.

'There. A little more *arak*, I think, to help you on your way,' and Akbar reached across and poured a small glass, which Ali-Said held as they trickled the sweet liquid down Eduard's unprotesting throat.

Eduard remembered nothing of the drive back, but woke the next, last morning with a sense of wellbeing, no aches or pains, and a clear head. Wladek was already awake, setting out the pay-bench for the final pay-off.

'You were pissed as an owl,' he remarked. Eduard grinned and poked his friend in the groin.

'And you were randy as hell. Did you get your end away? Of course you did. Hope she was nice.'

Wladek squinted at him: 'And you, didn't you?' He did not wait for an answer, for the van appeared at that moment and for the next hour it was dinars and goodbyes as the reduced workforce dwindled away.

Back in the hut, Akbar had arranged two boxes of fruit and a crate of pils – 'for your journeys' – and shook their hands. As he retreated, Ali-Said bowed to each of them, then reached down into his soft leather boots, withdrawing in each hand a curved blade surmounted by a gold-chased hilt.

'To arm you well for the wars to come,' and he too bade them farewell.

As the two brothers climbed into their car, Abdullah spoke quietly to Wladek, then turned to Eduard.

'I should like to see you one more time. I have the car here.'

He seemed to make a decision, straightened and said, 'If you will excuse us, sir,' to Wladek, who nodded and sidled out of the room.

'My friend, come with me. I wish to take you to my wives.'

As Eduard and Wladek bounced in the jeep across the desert on the first stage of the journey to Palestine, Eduard thought back on that final visit to Abdullah's desert home. Strangely silent in the daylight, the fountains stilled, the lanterns out, the shadows shorter, the house was still the caliphate of Khanaqin. Abdullah had led the way across the courtyard, into the terrace, and through a doorway into a curious chamber – panelled with intricately pierced rosewood, protected from the harsh sun by shuttered windows and strewn with cushions, it was a simple room, with plain polished wooden floor, and a single, central table of red mahogany.

Eduard heard the click-clack of clogs as four ladies entered, veils draped across their faces, so that Eduard could discern their features, yet respect their privacy. Abdullah introduced him to each in turn, leaving until the last the youngest.

'And this is Shirah.'

Eduard bowed, placed his fingers together, bowed again.

'M'sieu,' she whispered.

Abdullah smiled, poured two glasses of *arak*, raised his to Eduard's and said, 'A toast – to your future, to your war, and to your peace. I am proud to have known you and glad to have been of service.'

Eduard raised his glass, and because he could think of nothing else to say, said, 'Thank you,' drained it dry and then added, 'And tickle your toes!'

It was time to leave, time to move on, time to go – just as it would be when the gold was stowed and they slipped away from England, Warsaw bound.

WAR III: 1943–1944

OFFICIAL SECRETS

The road to Damascus was long, weary and hot. It was also strangely uneventful. For much of the time, the jeep was accompanied by erratic, attenuated trails of trucks in convoy, transferring materiel and occasional stragglers like Eduard and Wladek, from Khanaqin and Baghdad. When they overtook a convoy and were alone, the sand and basalt rocks, pitted and pocked, achieved a monotony that left them lightly dazed and silent, each wrapt within his own thoughts of the war to which they journeyed.

After Stalin had released his Polish prisoners, the 3rd Carpathian Division was formed, its core in Palestine, to become part of the British Eighth Army for Italy, while the Polish Home Army looked to London for support, intelligence and the signal to move against the Boche from within. Eduard little thought, as he nursed an increasingly sore backside, bumping over the ridged and rutted tracks, that he would become part of both those armies.

In Damascus, their stay was brief and, as Wladek wryly observed, 'You weren't converted on the way, then.'

Eduard grimaced, saving his riposte for when they crossed the Jordan, breaking out into a poor parody of the negro spirituals he remembered from the pre-war wireless, adding his own stanza:

'Oh my Lord, the river is cross –

What a way to live.

Simple soldiers, at a loss;

Why we goin' to Tel-Aviv?'

'Why indeed,' mumbled Wladek, irritably tugging at his makeshift topee, jammed down over a torn handkerchief. 'God, it's hot.'

Rechovot was just inland of the city, another transit camp, hutted on the edge of the settlement, on the rim of the desert. One of the huts was the wireless station, equipped with British transmitters, and that was where Eduard and Wladek found themselves the next morning, standing to attention before a young, pink subaltern, immaculate in khaki drills, impeccably ironed shorts, gleaming brogues, Sam Browne and glistening brass, a willowy sapling with a nonchalant manner, and a light, blond moustache perched temporarily upon his otherwise downy lip.

'Chumley-Da'npor' – IC signals. You'll report to me daily, eight ayem. Practice for the real thing. Need to know your codes, language, that sort of thing.'

He paused, looked down at his papers, then glanced back at them both.

'Oh, at ease, men.'

Wladek glanced surreptitiously at Eduard, but Eduard was staring straight ahead.

'Question, sir.'

Cholmondeley-Davenport looked up at Eduard.

'Yes, Corporal?'

'What's the real thing – sir?'

'The real thing? War, man, war. You'll see soon enough, when you've got some service in.'

'Question, sir.'

'Well, what is it this time, Corporal?'

'Does that mean fighting, killing people?'

'Of course it does. What d'you think war's all about, for God's sake?'

'Sir.'

Eduard paused, looked down at his hands, then leant forward, placed them squarely on the officer's table, and looked up into the other man's eyes.

'Question, sir,' and he did not wait for approval before he went on to ask, 'Have you killed anyone – sir? I mean, fought them close up, stuck a knife in their belly, shot them in the face, thrown a grenade and watched them spill out, their guts hanging one way and their limbs torn off and their eyes weeping blood? Have you – sir?'

He leant back on his heels, his eyes on the Lieutenant. Cholmondeley-Davenport, to his credit, glared back, his mouth clamped closed, his hands still.

'As a matter of fact, no. I haven't. But I will.'

He looked briefly at Wladek, then back at Eduard.

'Have you?'

'Perhaps I have, sir, perhaps I have.' Eduard pulled himself to attention. 'Permission to leave, sir.'

'Dismiss. Oh, and Corporal.'

'Yes, sir?'

'I hope we're not going to have any trouble, are we?'

'Sir? No, sir. No trouble.'

Back in their hut, Wladek could not stop laughing.

'God, you told him. I wish I could see his face now. He must be wild. My God, you told him.'

Eduard shrugged.

'He annoyed me, that's all. Poor bastard's going to find out the hard way. Just hope he's not my CO when it happens.'

Wladek busied himself with arranging his sparse kit, then turned and said, 'Have you killed anyone, Eduard? I mean, fought?'

'Yes, I have, but I don't want to talk about it.'

'But you haven't been out there fighting, I mean, in battle or anything, have you?'

'There's other wars, other fighting.'

246

Eduard swung his legs over the bunk, and brushed down his tunic.
'Change of subject. Let's find something to eat.'

'And drink.'

'Yeah, and drink. Good idea. I'm parched.'

With boring British efficiency, Rechovot boasted a NAAFI with solid staples – anaemic baked beans floating in sickly red sauce, brittle bacon more fat than meat, bloated sausages, evisceral pink within cremated skins, and pallid powdered eggs, scrambled in a pool of piss-pale water, all served with glutinous slices of soggy bread, and accompanied by a range of Blighty booze – Vimto, Tizer or fizzy lemonade and, if you were lucky, genuine stone-bottled ginger beer. Dessert ranged from imitation cream eclairs that stuck halfway down the throat, to thin custard-laced pastry turnovers – London stock brick colour. And there were Eccles cakes, sticky, sprinkled with chewy raisins and as dry as the desert sand. There was no alcohol except a pallid beer masquerading as English mild and bitter, which simulated an uneasy coalition of vinegar, warm tap water and syrup of figs.

After one such meal, Wladek and Eduard determined to find an alternative, and enquired after transport to Tel-Aviv. A friendly SP offered them a lift the next evening, and left them outside a crumbling concrete Bar-Taban, 'Englitch spoke', where they descended a short flight of broken steps to find themselves in a dusty subterranean chamber with a makeshift bar comprising a table raised on several bricks. Behind, a heavily moustached, pockmarked Arab lounged, sipping from a tall, chipped glass.

The room was furnished with upended crates and metal stools, at several of which sat groups of similarly hirsute citizens, also sipping from tall glasses. Smoke hung heavily along the ceiling, absorbing most of the sparse light from a series of low-wattage bulbs. There were no women.

Wladek identified an empty 'table' and sat, while Eduard approached the man behind the bar.

'Have you any beer?'

The man looked at him without comment, reached under the 'bar' and produced two more chipped glasses. He swung round to the shelf behind, and hauled down a jug of sticky red liquid, which he poured into the glasses, pushing them across the 'bar', without comment.

Eduard pulled a selection of coins out of his pocket and spread them on the seamed surface. The Arab gathered them up, contemplated them, put two back down again, and pocketed the rest. As Eduard collected the glasses, he pushed the jug towards him.

'Friendly lot,' observed Wladek.

'Perhaps they don't speak "Englitch" after all.'

'Perhaps they don't.'

The drink was cool, sweet and plainly high octane for, after two glasses, Eduard felt his eyes unfocus, his head dissolve, and his hands tremble.

'Powerful shtuff.'

Wladek nodded and smiled stupidly as he poured himself a third.

'Certainly ish.'

When they finished the jug, the 'barman' walked slowly over, looked carefully at them both, took the jug, and then returned with it, refilled. Eduard put his hand in his pocket, but the man stayed him, a cool brown hand on his sleeve.

'Not necessary, my friend. Just drink up. Enjoy yourselves.'

The evening gradually dissolved into a warm haze, people moving in and out of focus, nobody troubling them, until at last they finished the final jug, and Eduard stood, or rather, he tried to stand and failing, toppled over onto the dirt floor, where Wladek was already asleep.

The rippling racket of a pace-stick dragged across the tongued and grooved boards of a desert-dried hut wall is not a pleasing manner in which to start the day in the ordinary way. Given a head the size of a Tashkent melon, gritty teeth, torpid tongue within a mouth incapable of movement, and a hand sufficiently tremulous to suggest a permanent palsy, such a reveille sounds like an act of outright hostility. Wladek moaned and Eduard tried to breathe, momentarily believing he was in danger of oxygen starvation. An hour later, they reported to the wireless hut.

'Late, Corporal. You're late.'

'Sir. Sorry, sir.'

'Why are you late?'

'Not well, sir. Not at all well.'

'And you Wladek? Are you unwell too?'

'Sir, yes sir.'

'Very well. In that case, you had better concentrate on your codes.'

He shoved a folder across the desk, and Eduard listlessly picked it up, and then promptly dropped it.

'For God's sake man. Never had a hangover before?'

Eduard regarded his superior officer blearily. So the damned man had a heart after all, and obviously some experience, for now he was grinning.

'May not have fought, Corporal, but I know a bloody hangover when I see one. Had a few of those in my time. Hah!'

The officer bent and picked up the folder.

'Right. Well you lot are absolutely no use today, obviously. Back to your billet, and report at two pee-em sharp. Understood?'

'Yessir.'

'And Corporal.'

'Sir?'

'I suggest plenty of water and some bicarb of soda. See the MO. Say I sent you.'

'Bumly-Chumly's not very pleased,' observed Wladek.

'Too bad. His class is a waste of time anyway. We all know that stuff.'

Wladek contemplated his friend.

'Your trouble is you're bored.'

'My trouble is that I don't like wasting time. This isn't war, not what we came for – is it?'

Wladek spread wide his hands.

'Eduard: you take it as it comes. I keep on telling you, war'll be with us soon enough.'

'Well, it can't be soon enough for me. Wasted enough time as it is.'

'Like last night for instance?'

'Don't remind me.'

Eduard rummaged in his pockets.

'Oh shit! They took all my change, *and* my wallet.'

He fingered the silver watch.

'But they didn't take this.'

Wladek waved his wrist about, the bracelet jangling.

'Nor this either. Wonder why?'

'It's written there – that's why.'

Wladek looked at the short inscription on the back of Abdullah's gift.

'I thought it was some Ay-rab trademark.'

'It says "The gift of God", like mine.'

Eduard slipped the watch off his wrist, turned it over and showed Wladek the identical, scrupulously scripted, tiny Arabic letters, then said again, 'The gift of God, not Abdullah.'

The Medical Officer was an NCO from the RAMC, unexpectedly detached from active duty after an arduous spell in Libya, with an acting commission. He was permanently bemused, trying to adjust to his superior status as the only expert in Rechovot on everything from crabs to dislocated thumbs, non-specific urethritis to desert colds. Most of his charges suffered, some from the unremitting, dry heat, some from the debilitating diet, and a few from accidental damage. Hangovers were 'a piece of cake, Corp'ral. Drink plenty of water and take these antacid tablets before eating.' He felt expansive towards these junior suppliants.

'What's that rash, man?'

Eduard fingered his throat.

'Oh, nothing. It's a shaving rash, sir.'

'Shaving rash? Indeed, indeed. The water's very hard. Not very hot either.'

Eduard nodded his agreement, and turned to go.

'Here. Use this ointment.' He pushed across a small pot. 'And you may as well be excused shaving too.'

He scribbled a note, and flicked it across the table. Eduard picked it up and glanced at it.

'But beards, sir. They're against King's Regulations.'

'So they are, so they are. Never mind. That'll cover you. Off you go.'

Within a week Eduard's beard had sprouted, unevenly, strong on the throat if weak on the chin, while his moustache was a never-ending cause for comment by his friend.

'Looks like a woman's eyebrow to me, all soft and plucked.'

Cholmondeley-Davenport was unimpressed.

'What's wrong with your face, Corporal?'

'Shaving rash, sir.'

'Doesn't suit you.'

'No, sir.'

'Shave it off then.'

'MO says let it grow, sir.'

'Ah. I see. Well, I'll have a word about that.'

The second week, Eduard made up his mind.

'You want a transfer?'

'Yes, sir.'

'But you haven't finished your training, acclimatisation exercises etcetera.'

'No, sir, but I would appreciate a transfer to an active unit, sir.'

'Well, we'll have to see about that.'

In the wireless hut, Eduard pulled the earphones off and flung them down with disgust, pushing the transmitter away. Thirty-six men were sitting at the tables variously tapping, tuning, scribbling or just daydreaming. The afternoon sun scythed through the ceiling, where two fans sluggishly revolved, stirring the still air, but creating little breeze, some dust and no reduction in temperature. Eduard nudged Wladek.

'Got any cards?'

'Yeah.'

'Come on then, let's set up a school of brag.'

Within ten minutes, four wireless operators were huddled together at the end of the hut, two of them smoking Park Royals, when in strode Cholmondeley-Davenport. Eduard scuffled the cards under his keypad, Wladek pushed his chair sideways, and the other two players made their ways back to their stations.

'Corporal!'

Eduard looked back at the officer.

'Come with me.'

Outside, the lieutenant walked a few paces away from the hut, then wheeled, and glared at Eduard.

'I'm going to have to report you, Corporal.'

'What for, sir?'

'What for? You know damn well what for. You get drunk, you're always late, you complain about your training, you won't take no for an answer, and you don't shave. Now I find you running a school of cards on duty. You're a disruptive influence, a downright nuisance and a disgrace to the uniform.'

Eduard said nothing.

'Right. Well man, get on with it, get back in there, and get to work.'

Jerzy Kostka was a reasonable man. He had had a hard war, in the camps, and briefly with the Russians, before he was wounded, then seconded to Rechovot to oversee the training and transit of the 3rd Division.

Ranked as a full Colonel, his only wish was to return to the war, to the front line, but in Europe, against the Hun. Until this happened, he saw it as his duty to facilitate the return of others, that they might fight where he might not. He wanted men to be fit and professional; he wanted his countrymen to honour their past and secure their future. He wanted men like Eduard, hardened, capable and properly trained. He did not want failures, and he did not welcome fractured relations between his charges and their mentors.

He rested his aching leg on the footstool concealed behind the courtesy panel of his desk, and shifted his shrapnel-stippled back against the soft cushion of his swivelling chair, adjusted the glass of water on his desk, and for the third time, read the British subaltern's memorandum of complaint against Eduard Cjaikowski, Corporal, Signals, flipping the sheet over to remind himself of the soldier's other past.

Captured at fourteen, escaped, recaptured, released, recaptured, escaped, adept at signals, with an apparently natural gift for electronics, several languages, and an aptitude for command, ability to work with a team, coolness under pressure, and a certain innocence. Ideal. Now there were signs of rebellion, discontent, and a second request for transfer. Perhaps the man was ready, but he had not been passed ready.

What a weary war this was, when able enthusiasts had to suffer tedious training – and protracted convalescence. He leant forward and pressed the buzzer. The door opened and his ADC looked in.

'Bring Cjaikowksi.'

Eduard stood to attention, staring past the man at the desk.

'At ease, Corporal.'

Kostka recognised him. That day when the lines came down. He had scaled the latticed mast and single-handedly secured the right cables, without any supervision. It had not seemed out of the ordinary at the time, but now the Colonel realised it must have been the first such call on this young man's talents. And he had not failed. Ideal.

'Well Eduard – you don't mind if I call you Eduard?'

'No, sir.'

'Good. Well, my officer tells me you have been mucking about a bit – I think that's what the English call it?' and he smiled encouragingly at Eduard.

'I believe they do sir. We were playing cards.'

'Did you win?'

'Too early to say, sir, but yes, I think we were winning.'

'So I should think. Got to show these Anglos what we're made of.'

Kostka shifted his rump again, and raised his glass, sipping slowly.

'What's going on, Eduard?'

He did not wait for an answer but continued.

'You play cards, you don't shave – yes, I know the MO gave you permission, but that's hardly the point – you get drunk, you're always late, and you hardly ever complete the tasks you're set. That's not like you, not according to your record, anyway.'

'No, sir.'

'Well?'

Eduard clamped his lips and resisted the temptation to shrug. Kostka pushed against the desk, and arched his back to relieve the ache, then stroked his face. He tapped the file.

'You asked for a transfer.'

'Sir.'

'Why?'

'Because I'm fed up, sir.'

'We're all fed up, Corporal. We're all fed up with waiting. But that's war. Most of it's waiting, then there's the burning hell of battle. Then we're waiting again – or dead.'

He rose, pushed the chair back, walked round the desk, and stood in front of Eduard. He put a hand on his shoulder.

'You're a good soldier, and an able man. But you have to wait. You're too valuable to be wasted in the wrong place. Finish your training. Then you can really make a contribution.'

Eduard held the officer's gaze.

'Sir. I am not learning anything. I'm bored. Please. I need a transfer.'

The Colonel dropped his hand, looked down and shook his head sadly, returning to his seat.

'Eduard, I have to reprimand you, because you were neglecting your duties, and this was in front of an officer. I have no choice. And you have no choice. You have to do this for as long as it is deemed to be necessary. It's what the Army's about – doing what you are told, even if you don't understand it.'

He opened a drawer, dropped the file into it, and looked up at Eduard.

'Try to understand, because if you do it again, or anything like it, you'll be on a charge. You have a reputation now – someone who doesn't like authority. That could stop you ever going to war. Look at it this way – it's just one more challenge. Then I promise you, you will go to war. OK? Dismiss.'

Eduard tried. He went to the wireless hut and went through the motions. He resisted Wladek's blandishments to return to the Bar-Taban. He contrived to be on time, every time. The only concession he refused to make was the beard. He calculated that to shave would be to admit ultimate defeat. The beard was his signal to the subaltern: 'I'm independent. I have a right. I'll play your game but I will not give in.' If that meant jankers, so be it.

In the heat of the early afternoon, after what passed for lunch, the wireless operators were allowed an hour of freedom, to rest, play cards, read, listen to the BBC if they could tune in to the overseas broadcasts. Eduard and Wladek were playing patience when the door banged open and in marched the Colonel's orderly.

'Corporal. Colonel Kostka wants you. In his office. Now.'

Eduard buttoned his tunic, pulled on his forage cap, and scuffed his boots against his trouser legs, following the Lance Corporal out of the hut, and into the waiting jeep. Two minutes later they slid to a halt outside the command building.

'Wait here, please.'

The orderly disappeared into the Colonel's office, and Eduard stood, waiting. A moment later the Lance Corporal emerged.

'He'll see you now,' gesturing towards the half open door.

Eduard marched across the outer office, knocked, waited, heard nothing, so pushed the door, and marched inside.

'Close the door, please.'

Reflexively, he turned to close the door, and then, for the first time, realised he was alone, not with the Colonel, but with a stranger, in civvies, sitting in the Colonel's chair.

'Sit down, please.'

The man opposite him was clean-shaven, hatless, dressed quietly in a pale blue shirt with a dark blue tie striped in maroon. His jacket was draped across the back of the Colonel's chair, and his hands were loosely clasped and resting on the desk. There was a heavy signet ring on one finger.

The man's hair was parted on one side, an ambiguous dark blond, almost but not quite brown in colour; his eyes were pale and steady, cheeks lightly tanned, with a slight flush along the bones, features calm and friendly but otherwise expressionless. The only distinctive feature that Eduard noticed was that one ear was lobeless. Otherwise this man was impossible to read.

'My name's Teichmann. Lieutenant Teichmann. I am an English liaison officer. Would you like some wine?'

'Thank you, yes.'

Teichmann bent to one side, and lifted a bottle and two glasses onto the table. He produced a corkscrew, and handed that and the bottle to Eduard. Eduard implemented the unspoken order and handed them back.

'Thank you.'

Teichmann poured two equal measures, and pushed one towards Eduard, raising his to eye level.

'Cheers.'

'Prost,' responded Eduard and Teichmann smiled.

'The name is Dutch, not German. My ancestors came over to England in the seventeenth century. We never saw the need to anglicise the name.'

He sniffed the wine appreciatively and drank some more.

'Quite a good claret – useful in these warm afternoons. Room temperature of course.' Then he laughed. 'You are wondering what all this is about. Well, let me explain.'

He put down the wine glass and folded his hands once more.

'Your CO tells me you are disobedient, not too keen on authority, good at languages, find signals a bit of a bore and anxious to get on with the war.' He paused. 'Am I right?'

Eduard: 'Yes,' vehemently.

'I am a sort of a scout. Looking for special people. For special tasks.'

'What kind of tasks?'

'Well, if you pass the tests, when you're fully trained – oh yes, more training, I'm afraid – when you're fully trained, it'll be underground.'

'Underground?'

'France, Poland, Germany, anywhere.'

'Fighting?'

'Well, yes, not exactly, but yes, you would be in the thick of the fight, as it were.'

Teichmann picked up his glass and swirled the wine around, then set it down again, leant forward slightly and asked, 'Would you accept it if you had to be dropped behind the lines – anywhere? You've got till tomorrow to give me an answer.'

Eduard raised his glass, and swallowed the contents, placed it carefully on the desk beside the other one, stood and asked, 'Where do I sign?'

Teichmann rubbed his hands briskly, smiled warmly, and rose too. He extended his hand and Eduard took it.

'Men like you are exactly what we want – quick, straight, decisive. If you'd hesitated, you'd have been no use to us. Now go back to your unit, and I'll be back to you – within two or three weeks.'

'Will I be accepted?'

'We'll let you know, but I think we both know the answer to that.'

As Eduard opened the door, Teichmann added, 'Just one thing.'

'Yes?'
'Official Secrets – say nothing to anyone about any of this.'

Sometimes we play games – simple games. She gets out the snakes and ladders and shows little Anna how to roll the dice and move the counters. Up the hill and down the slope. There's no risk, because there's nothing riding on the result. I suppose I was playing games because there was no risk and no result. Then again, after the hedonism of Iraq, Rechovot was a vacuum – we had come from nowhere and were going nowhere, and my war was a misty mirage across the endless desert.

I can play simple games, because you don't need to speak – the action's all on the board, and anyway little Anna is utterly ruthless, whereas I want her to win. It wasn't like that then. I would not have known what ruthless was, since I had no criteria by which to judge myself, and the games were just games – something to while away the pointless hours.

Then this real game emerged, tantalisingly out of sight, just hinted at, with a mysterious title – Official Secrets. It was difficult to differentiate between the superficial games at Rechovot and the suggestively 'real' game on offer.

I suppose this was the fulcrum of my war and of my youth. I sensed I was on the edge of whatever it was I had been awaiting. Was this the endgame? Or was it yet another episode in what seemed to be a petty odyssey of little ladders and small slopes that epitomised my less than satisfactory life?

Whichever it was, I accepted the die and rolled it without hesitation, because I had a secret too. I knew I had prepared for something, that all that effort and energy was to some purpose, and all that remained was to discover what the purpose was, what my war was about, and where.

The climax is always when you are on the cusp of completion, not when you are complete; life was living on the threshold of the stroke – now it is death within. My war is never-ending and I have to say I preferred my peace.

CLEOPATRA'S NEEDLES

Eduard packed his bags – a single rucksack, knife and money belt, water bottle – and hesitated, then handed Ali-Said's gift to Wladek.

'If you have them both, you will remember me as one of a pair,' and he clapped him on the shoulder. 'After all, I've got one of my own.'

Wladek's eyes were welling, and Eduard pulled him close in a brief embrace, then pushed him away.

'Come on – you're the one who takes life as it comes.'

'And you're the one who's going.'

'Well, that's the Army for you, mate.'

Wladek sank back onto the bunk.

'Wish they'd hurry up and send me somewhere.'

'They will, they will.'

Eduard held out his hand.

'Take care of yourself.'

They held the handshake for a long moment, then released each other, and Eduard jumped onto the jeep, waved and slapped the facia. As they pulled away, he glanced back once – Wladek stood, his hand raised in salute, then vanished in a cloud of dust as they accelerated.

Teichmann told him that six of them had been selected, fast track, train across the Sinai to Cairo, then ship from Alexandria or Port Said to Gibraltar, and convoy to England. When the Germans stepped up their attacks on Mediterranean convoys, the designated ship was holed up in the harbour and the arrangement was deferred. On 11 May 1943 the Axis had conceded defeat in North Africa. Now, later that same summer, Eduard was diverted to Algiers.

At the Red Cross Hostel in Cairo, Eduard waited in line outside the refugee office. No-one knew an Audrey.

'Sorry, Corporal. No-one by that name here.'

'She served in Kermener.'

'Kermener? Where's that?'

'Asia, Russia, near Afghanistan.'

'Sorry, mate. Never heard of it.'

Eduard was not at all sure why he had bothered, what had prompted him to ask after the English girl. Perhaps it was just the thought of England that reminded him, brought back an image of sweet sensibility, and her calm efficiency. He shrugged and stepped out into the arid afternoon.

Three weeks in Cairo. The Pyramids, the Sphinx and Cleopatra's Needle – or was that somewhere else? Perhaps it was like the Egyptian camels, difficult to find when you wanted one, always snorting and crapping in front of you when you did not.

The Special Pass, signed by an indecipherable General, opened most doors. Yet the attractions of bars and brothels were scant consolation. To be selected for special duties, to be promised special training, to be guaranteed special shipment, and then to be faced with yet another delay was not conducive to party-time. Eduard was bored.

Somehow he contrived to fill the hot, dusty days with visits to ancient sites, endless hours sipping cool, often gritty drinks, tuning in to the BBC on the battered radio in the sergeants' mess, and keeping himself to himself. After five days, he was seething with impatience, constantly reminding himself that he had waited this long, another few days would make no odds, when a call came. 'Report to the landing strip by the Pyramids.'

The twin-engined Dakota looked somewhat lonely, parked on its own when Eduard arrived. Inside, the fuselage was stripped bare, with miscellaneous crates and bundles dispersed along its length. The aircraft was ticking over, and the pilot shouted back over his shoulder, 'Find yourself somewhere comfortable, and don't touch anything you don't understand.'

Eduard wedged himself between two rolls of tenting, and braced his feet against a metal rib, shouting back, 'Where're we going?'

The pilot ignored the question, yelling, 'Sorry, no 'chutes. We're flying fairly low, so you won't drop far.'

Eduard muttered 'Thanks' under his breath, and pulled his rucksack round his neck to rest on his chest.

A Flight-Sergeant emerged from the cockpit, and leant over Eduard 'You have company,' jerking his thumb at the open hatch.

Eduard glanced up, just as the sky disappeared behind a massive figure in khaki shorts and shirt, with a black beret, no badge, and sergeant's stripes on the sleeves.

'I'm Johnnie – and who are you?' he asked as he stumbled forward and collapsed beside Eduard.

'Cjaikowski – Eduard.'

'Thank God for that – I've had enough of Yankees and Brits and bloody Frogs for the past ten days. Now at least I get to fly with one of my own,' and he leant across and proffered a massive, heavy fisted hand.

'Johnnie who?'

'For the record, Zbigniew Makowski, my friends call me Bish, but since we're going to England, I've decided to call me Johnnie. OK?'

Eduard laughed and agreed, 'OK.'

There were two transit camps – one in Algiers itself, on the old racecourse, the other twelve miles distant, at Capmatifu, virtually on the beach. At the first, there were French, Belgians and Yugoslavs, and at the second, Poles. The town itself was host to what Churchill called 'horribly bloated staffs which are lurking there'. Officers were abundant, busy-busy and uninterested in the Polish resort on the sand, where Eduard and Johnnie merged with the other NCOs destined for the Italian campaign. By tacit consent they avoided discussion about England and why they might both be going there and not across the Mediterranean. Instead they set out on the second day to reconnoitre the coast and the city.

Not far from Capmatifu, they were turned back by SPs manning a barbed wire barricade, beyond which tractors and cranes laboured day and night. In the bar behind the camp, they found out why.

'False premises.'

'What?'

'Fake, false, unreal, c'est un illusion,' explained their informant.

They were sitting on either side of a trestle table under a frayed awning, flapping above four pliant poles, sipping imported beer from America. The speaker was a berry-brown lined and lean Frenchman, or so he seemed, until he introduced himself.

'Felix Terlecka, born in Algiers – French mother, Polish father, been here ever since.'

Felix owned and ran the local glass factory, and was the eyes and ears of Capmatifu. He explained that the French and British were completing a fake harbour as a decoy against German raids, for Algiers was temporarily the centre of the universe.

'Now we have North Africa, and will take southern Europe, everyone comes here: de Gaulle, Churchill, Roosevelt; the Generals have their mission here too; this is where they plan the Mediterranean war – and I make glasses. Drink, gentlemen?'

One drink led to another, and then to Felix's ancient Chevrolet, its buxom lines scratched and dented, its chrome bubbled and its whitewall tyres a dirty grey. As the afternoon waned, they jolted and jogged their way through the narrow streets and curdling crowds, abandoning the car to climb a short hill path to a dirty concrete block, with a black Pharaonic cat painted on its wall.

'Le Chat Noir – en effet the Sphinx of inimitable smiles,' commented Felix, as he ushered them through an anonymous door, down a flight of detritus-free steps, and into a dimly lit and sweetly scented interior. As their eyes adjusted, they gradually defined tables, chairs, a small dance floor, and a neatly arranged, small bar. Surprisingly, at least to Eduard, used as he was to clandestine rendezvous in towns and cities across the Orient, this bar was clean. A scattering of customers took no notice of the new arrivals, apart from sundry nods to Felix, and a white-tunicked youth with baggy trousers tucked into pale socks above moccasins inclined his head as he paused by their table, the tassel from his red fez gently swinging.

'M'sieu Felix. Normale?'

'Oui. Normale, et aussi pour mes amis.'

'What's normale?' asked Eduard.

'Kir – French drink. Blackcurrant juice and wine. You'll like it.'

'Mehla.'

The youth turned.

'M'sieu?'

'Quelle heure?'

'Six heures, m'sieu.'

Johnnie lifted his glass, and squinted at the pale red liquor.

'French or Algerian?'

'French cassis, Algerian wine.'

Without pausing, Johnnie sank the glassful, and licked his lips.

'Bit sweet for my taste, but not bad. Not at all bad. Let's have some more.'

Eduard peered at his wrist. It was nearly six. What happened then? As if on cue, a trio of musicians appeared quietly alongside the bar, mounting a low platform, and started tuning their instruments – a viola, double bass and saxophone. As the hour arrived, they struck up 'The Red Flag'. Eduard spluttered as the drink went the wrong way, Felix clapped him on the back, and Johnnie half rose.

'What the hell...?'

'Don't worry my friends. It's a joke. The owners are Russian – White Russian.'

As he spoke, the band broke into 'The Marsellaise', to groans from the predominantly Arab customers, then moved smoothly into a Tin Pan Alley routine. Eduard was about to speak, when Felix put his fingers to his lips, and pointed to the other side of the bar.

Two robed figures glided swiftly onto the miniature dance floor, and slowly gyrated, letting their garments float down, to reveal a close-cropped petite brunette in leather shorts, high-heeled boots, brown shirt and high-peaked officer's cap, complete with swastika armband, and a lanky blonde, brassy locks hanging on her shoulders Lamour-style, in red boots, white pleated skirt, crimson blouse and a red star on her forage cap.

The dance reflected a stylised duel, each close encounter eliminating clothing, until only the boots, belts and headgear remained, along with vestigial underwear. When the music climaxed, the girls took a bow, and Mehla returned with fresh drinks. Felix thanked him, and turned to his guests.

'Five minutes – then we have the second act.'

This time the lights dimmed, and a single spotlight illumined the floor. The two girls appeared, each concealed as before but, as they let drop their flimsy robes, it became clear that they had also removed all except boots and belts. With a flourish, each produced a short whip, and simulated a short-distance duel. As the 'Russian' executed her final flourish, the 'German' cried out, dropped her whip, and bent in

259

submission. The music paused, then recommenced, as the beaten girl bent before the dominatrix, who produced a black rubber dildo and caught and held aloft a black jar. Plunging the dildo into the jar, she withdrew it, glistening with gelatinous cream, and swooped towards her victim. The audience started to clap and, as the handclap steadied into a slow rhythm, so she pushed and pulled, pushed and pulled, and the 'prisoner' sobbed and moaned. The band broke once more into 'The Red Flag', and the victor took the dildo with both hands, hauled it out, held it up, squeezed it, and a fountain of liquid shot five feet into the air. The lights came up, the two girls bowed, the audience applauded, and a voice could be heard above cries of 'encore, encore' with 'Vive la difference!'

Felix smiled at his two guests, ordered a fresh round and enquired, 'You like?'

Johnnie grinned.

'It's certainly different, but what about the real thing?'

'You want real girls? That can be arranged. And you Eduard?'

Eduard shrugged. He was in two minds. The show had amused, but not aroused him. Then he looked at Johnnie, and realised his new friend needed some release for his massive physique.

'I don't mind. We can have a look anyway.'

'Come. I take you somewhere else.'

Felix stopped the car outside a two-storey, whitewashed house set back within stone walls, punctured by a solid oak gate within an arch, beyond which were quiet gardens. Across the front of the house ran a verandah, and within this the windows were all shuttered. Slivers of light escaped through the vertical cracks between the shutters, and soft music could be heard as they approached. Felix knocked twice, and the door swung back as a turbaned head looked out.

'Ah M'sieu La Fenetre,' and the door swung open to reveal a corpulent personage, with a broad yellow sash across his jellabah, and pointed shoes. Beringed hands clasped as he gave the customary bow, and he ushered them across a small central hallway into a salon.

In the centre of the room stood a sedan chair, caparisoned with silk fringes, embroidered cushions and ostrich plumes. In the sedan sat an ample figure, robed in satins, with white hair piled high and fastidiously arranged with jewels and peacock feathers. One braceleted hand slowly bisected the carefully rouged and powdered face with an ornate Japanese fan. The other lightly held a sheaf of banknotes.

'Ah! Our wonder of the windows.'

Felix approached the sedan and bowed deeply.

'Allow me to present my compatriots from Poland – Monsieur Johnnie and Monsieur Eduard.'

'They sound English to me,' observed the chatelaine somewhat tartly, then allowed her careful face to crease slightly in the semblance of a smile.

'They are of course welcome to our house of pleasures.'

She extended the hand with the notes, and Felix discreetly increased its contents. She closed the fan with an audible flick, then opened it again; the gentleman of the door appeared at her side.

'Three tokens for our friends – gold standard.'

The usher bowed, and from within his jellabah produced three gold-coloured circular tokens, and handed them to the three guests. He then produced a rubber stamp, bent his head towards the chatelaine, listened and nodded. Straightening up, he took each of their hands in turn, held the token, and stamped it with a number.

'Thank you,' said Felix and then, 'Follow me,' as he led the way across the salon, into an antechamber, and up the stairs. At the top he directed them into another room. Several veiled and gossamered girls sat in groups, talking quietly, taking no notice of the visitors. Felix gathered their tokens, and indicated the doors off the room, each with a corresponding number.

The senior girl approached them, smiled at Felix and addressed the other two.

'There are nine girls and three nationalities, and each girl is different. Here are their dimensions.' She snapped open a ledger. 'If you will say which you prefer, and go to your room, when the bell rings, it's your turn, and your choice will come to you.'

Johnnie and Felix made their choices, and Eduard said he really did not have a preference, so long as the girl was healthy.

'They are all healthy girls here. Madam insists upon it. We pride ourselves...' and with that she snapped the ledger shut, and each went to his allotted room.

Eduard's was plain but clean, with gingham curtains, close-fitting pale rose carpet and a single, low light. There was a wash basin, with a clean towel, and a small fan rotated slowly in the centre of the ceiling. The bed was anonymously sheeted, the corner turned back. When the bell rang, Eduard sat up, and reflexively smoothed his hair. The senior girl closed the door quietly. She sat beside him.

'You aren't really interested, are you?'

Eduard looked away and muttered, 'Please don't think...'

She interrupted him: 'I don't think anything. I'm not paid to imagine what our clients think. Would you like to talk?'

'Not much to talk about, really.'

'Alright. Then I suggest you just close your eyes, and think of England.'

Eduard froze. His eyes flickered and he stood, trembling.

'I don't think this is at all a good idea.'

'Relax. It's only a turn of phrase. I'm half English, and we were always told to lie back and think of England. I just thought it was slightly amusing, that's all.' She paused. Then added, 'Why did it startle you so? You're Polish, aren't you?'

Before Eduard could reply, the bomb exploded.

Plaster sprinkled them. The light went off and back on again. The building trembled. Then there was a total stillness. The rise and fall of the enemy's engines could be plainly heard, and the ack-ack, ack-ack of the anti-aircraft guns; searchlights criss-crossed through the slatted bands of the shutters.

Then the next bomb fell. The light went out. More plaster fell. One of the shutters clattered open, slammed shut, then fell open again, hanging half off its hinges. Eduard found his arms wound protectively round the girl. She held onto him. The drone was above them now, the guns firing frenziedly, the searchlights flooding the room as they passed.

The third bomb fell without any warning apart from a sudden vacuum of sound before the rushing air made their ears pop, and then the hesitation of a split second before the catastrophic crunch and the timpani blast sucked the shutters off their hinges, ripped the curtains out, lifted the bedclothes and hurled them across the room, drawing the bed halfway towards the door, and then shattered the inner wall, splintering the floor, and hurling them down the new gradient, straight into the salon. Eduard and the girl lay alongside the sedan, dazed until he looked up to see the Madam looking down, fanning the dusty air away from her immaculate maquillage.

'You came quickly,' she observed.

The damage was limited, for the raid was mostly concentrated on the harbour – the false harbour, which was virtually destroyed as Johnnie and Eduard discovered, when they walked along the beach the following day.

'Did its job well,' commented Felix that evening, 'and just as well, since M'sieu Roosevelt was in town last night.' He turned to Eduard. 'Tonight we go to the real harbour, where the real shows are.'

The night club was in the shell of an old theatre, rendered roofless in a previous raid. The circle was packed with British soldiers, some even sitting on the balcony, their legs swinging over the edge. South African soldiers crowded the stalls, or what was left of them, and a small group of Scottish infantrymen were huddled in a corner, under the circle overhang.

A bar operated in the foyer, and waiters hurried to and fro between circle and foyer, foyer and stalls, distributing drinks. Independently, bottles of vodka passed from hand to hand – a contraband consignment circulating among a contingent of sailors, on liberty from the presidential presence.

The show was a ramshackle parade of scantily dressed girls clearly secondary to the sustained intake of high octane alcohol. The Tommies catcalled and threw an occasional bottle, while the South Africans and the Scots traded insults. The sailors watched and waited.

When the curtain came down for what the compère needlessly called 'a toilet interval, gentlemen', a bottle from the circle landed at the feet of a South African soldier, who bent, swept it up, and hurled it back. 'Fuckin' Boers,' shouted someone, and that was the signal for a stampede into the foyer and up the stairs, where a fracas developed, inhibited by the inconvenient ranks of seating.

The sailors downstairs eyed the Scots, and the Scots eyed the sailors, and by some chemistry of pragmatism, both groups turned away and together eyed Johnnie, Eduard and Felix. Johnnie was describing, with considerable enthusiasm, the charms and propensities of the French lady with whom he had shared the raid and its aftermath, not returning until early the next morning. As he spread his great hands wide, to illustrate the grandeur and scale of her mammary assets, a Scotsman, leaning against the front row of seats, observed with a leer, 'Futckin' Pules, couldna futck a bent bint if they saw one.'

Johnnie paused to look at him, then turned back, and continued to tell his tale.

'Stupid cerntry, Puland – futckin' thick, let the Jeermuns tek theur wimmin.'

Johnnie dropped his hands, and glared.

'If he says anything more, I'm going to pulverise the bastard.'

The Scot warmed to his ribaldry.

'Hey, Pulishmun. Dy'evair futck a chickun?'

'That's it,' and Johnnie hurled himself across the seats, grinding the Scot's face into the back of the plush seat squab. Instantly, three fellow Scots threw themselves at Johnnie, and Eduard clawed at one of them. The sailors sat and roared encouragement impartially, hurling empty vodka bottles.

'Give the shithouse 'ell, Polish,' and, 'Stick 'im one, Glasgow.'

Felix slipped quietly away and, once outside, peered up and down the street looking for SPs. There were none. Eduard stumbled and fell, put his hand down to push himself up, and felt it close on a bottle. He smashed it against the iron seat leg, and drove it into the nearest Scottish limb. Johnnie brought his hands together like mighty buckets and clapped two bullet heads between them. In the hiatus, Eduard grabbed his shirt, and yelled, 'This way,' running down towards the stage.

The sailors, not to be robbed of a joyous rumble, now that two protagonists were leaving, approached the Scots, and offered their own spirituous challenge. The fighting spilled down towards the stage, and Eduard leapt up, dragging Johnnie after him. As they ducked behind the curtain, the French proprietor appeared from the wings, brandishing two wine jugs, which he brought down smartly on their heads.

Drenched in red wine, with glass shards stuck in their tunics, Eduard and Johnnie ran down a narrow passage, towards a small

263

window. Eduard kicked the glass out, hurled himself backwards and squeezed through but, when he tried to follow suit, Johnnie's bulk stuck fast, just as two SPs skidded round the corner in a jeep, braked, and leapt out running towards them. 'Go! Go! Go!' yelled Johnnie, and Eduard, realising he had little choice, went.

The theatre stood next to a sombre block of flats, brooding behind iron gates. Eduard pushed at the nearest gate, it gave, and he ran into the building, racing up the stairs. After two flights he paused, heard the front door bang, and swivelled round, looking for a way out. The door was locked shut against him, so he leapt up the next flight, to find the door there locked too.

Breathless, fearful and desperate, he hurled himself up the final flight, and against the door. It slammed back and he fell into the fourth-floor landing. There were six further doors, three on either side.

Eduard took the first, and knocked urgently. It too was unlocked and gave as he knocked. He pushed it open, slipped inside, closed it quietly, and stood for a moment, trying to bring his breathing back under control.

A small voice whispered, 'Qu'est ce va? Who is it?'

He bent forward in the gloom, and could just make out a shawled figure in a low rocking chair.

'Pas de problem. Don't be frightened. I won't hurt you.'

A torch flashed in his face, then was as abruptly extinguished.

'You look to be a nice young man. What do you want?'

'To hide.'

'What from?'

'The police.'

'Oh dear, what have you done? You haven't killed anybody have you? There's so much killing going on, you know.'

'No I haven't killed anyone. My friend and I were in a fight. Someone called us filthy Poles.'

The tiny figure unfolded itself, and a fragile, wrinkled face peered out from beneath the crocheted shawl, as she approached Eduard, and once again played the torch across his face.

'You're Polish?'

'Yes I am.'

'You'd better hide then.'

She pointed at a Japanese screen in one corner of the room, and Eduard went across and crouched behind it, trying to still his breath, and steady his shaking legs. The Frenchwoman returned to her chair.

There was a peremptory knock on the door, then another, then it opened.

'Entrée.'

Two SPs stood just inside. One buttoned his torch and played it over the walls, bringing it to rest at last on the old lady.

'Pardon, Madame. Have you seen anything, heard anything?'

'Non.'

'No-one disturbed you? Your door was open you know.'

'No, no-one. Yes, silly of me. Perhaps you would close it when you go.'

'Sure you've seen nothing?'

'Yes, M'sieu. Nothing.'

They took another look round and at each other, nodded, then quietly backed out, closing the door behind them.

'They've gone. You can come out.'

The old lady moved slowly and arthritically across the room to an alcove.

'Would you like some coffee?'

They sat facing one another and Eduard began to express his thanks.

'Not necessary, young man. Let me tell you a story.'

She paused, and looked closely at Eduard, then away, as she remembered.

'Once, long ago, in 1914 I met a Polish officer in Marseille. I was a young woman in those days, and war was upon us. He was the kindest, sweetest man I had ever known. We were going to get married, after it was all over. But he never came back. I believe he would have if he could.'

For a moment she was silent, then: 'He was the love of my life.' She stopped, and they remained still, disposing of her memory. Then she smiled at Eduard.

'Of course, I got married, had children, and here we are, another war, and my husband is gone, and my boys are somewhere, fighting no doubt. And one day I shall see them again. So you see, young man, I could hardly keep a Polish man almost as handsome as my dear Stanislaw away from his war, now could I?'

As Eduard held her hands, and thanked her, she released one hand, and made the sign of the cross, whispering, 'Bless you,' and he left her there, sitting in the rocking chair, her shawl pulled tight, her mind loosely running back down the years to that other war.

Outside he jumped an Air Force lorry as it slowed to negotiate a narrow bridge, and jumped off as it approached the smouldering false harbour. At the camp, Johnnie was asleep. Eduard woke him.

'What happened to you?'

'Put on a charge. And you?'

'I met somebody else's sweetheart.'

I am not what you might call an impatient man. I do not rise to the bait. My fuse is long. When it is lit, there is usually time to consider, diss the words of discontent before they are spoken, and so recompose the paragraphs of pragmatism as to sidestep other people's ill-tempered tempests. But just sometimes, wrath transcends wisdom, and I strike out, and I always regret it. On those occasions I choose the wrong fonts – the italics and the bold Bodonis where I might be better advised to use softer serifs and a smaller point-size in pale Perpetua. Usually I do it on my own, and nobody reads my murderous mind.

Not until now have I wondered whether this is an acquired skill or an inherited trait, something made or received. My little Mamita was a patient soul, whereas my Papa was a strong-headed man of instant opinion and certain invective. So the genes are mixed. My childhood was stabled by the Seret in some tranquillity, yet I enjoyed the impulses of rebellion. So those signs are crossed too.

Inevitably I look to my war for the explanation, for the formative, the *bella causa* of the conjunction of irritation and ointment, rage and salve, outrage and insight. The waiting – that was the magisterial test of patience. Not the conflicts, not the brawls, not the insults, not the insensibility of the formatted discipline of the military on inactive service. None of those things lit the fuse, but the waiting did – the attenuated justifications of extenuated circumstance which strangled the spirit and dulled the mind.

Original pain of family parted, agony of country despoiled, chronic affliction of captivity, stress of survival, disease of deprivation and the testing torments of the road to war – none of these roused my wrath, other than with a detached, rational, academic sense of simple right and wrong, but the waiting did, yet not so much the waiting itself as the emptiness of each minute when the waiting was supposed to be over, and the war begun, the disappointment, especially when it seemed blindingly obvious that it could have been prevented but for the stupidity or ignorance or indifference of the disappointer.

That was what made me angry, blind with incandescent ire so that, within my external composure, I seethed, was within an iota of losing that control which prevented my fists from flying through walls, boots into heads, knife into any available gut. At such times, one is within a skin's width of massacre, of violence to the first unexpecting voice, unseeing glance, unfeeling touch. Frustration is the needle that pricks restraint.

And when this happened, my salvation lay in the intact vision, the remaining dream, the certainty that, whatever happened, the time would come, my time would come, and my country, my family and I would be avenged.

Yet, when the time did come, I thought not of such things, but only of the work to be done, and perhaps that itself was the measure of my wrath, that it was always a small rage, focussed on small targets, to be destroyed with the small arms of my insignificant self, patiently and without malice aforethought.

I have always been good at waiting. Just as well, now that waiting is all that is left.

THE SAVOY GRILLE

The orders were plain: convoy to Gibraltar, the Azores – and Scotland, to avoid the U-boats. The reality was otherwise: transfer to Catania in Sicily via Malta and thence to Brindisi on the Italian mainland, to join the first Poles, 100 miles behind the front line. Eduard was bemused; this was not what Teichmann had proposed. In the Englishman's absence, he decided to break his silence.

'Have you got your orders?' he asked Johnnie, as they sat on Capmatifu beach on the morning of departure.

'Yes. You too?'

'Scotland, but the boat's going to Italy.'

'The same.'

They looked at each other.

'You thinking the same as me?'

'Who do we see?'

It made no difference. Wherever they probed, separately, carefully, without revealing their supposed missions, it was the same. Orders were orders and transfer was transfer. If the orders said Gib and transfer was to Sicily, then that's the way it was. 'There's a war on, you know' became a repetitive mantra, such that, after several hours, they met again on the docks, and admitted defeat. 'Well, at least we get to go to war, my boy,' and Johnnie laughed. 'Isn't that what you always wanted?'

'Welcome to the Savoy Grille, lads – best caterin' course in Italy. Pasta, vino, bags of olive oil and if yer 'chute don't open, Perlahmi sand-witch.'

They were seated in a spacious tent in the makeshift camp set up on the eastern seaboard, as the Allies pushed northwards, striving to pierce the Gustav Line south of Rome – within months Wladyslaw Anders' II Corps would be pitting Polish battle skills and persistence against the German Panzergrenadiers and paratroopers at Cassino. Eduard and Johnnie listened to the instructor, as he explained the rudiments of jumping out of aeroplanes. 'Would you accept it if you had to be dropped behind the lines – anywhere?' Eduard remembered Teichmann's words, and realised – this was the beginning of his war, training to be dropped, anywhere.

'Me nime's Charlie. I'm yer muvver, bruvver and bleedin' farver confesser fer the next four weeks. What's yours is moine, and what's moine's me own, so remember this – you might come from Gawd knows where in 'a middle a' nowhere, but as far as O'im concerned, yer 'ere to listen, learn and leave wiv yer wings. Any bleedin' failure is dahn ter me, an' Oi don't 'ave failures. OK? Moi wings is your wings, so let's gerron wiv it.'

On the tables in front of them were piles of silk and tangled cords. On the blackboard were diagrams. For the rest of that day and most of the next they learnt to fold and pack, fold and pack, fold and pack.

'If yer bleedin' chute's up the spaht, it don' open, see? It's dahn ter you lot. Pack it good, and it opens good. Cock it up and you're cock'd up.'

The rest of the week was spent on the theory of flight, slipstream and wind flow, rules and regulations, patterns and programmes of paratroop life.

'This 'ere's what we calls a sim-u-later. If yer don't do exackly as Oi says, it wont be a case o' sim-u-later, but see-u-later, in the morchary. Roight? Roight.'

The simulator was a 100-foot mast, with a lattice of ladders and intermediate platforms, and a final launch pad and projecting gantry with a harness, at the apex.

'Roight, then. Let's get yer in the 'arness, and see what 'appens when yer jump orf.'

Charlie strapped Eduard in, shoved him none too gently towards the edge, and added, 'On a'command, when Oi says "Jump" yer jump, OK?'

Eduard looked down, pulled on the straps to make sure they were secure, checked all the points he had been told to check, and waited.

'Jump!'

The elasticity of the straps pulled him up with less force than he expected, and Charlie yelled, 'Well done, mate. Tha's what i's all abaht,' as the other instructor grabbed him and hauled him back onto the lower platform. Each jump was longer, deeper, demanding more control, until the fifth jump brought him within a hand's length of the ground.

'Nar's the 'ard bit,' and Charlie demonstrated the fall and roll, arms parallel to the harness, firmly held, legs cycling. Eduard fell awkwardly and winced. The second time was easier, and the third perfect.

'This 'ere's a useless airypline. As yer can see, it ain't got ner wings. It's an 'Alifax, which is one of yer great British airiplynes and in this 'ere, we 'ave another sim-u-later, only this one's the real fing, like it's got a fewz-i-large and proper 'arness etceterah, etceterah.'

Eduard lost count of the number of times he sat with the others as they rostered their jump routines, moved one after the other to the jump door, leapt out, pulled the ripcord, rolled, somersaulted, and rose to their feet, running.

'If yer under foire, and yer not bloody well runnin' when yer 'its the grahnd, yer undergrarnd – dead, see?... Not loike that Farnes Barnes. 'Ere. Come 'ere an' do it agyne.'

They were back in the instructor's tent. Charlie looked at them appraisingly and moved from one to the other, checking their 'chute packs, helmets and general equipment. Each man carried a rifle, knapsack, water bottle in full battle kit order.

'Roight you lot. Up ter nah, yer've done awroight. Nah comes the 'ardest bit. Nar it's fer real. And this is where yer meets the Savoy Grille. Ahtside, and 'op to it.'

There were three trucks drawn up outside the tent, and the squad scrambled aboard, Charlie slapping shut the tailboards and running round to the final truck to swing himself up as they moved off. On the airstrip was a tri-engined monoplane, its RAF roundel as new as its aluminium bodywork was old and worn.

'This 'ere's yer Savoy. It's an Eye-talian airypline, which is Polish fer fuckin' useless, so the sooner yer aht of it, the better fer you and me and the poor old airiplyne. And I don't want any blood on the carpet, so check yer chutes, check yer 'arness, check everybleedin'thing, and then check it all over agyne. Roight? Roight.'

Eduard's first jump was perfect, and he had time to enjoy the sensation of floating free, controlling the direction of descent, watching the world unfold towards him. He fell well, in a patch of damp grass, somersaulted twice, and gathered the chute, rolling it up, detaching it, and moving swiftly under the cover of some trees, where he found himself staring straight at an unsurprised cow who, after a desultory inspection, turned away and continued the more interesting business of chewing cud.

On the second trip, Eduard fell badly and twisted his ankle. As he rejoined the squad, he feigned normality and only when they were safely in their billet did he confide in Johnnie. 'I think I've sprained my ankle.' The big Pole swung his bulk off the bunk without comment, and disappeared. Ten minutes later he returned and tossed a small bottle onto Eduard's bunk.

'What's that?'

'Olive oil. You don't want to be a Perlahmi sand-witch, do you?'

The third jump was awkward. Eduard judged the landing as carefully as he could, and favoured his left side as he rolled, fortunately for him, in a water meadow. Soaked and muddy, he staggered back to the truck, once more avoiding Charlie's narrowed eyes.

The fourth and fifth jumps were straightforward, and his ankle was easing by the sixth, when he misjudged his descent and fell into an olive grove. As Charlie stood by and watched, Johnnie and two others helped to cut him free, and eased him to the ground.

'Banged yer ankle, didja?'

Eduard smiled weakly, and minimised the discomfort.

'Just caught it on a branch. Nothing much. Really.'

'Day afta termorrer. Three more jumps and tha's it.'

Eduard rested on the seventh day and, in the final week, approached the seventh jump with some trepidation. This was onto water, and water, he had been warned, was like concrete if you hit it too fast.

The Adriatic was in a benevolent mood as they flew across the coast, banked, and climbed. Then the jump began. Eduard manipulated the 'chute as the water began to surge towards him, curling as he fell, and glissading along the surface until his momentum slowed, and he was sucked under, the 'chute reluctantly slithering across the waves, pulling him up, his goggles misted, and his lungs bursting. He was 20 feet from the strand, and gathered the harness and silk, striking out for the shore, when the high-prowed fishing boat pulled alongside him and Johnnie's strong arms reached down and hauled him over the gunwales. 'How's the leg?' and as he could feel nothing he shouted back, 'Fine.'

After that, the penultimate and final jumps into woodland and a bare hillside were comparatively simple affairs, and Eduard made no pretence as he limped into the tent for the final debriefing.

'Well, gennelmun, we seem to 'ave a 'undred per cent pass rate. Which is bloody amazin', seein' yer all Perlahmis.'

Charlie paused, and grinned at them all.

'Prahd of yer, the lot of yer. Best lot ever. 'Ere's yer wings then.'

The convoy left for Glasgow via Catania, Valetta, Gibraltar and the Azores the very next day. The Polish contingent embarked on an armed freighter. The 20mm Oerlikon with its round drum was shrouded in tarpaulin, and mounted in the bows was a 12-pounder cannon. As they left Valetta, they were summoned on deck. The Master was a short, stout, tidy figure with a full set, his hair and beard white, his cap set square, his hands tucked into his jacket pockets.

'Gentlemen. This is a Trade Division freighter, under naval protection, manned by the merchant marine. Our gunners are young ratings and some recalled to service, all naval men and otherwise you, gentlemen, are the rest of the ship's complement. You are our cargo. We intend to see you in Scotland, safe and sound before the month is out.'

The Master scanned the assembled Poles.

'I know you all want to serve. I am aware you have had a hard time getting this far. However, on my ship, you are in the way, unless you make yourselves scarce or useful.'

He withdrew his hands, and ticked off the points on the fingers of one with the other.

'One. You at all times follow orders from my officers and remember, on my ship I am God. Whatever I require of you, that's what you do. Two. Unless you are otherwise required, you stay in your quarters except for designated mealtimes, exercise periods, organised recreation and any duties. Three. Complaints. If you have any, you hand them to your senior officer, and he hands them to me, and I rule on them. My decision in that, as in all else, is final. Four. In emergency, you stay below, unless called upon. Five. Duties. You clean your quarters by rota, you attend emergency drill, and you learn how to fire the ship's armament.'

He looked around.

'Any questions?'

There were none.

'Thank you, gentlemen. You may dismiss.'

Back in their makeshift quarters below decks, Johnnie complained.

'What the hell're we going to do for the next few weeks?'

'How to fire ship's guns, by the sound of it.'

'What the hell use is that?'

'You never know – you might find yourself grateful one day.'

Captain Albert Bytheway was a Master of the old school, at sea since his teens, and a stickler for precision and practice makes perfect. With a slight crew, many of them young Vindi-boys, fresh from their twelve weeks at Sharpness, he made the most of what the Admiralty served him, whenever he set sail. With 120 Polish soldiers, enthusiastic, young and in many cases skilled, he determined to make them earn their keep.

The Poles were divided into squads. Those with practical skills were set to repair and maintenance; signallers assisted the radio room; clear leaders were taught emergency procedures and the fittest were assigned to gun drill. A stray complaint about food found the complainant in the galley, a casual comment about holiday sailing sent the sailor-manqué to the lifeboats, and an argument about athletics formed the foundation of a gymnastics and boxing class. Master Bytheway fitted effect to cause.

Eduard and Johnnie found themselves in the radio room. They knew about Enigma. Their country had details of the German code-maker in '39. Poland shared what it knew with the British but it still took time to catch a signal, make sense of it and warn the prospective victims. By 1943, U-boats worked not in oceanic formation but lurked in-shore, darting out as opportunity knocked. Their signals were shorter, their actions faster. Master Bytheway's response was vigilance and caution.

Eduard was standing by when the signal came through.

'To the Captain, please.'

He trotted down the gangway, and hauled himself up the rails and steps to the bridge.

'Message, sir. Enemy intentions.'

'Thank you, Eduard.'

The Master read the signal.

'The Commodore wants us to hold course, but be ready.'

Bytheway issued commands in a steady stream, to gun crews, and their Polish auxiliaries, the netmen, mortar crew, medical staff, and sent Eduard back to the radio room. Half an hour passed, and another message from the Commodore.

The Master scanned it, folded it, and glanced at Eduard.

'Nothing new, Eduard. Back you go.'

An hour, hour and a half, two hours passed. Eduard scuttled onto the bridge with a third signal. Bytheway read it twice, smiled, and tucked it under the flange of his chart table.

'You can return to the radio room, Eduard – and relax. Nothing's going to happen.'

It was a false alarm, and set the pattern of the days aboard their anonymous freighter, but it taught Eduard a useful lesson.

Johnnie was complaining.

'Waste of bloody time, those damn guns. He had me firing practice rounds and the bloody drum kept getting stuck. Don't see the point.'

'Yes you do. If we had been attacked, we'd have been ready. You'd have unstuck the drum, I'd have handled the signals, and Mister Bytheway would have, has got an effective crew, in any emergency.'

He waved his finger at his friend.

'It's not a waste of time. We've been learning, ever since we came on board. What a waste it would have been if we'd had nothing to do.'

On the eve of their arrival, the Master toured the ship, talking quietly to groups of men. The words varied but the message was the same, as he said to Eduard, on his final visit from the radio room.

'It's been a privilege to have you on board. And I hope you find what you're looking for.'

He shook Eduard's hand, looked out of the bridge and added almost inaudibly, 'To Poland the brave, be honour and glory.'

Eduard stood, uncertain that he had heard the words, as Bytheway said, 'You can go now. Goodbye.'

The train from Glasgow was noisy, dirty and slow, the truck from King's Cross to Kingsnorth, Kent, crowded, cold and uncomfortable. It was an irritable, tired, colic collection of Polish military immigrants who arrived at the Big House in a village near Ashford. There were no road signs, and even names on the larger houses had been removed – a legacy of the early war months of invasion fear. 'Careless talk costs lives' was still an article of local faith, as Eduard discovered whenever he enquired after the owner of the house they now called home.

There were captains, majors, privates and corporals, without acknowledged rank or distinction, not that anyone cared on arrival, when they were allocated rooms, beds and lockers. Eduard unpacked his sparse rucksack, relieved to be at rest, even temporarily. The first day was devoted to familiarisation – with the rambling part-Tudor old house, its sanitary ware and canteen. The inquisition started on day two. Eduard faced four British officers.

'At ease, Cjaikowski.'

'That is your name?'

'Yes, sir.'

'Where were you born?'

'Where's that?'

'School?'

'Where?'

'Brothers and sisters?'

'Names.'

'Your father – what did he do?'

'Where were you born?'

'What river? What mountain? How far from the border?'

'And your father – what was his rank? In the police.'

'Your younger brother was shot?'

'Why? Was he a traitor? Answer the question, please. Who did he betray?'

'Did you betray him?'

'What did you say when he was arrested?'

'What did you do?'

'Where did you say you lived?'

'What was the address?'

'Was that the town where you were born?'

'Where's your father?'

'Who killed him?'

'Did your brother betray you?'

'Do you want to go back?'

'What will you do when you go back?'

'When will you go back?'

'Why are you here?'

The questions were designed to confuse, to raise emotions, to generate anger. Eduard answered them calmly and quietly. He was not confused, he was angry but only coldly so, and he refused to allow himself to be upset. There was a short silence, as the officers quietly conferred, then one looked up.

'Dismiss, and thank you, Cjaikowski.'

The third day they played games. Eduard shared the room with nine other countrymen. The British Captain handed out folders and pencils.

'Open your folders.'

Inside were crosswords, one with clues in English, another in Polish, a third in German and a fourth in French.

'English first, gentlemen. Take your time, but you will be timed. Hand them in when you have finished.' He clicked his stopwatch.

Eduard struggled. He was the last to complete the first puzzle – with two gaps. It took him just over an hour.

'Now Polish.'

They all handed their folders back within 20 minutes; Eduard's was complete, though he was unsure of at least one answer.

'French.'

This was more difficult; after the first hour, only one folder had been handed in. Eduard's was the second.

'And now the German one.'

Hard as it was, Eduard smiled grimly. This was the real test – beat the bastards at their own game. He could not tell if it was luck or sheer resolve, but he finished within the hour, and was sure he had made no mistakes.

That afternoon, they played Kim's Game – 20 seemingly innocuous items on a tray: a cotton reel, key, coin, ticket, cap badge, biscuit and brooch; a ring, glass stopper, screw, needle, knife and a ruler; a pencil, a pepper pot, visiting card, light bulb, stamp, booklet and purse. They were given five minutes, a pad and a pencil, then told to write a list of what they remembered when the tray was withdrawn.

The second tray seemed the same, or similar: key, coin, ticket and pencil; stamp, booklet and purse; ticket, light bulb and visiting card; a screwdriver, identity card, bar of scarce chocolate, battery, another, different coin and a button; a card case, lighter, cigarette and tablets. The test was the same.

The third tray contained echoes of the second, but was somehow different: a key, coin and ticket; identity card and pass; screwdriver, battery, lighter and a cartridge; a knife, bandage and pad; a valve, red light bulb, packet of fuse wire, two screws, a pencil and a pillbox. As they completed the test, the tray was brought back.

'Form yourselves into two teams. First team stay here. Second team outside.'

Eduard was in the first team.

'You have fifteen minutes to utilise what you see. What can you make, using all or some of these items?'

Johnnie looked round at the others, then at Eduard.

'You take charge.'

'I'm not an officer.'

One of the others spoke up.

'What's that got to do with it? Someone has to lead, there isn't much time. You're it.'

After ten minutes, they agreed – a small explosive device, or a transmitter. The other team took over. They offered one solution – a signalling device.

'Thank you gentlemen. You may dismiss. Get some sleep. You'll need it.'

On the third day, Eduard awoke with a start. The room was still dark. He glanced at his watch. Six o'clock. He leant on one elbow, drifting over the events of the past two days when the bugle shattered his reverie.

'Wikey wY-key.'

The door slammed open, and a diminutive figure stood squarely in the opening.

274

"Tis the toime to roise and shoine, me dears. This is your coach, second and manager. Me name's Moikle, and Oi am risen from de rock of me feythers to bring you the tablets o' Moses, whom I've known since he was in the bulrushes. The first tablet says honour thy father and mother, and the second says get yer arses outer them beds, and yerselves op, dobble quick.'

Within minutes the entire contingent was dressed and downstairs, where coffee and cold sausage were doled out. They were commanded to form up outside, and marched across the drive, behind the house, through an orchard to a paddock, where they were confronted by an array of instruments of torture – or so it seemed to Eduard.

There was a wooden frame with ropes dangling, old tractor tyres hanging on their ends, assorted fences and railings, high, low, barbed and spiked, long sewer pipes, coarse nets laid across battens, a water-filled artificial ditch, a rolling bank of turves beyond it, a series of low brick walls, and a circular barrage of sandbags.

'Phwell now, me darlins. 'Tis a moighty foine soight ye are an' no mistake. Will ye all survive, Oi ask meself? And me answer's yes! So let's be havin' yer, whon at a toime, if yer please, after me.'

Saying which, Michael O'Connor, instructor extraordinary, ran to the first rope, corkscrewed through the tyre, hauled himself up, balanced on the cross-beam, laughed, and jumped down, rolling in a neat ball before leaping to his feet in one smooth motion, scaling a wooden fence, ripping off his jacket, laying it across the barbed wire, then literally climbing up it, rolling it up as he landed on the other side, then hurdled the railings, clearing the lethal spikes by an inch, wormed and wriggled through a length of pipe, emerging with a wide-eyed grin, slid under the nets, and turned on his back, hand over handing himself down its length without any apparent effort, leapt the ditch, somersaulting up the bank, landing on his feet on the other side, and running towards the brick walls, zig-zagging between them, and finally, throwing himself flat, crawling on his belly up to the sandbags, before hurling himself over the top, and crying inexplicably, 'Caramba!'

He sauntered back to the squad, grinned again and commented, 'As you c'n see, 'tis not Spanish Oi am, but 'tis me battle croy. Yer choose yer own, startin' with you, me dear,' and he tapped Johnnie on the shoulder with one hand, giving him a shove with the other.

Johnnie was a good choice. His physique ensured a good performance, almost as good as Michael's, until he fell in the ditch, but he received a round of applause when he finished. Ten minutes later it was Eduard's turn, by which time several contestants had failed to finish the course, and one or two had fallen at the start. Two soldiers limped away to the sick bay. After lunch, a reduced squad tackled the assault course again, this time with officers attending, stopwatches in hands.

The fourth day was a comparative relief for Eduard. It was spent in an improvised radio room. The Morse transmitters were set to full volume, and the messages were slow and deliberate. As they scrawled what they heard on their pads, transcribing as they went, the volume reduced and the speed increased until, by the end of the morning, the messages were barely audible, and staccato. Johnnie was in despair.

'I can't keep up with them.'

Eduard was philosophical.

'You can't be expected to get it all down. Just do the best you can.'

Then he observed, 'It's probably just like that out there,' and they both realised that these were not just training, but tests.

After the Morse test, first aid was almost recreational. They were shown how to dress wounds, splint broken bones, revive victims of shock, and then told to do it all over again, without instruction. Observers noted their actions and the time they took.

'Have you noticed, how they time everything?' asked Eduard.

'I have – and it's a good job we're quick off the mark.'

The lessons continued, from first aid to writing, and codes, and decryption, and maths, and map-reading, and more maths, and aircraft recognition and rifle practice, and yet more Morse.

The four officers sat opposite Eduard.

'It's been a difficult week?'

'Yes, sir. Well, not difficult, but hard work, sir.'

'Yes. Good. Well, Cjaikowski, I'm glad to tell you, you've passed. You'll be sent on for further training. That'll be all.'

Johnnie passed too, but of 120 intake, 84 Polish soldiers returned to their units for active duty – as soldiers. Only 36 were sent on to Audley End, the University of Special Force Advance, where SOE Polish operatives learnt their secret trade.

I have time to think now. I had no time to think then. It is humbling to find that you have little control over your destiny, that others hold your life in their indifferent hands, for their purposes, not yours. If you think about it, that can destroy you. The trick in controlling others is to remove the opportunity for question time. No time to think, and no-one questions what is happening to them. If I had had the time to think, I might have challenged the sterility of the tests, the futility of the obstacles, the senselessness of the questions. On the other hand, I might have been convinced of all their reasons, and felt myself unnecessary and impotent. As it was, I thought little, felt nothing, and questioned not at all.

That is the Army way, and it works, I suppose. Now I have the time to think, I am less disciplined, but then, I have nowhere to go and nothing to do, whereas then I had a purpose – not theirs, but my own. And they made me ready. I doubt that I am as ready now.

BY DEGREES

The Dakota circled twice, then dipped its wings, waggling left, then right. The pinprick appeared once, twice, then darkness; once twice, darkness; once, twice. The 'plane banked, and levelled out, throttling back, as first one, then two, four, seven, ten, fifteen miniature beacons flickered against the anonymous black backcloth. Eduard tensed, the slipstream slicing past the open hatch. The red light remained steady, then blinked; green light and 'Go!' hissed his despatcher.

He stepped out into the night, felt the visceral tear of the slipstream as he was ejected from the 'plane's passing, then the slow, whistling fall; he braced his fists round the harness, felt for the safety tab but the jolt came like the volume on a radio, an instant afterwards, as the automatic device opened his 'chute; then he was floating. He looked down. The flare path was off to his right and slightly behind. He adjusted and felt himself slowly revolve, as the flares rose to meet him.

As he brushed past the treeline, they disappeared, one by one, except one. Then he was down, rolling, the 'chute dragging, bundling, scraping him along the grass. His wrist snagged an outcrop, and he grimaced, as he stopped, rose to a crouch, and softly gathered up the threads, automatically packing and folding the canopy into a manageable carryall. He checked his pouches: knife, water, gun, first-aid kit, maps and papers. All correct.

'Grybos?'

'Yes.'

'Follow me.'

The flares had gone; his shadowy host led him across the field to a gate, across a road, into another field, and down a path towards a dimly outlined shed. As they neared it, Eduard saw it was a barn.

'Leave everything here, under those bales.'

He turned, but could only make out the outline of his guide. The bales were piled to the left of the door. He slipped out of the coveralls, emptied the pouches, secreted them, the 'chute, the gun and the maps underneath, unstoppered the water bottle, took a long, quenching draught, hesitated, then added that to the treasure trove for his return – or a future historian. On a whim, with an after-prayer, he tucked the first-aid kit in with the rest, and smoothed the jacket of the suit, checking his knife, underneath his sock, against his calf.

When he rose, and straightened, there was no-one there.

He had memorised the route from the barn, and set off round its leaning flanks, until he found the path, then the rutted country track, and started the ten-minute walk to his destination.

The searchlight was blinding.

'Halt!'

'Who are you?'

The ride was short and uncomfortable, with two guards in the back of the short-wheelbase truck. He was roughly manhandled out and up steps into a brick outbuilding, down a passage, and into a stone-walled room, where he was left.

After what seemed an hour – his special issue second-hand watch had been stripped, along with his money, pen, photos, papers and handkerchief (but they had not found his knife) – the door slammed open, the same two guards collected him, and he was marched across the passage into another, similar room, with a table and two chairs. He was told to sit on the one nearest to the door. He was left for another hour.

The door opened. An officer strode past him, bent to switch on the light on the table, angled it towards him, then disappeared behind its penumbra. Eduard could see nothing, except the second figure, which hurried past him and disappeared behind the light too.

'Your name?'

'Jozef Grybos.'

'Where do you live?'

'Gorzow.'

'Where's that?'

'Near Prazska, not far from the river Prosna.'

'Not far? How far?'

'Thirteen kilometres.'

'And your father?'

'Andresz Grybos.'

'Where is he?'

'Dead.'

'Dead?'

'Yes; killed in the fighting, near Moskva.'

'Ah – a patriot.'

'Yes.'

'Where is your mother?'

'Dead.'

'She is dead too – you are an unfortunate man.'

'Yes.'

'How did she die?'

'In the shelling.'

The interrogation was relentless.

'We don't believe you.'

'It is true. I have papers.'

'Yes. We have seen your papers. Very good papers.'

There was a pause, and the light flickered as the officer touched it inadvertently. Another voice spoke.

'Where did you get these papers?'

'They are my papers, official.'

'Why are you here, and not fighting for the Fatherland?'

'Essential duties.'

'Essential duties?'

'Repair, maintenance. I repair wireless equipment for the Reich.'

'What equipment?'

'Receivers, transmitters, amplifiers, speakers, resistors.'

'Where do you do this?'

'In my workshop.'

'And where is your workshop?'

'Gorzow.'

There was a pause, an undertow of brief exchanges. Then it started again.

'Your name?'

'Grybos.'

'Where are you going?'

'Home.'

'Where is home?'

'Gorzow.'

'Do you live with your father?'

'No.'

'Why not?'

'He is dead.'

'How did he die?'

'Fighting, near Moskva.'

'A patriot.'

'Yes.'

The light went out. Eduard closed his eyes. When he opened them, the room was empty. An hour later, he was taken back to the first room. An hour after that, he was once more under interrogation.

'What is your name?'

'Jozef Grybos.'

'And what is your father's name?'

'My father is dead.'

Eduard lost count of the questions, the hours, even the days. He would fall asleep, only to be awoken, and the whole process started all over again. He needed water; his throat was dry, his voice creaking. When he could hardly speak, he was given a beaker and told to take a sip, then it was dashed to the ground, as the questions recommenced. On what he took to be the second or possibly the third day, he was led, once more, down the passage, and into the open air. The sun was shining, and the great house looked as serene as the day he had left it.

'You had better get yourself some proper rest, clean up, change, and report for debriefing this afternoon, fourteen hundred hours.'

His instructor smiled.

'Worse than you thought?'

The aerodrome near Cambridge was featureless and flat. The wind rippled the tents and flattened the grass in metallic waves as they trudged back to the dispersal bay. It cut through the thick serge uniform. Blackout restricted vision to a few yards. It was the sixth jump that week, in the dark, in the wind or the rain or both. They were accurate to within 20 feet of target, and for that they received a weekly bonus, and were told they would now embark on a test flight and drop. This had been the test drop.

Eight weeks before, Eduard had arrived at Audley End, and met his new CO. Colonel Kennedy, late of the Indian Army, reflectively twisted the end of his moustache, a luxuriant growth of which any fighter pilot would have been proud. His smooth dark skin was darker beneath his eyes, and his carefully ironed uniform set off his satin epidermis to perfection.

'Sergeant Cjaikowski. Your acting rank is Lieutenant. You will be allocated a room, and a batman, whom you will share. The rules here are few. You are on one of two courses of 35 men; throughout you will be assessed; if you get through, you will go home – to fight for your country.

'You are here to learn, within reason, at your own pace. The sooner you are fully trained, the sooner you can go over. Schedules of seminars are posted on the board; you can apply for a pass off camp, which will be granted at any reasonable time. And finally, you will sign this. Read it first.'

He swivelled a document across the desk – the Official Secrets Act, agreement to, operatives for the signing of. Eduard signed without comment.

STS43, the University of Polish Military Intelligence, was at Audley End, in Essex, near Saffron Walden – a Jacobean mansion, once owned by Charles II, remodelled by Adam, and requisitioned in 1941. Executive Officer was Major Hartmann, Josef Hartmann, once ADC to Marshall Pilsudksi, too well- known to fight on home ground, sublimating his rage against the Reich through his fellow countrymen, training them to wage a secret war of sabotage, infiltration and espionage, working alongside them on each course.

Lord Braybrooke's dynastic home was initially occupied by the wounded and medically unfit. In May 1942 the Poles arrived to train, primarily for underground work behind German lines in occupied Poland – 2,000 miles away. By the time Eduard arrived, the proud house's alien complement was declining, as gradually, more and more operatives were posted to Italy, to infiltrate their homeland from there. The great house was gated and guarded, the grounds walled against prying eyes, the outbuildings converted to workshops – and simulated interrogation rooms, to prepare tomorrow's operatives for the trials ahead.

'Behind that screen is the main staircase – boarded off to save it from the likes of us.' Jardine was an RASC sergeant assigned to Eduard and Johnnie. They climbed the south stairs to the top of the house.

'Basic Course is taken by Captain Mackus. Lectures up here in the north wing of the second floor.' They glanced into the rooms, sparsely furnished with tables and chairs where once servants slept.

'Your rooms are on this floor too. You can drop your kit there. Everyone sleeps up here, including me and your instructors. Only Colonel Kennedy and Major Hartmann get to use the good bedrooms – one floor down.' He grinned. 'Privileges of rank.' He clattered down the servants' staircase.

'They're here – and so's Our Alfred.' He knocked, then opened a door marked 'Private'.

'Lieutenant Wisniewski, sir? Two new candidates. Cjaikowski and Makowski.'

An officer in shirtsleeves came to the door and looked them over gravely, nodded, looked briefly at Jardine, turned and was gone, the door closing softly behind him.

'That's where your papers'll be manufactured – out of bounds, OK? In fact all this floor's out of bounds in the normal way, except for this.'

Jardine led the way into a magnificent room, with soaring ceiling, fretted with plasterwork, enclosed by friezes, commanded by double columns, and dominated by ornate fireplaces. The serviceable tables and chairs were in utilitarian contrast.

'Robert Adam, one of our great architects, designed this room specially for chaps like us – this is where you come to meet and chat and take a rest.' Jardine turned outside the rest room and pointed at what was once the library – 'and that's where you sit your exams.' Jardine put a cautionary hand on Eduard's sleeve. 'If you pass, you will come here for your Dispatch Course.'

They marched down the length of the house, along the old picture gallery and down the north stairs, back into the entrance hall, Jardine flinging open double doors on the left. The room they entered was not so much a room as a vast chamber, its ceiling criss-crossed with timbers, within which heraldic beasts were set in plaster within roundels within each square. Carved finials descended from alternate cross-beams, and pale rectangles disclosed the shapes of great paintings once hanging there. Five windows punctuated the west wall, the central one a jutting bay, above bland ply panels, which surrounded them. Behind and above the doors through which they came, rose a complex fretted screen.

'Behind those plywood sheets are original panels,' and at the other end was a magnificent stone screen, backed again by plywood.

'The main stairs are behind there.' Jardine paused, centre stage. 'This is the mess – we all eat here, including the Colonel.'

Outside they toured the outbuildings.

'This is the wagonhouse, where we keep the vehicles, and learn how to go "bang", and these are the stables, where you'll learn to shoot straight, and about mines.'

His wave encircled the view from house to river.

'This is all for wandering about in, but you aren't allowed past the fence. River's out of bounds too.'

He shepherded them back into the house, just as a gaggle of young women, laughing and talking, flooded through the entrance hall and spilt out into the grounds. 'Fannies,' announced Jardine. Eduard looked at Johnnie, and they raised their eyebrows.

'F-A-N-Y-s – FANYs; First Aid Nursing Yeomanry, stationed here to look after us all, and look after us all they do – bloody well. They're not here for romance, or jiggery-pokery, but to make you comfy and see you have a window on the world. They've earnt all our respect.'

In some ways, it was like going back to school. The lessons were more intensive, but the requirements were the same – listen, learn and above all, remember. Remember German rankings, from Feldt Marschal to OberGruppenFuehrer; learn the difference between Gestapo and Wermacht; learn their command structure, recognise their equipment, from Messerschmidt FE110 aeroplane to Balda Jubiletta 35mm camera, and how to dispose of it; learn the language – which was less of a problem for Eduard than for Johnnie, who was sometimes impatient.

'I don't like the bloody Krauts, how can I be expected to *like* the bloody language?'

There were French lessons too, which Eduard enjoyed, because he found an outlet for occasional theatrics.

'Est-ce que c'est possible? Merde, c'est im-poss-ible,' with a great Gallic flinging of the hands and a twitching of the eyebrows.

They underwent a crash course in behavioural psychology.

'Cause and effect, gentlemen. Always give the adversary an escape route – preferably one that leads to extinction,' and they all laughed.

Then there was a course in explosives.

'TROTIL is extremely volatile. It may seem like cotton wool, but it is plastic explosive, and the Germans use it, which is why we do, when we are their uninvited guests. UK808 is highly poisonous – always use gloves.'

Johnnie was in his element on their weekly excursions to the quarry for practical demonstrations and a little practice themselves, blowing up railway tracks balanced on spare timber sleepers. Johnnie always volunteered to crawl through the broken stone, to place the detonators – small caps with tremblers, balanced on the rails – with precision and infinite sensitivity for such a big man.

'That's why I am such a good dancer,' he told Joyce, a FANY who had taken him under her wing, 'light on my feet, and tender with my hands,' as she pushed him away gently, to resume their sedate circumnavigation of the floor at the weekly *thé-dansant*.

The best outside activities involved the new PIAT bazookas, targeting redundant Churchill tanks. At Eduard's suggestion, Jardine had arranged crude Prussian crosses on their superstructure.

'Something to aim for,' explained Eduard, when instructor Ihnatowicz asked why.

'You mean aim at,' he suggested.

'No,' insisted Eduard, 'aim for, not at, because we need to have something to aim for, don't we, if we're ever going to go back?'

Aleksander Ihnatowicz was perhaps the best marksman in the Polish SOE, and he imparted his expertise to his charges – with Bren, Spandau, and in particular, small arms: Luger, Colt, Biretta, Browning. He understood Eduard's 'aim' for, in the stables range, the targets were human figures, and they were rigged in uniform – StatzPolizei, Schupol, SS, Wermacht, and he applauded Eduard's persistence and increasing skills with pistol – and with knife.

'Shoot from the hip, with one hand, lean forward, your body is the pointer, your head aligned with your hand – you have two chances, two bullets. After that, you're dead.'

Eduard rarely missed with the first.

'And don't forget – leave a bullet in the chamber if it's an automatic, *before* you change the magazine: that's when you'll need it,' and the target suddenly loomed, close to hand.

'Well done, Eduard, but next time, get the magazine in your mouth before you need it,' and another target shot up as Eduard shot, and another.

'Hit the floor, Eduard, down, down – too late. He would have hit you.'

It was worse in the dark. They were given five minutes to accustom sight to shapes in the gloom, and then up came the targets, frequent and fast. They came on cables, often two at a time; it was a case of 'Be ready, target/fire, target/fire, down, magazine in mouth, target/fire/ miss/fire, target/fire, roll over, change magazine, target/fire,' and, 'Well done, Eduard, you have to get the rhythm, understand?'

As they handed in their pistols, Ihnatowicz collected their fines – half a crown for each miss to the Red Cross. Johnnie spent 7s 6d on the first day, Eduard five shillings. By the end of the course, it was often nothing, but on the last day, by tacit agreement, they each dropped a ten shilling note in the tin.

From stable range to open range, the course moved into the fields and the caves near the quarry, where the machine guns were mounted on a slight rise, and the targets triggered at varying distances, to be attacked, first with a grenade, then two short bursts.

'If you don't scatter them with the grenades, you won't finish them with the tracers. Get them out, then strike them down.'

The knife was a different matter. The cellars under the house were equipped with dummies, suitably clothed. Standard issue were flick-knives, though Eduard practised in his own time with his own knife.

'I've killed with it before,' he explained to Johnnie, 'so I feel it best to keep it in the family, so to speak.'

Unarmed combat was yet another matter and it was this part of the course that frequently removed candidates from the active list for days on end. They were shown how to kill, and how to avoid being killed. It was a smooth transition from Alan Mackowiak's fitness sessions to the first lessons in defending themselves in hand-to-hand combat.

'Breathe – out, then in, count to ten – and out again. Now feet apart, one leg forward, elbows in, hands UP. The old adage – attack is the best method of defence.

'Go for the eyes – both fingers, or clap the ears and remember, knee them in the balls, but get your foot firmly on the ground again.'

There followed the bear-hug, twist and chop, neck-lock, dead-leg, until the lessons moved to more lethal moves – the neck-scissor, pressure points, knockout chops, and how to break a neck or a back. In the second week, the two courses met on neutral ground in the cellars.

'An element of competition in your quest for graduation,' commented Mack the Knife. Eduard and Johnnie were casually flicking each other over on the judo mat when the door opened and the other intake sauntered in.

The first man through the door was Wladek.

'They called me three weeks after you left – made me an offer. Wonderful!'

'So where did you go?'

'They shipped us off to Scotland, place called Leven, for paratroop training. We called it Monkey Grove because of all the weird towers and apparatus we had to swing about on. It's the HQ of the Polish Parachute Brigade, Eduard – crème de la crème, as the Froggies say. And I was there! Then we went to a dreadful place, Manchester, with an airport called Ringway – except for the girls, who were excellent – where we had more jumps, from bloody balloons, and finally from 'planes, and then back again to Scotland – a beautiful place, Loch Morar near Fort William, where we messed about with explosives, then here. What about you? I thought I'd never see you again.'

Eduard put his hand over his friend's.

'I told you, didn't I? Oh ye of little faith. I told you we'd meet again. I knew it.'

He held his friend's hand, then released it.

'Me? I've been hard at it, learning how to shoot, blow things up, kill people. Soon I'll know if I've graduated. Then it's the serious stuff. Dispatch Course, for my first drop – and then, Wladek, home! Home to fight the sodding Germans.'

He patted his friend's hand again.

'At least you're on the other course, so you get to go home on your own account, without my help,' and they laughed together.

'...Cjaikowski and Makowski. The rest of you will receive your postings in the morning. You have all worked hard, and done well. Only a few make it; that does not mean that those of you who have not are any less valued. You will join an active unit shortly, and I warrant you'll find yourselves in mainland Europe before the year is out. Dismiss.'

The Colonel hated this part of the job – telling four fifths of the original intakes that they would not go home to Poland to join the Armia Krajowa, the Polish Home Army, fighting clandestinely against the Hun. Yet he also knew that not all of the successful ones would reach Poland, and of those that did, many would perish in the undertaking. Of the final 527 graduates of STS43, 346 would be dropped in their homeland, and 108 would die. Their courage would be matched by the airmen who took them in, of whom 62 aircrew would lose their lives, with a loss of 70 aircraft.

The Dispatch Course started the next week, after Eduard took a 48-hour pass to train to London, where he found the Headquarters of the Red Cross.

'Audrey – I don't know her other name. She served in Kermener.'

'Wait there, please.'

Five minutes later a pale, elderly man with a slack suit, shiny from office use, beckoned him to follow.

'We do have an Audrey de Croix Richardson, who was stationed at Kermener.'

The old man looked permanently tired, and Eduard hesitated before pressing.

'And she is where, now?'

'I'm afraid I can't help you there. There are forms...'

He trailed off, looking sad, dispirited and apologetic all at the same time.

'If I fill them in, can you try to, I mean, could you find her?'

The old man sighed, examined his cuticles, and picked at them absently.

'I don't know. We have so many things to do, and there's so much interference. The pressures...' and again he trailed away into sombre silence.

'How old are you? I'm sorry, I didn't mean to be rude, but isn't this rather a lot for you?'

'Thank you. No, it's not at all rude of you. You're right. I am in fact over seventy, but we all try to do what we can. There's a war on, after all.'

The old man seemed to collect his back, hands, even his wispy hair as he smoothed his head, and leant forward, fiddling with his fountain pen.

'Look. Leave it with me. Let me make enquiries. I'll see what I can do. Really. Then you can come and see me again. In about a month.'

As Eduard got up to go, he stood too.

'You must be frightfully interested to come all this way.'

'Yes, well, she was very kind to me. I'd like to find her.'

As Eduard turned to go, the old man said a soft 'Goodbye' then added, 'Ask for Arthur Mortimer. That's me.'

On his return, he had an evening free before the course began. One of the FANYs had made a point of looking after him, and he found her in the kitchens.

'Margaret, would you join me at the flicks?'

They sat watching *In Which We Serve*, with Noel Coward, hands demurely in laps, and then afterwards went to the British restaurant for beans on toast and a cup of what Eduard lightly called 'strong, British tea' before returning in her Morris Eight to the great house in its dreaming grounds. They sat side by side, and Margaret spoke first.

'We see lots of you chaps, you know, and we try not to care, but it's difficult.'

Eduard stared through the windscreen as tiny drops of rain started to pattern the glass.

'We do care though,' and she leant over and gave him a light kiss on the cheek, then pressed the handle down, pushed the door open, and stood outside while he joined her, and together they walked into the entrance hall.

'Thanks for a lovely evening, Eddie.'

Eduard looked down at her, and unaccountably a vision of Sara flushed his mind, his heart throbbed, and his hand shook. He instinctively raised a hand, and touched her cheek, his hand dropping away suddenly, but she caught it, lifted it again and held it against her face.

'You're a good man, Eddie. I hope you find what you're looking for.'

It was the last time Eduard saw her. When he tried to find her the following week, he was told she had been posted but, some long time later, on the eve of his mission, he learnt that Margaret lived at Dagenham with her bank manager father. In late 1944, Hitler's pilotless V1 doodlebugs were droning over London when an occasional stray went wide. One such stray hit Dagenham and demolished the banker's house. Margaret was at home.

Identities had to be chosen, papers prepared. The paper had to be German, or seem to be. Shaving brush, soap, money – all German, or counterfeited to seem so. There was the Arbeitz, or work permit, the Bischaine Gung, or travel pass, and everything had to be aged under infra-red lamps. The two portraits impassively stared across the small room – Marian Jurecki and Andresz 'Afgan' Swiatkowski, their heroes and exemplars, who had been dropped in the wrong place and died.

'Choose your own names. Eduard?' Colonel Wieronski waited. 'Grybos.'

'The drop's near Gorzow; that's where you live.'

I don't know why I chose Grybos. I suppose it was a sort of memorial. I would take Grybos with me, and together we would hammer the Hun.

In that in-between world at Audley End, nothing was real. The preparation was a rehearsal; the house was only waiting to get rid of us and revert to its natural nobility, the girls were future housewives who had put life on temporary hold, and most of us there wished we were somewhere else, which is why we were there.

Have you ever felt like that – out of place, out of time and sometimes out of mind? Not out of your own mind, which is exactly the opposite of my condition, where I am very much in my mind, but out of mind in the sense removed from others' orbits. I was out of Sara's mind, of that I am positive, for how could she envisage my return when I had so simply chanced in, and swiftly chanced out again?

I was out of Audrey's mind, for was I not simply a soul to be helped on its way, as I searched for my mother – and myself? I was out of my friend Wolski's mind, for was he not single-minded, seeking his dear daughter and his longed-for grandchild?

Out of place certainly – for this was not my milieu, not my home, not my style. Out of time, indisputably dislocated for how could a young adult be in his own time, and yet in times of great moment, in time with his compatriots, most of whom were old enough to be, if not my father, my considerably older brother. Yes, I was out of everything, and most of all, out of joint.

This was not what I wanted. Yet it was essential to what I wanted.

It's like the tablets – banked and ranked in the little plastic case they give you. So many here, so many there, to be taken at such and such a time, at so and so intervals, to thin the blood, regulate the pulse, oil the digestion, ease the aches, and of course, those that counteract the reactions to all the actions of the others. Essential to what I want – release from this rehearsal for the performance which may never happen. I am my own understudy, ever in the wings of performance, learning my lines, making my moves, entirely familiar with the plot, the cast, the *mise en scène*, even the bloody audience, yet constrained from participation by the old dog who plays the part I seek, and so badly, because he cannot speak, or make himself understood. If only, if only – I could do it so much better if they would let me try. But they stroked me, and I cannot.

It was like that at Audley End. I was ready when I arrived, and I was ready when I was there, and I was ready when it ended. And the curtains remained obstinately down throughout the whole run. They even gave me a trial run out of town. I had one of those after the first stroke too, then the curtain came down again. The one difference then was that I got to go to a new theatre, not once, but twice, and I tried to give the performance of my life.

AGAINST THE LAW

It was one of those days – still, silent and grey, engendering neither menace nor joyous expectation. Yet Eduard was tense, and Wilfred Webb was angry.

'Objective: five thousand pounds in used notes. Location: small town bank. Date: next Tuesday – market day. Guns, but no ammunition, no violence. ETA mission accomplished seventeen-fifteen hours. Back here for debriefing nineteen-hundred.'

Eduard pointed at the map on the blackboard, and explained Scheme 5 – because Poland was as far away as ever.

Prime Minister Stanislaw Mikolajczyk was adamant. He told Churchill it was essential 'that a British Military Mission be sent to Poland' to liaise between the Home Army and British Forces in the 'decisive phase [in] the struggle for the destruction of Nazi tyranny'. That was in February 1944. He also wrote to Lord 'Top' Selborne, Minister for Economic Warfare and the SOE. From that moment SOE's plans were laid, yet the Foreign Office vacillated. The Russians were against the Home Armia Krajowa, favouring the Communist Armia Ludowa, and the Russians were poised to retake Poland. They were Allies. The FO's catchword: caution.

Even so, personnel were shortlisted, including two SOE signals experts. Eduard was one. His instructor Antoni Pospieszalski was the other.

Gorzow was the initial drop zone. Week followed week, as the summer approached – and with it D-Day, Anzio and the Warsaw uprising. Still the mission was on hold, as the Dispatch Course ended and rehearsals began.

'Johnnie, leave your vehicle across the river under these trees, take your unit, assemble outside the farmers' tavern at 1640. Unit two will come with me, scatter, then gather in this alleyway at 1645. Unit three will drive up to the bank, park outside, leaving one man on board, engine running. The others will go in at 1650. Remember, everyone, the bank closes at seventeen hundred, when the last traders have deposited their takings.'

Eduard paused. 'Any questions?'

Some shook their heads, most just stared at the blackboard.

'Unit three tackles the manager – two of you over the counter, two of you in the public area. Unit two empties the safe, takes the money, leaves the building and Johnnie's men lock everyone up in the manager's office, back to the vehicles and away.'

Eduard wiped the dust-block across the blackboard, dropped it, and then rolled down the map. He picked up the pointer and tapped the map.

'Rendezvous at this town here at 1720. Then convoy back to base. Any questions now?'

'What if someone objects, attacks us?'

'Minimum force – you've learnt how to disable without permanent injury. Use what you've been taught.'

'And if the manager refuses to co-operate?'

'Fall-back allows the use of small explosives – on the safe, and as long as there's no risk to civilians. But only by me or Johnnie.'

'Are there any guards or anything?'

'No. Banks here are unguarded. Nearest military unit's a small airfield – we'll have cut the phone lines anyway, once we're inside. Army unit in the next town – twelve minutes away. Contingency. If you are tackled by anyone armed, try to neutralise them. If you can't, surrender. We're not there to hurt anybody, but to practise what we've learnt. That's all.'

Everyone started murmuring to his neighbour, when Wladek's voice cut through the background buzz.

'Do we get to keep the cash?'

Everyone laughed, and Eduard turned to Wieronski. The instructor was smiling too.

The bank was in the main square of an unidentified Home Counties market town – a classically porticoed single-storey building fronting the main street, with the marketplace alongside. The approaches were all relatively open. Market Hill ran from the crossroads directly past the bank, but a narrow alley, the Chewar, ran parallel, behind the buildings behind the bank. It was this alley Eduard chose as the main way in.

The jeep idled by the kerb, as they waited. Inside the bank, the five late customers cowered in one corner, and the staff in another, as the men in overalls calmly went about their business.

Wilfred Webb was thick i' the arm and strong i' the head. He had left school at fifteen, joined his father in the family business, tenants at the glebe farm, taken over on the old man's premature death from TB, contracted that hot, hard summer, and always carried the family twelve-bore in the old Ford jalopy on market days – 'just in case of invasion, do well.'

His was a long, hollow-cheeked, grizzled, hard-jawed face, tight-curled straw-dust hair spinning diagonally across his brow, his stance sturdy, his old cord jacket pocket-proud with knife and binding twine, wire trap and corn pellets, his hands creased, calloused and dirt-driven. Under tangled shrubs, his eyes missed little, periwinkle blue, unblinking.

No-one spoke. Two 'soldiers' stood apart, back to back, their sten guns trained on the captives, their faces inscrutable behind the smeared black masking camouflage. The shadow of what was obviously another of them obscured the entrance.

The door to the manager's office was ajar, and the frightened townsfolk could hear the sharp commands, as others supervised the opening of the safe. Two men emerged, carrying fibre cases, and a third, clearly in command, rapped out a series of brisk orders.

'Door. Disperse. Bring them here. Two minutes.'

The staff were herded into the manager's room, then the traders. The first 'soldier' emerged from the bank, carrying a case.

Wilfred Webb regularly attended market on Tuesdays, and banked at the same time, to save precious petrol coupons. He had watched the group of strangers, all in khaki overalls, approach the bank and disappear inside; he had seen one standing outlined against the glass door. He had noted a jeep parked outside, engine running, its driver apparently reading a newspaper. He had heard what sounded like frightened cries and he thought 'That's not right, something's up' and had gone back to the car to fetch the gun, slipping it under his shapeless duffel coat, and two cartridges into each pocket. It was two minutes to closing time.

Eduard had been watching staff and customers; the manager was no problem. He recognised superior forces, had no illusions of heroism, and his staff took their lead from him. The customers were mostly women, with two men, one a slight, bemused shopkeeper. The other, a latecomer, looked like a farmer, a man of considerable physique, and with a determined air.

He had moved slowly through the front door just as they were about to secure it, but not from stupidity so much as calculation, and had positioned himself nearest to the door within his group. Eduard had seen him weighing up the odds, and conceding twice – when first told to move, and again, when told to sit on the floor. Now he fell back as the soldiers shepherded the customers across the room.

Johnnie had left with the money, unit two had gone too, locking the front door first. The rest of them were split, one man inside the captives' room, one on the door, and a third bringing up the rear behind the customers. That was when the farmer made his move, suddenly stopping and, as one soldier collided with him, turning, tearing his sten from his hand, swinging it high into his jaw. As the soldier reeled, the farmer turned, and raised the gun, aiming at Eduard, who smiled to himself, knowing it was unloaded, then cried out as the farmer plunged to the right, let go of the butt, swinging the weapon by its barrel, the butt gathering speed, striking Eduard across the face.

He staggered slightly, and the farmer was upon him, kicking his own sten aside, encircling his body, lifting him bodily off the ground, and pivoting sharply so that Eduard found himself facing the other

290

soldier, as he jumped towards them both. The farmer charged him, using Eduard as a shield, his arms pinioned, the other sten uselessly trapped between them. The momentum sent Eduard's would-be rescuer sprawling.

The man on the door had momentarily gone inside to check their captives. Now he emerged, his colleague immediately behind him turning to lock it, as he yelled out, 'Team Leader in trouble!'

For a moment both men froze. The farmer kicked the man on the floor, threw Eduard at the other two, and turned, sweeping his coat open, to reveal the shotgun. With a seamless blur, he broke it and, balancing it on the crook of one arm, reached into his pocket and extracted two cartridges, slid them into the breech, snapped it closed, and with both hands raised the gun until it was pointing straight at Eduard's midriff. No-one moved.

He walked slowly forward, then raised the gun in his right hand, fingers on the trigger guard. Eduard had time to notice the cocked hammers, as his left hand drew back, fist curled.

One man took two paces towards him, and was felled with an accurate and powerful punch, the second stumbling as they collided. Momentarily freed from the farmer's gaze, Eduard scooped his sten up from the floor, and threw it in one continuous, sweeping movement. It span towards the farmer, butt over barrel, and he instinctively turned his body against it, fending it off with his left hand as his right swung wide, both barrels exploded, the pellets scouring a ragged sore in the wall below the ceiling.

Eduard reached him at the same time as the second man, and they each grabbed an arm, the shotgun clattering to the floor. The three stood stock-still for a moment, breathing hard, teeth clamped shut, glaring at one another.

Then Eduard looked directly into his eyes and said, softly, 'Well done,' pulled his arm back in a half-lock, and nodded at the manager's room.

The other soldier scraped the key up off the floor where it had dropped, unlocked the door and eased it half open; Eduard shoved the farmer in, and they slammed and relocked it, turning back to the others. One was leaning against the wall, nursing his cheek, and his partner was kneeling, moaning and holding his ribs where he had been kicked.

'On your feet. Collect the guns. Out and don't stop until you get there.'

The first man hauled the second up, and they moved out, the third behind them, only pausing to scan the street left and right before signalling to Eduard 'All clear' as he followed. The shotgun lay where it fell.

'Lessons learnt, I hope,' commented Wieronski at their debriefing. He had listened to Eduard's report without interruption and now offered no comment beyond, 'You used your initiative. You won.' Then he added, 'I'm glad you kept the violence down,' and smiled. 'We don't want to lose any farmers – dig for victory and all that.'

He tapped a file.

'Your next assignment – a good deal more dangerous.'

The target was an RASC base, with 120 armed men, half an hour from Audley End. It was well guarded, and the men guarding it carried live ammunition.

'You will have stens, blanks, thunderflashes, smoke bombs. Your target is the Commanding Officer, who knows you are coming. He has told his men there may be an exercise. They don't know when or why, so they won't know if it's you – or someone else.'

Wieronski looked around the briefing room.

'It only needs one trigger-happy, tired, stupid soldier to jump to the wrong conclusion, and one of you could be coming back on a stretcher, or in a box. Think about that, and make a success of Exercise Petada.'

In April, Minister Selborne wrote to Foreign Secretary Eden: 'As I told you last spring, I would welcome such a mission.' SOE was still pressing for the drop at Gorzow and Eduard was still waiting.

He had studied the plans provided. This was surely the final trial before he left for Poland. The problem was how to reach the CO and his papers without alerting the guards. The base was well protected and by professionals. The keys were surprise and speed. The solution was to neutralise the guards – simultaneously. Eduard decided to alert the entire camp, confuse them and keep them busy, while infiltrating the core. He briefed his team carefully, requisitioned four jeeps, and timed the assault for dusk.

They set off in convoy, four to a vehicle, watches synchronised, stens loaded with blanks and engines muffled. The camp was set back from a secondary road, in open countryside, flanked on one side by a narrow belt of beech trees, and by a perimeter track on the other.

Johnnie's jeep bumped along the track until it reached a gated field. Once through the gate, the jeep bounced across the leys until it was in a fold in the ground, some hundred yards from the perimeter fence. Wladek's jeep continued until it neared the back gate, with its paired guards. The third jeep skirted the beechwood, and parked behind a low bank of shrubs. The fourth approached the main gate, lights doused and Eduard checked his watch.

'Slowly does it.'

They eased towards the barrier. As they approached the guardhouse, Johnnie reached the perimeter fence and blew his whistle – twice – then threw the first false grenade. Each of the others to his left and right did the same.

The four men who had scrambled through the beechwood opened fire briefly, then crouched by the fence on the other side of the camp.

Wladek's jeep was standing in the back gateway, on the wrong side of the weighted pole, as a guard examined their papers. There were two flashes, and a short burst of firing. He looked up in disbelief. Wladek jumped him, the driver gunned the vehicle, one man leapt out and raked the guardhut as the fourth crawled round behind it.

At the main gate, Eduard was standing by the guardhouse, talking to the MP sergeant. As the grenades exploded, Eduard grappled with the NCO and, when the guards ran out, the two men from the vehicle overpowered them.

Camp troops raced towards opposite fences as Johnnie's unit fell back into the field, firing short bursts towards the advancing soldiers before circling the perimeter to the back entrance. The beechwood contingent also fell back, behind the trees, detonating two more explosions, then raced towards the main gate.

The two guards at the back gate sat sullenly hogtied, as Wladek crouched in the back of the jeep, and his driver gunned it across the grass, diagonally away from the access road. Eduard and his driver drove the lead jeep at a measured pace towards the core complex. Wladek's vehicle had reached the buildings, and now Johnnie's appeared, cutting across the far corner.

Eduard risked a quick backward glance to ensure the fourth jeep was following down the main camp road. He looked down at his watch, murmuring 'Now!' under his breath. At that precise moment, Wladek laid a series of smoke canisters in an arc before the buildings, just as Johnnie did the same behind. Eduard could see the barrack block diffuse and disappear as he reached the main square.

The jeep swung left towards the officers' quarters, driving smoothly and slowly. Explosions ripped the sky behind them, where the fourth jeep had veered off the main camp road to seed grenade after grenade in a random pattern.

In each quarter of the camp, bang followed flash, as Eduard and his driver approached the core. The defending troops had flattened themselves short of the perimeter, on opposite fronts, and were advancing in echelon, crawling towards their supposed enemy, as tracers scoured the night sky behind them. Startled, they stopped, not sure whether to retreat or to advance.

The buildings round the main square emptied as the remaining troops spewed out, and took cover. Eduard's driver slowed, braked to a standstill beside the CO's house, jumped out and ran, half crouching, to the front door as Eduard slipped round to the rear of the house and the kitchen door he had earmarked as his port of entry.

He forced the lock silently, crept through the kitchen, and into the hall just as his driver reached the foot of the stairs, then stepped, two stairs at a time, up to the landing. Outside the CO's door, he checked his watch and nodded to himself as the camp fell strangely silent.

Wladek had withdrawn to the rear gate, collected his men, and was driving down the perimeter track; Johnnie had followed suit, gathering the guardhouse unit on the way, the guards now bound and harmless, while the beechwood boys were halfway across the meadow behind. The only assailants left onsite were Eduard and his driver. He knocked on the door.

'Come in.'

'Sir.'

The CO was standing by the window, contemplating the pall of smoke. A distant fire bell sounded. He turned as Eduard saluted.

'Exercise Petada, sir. May I have the papers?'

'I've been expecting you.'

The half-Colonel looked up at the clock on the study wall.

'Half a minute early. Very good Lieutenant. Congratulations,' and he pulled the phone towards him, punched the bar and said, 'Stand down, John. Cease fire. Exercise Petada is over. Oh yes, and tell the fire brigade it's a false alarm.'

He leant across his desk, handed Eduard a file, and hesitated. Then he spoke, quietly.

'You know, I'm far too old for action, so I envy you in a way, but I don't think I would relish what you're going to do.'

He held out his hand and Eduard took it.

'Next time you'll be facing Jerry, and he will be armed.'

Eduard frowned and the officer laughed.

'You don't think I'd risk live ammo, do you?'

One week later, the orders came through. Gorzow. Sixteen-hundred hours at an anonymous aerodrome outside Cambridge. Eduard had two hours to prepare. Poland! At last.

He wore a civilian suit under his uniform coveralls, a Colt 45 under his arm, his knife strapped to his leg, money belt, a leather bag on his backside with his documents – identity card, travel pass, work permit – and in his head the plans of the town, the streets, cinema, theatre, schools, who to contact, in particular the man who ran the glass factory – shades of Felix and Capmatifu – communications officers with AK, the codes, the signals, the agents and, above all, the mission: to create the essential links between the Home Army, the Allied forces in Europe and the advancing Russians. It might not be fighting the Germans head to head but it was arguably the most significant SOE mission to Poland of the entire war.

He could have gone to France or to Germany, as some had done, but here he was, two flights from Poland – first Italy, rendezvous with Antoni, with the British officers, and then the drop, to Gorzow.

At the airport, the civilians said little. At 1600 there was a 'slight delay'. At 1700 he was told to stand down and await instructions. At

1800 'aircraft due', then 1900 'another delay'. At 2000 hours the door opened and a civilian entered, closing it behind him. He stood with his back to the door, contemplating Eduard. Then he spoke.

'I'm so sorry. Mission aborted, I'm afraid. Car's waiting.'

He pulled the door open behind him and stepped aside as Eduard, numb, and near to tears, walked listlessly away.

Wilfred Webb cared less about the mild bruises on his arms than the ones to his pride – to be outwitted by some bloody foreigner was not good enough. He told Inspector Pearce, 'Couldn't place it Tom, the accent. Not French, more like German, but that's impossible, en't it?'

There was a paragraph in the local rag, headed 'BANK THEFT FOILED', and a vague report about escaped PoWs, stolen army jeeps, and the bravery of local farmer Wilfred Webb, who had 'foiled the raid' by quick thinking and 'exemplary British courage'. Nothing was stolen, no-one else was hurt.

That week, the bank opened as usual, the authorities said little, beyond 'Enquiries are proceeding' and life went on much as before. There was a little muttering behind closed doors, but no public fuss for, as staff and customers on that particular afternoon were advised, 'Careless talk costs lives', while the men from the Ministry smiled, and left as imperceptibly as they had arrived.

Down the following years, details became blurred, and 'the day they robbed the bank' and 'farmer Webb foiled the foreigners' went into local lore as 'the battle of the bank' and 'Webb's victory' until, decades later, a local historian wrote about a 'local farmer's wartime courage on market day, when the late Wilfred Webb single-handedly fought off five desperate men from a German PoW camp'. Unaccountably, the archive edition of the local paper for the relevant week was damaged, with part of the news pages missing. And that was literally that.

'There's every reason to believe you will recover. It will take time. Your speech will improve, and your right hand will be useful again.'

The consultant was benign, benevolent and encouraging. He was also correct, insofar as my speech did return, and with exercise I regained the use of my hand – that time. What he did not tell me was that I could have another one. When that happened, he said much the same things: with patience and exercise and luck, I would recover – again. This time he said there was always a risk of a recurrence, but then I knew that didn't I?

When the third stroke came, he almost said 'I told you so' and he was even more benign, almost as if he needed to compensate for the increasing frequency and debilitation of my afflictions. By the fourth stroke, I realised that he could never be wrong, and that it was always a question of degree, and recovery became his lodestone for optimism, but never a guarantee.

It was the same with Gorzow. Every time the mission was deferred, it was promised anew. I was stricken from Poland, then told I would recover the chance. Today we would call it a window of opportunity, albeit one that remained obstinately closed.

When Gorzow was postponed the third time, I gave up in the sense that I forced myself to concede that it was a dream, whether it was called Gorzow or Warsaw or Cracow, that I was unlikely to see Poland in wartime, that there must be other ways to fight.

I wanted my war. I needed the catharsis of battle. I had to strike back at those who had riven my family and my life. I knew that there were other missions as D-Day approached. I let it be known that I was game for anything, as long as it offered action and results. I appreciated I was needed for Gorzow, but just in case, should the opportunity arise... I think they understood.

It was the same with the consultants, for my original guide had been replaced with minor mentors as I retreated down the road from recovery. I let it be known I was prepared for comparative mutation, to a dribbling savant with a trembling hand who could still be trusted to live a life and fight another year.

And in the end, I got both – my version of Gorzow and my version of a life.

THE NORMAN HOLE

'. . . if you had to be dropped behind the lines – anywhere?'

It was six days since Rome was freed and six days since the Allied armada assaulted the Norman strand. Rommel was in France – somewhere. The Desert Fox was now the Norman wolf, and Military Intelligence wanted to know where he was.

'The Resistance suggests he is on the move, and not tucked up in HQ. We want you to find him.'

Teichmann played with the paperclip, bending it, then straightening it, then bending it again. He looked at Eduard, tense, angry, resentful.

'I know you were geared up for Gorzow. It may still happen, but this is equally important.'

He pulled the paperclip out and twirled it in his fingers.

'Nobody expects you to get that close.' He paused, then added, 'But if you do, you know what to do. . .'

There was a moment of silence.

'He'll be too well guarded. But if you can find a pattern, places he visits, regularly, then we can send in the heavy brigade.'

'Heavy brigade?'

'Bombers.'

'You can't just bomb one man.'

'True. But we can bomb his front-line headquarters – if we can find them, if you can find them. We might catch him. We might not. But we'll have disrupted his efforts, and we're bound to catch significant people, if it is his alternative lair.'

Teichmann put down the paperclip, and opened a slim file.

'We know he moves about a bit, behind the lines. We know he has a forward base he visits regularly. The only trouble is, we don't know where it is.'

'Why don't the Resistance know?'

'We don't know that either. We suspect he comes and goes incognito.'

Teichmann leant forward, tapping the file.

'We know there's a German presence in a particular town. We want you to go there, see what you can find. Everything suggests it's the most likely place.'

Teichmann stretched, put his hands behind his head, and studied Eduard.

'There is an SS Wermacht outfit there. That we do know. If it's as big as we think, it might be worth bombing anyway.'

He unclasped his hands and closed the file.

'How's your French?'

'Good enough.'

'Good enough?'

'Good.'

'Good? Good. See what you can do.'

Eduard checked his equipment. Usual papers, suit under uniform, Colt, demountable French sub-machine pistol, the suicide capsule in his signet ring, money, and in his head, the memorised map of the Vallee de la Vie, in Calvados country, in Normandy, the rendezvous point and his contact: Ammeville and Le Puy. Eduard's codename was Le Loup – the wolf.

The night flight was short, bumpy and chaotic, as the Dakota contrived to mask its passage above the flotillas of Bomber Command. There was one uncomfortable moment when stray shrapnel pierced the fuselage aft of Eduard and his despatcher, but the damage was slight, and they droned on over the Norman bocage.

'Five minutes.'

Eduard tightened his harness, checked everything for the umpteenth time, and took the proffered thermos, sipping the sweet, acrid ersatz coffee to ease his closed throat.

'Two minutes.'

His mind raged across the twisted tale of Russian intransigence that had denied him his Polish war, after so long, so much effort, so many years.

'One minute.'

He stood by the hatch. France! What difference would he make? As he jumped, he told himself, 'I will make a difference. I bloody well will.'

The barns crouched beneath him, as he hauled on the line to swerve past them, and tumble into the ripening wheat. It slashed and tore at his face as he was dragged across the furrows through the still stalks and bumped against a small tree on the edge of the field. He lay for a moment, adjusting to the night sounds – the crickets clicking, the far-off call of a questing owl, and the ceaseless rustlings of small matters in the cultivated earth.

He pulled the 'chute together, and loosely bundled it, tucking it under his arm as he cautiously rose to one knee, and peered across the crop. The farm buildings were to his left, about a hundred yards away; there was no light to indicate the house. He closed his eyes and visualised the map. The farm, if it was the right one, was on a bend in the road, just beyond a Y-junction.

Find the road. Then check the layout. Then the buildings. Cautiously, he rose to his feet, and stepped clear of the wheat, walking quickly between that and the hedge until he reached a gate.

The gate was little more than a few strands of wire hooked over a post. He unhitched them, moved slowly onto the verge, and replaced them. He could see a junction, vaguely. This must be the place. A narrow beam of light flashed across the right-hand road.

He fell to the ground, rolled over and over, into the shallow ditch, and froze. The car laboured towards him, passed, and continued until it could no longer be heard. His heart was throbbing, and his hand shaking as he expelled a long breath, suddenly aware he had been holding it without breathing. Once more, he got to his feet, and walked along the verge towards the buildings.

The arm-lock was as painful as it was unexpected.

'Prenez les choses,' in a rasping, hoarse whisper, and the 'chute was ripped from his other hand, his document pack was wrested from his uniform and hard, questing hands invaded his clothes to seek, find and remove the guns. Then he was pushed, none too tenderly, and told, in an urgent whisper by the same voice, 'Marche.'

They walked towards the farm, into the farmyard, and across between great, squat, dark shadows of buildings, to a solid, square farmhouse. A door opened, a glimmer of low light filtered out, and he was pushed inside.

The door closed, and an oil lamp was thrust so close to his face that he could distinguish the taint of the burning wick from the fumes of paraffin. The arm-lock was released, and for a moment he could not straighten his arm. He was in the salon, a massive oak table running the length of the room, benches on either side, and a solid oak carver at one end.

The embers of a wood fire glowed in the cavernous hearth, beneath a great curving oak beam, the Caen stone blocks clambering up from floor to mantel. There was a side table, an ornately carved black beast, crouching on sinewy legs, across the surface of which marched stone flagons, grizzled bottles, brass tankards and frosted glass.

'Asseyez-vous.'

The speaker was seated in the carver, pipe in mouth, hands resting on the table, a tankard between them. Several men sat on the benches, all heads turned towards Eduard. He was pushed, none too gently, towards the vacant seat at the end furthest from the speaker. His captor sat beside him. The *chef de resistance* took his pipe out of his mouth, and contemplated the bowl, a thin trickle of smoke quivering above it. He was, for a moment, entirely still, and Eduard studied him. Black beret, white stubble; thin, curving nose, pinched below the bridge, and long, seamed cheeks, gullies running into a narrow mouth; Eduard could not see his eyes beneath sparse, tufted brows.

The hands that held the pipe were pale, slender, and terminated in curving talons, contrasting with the roseate velvet of his cuffs, folded back over a black tunic, brass-buttoned to the throat, with a Lorraine cross stitched in gold wire on the left breast, to match the one just visible on the side of the beret. He looked up, and held Eduard's gaze, without malice or welcome, the eyes strangely flat, dull grey, and lashless.

When he spoke, it was in English.

'My friends want to know why you're here.'

Eduard thought swiftly. If it was a trap, he was doomed. If he dissembled, he was doomed. Better to find out quickly, and prepare for the consequences.

'I have come to Ammeville, to meet Le Puy.'

The eyes did not waver.

'Bon. And when you have met your M'sieu Puy?'

'Le Puy.'

'Just so. M'sieu Le Puy.'

'Le Comte Le Puy.'

The eyes flickered for an instant, but remained locked on his.

'Le Comte you say. Is there a Comte Le Puy?'

The question was clearly addressed to the room at large, but the eyes were constant. Eduard began to tremble, tensed to still himself, and answered nonetheless.

'So I am told.'

'By whom are you told?'

'By his friends.'

'What friends are those?'

'Friends in high places, far from here, friends who seek the spirit of the mill.'

'Aaaah.' The breath was expelled soft and lingering, and then there was silence. Eduard waited. The room became restless with the shuffling of feet and scratching of beards, the susurration of a small gathering held in tight accord, which reaches a moment of relief, and relaxation.

The eyes were once more contemplating the pipe, which no longer smoked. Without looking up, his inquisitor asked, 'Aimez-vous le trou Normand?'

Eduard sat back, his arms aching, his palms scored by the pressure of his clenched nails, his hair dank with sweat.

'Je l'aime,' and then he added, as he leaned forward again, his hands clasped before him on the table, 'J'aime vous donner liberté, fraternité et egalité dans le trou Normand.'

The room erupted with a subdued roar of approval, and the door opened. A young girl approached, and bent towards the table, slipping a tray of *petit balons* and an anonymous dark brown bottle onto the scarred oak.

Setting the pipe aside, the slender hands reached for the bottle, removed the already drawn cork, and poured. Glass after glass was quarter-filled with viscous, bark-brown liquid, and pushed across the board, as hand after hand cupped each *balon*.

The inquisitor stood. They all stood. He raised his glass.

'La France, et notre liberté.'

'La France. Liberté.'

As they lowered their glasses, he beckoned Eduard and Eduard walked towards him, round the table, behind the standing men. None spoke, none turned. As Eduard reached his side, the inquisitor moved aside, so that they were standing together, turned to him, raised his glass again, and touched Eduard's, as he gave the traditional Norman toast:

'Le trou Normand!' and every man drained his glass, then sat, only Eduard and his host still standing. They faced each other as he said, 'Le Puy, a votre service,' and bowed lightly, indicating that Eduard should be seated, as the girl drew another chair up to the end of the table.

Le Puy smiled, his entire face animated, the cheeks lifting, the mouth apart, the eyes half closed and merry.

'Not many can dig the Norman hole without falling down it, my friend, but then, you come from a country with a prodigious reputation for an equally ambrosial brew. I believe that your wodka and our calva are closely related, no?' and he roared with laughter, draping a slender arm round Eduard's shoulders, and gesturing to the girl to replenish all their glasses.

'And now to business. You, of course, are Le Loup, yes?'

'That's right.'

'And you seek Le Reynard.'

Eduard nodded.

'The trouble is, we have no idea where your quarry is. Our people have probed and pried, but to no avail. The fox has gone to ground.'

Eduard was shown to an attic room, shown the window, the vine that climbed the house, the lean-to roof below, and the simplest escape route. His equipment was returned, his stomach filled with bread and cheese, and his mind with advice, conjecture and suggestions, but nothing that might lead him to the object of his mission. As Le Puy bade him goodnight, he proposed a reconnaissance the very next day, to Vimoutiers, over the hill from Ammeville and Le Parc du Moulin, where Le Comte would meet him at first light.

'I leave you with your host and his daughter. I shall see you in the square, before the church, near the Hotel de Ville, where the Germans are. It's market day, so we shall be setting up our stalls. A bientôt.'

The town hall and its adjoining courthouse dominated the square, yet somehow failed to control it in the way that the church of Our Lady managed without difficulty, gazing benignly down the length of the market, with its carts and bicycles, stalls and produce, the occasional ancient truck and tethered horses. Le Puy strolled from stall to stall, shaking hands, listening, and occasionally offering an encouragement, commiseration or cautious comment. Eduard walked beside him.

'This is our living – cheese and cider, fruit and vegetables, fish and bread. It is also our command centre. Here we can listen and learn, warn and advise, plan and report.'

He turned to Eduard and steered him past a poultry stall.

'We can also avoid and take heed. The chickens can be dangerous. We will not speak with him today.'

'A collaborator?'

'Mmmm, peut-être. Who knows? But there have been rumours, signs, and, well, it pays to be careful, my friend.'

'Ammeville? Is that careful?'

'Aha. Ammeville. Now, you see, that is exactly the point. We have never met there before, and we shall not again. Just for you, as arranged,' and he pinched Eduard's arm.

'This is our rendezvous, le marché, where everything is fresh, for sale, and of good provenance.'

They stopped alongside a butter stall.

'Madame.'

'M'sieu.'

'Allow me to introduce my young friend, from the country.'

Le Puy emphasised the 'the' and the stallholder wiped her hands vigorously on her smock, reached across the pans of butter, and took Eduard's hand.

'Welcome, mister wolf. I hope you find your fox. He's not here today,' and she raised her eyebrows as her eyes swivelled briefly towards the town hall.

Eduard followed her gaze, as the double doors opened, and two officers strode out, followed by a contingent of helmeted soldiers, rifles held at ease. A low-slung Mercedes tourer purred up to the entrance, and a soldier jumped out, saluted and opened the rear door. One officer stepped back, and gestured to the other, but his companion shook his head, removed his cap and flung it in the back of the car, walked round, and took the driving seat. The other officer wheeled, and gave a series of commands, two soldiers dutifully slid across the rear seat, and their officer joined his superior.

'No fox among those chickens,' observed Madame.

'No, but perhaps another wolf, and not a junior one either,' rejoined Le Puy.

He turned to Eduard and gently pulled him out into the melée of townsfolk, moving back and forth between the stalls. In a low voice he murmured, 'Back again. Looks like an SS man. I shall make enquiries.' He looked at Eduard and asked, 'Will you be alright for a few minutes?' and was gone.

Eduard strolled along the stalls, stopping now and then to inspect the merchandise, and to smile at its vendor, until he reached a cheese stall, and glanced up, straight into the eyes of the girl from Le Parc du Moulin.

'B'jour, m'sieu.'

'Mamselle.'

She smiled, and sliced a sliver from the squat round goat's cheese which predominated, proffering it on the end of the blade. Eduard took it, tasted it, found it good, smiled back, and was about to ask for some more, when he felt himself pushed aside. Half turning, he glimpsed the grey uniform before he heard the rasped 'Allez-vous s'en' and watched as a group of German officers jostled each other and picked at the cheeses. The one who had pushed him addressed the girl.

'Where is your Camembert?'

Before she could answer, her father gently moved her to one side, and reached under the table, producing a tray of round rinded cheeses, and quietly commenting, 'Reserved for you especially, Herr Oberst.'

'Danke, danke,' said the German, signalling to a colleague to take the tray, as the group crowded round to see what was on offer.

'It is appreciated, mein friend. Please to join us for some wine when you have finished.' The officer delved into his pocket, and produced a bulging purse. He shook out several coins, and placed them on the stall.

'I trust that is sufficient?' and when the stallholder nodded assent, added, 'We Germans pay for what we buy, nein?'

As they moved away, Eduard glimpsed the girl in the background, and the rage on her face, as her father brushed past her, and through the flaps of the stall canopy. Just as he was about to speak to her, Le Puy rejoined them, quietly observing, 'Our host has worked hard and long for this. Now perhaps we shall see, after the wine.' He pulled Eduard closer. 'We will join them in the café, and then join Maraud – later.'

The café was on the corner, and quietly seething. The German officers were nowhere to be seen.

'They're in the back room,' explained Le Puy.

He and Eduard sipped the coarse, dry cider and surveyed their fellow topers. Le Puy gave him a guided tour of Vimoutiers' traders and teachers, farmers and fabricators, lawyers and layabouts and was halfway through a succinct breakdown of the convoluted relationships between two men and three women at a certain table, when the girl joined them, hovering behind Le Puy until he pulled out a chair and rose to fetch her a drink. Eduard smiled, and she smiled back.

'You have finished for the day?' he asked.

'Oui. Maman is here now. She will continue.'

Le Puy returned with a glass of clear liquid and chuckled as he put it before her.

'No, my friend, it is not water. Genie likes something a little stronger, don't you, cherie?' and the older man's hand closed on the girl's for a moment before he busied himself with his pipe and she lifted the glass – 'Sante' – and drank. Eduard noticed a slight frown, and a momentary flush when Le Puy touched her.

At that moment, a door opened at the end of the room, and voices raised in bonhomous accord preceded the German officers, as they gentled their way through the crowded café, and out into the street.

'Who would imagine their countrymen are dying and they are doomed?' muttered Le Puy under his breath, just as one detached himself, and strode over, planting his hands on their table, and looking at each of them in turn. Then, as he straightened, wiping his mouth with one hand, and putting the other between his tunic buttons, the Obersturmfuehrer struck a Napoleonic pose. He smiled down at Le Puy.

'Monsieur Le Comte. I believe we have the honour to be fighting to stay in your excellent country. I look forward to maintaining our agreeable accord and' – he waved a hand round the suddenly subdued bar – 'to more of your country's splendid hospitality.'

He bowed slightly, and Le Puy half rose, his head partially inclined; the German span on his heel, and caught up with his colleagues as they spilt out of the door.

'Arrogant bastard,' grated Le Puy, lifting his drink and swallowing it, then angrily banging his pipe out on the table leg. Genie looked at Eduard, pursed her mouth, and sipped her drink. Le Puy stuffed tobacco into the bowl, rammed it down and set flame to pipe, exhaling dense clots of gritty smoke. 'Time to go.'

Outside, the market had thinned, and several stalls were already broken down, their holders packing unwanted produce on their carts. Maraud was sitting at one end of his stall as his wife dealt with the occasional customer. Le Puy joined him, spoke once, listened, interjected once, listened again, nodded vigorously, waved Eduard over, shook Maraud's hand, lingered by Genie for a moment, one hand tenderly poised on her arm, then pointed with his pipe.

'Off to the Halle to choose some apples,' adding cryptically, 'the fruit is ready to pick.'

The tables were empty. There was not an apple to be seen. The hall was empty. Le Puy motioned Eduard to wait, and disappeared behind a low door. Eduard wandered round the cavernous room, idly running his hand along one table after another, when he heard the door open, and looked round. Genie walked towards him and stopped, felt in her apron pocket, and produced – an apple.

'I thought you should have at least one. Le Comte is fond of his jokes. There aren't any here. It's out of season, of course.'

She perched on the table as Eduard produced his knife, and pared a slice, offering it to her. She shook her head and watched as he sank his teeth in, grimaced slightly at the sharpness, then cut another piece.

'It grows on you, that kind,' she observed. And Eduard thought, yes, and you grow on me, my little French fruit. Or was she Le Puy's choice dish? As if she read his mind, Genie, swinging her legs, cocked her head to one side and commented, 'He's my father's friend. Fond of me, but. . .' She let the words hang out to dry and Eduard began to mildly fantasise when Le Puy returned.

'Right. Genie, you take M'sieu to the Father. I'll see you both later.'

He glanced at a large, silver watch extracted from an inside pocket.

'Your belongings are at the Hostellerie. You will need them tonight. I'll explain later.'

He glanced about him, then moved closer to Eduard and murmured, 'Your fox is not far away. We go hunting tonight.'

Genie led the way out of the square along the old Grande-Rue, now the Rue Sadi-Carnot, its once bustling shops lack-lustre, its ancient façades in need of paint and stain and creosote, the timbers parched and bleached, its colombage crumbling, its classical interruptions, where prosperous merchants had refronted the old mansions, peeling and blotched with damp.

'After the war, we'll have a tremendous clean-up.'

Genie swept her arm round to take in the high sentinels of the past, their dormers capped, eyes closed, the jumbled timbers and the occasional turrets.

'We'll brush it down and paint it up and it'll be just like new.'

Her eyes lit up, her lips danced and her hair bounced as they walked along and she shone with pride in her heritage. Eduard envied her, at home, free at least to walk the streets, and wait. Her war was being fought, and won.

Genie took them between tall houses, down crooked alleys, over random cobbles, never looking back, but moving inexorably round the town. If anyone had bothered to follow them, they would have given up by the time they reached the house called the Hostellerie of the monks of Jumièges. Hostel, hotel, decayed, restored, and revived as the cantonal museum, it was closed for the duration, its sixteenth-century timbered windows shuttered, its two great doors shut, its broad steps weed-strewn.

The adjoining high palisade contained a panelled door, its sign proclaiming 'Agent General' but for what, no longer apparent. Genie turned her back to the door, surveyed the street left and right, and pushed. The door gave and she beckoned Eduard through. Round the narrow flank of the Hostellerie they scurried, to the rear of the building, where a faint light faltered behind a grimy window in a recessed door, below ground level, and old railings, bent and rusted, their gate padlocked.

Genie slipped the lock, lifted the chain, clattered down the steps, rapped twice, paused, then again, the light faded and disappeared and, after a moment, the door grated open a few inches.

'Comment?'

'C'est moi, Père.'

'Qui?'

'Maraud's daughter.'

'Entrée. Vite, vite.'

The door closed before Eduard could follow, and he stood uncertainly in the shallow basement area. He sensed the footsteps before he heard them, and scuttled under the overhanging flagstones, crouching in the shadows. There were two of them. They were arguing – in German.

'It's closed, Ernst. It's been closed since we arrived. We closed it. That is, the SS closed it, when they found nothing of value.'

'Closed it may be, Oberst, but closed the outer door was too, until this afternoon. When I pushed, it opened.'

The voices were directly above him.

'So?'

'So someone must have opened it.'

'Perhaps it blew open. There was a strong wind last night.'

'Well...'

'Well, there's no-one in there. The front's shuttered, the back's padlocked. Look.'

Eduard heard the chain rattle.

'As the Oberst wishes.'

Footsteps receded, and Eduard heard the fence door open, and close again. He relaxed, started to move, when he heard the door creak once more, and this time, stealthier footsteps approached. The chain rattled, clattered to the ground, and he saw the hard black leather boots start to descend. In desperation, he shrank back again, as the legs followed, then the tunic and –

'Ernst!'

'Ja. Mein Oberst.'

'What the hell are you doing down there?'

'Just checking, Oberst.'

'Well come and check my supper, damn you. I wondered where the hell you'd gone.'

Ernst hesitated.

'Come on, man. I haven't got all day.'

Ernst turned, hesitated again, then bent down, and peered at the door. At that moment, Eduard knew he would have to fight. Ernst straightened, and Eduard saw his body swerve as his gaze presumably swivelled, to check the entire area. He eased the knife out in the palm of his hand, and tensed, holding his breath.

'For God's sake, ERNST!'

Ernst sighed, two hands appeared, straightening the crumpled tunic, and the legs, then the boots, climbed up out of sight. A moment later the outer door clacked shut, and there was silence.

The silence lasted for a few seconds.

'What are you doing out there?'

Eduard lunged forward with the knife, and a thick, white haired wrist clamped his, a large, dry palm hit him full in the face, and he stumbled, straight into wide, swinging folds of black cloth. The large hand held him under the chin, and brought his head up, and his face close to the cloth.

'God bless you, my son, and lay all your fears to rest.'

He looked up, and the broad, beaming, stubbled features smiled down at him.

'Father Bazile, and you must be the wolf. Alone, if not lone.'

The cleric laughed.

'You should see your face. Bon Dieu, you look as if you could do with a drink.'

He turned, and led the way into the basement of the Hostellerie. The room was cluttered with broken furniture, old pots, empty chests and a stack of old picture frames, shorn of their contents and their painterly purpose. Father Bazile pulled the edge of one, and the entire stack lifted, to reveal a low door.

'In here.'

As he bent to enter the cellar, Eduard smelt the musk of old casks and beyond it, a faint and familiar scent. The Father closed the hatch, and a flame flickered, held, wavered, and was still, and there was Genie, holding a lamp.

'Hallo. You got left behind.'

Father Bazile added, 'We saw them coming, just as you arrived. There was no choice.'

He looked at Eduard without the glimmer of an apology in his eyes.

'In war, you take your chances. It was a good test. You did well. Come.'

The door beyond opened into a narrow, brick-vaulted passage, creamy mortar oozing out at intervals, between spauled bricks, some coated with wet green moss. The cobbled floor was slippery, and Eduard stumbled twice, the second time falling momentarily against Genie's slender back. She glanced back at him, smiling, and offered her hand.

The passage led imperceptibly down, until the bricks above them dripped sullenly on their heads and shoulders, and Eduard thought he could hear running water not that far away. 'It's the river,' murmured Genie, pointing up at the sodden vaulting. 'We're crossing under it now.'

Without warning, the passage turned sharp left and ended, apparently at a blank wall. Beside it was a narrow handcart, shafts uppermost. The priest pulled it away to reveal a small aperture. They crawled through, into a long, low chamber, stone vaulted, with tombs and wall plaques. 'The crypt,' announced the Father, propping an upended table against the hole. Genie collected some dusty sheaves of long-harvested corn, and scattered them by the table.

Across the chamber was another door, two steps up, heavy oak, and dry – fresh air ruffled Eduard's hair from the grille in its upper panel. Father Bazile pulled his cassock aside, and fidgeted within its folds, bringing forth a large iron key, which he inserted in the massive rectangular lock-case, and turned anti-clockwise, twice. The door swung outwards towards them noiselessly.

The Father beckoned, and Genie, stil gripping Eduard's hand, led the way up a flight of stone steps, sculpted into concavity by countless foregone footsteps, to an archway. She stopped, slid open a small panel, and peered through. Sliding it back, she stepped aside to let the Father through, whispering, 'I can't see anybody, but I'm not sure.'

Eduard started to move forward, but she checked him.

'A moment. Wait. Let the Father check.'

They stood, close, their hands held loosely, the door ajar, the priest's cassock fluttering across the floor beyond.

The sharp report made them both jump. It was followed by a confused murmur, and then a single voice.

'Is that you, Father? Are you hurt?'

The speaker was invisible. Genie put her hand to her lips, released Eduard, and, with infinite care, pushed the great door to. She bent close to him and breathed into his ear, 'I have no key.' Eduard felt in his pocket, located his knife, and brought it out. Gently, he pushed her aside, and motioned down the steps. She shook her head.

Through the door they could hear voices. Genie slowly eased the panel back, and they heard Le Puy.

'What have we here? Oh dear, oh dear. What have you done?'

Then they heard another voice, and Genie murmured, 'Merde. It's the chicken.'

'I found him like this. I heard a shot, and rushed in. Is he alright?'

'Of course he's not alright. Ask the officer to join us, please.'

There was the sound of a ringed curtain skittering back along a rail, and then the familiar tones of, 'Ach. That Ernst. He is paranoid. First he sees ghosts at the museum, and now he's shot a priest in the vestry. Whatever next?'

Hurried footsteps preceded Ernst's 'But, sir, I was told —'

'Never believe what you're told, Ernst, especially by market traders.'

There was a malicious timbre to this last and Genie's eyes narrowed.

'Anyway, no harm's done. It's only a flesh wound, perhaps a broken finger. We'll soon get it mended.' There was a pause, then, 'Are you able to walk, Father? Good. Well, M'sieu le Comte, if you would be so kind...'

There were sounds of movement, then silence. Eduard strained his ears, and was about to move when the door shuddered.

'Where does this lead, Father?'

'To the crypt,' growled Bazile.

'Is that all?'

'Certainly – though there are old drainage tunnels into the river.'

'Ah. Well, Ernst, since you're so minded to find spies and traitors and the dreaded maquis, you had best descend into the crypt. Who knows? You might find somebody's body.'

And the Oberst spluttered with merriment at his own macabre sally. It was Eduard's turn to swear.

'Oh shit. We'll have to get out, fast.'

'No. You go. Now.'

'I can't leave you.'

'Don't argue. There isn't time,' and she ushered him past the dead harvest as she swept it to one side, and through the hole in the wall, shoving the table back before he had barely gone. He saw the sheaves scattered against the other side of it as he turned to push past the handcart, replace it, and start down the tunnel, back to the Hostellerie. As he went, he thought he heard Genie and his overwrought brain imagined the exchange.

'Who are you? Why are you here? Come with me,' and the interrogation that would surely follow.

It seemed to take a lot less time to reach the Hostellerie cellar than it had taken to leave it. Eduard stopped, and leant against the outer door, his heart thudding and his breath short. Then he slumped onto one of the old chests, and considered his options. If he stayed, Ernst might find him. If he left, he risked exposure before he reached the street. And when he got there, he would be disoriented and lost, and vulnerable. On the other hand, if he waited, and Ernst did arrive... Eduard fingered his knife. Perhaps the time had come to act, to take the initiative, some initiative. He had been in the place nearly a day, and so far, had achieved nothing.

He passed the day's events across his mind's eyes, seeking truths and needing answers. Ammeville and Le Puy; Le Puy and the market; the Halle – and Le Puy. Then the girl, the priest and the ubiquitous Oberst. Eduard stiffened. The Oberst. It was not Ernst who came to mind. Why should that be?

He reviewed the facts again. The Hostellerie, then the church. Ernst at both places – and Herr Oberst also. And where had he seen him before? In the bar. And before that? At the stall. And before that? In that damned Mercedes car. At the time he had thought nothing of it, but the more he recalled, the more odd it seemed. The man who slung his cap in the back was not the senior officer, a Standartenfuhrer, or, if he remembered rightly, a full Colonel. It was Herr Oberst, a mere Lieutenant. How could, would a junior officer behave like that in, of all armies, the so-correct Reichwar, the highly disciplined Wermacht?

It made no sense, unless, yes, unless Herr Oberst was not Herr Oberst but something infinitely more significant, a senior Waffen SS officer, masquerading as a junior army officer.

The picture-frame door shivered, and started to move. Eduard spreadeagled himself against the wall alongside, the knife ready. A small, square-nailed, capable hand appeared, followed by familiar tresses, falling forward, as Genie stepped through the opening, and straightened up.

'I thought you'd be here.'

They sat on the chest as Eduard plied her with questions. Her explanation was short and simple.

'He came down, and found me cleaning the crypt. He knows who I am. He asked me if I had seen anyone, and I shrugged and got on with my work. He poked around a bit, but didn't give a second glance at the old table and the mess on the floor in front of it.'

Genie laughed. 'He did seem a bit disappointed.'

Ernst had returned to the vestry, the officer had gone, she had checked, and found a brief note from Le Puy to say he had taken the Father to the presbytery for a rest and a bandage, and a trou Normand.

'Which means that we should meet there tonight.'

'And the other man, the chicken, as you call him?'

'Oh he was there. He gave me the note.'

'What!?'

Eduard jumped up, and started to prowl around the small room.

'But he's probably why the Father was shot.'

'Yes.'

'So he'll know that's where we're going.'

'Definitely.'

'Well?'

'But we aren't going to the presbytery.'

Eduard sank onto the floor, bewildered. Genie crossed the room, and crouched beside him. She stroked his hair for several seconds, kissed him lightly on his brow, stood up, smoothed her skirt, and opened the basement door.

'He's going to the presbytery, and the Oberst's going too, no doubt, with the ever so earnest Ernst, and there they will find the Father resting, and they will start to search, and they will be surprised at what little they find, but it should keep them busy' – and she went through the door, and held it for Eduard – 'while we shall be somewhere else.'

Genie closed the door, peered cautiously through the railings, lifted the chain, and pushed Eduard through, before returning the padlock, and walking swiftly in the gathering dusk to the palisade door. The street was quiet, and when they closed the door, empty.

'Hold my hand,' commanded Genie, as they set off towards the centre.

The market had gone, the square empty of all except some bicycles, propped against a kerb, a German truck outside the town hall, and two military motorcycles. There was a low light in the Café de l'Equèrre, and they could see a group of traders inside, gesticulating, while smaller groups sat at tables, playing dominoes, or exchanging gossip.

Inside, the Halle was empty as before. The door at the end was ajar. Genie led the way. The small kitchen smelt of apple juice and coffee. Le Puy sat on a bench, a smouldering pipe in his teeth. He did not look up.

'Did you find your equipment?'

Eduard looked at Genie and she shrugged.

'Where was it supposed to be?'

'I told you, in the Hostellerie.'

Le Puy took the pipe out of his mouth and contemplated Eduard.

'You did go to the Hostellerie?'

'You know we did.'

'But not upstairs?'

'Not upstairs.'

'Right. We had best go there straightaway.'

'But won't we be seen? And isn't it dangerous – after this afternoon?'

Le Puy shuffled in his pockets, found a silver match case, and struck a match, holding it to his pipe. Between puffs, he peered at Eduard.

'Not at all. Our little diversion has diverted attention.' He tamped his pipe. 'You don't understand? Ah you English – I'm sorry, I forgot, you're not English, are you?'

He sucked in a draught of smoke, and expelled it with obvious satisfaction, removing his pipe to examine the glistening mouthpiece, shake it free of spittle, and replace it between his lips.

'You Polish are different, of course, but you are still romantics. You expect a certain inevitability. But here we do not think in straight lines, like the Anglo-Saxons or the Slavs. We are, as the English have it, more devious.'

He chuckled.

'Let me explain. The chicken is a guinea fowl, the apples are sour, the wine is the blood of our Lord, but in reality we know it is wine, and in short, nothing is quite how it seems.'

Eduard looked puzzled. Le Puy placed a friendly hand on his shoulder, and an even friendlier one round Genie's, as he drew all three of them into a collective embrace.

'The Father was shot – sadly, and badly. Ernst thinks he shot him. The Oberst thinks Ernst shot him. Ernst shot at him, because the chicken egged him on, but in reality, it was the Father who shot himself. This little charade focused attention on the crypt, having focused it already on the Hostellerie. Now both are clear. And our principal objective is secured.'

Eduard was frowning.

'You don't look happy.'

'Yes, well, but how is all this supposed to help us find the fox?'

Le Puy drew them even closer.

'By sending the cubs out foraging for themselves tonight.'

'I don't understand.'

'You will once you're inside the town hall.'

Eduard pulled apart.

'We can't go in there.'

'Why not? We're citizens, reporting unusual goings on at the Hostellerie, which we have just left, on our legitimate, my legitimate business, as custodian, for the duration, of all our treasures.'

Le Puy beckoned Eduard back into his magic circle.

'And while some of us are occupying the much-depleted resources, of an anyway off-duty establishment, in the little hours, you, my friend, will be taking a closer look at the records, their records, to see where Le Reynard might be.'

Le Puy slapped them both lightly on the back, and stepped away, recharging his pipe.

'Now do you understand?'

As Eduard shook his head, Genie smiled uncertainly and Le Puy erupted with great gouts of smoke, the door opened and the Oberst strode in.

'I thought I might find you here.'

Great expectations – a good title. The story of need and greed, of sad and bad, and the desperation against all odds to achieve a goal. That is how I feel – sad, bad, needy and greedy for what I once had, but no longer desperate, for there is no realistic goal. But then – ah, that was different. I had a goal alright – to smack Hitler in the eye and it began to look as if I might, for was not Rommel the most feared and effective of his generals?

I sit here in the empty hall of my fruitless existence, and I marvel at the way in which I aspired to greatness. Eduard the teenage rebel, now barely twenty, and stalking the mighty Erwin. What puzzles me now is that I never realised then quite how ambitious, if not presumptuous I was.

Yet the answer is simple, and lies in the distortions that war creates. Rommel was weakening and, as a good soldier, must have known it. I was like the man whose adrenalin flows instantly and unexpectedly when someone wrongs him, and is momentarily all-powerful. I had the mental strength of ten men, and fortunately for me, not even the egotism of one. Had I realised how important was my mission, I would have failed through self-importance. Pride was not then one of my sins.

I have regressed since that sharp time, and now mourn what I presume to think I was – of value, amusing, effective, and important to others. Then I was nothing but a man with a mission – both the one for which I was trained, and the one I had learnt within.

If I recover, and that I doubt, it will be despite myself, for I have no mission, only a longing which is for self, not others. I deserve no great expectations and I have none, only small desires.

Then I was a giant, and I did not know it. But then I was someone else, and not me.

A LETTER FOR LONDON

The single guard was reading. He looked up. He dropped the paper and saluted. The Oberst nodded, and strode past him. Ernst followed, Eduard alongside, as they climbed the stairs.

'In here.'

They filed into the office of the Mayor. The Colonel rose, saluted, and the Oberst nodded and, with a minimal gesture, returned the salute, wrenched his cap off, and flung it onto a chair. It missed, slithered to the floor, and Ernst retrieved it. Eduard stood, waiting. Ernst bowed slightly, murmuring 'Mein Herr', and left the room.

The Colonel excused himself, and Herr Oberst subsided onto the captain's chair, swivelling it to and fro, his hands steepled, just touching the tip of his jutting nose. Eduard had time to observe him for the first time. Hard, dark eyes appraised him in turn, the almost blue, close-shaven chin in contrast to the crimped blond hair, a short quiff falling over the high, bony forehead.

'So. Your papers are in order, but are you in order, I ask myself.'

Without waiting for Eduard to reply, he continued.

'Le Comte speaks warmly of you, doesn't he? An old friend, or rather, the son of an old friend, from Caen, but we can't check that, can we, because your home has been obliterated by the enemy's shells.'

He stared at Eduard.

'Convenient, or rather sad? I wonder which.'

His hands left his face, patted his pockets and reappeared with a silver cigarette case and a slim lighter. He flicked the lid, thumbed the wheel, at the same time as he shook out a black cigarillo, and placed it centrally between his teeth. Eduard noticed they were small, neat and sharp. The flame flared, with a wisp of black smoke, and he put it within an inch of the little cigar, which glowed, burnt, and jettisoned a fluff of ash as he inhaled.

'My name is Jodl with a soft J – Helmut Jodl.'

He put the lighter precisely in the centre of the desk, on top of the packet of cigarillos. He gestured towards them.

'Would you like one?'

Eduard shook his head. Jodl jogged his head up and down in small agreement.

'No. Difficult to find – in France.'

The Oberst leant forward, picking up the lighter and turning it over and over between thumb and forefinger.

'Now. If you're who you say you are, we can all relax, perhaps have a little kir in the café, go home, and forget about the war.'

He dropped the lighter suddenly, and it clattered across the desk.

'If not, we have a problem. Or rather, you have a problem.'

There was a discreet knock at the door.

'Come.'

The Colonel opened it and stood in the doorway. The Oberst glanced at him, without expression.

'Walther.'

'Helmut. The parties are ready.'

'Yes. Good. Just give me a minute, will you?' He added 'Please' after a short pause; the Colonel nodded briefly, and withdrew.

Jodl picked up the lighter again, looked down at it reflectively, then pocketed it, gathered up the packet and slipped that in another pocket, and stood. He walked round the desk, right up to Eduard, and looked into his eyes. Eduard could smell the faint echo of what seemed to be a woman's scent.

Years later he would remember that moment whenever he smelt Chanel No. 5 on a lady customer. It often put him off. Almost inaudibly, Jodl spoke, slowly and deliberately, without menace or, indeed, any discernible inflexion.

'I like you very much. You are very much my type.'

He raised a slim, white hand, the veins pulsing softly beneath the surface. He stroked Eduard's cheek, caressingly.

'I would hate to have to hurt you.'

His hand rested lightly on Eduard's face.

'I hope I have no cause. I would rather you hurt me, but in a gentler way than I might have to hurt you.'

His hand dropped. He remained, standing so close Eduard thought he could feel the air move between them with their heartbeats.

'Don't make me hurt you, Eduard. Stay out of trouble.'

For a brief moment, Eduard had the impression the German was about to kiss him, then Jodl stepped quietly back, smiled, wheeled, bent to retrieve his cap, deftly donned it, glanced in the mirror beside the door, adjusted cap, tie, belt, and smoothed his jacket, before walking out of the office without another word.

Eduard stood, his mind misted, his stomach contracting with revulsion, as disgusted with his own perverse pleasure in the German's overture as he was appalled at Jodl's seductive approach. Despite himself, he knew he was tempted, just for a moment, to wonder what it might be like to return the Oberst's touch. He felt immediately and overpoweringly sick, and sat down, holding his belly, his other hand to his mouth.

He did not hear Ernst's knock, or see the man enter, until a rough hand clamped on his shoulder. He looked up, and the soldier jerked his head at the door, adding in German, 'Wait outside.' Eduard's reflexes took over. He looked suitably puzzled, raised his eyebrows, and asked in French, 'What do you want?'

Ernst took his arm, and pulled him to his feet, pushing him towards the door. Once through, he indicated a leather bench against the wall, and Eduard subsided, folding his arms, and looking innocent. Ernst grunted, and clattered down the stairs. In the hall there was a flurry of movement as soldiers appeared and disappeared, and the guard was hard put to it to move his saluting arm up and down as the Colonel, the Oberst and at least two other officers hurried to and fro.

Outside lorries were revving and, as the last contingent scurried out into the night, followed by the Colonel, Eduard heard the hesitant flutter and series of backfires of first one, then a second motorcycle starting up. Within seconds, trucks and cars and motorbikes joined in a concerted crescendo, and moved off. The town hall, deserted, echoed to their vanishing revs, and there was a moment of complete quiet.

'Colonel Hirsch, if you please.'

Le Puy's most emollient tones were instantly recognisable.

'Not here, sir. Colonel – not here.'

'Then I'll wait.'

Le Puy was wedged in the doorway between the uncertain guard and the half-open door.

The guard was in difficulty. Here was the most senior citizen, a confidant of the Commandant, someone who drank with the officers, for God's sake, not your average Frog, wanting to come inside, and there were his orders, which said nobody could do that without the officers' permission. As if he read his thoughts, Le Puy flourished a piece of important paper – stiff, cream, embellished with a swastika, and the two folded flashes of the SS, with a signature and a dense paragraph of type.

'Permission to enter, my friend. Indeed, orders to report.'

The guard capitulated, and Le Puy glanced behind him and waved peremptorily. Maraud and Genie appeared as if by sleight of hand. The guard saluted reluctantly, and opened the door, stepping aside as they entered.

'We'll wait upstairs, in the Commandant's office,' announced Le Puy, as he walked sedately towards the stairs. 'They can wait here,' he added, as two more appeared, and Eduard recognised the man who had apprehended him at Ammeville, and the woman in the market.

The guard nodded, and resumed his station, picking up his book, but glancing from time to time at his unexpected companions, as they settled comfortably on the hall bench. Le Puy and Genie mounted the stairs, ignoring Eduard, and disappeared inside the Colonel's office.

After a moment, Le Puy appeared, his talons gripping the door, as he spoke, a note of command in his voice.

'My friend!'

The guard started, looked up from his book, and half rose, a query on his broad face.

'Some water, please. We may have a long wait.'

The guard looked about him in agitation, stood, sat, stood again, and finally waved his hands.

315

'Not possible. Not possible. The door. I stay.'

'Of course,' responded Le Puy, 'but is there nobody who can fetch us a carafe?'

'Not possible. All not here. Not possible.'

'Aaaaah. Very well. I understand.' Le Puy smiled a reassuring smile, and beckoned Eduard. 'Perhaps you would fetch us some water.' He looked down at the guard, raising his voice. 'Is that alright?'

The guard, again startled, stood again, wretchedly. The poor man was clearly out of his depth. It was easier to agree. As he sat down, he smiled uneasily and pointed at the door along the landing.

'The water. It is there. Please. Thank you,' and he buried his head in his book, a clear signal that he would be grateful, very grateful indeed, for no further interruptions, thank you very much.

Le Puy waved Eduard away.

'Go on. Get some water. It is in the officers' cloakroom, the door beside the Commandant's private secretary's office – that's the one with the padlock.'

This last was said quietly, and certainly out of the guard's hearing. Le Puy disappeared as Eduard walked along the landing and through the swing doors. Beyond, he paused, and assessed the lobby in which he found himself.

There was a frosted door on one side, and another, with a chain and padlock, beside it. One other door was ajar. He pushed it slightly, and peered inside.

'I'm sorry.'

The man inside was sitting at a circular table, covered with maps, and with a wireless set behind him, on a small table. He wore earphones, and was holding a heavy microphone. He looked slightly annoyed, somewhat surprised, and clearly preoccupied. He rapped out in German: 'Yes? Who are you?'

As he spoke, his hand moved to his side, and Eduard guessed he was feeling for a handgun. He walked straight inside and stopped, well away from the man. In precise and unaccented German he replied, evenly and quietly.

'Vidler. Headquarters. Carry on. I am in the Colonel's office with our French people. Please stay here.'

Eduard looked round the room with what he hoped was a proprietorial air.

'Good. Very good. But please stay here until further orders, ja?'

'Jawohl, mein herr,' and the man started to rise, his hand coming up in a salute.

'Not necessary. Please sit. Finish what you are doing.'

Eduard turned, walked slowly to the door, and closed it behind him. Outside he closed his eyes, and breathed in and out, stifling an insane desire to scream and run. When he opened them, Genie was standing in front of him, holding out a small leather bundle.

Inside was a set of delicate tools – picks, screwdrivers, narrow blades, pincers. Genie pointed at the padlock and Eduard crouched and inspected it. Simple enough, he said to himself, mentally adding that Le Puy was right, they were arrogant bastards if they thought this was security. It took a moment to unpick the tumblers, the padlock dropped open and, carefully easing it out of the hasp, Eduard handed it to Genie, and turned the handle.

They stood still for a second or two, waiting for a non-existent or shut-down alarm, then Eduard pushed the door open. Once inside, Genie beckoned, and he bent towards her. Her mouth against his ear, she murmured, 'I will fetch the water, stand outside and, if he comes out, I'll say I was just fetching it, and try to get him back inside. If not, I'll take him to Le Puy.'

Eduard nodded agreement and drew her to him, whispering in turn, 'If there's a problem, just drop a glass or cup or whatever you find, and I will be prepared.'

Left alone, he stood in the centre of the room, and assayed the contents, moving round in 360 degrees, making a selective inventory: desk, drawers – inspect; filing cupboard – most likely; boxes – probably longer-term storage; a leather attaché case – priority. He walked over to the desk, and picked up the case. It was locked. It took several minutes to manipulate the single lock, which was more sophisticated than usual. Inside there were two folders. One was marked with coded symbols; the other was blank.

Without the equipment still at the Hostellerie, he could take no film. He cursed Jodl for waylaying him before they were ready, as he opened the other file, and his hand shook slightly. Several papers fell to the floor. One was signed. The name beneath was Erwin Rommel.

It was addressed to VS (Jodl), 12th Schutzstaffel Panzer Division, Town Hall, Vimoutiers. It was a short letter, and to the point. It acknowledged previous signals, and confirmed unspecified arrangements. The other papers were in code.

Eduard sat down, and replaced the papers in the file and the file in the case. He locked it. He had memorised the two salient facts. The letter was dated 7 June and referred to a week hence – the 14th – and a time – 0700 hours. Whatever was the substance of the signals was going to start to happen at that time on that day. If it was significant enough for Rommel to confirm it, then the 14th would be a significant, German event.

The letter was addressed to VS (Jodl), 12th SS Panzer Division. Eduard's mouth dried. He tried to swallow. His mouth closed, his tongue cloved to its roof, and he thought he heard his teeth rattle. 12th SS Panzer – Hitler's crack armoured division, led by the legendary Fritz Witt, the so-called Hitler Jugend. It had blocked the Allied advance on Caen a week before. Was it now in the Vallee de la Vie, poised to wreak more havoc under Rommel's baton?

And what was the VS? He wracked his brains. It could reflect Jodl's job, his mission, his status even; then again, it could simply be initials. But Jodl called himself Helmut. Could it mean a unit – Forward Station, perhaps?

Eduard ran through the possibilities. The Allies had landed the day before it was sent, so there must be a connection. Something was scheduled for Vimoutiers tomorrow morning. But what? Eduard looked again round the room, and got up, walking over to the boxes. Inside the first were bundles of papers, neatly tied with black tape. Old stuff. It was the same in every box.

Not worth the trouble. He turned to the cupboard. Double doors, unlocked. That suggested routine bumf. Inside were marked files. He glanced at the first half-dozen – all average military material. Nothing in code. A random check on each shelf yielded nothing but mounting irritation. He walked back to the desk. The first drawer was empty, save for a tin of cough pastilles, a small pennant with the Reichstandard furled round a bronze stem. He pocketed that without thinking, beyond a sense of potency that he had such a symbol of the enemy in his possession. The second contained blank paper, pins, elastic bands – all the paraphernalia of a clerical life. The remaining drawer was locked.

It resisted all his attempts to open it, for there was no keyhole, only a revolving handle, which went round and round without apparently doing anything. He tried to pull it, push it, shift it sideways, all to no avail. He sat contemplating the drawer, asking himself what he would have done at Audley End had he been faced with such a conundrum, when the glass fell.

The first bounce was followed by a splintering, the tinkle of glass shards scattering, and an audible 'Merde' followed immediately by an 'Oh! Pardon' as a door banged against a wall and a German voice, the wireless man's voice, exclaimed, 'What the hell?'

Eduard slid under the desk, and thanked the manufacturer, presumably French, for his prudery in providing a courtesy screen to conceal feminine legs. He felt for, found and palmed his knife.

The voices were more muted, and he could only make out an occasional word. Then he heard a door close, less noisily, and there was nothing. Eduard was uncomfortable. His legs were twisted sideways, and his knees were jammed between his face and the pedestal. His head was forced onto his left shoulder, and his neck ached. He knew he could not stay in that position much longer. Cautiously, he shifted the angle of his head, and felt something hard and round press into his temple. Slowly he backed out of the kneehole and lay on the floor, looking up at a small, round knob.

Tentatively, he twisted it, and above him, the drawer sprang open. He caught the back of his head on its underside as he scrabbled out of his hiding place. Rubbing the sore spot, he looked down and, beside a

Walther P38 automatic, saw a clip of silver-nosed bullets and a sheaf of square papers, obviously torn off a notepad.

He put them on the desk, and pulled up the chair. One by one, he examined them. They were covered in symbols – code. Except one. The twelfth note was in German. All it said was: 'My lovely man. I am so jealous. He is AMAZING! Never mind. See you on the 15th.' It was signed Kurt and it was addressed to Helmut.

Eduard dismissed his VS quest and focussed on the inescapable. Helmut had cancelled a tryst, because Rommel himself was coming to Vimoutiers on the 14th of June – tomorrow. Teichmann was right. With or without the Panzers, the heavy brigade could strike, the wolf would die, and the Nazis would reel, without their most mercurial, effective and, as far as the Allies were concerned, dangerous soldier.

The priority now was to get out, find a wireless, and tell London. He put the papers back, and slightly disarranged them, pushed the drawer in and heard it click, checked that it was once more locked, and pushed back the chair. The door opened.

'You again!' The German was still for a moment. Then his hand rose, the gun pointing directly at Eduard's head.

'You come with me. I want to ask you a few questions.'

Eduard shrugged, and spoke quietly.

'You know who I am. Put the gun down. It will only get you into trouble.'

The German waggled the gun, grimaced and, with his other hand, made it clear that Eduard should walk past him and out of the office.

'I do know who you are not – you are not Vidler. There is no Vidler at Headquarters. I checked.'

Eduard shrugged again, and walked past, the knife in his palm, but the man moved back as he approached, and put the desk between them until Eduard was outside.

'In my office.'

Eduard pushed the door open, and the man followed. He sidled round Eduard and took his seat behind the table.

'You kneel, on the floor, there.'

Eduard did as he was told.

'Now.' The man placed his gun carefully on the table and folded his arms. 'Let us begin with who you really are.' As he finished, the man looked past Eduard, then back to him, picking up the gun, and waving it about.

'Keep your eyes to the front.'

The door was open; someone was standing there, but who, Eduard could not tell, until he caught the trace of a faint scent, and tensed.

'Yes?'

The question was filled with uncertainty, and Eduard eased the knife down his palm, into his fingers, the blade slick with his sweat.

'Le Comte is unwell. Can you help?'

319

As Genie spoke, the man's eyes flickered between her and Eduard and, as he hesitated, Eduard swung his right arm with a speed beyond anything he had achieved in those sessions at Audley End. The knife left his hand like an arrow from a crossbow, Genie kicked him sideways, falling on him, as the German fired, but too high and too late. The knife lodged in his throat, and the blood surged out.

The gun dropped on the desk, end over end, and fell to the floor, the bullet embedding itself in the architrave above the door. Eduard shoved Genie to one side, and leapt across the room, pulling his handkerchief out, grabbing the German, retrieving his knife, and staunching the flow.

'We must not leave a trace,' he gasped as Genie joined him, ripping off her blouse, and winding it round the German's neck. They eased the man onto the floor, and tied the material. Eduard turned, and walked rapidly to the door, extricating the bullet with the blade, and pocketing it. Genie had stuck the gun in her belt and, as they leant against the desk, breathing heavily, Le Puy appeared. He took in the *mise en scène* with a single glance.

'Right. We have to leave. Can you carry him?'

Eduard nodded, and asked, 'What about the guard? Didn't he hear the shot?'

'Of course he did. He came bounding up the stairs, and I asked him what was going on next door. "Next door?" he asked me, and I said I heard a shot, so he ran back downstairs and disappeared towards the courthouse with Maraud and Madame.'

'Thank God for that.'

'Yes, but he'll be back, so we've got minutes, if at all.'

'We've also got information, and I need a wireless – now.'

Le Puy made no comment, but instead, held the door open, as Eduard humped the German over his shoulder, and Genie followed, steadying his burden. They made their way across the landing, looked over the banisters and the now empty hall, then moved down the stairs in single file. Le Puy beckoned them away from the front door.

'Round the back – no lights, nearer the Hostellerie. Come on.'

Once outside the town hall, Le Puy and Eduard slung the dead German between them and walked swiftly down the narrow alley, to the lane that led to the back of the ancient refuge of the monks. Genie lifted the chain, and they quickly made their ways into the main cellar, Le Puy leading. There he removed several old crates, to reveal an arched door. Beyond were spiral steps.

'Leave him here,' suggested Le Puy. 'We'll dispose of him later.'

'So long as he isn't found,' offered Eduard.

Le Puy's usual calm slipped slightly as he snapped back, 'He won't be found in a tomb, in the crypt, in the church, will he? Now let's get on with it.'

The body was propped against the wall and, as Eduard arched his back to relieve the strain, and Le Puy vanished round the curving stairs, Genie spoke quietly, her hands on his face.

'I must go. I will put the crates back. In the morning you must go too.'

She leant into him, and kissed him softly on the lips.

'In case I don't see you again.' Eduard pulled her close, and kissed her back, restraining a mounting surge of passion. As they parted, they took each other's hands and Eduard saw in her eyes something of Sara's longing, and she saw his.

Abruptly, she released him, turned, and was gone. He sighed, then made his way up the stone steps.

'Your equipment is all here. If you need it, use it – quickly. Then you must go. You are too dangerous, my friend, and you are in danger too.'

Le Puy had found his pipe, and was tamping tobacco as he spoke, his eyes probing Eduard's as his talons clicked on the bowl.

'Wireless. Where is it? I must tell London what I have found.'

'There.'

Le Puy pointed his pipe stem at a table in the corner. On it stood a familiar sight – a portable transmitter. Eduard sat, pulled on the headphones, and drew the key towards him.

'What about the codes?' asked Le Puy.

'In here.' Eduard tapped his head and tuned in. Then he started tapping his message.

'Wolf says fox in lair, Vimoutiers. 14 June 0700 hours. 12 SS Panzer connection.'

In war, timing is critical. Sometimes opportunities are lost through the bureaucracy of the military machine but this time SOE moved quickly. The USAAF was informed. The 9th Army Air Force looked at its missions. Highway command centres south of the beachhead were part of the schedule.

Two Combat Bombardment Wings comprising 32 Bombardment Squadrons, with over 500 aircraft, were poised to strike. Now Vimoutiers was logged on as well. The fourteenth of June would become its Armageddon.

Obersturmfuehrer Reinhard of the Schutzstaffel was not pleased. Vimoutiers came within his purview at area HQ Alencon and now there was someone called Jodl of the same rank, countermanding his orders, and seemingly on terms with Feldt Marschal Rommel himself. This upstart had wheedled his way into some sort of relationship with Witt's Panzers, and now he, Richard Reinhard, was summoned to a meeting in this wretched cheese town early next morning.

Nobody would tell him what it was about, only that it was important. Important! Good God above, what could be more important than manning the barricades as the barbarians battled for Caen, on their way south no doubt, to Falaise, Argentan, Sees and then, God help us, Alencon. There were paintings to crate, silver to pack, wine to transport, and these bloody generals and their SS infiltrating lackeys wanted meetings? He would see about that.

He was not going to be outgunned by some newcomer, just because his name was Jodl, his status probably guaranteed solely through family influence. Well, Colonel General Alfred Jodl was a long way away at Overkommando der Wermacht – operations staff HQ in the Reich – so he was not a local factor and, so far as Rommel was concerned, well, Richard Reinhard was not impressed by a Field Marshal who had lost two battles already. Not for nothing had he spoken personally with Reichsfuehrer Himmler about the need for control, respect for authority, implementation of orders without question. He picked up the phone.

'Get me Colonel Hirsch, at Vimoutiers. Yes now!'

The conversation was commendably brief. The Colonel understood how these things work. He would speak to the 'other' Oberst. The arrangements would be made 'as you suggest'.

Reinhard smiled as he replaced the receiver. These superannuated Army officers they were sending west these days – absolutely hopeless, but they did understand the politics, and they always jumped to attention where security was concerned, especially their own.

At USAAF Great Dunmow in Essex, England, the flight was ready. Sixteen B-26 Marauder bombers of 386 Bombardment Group (Medium) were bombed up and ready, engines turning, as the first wheeled and taxied onto the main runway.

On the road out of Vimoutiers, Jodl fidgeted with discomfort inside the small 256 half-track. The raid on Ammeville had yielded nothing except a little gratifying fear on the part of the mill owner, hardly worth the broken arm and the dishevelled wife. The men had stopped as soon as he realised there was nothing for them there. She was hardly attractive anyway.

Back at the town hall, there was little more satisfaction. There had been some sort of a fracas. The man Eduard had gone. Wirelessman Stiffell had gone too, which was inconvenient. There was a bullet hole above the doorway and that was Stiffell's, yet the guard swore there was a shot next door. There was no bullet there. Le Puy had suggested that all was not well; then he, too, had inexplicably disappeared. That was especially inconvenient, since Le Puy's information of late had been somewhat incomplete and increasingly misleading. One might be forgiven for wondering if, after all, he was on the other side, despite his Prussian wife.

ERWIN'S ACCIDENT

It was not discomfort that itched. It was irritation. Someone was playing tricks and Jodl was not amused.

He had three men apart from the driver – and Ernst, the stalwart, steady sergeant who had been with him in Poland, in Russia and later, in Rome. Only Ernst knew his secrets, and Ernst only knew some of those. He knew Jodl's real name was not Jodl, but he did not know what his real name was.

He knew his rank was not Obersturmfuehrer, and he also knew, because that was essential, where Jodl's real interests lay, and their secret nature, but he did not know where his 'secrets' were buried, and he did not know Jodl's real rank or his personal antecedents, though he had long ago guessed that he was part of a quite different arm of the Schutzstaffel, which Ernst, being Ernst, never articulated, but kept to himself, against a day of personal need.

He was not the sort of man who worried about such trivia anyway, which was one of the reasons he was Jodl's man. The other – he was the sort of man who relished the chase, and now he was sniffing the air appreciatively, like the terrier he was, as they embarked on the manhunt that would end in the chambers of persuasion for those of the Resistance they found with the man they now knew was a British spy – the man who called himself Le Loup – Eduard Le Loup, lately of Caen.

Eduard had not yet left Vimoutiers, but he had slipped away from the Hostellerie, left Le Puy at the Halle, and was sitting quietly in the back room at the Hotel Soleil d'Or on the main square, with Maraud and the man they called 'the chicken', who wiped his mouth as he set down his glass of cider, sucked his teeth, then said shortly, 'We leave at midnight. Your rendezvous the estuary, off Honfleur.'

Maraud ground his cigarette into the cracked saucer, drained his cider, rose and buttoned his jacket.

'It is good that we go now, to collect your equipment.' He turned to 'the chicken'. 'You will be at Honfleur?'

'But of course.'

Hands were shaken, without smiles, for this was no fond farewell, but the business of several departures. As they walked away from the square, and skirted the church, Maraud nudged Eduard.

'I think perhaps we send someone else ahead.' He paused and added, 'Just to be sure.'

555 Bombardment Squadron droned above the clouds, the heavy overcast inhibiting the German defences, so that Captain Barney 'Basher' Labovitch felt secure enough to 'talk' 'plane-to-'plane.

323

'Green Leader to squadron, ten minutes to target. Repeat. Ten minutes to target. Roger and out.'

One by one the others called back, 'Ten minutes to target. Roger and out.'

As they crossed the bocage, the clouds parted momentarily and, not for the first time in these Norman sorties, Barney wondered at the tapestry below, wooded, woven with boundary and stream, a green plainsward, tranquil through the pale blue lens of distance, where the only evidence of war was an occasional smudge of smoke. It seemed unbelievable that on the ground men and machines ground mercilessly to and fro, churning the rich earth, flailing each other with shell and grenade, killing and crying and dying. It seemed as always on these missions, entirely unreal that he would add to that threshing turmoil without ever witnessing the indelible scars his will inflicted upon lives and livings.

'Two minutes. Start descent.'

As they broke through the cloud cover, German radar 'collected' them, and the anti-aircraft barrage fluffed among them, lethal shrapnel disguised as cotton-wool tufts. The squadron jinxed slightly and, as suddenly as it started, the flack stopped, the cloud receded, and ahead of them lay Vimoutiers.

'Five degrees and turn.' The squadron veered in for the kill. Labovitch's bomb-aimer opened the bay, his leathered hand closed on the levers. 'Bombs away,' and the aircraft banked and rose. Twenty-nine tons of high explosives lazily somersaulted down to earth – 'with excellent results', the War Room noted the very next day.

Barney glanced over his shoulder as each 'plane released its seed to pollinate the rich rooves below and the first fungal brolly opened and flowered beneath them. Seconds later, the rigid birds were sucked into the clouds, and gone, as if they had never been.

'Mission completed. Well done everyone. Roger and out.'

The Hostellerie shuddered as the ground reeled, metal burst and blast gathered, grew and reared over the tiles, sucking a random few into its maw as it careered across the rooftops, to sway, then swallow whole terraces beyond. Windows were sucked out, their curtains with them, then blown back in again, the material trapped 'twixt frame and casement. Glass survived within feet of contact, yet shattered a hundred yards away.

The square echoed to the roaring roll of the first cluster as bomb after bomb hurtled through the cobbles, and blast sucked brick from timber, tile from rafter, stone paving from neighbouring steps.

Then hell's angels stalked the streets of Vimoutiers, their wings sweeping shop and house and hall and café aside, walls crumbling, their horned feet crushing people and produce alike, their careless hands brushing aside children and their mothers.

The Hotel de Ville defied the first onslaught; while blast sucked the contents dry, its walls trembled, slipped, but stood fast. The Hotel de Soileil d'Or collapsed. The Halle disintegrated. The Café de l'Equèrre slipped into memory's labyrinthine paths. The monks of Jumièges long gone were not there to see their Hostellerie demolished. The Pincons and the Cochets were oblivious, for they too were dead.

At 7.50 am on that morning of the 14th of June, nine weeks before freedom followed, Vimoutiers was destroyed. Two hundred Vimestrians did not survive to greet their liberators – the comrades of the men who closed their lives. Alone in the centre of town, stood the church of Notre Dame – Our Lady's House was safe, and so was Erwin Rommel, for he had gone to another place to meet, not his doom, but Oberst Reinhard and some other, more important men.

His only regret – Jodl, who led Five Sturmtruppe, the 'secret' weapon, the death squad born of the blitzkrieg, would not be there. He had no illusions about the man, his concupiscence or his finely balanced focus on pain, but his unit was fearless, ruthless, superbly well-equipped, and integral to the battle plan. VS would still play its part.

The man himself was also safe. Helmut Jodl was in his half-track, parked in the woodland, above the cliffs, not far from Honfleur, satisfied that his informant on the beach below at Vasouy was sufficiently fearful not to mislead him.

Safe but not sound was Le Puy who, with Father Bazile, lay dazed in the crypt of the church of Our Lady, their ears and eyes and throats crusted with sweat and dust and mucus, their thoughts chaotic and their fears shadowing their cries as they crawled to the great door, and found it jarred and jammed. Le Puy slumped down on the step, and closed his eyes. The priest staggered to the back of the crypt, and reached under a low table. He turned, his arm trembling, as he held aloft a bottle of communion wine.

''Tis not yet blest, as we are curst, so let us cleanse our minds of this horror.'

He smashed the neck against a tomb, and glass splattered among the small spurts of wine, as he thrust the bottle at Le Puy, startled by the sound of breaking glass. Le Puy took the bottle, upended it, and let the red liquid splash on his face and stream into his open mouth, then reversed the bottle and passed it back to the Father. As Bazile in turn poured the wine down his caked throat, Le Puy fumbled in his pocket, produced a pipe, tobacco and a battered box of matches. They sat together on the step, sharing bottle and pipe, silent and infinitely sad with their conjectures, the balance sheet of their future freedoms, and the impotence within their incarceration.

'The angels of death, Father. Our liberators.'

'You speak with bitterness, my Count. Think of the lives to be saved.'

Le Puy passed the bottle and the priest trickled the last of the wine past his lips.

'And those doubtless lost, above our very heads.'

He took the pipe out of his mouth, and looked down at it.

'Their embers are extinguished too, and for what? To reach an old soldier who is himself lost, even if he does not yet know, or recognise it. They should have waited.'

He knocked out the dead ash, and started to refill the pipe.

'I am weary of this war, Father. Tired. Really tired.'

The priest propped himself up on one hand, and raised the other.

'Forgive me, for I too am tired, so I shall not stand. But you have done what you could, and what you should have done, and you will be thanked when the time comes, by Our Lord in Heaven,' and he made the sign of the cross over the old man's head.

Genie stood on the cliff path, watching the tide riff across the shallows, as it reached the slabs of rock at Vasouy, on the estuary of the Seine, and strained to see the cliffs and the carcase of Le Havre across the straits. Below her, 'the chicken' sat alone, his arms around his knees, staring out to sea.

Eduard and Maraud knelt in St Margrethe's in the square above the port of Honfleur, praying not only to their God, but for their courier to appear. There was a scurry of salt air as the door opened, then closed. Footsteps clacked down the wide timber floor and stopped beside them. A grey envelope of cloth settled beside Eduard, and the sleeves fell back to reveal solid wrists and calloused hands, clasped in prayer.

Madame murmured, head bowed in devotion

'There is company at the beach. Genie is there. There are others too, in the woods above.'

Eduard stiffened. 'Others?'

'Of a certainty. Your blond friend, his lackey and perhaps four others.'

Maraud murmured quietly, 'We should return home. Perhaps another day.'

Madame: 'Not possible.'

'Not possible?'

'There was a raid. Many died. Best to stay away. Our town is no more.'

She turned briefly and spoke slowly, but clearly.

'We are invisible, for now we are truly dead.'

They stayed, prayed, then one by one, left the church.

Outside, Eduard, the last to leave, watched Maraud, then Madame walk down the curving lane towards the harbour. Then he followed. The unrelated procession of three solitary souls wended its connected way past the custom house, and along the harbour wall, then onto the inshore path alongside the outer haven, until first Maraud, then

Madame, slipped into the scrub below the lighthouse. Eduard hesitated, then plunged into the desiccated brush, following a meandering, sandy path until he reached a small clearing, an upturned boat, and a leaning hut.

Inside there was a third party. Maraud shut the door.

'Jean-Pierre – Le Loup.'

They nodded, the tension inhibiting handshakes.

Jean-Pierre, a sullen, unshaven, short, square slab in sailcloth pantaloons, clogs and an unravelling sweater, pulled a shapeless knitted hat over his brow. His cigarette was dead between his lips, his hands restless on the notched knife he held, and twisted and turned and weighed and stroked.

'We cannot sail from Vasouy now he's there.'

Maraud twitched.

'Where then?'

'With the fisherman, tonight.'

Madame was restless too, frightened, Eduard decided, but not for herself.

'What about Genie?'

Jean-Pierre shrugged.

'What can we do? They are there; she is there; he is there. Impossible.'

Maraud chewed his mouth, then wiped it with one hand and, with the other, reached into his battered shoulder bag. One by one, he placed the grenades on the shelf beside him, until there were six lined up. Then he opened his palm towards Eduard and his scrubby eyebrows lifted in expectation. Eduard smiled a mirthless smile, and unfolded his bedroll. Inside lay the machine pistol and the German's handgun. He waved a finger at Maraud.

'Take it. He has no use for it any more.'

Maraud reached over and lifted the gun, flapped it from one hand to the other, nodded, and then he too smiled.

'Good enough for this evening's work.'

He checked the mechanism, counted the bullets, then snapped it shut and handed it to Madame. Without a glance, she folded it within her skirts.

Maraud replaced the grenades in his bag, and Eduard rolled the pistol into its temporary holster.

'What next?'

Jean-Pierre stood, eased the door ajar, and cautiously looked outside.

'We leave now. Rest, eat. Then we meet again, tonight.'

Maraud nodded his agreement, turning to Eduard.

'For you, this is acceptable?'

Eduard was studying his hands. Without looking up, he asked, 'What about Genie? She can't be left there all day. They'll find her.'

Maraud grunted, but it was Madame who answered.

'I shall go to her, and we will wait, for the rest of the day if necessary. They will not find us.' She put a hand lightly upon Maraud's arm. 'You go, with Eduard, and eat with cousin Thérèse. Then you can visit the wrath of God upon the German, from above.'

'What about "the chicken"?' asked Eduard.

Jean-Pierre gripped his knife, then he stabbed it into the wooden wall.

'Leave him to me.'

In the half-track, the atmosphere was rancid, and tense. Jodl was tired, irritable and hungry.

'Ernst. Nothing is happening.'

'No, my Oberst.'

'Go outside and see what you can see.'

Ernst pushed past the seated soldiers, and raised the hatch.

'Nothing, sir.'

'Right. You two – out. Stand guard, and keep quiet. Anyone makes a noise, I will personally ram his rifle up his arse.'

Two of the soldiers extricated themselves, and Jodl turned to the others.

'You two, you can go too, and I want you to patrol from here to the road, without being seen – or heard. Your arses are not immune either. Go!

'You two,' he continued, addressing the remaining rank and file, 'can climb this stupid hill until you are well clear, then you can find us some food and water. No alcohol. I expect you back in an hour. Get out, then.'

He tapped the driver on the shoulder.

'Sir?'

'Stay here. If anyone comes, stay still and silent. The guards will deal with them. Understood?'

'Sir!'

Jodl stretched, then poked his head clear of the hatch. In every direction trees swayed gently in the onshore breeze. Apart from the two guards, there was no sign of anyone. He opened the rear door and eased himself out, then sat on the front offside. He glanced up at the Mauser machine gun above him and smiled grimly, his teeth bared and clenched, as he contemplated the short engagement ahead.

Eduard he would handle separately, with relish. He loaded the silver bullets into the Walther, then stuck it in his belt and took out the slim, thin-bladed stiletto, and stroked its shining spine.

Genie was sitting, concealed in the scrub, directly above the beach. 'The chicken' was walking aimlessly along the waterline, scuffing the occasional strand of seaweed and the wrack of seashells. He had walked up and down a hundred times, and Genie was weary of watching him. She shrank down, and flattened herself as she heard the snap and crackle of twig and root.

Someone was treading slowly, carefully, deliberately, within feet of where she lay. The boots paused within arm's length. She could have reached out and pulled, and he would have fallen, but she might not be quick enough. She heard the match strike, and saw it twirl to the ground, trailing a thread of smoke. Then the bitter swirl of black tobacco curled down towards her.

The boot shifted, and its owner coughed, cleared his throat, and hawked. A slub of glottal snot landed on her arm. She winced. The boot shifted again, then moved. As the movements receded, she relaxed, then froze.

'Who is there?'

Jean-Pierre left the harbour on his ancient, mudguardless, upright bicycle, sweating with the effort of pedalling up the hill out of Honfleur, the estuary below him on his right. Halfway up the hill, he put his clogs to the ground, and grated to a halt, swung himself off the 'bike, and started pushing. Long before he left Honfleur, Madame had begged a ride on a donkey-drawn cart, and dropped down off the tail at the turning to the sands of Vasouy. Ignoring the beach route, she trudged along the cliff path towards the scrubland above the rocks. As she cleared a corner, she sensed a presence, and stepped noiselessly off the path, her hand within her skirts, her finger releasing the safety catch.

She smelt the smoke before she saw the guard. His rifle was propped against a twisted treelet, as he shifted from one tight boot to the other, and dragged on his cigarette. He must have sensed her too, for he turned sharply, his hand wresting the rifle, then weighing it, balancing it, as he scanned the path before him and behind, and peered across the scrub towards the sea, and back up the hill. After a moment, he dropped his cigarette, twisted his heel, then started up the path, his rifle swinging in one hand. When he was out of sight, Madame emerged and, as she did so, heard the faint sigh. Finger on the trigger, she wheeled about and about, and murmured, 'Who is there?'

'Maman! Thank God.'

Genie materialised almost between her mother's feet, and the two women embraced. Genie pointed through the scrub.

'Look. He is there. He's been doing that all afternoon.'

They watched 'the chicken' as he paced back and forth, and the sun settled. They watched the soldier who watched 'the chicken', standing immobile behind the overhang, beneath the scrub.

Jodl threw the bread on the ground.

'You call this food, man? It's stale.'

The soldier stood nervously, fidgeting.

'Sorry, sir. That's all there was.'

The second soldier held out a bundle.

'What's this then? More shit?' snarled Jodl.

He unwrapped the rags, to reveal a fat sausage and a square of local cheese.

'That's a bit more like it. What about water?'

The soldier shrugged.

'No water, sir, or rather, nothing to put it in. We got this, though.'

He signalled the first man, who unhitched his rucksack, unstrapped it, and brought out a fat bottle.

'What the hell is that?'

'They said it was raw cider, sir.'

Jodl uncorked the bottle and sniffed, and fell back coughing.

'Jesus Christ almighty! It's not cider, it's schnapps.'

He sipped, and coughed again.

'Bloody raw schnapps as well.'

He took a draught of the calvados.

'Alright. But only one mouthful each – after you've eaten.'

He pointed at the bread.

'That's for you and leave some for the others when they come back.'

Jodl pulled the rear door open, and slid inside, and Ernst followed him.

'Here you are, then.'

He offered Ernst a slice of cheese on the end of his knife blade, and tore a piece of sausage off.

'Take this too.'

They sat, eating and sipping calva until they had finished the food.

'Take this bottle outside, and supervise. One sip each. OK?'

'Yes, sir, Herr Oberst.'

The bicycle bounced down the stony path to the strand, as the light faded. Jean-Pierre slid off just before the bottom, and carefully laid the 'bike in the long grass, where it was hidden from casual eyes. He crouched down, and crept towards the edge of the overhang. 'The chicken' was within feet. He eased back, and crept quietly into the grass, and lay there.

Eduard and Maraud had set off immediately after a lunch of fresh mullet and clear spring water, served by cousin Thérèse in her cottage behind the tall harbour houses. They had walked up the winding hill, behind the buildings, along the woodland paths, until they reached Vasouy. The track wound down to the cliff road, but instead they struck out across the hillside, beyond the hedges above the woods.

'How far?'

Maraud tapped his nose.

'Far enough.' He pointed at the sky. 'Dark soon. We'll be there before the sun sets.'

Genie and her mother saw Jean-Pierre arrive, watched him reconnoitre, then go to ground. Like him, they watched 'the chicken', and waited.

The other guards were relieved, then Jodl called the small platoon back to the half-track.

'Now listen, and listen carefully.'

He looked at the men, appraising them.

'Two of you will stand guard – there, and over there. Keep behind the trees.'

He waited while the soldiers reached their sentry posts, then continued.

'Four of you will sit inside, with the flaps down, and be alert. I don't want any misses. When you hear my command to fire, open the flaps, and fire.'

He waited while the four men crawled inside the half-track.

'Ernst. You stay with me.'

Jodl rapped on the hatch and the driver raised it. He spoke softly into the interior.

'When the firing starts, you rake the clearing with the Mauser. Try not to hit our men, but if you must, you must. Just don't miss any of theirs.'

The hatch closed, and the half-track squatted, like some reptilian beast, half asleep.

'Right, Ernst, let's try to hide this damned thing.'

He sighed, muttering, 'I wish to God we had Five Squad here.'

With their knives, they slashed at small saplings, slicing branches, and cross-hatching them across the already camouflaged monster. As the light went, outlines blurred, and the vehicle faded until it was but a vague shape within the shapeless wood.

Jodl started up the hill, Ernst a pace behind. At the edge of the wood, Jodl cautioned him. Ernst leant towards his officer and listened intently.

'Ernst. They are here. I feel it. We shall stay just inside this wood, but move slowly over there.'

He gestured to the junction of wood and downward sprawling hedge.

'We have cover behind that hedge, and can see both up the hill and into the wood. When they attack the 256, we will wait. When they stop, we will have them.'

He pinched the other man's arm.

'And Ernst, I want that Eduard. He's mine. Understand?'

The tide was almost up, the night sky flickered with far-off flame, as the Allies pounded coastal targets; a constant crumple of growling guns told of distant danger, and the Seine ebbed and flowed, the waves softly surfing Vasouy's rocks as Honfleur slept. Jean-Pierre waited in the grass. Genie and Madame waited in the shrubs. Jodl waited in the ditch by wood and hedge, and Maraud waited with Eduard just below the skyline, in the striding wild wheat above the field beyond the Germans' wood. Within the wood, the half-truck slumbered, its occupants clammy as the summer's air condensed on cold metal, while the two guards stood apart, immobile, waiting for they knew not what.

Jodl heard it first – the stealthy slither of foot through leaves, the sibilant scurry of night creatures disturbed, the occasional, almost inaudible tick of twig released from cloth or careful hand. His head inclined, his hand snaked out as he pointed down into the wood, to the Cricqueboeuf side. He willed Ernst to read his lipless words.

'They're coming across the scarp, the wrong way, cunning bastards.'

Ernst started to move; Jodl grasped his arm, softening his grip as the man gasped involuntarily. Not yet, thought Jodl; not yet. Let them get too close for flight.

Ernst nodded, stroked his officer's hand away and drew the long, glittering blade from his jackboot with his right hand. The Luger was in his left. 'Each-way Ernst' smiled Jodl to himself. The wood paused in stifled silence.

Even the night creatures were stilled, fearfully aware that predators were near. There was no onshore breeze. It was as if the land was scaped in deep oils, waiting to gain value against imminent auction. Jodl looked away from the wood, scanned the dark field against the darker hedgerows, seeking shadows that should not be there. Cloud concealed the moon, whose lustre might have reflected on gun or blade.

Jodl glanced up – there was no sign of a rift. If light was needed, they would have to kindle it in violence. It was simple enough. Either Gratz would see the boat, kill the spy, and take Eduard, or Eduard would choose the woodland path, and walk into their holding pattern. Then Gratz could kill the spy. Either way the Frenchman's usefulness was at an end, and the fun could begin with the new man, this sweet Eduard the gods had sent. Jodl's teeth gleamed as he contemplated the exquisite jewels of desire and damage, the twin pearls of pain and penetration, the sheer creativity of the ghouldsmith as he fashioned fear through lust. All that was lacking was the signal – and the sheer silken subtlety of it all was that the signal would be given by the other side, as they fashioned their own destiny. Escape? There was no escape.

We are here, there and down there too. They have to come to us across the water, down the hill, or through the wood. They are doomed, for someone has chosen the wood. Jodl nudged Ernst, and they held themselves taut and tight and ready.

A single gunshot broke the spell. A sharp cry. Silence. There was no footfall. The wood was riven with the absence of sound. Then they heard a strangled 'Ach!', instantly followed by a scatter of shots, shouts, and the stutter and cough of the Mauser as it raked the trunks and branches of men and trees.

'Stay!' commanded Jodl. 'There will be more. This is a feint, to draw us out.'

The firing died away, then twin gouts of flame momentarily blinded them as 'Mein Go-o-o-o-o-ott' rose to a screaming propeller pitch, then abruptly stopped.

'One of the guards,' muttered Ernst.

'The other one, you mean – the first one went at the beginning,' hissed Jodl.

Again, stillness, then a withering, continuous blatter of fire, and several screams. More silence. The flaming twelve-bore fired again, this time much closer. There was a pause, then a splattering of pellets to their right, as they fell on leaf and ground.

Jodl turned to Ernst. He was not there. Jodl crouched against the tree, his hand steadying himself against its bark. He felt the tremor, and looked up. Ernst was ten, fifteen feet above him, his Luger poised, the blade under his other arm. Ernst pointed beyond the half-track, then down the hill, and finally, to the right. Then he slid down. Jodl crept along the shallow ditch, towards the right hand; Ernst moved away, a shadow among shadows.

On the beach, 'the chicken' strained to see a darker shadow against the tidal flow. He heard nothing, until the arm encircled his throat, and the knife went in. Jean-Pierre eased him down onto the rocks, and turned him round, so that he could meet his death and his killer together. He wiped the blade, then looked up suddenly, startled, one hand convulsively seeking the heart that had stopped the bullet, as he slid down, across his victim. The whiplash of the pistol shot reeled Gratz in, just as he lowered his rifle in single satisfaction, and sank, surprised, to his knees, then fell forward onto the cigarette he had just extinguished. As he rolled clear, the black ash-mark on his forehead made a ragged cross. Madame moved closed, prodded him with her foot, and nodded to herself. 'The iron cross, eh?'

Genie held Eduard's revolver, and the two women, incongruous with their hand arms, clambered cautiously through the scrub and towards the road. The wood above had erupted with gunfire, shouts, screams, and the unmistakeable stutter of a heavy machine gun in that first onslaught.

At the road's edge they hesitated.

'Wait here,' whispered Madame, as she tucked the gun into her skirts, and extracted a baguette and a small canvas bag. Into the bag went the baguette, along with stones, weeds and twigs, until the late home-coming housewife, weary and footsore, emerged onto the road, trudging, bent and troubled by the proximity of conflict.

Jodl stood behind the hedge as Ernst speared his blade into the ground, holstered the Luger, and marched across the broken tarmac.

'Woman. Why are you out at this hour?'

'Late from work, sir.'

'Your bag?'

'Bread and a few greens – weeds really, but you know how it is, vegetables. So scarce.'

Ernst poked the bag. The first grenade opened the skies. Then another, and another.

'What was that?' gasped Madame in simulated dismay.

'On your way, woman,' rasped Ernst as he started to run.

Jodl and Ernst sprinted up the path, back towards the half-track, as the smoke billowed downwind, downhill. As if the cliffs and waters, woods and meadows had all erupted together, the clouds rolled back, the moon's sliver reflected wanly through the trees, and Ernst slid sideways behind a dense thicket of evergreens.

As they neared the clearing, Jodl was nowhere to be seen. The half-track had burst open, its metal skin blistered and peeling, the mangled remnants of its occupants slathered in blood and powder, blackened and steaming.

The driver's head was balanced on the rim of the hatch, grinning idiotically, his body out of sight. The guards lay where they had fallen, and among them lay several partisans. Behind Ernst, Madame drew closer, her pistol drawn.

His blade curved up and over his shoulder as he hurled it at her, and she twisted. Too late, the blade, wheeling hilt over point, caught her across the shoulder, severing her arm, the pistol reflexively firing as her disconnected fingers snapped open and shut. Madame fell, lifted herself with her other hand, subsided, and was still. Ernst looked round. Genie faced him, her back to the next tree, not two yards distant. She held the revolver low in one hand, steadied her wrist with the other, and fired, once, twice, three times, the heavy-calibre bullets tearing into Ernst's trunk as he slid, transfixed, down the bark, to sit, puzzled, among the roots, speechless, then sightless. Jodl was nowhere to be seen.

Two more grenades burst the trees apart, and Genie glimpsed a figure flitting across the clearing behind the half-track.

'Eduard?'

Clouds parted were reunited, and the moon went out. Genie stealthily crept up the wood, diagonally away from the half-track, in the same direction as the half-glimpsed figure. Pausing for breath, she looked back at the half-track, half a hundred metres away. She thought she saw a movement, and started back.

'Eduard?'

Now there were only two trees between her and the carnage, when she saw the movement again. Looking left and right, behind and forward, she crept towards the wreckage. Two yards away, she recognised the boots.

Maraud tried to lift himself, but failed. He managed a wry smile, and opened his hand. In it lay the remaining grenade. As Genie bent towards him, the grenade rolled from his grasp, and she automatically reached for it.

'Not a good idea.'

Maraud's eyes closed, as she straightened, her back to Jodl. The Oberst tapped her with his gloved hand.

'Look – no hands,' he said, and chuckled.

Gently he turned her to face him. He held out his hand and she relinquished the revolver. Jodl flicked it open, his eyes on hers. Without looking down, he checked the chamber – empty.

'When the chamber's empty, my lady's gone.'

She stared at him, and he smiled at her.

'Don't you think?'

One black gloved hand held her shoulder. The other rose, the knife gleaming. She felt her neck muscles tense. She closed her eyes. Jodl's lips parted, his teeth gleamed.

The hand on her shoulder slithered up and the supple soft leather closed round the tress of hair falling across her face. The knife neatly trimmed the locks away, and Jodl looked down at his handful, raised it delicately to his flaring nostrils, and breathed deeply, his eyes half closed, a hand once more gripping her shoulder, the knife balanced across his smiling mouth.

'Aaaaah... one of the few truly exotic aspects of femininity, the faintly acrid smell of hair.' His eyes opened, inches from hers. 'Don't you agree?'

He stepped back, his hand slipping down her arm, to grip her wrist, as he appraised her body.

'I suppose one man's entry is another man's exit,' and he turned her swiftly, so she faced away from him. The knife hand dropped, and he bent slightly, tucking it beneath her skirt. The knife ripped the skirt apart from hem to waist, and exposed her calves, thighs and her back above her hips. He pulled her round again, and ripped the skirt away.

'Aren't you glad I am not a ladies' man?' as the knife slowly and deliberately parted the front of her blouse, severing her undergarment, allowing her breasts to fall apart. Jodl raised the knife to her throat.

'I would never harm a woman,' and, as his grip tightened, and he pulled her closer, the knife pressed against her throat and a glistening bead of blood appeared at its point.

'But then, you're not so much a woman, as a fighter for others' freedoms, aren't you?' and she closed her eyes against the tension she sensed in Jodl's grip.

'Goodbye, little lady.'

The hand hovered, moved – then the knife fell. Jodl released her, and she stepped back, reaching behind her. As her hands felt for the armour, she touched a mess of bone and flesh, and screamed. Jodl was still smiling as he staggered slightly, fell against her, then pushed himself upright, and slowly turned his back.

Eduard's knife was buried just below his left shoulder blade. Eduard stood absolutely still, stiffly to attention, and brought his hand up in a sardonic salute.

'Heil – fucking – Hitler.'

Jodl's smile remained. He brought his right hand up to his forehead. As he swayed slightly, Genie pushed herself away from the half-track, gathered her tattered clothes around herself and leant against a tree. Jodl ignored her.

'That really hurt.' He looked longingly at Eduard and added, 'Wonderful,' and crumpled slowly, his smile undisturbed, subsiding onto the ground, twitching once, and then relaxing, one hand still in perpetual salute.

'Run!'

Genie ran, Eduard standing alone in the clearing, until she was gone. Then he squatted by Jodl, pushed him over, and pulled out the knife, wiping it on the German's tunic as he said quietly to himself, 'My first fascist, but not my last.'

Off the strand at Vasouy the low boat with the high prow rode the turning tide. Eduard waded out to his homecoming. Concealed in the scrub above the strand, Genevieve raised a small unseen hand in farewell to the man who almost loved her.

Four weeks after Eduard left the Normans, Erwin Rommel climbed into his staff car amid the ruins of Vimoutiers at five to six. The old fox was tired. His luck was running out. Once more the gaunt Montgomery was chasing his ageing quarry, this time through the summer fields and not over the desert sands. Only two days before, Rommel had told Field Marshall von Kluge: 'The unequal struggle is drawing to a close.'

The car pulled up the hill, and veered left, through the trees, on the road to Livarot, behind its motorcycle escort.

On 17 July, South African Squadron Leader Johannes 'Chris' Le Roux DFC led twelve Spitfires of 602 (City of Glasgow) Squadron on armed reconnaissance, with 500lbs bomb-load. 'Bounced' by six Messerschmidt Bf109s, they jettisoned their payloads, scattered, and Le Roux foraged for targets of opportunity as he started home.

At la Gossellinaie, less than a mile from Vimoutiers, the road curves, and the heavy car slowed to take the bend. Out of a clear sky screamed a vengeful Spitfire IX, its cannon clattering. The escort skidded, the car swerved, but it was too late. Rommel was lifted from the wreckage, his face shattered, his skull fractured, unconscious, his destination, by a strange quirk of fate, the namesake of his nemesis – Ste Foy de Montgommery.

Erwin's accident was tersely enclosed in Churchill's words: 'An important event.' VS was never called to arms.

I suppose France was the turning point.

There love died stillborn, unseasonal lusts drowned in blood and I made and lost more friends more quickly and more sadly than ever I did before or since.

There I saw war. Real war. Not the war I imagined, nor the one you see on your screens – with special effects and round-the-room sound. For the first time, I saw the war at first hand, in close-up, nasty, brutish, and largely pointless.

We could have caught the tide and the boat without killing those men. We killed them because they were 'the enemy'. Jodl apart, of course, but then, Jodls are alive and well and among us in our own society today, tormenting, torturing, taking lives and their pleasures where they will, and not all of them are caught, as was Jodl, in the act, so to speak, and executed as I executed Jodl, very much on the tooth-for-tooth, blade-for-blade basis, which is what war allows, I suppose, justifies, condones and exonerates.

All's fair? I think not. Certainly, Genie would not agree with that. Then again, Stiffell was not a Jodl, but an ordinary man, doing his job, and he was only following orders too – reasonable orders, if you think about it rationally. Yet I cannot truthfully say his death affected me, other than with the relief of a danger dismissed.

Thus are our instincts transmuted from survival to action to justification to indifference, as the occasion demands.

And Vimoutiers. What possible basis of rational cause and effect could justify that bombardment, the carnage, the loss of lives and livings, and the clearing out of centuries of lives' echoes in those ancient buildings, the very dust and detail of a town's past, families' pasts, the past of a very present community?

None. How cruel is a clock. A matter of hours, and a matter of pride, and a matter of fact – the fox changed his mind, or his mind was changed, and yet, one month later, he is there in the same place, and by accident, mark you, that is achieved which was determined, at no peripheral cost.

I mourn for the Vimestrians, for all the Vimestrians who fell victim to men's pride and folly, and reliance on the word of mouth – in that case, my mouth.

I have often asked myself if I was the town's executioner; if I had only known what those two letters meant, and if I had stopped to consider how

337

fragile was my information and my conclusion... I have told myself I was doing what I was trained to do, told to do – but did we not tell those same Germans that following orders is no excuse? That ignorance is no excuse?

For sanity's sake, I determined that I did my best. I tried to stop one man from withholding the freedom of thousands. That I failed, and I suppose that is what principally rankles, the failure, is a small fault alongside the larger failings that put that town in the way of such monumental change. I only pray that there lingers less bitterness than fading pain, that the chance to rebuild revitalised as well, and that the survivors and their successors can at least feel they offered a sacrifice to freedom that was not entirely in vain, for freedom surely followed.

Whether Genie was freed by her experience, I never knew – I do know that I watched her run from those deaths and I felt her taking my life with hers. As I turned in that little boat for one last look, I thought I saw a small hand flutter in shared life and nascent love – but I was probably mistaken. I lost her as I lost Sara, and in that loss and the greater losses in that poor town, lay the beginnings of the doubts that stayed with me most of my life.

HOME RUN

The long estuary curved slowly away from the flat leaden skies and sombre wastes of offshore Essex. The Crouch was aptly named, thought Eduard as he watched the Frenchmen prepare for landfall. Burnham was battened down against wartime exigencies, barbed wire rolling along the quayside, a narrow gap between the metal nets across the waterway, and ack-ack guns silhouetted against the flaccid sky. They banged against the landing stage, warped bows and stern, then turned to Eduard: 'Bon voyage' and 'Au fin de guerre'; 'Merci' and 'Rien de tout'.

Eduard jumped ashore and turned to wave a final farewell. The Normans busied themselves about the short, curved deck, perhaps glad to be rid of their cargo, perhaps sad, but certainly uninterested in the British Military presence and its Intelligence counterpart, for there, stepping forward as Eduard turned back, was an anonymous officer in civvies, black homburg doffed in his left hand, his right extended, his pinstripes and bright shining shoes in contrast to the nondescript, scarved and trilbied, slightly bent figure, hands in pockets of his British warm, scuffed brogues crossed, who silently regarded them both, then nodded, and loped away.

'Welcome back,' said one, and, 'Car's waiting,' said the other.

Homburg sat in the front, the soldier drove, and trilby waved to Eduard to join him in the back. The black Humber drew smoothly away, clittering across the cobbles, before turning onto the road to Cambridge.

Nobody said anything for several minutes. Then the man in the trilby took it off, revealing sparse, sandy hair, delved in his pocket and brought forth a packet of Players and from the other, a box of pink-tipped matches.

'Smoke?'

'No thanks.'

'Barrett?'

The man in the front shook his head without turning.

'Mind if I do?'

Nobody demurred, so he lit up, dropping pack and box on the seat between them and replacing the hat on the back of his head, almost as if it was necessary to remove it as a precursor to recreation, and then replace it for business.

'You made it then.'

It was a statement, and of the obvious, so Eduard said nothing. Smoke gathered and hung beneath the car's roof, and Barrett discreetly wound his window down a fraction. Throughout, the driver kept his eyes away from the mirror.

'Not many do.'

'No, I suppose not.'

"S'a fact. Not many do.'

Eduard shrugged. Jeffries looked out of the window, as he added, 'Not many go out again either.'

The flat landscape sped past, interrupted only by an occasional lorry lumbering the other way. Eduard's heart thudded as he contemplated a return to France, and fear, and war – and Genie?

Then the view disappeared altogether beyond a continuous stream of Army trucks and jeeps and despatch riders and bowsers. The soldier looked into the mirror.

'Station XDS, sir?'

'Yes please, Matthews. Usual route.'

'Sir.'

They drove on for several minutes, then slowed for a crossroads. Matthews swung the wheel over, and they drove down a narrow lane, flanked by open fields and barricades of high wire fencing. Gradually fence replaced hedgerow, and Eduard glimpsed the dull gleam of airstripped aluminium. As they slowed, he heard the crescendo of multiple engines, then a great shadow passed over them.

He twisted in his seat and looked back, as the Flying Fortresses rose awkwardly across the fields. The car stopped. Matthews wound down his window. An American SP looked in, took the pass from Matthews, handed it back, and the car gathered way. They continued between hedges, until the fences appeared again, and again they slowed.

The car turned sharply to the right, and lurched through a field gate, across a rough, rutted, cindered track, until it came to rest outside a featureless Nissen hut, corrugated flanks buried in flettons, a single, central smokestack belching grey smoke.

Matthews opened the door, and they clambered out. A sentry walked slowly past the single door, his sten held across his body in what Eduard recognised as the 'ready' position. As they approached, he paused, turned, and waited for them. Matthews proffered a pass, which was speed-read; then the man nodded, inclined his head, and they filed past him into the hut. Matthews stayed outside.

'Sit.'

Eduard sat and the other two disappeared through an internal door. The 'room' was a partitioned cubicle, an ante-room to whatever went on behind the clearly well-insulated wall, for he could hear nothing. Moments later, the inner door opened, and he was invited through. Inside the two men sat at a long table with four chairs. At the head sat Teichmann. Despite the summer temperature, the cubicle had struck cold, and Eduard was glad of the stove, its waist glowing cherry-red.

'Morning Eduard. Hope you had a good journey.'

Teichmann rose, stepped forward and shook Eduard's hand briskly.

'Thought you might not make it. Glad you did.'

He indicated the other two.

'You've met the man from the WD – Bernard Barrett. And this is Colonel Jeffries, also down from Whitehall, but a different patch.'

They nodded.

'Do sit down, Eduard. Tell us what happened.'

After two hours, Eduard sat back, drained. It was only three days since he had flown out, yet it seemed like weeks. He felt as if he had earnt his leave.

Teichmann cut across his reverie.

'Like to give you some leave, Eduard, but it can't be done.'

Teichmann tapped the table and Eduard remembered how his hands were never still, turning a file, twisting a paperclip, always moving, whenever he had something difficult to impart.

'Gorzow.' He looked down at the paperclip, tossed it aside, and folded his hands, the whites of his knuckles betraying his tension.

'Gone, Eduard, gone. I'm so sorry, but the whole exercise had to change. Different drop, different date, different folk. Pretty well all Anglos now – except for Toni, of course. Can't tell you much about it, but one day you'll find out, I expect.'

Eduard wiped his face with his hands, brushing away an imaginary tear, his mind a turmoil of resentment, relief, resignation.

'I wanted to go home, sir, to fight them there.'

'I know, I know. All that training, all those false starts. Not fair, is it? But then, war isn't – fair, that is.'

Teichmann leant over, and touched Eduard's hand.

'The lads who've gone won't fight anyway – they're liaison, with the Russians. And anyway, you've done just as much good already.'

He leant back again, tapping the table.

'You can do some more. Help your country that way.'

He glanced at Jeffries.

'The Colonel will explain. We'll leave you two together.'

Jeffries lit up, blew a thin cannonade of smoke across the table, then peered at Eduard.

'Think you're up to it?'

'Up to what, sir?'

'Another mission, so soon. After all, you've only just got back.'

'As you said, sir, not many do, and not many get to go again. When?'

'Ah well, not immediately, and' – he took the cigarette out of his mouth, dropped his hand, and tipped the ash discreetly on the floor – 'and not to France.'

The waiting station was beyond the SOE hutments in a nondescript, Edwardian villa, stuck for some historic reason at the end of a rutted lane. It was isolated, and empty, save for Eduard, and the Anglo-Polish staff. They left him alone in his anonymous room, complete with iron-frame bed, locker, wash handbasin, bookshelves with Daphne du Maurier, Dorothy L. Sayers, Dickens and a Bible – Authorised Version. In the locker drawer was one concession: a rosary.

Supper was a desultory affair, palatable enough, with spam, fried potatoes and baked beans and halfway through, Jeffries appeared, clutching a bottle and two glasses. The two instructors made their excuses, gathered up their plates, irons and cups, and quietly closed the door.

'Drink?'

'Why not?'

'Thought we might celebrate your return, safe and sound, eh?'

Jeffries poured the wine, tipped his glass, peered at it, took a sip, batted his lips several times and pronounced it 'Good, very good' then lifted his glass.

'Cheers.'

'Cheers.'

The wine glinted golden. Eduard lifted the glass to his lips and tilted it. The sure, sweet, clean, shivering taste assaulted him gently, its scented bouquet drifting past as the aftertaste lingered, and he was back on the banks of the Seret, with a purloined bottle from Grandpa Luke's cellar.

Jeffries smiled.

'Aszu from Tokay, the '37, I believe. Remind you?'

Eduard smiled.

'Yes, it reminds me. Thank you.'

Jeffries dug his hands in his pockets and brought out a battered pack, lit up, leant back, pushed the chair away from the table, and hoisted his feet on the rail.

'I expect you want to know where it is.'

He inhaled, drew the smoke deep down, and let it trickle out as he added, 'The mission.'

He expelled the rest of the lungful, examined the cigarette and blew on its end, making it suddenly glow and grow a grey dribble of ash.

'Ought to give it up. Bloody things. Not good for you, you know, but do help to concentrate the mind – and I enjoy them, dammit.'

He dropped the cigarette, and stamped on it, grinding his heel into the wooden floor.

'Right. There'll be three of you. The soft underbelly of Europe. We want information. Equipment, 'planes, artillery – what have they got?'

Jeffries stood the pack on end, and balanced the matchbox on top.

'We have a good network out there – partisans, but they're not expert at assessment, and their signals leave something to be desired. Want you three to gather it up, and send it back – Cairo, London. OK?'

Eduard nodded, as Jeffries absent-mindedly extracted another Player, the match flared, and another stream of smoke eddied over the table.

'We're going to drop you in the triangle between Albania, Greece and Yugoslavia. At night. Fourteen days.'

Taking another pull at the rapidly shrivelling cigarette, he added, 'And while you're there, you can train the natives too.'

He tipped forward again, the chair snapping down onto the floor.

'Have some more wine.'

Eduard slept badly. He put it down to the occasional roar as aircraft swept across the flat countryside, yet he knew it was not that, but the questions – who? Who were the other two? And how long would it take? Where exactly were they going? A triangle between three countries was a bit vague, after all. At around four, he gave up, got up, washed, shaved in cold water and dressed. There was no atlas in the bookshelf. So he stepped outside the room, and started down the stairs.

A door creaked, and he froze reflexively, then laughed softly to himself. Idiot. Who was going to hurt him in the middle of the night in an SOE safe house? How stupid could one get?

The arm encircling his neck was firm, the hand across his mouth warm, the knee in his back sharp. He relaxed – first lesson; then he gathered himself for the response, when he was deafened by the gust of uproarious laughter right into his ear, and immediately released.

'You should always watch your back,' said Johnnie.

'Bish! Where have you been? What are you – you're not?'

'Yes, I'm on the same team. And so's he.'

Eduard followed Johnnie's quick gesture, as another door opened and, outlined against the weak electric light stood Wladek, grinning.

'Told you I'd catch up with you, you old bugger you, did'n I?'

Johnnie put his great arm around Eduard, beckoned Wladek onto the landing, and encircled him too.

'What we need is some sliv, and what I've got is some sliv, and what we are going to do is to get that sliv inside ourselves, now!' and Johnnie released them, burled past them, his bulk filling the doorway as he reached inside and turned triumphantly, clutching a fat bottle of white plum spirit.

'Got to get used to it – they drink it all the time where we're going.'

The courses were intense, densely documented, and meticulous: maps, codes, contacts, communications equipment and, paramount, the detailed information required of troop movements, strategic sites, railheads and their state of readiness, ammunition transit dumps, armour, artillery and aircraft. All this was absorbed against a background of international politics, for the Russians were intriguing in Yugoslavia, Italy and Greece and, as Churchill recorded, 'We do not of course want to carve up the Balkans', but 'are we going to acquiesce in Communisation?' The partisans of Macedonia, in the most southerly part of the royal Yugoslav realm, were almost certainly communist, their loyalty to Lenin, and their inspiration, Tito.

After fourteen days of unremitting instruction and catechisms and isolation, Eduard was bored with people and politics, and craved action, the more so after the depressing deprivation of Gorzow. Wladek proposed a trip to town, and Johnnie produced yet another bottle of slivova to 'liven us up on the journey' and a pack of cards.

'Where d'you get the damned stuff?' got a simple answer

'Sliv's from spivs.'

Eduard asked Jeffries for a 24-hour pass.

'We're in need of a break – before we go "into battle" – sir.'

Jeffries contemplated his usual cigarette, dripping ash onto his threadbare hacking jacket.

'Your files say you're a bit of a rebel, Wladek's a troublemaker, and Makowski's a hellraiser. If I let you go to London, what guarantee have I that I'll still have a team when you return?'

Eduard smiled, grinned, then laughed.

'None whatsoever, sir. No guarantees. But then, that's why you chose us, isn't it?'

'Bloody Poles. Don't know what we'd do without you. Go on. Bugger off to London – and try to come back in one piece.'

'First stop Red Cross,' announced Eduard.

They were walking down the platform at Liverpool Street.

'What d'you want with the Red Cross? They're for when you're wounded.'

'Yes, well, my heart's wounded, and that's why I need the Red Cross,' and despite all Wladek's attempts, Eduard would not be drawn and Johnnie just smiled to himself.

'Arthur Mortimer, please.'

They stood in the panelled waiting room, its walls scratched, the muddy brown linoleum cracked and concave, where thousands of boots had beaten their way to relative enquiries, scuffed by the dragged heels of the hopeless, and pitted with cigarette burns, light filtering through a criss-cross of brown windows, taped against bomb blast. As they waited, they heard the distinctive drone of a doodle-bug. The flying bombs were claiming lives and homes – thousands of one and three-quarters of a million of the other. People started walking briskly outside, to join those pedestrians peering up at the sky. A small boy in grey flannel shorts, oversized socks and a cut-down grey flannel shirt pulled Eduard's arm excitedly.

'Come on. You'll miss it.'

'Miss what?'

'The buzz-bomb. Come ON.'

He jerked at Eduard, dragging him to the door. Outside, they stood on the pavement, all eyes skyward.

'If it stops before it gets 'ere, run like 'ell. If it don't, wait fer it ter drop. Then yer cun guess where it's 'it.'

The youngster's eyes were bright with the thrill and the fear and the mystery. They listened, heads on one side, straining for the silence, but the engine droned on, louder and nearer, until it was almost overhead, and someone screeched, 'Look! There it is. Bastards,' and waved a clenched fist at the pilotless 'plane, as it started its dive. Nobody made any attempt to flee, as Eduard tugged the small boy.

'We must find a shelter.'

'Nar. S'not gonnar 'it us. Be 'Ampstead, more like.'

Fear gone, fun dissipating, he let go of Eduard's hand, and wandered back into the Red Cross building, just as the crump and crackle reached them, and they saw a plume of smoke and debris rise above the skyline.

'Mr Cjaikowski?'

Arthur Mortimer wobbled slightly behind the counter, the file trembling in his left hand, as he pushed his wire-framed spectacles up his nose.

'I think I've found your Audrey.'

Eduard's mouth was suddenly dry and he looked round for Johnnie, but the little boy was sitting between him and Wladek, and they were all engrossed in Johnnie's cards.

'Yes?'

'An Audrey Richardson was at Kermener, and is now serving somewhere else.'

'Where?'

Mortimer rubbed his nose, and the spectacles fell half an inch or so. He pushed them back, blinked, and tapped the file.

'Doesn't actually say. Well, it sort of says, but you know, everything gets classified these days. Silly really. Still,' and he brightened momentarily, 'doesn't matter now, because I have found out where she lives,' and a quite different smile, of triumph, beamed at Eduard, lighting up the old man's features, so that Eduard could see, for just a moment, the once handsome, confident young man that lay within this weary, war-worn and perhaps unloved bachelor.

As if he translated Eduard's thoughts into words, Mortimer softly remarked, 'I hope you find her. I had someone once, but...' and his words drifted away on a wistful note, carried off by the eddying winds of sad memory.

'My war was harsh too, you know, perhaps not like this one, but we never knew if we would return, or if they would wait for us if we did, or what would happen if we came back shot up, and...' He hesitated, then added, 'and in some way spoilt.'

He looked down at the file.

'Perhaps I should have had more faith – and fought for her too.'

He opened the file, and extracted a slip of paper.

'I took her address. Here it is. You keep faith with your desires. Who knows, perhaps she will have you if you are not too late.'

Eduard took the wisp of paper, and unfolded it.

'Audrey Richardson, Sunnyside Road, Chesham, Bucks. That's a good omen, Sunnyside,' but, as he looked up, Arthur Mortimer was gone, behind the swing door beyond the counter, back to his files and his memories.

The journey to Manchester was uncomfortable. The train was cold, Johnnie had run out of slivova; they had started with poker, tried brag, changed style and pace with pontoon, then lost interest, and rehearsed the mission, but first Johnnie, then Wladek, fell silent, and Eduard tried to sleep, but could not, the train pulling and pushing him from stiffness to cramp to pins and needles, until he got up, slid the compartment door open, and walked down the corridor for the fifth time, to the acid-smelling toilet, pocked with belligerent graffiti – 'Fuck the Nazis' and 'Itler's an arsole'. Then he stood, listlessly swaying with the clackety-clack rhythm, pressing himself against the grimy window every time someone passed.

He thought about Audrey and her soft kindness, her dimpled arms, and her open smile. He thought about Sara, and Genie too, and immediately wiped them from his inner eye. Waste of time. Long gone. Another world.

And thought again of Audrey, and of Mortimer's words. 'Keep faith with your desires.' But what were his desires? He glimpsed his own lank hair, pale features, brown eyes, and laughed without warmth at his own reflection. 'I honestly don't know,' he told himself.

'Don't know what?'

He swung round, one hand against the rail, back to the window and his thoughts and his doubts and, if he admitted it, his fears, and punched Wladek lightly on his chest.

'Don't know what I'd do without you and old Johnnie. Off to war, my fine frolicsome friend – and I bet you find some Balkan bint when we get there.'

The flight was less tiresome, for they slept much of the time, lulled by the steady throb of the engines, landed in Gibraltar, had time for a fast shave, quick wash, some short relief, and took off within an hour for Brindisi. Once on the Adriatic coast, they came to life, and eagerly set to, scouring the base for extra equipment, as they prepared for the flight to Florina – or rather, to the nearest point across the Macedonian border from that Greek town.

The radio equipment was Polish. The stage container held that and a bicycle generator. Eduard insisted they had the same armaments – Colt 45 and French sub-machine pistol, because he was familiar with them, and they worked. The pistol was demountable, which made it easier to carry. They were each issued with a cheap signet ring, its false stone concealing a cyanide capsule, documents, money, and a tailor-made suit, though nobody seemed to know how an absent tailor could cut a suit for unknown clients without measurements. Eduard's fitted perfectly under his uniform, and was duplicated in his equipment pack. Their parachute overalls had pockets for gun and knife, but Eduard preferred to secrete his knife, as usual, against his leg.

They were instructed to pose as Anglo-Slavs, to dispose of their uniforms, and warned that, once they did so, they would be outside the Geneva Convention, and liable to execution as spies.

'Have we any choice?' asked Wladek.

'None,' responded Jeffries. 'I was just warning you, that's all.'

Wladek laughed. 'You mean orders is orders?'

Jeffries, shortly: 'Right.'

The flight from Brindisi was short, across the Adriatic, the Albanian coast, the rising hills of the interior, and into the southern tip of Macedonia, where the mountains rose 10,000 feet above sea level, skirting the Prespanska lake, and hill-hopping between Bitola and the Greek border. The old Dakota workhorse dropped, levelled off, and wheeled, coming in against the updraughts from the stony terrain, flares winking and blinking in the middle distance. Eduard held Wladek's shoulder, then lifted his hand, clapped it down once as the green light flashed, and Wladek disappeared into the darkness towards the flare path, followed within seconds by Johnnie.

Eduard stepped out, felt the suck of the 'plane as it banked up and away, then the jump-jerk as the 'chute unfolded, flowered and billowed above him. The flares were now to his left, as he slowly circled, descending in the thin, cool air. He could see what appeared to be a small army of small figures moving in ragged lines towards the flare path, with another clump of figures, somehow isolated and separate, at one end.

They were closer now, and he could make out individuals and, as the ground rushed to meet him, a bristle of rifles, sub-machine guns and bandoliers of ammunition. He slipped as he touched down, fell and rolled, the 'chute floating alongside him, then rising in an eddy as hands grasped him, set him upright, and gathered the silken strands. The first words were incomprehensible, then someone said, 'Welcome to the real war.'

Wladek was standing on the other side of the flares, cursing as he tried to unravel his harness, which had somehow caught in his overalls. Eduard looked round for Johnnie, but then he was surrounded by partisans, and could see no-one beyond the circle of dark, mostly bearded men, silently regarding him with a mixture of suspicion, resentment and curiosity. An inquisitive hand pinched the material of his coveralls and rubbed the cloth reflectively.

'Nylon,' offered Eduard.

'Ny-lon?' and the man stepped back, relinquishing it.

'New material – synthetic.' Eduard was speaking in English, but none of the faces registered comprehension. Then the circle parted to

347

make way for a taller man, moustached but otherwise clean-shaven, without the beret or peaked cap of his compatriots, smiling sardonically, his mouth twisted to one side by the concealed harelip, his head close-cut, bristling and uncovered, his tunic blouse buttoned to the neck, a long-barrelled revolver stuck through a wide leather belt on either side, his hands extended.

'Milosevic Kradask – welcome, welcome. My friends call me Milo,' and he advanced on Eduard, enfolded him and crushed him to his chest, his smooth cheek nestling against Eduard's as he murmured quietly, 'They don't trust you – yet. Be calm, my friend. I am here. You are among friends with Milo.'

He released Eduard, held him at arms' length and regarded him with the same twisted smile and announced, 'Here is our saviour – come to lead us to the promised land of victory and revenge. Greet him well, comrades. This is Eduard,' and one by one the comrades stepped forward and shook his hand. Milo turned and gestured behind him.

'Come. Join us. You are?'

Wladek walked into the circle and stood close to Eduard, their shoulders touching.

'I am Wladek.'

'Then the other fellow must be Makowski.'

They all turned, and in the gap they had made for Wladek to walk through, he saw an elongated figure, seemingly eight feet tall, strangely bent, and with a cylindrical 'head'. Johnnie strode among them, bent down, and set the canister beside them. He surveyed the gathering, pointed at his mouth, licked his lips, and then asked, 'Has nobody got a drink?'

The circle had dissolved, to reveal blank terrain, the flares extinguished, and the long, thin line of partisans formed up in a close-ranked group, rifles held across crooked arms, ammunition belted in loops, faces impassive as Milo quickly counted them off, spoke sharply, clearly, but quietly, whereupon they were joined by one of the bearded comrades, given a murmured order, and marched away.

'We always check, to make sure none of them have slipped away. Youngsters, you see. Never can be too careful,' and Eduard realised what it was that had puzzled him – they were all clean-shaven, and much younger. They were the 'troops' and the others were the comrades.

A short, squat, bearded figure sidled up to Milo, and muttered to him. Milo pulled him over to where Eduard, Wladek and Johnnie stood.

'This is Irman Laszazek, my number two. He will find you a drink.' Milo's permanent smile twisted even further and his voice softened as he added, 'A little grk for Makowski!'

He turned to Johnnie.

'You'll like it; it's our best wine, from Korcula, but I fear you may find it over strong,' as the aide produced an anonymous flask from his knapsack, uncorked and proffered it. Johnnie snorted, and tipped it up, closed his eyes, letting the liquid slide down his throat. He opened them, looked straight at Milo, and was about to speak, when they closed again, he swallowed twice, and held his breath. Then he smiled a beatific, spreading smile and tipped the bottle to his lips once more.

Handing the bottle back to the surprised Irman, he remarked, 'A little dry for our taste, but exactly right for the night. Thank you.'

He looked at Eduard, his eyebrows slightly raised and in Polish added, 'Dragon water. I hope that's not standard stuff. I'd rather have sliv.'

He glanced around the rocks and shook his head.

'Looks a bit bleak.'

'It'll be autumn soon,' observed Eduard. 'You can't have everything.'

When they woke the next morning, his assessment seemed generous. The buildings were low, stone structures, with tin rooves, rudimentary hearths and a hole for a chimney. Furniture was limited to wooden tables and benches, with palliasses stacked in the corner. Food was simple, but hot – a sweet gruel, accompanied by warm wheat cakes with honey, and rich red tomatoes. The coffee was black, sharp and thick in texture. Eduard added honey and found it strangely soothing. He glanced up as Johnnie came in.

'Where have you been?'

'Checking. The camp's a collection of these stone shacks. Stony fields with a few goats, an occasional pocket of crops, stunted cereal mostly, no trees that I can see, and over there' – Johnnie waved his hand behind them – 'the mountainside is dotted with caves.'

'What's in them?'

'Don't know, but I wasn't exactly encouraged to find out. They're well guarded. And the kids we saw last night...'

'Yes?'

'They're practising hand-to-hand stuff in the fields.'

'A regular training camp, then.'

'Looks like it.'

Eduard poured another coffee from the lidded jug.

'Where's Wladek?'

They had just drained their mugs, examined the Colts and pistols, checked the ammunition, and rolled up the uniforms, when the door slammed open. Irman lurched through, and slumped on the nearest bench. Behind him stood Wladek, grinning, a red weal scoring his cheek, his clothes dishevelled.

'What the hell...?'

'A little contretemps.' He wagged a hand at Irman, then laughed, joining him at the table, and pulling Eduard's mug across. 'Here, have a drop of this,' and he pushed the mug into Irman's hand. The Slav glared at him.

'Interesting.'

Wladek took the mug and drained it.

'They've got bints here, you know.'

Eduard groaned.

'You haven't been molesting women again?'

'Molesting? Don't be silly. Just ententing the Macedonian cordiale.'

Wladek slapped Irman on the back and the stocky Slav spluttered.

'He thought she was his, until I pointed out the Marxist dictum – equal ownership of the means of production. We had a little difference, then decided she wasn't really worth it, and here we are.'

Eduard rose, indicated the empty canister, the transmitter and 'cycle.

'I think it's time we went to work.'

The path wound up the close-shaven green mountainside, criss-crossed by the tracks of goats and sheep. They climbed to the rounded summit. In the lee of a grey stone overhang, they set up the generator and wireless mast. Eduard lodged the transmitter on a convenient ledge. Johnnie bestrode the 'cycle and started pumping his legs as Eduard adjusted the set. Wladek stood and watched.

'Does it work?'

Eduard glanced down at him, and returned to his calibrations.

'Not yet, but it will.'

'Bit exposed,' observed Wladek.

Eduard ignored the comment, and continued fiddling.

'Got it!' and without looking up added, 'Of course it's exposed. I have to find a signal, send a signal. Once we're set up, we can move down until we lose the signal. Nearer we are to the others, better for us. Here.'

He threw a spool of wire at Wladek, who fumbled and dropped it; it started rolling and bouncing downhill, the wire spilling out, until he caught up with it. Eduard yelled at him: 'Leave it there, and run the cable here. I need an aerial.'

With the cable attached to the mast, Waldek 'walked' it back and forth as Eduard experimented.

'Stop! Got it. Now, little further – over there, no, to your left. Stop!'

He started tapping, then held the earphone to one ear.

'Yes! We've got Cairo. Now we need London.'

It took all afternoon, until Eduard was satisfied, as they moved a few yards at a time, finally settling on an elevated site above a series of caves, with a clear view to the horizon, across the Greek border.

'That's it.' Eduard disconnected the transmitter, and Johnnie dismounted from the pedal-powered dynamo. 'We'll set up a guard detail, then start tomorrow.'

The long, stone hall reverberated to the thud of stamping feet, thumping fists and clapping hands, as the partisans sang songs of love and war, of death and freedom. Irman stood in the centre of the long pine table, and stamped the rhythm, leading the chorus, as Milo hurled the verses at them in his tearing, nasal tones. Thick bottles of grk and slivova passed from hand to hand, their necks from throat to throat. Women, dressed like the men in trousers and tunics, or thick, shapeless sweaters, sang with equal gusto and swayed with relish, arms interlinked with those beside them.

Wladek sat demurely beside a shawled girl with startling ash-blonde hair, straight as steel, and pale blue lashless eyes. From time to time Irman glanced at him and grinned, his yellow teeth bared between his tufted beard and moustache.

'And now, a song for Poland,' Milo exclaimed, launching into the Marseillaise.

'That's French,' yelled Johnnie.

'I know, my friend – that's why it's for Poland!' and he laughed and Eduard joined him, and Wladek looked at Irman and they both erupted, until the entire building rocked with crazy mirth. Without warning, Milo produced a gun, and fired into the roof. The singing and laughing and thudding stopped. Everyone looked up at the leader. Irman jumped down and sat on the other side of the blonde girl. Beating one fist into another, Milo declaimed: 'Tomorrow we go back to war.'

Cheers billowed up and round the stone house. Milo threw wide his arms.

'Tomorrow we seek trains to seed with death, soldiers to interrupt and send to Nazi hell, if there's a hell that will have them.'

The entire assembly rose and beat the table, clapped their hands, shouted, cheered, then fell silent as Milo raised his arms and bellowed: 'Tomorrow we find trucks and guns to fire and destroy.'

'YES!'

Milo looked round the stone house, dropped his hands, and spoke softly, yet clearly.

'Tomorrow we also find out what we cannot do ourselves, and we tell Eduard and Johnnie and Wladek, and they tell London.' He paused, then flung his arms out and cried: 'And London sends death and destruction to all our enemies.'

The partisans' voices swelled as they cheered and cheered again. Milo's voice dropped back.

'Tomorrow we learn to do more, to fight better, to fasten our eyes and ears more and more often and with more and more results.'

The room was silent. Milo raised his arms again, his voice gathering volume.

'Tomorrow we start the final fight,' and with hands clenched aloft, he roared the final words: 'FOR VICTORY!'

The stone house trembled with the force of the explosion of 'VICTORY!' as the partisans took up the cry: 'VICTORY! VICTORY! VICTORY!'

Milo jumped down from the table, and strode through them, collecting Eduard as he passed, and was gone. Irman beckoned Wladek to follow and, arm in arm in arm, they forced their way through the throng with the blonde girl.

Outside Milo pointed at a small stone shack, set apart from the rest, close to the caves.

'In here, please.'

They sat round a pitted, scarred old table, and Milo produced a bottle and a handful of small glasses. They sipped as he talked.

'Tomorrow I will arrange for the young men to attend your classes, every morning. In the afternoons, I will provide one dozen men to guard your transmitter. In the evening, some of us will cross the border, as usual. There will be action, but also I will send Irman and other trusted men back with information, for you to tell London.'

He raised his glass.

'To us all, and may God have mercy upon our endeavours.'

I had a premonition, that day with Milo. I had a feeling that we were not going to get through this time. I prayed, because I did not believe in 'Fate', but in God and His will, and I did believe in the power of prayer, not to alter the facts, or as a means to personal safety, but as a matter of salvation, and I knew that I had to survive to complete my task, my mission, my commitment to my country and my family – and to myself.

It was not a question of seeking time to salve my need – though that, too, came into my calculations, and I had to wrestle with myself to free my desire for revenge from my faith in the rightness of what I had chosen to do – so much as a plea to be granted the freedom from fear and other men's hate, so that I could be whole and thus shriven.

As I prayed, I wondered if I was a fool to pray, and examined my doubts. I decided I was a fool anyway, but that war was not a folly of my making and I would be wise to cleanse my mind of fear and therefore of doubt. God's will be done, but please God, let it be done after the event, and not before the prospect. So I simply sought His mercy – for the time being.

God listened, let me start, then struck me down when I was not looking. He left me alone after that until He struck me down again, when I had almost forgotten Him, and certainly stopped my prayers. It would be presumptuous to seek His help now – for I have no mission, and I seek no salvation, but just wait, and wonder, and do my best.

I believe He understands.

THE SUM OF THE SIDES

They went by night. In small groups, walking, they seeped out of the caves and stone houses, trickling down the rocky slopes, through the same cleft, out of view. Eduard and Milo joined Irman and the final unit, as they wended their way towards the border, stepping cautiously yet firmly along the stony paths, round the smooth green flank of the mountain, into the Greek mainland. There were six groups of some dozen partisans, each spreading through the ancient villages on their ways to Ioannina, Thessalonika, Trikkala, to the Aegean and the Ionian coasts, their missions to seek, destroy and report.

Eduard clasped Irman's hand.

'Send me good tidings of your deeds, and Godspeed.'

The melancholy partisan nodded several times, then his mouth lifted as his eyes smiled, and he patted his sten gun.

'There will be good deeds, I promise you. I will send news soon,' and he merged into the night.

Only one man remained, standing by Eduard.

Milo stood, motionless, and Eduard moved away, pausing to look back at the silent figure, then started on the trek back to the camp. The quiet voice drifted through the night air, and he stopped to listen.

'Give me but one firm spot on which to stand, and I will move the earth.'

Eduard strained, but could see nothing. The voice was silent but, just as he was about to trudge back up the path, it floated back to him.

'Archimedes.' There was a short silence, then, 'Perhaps, like him, I shall cry "Eureka! – I have found" and you will tend that which we find, and turn it by wireless alchemy, to gold, and dust, and...'

The voice faded, and Eduard felt himself alone and within that solitude that only the greatest of burdens impose. He wished he was on his way to fight. Suddenly the night was cold; he shoved his hands in his pockets, and began the slow climb back.

For four days, they took classes in the fields, training young cadres in unarmed combat, small arms, explosives and fieldcraft. Some knew more than others, some were slow to learn, and some were unwilling.

In the afternoons, they set up the transmitter, sent brief confirmation to Cairo and London, in seconds' bursts, to avoid detection. For the rest of the day, they took the rearguard of older partisans through simple codes, transmission procedures and encryption.

On the fifth day, the guards reported a shepherd with one dog and a handcart, approaching the camp. The youngsters were banished to work in the fields, and dispersed. The dozen partisans split into two groups – the men in the caves, to guard the provisions, equipment and ammunition cache, and the women in the stone houses, cleaning, cooking, mending.

The mast was stowed, the transmitter concealed, the generator 'lost' within its protective stacks of wood. Eduard watched from the long stone house window, a mug between his hands, while Wladek and Johnnie stayed in the caves with the guards.

The shepherd walked slowly, with a limp, a cowled cloak and shuffling gait, straight to the long stone house. Once there, the cart was allowed to tilt on its short shafts, the dog lay between them, its head between its paws, its eyes questing. The shepherd knocked twice. The woman looked enquiringly at Eduard, and he nodded sharply, once. She opened the door, and the shepherd hesitantly took a short step inside, then slowly folded up, settling into an untidy cluster of cloth and slender limbs and caked blood, the almost silver, ash-blonde hair spilling out of the cowl.

'Get Wladek, quickly – and water, morphine, blankets, cushions.'

Gently, Eduard unfolded the cloak that bound the blonde partisan, and stroked the hair off her face. His hand felt the obstruction within the cloak and, feeling through the cloth, he found the stump of the machine pistol, neatly severed, and prised the girl's hand open to release it. The cloth was sodden on the inside and crusted with dried blood outside.

Wladek burst through the door.

'Danovka?'

'Yes. She's wounded – badly, I think.'

Eduard indicated the cloth.

'I found this in there.' He pointed at the broken weapon. 'I think she took a shell fragment or grenade in the side. We will have to be extremely careful.'

Three women now busied themselves about the body of the girl, easing a narrow plank beneath her, then slowly lifting her onto the table. One of them glanced up at Eduard.

'Come on. We're no use here. Let them get on with it,' and he took Wladek's arm roughly, pushed him to the door and out of the stone house. They sat on the stone step, saying nothing, until Wladek stood, looked down at Eduard and smiled a bitter, wistful smile.

'You know what you said – about finding someone?'

'Yes?'

'Well, I have. And this time it's. . .' He paused, then looked away and mumbled, 'I don't know, I can't explain it, but it's different. I feel as if I've been waiting and all those other girls, well.' He sighed and added, 'They're just girls, and now this is what I've been waiting for, and she's hurt and. . .' His voice trailed away.

Eduard said nothing, for there was nothing to say. Wladek sat down again.

354

'She may be dying and that's just not bloody fair.'

The two friends sat in morbid silence.

After a few minutes, Eduard got up and pushed the door open. One of the women noticed the cool air, walked across, and firmly, but quietly, closed it.

'I don't think we're doing any good sitting here. Come on.'

He reached down for Wladek's hand and hauled him to his feet.

'Let's find Johnnie.'

The cave was cool. Within its depths, along the familiar fissures, out of sight of the fields, the chamber widened and soared above them. A single oil lamp flickered on a narrow ledge, concealing within the shadows which it cast a niche which became a crude archway to a long, hand-hewn chamber, racked with uneven ledges, on which sat piles of oilskin-wrapped equipment.

At the furthest end, another lamp faltered in the eddy of their approach. There sat Johnnie, a rifle across his knees, a bottle at his feet, a rotund pot in his large right hand.

'Evening. Like some?'

He gestured towards the row of pots behind him on a scant shelf, and Eduard took down two. Johnnie filled them, and then his own.

'Is she alright?'

Wladek shook his head.

'Don't know. She's unconscious. Been hit pretty badly. They took bits of the gun out of her side.'

'Have you prayed?'

Wladek's head jerked up and the slivova spilt down his chin.

'Prayed? What the hell for? Don't be bloody stupid.'

Johnnie took a long, slow sip, then set the pot down beside him, put the rifle carefully on the floor, leant forward, and took Wladek's hands. A single, sudden jerk, and Wladek found himself on his knees.

'You too, Eduard, because I know you do.'

Eduard complied, bending one knee.

'Our father...'

When they had finished, they remained on their knees, eyes closed, pleas common but thoughts separate, ranging and apart.

A stone scuttled across the outer chamber, and they jumped to their feet, Johnnie clutching his rifle, Wladek bending to scoop up a handful of dirt, Eduard's hand on his knife, his other to his lips, as Johnnie extinguished the lamp. A blurred figure, uncertain in the fractured dark of the chamber, loomed. A woman spoke.

'Danovka's awake. She asks for Wladek.'

The women had finished. Danovka lay beneath a coarse cotton sheet, her arms outside it, her hair spread as steel wings upon the cushion, her bed a thick palliasse on the table.

'We could not move her,' explained the first woman. 'She has lost a lot of blood. But she seems better, calm – and awake.'

As Wladek approached the makeshift bed, the girl's eyes opened and she smiled up at him, a small smile with a clear shaft of need and care and want shining through it. Then her eyes closed again.

'Be careful – her side is badly torn, and tender.'

Wladek nodded, crouched beside the table, and took Danovka's hand in his, raising it to his mouth, and kissing it soundlessly. He held it to his lips, then gently replaced it on the sheet, and sat back on his heels.

'We prayed, you know. I prayed,' adding, 'Not a habit of mine, but – well, it seems to have worked.'

Eduard studied them both, and thought of Sara, and caught his breath, and left the room, muttering to Johnnie as he passed him, 'Find out what happened. I need to call London.'

For four more days they nursed Danovka, and each day she lay still as the women tended her, fed her, relieved her, and always summoned Wladek when they had finished. Wladek's unqualified adoration reinforced their care and by the fifth day the girl was stirring. On the sixth day she spoke.

She told Wladek that only he had saved her, that she had reached the camp solely because he was there, waiting for her, that this alone had sustained her. She told him that the unit had been destroyed, led into a Gestapo trap by a false informant, a Greek whom Milo trusted, and whose information had been passed to one, if not two of the other units as well. She had been left for dead, with the other dead, for all her unit had died. They had not reached their target. They had failed.

That afternoon Eduard and Johnnie set up the transmitter with Wladek, when Danovka was sleeping. The message to London was terse and to the point. 'Fifty per cent casualties. No hits. No news. One traitor: Skoros.'

On the seventh day, the guards reported movement in the valley. Eduard and Johnnie climbed the ridge above the caves and swept the terrain through their glasses. Figures leapt into focus. Grey figures. The Wermacht.

'Small platoon, I think. One infantry carrier, another, smaller vehicle, looks like a half-track, and some sort of machine gun. Nothing else.'

He lowered the glasses.

'Wonder what they want. There's nothing here for them.'

'Except us.'

Eduard raised the glasses again.

'Bastards. They're settling in by the look of it. Wonder where they came from.'

He turned to Johnnie.

'Know what I think? I think they know we're here, somewhere here, they know the partisans will return – those they haven't killed, and they're waiting.'

'So?'

'So the question is, what do we do about it? Let them alone, or...' and he let the alternative hang, as they contemplated the dilemma.

With guards concealed, but watching the Germans, they returned to the long stone house. With Wladek and the guard commander, they considered the options but, after half an hour's discussion, the dilemma remained. If they struck, there could be more. If they did not, Milo would walk into a trap. Then Eduard started to smile.

'I've got it.' He looked round the table at the bewildered faces. 'We'll move them, but with their complete agreement.'

Johnnie spoke for them all.

'How do you propose to do that?'

'I'll give them their marching orders – German to German.'

Before the others could protest, or articulate obvious objections, he was racing ahead.

'Uniforms – there are those captured by Irman last year. Language – all three of us speak it. Orders – we'll be vague, but make them check the next valley, and the one beyond that. That'll keep them away from base.'

'How do we get there? We can't very well walk up to them out of the blue. Officers don't spring out of hillsides. Not German officers.'

'We use the 'bike – the motorcycle and sidecar, the one Milo stole – paint it up camouflage style, and they'll never know.'

'And if they have radio? They'll soon find out, and then we're sunk.'

'Lado's department,' and Eduard grinned at the partisan. 'Once we get there, watch for a signal and then start your attack.'

Eduard turned to Wladek.

'In the confusion, take the radio to send a message, and disable it. Drop it in the excitement. When they find it – too late!'

Lado thumped the table, and they all looked at the bristling Slav.

'How can I attack without giving us away?'

'Two of you, with the bazookas, from down the valley – work your way round. They haven't the equipment to tackle the mountain. They'll use you as the excuse to do what we've told them to do, and go.'

He paused, looked down at his hands, then added, 'The signal – a blast on the motorcycle klaxon. OK?'

'But—'

This time Eduard slammed his hands down on the table.

'We're here to fight. This is what we're here for. We fool them, we hit them, we leave them. Trust me. They will not come back.' He stood, and added, 'Not yet anyway.'

ETD was dusk. Lado and his comrades had left three hours earlier. Johnnie had checked the 'bike. The three Poles were dressed as despatch rider, rifleman and Oberleutnant. Johnnie primed the carburettor and stamped down, hard. The engine spluttered and died. He tried again.

On the third attempt, it fired, and a thin croak emerged from the exhaust. Johnnie twisted the throttle and the croak became a series of barks, a cough, a hesitation, then a rasping roar. He swung a leg over, and bestrode the battered grey tank. Wladek jumped on the pillion, and Eduard eased himself into the sidecar.

Adjusting his hat, he pulled down his goggles, and raised his arm.

'Heil Hitler, and up Jerry's a-a-a-arse,' the final word juddering out of him as Johnnie let in the clutch and blipped the throttle.

The track led down into the valley and then levelled out. Two hundred yards from the German encampment, they were challenged. A guard reared up from behind a low outcrop. Johnnie slipped the clutch, the 'bike slowed and Eduard raised his hand – 'Heil Hitler' – as they slid past the guard, who shrugged, and sat down again behind his rock.

Johnnie slowed as they approached the half-track and the two tents.

'Oberst!'

Eduard returned the salute and lifted himself out of the sidecar. Johnnie dismounted, pushed his goggles over his visor, and stood at ease beside the 'bike. Wladek stood to attention behind Eduard. The three men who had been lounging outside the tent stood rigidly to attention as Eduard strolled up to them, then past each one, fingering a lapel, adjusting a buckle, and patting the last man's insignia as he noted the large personnel carrier, and a strange, half-tracked motorbicycle.

'Gefreiter!'

'Mein herr!'

'Who is in charge here?'

'Obergefreiter Ronstein, mein herr.'

'And where is he?'

The Lance-corporal looked embarrassed, coughed, and stared past Eduard.

'Over there, sir.'

Eduard followed the young soldier's eyes, just in time to see a portly figure pull up his trousers and step out from behind some rocks, buttoning his flies, as he sauntered towards the group, his eyes on his task.

'Ronstein!'

The Corporal, startled, looked up, raised a hand to salute, felt his trousers droop, caught the trouser flap with one hand, and froze to attention, his arm extended.

'Heil Hitler, Herr Oberleutnant.'

'Heil Hitler.' Eduard returned the salute. 'In your own good time, Corporal.'

The man rapidly reassembled his uniform, buttoning the tunic and donning his soft-peaked field cap. As he approached, Eduard noticed the paratrooper's badge.

'At ease.'

Eduard stood between the two NCOs, and contemplated the vehicles. Wladek remained at attention, and Johnnie was still. Eduard strolled slowly towards the carrier, realising, as he got closer, that it mounted a Mauser machine gun. He turned round and leant against it.

'You are looking for the traitors?'

'Sir?'

'Resistance, local renegades, saboteurs.'

'Mein herr, we have information.'

'Yes?'

'There are raiders, from over there.'

He pointed at the mountains.

'They come and they steal our supplies, destroy our transport, kill our people, and rape our women.'

Eduard's eyebrows rose a fraction.

'Rape your women? What women?'

The Obergefreiter looked confused, and mumbled something. Eduard snapped his fingers.

'Speak up, man. What women?'

'I'm not sure, sir. It's just that, we heard, that is, the Obersturmfuehrer told us that we must find these pigs, that they are nothing but barbarians, who do the most dreadful things, but, well...'

His voice trailed off, and he looked even more uncomfortable than when he was fastening his flies.

Eduard straightened up, pulling his greatcoat down.

'Quite so. Barbarians. Root them out.'

He waved his arm in a vague circle.

'You have mobility, weaponry, information. Why are you sitting here doing nothing?'

'Waiting orders, mein herr.'

'Ah. I see. And where are the rest of your men?'

The Corporal brightened.

'Yes, sir! I sent them on reconnaissance. They should be back shortly.'

'How many?'

'Sir?'

'How many did you send, man?'

'Six, sir.'

'You sent six of your soldiers out, without a commander?'

'No, sir. I sent the Funkmeister with them. They're all Hiwis, sir.'

'Hilfswilligers? Auxiliaries? Communists?'

'No, sir, not Russians – Georgians, I think.'

'Same difference,' snapped Eduard, despite himself. 'Stalin's a bloody Georgian. Can't trust 'em, you know. Can't trust 'em at all.'

He tapped the Corporal's chest.

'And did you send the radio with the Funkmeister?'

'Yes, sir. He is the operator, sir.'

'I know that,' snarled Eduard. 'So you have no communications?'

The corporal remained silent.

Eduard let him stew in his concerns, then sighed, turned to Wladek and commented, 'We shall just have to wait and see, then.'

Johnnie's hand was on the klaxon, and he let it drop to his side.

'When are they due back?'

At this the Corporal smiled and said, 'Now, sir. They're due now. There they are.'

He pointed to the track down which Eduard and Johnnie and Wladek had ridden. A file of soldiers, trailing their Karabiner rifles parallel to the ground, stumbled slowly towards them, the Funkmeister in the van, his portable transmitter slung between him and the next man.

Twenty minutes later, the forlorn band of pressed men approached and Eduard narrowed his eyes and imperceptibly shook his head at Johnnie. It was not yet time.

'Tell them to get some food, then rest; you can go too. We will wait here.'

Eduard waved his hand peremptorily.

'Get on with it then. When you have eaten, I shall decide what to do with you. Dismiss!'

The two NCOs and their three fellow soldiers moved over to the tents, where Eduard watched the Corporal explain the newcomers to the wireless man. When the latter bent towards his set, Eduard stiffened, Wladek stepped forward and Johnnie's hand came up sharply to rest on the klaxon. They saw the Corporal shake his head, and the other man straighten. Two disappeared inside the carrier, and the others dived into the tents.

'The Hiwis have all gone together,' remarked Wladek.

'And the NCOs are in the vehicle,' added Johnnie.

'Good time to start?' asked Wladek.

Eduard thought for a moment, sucked his lip, pulled his nose, and sat on the sidecar cowling.

'No. I think we should split them up. Send the Hiwis off with one of us, then tell them to disappear – we'll send them back to Milo. He can pass them on.'

'That leaves six Jerries,' observed Johnnie, 'and two of us.'

Eduard chuckled.

'Exactly. One for Wladek – the wireless man; and five gentlemen who are going for a long, long walk – in the wrong direction.'

Eduard looked at Johnnie.

'They should be reasonably relaxed now. Let's call the Corporal, show him the 'bike, and accidentally hit the klaxon.'

Wladek strolled over to the tent, pulled the flaps aside, and poked his head inside. Within seconds the wireless man appeared, Wladek pulled back the carrier's hatch, called inside, the Corporal appeared and the two men slung the transmitter between them, carrying it across to Eduard, Wladek in the rear.

'Now Funkmeister, can you reach base with that thing?'

'Ja, mein herr.'

'Good. Then' – and he turned to the Corporal – 'we shall send them a message.'

Eduard peeled a glove from his right hand, reached inside his tunic, and produced a notebook and pencil. As he started scribbling, he glanced briefly at Johnnie, who bent over the machine, appeared to stumble, and caught at the wireless man's arm. The Funkmeister fell against the machine, and the klaxon blared shortly and twice.

Eduard tore off a page and handed it to the Corporal.

'Alright Obergefreiter?'

The NCO read the message once, then again, looked up at Eduard with a worried look, then grimaced.

'If you think that's right, sir, yes, of course.'

Eduard frowned, and snapped back.

'You have a better idea? You have something real to report? You think you should wait?'

'Er, no, sir, mein Oberst, that is, well, if you feel we should...'

'I feel you should find the enemy, and destroy him. All you are doing is telling headquarters that you are widening the search.'

The Corporal was confused. He made one final effort.

'We are to move south? Your assistant will take the others north?'

'That's right. You take the carrier. The Hiwis can use the small tractor turn and turn about. My man here will guide them. We have sniffed out the barbarians' tracks.'

The Corporal nodded and Eduard buttoned up his greatcoat.

'My rider and I shall return to base.'

Johnnie started the 'bike as Eduard paused by the sidecar, leant across and murmured loud enough for him to hear, 'If Lado doesn't act soon, we must go, before they wake up,' and, as if he had read Johnnie's thoughts, added, 'Wladek can look after himself.'

As the motorcycle swung round in an arc, Eduard raised his hand in salute, and the wireless man started transmitting. Wladek leant over him, but no rockets came. He looked around. The Corporal had vanished inside the carrier, and no-one had emerged from the tents. Wladek spoke quietly, and the wireless man looked up at him, breaking transmission. Wladek grinned at him, stuck his thumb out towards the retreating motorbike, and said something else. The wireless man watched the 'bike recede, smiled, and took Wladek's arm. Together they started walking towards the tents. Eduard reached up and tapped Johnnie's arm. 'Slow down' he mouthed, then pointed down the track to an overhang just beyond the rocks which the

361

Corporal had made his latrine. Johnnie stepped on the clutch, and they stopped.

They saw the flash before they heard the whistle before the rocket erupted in the gap between the carrier and the tents. The wireless man fell flat on the ground, and Wladek fell across him, kicking the transmitter to one side. Then they crawled towards the vehicles. The Hiwis were spilling out of one tent, running wildly towards the cover of a loose scree of stones, the soldiers tumbling out of the others, to make for the carrier, where the Corporal's head shot out of the top hatch, as its engine crackled, and it started moving. Wladek jumped on the hybrid tractor, twisting the handlebars as he fired the engine, two Hiwis hurling themselves on the back. The wireless man scrambled into the carrier as it gathered speed, Wladek gunned the little tractor, and its treads started turning, accelerating, and then careering between the tents.

Wladek twisted the handlebars to full lock, and swung the machine round, heading straight for the transmitter. As the treads ground over it, the wireless disintegrated, and a second rocket landed, blasting the soldiers' tent. Wladek headed for the track, where Johnnie and Eduard waited, his Hiwis holding onto one another and the metal panels. The carrier had turned, and was speeding towards the overhang, its Mauser spewing rounds which chipped into the rock, splintering stone and clodding earth. The little tractor paused alongside the 'bike, where Eduard was standing in the sidecar, his hand to his eyes, shading them against the sky as he watched the skirmish.

No more rockets came. The carrier stopped, and the Corporal cautiously looked out of the hatch, then swivelled and looked back towards Eduard. Eduard raised a hand, and imperiously beckoned him. The Corporal disappeared, the carrier turned, and slowly motored back until it came to rest with its fellows. The back hatch opened, and the men crawled out.

'Anyone hurt?' asked Eduard.

'Nein, mein herr. Nobody.'

'Good. Good. Then we had better get on with it. We know they're there, to the south. Don't lose any time. Get after them.'

The Corporal saluted, hesitated, then asked, 'What about our message? Headquarters?'

Wladek leant towards Eduard and Eduard nodded.

'Too late, Obergefreiter. Your wireless was hit in the attack.'

He pulled on his glove.

'I will report on your behalf. Auf Wiedersehen and good luck.'

As the carrier pulled away, Eduard turned to Wladek.

'You'd better collect your Hiwis – they're over there,' and he pointed at the loose rocks.

'We'll see you back at the camp – if that thing goes that far,' and Johnnie roared with laughter as the 'bike scudded away, leaving

Wladek sitting in the unfamiliar seat of a motorcycle which did not know it was a half- track.

'What the hell do they call this bloody contraption?' he asked and one of the Hiwis answered, in broken Polish.

'It's a Kleine Kettenkraftrad – German for small tractor.'

'You spoke Polish?'

'Well, you did too just now.'

The man grinned, his arm linked with his fellow.

'Can we go home now, please?'

'Of course you can.'

It's a funny thing about war – it changes everything, yet it changes nobody. There were we, supposed to be transmitting essential information to our masters, and here we were, mucking about with the Germans, generally enjoying ourselves making fools of them and fun of our allies. The situation was absurd – and dangerous, if not potentially lethal for all of us; the people were, well, people: ordinary men with small concerns, limited outlooks and just a desire to do the job and get out of it, and back to normality, if that still existed.

There was not, if we were totally unprejudiced, which we were not, at the time of course, much to choose between us, except that small smidgeon of extra information we held – we knew we were fakes. Otherwise they were where they had been sent, trying to do what they had been told to do, and utterly bewildered by being told to do something different. We were where we had not been sent, doing what we had been warned not to do – mixing with the enemy, and abandoning our posts to attend to the probably negligible risks they posed. Why?

When I saw that corporal fastening his flies, I could not hate him. He had just the same needs as I did. When the wireless man wanted his radio, it simply reminded me of the day my shotgun jammed – a familiar toy was broken.

Wladek, faced with the hybrid motorbike, was just another man with sixteen left thumbs, confronting the mystery of mechanicals. The Hiwis were lost children, far from home, where they had no desire to be, with people they did not understand, fighting someone else's war without conviction.

Only Johnnie seemed to rise to the occasion, until you realised that he was a natural fighter, and responded positively to that which he enjoyed most – a good scrap, preferably with a twist of surprise. And me?

Well, I had changed so much, I was no longer sure of who I was, so I was atypical. I was change itself, so that, in reality, I was also unchanged, but simply evolving continuously, a captive-cum-fugitive who became a secret man – or was it a man with secrets; I was never quite sure of the difference, if there was one – who found himself in the van and then in the lead, and make no mistake, they are not quite the same thing.

Being in front, with the team following, is not the same as leading. One is folly blithely masquerading as captaincy; the other is wisdom, hesitantly seeking truths. In that mountain valley, for the first time I led others; I took the decision, and the responsibility, and the consequences would be mine, whatever happened. And the reason I realised?

I had stepped out of the world of pretence and into the reality of ordinary people in dislocated times, with intent, on my own, without compliance, determined to achieve something, admittedly small, but of value. The target was not the enemy, but me. I was, for the first time, face to face with my opportunities, and my limitations.

It did not happen again until recently. Then the limitations were subordinate to the opportunities. Now the opposite is true, but the challenge is still the same – to change the situation, because you can never change the people. They are always the same.

SKOROS THE GREEK

First came Zoran, then came Savic.

'Only two of you?'

Zoran slumped onto the bench; Savic leant against the stone wall, and reached over Eduard's head for the bottle. Johnnie wiped the neck and passed it. Across the room, Wladek sat close to Danovka, a hand loosely resting on her knee. It was the sixth week.

Twenty days after he left, Milo had sent word. One unit destroyed, no survivors – Danovka had smiled coldly when told. Another ambushed, but the partisans knew their ground. They had scattered, two men now returned. Of a third group, nothing was known. They had penetrated German lines on the east coast, then vanished.

The first good news came from Irman. He sent a courier. He spoke of trains derailed, convoys disrupted and a satisfactory raid near Trikkala, where the Germans stockpiled shells. The ammunition dump had been destroyed. No casualties – except Germans.

The second news came from Irman too. It was a man, Skoros, the Communist activist whom Milo had trusted, mistaking political allegiance for common cause. The Greek arrived bearing gifts: grovelling disclaimers blended with scraps of disparate information. Irman's couriers passed on the partisan's message, laconic, chilling and final.

'Irman says to find out what he knows, then kill him.'

'An execution?'

'That's what Irman says.'

'And Milo?'

The man shrugged.

'That's what Irman says.'

They put the Greek in a small stone hut, without windows, the single door secured with a timber baulk, hasped and padlocked. Each day he was extracted, to circle the hut endlessly, two men on guard, his legs chained.

On Eduard's insistence, he was fed at the same time and with the same food as the rest of them. Each day he was brought before Eduard, and interrogated. Where had he been? What had he seen? Who did he know? Eduard explained.

'I want to find out who he knows, so I can find out what he knows and whether it is worth knowing.'

After three days, it seemed clear that Skoros knew little of substance, but that he had travelled to the delta, had cousins in Athens, Communists connected to ELAS, the guerrilla army, through the National Liberation Front. In the wild and tangled skeins of Greek politics, the government in exile was ill-served by its fading Royalists, while ELAS far outnumbered its guerrilla competitors, and kept its intelligence to itself. London had come back to Eduard the same day he mentioned Skoros.

'Find the Greek. Is he ELAS? What does he know?'

On the fourth day, Skoros sat opposite Eduard.

'Take off his chains.'

None too gently, the guards complied, hauling the Greek to his feet, pulling the shackle so hard that he winced, then releasing it, backhanding his ankle so that he moved the other leg, then repeating the process, whipping the chain away so that it flailed against his shin, and he stumbled.

'Alright. You can sit.'

Eduard waved at the guards.

'Leave us.'

'But—'

'I said "leave us" and I mean "leave us". Now go!'

Eduard beckoned Johnnie.

'Give him a drink.'

The bottle was on the table already; Johnnie pushed it across.

'Wladek. Got any fags?'

Wladek smiled apologetically at Danovka, then fumbled the flap of his pocket, and flipped a battered tin down the table.

'Matches?'

Wladek sauntered over, leant past the Greek, tipped open the tin, extracted a limp, thin cigarette, put it to his lips, struck a match and lit it, expelling a stream of smoke, then placed it between the Greek's shaking fingers.

'Now leave us alone, please.'

Wladek took Danovka's arm, and then her hand, following Johnnie to the door.

'Are you sure?'

'Yes. I'm sure.'

The door closed. Skoros took a small sip of slivova, then set the bottle down, dragging on the cigarette, drawing the smoke deep into his lungs, before turning his head to blow it away from Eduard.

'I will try to get you a fair trial, but you know...' Eduard paused. 'You know what's going to happen, don't you?'

The Greek nodded imperceptibly.

'It'll be quick. I promise you that.'

There was no response, except perhaps a flicker of the eyelids, as the Greek took another sip. Eduard pushed the bottle to one side, out of reach.

'I need to know what you've seen.'

For over an hour Eduard asked and Skoros answered. As he spoke, Eduard made brief notes. Gradually, he built a picture of movement, of soldiers who were there one day, but not the next, of activity in

Piraeus, on the waterfront. The detail was opaque, but the generality was clear. Germans were moving north, but where exactly, and to what end? After two hours, Eduard was repeating himself. Skoros had nothing more to tell.

The bottle still stood to one side. Eduard reached over and pushed it in front of the Greek. He indicated the tin.

'Take another one. Light it yourself.'

He tapped the matches, idly picking two and breaking one. As the Greek lit up, Eduard snapped another match and, without thinking, put the broken pieces across each other, arranging them in the shape of a cross of Lorraine.

Skoros leant forward, studied the matches, then looked up at Eduard. 'Messerschmidts.'

'What?'

'That looks like a Messerschmidt – German 'plane.'

'I suppose it does.'

Eduard gazed down at the matches, then flicked them apart, tidied them up, and piled them together, pushing open the matchbox, and tucking them inside.

'They pack them like that.'

'Pack what?'

'Messerschmidts.'

'What do you mean, pack them?'

Skoros took a long, deep drag on the cigarette, then swore softly as the tobacco burnt down to his fingers, and dropped it, grinding it with his heel into the wooden floor. As he breathed out the smoke, he replied, 'In crates, on the trains.'

Eduard swallowed surreptitiously.

'Have you seen them?'

'No, but my brother did. He's only twelve. He plays by the railway.'

Eduard fondled the bottle, determined to conceal his interest.

'Oh yes. I suppose he watches the trains for something to do?'

Skoros nodded vigorously, his thoughts focussed on family, and his mind relaxed, now the serious part was over. For a moment he forgot his destiny, and the words spilt out.

'Alex, he's a dreamer, he dreams of travel, he dreams of the great trains, the Orient Express, trains like that. He's always watching the trains, keeps a little book with all the engines. Stuff like that. He's never any trouble, as long as he can go to the railway.'

'And Alex, he's at home most of the time? When he's not down at the railway, that is?'

'Yes. Yes, of course. He helps my uncle in the fields.'

Skoros seemed suddenly tired, and indefinably withdrawn.

'Something wrong?'

The Greek brushed his eyes with the back of his hand.

'No. Nothing really.'

'Your uncle perhaps? You're worried about him?'

Skoros looked directly at Eduard, reached across, and touched his hands. Eduard allowed the contact, did not move away.

'You have a family?'

'Yes.'

'They are at home, waiting for you?'

'Well, no.'

'Your mother perhaps?'

'My mother is somewhere else.'

Skoros's hands gripped Eduard's.

'My mother is somewhere else too.'

'Yes?'

'My mother is dead.'

The Greek released Eduard and sat back, seeming to shrink in on himself.

'My mother was taken, by the banditti. She was taken and beaten, and raped and then she was killed, and my father had to watch, and then they killed him too.'

The tears cascaded down the Greek's cheeks, and he shook, his sobs soundless, his head in his hands. Eduard watched with shared pain as the small spots on the tabletop soaked in and disappeared.

Skoros and Eduard sat in tacit silence. Then the Greek's hands parted, and he smiled bleakly.

'I don't care if I am killed. I have done what I could. I have sent some of the banditti to hell – for my mother.'

Eduard sighed softly, and persuaded himself that it was a waste of time to suggest that Milo's men were not the Greek's banditti, for he was not even sure of that himself. Instead he said, 'I would like you to take me to meet Alex.'

The Greek frowned.

'You can do that?'

'Yes, we can do that, if you would like us to.'

'So I can see him before I am shot?'

Eduard smiled.

'Let us go and see what can be done.'

On the fifth day Irman returned, with Marisa, Agim and Besnik.

'The rest are with Milo. They return soon.'

Each day Eduard called London. Each day he sent news. Irman's abrupt recital of hit and run also displayed an acute appreciation for numbers, concentration and armament of troops, so that London uncharacteristically added one word to the usual brief acknowledgement: 'Congratulations.'

That evening, Eduard spoke of Skoros.

Irman was adamant.

'He dies.'

Eduard reasoned, cajoled, appealed. It made no difference.

'He betrayed us. We lost good people. He dies.'

'Without a trial?'

'What trial? Why? We know what he did. He dies.'

Nothing would move the partisan, until Eduard mentioned Milo.

'Does Milo agree?'

'Of course he'll agree.'

'No. I didn't ask if he would. I asked if he had.'

Irman slammed the table.

'He will. The man will be shot.'

On the seventh day Milo returned with the rest of the partisans. Eduard staggered his transmissions, as he relayed the reports of trucks demolished, soldiers despatched and artillery destroyed. The volume of wireless traffic was beginning to cause him concern. He confided in Johnnie.

'I'm worried. The Germans must hear us. Law of averages.'

Johnnie laughed and replied, 'But we're not average, Eduard. We're above their laws.'

Wladek was less sanguine.

'You're right. I think you should think about leaving.'

The first time, Eduard missed the nuance. The second time he asked, 'You're staying?' but Wladek would not be drawn. He just smiled, tapped his nose, and laced his arm around Danovka.

'Irman is right. He's a traitor, my friend.'

'I know.' Eduard scratched his head. 'But I need to meet his brother. I need to see those trains.'

They were alone in the long stone house. Milo loped from one end to the other, his twisted mouth clamped shut in concentration. Abruptly, he stopped, swung round, and planted both hands on the table.

'If I let you go, you bring him back?'

Eduard stood, and put his hands on the leader's shoulders.

'Milo. The man's not a traitor, but betrayed for a reason. He loves his brother. If he takes me to him, he will not run. I shall have his heart in my hand.'

'Alright. But bring him back.'

Eduard released Milo, turned round and looked out of the window, his back to the wily partisan. Almost inaudibly he spoke.

'I don't know if you have your mother. I lost mine, then found her, and now she has gone again. I have lost my father. I have lost my brother.'

He pressed his head against the panes, his eyes shut.

'Skoros is like me. He has lost his mother too. He believes your men killed her. He knows you will kill him. But he has a brother, and he loves him. So he will come back, to die.'

Eduard turned slowly, and faced Milo.

'If he comes back, you will give him a fair trial.'

Milo nodded.

'If what he says is true, you will let him go.'

'If what he says is true, then I will kill the men who did it.'

Milo clenched and unclenched his hands, as if to dismiss the matter, strode to the door and pulled it open.

'I shall come with you. We will all go to Alex.'

They lay in the stiff, long grass, looking down. The scatter of hovels, washed off-white, tumbled down the hillside. Stunted and gnarled olive trees leaned against the remembered winds of winter, and skeins of goats tore and chewed at the available roughage. The sun stared out of a white sky onto the bleached grazing. Two goats paused and stood motionless a few yards from the partisans. Eduard murmured into Milo's ear.

'No sign of trouble.'

'No.'

He pushed himself up on his elbows and the two goats turned their backs, indifferently. Then, 'Right. Let Skoros go.'

Irman's eyes narrowed.

'On his own?'

'How else?'

Irman loosened the pistol in his belt.

'If he runs...'

Eduard put a restraining hand on his arm.

'If he runs, he'll not run forever. There's nowhere to go. We will find him.'

'You untie him. I cannot.'

Eduard rolled over, the grass stalks cracking and splitting and penetrating his sleeves. He reached Skoros, and spoke slowly, distinctly and without menace.

'If you do not come back, they will hunt you down. They will not be careful how they kill you. Understand?'

Skoros spread his hands as far as the cords allowed.

'I gave my word. I will come back.'

Eduard slackened the knot, then slipped the cord over the Greek's wrists and hands. He rubbed the chafed skin.

'Right. Half an hour.'

He squinted up at the Greek's face as the man rose, and stood over him.

'You be here. We'll leave a message, and we'll be watching.'

Skoros said nothing, turning, and gazing down at his village. Then he pointed.

'See that long, low house, the one with the black door?'

Eduard peered through the tops of the grasses.

'That was my home.' He looked down at Eduard. 'Only my uncle, and Alex, live there now,' and he stepped through the grass, onto the hollow, stony path.

As Skoros scrambled down, Milo signalled to the others, and the partisans scattered. Irman crawled up towards the first low ridge and scurried round it out of sight. Zoran followed Skoros, until he reached a small grove of olives, then slipped through them to a low walled enclosure. Savic wriggled through the grass along the flank of the hill while Milo cut up, towards an outcrop parallel to Irman's.

Only Eduard stayed where he was. When Skoros disappeared inside the small simple house, he stood, and began his descent. Almost on cue, the two goats reappeared, and ambled towards him, stopping short and regarding him with benign indifference, chewing slowly. As he moved, they moved, alongside and slightly behind him. Eduard swung the short stick he had culled, and whistled softly as he walked. One of the goats, more curious, or bolder, than the other, butted him gently when he paused. He stepped aside, and the goat bent down, snuffled the path, looked up, shook its head, stared at him, its amber eyes unyielding, then passed him. The other goat hesitated, then jinxed slightly as Eduard moved on, following at a cautious distance.

Thus the strange trio of goat, man, goat made its careful way to the first house, where Eduard could see that the picturesque detail of the creamy vista had soured to mildewed milk, the scabbed and pocked walls flaked, mould encrusting the once proudly daubed home. He began to realise the village was quiet, too quiet, as he slowly pushed at the dirty grey door.

Inside, the debris of a ravaged home lay across the dusty floor. Broken chairs, a three-legged table tilting awkwardly into the hearth and shattered crockery evidenced mindless destruction. Eduard unsheathed his knife, and crept to the back of the single chamber. There was a low doorway, and an open lean-to, corrugated iron rigged on makeshift poles, a crippled handcart resting on an axle stub, its single wheel still turning. Eduard shrank back into the doorway.

The dog barked. It stood, bristling, teeth yellow, tail erect. Then it snarled. Eduard tensed, and balanced the knife, waiting for the first run. The dog's tail dropped, then wagged, the snarl became a grin, and it went down on its belly, fawning, its tongue lolling. Eduard sensed the hand before it came to rest, on his shoulder.

'No-one here.'

He turned slowly, the knife ready. The boy was young, but quite tall. His smooth, brown face was sculpted by grief, his almost violet eyes shadowed by horror.

Eduard crouched before him, deliberately and carefully put the knife aside, and held out his hand.

'Tell me.'

The boy's English was incomplete, but vivid with the haunting.

'Murdered – mother, father. No brother – gone.'

He looked past Eduard at the dog and beckoned.

371

'Nana.'

The dog wriggled on its belly and lay between them, rolling over, its fawn underbelly quivering with expectation. The boy stroked it as he spoke.

'Uncle Mitri feed. We work. Then one day, I railway. Home, no Uncle. No people. No home. All broken – like this.'

He swept his arm across as he gazed at the damaged room, then looked back at Eduard.

'All peoples gone. I find. In olives.'

He pointed past the outhouse, towards the straggling olive grove.

'All hanging. Some shot. Some. . .' He struggled for the words, could not find them, then held his hands round his throat.

'Mitri nail to tree.'

The boy mimed the nails and the hands, and the broken skull, and Eduard shuddered as he saw the old man through the boy's eyes, forced to face the tree, to hug it, until he was brought to death, embracing his living.

'Who – did – it?'

'Banditti.'

They both stiffened as they heard the scrape of foot against stone. Eduard motioned the boy outside, where the dog followed. He sidled behind the small door, and waited. The outer door swung on its old hinges, half open.

'Alex?'

The voice was low, hesitant. Eduard remained out of sight, as Skoros pulled the door back and stepped inside. The boy stood framed in the other opening, the dog behind him. They stared at each other for a moment, then Skoros stumbled forward, and scooped the boy into his arms.

'Alex, Alex, Alex.'

They sat in the old house, where Alex had gathered the best of the detritus from the village homes and goats' milk, Mitri's olives, dead neighbours' small cheeses, the dried grapes of last year's harvest, tomatoes and his own bad baked bread, unleavened and leathery. The village well slaked their thirst.

'Banditti,' said Eduard.

'Yes. The same bastards.'

'But not Milo's.'

'I don't know.'

Eduard shrugged.

'You made a mistake?'

'It's possible.'

'We may never know.'

Skoros agreed. Eduard threw the remnant of his bread at the dog.

'The railway.' He turned to the boy. 'When do the trains run? The ones with the boxes with the aeroplanes?'

'I see twice. Beginning day. Early. Boxes.'

'Right. We sleep here tonight. Then I'll tell Milo.'

He pushed back the stool, and wiped his hands on his trousers.

The sun slanted across the open doorway, rainbowing the dust motes, which suddenly broke up into a cloud as a shadow bisected them, and the door slammed against the wall.

'No need. We're here.'

The partisans followed Milo into the room.

'You didn't come back, so we came for you.'

That night, as the partisans slept and kept guard turn and turn about, Milo and Eduard sat in a store shed, cool and clean, and somehow overlooked when Death visited Nethos, chewing olives and drinking retsina.

'So, he was right about the banditti.'

Eduard explained what Alex had said and Milo stroked his lip.

'It was not my men.'

'Are you sure?'

'No, I am not sure, but I am almost sure.'

Eduard poured more retsina.

'It will have to wait. We need to know where those 'planes are going – if there are any 'planes.'

'We leave the others here. With Skoros. You, and I, and Alex, we will find out.'

The railway came from Salonica, via Kiklis on its way to Petritsi, then plunged back down to Drama and to the east. There was a siding near Nethos, where Alex watched the trains crawl past. One day he had arrived to see flat trucks with crates sitting there. They were guarded by German soldiers, but it was a quiet place, with no other buildings except the footplate shed, and, when the guards disappeared, Alex had crawled down the embankment, and crept along the trucks, and tried to see what was inside. One crate was damaged, and through the gap he had seen the wing of an aeroplane. Skoros had imagined the rest.

Now Milo and Eduard followed the boy as he navigated the scrub along the embankment. Alex put his finger to his lips, as they approached the siding.

When they left at dawn that morning, Milo had warned Eduard, 'We'll be lucky to find anything,' and Eduard had agreed.

'Probably all gone by now.'

As they neared the boy's vantage point, Eduard tensed. He could hear the sibilance of valves leeching steam as a train stood in siding or on track, and he wondered which it was, and whether it was 'their' train or not.

The whistle was harsh and piercing, and they all jumped. The train groaned, spat steam, cackled and coughed, then began to grind along the gradient. They gradually raised themselves above the shrubs, and watched what appeared to be a series of closed carriages pulled along the line back to Salonica. Then Eduard spotted a lowered window, and raised the glasses.

'Good God.'

'What is it?' Milo hissed.

'A General and at least two other officers. That's a staff train. What the hell are they doing here?'

He raised the glasses again.

'Their uniform's Luftwaffe, not Wehrmacht.'

'So there are aeroplanes, then.'

They waited throughout that day, and returned the next, but there were no more military trains. At Nethos, Eduard faced Skoros.

'We know where the trains go, but there's no military to the east. So where was that train coming from?'

'I don't know.'

Eduard gripped his sleeve.

'Your life's at stake, man. Think.'

Skoros buried his head in his hands, and Eduard half feared another temperamental Greek outburst when the spy lifted his head, and laughed out loud.

'Nowhere. It was coming from nowhere.'

'Don't be stupid, and don't make jokes. This is serious.'

'No, it's obvious isn't it? They got on at the siding. Where the 'planes get off.'

Eduard clapped his forehead.

'Christ! Of course. You're right. And that means—'

Milo finished the sentence for him.

'That means the 'planes are not far away. Tomorrow we take the road from the railway, and see where it goes.'

The road went down the hill into the valley, and then along the widening vale, and was plainly visible from their parallel route along the flanking hillside. Long before they reached it, they could see the asymmetric cross of runways within the flatland behind the high wire fences. Tucked into the lee of the hill stood four large metal sheds – 'Hangars,' said Eduard, and Milo agreed.

Savic, Zoran and Irman fanned out, moving stealthily across the lightly wooded slopes as Eduard and Milo followed Skoros along the ridge. Above the aerodrome, behind the hangers, the woods rose more steeply, forming a natural defence against marauding aircraft, but exposing the big sheds to more subtle infiltration. Hard against the wood, the high fence bristled with barbs, and uniformed guards patrolled constantly.

They waited on the ridge, behind the trees. Half an hour passed, then Irman appeared.

'It's too well guarded. We could plant some charges, but we have not got the right materiel, and it is very dangerous.'

Milo cursed quietly, then asked Eduard, 'What do you want to do?'

'I want to see what's inside those hangers, and then tell London.'

'I'll go.'

They turned as Skoros spoke, and Eduard asked, 'What did you say?'

'I said, I will go. I can get in.'

'How?'

'By telling them who I am.'

Milo was bewildered, and annoyed and showed it.

'I do not understand, and this is not a day for silly Greek myths.' He added, 'They will kill you – slowly, more slowly than Irman.'

Skoros smiled.

'They won't, not when I tell them about Athens.'

As he spoke, Eduard began to realise that this man was not quite the simple peasant he pretended to be.

'Athens?'

'In Athens I am an informant, one of their people in ELAS.'

He looked directly at Milo.

'You must forgive me, but I hate the Communists. I help the Germans with ELAS and then I tell you about the Germans. That way I serve Greece and stop the Reds.'

The Greek hesitated, then looked hard at Milo.

'The information I gave you was true. But after my mother... I had no choice.'

Eduard: 'Then why are you here and not there?'

Skoros: 'For my family – I told you.'

Irman: 'So go to the Germans, and return to Nethos. Then I believe you.'

Milo: 'We will trust you.'

Skoros: 'Of course you will. You have Alex.'

They watched as the Greek emerged from the woods, and walked along the road. Before he reached the entrance, two motorcycles appeared, and racketed out of the compound, to waylay him. Pillioned and escorted, he rode back to the camp. They waited. Ten minutes passed. An open car appeared from behind brick buildings. At the entrance, an officer got out, and disappeared inside the compound. Minutes later, he returned, and Skoros was with him. They got into the car and it went back whence it came.

Milo scratched his beard.

'It looks as if he was right.'

'And telling the truth,' added Eduard. 'Let's go back.'

'Yes, but let's lay traps about the place, and take the boy, and wait where we can watch and withdraw – just in case. I do not like to face Germans on ground of Greek choosing.'

Savic and Zoran lay concealed in the stiff grasses above the village. Irman sat beyond them, below the ridge on the other side of the low hill, the boy beside him.

'He is our insurance,' Milo had said, 'so you can act as agent, and hold him as surety against Skoros's return.'

Irman had said nothing, but eased his pistol ostentatiously. Milo and Eduard sat back to back at the higher end of the olive grove, where they could see directly across to Skoros's house, protected by the trees. They talked quietly as they waited. Milo was reaching for the rucksack where they had stored food and drink for the day, when they heard the truck.

Minutes later, it bounced into view, then disappeared again, as it skirted the fields below the village. Then it broke into view once more, belching black exhaust, revving in high gear, and careering wildly from side to side.

'They are drunk, or that truck's lost its steering.'

Milo stood by the tree, in the dappled shadows cast by its foliage. The truck was in fact a battered van, its rear door missing, grey with the remnants of a black cross on its sides.

'Germans?' asked Eduard.

'Probably.' Milo unhitched his machine pistol. 'That bastard Skoros, he's double-crossed us – again.'

He glanced up the hill. Zoran and Savic had seen the intruders, and were already moving down, first one, then the other, crouching, running, flattening themselves, running again. Milo and Eduard moved the other way, so that the two pairs formed a pincer movement; the van braked to an unsteady halt, swaying and juddering as its occupants emerged. For a moment there was silence, the engine off, two men standing on either side, their hands shading their eyes as they surveyed the village, the hillside, and the trees. They wore the uniform of the Waffen SS.

One turned to the other and said something, the other nodded, and walked to the rear of the van, reached in, and hauled out two panniers. Milo frowned.

'What the hell are they doing?'

Eduard trained his glasses on the driver.

'He's not an officer. I can't see any chevrons. Must be rank and file.'

He adjusted the glasses as he scanned the other.

'Same with the other one. Wait a minute.'

'What?'

Eduard adjusted the glasses again, lowered them, wiped his eyes, then squinted once more through the lenses.

'Bloody hell.'

'What?'

'They're changing.'

'What do you mean, changing?'

'They've removed their tunics, and they've got loose shirts underneath, and they've wound scarves, like bandannas, round their heads.'

He put the glasses down again, and looked straight at Milo.

'They're going to the storehouse.'

'So they've been here before.'

'Looks like it.'

Eduard stowed his glasses, and checked his magazine, hefting the short gun, and sighting it. He raised a thumb at Milo, and the partisan responded. They moved forward, stealthily.

'Not Skoros's friends, anyway. Wrong uniforms. Wrong motive. Wrong moves.'

Milo glanced at Eduard.

'You are perhaps right. We shall see.'

'So we shall.'

The two Germans strode straight to the storeroom, and disappeared inside. Savic had reached the van, and was crouching behind the bonnet; Zoran ran beyond, and stationed himself in the lean-to behind Skoros's house. Milo eased himself along the storeroom wall, until he was beside the door. Eduard waited on the other side.

The first German emerged, struggling with a full pannier and, grunting, took two steps before bending and letting it flop onto the ground. As he straightened, his hands in the small of his back, Eduard put the pistol to his head and hissed, 'Do not move, or speak, or even think,' and grasped his hands.

At that moment, a low, quavering voice rasped from the van's interior.

'Have you found the boy?'

Distracted, Eduard dropped the German's hands, and Milo stepped swiftly towards the storeroom entrance, then dropped onto the ground as the German jumped sideways, drawing a short, black automatic from within his shirt. Zoran and Savic were both halfway round the van as Eduard fired.

The German fell, his automatic spinning out of his hand. From within the storeroom a withering stream of fire erupted, catching Savic full in the chest as Milo wriggled forward and, angling his machine pistol up and to the right, fired three single shots. Zoran was spreadeagled against the van's side, within inches of the back.

There was no movement from within the van, and the storeroom was silent. Eduard and Milo were still, Zoran pinned in position. The German on the ground sat, rocking himself back and forth, holding a shattered arm with his other hand. Savic was lifeless.

'Stalemate' mouthed Eduard to Milo as they covered the entrance from either side. The shot was wide. It came from the van, and harmlessly embedded itself in the storeroom wall, several feet above Eduard's head. The next was low, and missed Milo by inches. The third was high again, the fourth equally low. The fifth was between the first two, the sixth similar. It dawned on Eduard that whoever was in the van could not see them clearly, and was stitching a logical shot pattern that would, sooner or later, find a mark.

Milo jerked his head towards the van, then described a circular motion with his left hand, inching backwards as he did so. He cleared the storeroom corner, got to his feet, and ran in an arc, out of sight of the van, which would bring him back to it on the other side. Eduard followed suit in the opposite direction.

As they circled the buildings, Eduard glimpsed a movement behind the storeroom. A blinding flash was followed by a gust of wind, curling clouds of smoke, and the blast of the grenade. The storeroom wilted, then collapsed, as a ragged figure staggered out and fell to the ground.

With Alex tethered to him by a long cord, Irman appeared fleetingly in the trees behind the ruined building, trotting sedately across towards the high ground behind the van. Milo and Eduard reached Zoran seconds later. They looked at one another and smiled grimly in accord. Zoran stepped back, his pistol cocked, as Milo and Eduard pushed, then rocked, then pushed, rocked, pushed, rocked, until the van slowly rolled over onto its other side. A feeble screech filtered out as Zoran peered inside, his pistol aimed directly into the interior.

'Raus!'

'Impossible,' was the response.

Zoran shook his head incredulously.

'It's a cripple, in a chair – was in a chair.'

Together they hauled the crooked figure out of the van, replaced him in the metal chair, and contemplated their prisoner. Capless, the man before them was dressed in black, with the lightning flash of the SS on his leather coat, but no insignia of rank. He was legless, and one arm was bent and useless. One eye was sealed shut, the skin seared and taut, the ears gone, his lips a mere membrane divided by darkness, the nose a vestigial ridge.

Zoran had fetched the other Germans, who sat, bound and dazed, the wounded man clutching his broken arm, his partner dabbing at the blood from multiple grazes, where jars had exploded, showering him with shards of pot and glass.

As Irman approached, the tethered Alex behind him, the boy suddenly screamed, and tried to pull away, hauling on the cord that bound them, pulling Irman off balance. They both fell to the ground; angrily, Irman jerked the rope.

'You stupid child...' but he got no further as Alex screamed at all of them, 'Banditti! Banditti! Those are the ones.'

378

ONE DOWN

As the boy screamed and writhed, Irman reeled in the rope, and struck him, once, hard. Alex stopped abruptly, caught his breath and started sobbing. Irman shrugged, undid the rope, and shoved the boy away. Eduard gathered him up, and held him close, stroking his head. He looked across at Milo.

'What now?'

'We wait for Skoros.'

Milo instructed Irman to lay guard above the village, in case more Germans arrived. In their own minds they knew this was unlikely and that the burnt man and his accomplices were a rogue band, working to their own agenda. The wounded man's arm was bound and splinted, he and his companion incarcerated in the small single-roomed house that Eduard had first broached. The cripple was put back into the righted van, with a single guard, Zoran, and bound to his iron chair. Eduard moved with Milo away from the settlement, to overlook the approach road. Alex sat on his own, outside the small house.

'We should interrogate them, separately. They may know something about the aerodrome, and about the 'planes.'

Milo gazed across the valley beyond the dusty track. At length, he replied, as if in a daze.

'I suppose we should.'

He was silent for a while. Then he rubbed his twisted lip, looked at Eduard, and sighed, with a certain sadness.

'When we find out, and I have no doubt we will, we will not be more wise.'

'Why is that?'

Milo made no reply, but instead rummaged in the small leather pouch he carried at his belt. He drew out a folded paper, and placed it on his thigh.

As he unfolded it, absorbed in the detail of it, he said nothing, and Eduard, sensing a significance beyond anything he had thus far elicited, maintained an uneasy quiet. Milo smoothed the paper, and Eduard saw that, slightly crumpled, torn across one corner, and creased many times, this was a photograph. In the midst of a group of young boys a younger Milo stood, his arms round those on either side, his twisted smile more pronounced for having no protective moustache.

'Before the war,' offered Milo.

Eduard fingered the picture tentatively. Milo traced each face.

'My brothers.'

'Comrades?'

Milo laughed shortly, without any joy.

'No. Family – my brothers.'

379

He stroked the picture then abruptly refolded the paper, and returned it to his pouch, rising and starting back up the track to the buildings.

'Dead. My brothers.'

He stopped, and laid a hand on Eduard's arm.

'We will soon know of the German's aeroplanes, and then your people will send them to hell.'

They stood side by side, the partisan wrapt in his reverie, Eduard silent in sympathy, waiting.

'Then, soon, the war will be over.'

The partisan's tone was neither glad nor bitter, but emotionless. He glanced at Eduard.

'You will return to Poland?'

'I expect so, yes, when I have found my Mamita.'

'I am already home, in my own country, but with no family.'

There were incipient tears in Milo's eyes as he gazed at Eduard.

'You are fortunate. You have something to look forward to.'

He looked away, his words so quiet Eduard strained to hear them.

'When it is over, there is nothing. I have fought for it, but there is no victory, not in the ending of it all, only an infinity of absences, for ever and ever.'

They stood, suspended within the partisan's sadness.

The night passed in discomfort. They salvaged sufficient food from the shattered storeroom, and Alex, truculent in the aftermath of his discovery of his family's murderers, drew water from the well. The need to maintain vigilance against visitors, and a guard over their captives, precluded sleep.

The return of Skoros seemed less likely the longer the day drew out, yet it was Milo who reassured Irman.

'He will be back. He loves his brother,' and Eduard knew exactly what passed through the partisan's mind.

Zoran and Eduard were carrying and helping the crippled SS man to relieve himself, when they heard the familiar crackle of a motorbike. They set the man down in his iron chair behind the house, and Milo ran, crouching, to join them.

'Irman's above.'

'And those two are alone, waiting. If they shout out. . .'

'Unlikely.' Milo grinned, his sardonic self returned as the tempo increased. 'They have no idea who it is – and if it is Greeks, they will wish to remain undiscovered.'

'I have no such fear.'

They both turned sharply as the SS man spoke.

'One word, and. . .' Milo ran his finger across the man's throat, but the German laughed.

'You think I am afraid to die? If I was afraid to die, I would hardly be here.'

380

He smiled a glacial smile.

'I am, like you, my friend, fighting for the sake of it.'

He gestured with his good hand at his body, circled his face and pointed at the useless arm.

'Without the fight, what is life worth? A pension? For what? To sit and wonder what could have been?'

Without pausing, Milo struck the German, then slipped the scarf from his throat and bound it across the other's mouth.

'I cannot stop him thinking. . .' was his enigmatic comment.

The motorcycle slowed as it rounded the final bend, and they could see it for the first time. The rider was in German despatch uniform, and the pillion passenger was clearly Skoros, despite the leather hat and goggles.

'He has returned,' commented Eduard unnecessarily.

'And with one of his German friends,' added Milo contemptuously, 'and I felt he was telling the truth.'

'First, let us see what he says,' protested Eduard.

Skoros slipped backwards off the saddle, pushed the goggles up, peeling the gloves from his hands and placing them pedantically on the petrol tank. The German stayed on the 'bike, still revving slowly. They consulted their watches, Skoros retrieved his gloves, then the German saluted casually, and swung the 'bike round, letting it freewheel down the track until he reached the bend, blipping the throttle in farewell, and ripping across the grass as if in bravado, waving a nonchalant hand as he disappeared.

Skoros walked to the house, peered inside, started towards the storeroom, then stopped as he appreciated for the first time its destruction. His hands went in vestigial prayer to his lips, he pirouetted, surveying the village overall, dropped his hands and returned to the house, sliding down against its wall, waiting. They listened as the motorbike's exhaust receded, occasionally hesitating in gear change, then disappearing altogether. Milo cautioned Eduard, and they waited a further five minutes. Skoros did not move, his eyes closed, his body relaxed.

'There you are,' he remarked as they approached him. He did not rise. Milo stood over him.

'You returned.'

'Of course.'

Skoros waved towards the storeroom.

'You had visitors.'

His eyes met Milo's.

'My brother?'

'Is safe, with Irman.'

'Safe? With Irman? Ha!'

There was an assurance about the Greek; no more the fatalist, he hoisted himself up and addressed Milo.

'May I see him – now that I have returned?'

His tone invited neither rebuke nor resistance. Milo pointed. Irman and the boy were clambering down the hillside. Even so, Skoros made no move, but simply stood, waiting until they reached him, and then nonchalantly drew the boy to him. Seconds later, he erupted, stepping up to Irman and glaring into his eyes.

'You have hurt him?'

'No.'

'Then why has he been crying?'

Milo put a hand out to restrain him, but Skoros uncharacteristically swept it away.

'So...?'

Irman sniffed, and walked a pace away but, before Skoros could move after him, Milo's words stopped him.

'The banditti. He has seen them. They are here.'

Skoros whirled.

'Where? Are they dead? Of course not. You said they were here. Why not? They should be dead.'

He hit his head with one hand.

'But of course. Of course they're here, because they are your men, aren't they?'

Milo gripped the enraged Greek; Eduard held his right arm and spoke with what he hoped was a mixture of assurance and conviction.

'They are not Milo's men. They are not dead. They are here, and we have kept them here until your return.'

Gradually he loosened his grip.

'We trusted you. Now you trust us.'

Skoros listened as they explained the arrival of the van, the actions of its occupants, the brief skirmish, and the discovery of the cripple. When Skoros demanded their execution, forthwith, Eduard reminded him of his own still unresolved fate, and Irman's similar demands.

'So if I let them go, you let me go?'

The Greek answered his own question.

'Of course not. I am to be tried, so they must be tried. Justice for all, yes?'

They were sitting round the tilted table, its missing leg supplanted by an empty olive cask.

Milo and Eduard exchanged glances, but it was Eduard who ruled first.

'Your trial has taken place. Justifiable homicide, and anyway you walked into the enemy's hands, and have returned. It is enough – is it not?' he concluded, his eyes on Milo.

The partisan nodded his assent, looking, not at Skoros or Eduard, but at Irman, who turned away, and kicked the wall softly, then spoke quietly, without venom, to the wall.

'Sometimes man draws the balance, sometimes God. I absolve the Greek. The Germans killed our people. We kill them.' He swung round and added, 'After a trial, of course.'

The two Germans were brought to the house and placed on stools, still bound, the SS man on his iron chair between them.

Milo began.

'You are accused of murdering innocent people in this place. Did you?'

The wounded man appeared troubled, as the other spoke.

'No. We came for food, that's all.'

There was no defence, only prosecution. Eduard led.

'Why the shirts and scarves, the change of uniform?'

'In case the villagers objected – we were just visitors, passing, like them.'

'Speaking German?'

The wounded man spoke.

'We were following orders – to find food. If we were prevented, we were to defend ourselves. That's what happened. We didn't mean to hurt anyone.'

'They just got in the way?'

'They tried to kill us.'

Irman intervened.

'Our men were betrayed and destroyed.'

The Germans looked at one another and then at Irman, confused. Irman explained.

'Because you raped a woman, mutilated her, then hanged her.'

'No!'

Eduard and Milo frowned, for there was sincerity in the collective cry, the automatic negative.

'Yes!'

The dry, rasping intervention startled them. The SS man sat, immobile.

'I used the woman, then I cut her. They hanged her as I required.'

Irman held Skoros. Milo gestured to the door, and Irman dragged the Greek outside.

'Why?'

'The Greeks did this.' The SS man pointed at his face, his twisted arm, his legs. 'I am no angel, but I was not one of those who hounded the Juden, nor am I interested in the Fuehrer's madness.'

He smiled icily at Eduard and Milo.

'In war, it is a matter of survival. In Hitler's war survival requires insurance. The Schutzstaffel offered the best policy. I joined. I perpetrated those acts I was unable to avoid – interrogation and so forth, but never more than the minimum.'

'So you tortured, beat, maimed and murdered?'

The German shook his head slowly.

'Not really. I applied discrete pressures, but never crippled – yes, that's the word for someone like me, isn't it – I never crippled anybody, and I certainly would not have killed. Then we went to this village.'

'This village?'

'No, a certain other village – "this" is a figure of speech, is it not?'

The German drew a deep breath, then expelled it in a long sigh.

'A village where we knew there was an informant, someone who was causing us difficulties. It was a trap. We were locked in a small house, somewhat like this one, and a woman stood at the window, mocking us, before she threw the petrol bomb.'

The German squinted at his good hand, then held it up, the palm inwards – for the first time, Eduard realised he had no nails left. No-one spoke.

'That was after they had tested us to see what we knew. Communists, you know. ELAS.'

He dropped his hand, and it rested on the twisted arm.

'This village was the first opportunity.'

Eduard asked the single question: 'Opportunity – for what?'

'To see if I still could. A Greek woman, because no woman of ours would look upon me that way ever again. Then the cut, to compensate for these.' He held up the same hand, then with it lifted the other arm. 'Finally, the execution, for a murderess.'

'And the others?'

'The husband saw the execution, so I sent him to be with her.'

Eduard persisted.

'The others – the villagers?'

'We expelled them. We told them to go, and not to return, if they wished to survive.'

The SS man smiled again, this time with some vestigial warmth.

'You see, I am not a murderer.'

Eduard spoke quietly to Milo.

'I think he is telling the truth.'

'Perhaps. He is still a murderer, whatever his justification.'

The German cut across them.

'Unfortunately, they refused. So we had no choice.'

'They would not go?'

'Oh yes, they went, but they returned, and tried to surprise us – when we were eating. So we had to defend ourselves. One old man in particular...' and the German tutted at the recollection. 'Such an obstinate fellow. Hanging was too good for him. One has to make an example, you know.'

They tied the two soldiers to the olive trees, and shot them. They left the SS man to Skoros, taking the boy with them to the railway.

384

'You can collect him there.'

Before they went, Skoros told them what he had found at the aerodrome: MK Messerschmidts, crated as described, moved in by rail for one last stand against the imminent onslaught, even as the German forces fell back into the north. In the great hangars, they were being assembled with customary Teutonic efficiency and made ready, as a lethal sting in the tail of the hordes of barbarians departing from the land of Democritus. Village deaths and German savagery paled. Of these greater threats London must be told.

The last Eduard saw of the Greek was starkly simple. The German was in his iron chair, still smiling, as Skoros placed the rope around his neck, then unsheathed his knife. Skoros knelt before the German, one hand gripping the rung of the iron chair, the other, with the knife, making the sign of the cross.

Johnnie pedalled the dynamo 'cycle as Eduard transmitted. The information from Skoros was detailed – number of 'planes, those still crated, part knocked down, and complete; numbers tested; armaments, ammunition, personnel. For the first time, he broke his own rule, and transmitted for three, sometimes five minutes continuously. On the first day there was no acknowledgement, so he perforce repeated the information on the second day. As he explained to Wladek, the stone of the mountainside was a hazard. It created a danger zone that bounced the signal, so that longer transmissions could and probably would be monitored.

Eduard staggered transmissions to compensate for the length of each message, and recommenced at random intervals. Thus it was the third day before the German listeners homed in on his signal, and well into the afternoon before they triangulated the source.

The young conscript guerrilla fighters had been moved back. Milo and Irman remained, with Zoran and Marisa, Agim and Besnik, while Danovka was beside Wladek. The rest of the partisans had departed, except five older hands, closing down the caves, sealing what could not be taken. When the first shell fell, nobody was in the long stone house.

It collapsed in a gasp of surprise, a cloud of dust rising slowly above it. Eduard tapped in a frenzy, determined to complete the transmission. Suddenly finished, he prayed that London answer before the next barrage.

The second shell was fifty metres nearer, as Johnnie leapt off the 'cycle and rapidly dismantled it. Dragging it back to the caves, he shouted to Wladek to haul down the mast. The third shell fell short. Eduard knew the next one was destined to find its mark. Yelling at Danovka, he grabbed the transmitter and attempted to drag it across the stony terrain. As Irman and Zoran lifted it between them, they heard the whine of the fourth shell.

Eduard fell to the ground, Irman dropped beside him, and Zoran across them. Eduard watched as Wladek released the mast, linked hands with the girl, and running, gathered her closer and closer, until his arm encircled her, the white steel of her hair rippling as a cloud of pennants behind them, their fleet feet soaring across the stones. They were one, they were fused, they were lifted into the air, spinning into the sky, a single shadow, gone.

Eduard lay there. The others staggered to their feet, and stood unsteadily, flailing at the dust and particles of stone embedded in their hair and clothes. Eduard raised his face, two dirty channels running down his cheeks.

His head fell back onto his arms, and his whole body heaved, wracked with the pain, the realisation, the dreadful vacuum, the loss of Wladek. He stumbled to his knees, Zoran reached down and grasped his hand, pulling him to his feet. Irman steadied him as he lurched against them both. His head went back, his mouth opened, his eyes closed and no sound emerged. He stood there, screaming silently. Irman struck him with his open hand, twice, and Eduard's mouth snapped shut; he looked round without comprehension, then glared at Irman, raised his hand for an instant, then let it drop. Half to himself, he mouthed 'Oh my God, what a waste' and then the need to survive took control and he started to run.

They all ran – for the caves. There Milo distributed the machine pistols, the one bazooka and the stens; each took as much ammunition as was consistent with rapid withdrawal. Then the fifth shell fell.

Eduard was standing just outside the cave, checking his coveralls, pouch, knife, the French machine pistol, and glanced up automatically as the shell shrilled in warning, its descending whistle an instant before the earth exploded. The cave billowed with whirling dust, small, sharp particles stung his face, he felt his left leg give, stuck his hand out to brace himself against the rock face, and the sharp pain arced up his shin and thigh. 'Christ! That hurt,' he exclaimed, as he reached down to feel his leg. The cloth was torn, and something sharp scratched his palm. He glanced at it – the blood was bright and fresh. Leaning over, he peered at the leg, and saw bone standing out at an angle. As he crumpled, Johnnie caught him.

They could hear the Germans now. Shouts, commands, answering shouts. As they left the caves and scrambled up the hillside, Eduard slung between Johnnie and Irman, another more staccato sound reached them – the yapping of dogs. But the partisans held the advantage of familiar terrain. Gradually the shouts grew fainter, the commands indecipherable, the yapping faint echoes.

Three days later, on the small plateau some miles back from the border, Eduard woke early. Aircraft droned overhead. His leg throbbed, and the splint chafed inside the tight bandage. He recognised the even piston stroke of British bombers and after half an hour fancied he could hear the soft crump as the bombs found their mark. The sting was drawn.

It was almost an anti-climax to welcome the small 'plane from Brindisi. Farewells were muted but, as Milo embraced Eduard, his soft cheek close, he murmured, 'You have been among friends.'

At the military hospital, his leg set in plaster, Eduard rested.
'You're young. It's doing well. You'll soon be back to normal.'
Three weeks later, he had a visitor.
'Ah Eduard. I hear you've been in the wars.'
Teichmann twirled his pencil as he sat on the other chair.
'But they tell me you're mending nicely.'
'Yes I am.'
'Just as well.'
Teichmann snapped the pencil and, startled, looked down at the two separate pieces. Then he placed them carefully, parallel one to the other, on the small table, beside Eduard's supper dish.
'You're wanted in London. Mr Eden's expecting you.'
Teichmann paused, clearly relishing the moment, swept up the broken pencil, stuffed it in his pocket, and patted Eduard's arm. As he buttoned his jacket, he smiled seraphically.
'Dinner in Downing Street,' and here Eduard sensed a moment's hesitation, 'where you'll be made most welcome.'
When Eduard still offered no response, he added in token assurance, 'You will be among friends.'

Among friends. I have been fortunate to have been among friends most of my days. Of course, I have lost some along the way. You wave goodbye and never say 'Hallo' again – that's a loss, but one you don't always notice until it's too late; the departing, parting friend, whom circumstance changes into a memory – when you remember. Like Wolski. Not like Ivan, whose very going was in our beginnings. And not like Johnnie, dependable, unchanging, direct Johnnie, ever there when needed.
 Then there's the severance of death. Wladek was my friend perversely, against reason, despite belief, yet his going was so entirely final, no time for 'see you later', no 'take care', not even a 'thanks for the memories' of beer and girls and risks shared, and laughs collectively engorged, just a riven present, joint enterprise sundered instanter as he fled our fellowship in love and oblivion.
 I have been among other fair-weather friends since then – the casuals on part-time social wages, playing games, sinking drinks, chasing birds; the sub-contractors, unwittingly sharing you because you shared yourself – with their wives; the principals whose principles stood stark alongside your own, provided you paid the priced percentage of pretended likes to bank the

asset of their friendship, so generously lent; the partners who presumed partnership in false endeavours, provided you put their hand in your pockets; the caring fellows in whose good ship you took passage to a smaller freedom, in their good time and name and works. I have been among such fine friends, and haven't you?

Some persist despite all, some haunt me still, some join me in this quiet chamber of perfect memory. It's one of the ironies of the struck mute that he cannot praise dead men past, having failed to praise them present.

Swift friends short-lived, such as undaunted Danovka, irked and irksome Irman, and overflowing, outwhelming, mighty Milo, were rare friends indeed to be among – the giddy gods of battle, fair in flux, rich in intervalled riot, stout in secret silence and ever mindful of the needs of others which, mercifully, included me.

But the rarest friends of all were Wolski, Bish and Wladek. To be with them was to be truly among friends.

That I would rediscover on the day of Our Lord, when we waited with the gold, in vain.

BON VOYAGE

'Among friends' Teichmann had said, and perhaps the best thing about that Downing Street dinner was the return of Wolski.

No-one had said much about anything, no detail, just that there was another assignment and we were the 'volunteers'. Obviously it was special, for otherwise why were we to dine in such august company, but we had supposed, I had supposed – we had not discussed it together – I had supposed it was another behind-the-lines suicide mission from which, as usual, we would extricate ourselves at the eleventh hour, with or without casualties; all in a week's SOE work. We didn't call it that then, mind you. It was Special Force Advance, and Very Secret Indeed.

Yet I knew this was the point, the climax, the *raison d'être* for all that had gone before. This was what I had been waiting for, the opportunity to take the fight to the enemy – not passing the buck to daylight precision bombers, nor winkling out the dying dragons of the disgusting Axis. This, I could feel in my racing pulse, was for Poland; this was the way home; this was for Papa, for Bruno, for the wasted years. And I have never thought differently since and, even if I am today disarmed and exiled, I shall never forget that delicate foreboding of redemption and recompense and return.

We were going home, but how, or when, where or why, we did not know. And then someone said 'gold' and we all stopped, stopped talking, stopped thinking, just stopped.

Suddenly it was gold – what gold, where and for whom, and for the matter of that, whose gold?

Eduard walked into the ante-chamber, saw Johnnie and, for a moment, ignored the short, squat figure, his back half-turned, then, 'Eduard,' in that curious flat monotone, avoiding surprise, and, 'Wolski!'

There was nothing more to be said. It was as if they were back sitting together on *The Angel of Omsk*, sipping the captain's tea. The questions 'Your daughter?' or 'You managed on your own, then?' and their answers left unsaid, set aside. That day Eduard was again among friends, and somehow, that was all that mattered.

Eden and they were guests of Mikolaczek. So was Bishop Gawlina. There were between twelve and fifteen there, as they sipped their pre-prandial slivovitz, most of them English. 'Na zdrowie.' It was late 1944, and the war was swinging their way. Everywhere the Krauts were in retreat. There was a certain jubilation in the overloud conversations, the braying laughter of the British overlaying the murmurs of the three Poles – warriors in the cause of winning back their motherland, civil decencies and perhaps their families. Premier

Mikolaczek gestured towards a side room, and closed the door. Then he turned to Eduard.

'You enlisted, yes?'

'Yes, sir.'

'That is good. We are proud of our people who fight with the British Army. We are proud of your patriotism. Most of all, we are proud of those who stayed behind and also fought – who resisted, and died resisting.'

Bishop Gawlina brushed his fingers across his throat, murmured softly, and raised an imperious index finger in static blessing.

'I too praise the fighters, the patriots, but most of all I praise the patriotism of this deed, of this assignment you are about to undertake.' He paused. 'And I bless you, in His name, and pray He will look over you and after you,' and he paused again, 'and deliver you safely.' He glanced momentarily at Mikolaczek and added, 'and the gold, of course.'

'Of course,' added Eden, who had not spoken until that moment, 'and the gold, which is why we are here.'

Johnnie looked at Eduard and Wolski glowered at Eden.

Mikolaczek was talking again, rapidly, quietly, as if he was afraid he would not have the time to finish, before someone would come in and steal his idea, and his gold, from the dinner table.

'If you are successful, this money, the money the gold will buy, will help rebuild our country. Our nation is ready for repairing; Warsaw is still under German control, but not for long now. The Russians are pushing this way...' – he gestured broadly, right to left, east to west – 'and we need, they need,' and Eduard could have sworn he winced, just as he himself would have winced if he could even contemplate the thought that they might 'need' the bloody Russians, 'to help the Resistance.'

He looked at Johnnie, then Wolski, and finally, at Eduard and added, inconsequentially, it seemed at the time, 'I'm so proud you enlisted. You see, so many had to fight. They had no choice if they were to survive. But you chose. That is patriotism.'

Eden delicately withdrew a handkerchief from his sleeve and gently blew his nose. Eduard wondered if he ever got any snot on his handsome moustache and, if he did, if he washed it afterwards.

'The steak is very good,' he murmured, 'don't you think?'

Gawlina smiled, Johnnie nearly choked and Wolski just went on chewing. Eduard smiled too.

'Very good, sir.'

'Yes, well I am glad you are going to have a go at this. You see,' and he waved his soiled hankie up and down vaguely, 'it's extremely important that we do get this money into Warsaw. We were a bit late last time...' and he tailed off mildly, smiling plaintively at Gawlina, who waved his busy index finger across his face dismissively, but said nothing, priests, especially prelates, knowing how to make a point while appearing to oppose it.

Mikolaczek must have read their minds.

'It is Polish money, here in England. We have been saving up.'

He smiled a withered, weary, winter's smile.

'It has been kept in Canada,' he said, adding, 'waiting.'

Eden rose, whittling a little spittle from his lips with the dainty kerchief.

'Well, it was kind of you to let me sit in on this, Prime Minister.'

He turned to Eduard, and a hard, desiccated, dry and Siberian look stole over his face and settled in his eyes. A politician's smile failed to light them, and his mouth was a thin, clean line before he raised that splendid moustache with the back of a manicured finger and added, 'Don't fail. Get there. Deliver the stuff. Safely.' He paused. 'And intact.' And then his early smile returned, the host country's secure, uninvaded, welcoming smile, and he added, as he leant down towards Eduard and touched his shoulder delicately, 'And try not to get killed.'

Then he was gone, quietly through the closing door. Mikolaczek stood, walked to a side table and reached into a walnut humidor.

'Cigar?'

As they shook hands – Eduard was the last to leave, after Gawlina and the other two – he looked simply, without cause or care, directly into his eyes and said, without waiting for a response, letting him go, turning, and starting to walk away on the last syllable: 'You are a decent man.'

The orders came as usual, through the intricacies of Army protocol and Intelligence obfuscation, and they were late – days after dinner in Downing Street. Eduard was summoned to an obscure address in Chelsea, a mews off Old Church Street, and told to wait in a nondescript outer hall, with shiny brown linoleum, pale green distempered walls, and an oak umbrella and hat stand. There was one upright chair, with a sagging rexine seat, and a makeshift, badly chipped plywood table with old and curling copies of the *Illustrated London News*. A surprisingly ornate cut-glass chandelier illuminated the windowless space, off which led three darkly varnished doors, with no visible handles.

After a 20-minute wait, the door on his right opened, a soft, pink face appeared above an impeccable grey flannel suit, terminating in burnished oxblood brogues, and smiled: 'Do come in – Sergeant.' Clearly an officer and a gentleman.

Eduard followed the officer into a long, spacious room, close-carpeted, with closed windows and drawn curtains, two even more ornate glass candelabra, a long, narrow, walnut table with curved ends, many chairs and a closed cabinet. The officer opened it.

391

'Now then. We've got your orders. Bit late, I'm afraid, but there 'tis.'

He shuffled a small folder of onion skin papers, with fuzzy blue type, extracting a single, small card.

'Usual stuff. No source, no identification, just a time and place.'

He reached into his inside pocket and extracted a gold-rimmed monocle attached to a thin black ribbon. Slotting this into a dilated eye socket, he scrunched his face up and peered at the card as if it had insinuated its way into his otherwise orderly life.

'Liverpool. The docks. I think we'll have to get you some transport.'

He riffled the papers, and pulled one out. Scanning this, he added, 'Wolski and Makowski – they're going with you?'

'As far as I know.'

'Mmm. Yes. I see the Foreign Secretary has stipulated all three of you. Seems urgent. Well, let's see if the transport's ready.'

He pulled open a small side door in the cabinet and lifted a phone. 'Put me through to Bob, will you?'

After a pause: 'Bob? Norris here. Is the Liverpool run ready?'

Another few seconds: 'Yes? Good. Thank you. We'll be there shortly. See you at the In and Out. 'Bye.'

He turned back to Eduard.

'If you'll just wait outside, someone will see that your companions are ready, and then we'll pop up to Piccadilly and get some grub while we wait.' He closed the folder and, as Eduard walked to the door, added, 'You are hungry?'

Eduard nodded, hesitated, thought about all the other things he needed, then thought better of it, and reached for the handle. The door swung open before he could touch it, and he returned to his sagging seat. He was about to dip once more into the redoubtable *ILN* when the door opened again and his guide reappeared.

'Come along then. Car's outside.'

They stepped out onto the uneven cobbles, towards a black Buick with the customary metal slits shrouding its headlamps, and unusual dark windows. No-one opened a door, until they reached the car. Then the rear nearside door swung back, and they climbed on board. The driver was screened by a smoked-glass window above the back seat, which the officer tapped. The V8 pulled away without fuss or engine noise, rippling over the uneven roadway. Within fifteen minutes they drew into a shallow drive across the front of an elegant stone building, and again the door swung open.

'Off we go, then,' and the officer led the way up the steps.

'Afternoon, sir.'

'Afternoon, Ralph.'

The officer forged ahead into the discreet chambers of the Naval and Military – home from home to officers and gentlemen.

'We've had our pre-prandial, so we'll go straight in, shall we?'

They entered a large salon, with quiet furniture, crisp napery, spotless silver service and low lighting. A tall, blank person approached.

'Sir Norris.'

'Stevens.'

'Your table's ready, sir. The General's there already.'

'Thank you, Stevens.'

'Sausages, sir?'

'Certainly, Stevens.'

'Very well, sir.'

They were shown to a table against the window wall, heavily curtained. A short, pale, elderly man in dark tweeds sat ruminating, a plain and slim glass twisting slowly in his fingers as he watched them approach. As they got closer, Eduard noticed his eyes – shallow, grey, lifeless – below hard grey eyebrows and a vestige of pepper and salt hair laid delicately upon his scalp. Eduard recognised the eyes – he had seen them before in other faces. This General had seen action.

'Norris.'

'General. This is Cjaikowski.'

The General looked up and nodded.

'Glad you could join us.'

The General raised a hand, and Eduard noted the royal lion on his signet ring. The meal was generous while simple, hot and a good deal better than recent rations. The conversation was low-level domestic and foreign, and Eduard was politely excluded. By two o'clock, they had finished and the anonymous General excused himself. Eduard had passed the test. His mentor was visibly more relaxed as he commented, 'Glad the General could see us. Makes it all so much easier.'

He smiled, partly to himself.

'Care for a snifter?' as he signalled to the waiter.

Eduard thought, why not, and nodded.

'Armagnac?'

'Thank you.'

Moments later two fat glasses arrived, and they warmed them in their hands, each in his own thoughts, tacitly acknowledging by mutual silence the lack of mutual interest. Idly glancing round, Eduard noticed a lone diner in the corner who took out a handkerchief and rubbed his mouth clean as he stared at Eduard. There was something faintly familiar about him, but he could not quite place it. The man rose, and walked towards them.

'Norris...'

The officer jumped up, extending his hand, which the other took in a slow, supple way, and shook it slightly, as if the contact was somehow exploratory. Sir Norris, Eduard noticed, looked slightly uncomfortable, and retrieved his hand rather sharply, as if it might be contaminated.

'Bob – do sit. Brandy?'

Bob pulled out a chair, and lowered himself, languishing against the table, with one elbow on its edge, his hand cupping his tanned and softly moustached face, his hair brisk by contrast in its blond short-back-and-sides.

'This is Cjaikowski, but then, you knew that anyway.'

'Absolutely. Good afternoon, Eduard.' A pause, then, 'You don't mind if I call you Eduard, do you?'

Eduard shook his head, shrugged and lifted the glass to his nose. There was something familiar about the eyes. They were slightly Asiatic, reminding him of those guards at Tara, and the tan was not tan at all, but weathered olive skin. Bob was not all he seemed, and clearly Sir Norris knew more than he was telling. Eduard came to the conclusion Bob was not Bob at all, but probably Igor or Vlad and more familiar with the details of his past than he was admitting.

'A moment with Eduard, if you please, Norris.'

'Certainly,' and the officer excused himself with, 'Must pop round the corner. Back in a mo.'

As he left, Bob watched him, then pulled his chair forward, dropped his hand on Eduard's, and said, slowly and carefully, 'You are going to face some difficulties. Be prepared for trouble – on the ship certainly, and without doubt, when you reach Naples.'

He smiled at Eduard's obvious surprise.

'Yes, Naples. That's where you are going. Slight change of plan. The consignment will be moved on from there.'

He smiled directly at Eduard, then the smile died.

'You will be armed, you will have your companions, in whom you – and I – have every confidence, but that is all. There will be attempts to change the plan again, and to divert you. There will be dangers.'

He released Eduard's hand, put his in his inside pocket and drew out a manila envelope marked OHMS. This he passed across.

'Open it when you get to Liverpool. It's not marked "Top Secret" – far too melodramatic, and anyway, draws attention. Having said which, it is, top secret, that is. I suggest you read it, memorise it and then get rid of it. You can give the other two the gist, but not the names.'

He paused, and studied Eduard carefully.

'One more thing.' His words hung in the air, and Eduard felt bound to ask:

'One more thing?'

'Yes. One more thing. There's a man, an advisor, one of our' – he hesitated, almost stumbling over the word – 'Russian allies' people. We know he's involved. We don't know how. He's not one of ours. Keep an eye. Watch out for him. Name's Kolanski.'

The images came back too sharply and so suddenly that Eduard's mouth dried; he felt cold, shivered, and sucked in a deep breath, trying not to exhibit the hard, tight, chilling fear he felt.

The other pushed the chair back, and leant across, both hands planted on the table. He stared into Eduard's eyes, his narrow and cool, as if he was out-facing the winter sun on the steppes. Then he straightened, patted his jacket, extracted a silver cigarette case, a du Maurier cork-tipped cigarette, flipped a gold lighter, lit up, and drew the smoke in with a steady, slow intake. The smoke curled out as he added, 'Go with God, leave the gold, and come back in good health,' and he was gone.

Eduard finished his armagnac and sat, the envelope balanced on his palm, before he put it away. As he did so, Sir Norris strode briskly across the room, beckoning.

A bulky Austin 16 waited by the steps. Sir Norris shook his hand, wished him good luck and turned away. Suddenly he wheeled, lifted a finger to his head, looked quizzically at Eduard and, as his hand dropped, added, 'I hope you find what you seek, and that you succeed in your mission. I don't know what it is, and I don't want to know, but whatever it is, you must be a brave man' – he hesitated, then smiled bleakly – 'or a fool.'

He paused, held the car handle a moment, then slammed it shut as he murmured, 'God bless you.'

The car swung out of Pall Mall, across St James's Park and into Buckingham Palace Road. Within minutes it drew up outside the Rubens Hotel, where an armed guard with Polish insignia ushered Eduard into the foyer. This was the headquarters of the Polish Government in Exile, opposite the Royal Mews behind the Palace – the heart of Empire.

'Wait here – please.'

Half an hour passed, then the soldier returned.

'Follow me, please.'

He took Eduard rapidly through the public rooms, through an unmarked door, down a passage, into what appeared to be a storeroom, and out of that into a quiet narrow street. There were two jeeps waiting, with two, armed and uniformed sergeants in each, without any insignia. They said nothing, but one beckoned Eduard to join him; he slid into the passenger seat, and they sped off.

They dropped down to the Embankment, and bustled along to Upper Thames Street, swinging away from the river up Dowgate to Walbrook and there the jeeps slowed, moving past the Old Lady's façade down Threadneedle Street, and round into Throgmorton Avenue, juddering over the cobblestones, until they reached an archway, swinging into the heart of the City's financial centre, the Bank of England. As they pulled up, a uniformed attendant approached, and bent towards Eduard.

'Excuse me, sir, but would you mind waiting a moment? The silver collection's due, and we don't like to keep them waiting.'

He straightened, looked behind, then leaned in again.

'Here we are, sir. Won't take a minute. Matter of security, you see.'

Eduard heard them before he saw them. Two smart-stepping shire horses drew a canvas-covered four-wheeled cart, and came to a halt in the yard. Bank of England messengers jumped down, and a youngster of around seventeen, with an older, bowler-hatted gentleman, clambered after them, long, silvery police whistles dangling from their necks.

'Who're they?' Eduard whispered, and the attendant put his finger to his lips.

'Top secret, sir,' then he smiled and pushed his head close, murmuring conspiratorially, 'like you,' and went on, 'Junior and senior clerks from the Inteller's Office, bringing half a week's silver from the Mint, for distribution round the country.'

The messengers were unlashing the canvas top, and furling it back. There sat two ironbound, padlocked chests.

'How much is in them?' Eduard hissed at his informant and he, perhaps revelling in the opportunity to unroll secrets of his own, murmured, 'Two thousand five hundred pounds – twice every week!'

As he spoke, the chests were lowered onto trolleys, and trundled down the slope. The canvas was neatly stowed, the horses stamped and wheeled, and the cart turned and lumbered slowly past, on its side the legend 'Charles A. Wells, Bonded Carman'.

'What's a bonded carman?' Eduard asked, but his man had gone, ushering the country's silver into the vaults as Eduard followed – to collect his country's gold.

The sergeants escorted him from the jeeps across a lobby and into a lift. The doors closed, and they started the descent. When they opened again, they marched down a passage until they came to a chamber at the end of which was a massive door. It was open. They were ushered through.

In the vault was a row of metal tables. On the tables were rows of large suitcases. They appeared to be quite ordinary suitcases, until one of the ushers clicked one open – inside they were zinc lined.

Then another wheeled in a low trolley, and on the trolley were many packages, wrapped and bound in dark, greasy brown paper and waxed twine, with irregular daubs of sealing wax on the joints.

Eduard was escorted to the table, where the ushers were loading the packs into the cases. They paused, and one indicated a pack to Eduard, who looked more closely, and there, embossed into the wax, was the symbol of his country – the spread eagle The last pack proved troublesome. The usher lifted it, and it started to split open. He hurriedly put it down again, but the twine snapped, the paper strained against the weight of the contents and, as he tried to lift it again, the folded paper unfurled, and a cascade of gold coins clattered onto the metal surface, sliding across the table. Eduard leant forward, and caught his breath – solid gold US dollars, international currency par excellence.

'Damnation!' was the only word he heard throughout the whole procedure, including this 'incident'. An usher walked to the side of the vault and lifted a phone, quietly murmuring into the mouthpiece. Moments later, two gentlemen in dark double-breasted suits strode purposefully into the vault. A weighing machine was produced, and the contents of the package were carefully assayed, noted, countersigned, and repacked.

Sealing wax was produced, and one of the officials bent to embed the little finger of his left hand into the hot wax. As he straightened, Eduard saw the heavily eagle-embossed ring. The sergeants stood to one side throughout, but now the official beckoned one forward, and proffered the document for his signature too.

The last case was snapped shut, strapped up and padlocked, and they moved out, the sergeants on either side of the trolleys. The lift was full for the ascent, and upstairs the sergeants silently supervised the loading of the cases into an unmarked, grey, covered truck.

They left Threadneedle Street and moved off back to the Embankment, until they once more swung away from the river, up to Hyde Park. Five minutes later, they paused outside a block of flats in Marble Arch. The door opened, and there were Johnnie and Wolski.

Wolksi: 'You're late,' and they jumped into the jeep. There was little conversation as they stowed their rucksacks and tried to make themselves comfortable. They dozed, woke, watched the towns come and go, and dozed again.

At Liverpool, they were met by two SPs in another anonymous jeep, and whisked through the bomb-damaged streets towards the waterfront. They slowed, and stopped outside a high mesh fence bounding a desolate yard in front of a tall, brick warehouse, with no signs or other identification, but two policemen strolling, apparently aimlessly, kicking an occasional loose brick, criss-crossing the yard, and exchanging a word each time they passed the entrance, which was secured with a heavy bar.

There the three of them sat for at least ten minutes until a door opened and they glimpsed someone just inside; the police stiffened, then walked smartly to the gate, slid the bar to one side, and pulled the gates open. They drove in.

The police sergeant – Eduard could see his stripes now they were closer – raised his hand, the jeeps stopped short of the entrance and the SPs jumped down, standing on either side, stiffly to attention. The man in the door emerged. It was Mazloff.

Eduard hurried forward, hand outstretched, then faltered. Wolski was beside him, and glanced quickly sideways.

'What's the trouble?'

'I thought it was Mazloff. It looks like him, but. . .'

By then, it was too late. They had met in the middle of the yard. It was indeed Mazloff, but a much older, slighter Mazloff, with less light in his eyes, and no pipe in his hand.

'Hello Eduard.' And he took his hands in both of his, squeezing them. 'Surprised to see me?'

Eduard nodded, too surprised to speak.

'Come along inside. We have to talk.'

He led them into the empty spaces of that dark brick warehouse, where the truck now stood in the centre, its back open and guarded by four armed men, stens crooked in their arms, their faces impassive. None of them were in uniform. To one side was a table with thermos and cups, and beside it a bench. They sat.

'You look anxious, Eduard. That is not like you.'

Eduard looked into those sleeping eyes, and wondered what torment, what agonies had they witnessed that calm, careful, knowing Mazloff had tried to absorb, and what reserves he had spent containing them.

'One day, Eduard. I will tell you one day.'

He smiled, and the old Mazloff was there again for a brief moment, as he looked up at Wolski and added, 'It's good we are together again – old friends. It's good, yes, very good.'

He reached out for the thermos, unscrewed the top, and poured four mugs. The coffee was black and strong and hot. He handed the first one to Johnnie.

'I'm sad Vatek isn't here today.' He paused. 'But you are just as welcome, my friend.'

They drank their coffee. Eduard said nothing, but he wondered, and Mazloff knew what he was wondering. He turned to Wolski.

'I asked for you – I knew you'd come.'

Wolski grunted. Then Mazloff turned to Eduard.

'Another day, Eduard. Another day I will tell you of those things that I have seen, and you can tell me about your adventures too.'

He looked kindly at the younger man.

'I don't think I have quite as much to teach you as I did at Tara and on that train. You are no longer my young Eduard, are you?' and he laughed, a warm, embracing laugh which culminated in a series of hacking coughs.

'No more pipe for me, until all this is over.'

He stood.

'Eduard. I am told that these are your responsibility.'

His hand, palm up, swung across the back of the truck, indicating the cases.

'A million pounds worth, or so the Englishmen tell me.'

Wolski looked at Eduard, Johnnie looked away, and Eduard looked at the cases.

None of them had the least idea what a million pounds would look like, and none of the others had seen gold dollars. The cases were designed to look like tough fibre suitcases at first sight, until they bent to examine them. Then it became clear they were made of metal, finished to look conventional, with straps around them which were genuine frayed and worn leather, with dull steel buckles. The hasps were fused together, and the lids overlapped the bodies of the cases, themselves sealed with some bitumastic material.

Eduard decided to keep his counsel. They were not going to see 'their' gold. Mazloff took him by the arm, and led him to one side.

'Eduard. Have you read your instructions yet?'

'No, not yet.'

'I suggest you do so on the boat – alone.'

He turned to the others.

'Time to go. These men will see to the consignment.'

The four guards paired off, two to the back, two to the front, as the truck doors slammed shut and Mazloff walked to the door.

Outside a single jeep waited. Mazloff signalled the truck behind. The sergeants had gone. Mazloff returned to the table, reached underneath, and withdrew a heavy attaché case, navy blue, with chromed locks.

'You'll need these,' he said, as he handed it to Eduard. 'Guns, knives, ammunition. Hand them out on board.'

They climbed into the jeep, the guards fell back, and Mazloff approached.

'Be careful, Eduard, and you two.'

There was a moment's silence, then the guards marched into the yard, the jeep revved up, Mazloff waved, the policemen swung back the outer gates, and they drove out, swinging left to the docks.

The streets were quiet, but the docks were busy. Gantries moved over merchantmen, lorries loitered alongside, crates moved up and over, and everywhere stevedores hauled and lifted, pushed and tilted, pulled and manhandled goods inward from the convoy ships that were the country's lifeline.

The small convoy slowed at a plain pole barrier, manned by two more SPs. Their driver showed his pass, and the barrier lifted. They moved alongside the waterfront, past freighters, many of which had seen much better days, some dented by use, others dashed and dotted by the malice of the enemy. At the end of the wharf there was a single-stacked steamer, without a name, riding close to the pilings, gently bumping and grinding, with wisps of steam dissipating in the grumbling late autumn cloud base. Its lines were rakish, its skin scarred with pockmarks, and scabbed with rust. In the stern was a menacing piece of artillery – an Oerlikon. The deck was stripped of all but essential equipment, and there was a small thicket of antennae on the bridge. The ship was old, but lean, light and clearly experienced in the ways of war.

The truck doors opened, the guards jumped down, and they began to haul their responsibilities onto the dockside, and thence up the gangplank and onto the deck, with the SPs' help. Eduard looked about for any sign of crewmen, but the deck was deserted. He glanced up, and saw a neatly bearded officer with a badged beret and immaculate khaki drills surveying them. After a few seconds' appraisal he slipped down the forward ladder, and strode across, extending his hand and briskly shaking theirs, one after the other.

'Bo'jour, messieurs. Welcome aboard.'

'Merci.'

'So, we make the sail soon.' He surveyed the squadron of cases. 'These we will take below.'

'Ah, no thank you. That is, we will take them,' Eduard said quickly.

The Captain dipped his head to one side, a heron smelling something fishy.

'As you wish. Follow me.'

Eduard asked Wolski to guard the cases, while Johnnie and he struggled with the first, following the Captain round the superstructure. He led the way into a narrow gangway, moving for'ard, stopping beside a heavy teak door, which he pushed open.

'Voila! La suite conjugale!'

The cabin was spacious, embellished with polished teak panels, trimmed with brass, and heavy mirrors. The floor was planked and strewn with Moroccan rugs, in the centre a long mahogany table, with leather-topped stools, set on gimbals. A long settle in maroon hide flanked the starboard wall with its two oblong ports. There was a ship's decanter, half full, and four glasses set on a silver tray.

They pushed the case to one end and Eduard turned to the Captain.

'Splendide. Is there another room – for the cases, and a lock?'

The Captain reached behind and pulled a heavy key from the door, handing it over without comment, but an ironic twist to his bearded lips, and pointed to the inner door. Eduard locked the cabin as they left to fetch the next case, and then again on each of the remaining journeys.

Finally, all the cases were neatly stacked in the adjoining space, and the Captain stared at them quizzically.

'Like the Yanquis, you 'ave the Fort Knox, uh?'

Near the mark, Eduard thought, as the Captain smiled back, and sat, pulling the decanter towards him. He filled all four glasses, and pushed them towards each of them, as they joined him on the plush stools.

'Messieurs. Santé, au trou Normand et bon voyage!'

RICHER DUST CONCEALED

I never asked Johnnie what he made of our mission, nor for the matter of that did he volunteer, but then, that was Johnnie, ever mindful of the need for silence if there was nothing much to say. As for Wolski, he grumbled, but that was just his way, hiding his true feelings, and his times since Tara. I suppose none of us really wanted to talk about it, because it was too large to comprehend, this burden of bullion – our country's savings, and perhaps its salvation.

We knew its intrinsic worth, but beyond that we just shut our minds. I think we were more concerned with ridding ourselves of the responsibility as fast and efficiently as we possibly could. Time enough then to contemplate its true value. At any rate, we reacted as we were trained, to guard and protect, survive and deliver.

I know I just concentrated on the moment, the dispositions, the linkages, the steps to be taken, the what-ifs, and the so-whats, all in the certain knowledge that I was part of the best possible team to get the job done. Johnnie, Wolski and me. Unbeatable, or so I thought.

The three Poles raised their glasses. The Captain tapped each of theirs in turn. He drained his in one, a single swallow, brushed his beard with the back of his hand and reached across for the decanter. 'Encore?' Eduard glanced at the other two, shrugged and said, 'Why not?' and he refilled the glasses.

'So, you join the convoy,' and this time sipped his calva. They sipped theirs, and waited. It was only a matter of time.

'So – what is it you take in the cases?'

Johnnie sat imperturbably. Wolski fidgeted, and Eduard scratched his head. If they were to travel with the man, they needed his protection.

'Confidential cargo – very special, valuable.'

'Eh bien. C'est monnaie?'

Eduard hesitated, then thought, what the hell – he needs to know. 'Oui. Monnaie.'

The Captain expelled a long, whistling breath.

'Voila! You 'ave the convoy, the escorts, the Royal Nav-ee. It is good, no?'

Johnnie looked down at his hands, and Wolski coughed irritably. Eduard got up and walked across to the porthole, looked out, turned, and bent over the man.

'We need protection. Armed protection. Guards.'

'Ah! Non, non, non. Ce n'est pas nos responsabilité.' He turned, drained his glass and stood up. 'C'est à vous, mon cher.'

Thought Eduard: 'Bloody man. Typical French. And they talk about perfidious Albion.' Aloud: 'But there are only three of us. We need help.'

The Captain was courteous. He was quiet. He was pleasant. But he was adamant. It was not his problem. It was theirs. They were on his ship. His ship was in the convoy. The convoy was going to Gibraltar, then Malta, then Augusta in Sicily and finally to Napoli. His job was to get her there. His ship was not a straggler, it would stay in the convoy. It was not a romper, in a hurry to beat the blockades of German U-boats. It was in a convoy, safe, protected. That was as far as it went. The rest was up to them. Did they really think his sailors would steal their monnaie? Eduard hardly dared state the obvious. In a state of war anyone would, did steal anything. And monnaie, well that was eminently stealable. My God, if he knew what they really carried, he would probably steal it himself. The Captain excused himself, and Wolski slammed the door after him in frustration.

'Bloody Frogs. Can't trust them an inch.'

'Yes, well. What are we going to do?'

Johnnie paced back and forth, until Eduard began to feel like shouting. The tension was palpable. It was Wolski who made up their minds.

'Let's leave.'

'Leave?'

'Yes, leave. Get off the ship. Find another one. Ask Mazloff for some guards.'

At which point there was a knock on the door.

'Yes?'

'M'sieu, compliments of M'sieu le Capitaine. You will attend him on the bridge?'

'Wait here,' snapped Eduard, 'and lock me out when I've gone.'

He followed the sailor to the companionway, then up onto the bridge.

'Aha; Lieutenant. We 'ave the orders – to sail.'

'Yes, well, we've decided to leave, find another boat. One where we can have guards, protection, security.'

The Captain's hands were stuffed deep into the pockets of his double-breasted jacket. He regarded Eduard with a placid, almost sympathetic gaze.

Then he took his hands out of his pockets, clasped them loosely together, turned to gaze out of the bridge towards the quayside, then turned back slowly.

'Je regrette. Ce n'est pas possible.' He smiled. 'We 'ave the orders too. You stay. We leave – soon.'

He touched a chart on the navigation table, then glanced up, almost ruefully, it seemed, and added, 'After all, you 'ave your guns. Once on

402

board, you cannot get off. You 'ave to protect your own gold.' He waited for Eduard to recover before adding, 'You 'ave the room service. You need anything, you only 'ave to ring.'

The convoy was due to divide at sea, the reduced complement then to steam at a steady seven and a half knots into the Mediterranean: two MACs – merchant aircraft carriers with rocket-armed Swordfish biplanes – two ageing light cruisers and four smaller frigates and sloops accompanied the fleet of merchantmen, armed with diverse depth charges, radar, Asdic and Oerlikons. All that Eduard knew from the briefing papers and what he had picked up from Mazloff. He also knew that the main threat came from the ubiquitous U-boats, and their torpedoes, 30-knot underwater explosive sharks. He prayed that the enemy would be so preoccupied with defence that they would be spared his attentions once they passed the Rock. But first they had to reach Gibraltar, and to do that they had to run the Atlantic gauntlet.

Eduard knocked twice, then again. He heard the key scrape in the lock. Wolski peered out, then opened the door.

'Well?'

'Too late. He has his orders too. We're stuck.'

'Typical,' muttered Johnnie.

'Yes, well, we're going to have to manage. One of us here at all times. All of us armed at all times. The cases are in the other room, we'll shove the table against the door, and well, we'll manage.'

It took but a few moments to check the cases, shift the heavy mahogany table, to check the stens, ammunition and handguns, and then Wolski laughed.

'Well, Eduard. We've seen worse than this. At least he's supposed to be on our side.' He pulled the decanter across, and tipped the remnants of the calva into his glass, lifted it in mock salute, and drained it in one short gulp. Johnnie lay back on the settle beneath the portholes and closed his eyes. As if his voice was disembodied, he murmured, 'As our Capitaine said – "bon voyage".'

Eduard looked out of a porthole, leaning against the brass rails. In the grey afternoon light, the Pier Head reflected the devastation of the Heinkel raids of four years before – the wasteland by the Liver Buildings. Perhaps this was how Warsaw looked. Slowly their ship eased away from the dock.

The convoy gradually shook itself into some semblance of order – the freighters and their escorts at four cable lengths, misty outlines in an untidy sea. The three couriers shook down into a semblance of routine, punctuated by the occasional call to mock 'Action Stations', which Eduard had negotiated with the Captain.

'Two of us will respond; one stays below,' he said, to which the Frenchman replied with Gallic acceptance: 'Pas de problem.'

Day followed day, the weather relatively calm, the sea-lanes seemingly deserted, their fellow freighters mildly tacking, practice net defence booms lowered every other day as they went to Action Stations, the Captain mildly swearing as he strove to make up the inevitable lost way. Apart from forays to the bridge, where they were ignored by crew and officers alike, and occasional brushes past sailors in the gangways, they saw no-one, made no friends, except Le Petit.

'La guerre, she changes many things, but not la priorité,' explained the Captain. La priorité was food. Capitaine LeGallo liked his food, and how he contrived his supplies was never explained, but the kitchen was the centre of his universe, and there his personal chef prepared miracles from the black markets of whatever ports they touched. Liverpool yielded fat bacon, fresh vegetables, cans and packets, plentiful potatoes and the basic necessities of oil and flour and sugar and even eggs. After powdered British omelette, tins of spam, ersatz coffee, dry biscuits and a diet of cinnamon sticks, liquorice root and lemon crystals for sweetness, the Captain's cuisine was a revelation. That first lunch set the tone.

There was a discreet tap on the door, Wolski unbuttoned his holster, Johnnie stood by the door, and Eduard opened it. Perhaps they were paranoid, but only hours after departure, with the Captain's reluctance to afford protection, they were wound up to a state of exact preparedness.

'Yes?' snapped Eduard.

He was confronted by a rotund dish of white metal, steam wisping around its perimeter, behind which he could just discern a slight figure with a tilted chef's hat, incongruous in the extreme.

'B'jou, M'sieu. Votre diner, si vous voulez.'

Eduard pushed the door wide open, and stepped aside. The miniscule, four-feet-something little chef stepped daintily inside, half-turning, and smiling a crinkled, conspiratorial smile, somehow contriving to bow slightly behind his gastronomic burden.

'What the hell is this?' grumbled Wolski as Eduard shut and locked the door.

'Eese deenay,' responded their visitor, setting the dish down on the mahogany table, and stepping back respectfully.

'Who the hell are you?' asked Wolski.

'Votre petit cuisinier.'

'Cook,' added Eduard, as Wolski looked blank. 'Little cook.'

'Oui, Le Petit—' but he got no further because at that point Wolski went to lift the cover off the dish, and immediately dropped it, waving his hands wildly as he squeaked, 'Christ! That's bloody hot.'

Johnnie retrieved the rolling semi-sphere, and set it on the table, beside the steaming platter. They all bent forward to examine the contents, intrigued by the prospect of hot food, and bemused by its fragrance.

Wolski poked the corner of the creamy confection with a tentative forefinger.

'Get your mucky paws off it,' commanded Johnnie, pushing Wolski aside. Le Petit dipped into his apron, and brought forth knives and forks, laying them down quietly beside the dish.

'Confit des fleurs des champs avec des cerveaux.'

Wolski raised his eyebrows, so Eduard translated – literally.

'Marmalade of field flowers with brains.'

'Eugh!'

'Try it.'

'Not bloody likely.'

Le Petit cleared his throat.

'Messieurs...' They all looked at him.

He leant forward, opened a door beneath the settle, and extracted several plates, dealing them like cards across the table, skilfully aligning the cutlery alongside each one, with a serving spoon delicately laid along the rim of the dish. He stood back, surveying the banquet.

'Du vin, peut-être?'

That Wolski understood, smacked his lips and announced, 'Well, even if I starve to death, I can get pissed in the process.'

Eduard nodded, and Le Petit stood aside as he unlocked the door. Within minutes the little chef was back with an unlabelled bottle, corkscrew and trio of glass goblets. The cork emerged with a satisfying slurp, and Le Petit produced a smaller glass from his capacious apron, pouring a measure, lifting it to the light, admiring its golden glow, then tipping it carefully down his throat.

'Superbe. Le Capitaine's favorite,' he said, pouring it into their glasses. He hefted his glass, waiting while they lifted theirs, grinned and added, 'Bon appetit,' as they all drank deeply.

That was the first of a series of midday meals, each different, each composed of apparently unrelated raw materials, and each an outright delight. Other bottles appeared each evening, accompanied by small cheeses and occasional fruit, while each morning they became accustomed to a wake-up call from Le Petit with coffee, sweet biscuits and an invariable apology for the lack of 'Les Oeufs Anglais'.

In the grey swell, the indistinct shapes of the two flanking cruisers dipped and rose as they flayed the waves off the Azores. The bell rang, whistles blew, and the ship seemed to tauten as the call came to 'Action Stations'.

'Another bloody practice,' moaned Wolski. Johnnie grimaced as he strapped on his Colt, and checked the action and magazine of the sten.

'My turn, I think,' he sighed, as he moved from the corner of the cabin, and Wolski and Eduard lurched into the gangway, swaying along to the companionway, and onto the bridge.

The 'mortar squad', as Wolski called them, was manning the antiquated Hedgehog depth charge in the bows. The Oerlikon was traversing, and a team was deploying a Foxer torpedo decoy astern. Clearly they were under threat, if not attack.

'I 'ope you 'ave the Mae Wests on your cases – in case we are 'it.'

The Captain was enjoying himself. Action was his metier, and Eduard realised how frustrating it must be for the invaded Frenchman not to be able to fight. This was the nearest he came to putting his fingers up to the Kraut – positive defence. He grinned.

'Maybe you get a chance to give 'im the fusil, eh?'

He gestured at the sten gun loosely hanging from Eduard's belt. Eduard turned away, embarrassed by the insult of a loaded gun on a friendly ship.

The escorts were manoeuvring, as the next merchantman ahead and slightly to the starboard tacked, then hesitated. Without warning a great gout of water erupted two-thirds of the way down her port flank, followed by a massive rumble, a splintered crack, a surge of thick black smoke streaked with guttering flame, a mesmerising pause, and then a shuddering shockwave which heeled the French vessel over. As it righted, the merchantman's bows lifted, her stern dipped, she lost way, and debris splattered her plates. The waters settled, and the wounded freighter lurched to port; they could see some crew scuttling across the sloping decks, preparing to abandon ship, as flames and smoke guttered from her aft hold.

Astern, the convoy's rescue tug was manoeuvring, and the flames receded, leaving blankets of smoke wreathing the now stationary vessel. The carrier wallowed helplessly as her rescuer closed, and their outlines merged in the manmade clouds.

'A direct 'it,' observed the Captain as he steadied himself against a stanchion, 'but they 'ave the fire under control, peut-être, and they 'ave le remorqueur to see them safely 'ome. She is strong bateau.' He peered through the port, then the starboard windows. 'I wonder, ou est le Boche?'

The thud-thud-thud of the mortars as their projectiles left, the stretched plates of the French vessel as she bucked and turned, and the crippled carrier combined to remind the Poles that they were at imminent risk, their mission now held taut as straining wire on the whim and will of an invisible foe and the skills and second-guessing of invisible escort commanders.

Mortar spouts were erupting in a pattern of criss-crossing search-and-destroy endeavours as first one, then another escort let fly. The convoy tacked and jibbed, the single-engined Swordfish pirouetted, as they searched the endless ocean for a sight of the enemy, and gradually, the mortar fire slowed, then ceased. On the bridge the radio operator was questing across the airwaves, seeking the momentary message that might declare the presence of the enemy.

'Huff-duff,' muttered Wolski.

'Huff-duff?'

'Huff-duff. It's what they call detection of the high-frequency signals subs give out when they talk to each other. On VHF radio. Split-second signals. HF/DF. Huff-duff. He's trying to find it. If he can't that's because there isn't any.'

'So?'

'So that means this is a lone wolf, and he's pacing himself, looking for an opportunity without risk. Because he's at risk now we know he's there.'

'Bon Dieu,' shouted the Captain, jabbing his finger at the Asdic. ''Ere she is!'

The sonar echo pinged on the green-static screen, and the mortars opened their throats once more, coughing their canisters of deadly phlegm into the depths. They watched and they waited. The Asdic stuttered, then steadied. The mortars spat in a steady stream, as fire was concentrated ahead and to starboard. LeGallo suddenly leant forward, and peered through the angle of the bridge glazing, exclaiming, ''Ere she comes!' and, as he spoke, a soft swell blew out of the water ahead, and the Frenchman swung slowly to port.

As it slewed over, the swollen sea subsided, only to be replaced by a froth of white foam and spray and dirty oil and, as it moved past, the bows, the shell, and the conning tower of the stricken submarine surfaced, slowly leaping out of the water like a lazy porpoise, settling back lopsided, as the Oerlikon pump-pump-pumped across its battered flanks. They watched as a frigate hove to, and the Oerlikon stopped in mid-cough, clearing its throat, the escort lowered boats, the conning hatch hinged open, and the enemy emerged, duty done, war over.

Eduard turned away from the railings, as detached mentally as he had been in fact, wondering if he should have hated them for the death they had dealt, then as quickly concluding it was the arms' length battle, the detached destruction, the suddenness of the onslaught, response, and reaction, all over in a matter of minutes, that left him so strangely undisturbed.

Back in the cabin Johnnie commented, 'Last time I hope,' and Wolski threw down his sten.

'Bloody war. We can't fight the Krauts like this,' adding, 'Sooner we get on dry land the better.'

Their introduction to naval warfare was once and forever. The voyage thereafter was tedious, uneventful and three weeks long, until they docked at Valletta. There the Captain visited them, armed with a full decanter of calva.

'We pause for a day – you wish to see the island?'

'Not possible; we have to stay with the cases.'

'Of course. Well, then, a little drink, perhaps?'

After two tots and some small talk, he excused himself, and they locked themselves in the cabin. There was a small radio, and Eduard twirled the knob to find the BBC. 'This is the nine o'clock news, and this is Alvar Lidell reading it.' The date: 16 December 1944.

The Allies had reached northern Italy, the so-called Gothic Line, but the fight for Mussolini's *terra fascisti* was not yet over. Like Warsaw, where the uprising had been crushed, the Germans had turned, cornered and lethal, and were on the offensive again. Now the three reluctant travellers had to get the gold to Italy, then find a way to Poland, for they were Warsaw's second chance.

Eduard opened the envelope. Inside was a single sheet of paper, no signature, no code. It simply said: 'Destination Warsaw, via Naples & Ostuni. Drop Boxing Day + one. Use Flinders; watch Peters; avoid Kolanski. *Find Duchnik. Make your own arrangements.*' The last four words were heavily underscored, in red.

Johnny was asleep. Wolski had, not for the first time, grumbled about the 'fancy food' as Le Petit cleared away, and Eduard commented how fortunate they were that no-one on board had questioned their mission.

'More to the point, no-one's made a move against us,' commented Wolski.

'All that protection you wanted, pointless. The crew either doesn't know, or doesn't care…' He looked at Eduard and added, 'about the gold.'

Eduard winced. Throughout the voyage they had, by tacit if unspoken consent, never once referred to their cargo as other than 'the cases', as if it was tempting fate to actually define the contents, reminding themselves specifically of the appalling risk they ran, and loss they risked, not just for themselves, but for their countrymen. Ever since they collected the cases, they had distanced themselves, deliberately ignoring the unreal nature and value of the assignment. Suddenly icy cold, he shuddered, whether from automatic reaction, or foreboding, he would never know, for at that moment, there was a knock on the door.

The knock was somehow too quiet, hesitant. Eduard looked at Johnnie and he heaved himself up, as Wolski grumbled into his glass. Johnnie opened the door, and they glimpsed a white hat and a red armband. Two military policemen strode in.

'Lieutenant Cjaikowski?' said one, in perfect English, but with a slight accent which they could not quite place – German? Polish? Russian?

Johnnie gestured towards Eduard and one of the men moved forward, the other standing just inside the door. Wolski reached for the decanter.

'Come with me, please, sir.'

'I'm afraid I can't do that.'

'Orders, sir,' and the policeman flourished a file under Eduard's nose.

'Makes no difference. I am not leaving this cabin.'

'Suit yourself,' and he flicked his baton from under his arm, striking Eduard a glissading blow on the side of the head, at the same time as his colleague slammed the door shut and tripped Johnnie, chopping him on the head with the side of his hand as he stumbled. Wolski hurled the decanter at the man who had struck Eduard, and Eduard in turn fumbled in his belt for the Colt.

The pain was immediate and stark. The gun clattered to the floor and the MP kicked it as Eduard fell, trying to hold his injured hand away from the floor. He slid across the cabin, and fetched up by the table just as Wolski head-butted the second man, who had thrown himself straight at him. The first MP stamped on Eduard's good hand, and then felt under the table for the handgun. Johnny was sitting by the door, dazed, while Wolski grappled with Johnnie's assailant. There was a quiet cry and Wolski subsided, slumping onto the floor, holding his groin. The first man shoved Eduard aside, collected the gun, and sat on the table. His colleague joined him.

'It would have been easier if you had come out in the first place,' he observed.

He nodded towards Johnnie.

'Tie him up.'

The second man produced some cord, and lashed Johnnie's hands together.

'Now him,' and Wolski was similarly bound.

'You we need.' He poked Eduard with the toe of his boot. 'You can get up.'

Eduard stood slowly, as the MP pointed the Colt without a tremor.

'Now. We can do it the easy way or the hard way.'

Eduard said nothing.

The man kicked the table; it shifted and a corner struck the locker. Eduard kept his eyes down, willed the man to ignore locker and door.

'You fetch the gold out, and you carry it on deck. OK?'

Eduard shook his head.

'Oh dear. Well, if you die, we'll just have to carry it ourselves, I suppose,' and he cocked the gun.

'If I die, you'll not find it, carry it, or get away with it.'

'Really?'

'Yes. Really. We have the papers.'

'Well, that's not a problem if you give us the papers.'

409

Eduard felt far from smiling, but realised his only chance was to bluff. So he smiled.

'The papers authorise me and me alone to deliver the gold.'

His captor looked at him warily; then he, too, smiled.

'Good. Then I shall have to persuade you to show those papers to whomsoever it concerns, shan't I?'

Eduard smiled again.

'Certainly. But there's just one other thing.'

'What's that?'

'I don't have the papers.'

'What d'you mean, you don't have the papers?'

'I don't have the papers. The Captain has the papers.'

Which was a lie, and also another bluff because, for all he knew, the Captain was in on the attempt to steal the gold.

'Right. Then we must go to see the Captain.' He stood up, waved the gun and added, 'All in good time.' He turned to his partner, curtly commanding, 'Tie him up too, and go and fetch Kruk.'

He sat on one of the stools, the gun on his lap, and considered his prey.

'Plenty of time,' he said, as if he had read their thoughts, adding, 'We shall be leaving you at Augusta,' which left them with a quandary. Did he mean to dump them at Augusta, and continue to Naples, or did he plan to depart there with the gold? It must be the latter for, unless he had LeGallo in his pocket, he would find it hard to explain their removal. How long would it be before he discovered the gold?

Eduard wondered, and tried to assess the options. They needed time. How to distract the adversary. Why was there no sign of Le Petit, unless LeGallo knew of their plight? As if on cue, there was a light knock, their assailant opened the door, and his partner and another man came in, bearing a typical Le Petit platter, and its cutlery complement.

'Intercepted this on the way,' he explained, setting the dish down on the table. 'Told him we had orders, were guarding the cabin and would need more food until Augusta.' He looked at Eduard and added, 'May as well eat well while we're here,' and lifted the cover. His English was also accented – with the inflections of their countrymen. These men were Poles, or at least this one was. They took it in turns to eat, then two of them left the cabin while the man Kruk remained.

The light faded, and Kruk was relieved. The second man was called Kress, and that was a German name. Eduard's mind raced – was this a conspiracy in the heart of SOE or were they the victims of some Russo-Polish initiative born of the Home Army's knowledge of the gold, or a leak to the People's Army?

What the hell was going on? He reasoned to himself that if only he knew, he might be able to turn the situation in some as yet unimaginable way. Of one thing he was certain – he would die before he relinquished the gold. And the more he thought about it, the more he realised he was probably right – he, they, would indeed die.

During the night Wolski complained, and was escorted to the heads. Johnnie was not long after him, but Eduard bided his time, trying surreptitiously to loosen his bonds. Eventually, bladder overtook desire and Eduard determined to exploit the opportunity, when he too went there. On the way he saw no-one, except the two men guarding the cabin in the gangway. That was their first mistake. In the heads, Eduard examined his bonds; they were expertly lashed and knotted, but he had some freedom of movement, which meant he could probably carry whatever he could find – provided they did not search him. There was nothing portable in the heads. Eduard scanned the tiny space as he sat there, leant back, and his back touched something.

He got up, turned and saw the plunger which activated the waste. When he grasped it, it wobbled. It was loose, it was threaded on a bolt, and it was heavy. It took a moment to unscrew it and, with some difficulty, secrete it in a pocket. Now at least he had a weapon. The only problem would be if someone else discovered its loss – Eduard thought quickly, and yelled.

'Need some help here.'

The door opened, and Kruk peered in. He cackled when he saw Eduard half- standing, hands bound, back bent with the rope that tied him in half, and the sheets of bum-paper on the floor.

'Can't wipe your own arse, then?'

'Not that well, but enough. Can't empty the bloody thing though, because the handle's broken.'

Eduard pointed at the protruding bolt, and prayed that his gaoler had not used the bog since he arrived. Kruk frowned, felt the bolt, and then gripped it with both hands, yanking it towards him. It flushed.

'Can't see the problem,' he grumbled, adding, 'better clean yourself up.' He then backed out of the door, leaving it ajar, as Eduard struggled to haul his trousers up and fasten the belt.

Back in the cabin, the leader listened as Kruk explained, then looked at his watch.

'Sit over there. I have to send a signal.'

Kruk sat by a porthole, and Kress leant against the door. Johnnie had moved back to the end of the cabin, near the table, and Wolski was in the corner furthest from the door. Johnnie appeared to be dozing, but Wolski was awake and alert. His eyes met Eduard's, but there was no message, for there was no opportunity.

Throughout the next day, they took turns, and from time to time the leader, who was never named, would leave the cabin 'to send a message'. The longer they remained bound, the more often he sent signals, and the more convinced Eduard became that LeGallo was involved or, at the very least, passively co-operative. Once again, Le

Petit delivered a meal, and once again, it was intercepted, and once again, it was shared, the three prisoners eating the leftovers after their captors had filled their bellies. They were reduced to eating with their fingers, not permitted to use the cutlery.

On the second night, Eduard tried to sleep, and must have dozed off, for it was dawn when he was woken by what sounded like an argument. The cabin door was ajar, and they were alone. The argument was just outside. It was in Polish. The leader spoke quietly, with conviction.

'If we leave them unharmed, it will be some time before they're found. LeGallo'll assume they are locked in because that's what they want.'

'Kill them. That way they'll not follow us.' Kress was adamant.

'I agree – we leave them, they'll not be long after us.' Kruk spoke slowly and without emotion.

'Fine. Kill them. Then what? As soon as they're found, we'll have everyone after us – SFA, the Americans, the Poles. Kolanski was quite specific. Get the gold and leave them alone. Those are our orders, and I intend to follow them.' There was a pause and, as Kress broke in with 'I don't...' the leader cut him short. 'And I'm in charge. Remember that.'

Kruk muttered something and the leader cut in sharply, 'What was that? You think you know better?' The sound of footsteps suggested a passing crew member, but then they receded and they heard Kress speaking alone.

'You should be careful with Kruk. He's a psychopath.' There was a short silence before he continued, 'I'll do as you say – but under protest, and only because it's what Kolanski wants. OK?'

The door opened, and they both returned, checked the captives' bonds, then shared the remains of the previous day's meal. As dawn filtered through the portholes, Kress switched off the single light and pulled out a pack of cigarettes. The other man lifted his eyebrows, but made no move to stop him.

Eduard glanced at Johnnie. He was wide awake near the door, and Eduard noticed his hands were clenched, at a slight angle from his body, between his legs. On the other side of the cabin, Wolski shifted irritably, raising himself on his knees and complaining, 'This bloody rope's a bit tight.'

The leader got up from the table, walked over to him, and checked the bonds, sucking his teeth.

'Tight enough, I'd say.' He straightened, looked down at Wolski and offered, 'Not long now.'

They could hear the engine note change, and realised that they were nearing Augusta. The door opened, and Kruk came in, closing it behind him, and leant against it, a small handgun idly dangling by the trigger guard from his forefinger. There was a knock. Out of the corner of his eye, Eduard saw Johnnie's hands clench again and a brief glimpse of something metallic between them.

'Bloody hell. What now?' and Kruk wheeled, pulled it open, muttered something unintelligible, and pulled it shut again, turning as he did so and stumbling across Johnnie's outstretched leg.

Then for no apparent reason, he grunted, clasped his stomach and slowly sank to his knees. Beside him, Johnnie rose up, as the knife left his hands, slick with the fluids of his first victim, but Kress ducked, and the knife hit a porthole, dropping harmlessly to the floor. At the same time, Eduard lurched sideways and struck him hard with the loo-handle, which was when Wolski bit the leader on the ankle.

'Christ almighty!' he cried, dropping his gun. Together they threw themselves at him, and he went down, as Johnnie leapt across the cabin and threw his considerable bulk against Kress. His head snapped back, and Johnnie grasped his shirt front with his still loosely bound hands, and hurled him at the table, which caught him in the small of the back. He went down again, and this time Johnnie threw himself bodily on him, hooked his hands over his head, held him and butted him. He fell back, unconscious. Eduard climbed off the leader as Wolski retrieved the handgun. His breath was short and shallow. Eduard went over to Kruk. He was dead.

The two remaining impostors survived intensive interrogation by the genuine MPs who came on board, and were removed onshore, their leader taciturn and unforgiving. Eduard watched as he was marched down the gangway. He turned at the bottom and looked back.

'Nearly, my friend, nearly. I am not the only one.' He smiled, and was gone. That night they set sail for Naples.

LeGallo was entirely contrite. It was debatable whether his contrition was for his lack of action or his inability to see through the impostors. It was clear that pride was pre-eminent.

'They were persuasive. I believed them.' His cheek muscle throbbed. 'Their papers were in order. 'Ow was I to know?' Then, 'Merde – to be fooled by such a man.' He brightened. 'But you were too, uh? At first, yes? No?'

Eduard had to agree.

The meal that day was exceptional, and so was the claret. A little later, LeGallo appeared again. The Captain sat back, rolling his glass between finger and thumb. Le Petit, at Eduard's invitation, hatless, sat opposite, and the three Poles were ranged along the porthole settle. Their glasses were full. In silence they lifted them, and silently they drank. The Captain set his down, and they followed suit. He clasped his hands and contemplated them.

'Naples.'

'Yes,' said Eduard. 'Naples.'

413

'The end of your journey.'

'No, M'sieu le Capitaine. The end of *your* journey. Ours has just begun.'

'Ah yes, of course. Warsaw.'

He paused, then stood, and walked across to Wolski, who rose awkwardly. The Captain extended his hand and Wolski took it in his.

'Bon chance, mon ami.'

He repeated the handshake and the words with Johnnie, and Le Petit impassively shook Eduard's hand, then Johnnie's, turned to Wolski and tapped the side of his head.

'Now you like les cerveaux, eh?'

Wolski nodded, and they embraced, as the Captain turned to Eduard.

'It 'as been an honour, for me and for La France.'

They shook hands, he bowed slightly, and abruptly turned and left the cabin, Le Petit behind him.

The three friends stood for a moment, each encased in a mess of sentiment and loss, until Wolski broke the spell.

'Time to go, Eduard.'

'You're right. Time to go.' He bent to slide the first case out into the cabin.

The dockside was seething, with GIs, jeeps, Italian stevedores, sailors, genuine MPs and a tangle of cranes and derricks and crates and shacks. They stood a few feet from the gangway, the cases between them, and Eduard felt exposed, vulnerable. Wolski had his sten across his stomach, and Johnnie was slapping his handgun from one hand to the other.

'Where the hell are they?'

Wolski expressed their concerns. Yet it was not reasonable to expect to be met the very minute they landed. Convoys were scheduled, but hardly to the day, let alone the hour. For the umpteenth time, Wolski asked, 'What's the arrangement then?' and for the umpteenth time, Eduard replied, 'Two Studebakers, lorries from Ostuni, to meet us, collect us, take us there.'

'And where the fuck is Ostooney?'

'Eastern coast, near Brindisi.'

'Bloody hell. It's miles away.'

'I know.'

They could see the transit camp on the hill above – overlooking Pompeii, they had been told. They had also been told that Vesuvius had erupted two days before, and a certain chaos had ensued, though how such an event could cause more chaos than an American army in wartime was hard to contemplate.

'So what are we going to do?'

'Wait.'

414

They waited for three hours, as afternoon faded, the cases accorded no scrutiny, and little interest apart from an occasional casual enquiry by passing American MPs.

'Wotcher gaht theyah, boy? Jools of the Ahrient?'

'Hi guys. Wanna hotel or something?'

'Hey man, gocherself some nylons?'

They ignored them all, and by and large they were also ignored, apart from sporadic offers of spearmint chewing gum.

As the light failed, Wolski became even more restless than normal.

'Eduard, we have to do something.'

'Can't stay here all night,' added Johnnie.

Eduard considered the options. They could make for the camp, but without transport, the cases were too heavy. They could try to commandeer a jeep, but that meant explanations, and complications. They could settle down for the night, and wait but there was no guarantee that that would produce the missing trucks. He decided to divide their labours.

'OK. You two stay put. There's a shed over there. We'll drag the stuff inside, and you guard it. I'll go to the camp and find some help.'

No-one stopped or queried them. Johnnie stood by the entrance, while Wolski sat on two cases, piled up, the others wedged behind him, against the wall. Eduard left them there with a considerable twinge of unease, and his sten.

The camp was loosely guarded, and the guard waved him through with only a cursory glance at his papers. The HQ was a stone building alongside the guardhut, and the CO was a US Colonel, accessible, relaxed, unsurprised.

'Have a cigar, Lootenant. Make yourself carmf'terble. What cin ah do fer yew?'

His office was comfortable – leather armchairs, carpets, chaise longue, some large oil paintings, probably looted, and an array of bottles and glasses in an ormulu cabinet – but overstuffed with furniture and disparate acquisitions. The Colonel himself reclined on a deeply buttoned settee, in dusky green leather with tasselled cushions and richly woven antimacassar. There was a brass inlaid trolley laden with ornate silverware, candelabra and more bottles, and a deeply carved baroque side table, incongruously piled high with cedarwood boxes of Havana cigars, a crate of bourbon and several pairs of leather boots. In a corner of the room stood a ragged palm in a ceramic jar, partly obscured by a cracked statue of the Venus de Milo, and stacked in another corner, two rifles and a bazooka.

'I have papers.'

The Colonel waved his cigar about carelessly.

'Yeah. Well, buddy, we all got papers. Don't mean nuttin'.'

Eduard tried again.

'My Government—'

'Government? What government?'

'The Polish Government.'

'Gee, you Pollacks did a wunnerful jahb. Your Genrul Anders – I fowt with his people. Great guys. Great guys. Have another drink.'

'Yes, well, my people sent me here to deliver a special cargo. A very special cargo.'

The Colonel nodded encouragingly, smoke veiling his permanent smile.

'I've left my squad at the docks – with our cargo. We were supposed to be met.'

'Yeah, well, nuttin's sart'n around heyah, boy.'

He pushed the bottle across and Eduard thought, what the hell, he might as well, and poured a third slug of extremely warming bourbon.

'Two lorries, Studebakers, supposed to meet us, from Ostuni.'

The Colonel nodded and poured himself his fourth, raised the glass, contemplated it with care, nodded again and downed it in one gulp. Eduard tried one more time.

'Very important cargo. We have to find the lorries. We've come all the way from England. We're tired, we need a rest, a shave, food, sleep – and we need transport. Can you help?' He added, 'It *is* Christmas Eve.'

The Colonel swung his legs off the sofa, hitched his trousers, stubbed his cigar out on the floor, and slowly rose to his feet. He looked down at Eduard.

'Well, buddy, I guess you gaht a prahblem. But it ain't mah prahblem. Ah cin give yew rest and a shave and ah cin give yew food and ah cin water yew, but trucks ah cain't give yew. Yew jest have ter find yer own way, boy.'

He unflapped his top pocket, drew out a wad of cards, handed one across, and took Eduard's hand in both of his, warmly pressing them together.

'Wish yew well, boy. This'll get you most anything – except trucks.'

Eduard looked at the pasteboard. Ornately printed, it read 'Colonel Harry StJ. Flinders MA – Objets d'art' with a Brindisi address and telephone number. Folded round it was an official letterhead, with a typed authorisation and the good Colonel's florid signature.

As he ushered Eduard out, he added, 'Try the Mayor – he's a new boy and anxious ter please. Appointed him mahself. Name's Cecchinato – Giancarlo Cecchinato.'

As he closed the door, Eduard heard him lift the phone, and his clipped order: 'Get me Kolanski.'

Eduard hitched a lift with two GIs out on the town, whom the Colonel deputed to be his guides, and they deposited him, with sparse comment and a packet of gum, outside a nondescript office building without any visible signage, which they assured him was the Neapolitan wartime equivalent of the district town hall. When he asked for the Mayor he was told he was out of town. The reception was a table in a corner and the Mayor's office was a room bare of equipment save for an old-fashioned candle-stick phone on a shabby desk, with a single, sagging chair. The staff comprised a handful of voluble but uncommunicative Italians in torn and patched uniforms.

When Eduard persisted, the receptionist explained in fractured English that it was, after all, Christmas Eve, and everyone was either at their devotions, or preparing for them, celebrating, or preparing for that. What did he expect? Even in wartime, Christmas was Christmas. When Eduard invoked the Mayor's name, all he got was a blank stare.

'Cecchinato? Niente. No Cecchinato.'

He tried again.

'Giancarlo Cecchinato?'

'Niente.'

The only Giancarlo was her sister's cousin's boyfriend, and he was a no-good *accessori*, *parasiti*, no-good-at-alla, and Eduard had to endure several minutes of considered condemnation of the hapless Giancarlo before they got back on track, and the question of a safe haven for the festive season.

He thought about the gold, about Johnnie and Wolski down at the docks, and decided they must find somewhere safe until after the festivities.

'Is there a bank?'

'Bank? Bank? Niente – all closed. Christmas.' She looked at him. 'You better off in prison. There you fed, safe, no need travel,' and she roared with laughter at her own simple humour.

'Prison? What prison?'

'Here. This building, is prison.' She shrieked with increased mirth and gesticulated at the gathering crowd of intensely interested onlookers, who seemed to be the entire staff of the alleged town hall. 'We all in prison,' and she dissolved into further fits of giggles.

A small, smiling man detached himself from the cackling throng.

'You wanta prison?'

Eduard spread his hands. Why not? At least there they might be safe.

'Luigi show you. Follow.'

He led the way down the steps, along the street, and into an alley. Eduard hung back, suspicious, but he waved him on.

'You come my volante,' and there, parked by the wall, revealed as he pulled away a dirty tarpaulin, was a stripped and spare military motorcycle and sidecar. He jumped on from the rear, kicked down on the starter and it fired immediately. Eduard clambered into the sidecar, his hand on the Colt, and his new friend let in the clutch. They wove through scattered groups of early celebrants, down the hill towards the harbour, veering off into a side street, and spluttered to a halt outside a tall, windowless stone block, with a deep-set double timbered door, strapped by a wide bar.

'You wait.' He knocked, and a small square of light appeared behind a metal grille, then a door within the door opened, and he beckoned.

They followed a capped and caped figure through an arched passage into an open courtyard, round which the gaunt walls rose up, as windowless as the exterior, save for regular horizontal grids at each of four floor levels. At the far side of the courtyard was a similarly arched passage, which ended in a similar door. Their guide wrenched this open, to reveal a steep flight of stone steps, down which they clattered, low-wattage bulbs recessed in the walls alongside them. At the bottom, another passage led between dank walls, slippery with glistening moss. The guide turned and indicated six doors.

'Interdictari.'

Eduard raised his eyebrows, shrugged and shook his head.

'You understand?'

'Not really.'

'These are cellars, not for vino, but for people. Interdictari.'

'You mean dungeons.'

'Dungeons? Not know that word. These are rooms for-a bad people, old days.'

'Are there any guards?'

The little biker turned to the guide and a low-volume fast dialogue ensued. They fell silent, and he turned back.

'No guards. Not necessary. No keys – only one. Come, we show you.'

They walked to the end of the passage, where there was an alcove, and in the alcove was a metal handle. The guide produced a leather folder from beneath his cape, opened it, and showed Eduard three tools. One was serrated with a series of complex indentations. He inserted this into the end of the handle, and turned it twice. Then he wound the handle, there was a grating and a grinding, and a bar appeared at the edge of the alcove, until it was at least 18 inches clear.

The guide pointed out into the passage, Eduard stepped out, and saw that the six doors were all ajar. He walked over to one, and pushed. It swung back, to reveal an empty, barrel-vaulted cell, without light or bench or anything except a single thick ring embedded in the centre of the floor. He pushed each door in turn and every cell was the same. The guide followed, pulling each door shut again, and they returned to the alcove, where he turned the handle, extracted the key and returned it to his leather folder, and in turn put that back beneath his cape.

'You want interdictari? For treasures?'

The guide's eyes were gleaming, and Eduard began to appreciate the purpose of his visit. Schooled by the exigencies of occupation, of which Colonel Flinders was presumably a prime example, he had guessed the need correctly, while assessing Eduard's cupidity with somewhat less accuracy. He thought that all Eduard wanted was a safe place for suspect loot, and he was prepared to provide it – for a fee. There was only one problem. If Eduard held a key, what was there to say there was no duplicate? How could he be sure his 'loot' would stay in place, once it was deposited?

'Yes. I want it.' Then he added, 'And both of you too.'

They looked at each other in alarm.

'You come with me and my friends, and we'll have a good time together.'

Eduard held out a hand. The guard reluctantly fished out his wallet, extracted the key and handed it over. They retraced their steps, and set out for the docks on Luigi's motorbike.

Wolski was standing just outside the shed.

'Where the hell have you been?'

'Later. I want you to meet Luigi, who has provided us with transport, and Cesare, who has given me a key to the dungeons.'

He stressed the indefinite. Initially Wolski was sceptical, but Johnnie was enthusiastic.

'It makes sense. So long as they're with us, they're not with the stuff. If one of us stays there, it'll be safe – until we find the trucks.'

And so it was. It took numberless trips behind Luigi's motorbike to haul the cases on a flimsy two-wheeled cart to the prison, where they left Johnnie on guard in the alcove, with two stens. As they left, he shouted, 'Have a good time!'

Naples in wartime was well served with bars and brothels. For the next few hours Wolski and Eduard were introduced to *la dolce vita*, Napoli style, at home with Luigi, in church with Cesare, on the town with them both after the children were abed and the wives, grumbling, let them go 'to show our friends our beautiful town'. Next morning, hour on hour they returned to the quayside, to make rendezvous with the missing trucks. Each time, they left none the wiser, then went back to the prison, to relieve Johnnie. Every time they were truckless in Napoli. When the MPs stopped them, which they did every hour, they produced their passes, courtesy Harry Flinders, Colonel and sometime dealer in objets d'art:

'Any assistance required at any time and any place to be given without any questions. Sgd Harry StJ Flinders. Allied Forces in Europe. Ostuni HQ.'

It was countersigned with the initials HK, and a smudged seal, which looked suspiciously like a hammer and sickle.

DIES DEOIUS

Christmas Day. Cesare went to church, Luigi offered wine, Wolski prayed, and Johnnie stayed on guard, as Eduard roused himself after a mere two hours' sleep, and persuaded his Neapolitan friend to take him once more to the dockside, though the incidence of lorries on this day of all days was as likely as Parma ham for breakfast.

He was wrong. There by the dockside stood two, admittedly battered, but sturdy Studebaker trucks, their GI drivers leaning against one cab, their MI carbines stacked carelessly beside them, simultaneously chewing gum and smoking. One detached himself and palmed his gum, strolling up with a 'You must be de Poe-lack'. The other, cheroot stuck up at an angle, out of the side of his mouth drawled, 'Who's the little guy? He ain't no Pallack'.

Anonymous J. – 'for Julius – call me Jools' – Bosch was a Harlem foundling. Dumped at birth outside the Metropolitan, he was discovered *en passant* by an art-lover who promptly stuffed him in a cruising cab with the comment, 'He's a child a hell,' adding, "minds me a Hieronymous Bosch,' so the cabman dumped him at the hospital with the comment, 'Abandoned minor: Anonymous Bosch,' and it stuck. Jools ran numbers for a living, was conscripted, wounded, and remaindered to truck-watch.

All this and more emerged as they churned their way through Naples to the prison gate. Luigi led the little cavalcade on his volante. By the time they reached the prison, they also learnt that Dexter Haagen was a frustrated fisherman who drove a 'bike for a living, delivering biscuits to dog-owners in Detroit. On that tenuous basis, he had been assigned to transport duties. Dexter was known as 'Dog' for, whenever mildly drunk, he would howl in return for free beer. Both men and trucks were seconded from Rome, on the request of one Captain Peters, USAAF Ostuni, attached to RAF Brindisi.

'D'you know Peters?' asked Eduard.

'Nar – never bin there.'

At the double-timbered door, Cesare hauled back the bar, and waved them through to the courtyard. Eduard told Jools and Dog to wait with Wolski, and followed Luigi down the steps, Cesare hard on his heels. Johnnie was waiting.

'At long bloody last. I hope you've got some wine. I'm parched.'

Within half an hour the cases were loaded, by tacit consent half on Eduard's truck and half on Johnnie's. There were already some crates on board.

'What's this?' asked Eduard, and Jools winked, tapped the side of his nose, pulling him to one side.

'You'll love it – jenn-u-wine vodka, mah man, from the guys in Rome.'

420

Eduard adopted what he hoped was a knowing look, and Jools added, 'Your guys, the Poe-lacks, guys who took care of Anzio, restin' up, need a dollar, so-a helped 'em aht.'

Cesare held out his hand for the key, and the two-truck convoy backed into the street. Eduard turned to Wolski as he climbed into the back of the truck.

'Hang on; I'm going to settle up.'

Norris had anticipated palms to be crossed, reasoning that crisp white British fivers would 'please the Wops' and that's what Eduard counted as they stood inside the courtyard. He handed Cesare £20.

'Whats-a this?' he asked, turning the notes this way and that, holding them up to the morning light, squinting through them, then rubbing them between his fingers, before finally producing a bent, steel-framed pair of spectacles, from which one lens was halved, the other a grimy blur.

'...promeeses to pay-a the bear-er?'

He pulled Eduard towards him, opened his hand, slammed the notes into it, and flourished the spectacles.

'Issa promees, no good. Issa money I need, not-a promees.'

Here was a little local difficulty which could prove a long-term hazard, so what to do? As Eduard pondered, he was overtaken by a stream of syncopating speech.

'Youse gotta lotta promise, Cesare, ma boy, and ah has a soe-lew-shun which will bring tears to yoh eyes,' and much more in the same vein, as Jools waltzed past, a hand of cigars fanned out, with three bottles of rye depending beneath them, skeins of nylon fluttering from the other hand, which also clutched a great, fat pack of chewing gum.

'Now, this heah's fer yew,' and he thrust a cigar in Cesare's gaping mouth, a bottle in one hand, gum in the other, wheeling and addressing Luigi. 'And fer yew, liddel man with a Gahd-given large heart,' he maundered on, stuffing the rest of the goods in Luigi's automatically upraised arms, and finishing with 'to keep yore light a flick'rin' in these hard ole times,' flaring a lighter right under Luigi's bursting eyes so that he had to suck the cigar smoke in, and immediately started coughing, his hands too full to extract it. Eduard took it out for him, helped him rearrange his booty, and replaced it between his broken teeth.

'Lezz go, mah good man,' and Jools bounded back up the steps.

Eduard shook Cesare's hand, and told him to keep the fivers anyway, stuffed four into Luigi's pocket and on an impulse, pulled him close and hugged him.

'Thanks for everything. Maybe one day we'll meet again.'

As they clambered back into the trucks, Luigi stumbled after them. He stood below the truck door, looking up beseechingly. Eduard lent down, and once more removed the stogie.

'You wanta know how to get outa town?'

Eduard turned to Jools.

'You know the way to Ostuni?'

The negro shrugged.

'Right.' Eduard smiled at Luigi. 'OK. Leave your stuff with Cesare, and let's get on with it.'

With the volante in front, they started the tortuous journey through the streets of Napoli, on their way to Brindisi. On the edge of the city, Luigi slowed, and the Americans slipped down a gear as they hauled past him. When the Poles looked back, he was standing by his 'bike, to attention, his arm raised to his forehead in rigid salute.

At midday they ground through Salerno and, by mid-afternoon, were labouring uphill, through quiet villages, along the flanks of towering rock, towards Potenza. As the two Studebakers rounded a seemingly endless bend, there was the hesitant stutter of an automatic weapon, and the first windscreen shattered.

'Shee-ut!'

Jools hauled the wheel over, as Eduard punched out the screen with the butt of his carbine. Nothing. The road was clear, there was nobody apparent on the crumbling verge, and no reasonable cover within yards. Eduard snatched a look in the square mirror which hung over the door pillar; Johnnie's truck was tight behind. Eduard stuck his arm out and revolved it rapidly – 'Keep going!' – and shouted at Jools, 'Change down, speed up, keep going,' and the driver grinned, his jaw chomping gum faster and faster as he spun the wheel.

The stutter came again, and this time they saw them – four men lying flat on an outcrop overhanging the road. They had shot across the corner, concealed by the overhang. Now they were visible. So was the overturned truck across the road ahead. They ducked beneath the bulkhead, as Eduard reached below the seat for the machine pistol and Jools grabbed his carbine.

'What the fuck do we do now man?'

'Keep down!'

Eduard looked in the mirror again. Johnnie's truck was reversing wildly, and vanished round the bend.

'Can you make this thing go back without getting shot?'

Jools smiled.

'Hang on, Poe-lack.'

As he engaged reverse, his eye on the mirror, Eduard risked a rapid glance over the bonnet. The men had disappeared. They lurched back, paused, changed direction, lurched again.

'Watch out! We're on the edge.'

Jools braked, and the now familiar stutter recommenced, this time from the right, Eduard's side of the truck. He slithered across the seat above Jools who was curled up in a ball on the floor, like a contortionist, one hand reaching up to grip the wheel, the other on the throttle, his knee hovering above the brake.

Poking the automatic out above the door, Eduard sprayed fire unevenly across the cab roof. Then they were round the corner, as the other truck careered out of sight.

'Can you turn it round?'

Jools's eyes glittered.

'Hold on mah man.'

In a flurry of fluid movements, a balletic sequence of throttle, brake, wheel, throttle, the truck lurched to one side, then sagged over, the mirror snapping as it grazed the rock. Jools thrust down hard on the pedal, and they were slaloming sideways whence they came. As they slid past another thankfully shallow corner, Johnnie's truck loomed, broadside across the road.

Jools saw it too, and forced the brake to the floor. They also saw Johnnie, and Haagen briefly, flitting past as they ran, doubled over, 30 yards from the edge, on the lower ground. Eduard prayed they were not visible to the men above. 'Out! Quick!' and he jumped, rolling over and over in the sandy dust, stones catching ankles and elbows, the machine pistol tucked into his belly. Jools was almost on top of him as they came to rest.

The road was invisible from where they lay. Eduard motioned to Jools to follow, and started crawling diagonally away from the trucks, so they could cross the road above them, as near as possible to the point of ambush. Eduard reasoned that Johnnie would do the same, and wondered how Wolski had fared, in the back of the truck. He wished he had him with him.

They edged past the outcrop, which was the only feature visible from their low field of fire. Then Eduard signalled to Jools to move away, and they approached the road 20 paces apart. At the edge, Eduard risked a quick look. Clear. Motioning Jools to stay put and cover him, he crouched, then ran across and stopped behind the ambush truck.

The road ahead was empty. Above there was a movement on the outcrop. Eduard sidled round the truck, and knelt behind its protruding cab. A man was suddenly silhouetted against the sky. He could not make him out – it could be Johnnie, it could be Haagen, or it could be one of their assailants. So he waited.

The brief cry was closed off as soon as it started, and the dark figure staggered, then fell. Stalemate. If that was Johnnie, Haagen was in trouble too. Jools was crawling rapidly towards Eduard, who mouthed 'I'm going up there' pointing at the outcrop. 'Cover me.'

Jools took up position, the carbine resting on the cab, as Eduard worked his way under the outcrop, back up the road, in the shadow of the rock. Within 20 yards, he found a rough track winding over the hill. Beyond lay loose rocks; he moved like the knight on the chess board, asymmetrically around and behind them, until he was above both track and outcrop, which was when the firing started again.

The field of skirmish was clear on all sides from where he knelt. A body lay awkwardly on the cleft surface of the outcrop, which fell away in several steps. Behind them crouched two men in uniform. Eduard could not be sure, but he did not think they were Germans. On the outcrop, spreadeagled on its lip, Johnnie lay with Haagen beside him. As they fired down, the men fired up. Stalemate again.

Eduard was helpless for, the moment he fired, he would be exposed. Jools was pinned down behind the ambush truck. Johnnie and Haagen were balanced by the men below them. Below the outcrop, 100 yards down the road, two more uniformed men advanced slowly. Beyond them, the trucks were parked, two men standing alongside, back to back, their weapons raised, alert. Of Wolski there was no sign. Perhaps he had left the truck, perhaps he lay inside, injured. Eduard's mouth dried when he thought of the third alternative. Perhaps he was dead. If those men reached the outcrop, Johnnie was dead too.

You can always tell the difference between the bark of the rifle and the snap of a pistol shot. Two single shots. Two bodies beside the trucks. Wolski. They watched him climb aboard the first truck, heard the engine fire, miss, fire, then rumble, cough as the gear engaged, and rumble again, and watched the truck heave itself across the road, back again, across, and forward, on its way up the hill.

The two men nearing the outcrop heard it too, and hesitated. One turned, signalled his partner to stay put, and started back down the road. He was carrying a bazooka. Eduard flinched in anticipation; with a range of 100 yards, it would tear a mighty hole in the truck within seconds.

Johnnie and Haagen were still firing, single shots, carefully. The opposition was responding, with automatic fire. Eduard was doing no good at all where he was, so started to work his way down towards them. Then he heard Jools's carbine, once, twice, and an exultant, whooping 'Bull's eye!' and the standing man sat suddenly, surprised, his head leant forward slowly into his lap, and he fell over, his rifle clattering across the road. Bazooka man wheeled, just in time for Jools's third shot, and fell back against the rock face, the weight of his weapon pressing him down, until he too sat, looking somewhat pained, and let the long tube tumble out of his grasp.

The firing had stopped. Johnnie and Haagen were standing, pointing down the slope. Their remaining assailants were fast disappearing, running towards the mountains, a diminishing blur.

They stood over the wounded man. He and his three dead colleagues were all wearing standard battlefield kit – khaki, without rank, unit or any other insignia. Their equipment, however, was American. They searched them all. No papers, no ID discs, nothing. Haagen was examining his truck, while Jools looked on. Johnnie had checked the contents.

'Vodka's still there.'

'What about the cases?'

Johnnie laughed.

'Priorities, eh? Don't worry. It's all there, safe and sound.'

Wolski poked the prone attacker.

'What's your name?'

Blood obscured the man's face, so it was impossible to read his expression, but for an instant, it seemed he smiled.

'Where are you from?'

Jools wandered over and looked at the man.

'Another one of us, ah guess.'

'What d'you mean? American?'

'Nar, man. Anonymous.' The wounded man tried to speak. Eduard bent down, then sat beside him, took his wrist and felt his pulse.

'He's not going to last.'

The man's eyes fluttered, and he tried again.

'Peters,' was all they could catch.

'Captain Peters?'

He nodded imperceptibly.

'He sent you?'

He nodded again.

'To kill us?'

He muttered something.

Eduard put his head close to the man's lips.

'What then? Why did he send you?'

'Because... Duchni... foun'... bad.'

Eduard could not catch the words as they trailed away.

'For what? Why?'

'Protect...'

He seemed to gather himself together, and a trembling hand touched Eduard's.

'Our... gold...'

His head drooped, his hand fell away. Eduard put his head against the man's chest. The beat was faint. Wolski lifted his hands.

'Try. Try to tell us.'

The wounded man's eyes opened. Quite clearly, he said one word as his eyes closed.

'Kolanski.' Then he died.

They retrieved the dead men's weapons and gave their bodies a makeshift burial – 'No point in taking them with us; nobody'd want to know them,' opined Johnnie – and set about shifting the barricade truck. It was early evening as they trundled into the piazza of a large village. The church bells were calling the people to Mass.

To everyone's surprise, Jools elected to attend. Dog demurred, and said he would prefer to 'see the sights'. They agreed to meet again at midnight and Wolski suggested they put the cases in one lorry, so they only needed one guard, but Eduard disagreed – 'Two lorries, half the risk.' Johnnie stayed with his truck and Eduard stayed with the other, until Wolski joined him in the cab.

'You want to go to Mass, don't you, Eduard?'

Unsure, he said, 'Yes,' more to give himself time to think than time for prayer, and left Wolski in charge. The risk of another attack seemed slight – perhaps a little prayer would help.

The church was decorated, and it was full. Censers swayed, music played, and the congregation muttered and fluttered, until the choral chant silenced them, and the Holy Virgin entered, borne aloft by dark children in white vestments, led by the Cross and the representative of Christ's Vicar. Despite himself, Eduard was consumed by the current of hope and clarity within the holy words, and found himself deep in thanksgiving and wonder until, in a moment of self-doubt, black thought invaded his mind.

As he knelt, he wondered what a million in gold might buy – plenty for each of them and the rest between the Yanks. It might buy mother's homecoming, grandpa's farm; it would buy horses and wine, it could buy a shop perhaps, or some other avoidance of toil, for what otherwise might he do when all this war was over? It could buy Wolski back his daughter, if that was possible, and give Johnnie a life; Jools could escape his origins and Haagen his drudgery. It would be a spoil of war and an act of retribution for the sins and sorrows they all bore.

'And he gave His only begotten Son...' The words jerked him back to remembrance of the mission, of all the lives that had been given, all the other sons who had perished, the sacrifices of fellow countrymen and, as he looked up at the impassive visage of the priest, offering the body and blood of Christ, if his holy beliefs wavered, his resolve did not, for he saw again Bishop Gawlina and heard again his words 'look after and over you' and knew he had no real choice. The gold was in his care, not his keeping. He was in the house of the Lord on His day and, even if He might fade from their considerations, the gold should, would, must get to Warsaw.

Outside, after the service, the villagers repaired to their homes for the Christmas feast; Eduard went back to the trucks.

'If we're going to drink sliv, we'd better go somewhere else.'

The vodka crates were intact, but it could not last. It was Christmas and the spirit was upon them. Two miles outside the little town, they found a disused track, took the lorries off the road and out of sight and Johnnie broached the first case. Everyone had a bottle. It was not what you might call a party. Jools was a loner and sauntered off to drink on his own; Dog became morose after two slugs.

The three Poles sat in the back of one truck, watching each other, slowly drinking themselves insensible. At least, Johnnie did, and Wolski was not long in following his example. Eduard wanted to, and got close to oblivion, but not too close and, as Wolski eventually slept, and Johnnie gradually solidified, he slipped off the back of the truck and inspected the other. Then he stood between the two and considered the future – the immediate future. Ostuni and Colonel Flinders; Brindisi and Captain Peters.

One was probably a fool, but they needed his help; the other perhaps a traitor, and they needed him foiled. Then his mind stopped, and that single, most unwelcome image engulfed him: five years before, standing there, condemning with words he thought his victim did not understand: 'Get rid of him.' Could it possibly be the same man? Was his destiny Kolanski?

Eduard looked at the empty bottle, and threw it away and, as it bounced once, then splintered, pulled himself together. Bugger Kolanski. They would do what they had undertaken to do, what should be done.

'Thinking about the money?'

Startled, he turned round to see Johnnie sitting on the tailboard, swinging his legs, as he tipped another lightened bottle to his lips. He laughed.

'I was, but it's not ours to think about, is it?'

He lowered the bottle, contemplated it for a moment, then span it away after Eduard's, and answered himself.

'It's Poland's gold, and Warsaw's hope, and we are going to see it gets there.'

He jumped down, like so many large men, light on his feet, gave the thumbs up and looked at his watch.

'Four in the morning, Eduard. Time you got some sleep.'

At seven, they were on their way. The drumming of the engine and the whine of the transmission sent Eduard to sleep again until a shearing, screeching slither of sound woke him. The truck was stationary.

'What's wrong?' he asked as he fumbled for the pistol.

'Relax mah bruther, 'tis not the enemy. We in the middle-a nowhere and this ole truck, he's given up on us.'

'Broken down?'

'This is true man. We's all outa clutch.'

'Spares?'

'Don't carry 'em on da Ostooney Ex-press.'

Minutes of frenzied examination, sundry kickings and a good deal of colourful exhortation on the part of Jools, Haagen and Johnnie, with no useful contribution on Eduard's part, left them speechless, until practical Wolski stated the obvious.

'Put the cases in one truck, abandon the other, and get on with it.'

'Very practical,' said Haagen, 'but I gottaraccount for my truck.'

'It's war, for God's sake. Forget the bloody truck.'

But Haagen was adamant. Wolski sighed in exasperation.

'Well, tow it then. But let's for God's sake go.'

427

At ten o'clock on Boxing Day evening, the two-truck convoy arrived at Ostuni, and at five minutes past, three weary Poles sat in the guardroom, surrounded by battered but still bound cases, the trucks gone, and with them dour Dog and the ebullient Jools: 'If you evah want any ole thing, you jest call on yoh brother, mah man.'

The SP outside the door snapped to attention 'Sah!' as the door swung open and in strode Colonel Flinders.

'Guys! You-all most welcome heah in Ostooney,' and as he hauled Eduard into a close embrace, he roared, 'Mah boys, you'all certainly dee-zerve a party. Chrissmass ain't over yet!'

A series of rapid orders followed, and the SP saluted again, moved out at the double, and returned within a squad of 12. The three couriers watched as they loaded the cases onto dollies, hitched behind jeeps, and jumped aboard, two to each.

'Follow me!' yelled the Colonel as he, too, swung into a jeep, and they joined him, clinging onto whatever metal they could find as the little convoy struck off into the night.

'Where're we going?' yelled Eduard through the slipstream.

'Mah em-porium,' he answered, flourishing a massive cigar, unlit, but well chewed.

The Colonel's office was less of an office and more of a warehouse. There were paintings stacked against one wall, rows of pots and vases and occasional statues against another, sheaves of swords and scrolls and walking sticks stuffed into more vases; pilasters and columns lying on the floor, more statuary between them, and a tangle of candelabra, fabric swags and bowls and cups and assorted silver in a corner. On several splendid tables stood an army of graceful glass and more silver, and against a third wall, a pile of rugs.

'Lib-ar-ated and in our good safe-keepin' foah the time bein',' explained Colonel Harry, as he pushed several boxes of Havana cigars to one side, and poured Bourbon from a crystal jug. As he did so, the door opened and a Captain walked in, without greeting or salutation, throwing himself into one of the numerous armchairs that sat uneasily among the assorted junk.

'Hi Malc. Howsa 'planes at Brindisi?' Flinders swept his guests into an introduction with a vague wave of his arm. 'These heah's the Pollacks I wuz tellin' you. Met this one in Napolee – coupla days since. That right, Ed-ooard? This heah's Peters, Cap'n Peters, mah aid doo camp.'

He did not wait for an answer before planting a glass in Peters' hand, and a cigar in Eduard's. Within seconds everyone was glazed and smoked.

Peters replied tersely, in clipped tones.

'No 'planes tonight, Harry. Weather's agin it. Talk to the Raff in the mornin'.'

Flinders inclined his head towards Eduard.

'Ah told yew nuttin's sartin, didn-ah boy? Let's have a party! Merr-ee Chriss-mass, everee-buddy.'

The door opened again, and two rankers entered, pushing trolleys. On the trolleys were silver salvers and on the salvers, cold cuts of beef and pork, sleek fat fish and plump tomatoes, bread and gorgonzola. Thick red wine was served and they ate as if this was the last day of the Holy Roman Empire.

Eduard was sitting on one of the cases when the Colonel walked over and sat beside him. He leant close and murmured, 'We got a spesh-ul unit heah, mah boy. Unit Two. In-telligence. They shadowin' Malc over theah. Think he's into the Black Market, see.'

Eduard said nothing, concentrating on the cigar, when the Colonel added, 'You-all want these cases to Brin-deezee?'

'That'd be a good idea.'

'Ah shall ay-range it. Now, smoke up, drink up, and have some more food. Ain't ev'ree day ah gets to entertain real hee-roes.'

With a flourish the Colonel produced a clipboard, ripped off a sheet of paper and stuffed it in Eduard's hand. Eduard skimmed it – USAAF HQ heading, close-typed officialese, space for consignment details, date, time, place. It all seemed in order. 'Held in safe keeping, OC consignment 2nd Lt Cjaikowski, E.'

The Colonel proffered a pen. Eduard hesitated, then read it again. It was quite clear. Polish Government... destination Warsaw... Brindisi... Ostuni etcetera, etcetera, and a space for him to sign, and print his name, rank, number. Still he hesitated.

'Prahblem?' The Colonel squinted at him. If he had smiled, Eduard would have handed it back, refused to move, stood on his proprieties, and demanded more. But the Colonel simply waited. So he signed, and handed the paper back. The Colonel read the paper, carefully, scribbled on his sheet, ripped that off and handed it to Eduard.

'Yoh copy,' he said, and added, 'and yoh stuff' – he looked at Eduard for a long moment – 'in safe hands heah.'

A contingent of SPs were left on guard and Flinders took them to mess quarters, some time after midnight. He promised they would be woken early next day and taken to the aerodrome, where the flight should be ready for the drop to Warsaw. The cases would be loaded onto a Liberator. Eduard would accompany them – alone.

At Brindisi, the Base Two radio transmitters were reputedly the biggest in the European theatre. Eduard sat down to the Borg key, the fastest key, like a machine gun, for was he not the fastest Morse operator out of Audley End? He eased the gun in his pocket – it somehow seemed superfluous now the mission was almost over. Within seconds, he sensed the power flowing through his wrist as he flicked the key sideways, and started the message, encrypted.

'Luggage in locker. Key with Flinders. Capital flight. ETD midday.'

Back came the answer.

'Capital flight no go. Red resistance. Contact Duchnik.'

Johnnie, Wolski and Eduard sat disconsolately in the mess.

'It's the same thing all over again.' Johnnie threw back his whisky. 'Hate this damn stuff. Wish we could find those trucks.'

The crates of vodka had disappeared with Jools and Haagen. It took little imagination to conclude what had happened. About Warsaw, Wolski was enraged.

'The bastards – they sat in the suburbs last August and watched Warsaw burn, watched our people die, and all for their precious Marxism.'

Johnnie: 'What do you expect from Russians? And it's not about Marxism, it's about power, about control, about them and us. Bastards.'

Several other Poles joined in and discussion raged across the uncertainties, for the Americans refused to drop supplies, the Russians sat back, and the Germans continued to decimate the Warsaw population. One man sat aside, sipping the vodka he had found, and shared with Johnnie. He beckoned Eduard over.

'You're the man with the money,' he stated. 'Don't worry. I know no-one's supposed to know about it, but the Colonel's not very discreet, and he doesn't usually have guards posted on his private store.'

'It's supposed to go to Warsaw.'

'I'm going to Warsaw.'

'When?'

'Today.'

'But the Russians...'

'Won't stop me.'

He extended a hand, and Eduard took it.

'Leopold – Leopold Okulicki. I'm a paratrooper, like you.'

He hesitated, as if undecided about telling more, then smiled to himself.

'I'm taking over from Bor-Komowski, the Armia Krajowa.'

'The Underground?'

'That's right.'

'Then you need the gold, I mean, money.'

'Indeed, but it's too risky. If we get caught by the Germans, it's lost. The Russians...'

He left the obvious unsaid.

'So what do you suggest? London seems impotent.'

'Find Duchnik. He'll know what to do – where to go, if it's not already too late.'

And with that, the General raised his glass in a silent toast, drained it, rose, touched Eduard's shoulder and left without even saying goodbye.

Within days, in mid-January, the Russians had crossed the Vistula, soon after 'liberating' Warsaw, driving the fearful before them, displacing all those who fought Communism. Eduard 'talked' to the British every day and tried to find the mysterious Duchnik, but none among the few Poles at Brindisi had heard of such a man, and none knew any more than he did – about Warsaw, the Russians, the Resistance or where to take the gold, now Warsaw was in Russian hands.

'Would you like to go to Rome?'

Captain Peters sat opposite Eduard in Flinders' office, the SPs on duty discreetly silent, the gold cases still stacked against the wall where the rugs were piled.

'Rome? What about the...' Eduard hesitated, then went on, 'the consignment?'

'Ah yes. The consignment. Not your problem, really, is it?'

Peters was relaxed, confident and confiding. He leant forward and in a low voice made him an offer.

'You go to Rome, and we'll see it gets to Warsaw. In Rome you can get some rest, they'll set you up with a professor, get some education, qualify – gee, the war'll be over before you know it, then what?'

Eduard looked at this smooth, suave fellow, and decided to take one more risk.

'I'd like to see Kolanski.'

Peters' hand flew to his mouth, his face pale, his eyes blinking. To hide his confusion, he rose, muttering, ''Scuse me – I gotta pee,' and left the room.

Eduard glanced at the guards; they seemed unperturbed. Clearly they were not involved in Peters' game, whatever that might be. As he walked to the door, the 'phone rang. The guards looked up, and he looked at them, eyebrows raised, as if to say 'Not my phone – you answer it' and one of them did.

'Yeah, okay, gahdit. Sure. Hang on.'

The soldier held out the instrument.

'You Cjaikowski?'

'Yes.'

'It's your call.'

Eduard took the phone, held it for a moment, then put it to his ear. It was the voice that was in all his nightmares, harsh, ruthless, totally devoid of personal interest, uncompromising and absolute.

'I told them to get rid of you. I knew you were trouble.'

'Kolanski?'

'Leave the gold. It's not your responsibility. It's not yours.'

The line was silent, but it was not dead. He could hear breathing, light, unhurried, regular, disciplined. He jumped when it spoke again.

'Its ours now. Go to Rome.'

FOOLS' GOLD

'So, Sergeant, you've come to Sappha and back to Signals.'

'That's right, sir.'

'Good. You ex-Intelligence wallahs are always welcome, especially when you're already halfway there, so to speak.'

The officer was barely older than Eduard, but he was British, superior, knew it and used it carelessly, as of right. Temporary officers were still sergeants. Officers and gentlemen were properly commissioned.

'All roads lead to Rome, eh?'

He was beginning to irritate, but Eduard reminded himself that the Carpathian Division owed much to the Anglo-effort, even to seconded subalterns like this, so he ground his mental teeth and promised himself he would not bite the man – not yet, anyway.

'So what *can* you do?'

'Well, sir, I can kill people, blow up bridges, rob banks, and that's just a start, apparently.'

The Englishman stiffened slightly, and straightened his papers.

'Well then, let's see what can be done with you.'

The villa at La Selva was a staging post, where Bureau VI missions paused before Poland. This is where the modified Gorzow operation had waited, and this is where Eduard was sent, not long after he met Okulicki. A jeep arrived at mess headquarters, a Polish-speaking SP sought him out and together they drove off the base.

'You know the General?'

'You mean...?'

'Okulicki.'

'I've met him, once – briefly.'

'A decent man.'

Eduard said nothing, but he remembered – that was what Mikolaczek had called him; the General and he had something in common, apart from the gold.

'Where are we going?'

'La Selva,' and that was all that he said.

They drove in silence, until they reached the village, and then the villa. The SP waited while Eduard got out, then reversed, pausing to lean out and wave at the building.

'You're expected.'

As the jeep scudded away, Eduard inspected the structure. It was clearly ancient, probably mediaeval, of a strange, beehive shape. He felt his knife through his trousers, comfortably sheathed alongside his calf and tightened up in preparation. Peters perhaps? Certainly not Flinders – he was obviously an opportunist, but no traitor.

Wolski, ever the practical one, had put it simply.

'The man's a buffoon, but he's not stupid. Probably make millions after this is all over, whereas Peters...'

Johnnie had snorted.

'Peters is an arsehole, the worst kind. All smooth talk and soft smiles. I don't trust the man.'

'Especially after the ambush,' added Eduard. 'And what about Kolanski?'

Johnnie grinned.

'You've got that man on the brain. Probably a different fellow anyway, and how do you know it was him on the 'phone. Give you his name?'

Wolski had stroked his beard thoughtfully.

'Do you think we should get the stuff moved, until it's all settled – where it's going, that is?'

Eduard shook his head.

'No. Flinders may be foolish, but he's safe. These CPs can't all be in some plot or other. There's too many of them, and they're constantly changing.'

He drained his glass.

'The gold's safe where it is, for the time being. What worries me is what happens when it's moved.'

Johnnie lifted the whisky bottle, and examined it.

'Must get another one – horrible stuff, but it'll have to do. Like Flinders. But you're right.'

It was Wolski who summed it all up.

'Not a lot we can do about it – until it goes to Poland. And anyway' – he shoved his empty glass away, and leant back, seemingly relaxed, yet with his constant tension still apparent – 'it's not our business any more – we've delivered, haven't we?'

But that *was* the problem, thought Eduard, as he walked towards the villa; they had delivered, but not all the way.

Inside, the villa appeared empty. Eduard cautiously tried one door after another. The rooms were sparsely but adequately furnished, much as one might expect from a requisitioned home: scuffed armchairs, tatty tables, stick furniture, and worn rugs on paved floors. There was, nonetheless, an air of expectancy about the place, as if it somehow knew it was significant, hosting the intrepid on their way to the unknown. A door creaked, and Eduard whirled.

A slight figure stood, still, contemplating him, then moved forward, hand extended. First impression was of a wiry whip of a man, economically muscled forearms in short sleeves, khaki trews tucked into shiny brown leather high boots, hair *en brosse*, eyes shrewd and calculating behind the gold-rimmed lenses. His grip was dry, firm and brief. He pointed to the table, and drew up a chair, sat and leant his elbows on the surface, his hands together, the forefingers pointing up, the knuckles close.

'Duchnik. And you're Cjaikowski.'

Eduard smiled.

'You sent for me?'

'Indeed I did. But first, thank you, and congratulations.'

Eduard was confused, but Duchnik continued.

'You brought the gold, our gold, our country's gold. You did well. Very well. You and your friends.'

Eduard put his hands in his pockets, and relaxed against the chair. It was clear that Duchnik had more to say.

'For the time being, it's safe. Flinders is well briefed – within limits.'

Duchnik folded his arms, and his eyes left Eduard's, unfocussed as he considered carefully what next to say. Eduard sensed he was being assessed, not for his face value, but for his deeper capacities – to handle knowledge, to keep counsel, to bear burdens.

'We do have a difficulty – Peters.'

Duchnik remained immobile, arms crossed and folded, eyes searching Eduard's.

'No proof. Just signs.'

The trouble was that nobody knew when the gold could leave, or where it might go; no longer to Warsaw, for the city was now in Soviet hands, and not yet to the Armia Krajowa, for that was 'like mercury, fluid, separating, joining, ever transient, until we know the future of our country'. So it was at risk, while it lay fallow, where greed and opportunity might come together.

'What about Kolanski?'

'Who?'

'Kolanski – his name came up in the ambush, in London and, well, I thought he might be here.'

'Kolanski? The name's not familiar, not here anyway.'

Duchnik seemed troubled.

'Wait a minute. Kolanski, Kolanski, let me see. Ah yes, I do remember. Russian advisor. Polish, but attached to Zhukov's Warsaw Front – came here just before they started their putsch on the 12th – part of the delegation that talked to Okulicki, tried to stop him. Not very perceptive.'

Duchnik frowned.

'You think he's connected?'

Eduard hesitated. Should he divulge the 'phone call? Perhaps not – after all, he had no proof it was Kolanski. Better to generalise.

'I think so. London warned me against him. I'm surprised they didn't tell you.'

'London doesn't tell us everything – there is some dissimulation; Prime Minister Churchill has problems with Comrade Stalin, I believe,' and here Duchnik clenched his fists momentarily, as if he might contain the problem.

'London wants Poland left alone. Russia wants Poland. While they argue, London is circumspect.'

'Can we check? If there's a link to Peters. . .'

'Of course.'

Duchnik's arms fell away and he stretched, before putting them behind his head and, apparently decided, his head leaning slightly to one side, announced, 'I'm closely in touch with Unit Two. They're watching. When it's time, we'll move. Until then, the gold stays where it is.'

Eduard had to ask. It was the only question worth asking.

'When it does go, will we take it?'

'That I cannot truthfully say but, if it's practical, I can't think of a better team.'

At Castello Tiburtina, lately occupied by Benito Mussolini, thirty Polish soldiers took instruction from exiled academics, grateful for the chance to teach, and the tranquillity of this transitory college. Eduard sat outside, idly flicking the pages of his manual, as he watched the fountains play. It was New Year's Eve.

After leaving Ostuni, Eduard resolved to keep himself to himself. There was little pressure at Tiburtina or in Rome itself, no special need for special people. He decided to focus on learning, or at least acquiring the appearance of having learnt, to equip himself for life after war. At home, what would he find? Would he find a home, a job, his family? Best to be prepared to stand alone, as he had stood so often over the past five years.

The men who shared the castle worked in groups of their own choosing, groups that were products of experiences shared. Eduard was alone. When he tired of the tutorials, he walked the city's streets and, if it grew late, he stayed at the Polish Embassy – there was always a room for those from Bureau VI.

Time and again he was drawn to the ancient city, the nexus of Roman empire, where he wondered at the warriors who had brought wealth and built wisely, but more often he found himself wandering the banks of the Tevere, crossing the great river, across to Trastevere, and in particular, to the little cobbled piazza hard by the church of Santa Maria, where he sat, nursing a glass of frizzante, on a wooden bench against an unstable table outside the shaded ostaria opposite the church, dreaming of peace, and Cjortkow – and Sara.

To begin with, others would offer to join him, or ask him to join them but, perhaps because now the need had gone, the gaol set met, he declined, and waited until he could make his own way, alone but not

435

lonely, to shoulder his way through his thoughts, to try to make sense of his past, to construct a future vision although, as he tried to visualise that future, his thoughts inevitably gyrated, sheered, back to Kermener and to Sara.

She was vivid and wild and bright as a star in his mind's eye, and he remembered her final borrowing of the poet's words: 'He jests at scars, that never felt a wound' as he laughed and said 'We two are bound to meet again', knowing, as he said it, that his farewell was the bond of their finality. He told himself that that time was dead, and blanked it and her out with comfortable considerations, of quiet nights prefacing calm, steady days, using even skills to earn decorous domestic evenings. He thought of Audrey, and smiled sadly to himself, for there was a prospect without wild ambition, of kind union, a simple psalm of hope and charity. Always he returned to reality, to the currency of his routine day, and counted his change in the small coinage of rise, eat, work, rest, walk and think and return, to sleep, and rise again.

He preferred it thus. But New Year's Eve? That was perhaps different so, when Jerzy Osak asked him what he was doing, he said 'Nothing – what about you?' and Jerzy told him about the Alexander Club and 'I know a girl, and she's got a friend and she's beautiful' so Eduard agreed to join him.

Rome's Alexander Club was on the fifth storey. The place was seething with men of many nations and many skills, all military, a few uniformed women, rather more local ladies of, to judge by appearances, flexible virtue, and a group of younger girls. As they looked around, one of the girls approached Jerzy, slipping her arm in his and pouting up at him.

"Allo Jerzee. 'Ave you gotta drink?'

'It's a bit early for that, isn't it?' and turning to Eduard, 'This is Lucia, and over there is the friend I told you about.'

Eduard scanned the other girls.

'Which one is it?'

They stopped talking, and examined him. One said, 'It's me,' and a dark-skinned, slightly stocky girl, dressed in black, joined them.

'I'm Maria; come-sta?' and she shook his hand.

It was mid-afternoon and tea-time; to war-weary, deprived and hungry Romans, the cakes and pastries were a luxury. Maria and Lucia despatched the first platter in short order. Eduard ordered more. Before he had finished his first cup they, too, had gone. Jerzy roared with laughter.

'Feed 'em up, feed 'em up!' and he ordered double portions. Eduard ate a pastry, drank more tea, and thought he heard his name called, but was mistaken and turned back, just in time to see Maria stuffing the entire plateful of meringues, rock cakes, fairy cakes and Swiss rolls into her handbag. She caught his eye, bit her lip, then smiled decorously, and snapped it shut.

When Jerzy returned and suggested a party, the girls were like puppies, jumping up and down and squealing with delight. Eduard began to realise how naïve and natural they both were. He thought to himself: there are going to be some sorrows and many regrets for some of these girls, and resolved to treat Maria as if she was his sister.

The party was in another club, the Pegasus, where the ambience was different, with dimmed lighting, lacquered tables, music, cabaret and drink – plenty of it. By the third glass, Maria was tipsy.

They danced, close but not too close, with affection, but not lust, and he relaxed and began to enjoy the easy music, his undemanding companion, and the respite from the anxieties of Ostuni.

At midnight, there was a great deal of root-a-tooting, much ardent kissing, and some sufficiently unrestrained behaviour for the thus far self-effacing stewards to eject the rowdies. Eduard encircled Maria in the slow, soft dance that followed, and kissed her again. The lights flickered, flared, then went out.

There were one or two shouts of derision but, for most of the remaining revellers, paired off and reaching towards the end of war through fond or frantic renewal, hands on soft places or hard, the lights were not needed and the candles that sputtered into local brightness a welcome necklace on the new year's flesh.

Half asleep, slumped against one another, Eduard and Maria barely moved, as the music pulsed in humid rhythm. Eduard's mouth brushed her fine, black hair, a faint perfume of burnt musk permeating his senses. His hands held her waist and he wondered, shall I sleep with her or shall I not?, for there was no urgency, nor need, in this, the hiatus between the old and new years.

The music stopped momentarily, and he looked round the room. Of Jerzy there was no sign, and of all the others, he knew them not.

'Shall we go?'

She murmured something, then she smiled up at him, a warm, affectionate smile and said, 'I cannot go home now.'

Eduard was unsure if she meant her house was locked, her father was difficult, it was too far, or simply that her presence there, in his present care, stopped her return. Either way, he reasoned it was time to go. If they were stopped, he would say she was his wife, for soldiers' women went straight to the compound, near the Vatican. As his wife, she could stay with him, in a room at the Polish Embassy.

Outside, the streets were deserted and dark, lightless in a moonless night. They walked, hand in hand, loosely held, quiet, she dreaming, he thoughtful. He thought once more of Sara and imagined her there with him, as they strolled the streets. The matt black and battered old Fiat was almost upon them, when Eduard realised it was a taxi, hailed it and handed Maria into the musty, dusty interior.

'Ambasciata Polska.'

The cab wheezed and rattled down the Via del Corso, then suddenly stopped, the exhaust farting indefinitely. There were three military police – one British, one American, one Polish as soon became apparent when they variously demanded his papers and his purpose.

'And who's the doll?' asked the Yank.

'My fiancée.' He reacted without thinking and, as he said it, realised he meant 'my wife' but it came out unformed, as if his wife must first be engaged.

'Heard that before,' commented the Tommy, adding, 'Think it's one of yours,' to the Pole, who stuck his head inside and leered at Eduard.

'Are you sure?'

''Course I'm sure.'

'When are you getting wed, then?'

'Two days.'

'Really?'

The Pole extracted his grinning face and spoke shortly to the others. Then he pulled the door open.

'Off to the "Vatican", and then you can go home.'

There was no opportunity to argue, for the door slammed shut, and the taxi trundled off, escorted by the international trio in their jeep, down the Corso, towards the river, across the Ponte Cavour, and along the bank to the compound. The soldiers waited while Eduard grudgingly paid the fare, or 'unfair' as he put it, though neither the gaitered Britisher nor the white-helmeted Yank saw the joke.

'If she goes, I go,' he announced, belligerently but, if he hoped to stimulate anger or argument, he was disappointed, for the Pole simply rejoined, 'Suit yourself.'

They were marched into the blank, stone building, bundled upstairs, and shown into a large, bare hall. Maria slumped down in the furthest corner. Eduard sat beside her, and took her hand.

'I'm sorry about all this.'

'That's o-kay,' she said, putting her other hand over his.

'Name, rank and number?'

The man standing over them was an American, a sergeant.

'I'm a Lieutenant in Intelligence, and I want to see the CO.'

'You cin be a gin'ral in stupidity and it ain't gonna do you no good, 'cos CO ain't here.'

'Then who's in charge?'

'That's me. Now – name, rank and number.'

Eduard complied, the sergeant gave exaggerated thanks, then left them. For several minutes they said nothing, until Maria started talking.

'We soon in charge. New ruler. Papa's part of it.'

'Your father's a politician?'

'Si.'

'Jesus – oh, I'm sorry, I didn't mean to. . .'

'Iss alright – don' worry. I get home in the morning.'

438

She laid her head on his shoulder and, within minutes, was asleep. In the morning, he woke, cold, itching, hungry and thirsty, rubbed his unshaven face, and hoisted himself to his feet. For a moment, he forgot, then looked down. No Maria. Outside, the Corporal on duty told him the women had been released.

'All of them?'

'All of them.'

'What about Maria?'

'Maria who?'

He never saw her again. Two days later, the call came. Duchnik wanted him back at Ostuni.

'How well do you know Colonel Harry?'

They were in the villa, at La Selva.

'Not well. Met him in Naples, then here. Why?'

'He's vanished, disappeared, gone. No trace.'

'The cases?'

'Safe.'

Duchnik pulled off his glasses, produced a hankie and started wiping them. As he concentrated on the task, he muttered to himself. Eduard caught the name twice.

'Peters? Is he still here?'

Duchnik held the glasses at arms' length and peered through the lenses, then put them on, looping the flexible ends round his elfin ears. He regarded Eduard absently.

'Peters? Oh yes, Peters. Yes, he's still here. Why do you ask?'

'Last time we spoke, he was the prime suspect – you said he was suspect, but you had no proof.'

'Eliminated. No proof. And anyway, with the Colonel gone, he's lost his job, so I expect he'll be transferred.'

Duchnik tapped the table, jumped up and paced across the room, standing at the window and staring out before turning towards Eduard.

'I want you to do something for me.'

'Yes?'

'Forget Flinders.'

'Why?'

'Because there's another problem.'

'And...?'

'Your friend Wolski's disappeared too.'

'Wolski? I don't believe it. You think he's with Flinders? Impossible.'

'Yes, well, I agree, but the fact remains, they both went the same day, or rather, night.'

'When?'

'Two days ago.'

Eduard rose too, and joined Duchnik by the window. They both stared outside as if, by sharing the view, they might come to some joint conclusion. Eduard hit the windowsill with a closed fist.

439

'Wolski would never betray us, or his country. He's indestructible and incorruptible.'

Duchnik put a light hand on Eduard's arm.

'Then we must find him.'

'First, I want to see the cases.'

The Colonel's room was exactly as he last saw it, trophies included. Eduard checked the more obvious items; they were all still there. In any case, the guards told him, they had never relaxed their vigil. If he had removed anything, they would have known.

'The cases?'

'Exactly as they were when you brought them,' the SP Captain told him.

'I want to interview every single man.'

The Captain was not pleased. The implied slur on his command rankled, but he agreed.

'You have Unit Two on your side. Not for me to comment, though I cannot say I'm enthusiastic.'

Man after man repeated the same mantra – they worked in pairs; they changed one on one; there was never the same pair two days running; no-one left the room without authority, and that meant the Captain. Standby guards took over even when one went for a meal.

The seventh man was truculent. Eduard was beginning to experience some frustration. He put the man's attitude down to his own behaviour, and shifted tack.

'Cigarette?'

'Don't smoke.'

'Gum?'

The man took the proffered pack and thumbed a spearmint out. He handed the pack back. Eduard unwrapped the long thin sliver and pushed it into his mouth, then the pack across the table.

'Keep it.'

They both started chewing. Just like two ruminant cows, thought Eduard, and caught the man's eye. They both smiled hesitantly, then laughed.

'Where're you from?'

'Montana.'

'Tell me about it.'

As the soldier reminisced, he relaxed, recalling his Mom and his kid sister, the local hardware store, his first girl in High School and the abrupt stop war had brought to home life and cookies, undemanding study and the movies, the fields round the homestead and the family's horses.

'You should be commissioned,' Eduard observed, 'with that kind of background.'

'Nope. We're poor folk, but we're proud. Hosses fer work.'

The man stretched.

'I'll have that smoke now, if it's still goin'.'

Eduard raised an eyebrow, but said nothing about the change of habit, fishing in his tunic pocket for the spare pack he always carried, spinning it across the table.

'Sorry I haven't any matches.'

The soldier grinned and produced a zippo with a flourish, and lit up, exhaling smoke in perfect concentric rings.

'There was one thing.'

'Yes?'

'Peters sometimes stayed when we went for a slash.'

Eduard tensed.

'You mean Peters was alone here, with the cases?'

The man shook his head.

'Ner. There's always one guy with him – that's the rules. Two of us, at all times.'

Eduard sat back again. If Peters was never alone, then that was that.

'I suppose he stayed just to help out, whenever one of you wanted to pee?'

'Oh not any of us, only Martini.'

'How do you mean, only Martini? Who's Martini?'

'He's one of the squad. Came with the Colonel, same time as the Colonel, that is. Been here ever since. Has family in Rome, I believe. Father came over before the war. You know, second generation an' all that.'

Eduard leant forward, his hands clamped together out of sight, below the table.

'Let me get this right. You're saying that Peters doubled for someone whenever Martini was left behind.'

'Yeah, suppose so.'

'Bloody hell.'

'What?'

'Nothing.'

Eduard got up, and walked over to the cases, standing exactly where they were when he was last in this room, still bound and padlocked. He kicked the nearest one. It did not move.

'OK. Carry on. And thanks.'

The interview with Peters was short, explosive and inconclusive.

'Are you im-plyin' that I have anythin' to do with Flinders' disappearance?'

'No.'

Peters grunted, as if to say 'well that's that then', when Eduard said the single word.

'Martini.'

'What about Martini?'

'So you do know him?'

'Of course I do. He's one-a the guards.'

'One you shared some time with.'

'Whaddya mean?'

'You spent time alone here, with Martini.'

'Yer.'

'And the cases.'

Peters was on his feet, bristling.

'You got anythin' ter say, say it. Otherwise, shut yer goddam mouth.'

Eduard's eyebrows flickered, and he turned his back on the aide.

'Know where Flinders is?'

'No I bloody well don't.'

'Know where Wolski is?'

'Not ree-sponsible fer yer friends, Lootenant.'

'Are you a rich man, Mr Peters?'

As he said it, Eduard wheeled round, and glared at the Captain, and the Captain glared back.

'My family cud buy yers any day, Lootenant. If you've finished. . .'

Eduard gestured towards the door, and Peters went, slamming it behind him.

Martini was a short, compact man with one of the smartest uniforms Eduard had ever seen, creases in all the right places, and in some he had not seen before; pockets pleated, braid brilliant white, cap neatly 'broken', brass scintillating. The man himself could have passed for an emperor, were it not for his short stature, for his nose was truly Roman, his lips thick and sculpted, his close-shaved cheeks blue with suppressed bristle, and his eyes a fathomless black. Then, when he spoke, the impression was spoilt by the stained and yellowed teeth. Martini was already smoking by the time Eduard extracted his pack.

'You've been helping us with the cases.'

'Guardin' them, yessir.'

'No problems?'

'Nossir.'

Eduard tapped a cigarette out of the pack, stuck it in his mouth and lit it with Martini's lighter, which reposed on his pack on the table. He let the unfamiliar smoke trickle out of his mouth, and turned away for a moment to wipe away an involuntary tear.

'You know Mr Peters.'

'We all know Mr Peters, sir.'

Eduard changed the subject and started talking about Italy, and Roma, and what it must be like to rediscover your roots, and Martini relaxed and agreed, and was describing his introduction to the Citta del Vaticano when Eduard leant across and took the cigarette from his mouth, stubbing it out alongside his own, standing and announcing, 'Martini. Mr Peters is in trouble. You are in trouble. I can help you.'

The soldier stretched his neck, fingered his tie, shifted in his seat and reached for the cigarette pack. Eduard flicked it out of his reach.

'Why did you leave Mr Peters with the cases?'

'I didn' – what – howdya know...?'

'You left the room, left him alone. Why?'

'It was only at night, when everythin's-a quiet. Just for a leetle time.'

'Why?'

'I'm a-not married, you know.'

'So it's a girl?'

'Yes! Yes! Rosanne. She's-a beautiful. I hope she come's-a home with me.'

'OK. How long was he alone with the cases?'

'Oh, notta long. Five minutes. OK. Ten, well twenty max.'

The Captain relieved Martini, and charged him, despite Eduard's protestations that the man was in love with his roots, and with a girl called Rosanne. Then he sent a detachment to apprehend Peters, as Eduard argued with Duchnik.

'We must open the cases.'

'We can't.'

'Why not?'

'They are sealed. Only someone in authority, in Poland, with Government approval, can unseal them.'

'That's ridiculous. By the time they open them they may be empty. We need to find out, here, now.'

'No, and that's final, Eduard. I'm sorry. But I cannot exceed my authority.'

The guard was doubled, and inspected at random. The Captain was not taking any risks. He was not taking any prisoners either for, when the detachment returned, they were empty-handed. They did not bring Peters back.

'Has he gone?'

'No. He's dead, Captain. Shot.' The soldier paused, then added, 'His own gun. I'd say it was suicide.'

Eduard saw the Base Commander, he signalled London, he even tried to reach the Rubens Hotel to speak direct to Mikolaczek, without success. His mission master had been deposed. Duchnik reprimanded him.

'I take no pleasure in saying this, Eduard, but you are allowing your reputation for rebellion to overtake your limited authority. You are not in charge of this investigation. I am.'

Eduard stared at the little man with the gold-rimmed glasses. He stayed his wrath and responded with a false calm.

'I'm sorry. I will go and find Wolski instead. I leave the gold to you.'

It took less than an afternoon to establish that Wolski had indeed left the same day that Flinders had disappeared. He had simply told his hut mates that he was unsure when he would return. He had given no indication of his plans, destination or purpose, but it had seemed that he was in a hurry, as if he was meeting someone or, as one soldier put it, 'accompanying some other guy'.

It was that comment which Duchnik had interpreted as collusion with Flinders. It might have meant something different – that he was following 'some other guy'. Eduard decided to return to Tiburtina.

The gardener at the Castello was a fecund father. His numerous children played in the grounds, except one – Francesca. She could be seen helping her madre, in the tied cottage, and she was the draw that brought the soldiers to the terrace every afternoon, to gaze upon her charms, for Francesca was not only seventeen, but beautiful, and endowed with a prow like a Roman galley, the which many a soldier fantasised grasping as he steered her to his lusty destination. Unfortunately for the Poles seconded to Tiburtina, Francesca's father was watchful. Eduard went to Mass, and sat beside her.

It was the third Sunday of his sojourn at the Castello. The service ended, and Eduard bid the Busolinis his usual brisk farewell, when Florio tugged his sleeve. 'Stay a while. Have some gnocci and insalata with Mamita and me – and Francesca, eh?' and the old man winked. Eduard was startled, but accepted, and found himself hugging a large, cold glass of pale red Nebbiolo.

The meal progressed; the Nebbiolo flowed and flowed. Eduard sat between Francesca and one of her siblings, the diminutive Tonti, but was beleaguered by the family at large, all practising their Americo-English, while he struggled to understand snatches of rapid Italian. Francesca spoke little, but when she did, in precise, though limited English, virtually unaccented.

'Please some bread,' as she passed the basket yet again. 'Fragole from garden – straw-berr-ies.'

After the meal, father Florio shepherded the children into the garden, while Mamita busied herself in the kitchen, leaving Eduard alone with Francesca on the family couch. Eduard started to say his thank-yous but the girl pulled him down beside her, and held his hands.

'Papa like you. Say you good man. Praise God. You please him.'

Whether the girl meant Florio or the good Lord, Eduard was unsure, but he had little time to consider the question, for Francesca pulled him across her and kissed him, pushing him away as suddenly as she had grabbed him.

Breathless with surprise and the immediate impact of her body, Eduard bent forward and pretended to adjust his shoelace, to conceal his heightened state. Before he could finish, the girl's arms were about him, and she was kissing his neck, his ear, his cheek. As he struggled to constrain himself and restrain her, the door opened, and a beaming parent stood, hands clasped in beatitude.

'Ah, my son, excellente, excellente.'

Eduard twisted round to respond, but the man had gone again.

'We go walk, yes?'

None knew the Castello gardens better than the Busolinis. Francesca led the way. Florio's potting shed was well away from the homes of the former staff, tucked into a fold in the ground behind an old stone wall. Sackings were neatly stacked, as if in readiness for a consummation. Francesca closed the door, jammed a large-tined fork against it, and pushed Eduard, so that he fell onto the soft, impromptu bed.

'You help please?'

She knelt before him, indicating the bow on the neck of her dress. Eduard fastidiously untied the ribbon, and then the buttons down the back, the flowered cloth falling gently away to reveal rib and vein lightly etched beneath her fair skin. The girl untied her hair, and shook it free, to feather onto her back, then turned, and stood as her dress slid away to her feet. Eduard blinked. She knelt again, this time her bountiful breasts tickling his nose as she undid him.

It was a long and languorous seduction, as he rediscovered the innocence he might have kept, had war and prison and happenstance not decreed otherwise. In Francesca he found the natural craft of instant fidelity, and he revelled in the joy and novelty of their tender tryst.

Every Sunday they made long love, and every Sunday Eduard prayed, the more loved, the more desperately that this maiden of the moment would tire, so that he could retire with honour, but throughout, he knew that their passionate routine would one day be destroyed and there would be regret and recrimination. Yet still she loved him and still he lusted kindly after her.

The messenger from Wolski arrived in church.

The stranger sat beside Eduard, so that he was forced to close up closer to Francesca, who giggled, and put her hand on him, beneath his missal. Then the stranger left during communion. There was a note on the pew, folded. Eduard slipped it into his pocket.

Nursery love, Eduard called it, as he walked back to the castle. It was a chill January night and he shivered as he thought of Wolski, pursuing the golden chimera. Once in the main building, he made for the nearest lavatory, and sat, his feet wedged against the door. Then he unfolded the note.

'Harry's here, with friend. I'm close. The raft floats – Hedgehog.'

Eduard's eyes glittered as he read the note the second time, then glistened at the memory of the landlocked raft that came to symbolise their hopes and their fears, and the first time he saw Wolski – and Vatek – on the train to Tara. He turned the note over, and there was a crude map: a dotted line, a square, a cross, and an arrow pointing to a question mark. Underneath and underlined was the name of a town – Fivizzano.

THE GOLDEN FLEECE

Over the next few days, Eduard placed random, discreet enquiries, through Florio and through Jerzy's numerous girlfriends. Fivizzano was the wrong side of the Gothic Line. Beyond, the German Army was entrenched along the Apennines. Fivizzano was not renowned for monasteries.

Eduard discreetly visited the local church more than once, in the hope of finding the stranger who left the note, without success. He cursed Wolski for his natural economy. The man never wasted words but just this once, it would have been helpful to have more information. Clearly, Wolski had no intention of seeking help – only of letting him know he was alive, and closing on the Colonel.

As Eduard wrestled with the options – stay put and wait, or take off and follow – the decision was taken for him. His class sat final examinations, and he passed both electronics and mathematics – well. Within days he was told he would be posted – to Cupra Marittima, HQ for Signals 3 on the east coast, near Ancona and complete with aerodrome. He wondered why. Francesca was inconsolable.

That Sunday they attended Mass as usual, returned for Mamita's usual feast and, as Eduard nursed his Nebbiolo, he started to tell her, how he had passed the exams and – but that was as far as he got, for father Florio exploded with joyous congratulations, enfolding them both in his brawny arms, then scurrying off to fetch a precious bottle of spumante. He rapidly returned, bottle frothing and glasses clashing as he bunched them together and spilt the wine, glass on glass, distributing them to Mamita and Francesca, Eduard and Tonti, and every other child, even holding his own glass to baby Pietro's lips, then raising it on high with 'Noi stessi, il famiglia – benediziones, moltissimi, moltissimi!'

The effervescence gone, Florio maintained the momentum with a fresh bottle of Nebbiolo and it was only when Mamita dried her eyes and retreated to the washing up, Tonti asleep on his father's lap and Florio snoring copiously, that Francesca dragged Eduard outside, and ran before him across the gardens, behind the stone wall and into the shed. Eduard was barely through the door when she snapped off her top button, wrenched the cotton dress over her head and lunged at his belt, ripping it away, unfastening his trousers and simultaneously pushing them down with one hand and a foot as she grasped him and fell to her knees, her mouth closing on him. Exalted like her by the wine and the immediacy, Eduard's mind drained and his body took over. As his excitement rose and lust flooded his loins, he pulled away and pushed her onto the sacking, kicking aside the clothes cloying his ankles, falling on her, snaking up and down her flushed skin, licking and fingering, as her hands worked between his legs and, with a sudden excess of Anglo-speak, she shouted at him, 'Take-a me, Eduard, take-a me!'

Later, they made proper love, with Eduard's fond affection and her simple devotion and, as they lay, exhausted, replete and loosely linked, he began to explain – about war, and orders, about postings and absences, about sadness and partings, of maybes and what-ifs, about young love, and future prospect, of hope and of doubt and how much he loved her, but—

'You go away?'

'I have no choice.'

'Where?'

'North, Signals HQ.'

'I kill.'

Eduard pushed himself up onto one elbow and regarded her fondly.

'You wouldn't *really* kill me, would you?'

'Not you, I kill me.'

'Don't be silly.'

'I suiciding.'

Eduard traced a trickle of dried perspiration down her left breast; she knocked his hand aside.

'True. I kill. Under train.'

He decided to try humour.

'The railway's miles away.'

She hit him, hard, her knuckles blinding him momentarily. Eduard grabbed her hands and forced them back onto the sacks. Then he slowly, deliberately lowered himself onto her, and kissed her. She bit his lip. He licked the blood away, still pinning her down.

'Better shoot yourself.'

'No gun.'

'I have.'

At that, she stopped struggling, her hands limp, and began to weep. Eduard fumbled for his tunic, found it, and tugged a handkerchief out. Dabbing at her eyes, he spoke softly.

'Francesca, Francesca. You're beautiful, and young, and so – so enthusiastic. You are kind and generous, and a good, good friend.'

'You no love me, then.'

'You are my lover; I will never forget you.'

Then she cried, and cried, and cried, the tears racked out of her, her body shaking, her hands trembling, and Eduard soothed and smoothed her, his hands fluttering over her tremulous frame, his words flitting between her tears and, as he spoke, Francesca found her womanhood, her sobs slackened, the tears diminished and at last, she looked up at her Polishman and smiled wistfully.

'You are my lover, and I never forget Eduard.'

447

She reached up and the tip of her forefinger tracked his lips, then she embraced him, and drew him down.

'Make love one more time.'

At 11 Via Sabatini, on the second floor, Eduard's room was clean, quiet and comfortable, and it was his own, unshared. He unpacked. With three weeks' back pay in his pocket, he found food cheap and wine plentiful in the bars of Cupra Marittima. For those three weeks he lived simply, without interference, and tried to cleanse his mind of Castello Tiburtina and the Busolinis, while he wrestled with the urge to cut and run after Wolski, to find Flinders, and what he was convinced was the evaporating gold. One evening, he was struggling to translate an Italian broadsheet when there was a knock. His hand closed on his knife, and he eased the door open. The man stood back, on the landing, and spoke in Polish.

'You've been here three weeks, Lieutenant.'

'That's right.'

'What have you been doing since you arrived?'

'Nothing.'

'Why?'

'Nobody told me to do anything else.'

The man was still in the shadows. Eduard beckoned him in and stood to one side, closing the door as he passed.

'Mind if I sit?'

Eduard indicated the bed, and leant back against the door.

'Curious. Can't make you out. You wear wings, jumping badge. You're a mystery man.'

'So are you. Who are you?'

The man ignored the question.

'I see you walking from bar to bar. Are you a signalman? That's what most of them are.'

'I was.'

'You were. I see. Where are you from?'

'Rome.'

The man fiddled with his pocket, and Eduard tensed, shifting slightly so that he was sideways on. The man laughed.

'I'm not going to attack you.'

He extracted a cigarette, and some matches and asked, 'Do you mind?'

Eduard shook his head, but walked across the room, and pushed the window ajar, then sat on the single chair. The man reached inside his tunic and Eduard tensed. He unfolded the piece of paper from his pocket, and smoothed it out. After scanning it briefly, he looked up.

'There's talk of trouble at Ostuni – some Polish chap.'

He glanced again at Eduard, turned back to the paper, murmuring as he read.

'Something about missing cases.'

Eduard felt for the knife.

'A complaint about a missing signalman too. Bit vague. Some Anglo-Polish muddle, I s'pose.'

He leant back and blew a thin stream of smoke across the room.

'Complaint's signed by one of those liaison blokes – name of Kolanski.'

Eduard tensed. He gazed at him.

'Know anything about it?'

Eduard shrugged.

'Well, you wouldn't want to be in the middle of that, would you?'

Eduard shrugged again.

'So you won't mind helping us out, staying here awhile, eh?'

It was clear; he had no choice.

Eduard shook his head.

'Good. Would you like to be a workshop supervisor?'

Eduard shrugged and the man continued.

'Handling transmitters for tanks. Twenty men.'

'OK. What do I do?'

'Strip them off, count to three, say bang, then write it off.'

'Sounds simple – and pretty stupid too.'

'Not really. They're all obsolete anyway. It keeps the men busy, and you keep the records. Start tomorrow. OK?'

For three weeks Eduard supervised the systematic destruction of obsolete equipment, laboriously noting it in a ledger and not for the first time noted how the task meets the need. As he continued to worry about Wolski, he was occupied with this useless, negative, bureaucratic nonsensical 'war effort' while soldiers with half his skills and experience sweated and struggled and screamed and died in the north of the country.

The party was in a large hall, all ranks, and local girls. Eduard missed Francesca, and was tense with the boredom of his destructive days. None of the girls with whom he danced reminded him of her; they bored him too, even those who strove to please, flaunting or flirting. He excused himself mid-dance after two hours, and went into the street to escape the foetid air, the rank smoke and stale bodies. Outside, the night was cool, but not cold. He decided to walk back to number 11. As he neared the house, he glanced across at number 24. The girl who lived there had nodded once or twice, and he imagined she might fancy him; she was often to be seen, elbows on the grille outside the first-floor window, watching the passers-by.

Whenever Eduard looked up, she was contemplating him with what he liked to believe was more than passing interest. He thought he might be interested too. As he swung across towards his house, he glanced back automatically, but she was not at the window.

'Buono sera.'

She was standing against the door.

'You like a glass of wine?'

'Why not? Yes, thank you.'

She stood aside as he approached, and followed him through the door.

'Up the stairs. Mother is waiting.'

The room was shadowed, with heavy figured drapes across the chairs, baroque, carved side-tables and chests and tasselled lamps, half covered with dark folds of velvet cloth. On the table stood a bottle of Barolo and three cut-glass goblets, dully sparkling in the half light. The woman who rose to greet Eduard was strikingly handsome, stately in her bearing, with a deeply cleft gown exposing pearlescent skin, long ringlets, and arched brow above a prominent and flaring nose. Her mouth was wide and surprisingly diffuse in such otherwise sculpted features. Her beringed hands were slender and her nails perfected with almost black varnish. She seemed hardly old enough to be her daughter's mother.

'Buongornata, even if it is the late night-time.'

Her English was immaculate and, when her daughter spoke, it was clear that hers was too.

'You will take some wine?'

Eduard inclined his head, and waited to be invited to sit.

'We have not been introduced.'

'Ah, si. I am Elsa, and this is my mother Elsevira.'

They solemnly shook hands, the mother first.

'Please be seated.'

Conversation flowed – the war, politics, the ridiculous self-styled Il Duce, the barbaric Prussians, what was it like in the Polish Army; one had seen dreadful sights, but yours must have been a far worse war. And so on. The Barolo was quickly dry, and another was brought. The third coincided with the deep, unhurried chimes of an ormolu clock at which Elsevira exclaimed, 'One o'clock. Time for bed.'

She looked at Eduard.

'Eddie. You don't mind if I call you Eddie?'

Eduard blinked.

'Eddie is not capable of climbing those stairs, down here, or up there. He shall sleep here – but not with Elsa.'

She wagged a mocking finger, and led the way onto the corridor and up the narrow stairs.

'We have two rooms. This one's yours. Elsa can sleep with me.'

Via Sabatini became Eduard's counterpoint to the ennui of the workshop. He admitted to himself that Elsa was the principal attraction, although the food was good and the wine superlative. The girl was a more sharply defined version of her mother, with one difference – her lips were slender, her mouth defined and as meal followed meal, and he watched the morsels move beyond those lips, the more he wanted to taste them for himself.

Each evening, Elsevira was gracious, but ever watchful. On the fourth evening, he found himself beside Elsa, for her brother had come to visit, the seating plan revised. As he reached for his glass, he felt a movement, then a flutter in his pocket. Elsa's hand. On the fifth evening, it happened again; this time he had cut the pocket out with scissors; the lack of material met a lack of inhibition, and Eduard felt himself blush as he maintained deep discourse with the brother while, as in a *conte drolitaire*, there arose that which was not called upon.

After supper, it was the habit of the household to remain at table, reducing the warring world to specifics, building blocks of futures, and passing judgement on the dramatis personae of the endgame, especially in Italy. Elsevira was a woman of conviction, strengthened by her missing husband's devotion to 'la resistenza'. Eduard learnt that Aurelio had been the town's youngest mayor, had organised the saboteurs and informants who harried the Fascisti, and latterly the Germans, and had left on a murky mission in Perugia, never to return. Her teenage son Lorenzo was by contrast a diffident young man, of slender build, fine features and thick, straight hair which fell across his left brow to give him the semblance of a posed model.

Eduard wondered as he watched his elegant gestures if he had inherited his mother's style without her substance. At midnight Lorenzo made his excuses, retiring to 'Eddie's room', but mother and daughter continued indomitable, glass for glass, and Eduard felt his control slipping as Elsa's hand wreaked delicate havoc and his own occasionally slipped between her knees. When Elsevira left the room for a third bottle, Elsa's hand burrowed and his rose between her thighs, as they resisted the temptation to turn to one another, until it overcame their caution, and they kissed.

'I think Eddie is now too drunk to travel across the street.'

Eduard mumbled an apology for his behaviour, their hands swiftly withdrawn, and Elsevira chuckled.

'I am glad to see you are a normal young man, Eddie.'

She raised the bottle.

'One for the night?'

Considered dialogue gave way to sporadic comment as the wine, the hour and the awareness generated by the break, the kiss and Elsevira's return inhibited them, and Elsa asked her mother, 'Where will Eddie sleep?'

Elsevira cocked her head to one side, looked penetratingly at her daughter, and replied, 'With us, of course.'

So it was arranged. When she was ready to retire, Elsevira disrobed, made herself comfortable, and called her daughter. Then Elsa told Eduard to wait until he was called, and disappeared. Five minutes later Eduard heard his summons. The door was open, but the room was dark. He stood, waiting for his eyes to become accustomed to the shadows and the faint wisps of fitful moonlight through the shutters.

'There's a screen over there – you can undress behind that.'

Self-conscious in his baggy pants, but nothing else, Eduard lifted the covers.

'No! You can sleep on top – it's not cold, and there is a blanket anyway.'

Elsevira lay on the far side, on her back, eyes closed. Beside her Elsa appeared asleep, on her side, facing Eduard, one hand outside the satin counterpane. Eduard lowered himself gently onto the edge, and drew the blanket up to his chest. He lay, eyes open, staring at the dim recesses of the high ceiling, wondering if he would ever sleep.

Eduard jumped. The room was thick with darkness. Her hand was on him. He could hear Elsevira's breath, deep and steady. Elsa's lips were against his ear as she whispered, 'Get out of the bed, onto the floor.'

He pushed the blanket down carefully, every rustle like scraping dishes, and eased himself out of the bed.

'You can get back now – without those terrible pantaloons.'

She was lying on the covers now and, as he climbed cautiously back, she drew the blanket across them. She, too, was naked. It was, by definition, careful sex, caring and achieved with care. When it was done, the blanket ballet was reprised. In the morning, Elsevira was awake and dressed when Eduard woke, alone in the bed.

'Would you like some coffee?'

He felt profound guilt, yet simulated innocence, telling himself it was not right to abuse his hostess's hospitality and trust. Yet, at supper the next evening, he felt again a questing hand, and knew that a small habit was forming, which would grow because he wished it to, despite himself.

On the seventh day, there was Mass. Elsevira and Lorenzo dressed for the occasion, in black. Eduard excused himself and returned to number 11.

Drawn to the window, he looked across, and watched as mother and son, arm in arm, processed down Via Sabatini, until they were out of sight. The low whistle drew his eyes back to number 24. Elsa leant on the grille, and her eyes seemed to glitter. She put a finger in her mouth and drew it out, slowly. Then she disappeared.

Every Sunday became a day of zest and frenzy, as if there could be no more Sundays, no more erotic evenings and no more surreptitious rendezvous beneath the careful blanket. It was perhaps because of the restraints of their nightly endeavours, Eduard reasoned in the hopeless throes of attempting to tell himself why he was doing what he was doing despite his best intentions and worst imaginings, that their Sunday couplings were so intense. In so thinking, he neatly sidestepped the real issue – the need and the novelty, the insidious addiction to physicality enveloping his days.

Only when he thought of Sara did he jolt upright, once during the midst of a close coupling in that quiet bedroom, so that Elsevira stirred, Elsa shrank away, and his desire evaporated. So he tried not to think about Sara, and to remind himself that he was single, strong, young, uncommitted and transient. He owed nobody justification 'except yourself' he told himself.

His addiction intensified, funding excuses for suppers at number 24, Sundays with Elsa, and casual attendance at the workshop, for he became tired more often, especially on Mondays, and throughout those suppers, he was conscious of the not-so-older woman, regarding him directly with those penetrating eyes, and reminding him nightly that he could 'undress behind the screen' as if it was an injection of desire. Eduard sensed that Elsevira understood his addiction, and supplied the drug at arm's length.

Early one morning, Elsa asleep beside him, Eduard drew with difficulty away from a dream into the dark reality of the room, the afterimage clinging to his inner eye, as he felt a hand on his face. 'Shhh,' and another hand felt for his and drew him slowly, inexorably from the bed. He rolled onto the floor, and pulled the blanket down with him, then felt those diffuse lips upon his own, mouths merged, tongues entwined. The tapered talons flicked against him as she guided him, and he was taken unto her, as she knelt over him. Eduard's being was entirely absorbed, as he began to learn new needs and requirements.

Suddenly he was called to Rome for consultations. Three weeks' intensive planning to pierce the Gothic Line involved the Division, and Eduard's skills and experience and training were focussed on possible infiltration behind the lines, to soften the supply chain, inhibit retreat and bring the Germans to their knees in final submission. Throughout, Eduard was stretched like a bass wire, taut and tensioned, battling through the questions and resolutions, the intricate creation of drop plans and combat scenarios, all the while yearning and physically straining for the sisters – for now he found them almost indistinguishable, mother and daughter, thirty-something, nearly twenty, two thirds of his entire being.

As never before, he wanted. He orchestrated his return in his feral daydreams, wolfing down Elsa's body, then sated, turning in renewed frenzy to Elsevira. He determined to return on a Sunday, to feast on flesh, the quest for Wolski suspended, his doubts about the gold rammed tight into the recesses of his inflamed mind.

Spring brought rural renewal; Elsa's demands intensified, and Elsevira took to calling at odd afternoon hours at number 11. Eduard's addiction was now absolute. When he was not directly involved, he was either exhausted or asleep. He began to long for some respite, yet could not halt or alter the evolution of his habit. Light-headed, he would sometimes fantasise about the next session as the last one finished. Relief came in an unexpected form.

The tank team had long since ceased stripping transmitters, and was engaged in testing equipment for the front. Eduard spent half-days checking and signing off, wishing once more he could take up the quest for Wolski, and once and finally check the gold. He was leaving when the telephone rang – a rare occurrence.

'Cjaikowski.'

'Duchnik. Time to go, Eduard.'

'Go? Go where?'

'To Tiburtina.'

There was a static thrum on the line and for a moment, Eduard thought Duchnik had gone. Then the voice returned, metallic, expressionless.

'There's been a development at this end. Tell you when you get here.'

'Where's "here"?'

'Oh, didn't I say? Sorry. La Selva.'

The same villa, the same room. Duchnik did not get up when he came in. Instead he waved at a seat on the other side of the table, and stared at his fingernails, as if they were somehow offensive to him. Then he stared at Eduard.

'I have a problem.'

He looked again at his fingernails, as if they required instant attention, execution perhaps. He was clearly displeased.

'A certain Florio called.'

'Oh yes?'

'Not a pleasant man.'

Eduard imagined the normally ebullient Florio when he had discovered Eduard's departure, or defection as he doubtless saw it. An angry Florio would not have pleased Duchnik.

'Wanted to see you. Refused to talk to me, except to be somewhat abusive about renegade Poles who seduce Italian maidens.'

Eduard sat.

'You surely didn't bring me here to talk about furious fathers.'

'No I didn't. Florio had a message for you. Has a message for you.'

'So?'

'From a stranger, and he wouldn't say what it was. Only to you. He insisted.'

I'll bet he did, thought Eduard.

'I don't think it is a sensible idea for me to see Signor Busolini.'

'I'm not asking you for an opinion. I'm telling you.'

Duchnik was up and striding across the room, back and forth, clearly agitated.

'I think this is about the gold.'

The gold, thought Eduard; I wondered when we would get round to that.

'I thought the gold was safe.'

'Of course it's safe, but we need to know what happened to Flinders, with Peters dead.'

'And you think this message might have something to do with that?'

'I know it does. Florio said it was a message from "Eduard's friend".'

'Wolski? You know where he is?'

'No I don't. But I believe Florio does.'

Eduard insisted on seeing Florio at La Selva, alone, refusing point-blank to travel to Tiburtina. Threats of charges, even court martial, availed Duchnik not at all. Eduard put it simply. 'You cannot charge me, since I have done nothing wrong, and have not refused orders. And you cannot order me to go to a civilian house to see the father of an ex-girlfriend. You'd be a laughing stock.'

He heard the jeep skid to a halt outside the villa, and went to the door to greet the gardener. Florio clambered out of the dusty vehicle and stood contemplating his lost son-in-law as the jeep backed up, and the driver called out, 'I'll wait over there, in the shade.'

The big chest heaved, the sigh a whole volume of regrets and resignations. Then the arms spread wide, and he advanced, enfolding Eduard in a great embrace, pushing him away, enfolding him again, then taking his arm.

'We go walk, my frien'.' Then softly, 'Vada, vada.'

They stepped down into the unkempt gardens of the villa, and Eduard wagged his hand at the ragged vines and writhing weeds.

'Sorry about this – can't get good servants these days.'

Florio guffawed, and slammed a great hand on Eduard's back.

'That's my good frien'.' He looked sidelong at Eduard, adding, 'We missed you. She missed you. She still misses you.'

Eduard linked arms with the gardener.

'I know. And I miss her. But it's not possible, Florio, not possible. Really. It's a war. I'm not. . .' He struggled for the right words. 'I'm not the answer, not the right person, not the right time.'

He pulled the older man round to face him.

'Florio. I love you all, but I am a soldier.'

They descended overgrown steps, grassed and mossed, until they reached a wild orchard, where they found a broken seat. Eduard wedged it against an ancient apple tree, and they sat, companionably, in short silence.

Then Eduard asked, 'You have a message for me?'

Florio dug into the pocket of his worn linen jacket, and produced a scrap of paper.

'Same stranger, in church. Francesca take it. Tells me. I know about gold – she tell me that too.'

Eduard was startled. He could not recall telling Francesca about the cases, but then, when a man's with his woman, he sometimes forgets what he says, even if it is supposed to be a secret, especially if it is supposed to be a secret. Secrets, after all, stitch together fond intercourse.

The paper was similar to its predecessor. The same sketch-plan, same word underlined – Fivizzano – and the message: 'Harry's here. Friend's gone. Raft's sinking – Hedgehog.'

Eduard folded the note, and pulled the small rucksack over his head. He undid the buckles, and pulled out the bottle and two glasses. He pulled away the foil, thumbed the cork, and the wine sprayed them both. He poured two glasses, handed one to Florio and stood.

'Quaccheros.'

'Quaccheros.'

This time Eduard succeeded. He went over Duchnik's head, talked to Bureau VI in Rome, who relayed his message to London. There it reached Teichmann and, when Teichmann had finished, Rome agreed the urgency of finding Wolski and Flinders. Eduard was instructed to stand by.

The drop was difficult. Fivizzano was close to enemy lines, in the Tuscan hills. They flew up the west coast, turned in near La Spezia, and tracked between the mountain ranges, where radar could not reach them.

'Only one pass,' warned the pilot, as Eduard readied himself, jumped, and dropped between two wooded slopes in a sandy valley, high in the hills. He rolled across the sparse grass, and came to rest against a pile of straw. This time there were no partisans to greet him.

Eduard detached his harness, and rolled the 'chute into as small a parcel as possible, and stowed it beneath some straw. Then he started walking, first along a rough path, then a red-soil track, and finally a pitted road. He scanned the roadside until he saw the land falling away, and a series of wooden rails.

Leaning over, he found what he sought – some large boulders, and swung himself down and under the overhanging highway. Once ensconced, he took off the coveralls, stowed the essentials in his pockets – handgun, map, emergency rations, and a small medical kit – checked his old knife, and settled down to wait for dawn.

Sunrise over the hills was spectacular, spreading a roseate backlight across the silky mist that rose from the valley. He could almost wash his face with the moisture suspended in the air. He started walking to Fivizzano.

The town emerged alongside a straight approach road, tumbling to his left, and he swung off it onto a winding path that struggled down the overgrown slopes to the backsides of houses strung along the old city walls. There he paused, to take his bearings. Early traders were setting up stalls, the church bell rang twice, and sundry women in universal matt black, hair coiled or scarved, walked the streets, exchanging greetings.

He paced himself, walking unhurriedly, but with seeming purpose to avoid undue notice, along the cobbled street to the Piazza Medicea. Alongside the church tower, he noticed a small bar, with three elderly men sitting outside, sipping muscat. He walked past them, and past the church and the hotel next door, into the upper square, where he stopped, leant against a concrete post and casually extracted and unfolded Wolski's note. The little sketch-map made sense now. The church in the square, and the cobbled street: they were all there in embryo, and the dotted line pointed straight at – the bar.

Shading his eyes from the rising sun, now slanting directly across the square, casting deep shadows, Eduard walked towards the bar. The three old men paused in their gossip, and one raised his hand in greeting: 'B'guorno forestiero,' and Eduard responded, 'Buon'guorno signore,' without pausing, entered the dark portal and hesitating only a second to take bearings, moved down the passage alongside the counter, into the back room.

A rotund woman in tight black, stretched across her seamless embonpoint, her arms dimpled and her chins numerous, looked up without fear or alarm. 'B'guorno, straneo.' Eduard smiled at her, swung his small rucksack down and onto the table, and replied, 'Buon'guorno, madre.'

She laughed, and put down the pestle with which she was beating small seeds. 'I am not mother, but you are stranger.' She pulled her tight dress down over her slabbed hips, and waddled across the room, knocking on an inner door. 'Caro, another stranger to see you,' and turning to Eduard, 'Sit down,' pulling a cup from a shelf. 'Caffe?' and, not waiting for an answer, she poured the slick, sweet liquid into a small, conical cup, handing it to him with a smile.

The back door creaked open, leaning out from its one good hinge, and the patrono bent his head to enter the room. He was unusually tall, almost skeletal, his cheeks sunken and seamed, his bald head ruched, ears tufted, and his mouth a crooked line, eyes almost lost behind drooping folds. He folded himself up and into a chair, his brown vest and trousers puffing dust as he settled, reached behind him to the shelf and poured himself a cupful, took a preliminary sip, and contemplated Eduard without comment.

The woman battered the mortar, and the men sat, drinking. Eduard reached into his pocket and fished out the two notes. He unfolded them, and placed them on the table, side by side, smoothing them out, then calmly, slowly turned each until they were facing the patrono. He was motionless. After a moment, he raised his cup, drained it, set it

457

down, and looked down at the notes. He touched neither. Then he looked straight at Eduard.

'Cotto. Casa del Monaco.'

Eduard nodded, gathered the notes, folded them, and replaced them in his pocket. In careful Italian he asked, 'Where is the house of the monk? Where is Cotto?'

The patrono rose, slapped his pants, raising a cloud of dust, which the woman waved away without complaint, moving her mortar beneath a handful of black dress, and pointed to the back. Eduard finished his coffee, muttered 'Grazie' and followed. The door led to another passage, narrow, of seeping stone, which fell downwards to an outer door, where an ancient motorcycle was propped against a broken concrete post.

The patrono turned a switch, pumped and pressed, then stepped violently on the pedal, and it fired instantly. He stepped across the frame, and sank down onto the tank, indicating the wired basket carrier behind. Eduard doffed his coat, folded it and fastened it with his belt, before straddling the flimsy 'seat'. With two feeble farts and an abrupt retort, the 'bike lurched into movement.

The road to Cotto was narrow, winding and precipitous, clinging to the hillside as it felt its way from town to country to comparative wilderness across tumbling stream and nauseating gorge, the crude bridgework wooden and tremulous. After half an hour, the patrono lifted an arm and pointed, and Eduard saw the outline of structures against the sun.

They clattered over cobbles, under a stone arch, through a narrow corkscrew access, past the static stone water tank, where already village women were walloping their clothes, and down a corrugated stone track by crumbling hovels into a small paved area, alongside the church.

The red clay-tiled rooves baked in the morning sun. The mellow stones sank into shadows, resting from the heat, but the church rose above the simple dwellings and the small, open-ended stocksheds, a masonry monster, gabled, pedimented, arched and arrogant, its copper dome gleaming with catholic assurance beneath its cupola, crowned by its own mini-dome; four pilasters flanked the door and the rounded apse hosted a single bell tower. Eduard was impressed. Close to the church on the tower side, a four-storey foursquare villa sat on the hillside, overlooking groves and plantings.

The patrono stopped the 'bike, and twisted in his saddle. He inclined his head towards the villa: 'Casa del Monaco.' Eduard ached. He rose with some difficulty, stretched, and collected his coat. He stuck out his hand. The patrono regarded it and him, nodded to himself and without comment or gesture, wheeled and started back up the corrugated street, Eduard's 'Grazie' lost in the puffballs and flatulence of the vanishing 'bike.

The villa was shuttered. As Eduard started clambering down the narrow steps to one side, the bells started – four dissonances, striking and clashing the hour. His heart pounding, he looked up at the tower. On a narrow wired walkway between tower and dome, he saw a figure. It waved, then vanished through an invisible door.

Eduard stepped inside the church. It was cool and spacious but, before he had an opportunity to inspect the altar, a small door opened, and a cassocked figure emerged, its back to him as it bent to secure the lock. Eduard waited. The priest turned.

'H'ow you-all, Ed-ooard. Sure glad ter see yew.'

Flinders led the way to the villa, and inside, ushered Eduard to a wooden bench, with integral counter. Eduard looked about him. The room was sparsely furnished. There were no signs of Flinders' entrepreneurial kleptomania. Flinders passed him an earthen pot. Eduard tasted it.

'Good ole-fashioned lemonade,' explained the Colonel.

He undid the black belt, loosened the cassock, and hitched it up.

'Goddam uncomfy, this heah, but ah'm kinduvva recluse in Cotto – sortuvva saint – browut some sunshine to theah lives.'

They sat through the morning, ate a simple lunch, then through the afternoon as Flinders unfolded his story. It started with the despatch from London, the one that told him to expect three Poles, with a consignment bound for Warsaw, and to make all necessary arrangements.

'Then Kolanski came. I don' like that fellah.' The renegade Pole seemed to know more about the consignment than Flinders.

'But he's one-a yower people, so I thouwut he's o-kay.'

Peters was Kolanski's sidekick, ostensibly his American minder – 'Ivy League arse-hole, know whaddah mean?'

Then the cases came, and the guard was set, and Peters 'sorta took over' and 'Kolanski said he wuz gonna go on ahead and kinda sort things out foh the drahp.' They waited until Eduard and Wolski and Johnnie had left, then Kolanski returned. 'He was kinda nice, alluvva sudden.'

It was a simple scam.

Kolanski assayed the Colonel's hoard of 'antiquities' and made him an offer, an outstandingly good offer, on condition.

'On conditiona what?' asked Harry and Kolanski explained.

So Colonel Harry had accepted the offer, some now, most later, in Swiss bank accounts – he had the number, he had checked, it was there – on condition he left the guard detail to Peters, and 'got the hell outta there'.

The third condition was the toughest. He had to go where they could not follow – behind German lines. Kolanski would help him, and he had to stay where he went until the war was over – or the Swiss would move the money, back to Kolanski. He checked that too, and it was true: a legally enforceable currency transfer if he was not where he was supposed to be – the monk of Cotto and, to reinforce the point, Kolanski arranged for his stipend to be paid through the bank, at Fivizzano, half to him, half to the church and village of Cotto, in his, Flinders' name.

'So when d'ya guess this'll be through? I ain't plannin' to stay heah all mah life.'

Eduard laughed, and told him that the Gothic Line was bending, and by May it should be broken. After that, who knows? Not long, but this year, surely. Then Eduard turned to the other matter.

'Where's Wolski?'

'Is that your guy with the beard?'

'That's right.'

'Not far behind me. I guess he snooped around a bit, and you-all know how it is – someone hollered when they shouldn't, an' he was heah 'fore yew cud say "Colonel Harry".'

'And now? Where is he now?'

'Strange guy. Talked nahn-stahp abowut his dowter. Said he'd send a friend but nuthin' else, ef ah gave him parta mah winnin's, so ah did.'

'You gave him money?'

'Nah. Gave him gold.'

Eduard choked on his drink, and got up hurriedly, coughing and spitting until the Colonel handed him a glass of water. He gulped it down and asked incredulously, 'Wolski. Took the gold?'

'Nah. Only jokin'.'

On 27 April partisans killed Mussolini and two days later the Germans in Italy surrendered. Eduard left Cotto for Ostuni. There he was met by Duchnik.

'You've got your wish.'

'My wish?'

'The cases. They're to be opened.'

'When?'

'As soon as Colonel Teichmann arrives.'

They stood in a semi-circle – Duchnik, Teichmann, the Base Commander and the SP Captain. With an irony that Eduard admired, Martini was marched in and ordered to break open the first case. As the padlock snapped, he sliced the bands with his bayonet, then knelt and undid the hasps. He lifted the lid. Inside lay row upon row – of dull golden bars. Duchnik smiled triumphantly.

Eduard thought: what happened to the paper, the seals, the coins?

'That's not right,' he said.

Teichmann did not even look at him as he snapped, 'I know. No paper, no seals – and no dollars.'

Teichmann tapped Martini's shoulder.

'Hand me that.'

The soldier passed the bayonet across and Teichmann crouched on his haunches before the case. He brought the bayonet up and then brought it down in a swooping curve. It sank into the first bar.

'Jesus Christ, it's lead.'

'Yes, Eduard, it's lead. You were right.'

Teichmann ordered Martini to break open all the remaining cases. They were the same. He turned to Eduard and softly said, with a terrible regret, 'The gold has gone.'

In Rome I did somewhat as the Romans do. I returned to Tiburtina, but Florio was gone, and with him Francesca and all her siblings. I saw my time out there, in a world of dreams. My war was done, my rage removed, my gold was gone, my loves diminished but not forgotten.

I met the Baroness at the lido, on the beach, or rather, in the sea, about one hundred metres off the beach. Skin's slippery in salt water, but none the less tasty for that. There were those little cabins for changing, and it did not take long for us to change into something simpler – nothing. She would insist on wearing this funny little hat, and she liked to play around under the umbrella in the afternoon sun. Great fun. She called herself the Baroness, she was married to a surgeon, twice her 30 years, and always operating – in Roma. Others called her Signora Catarina. I called her Caro. We had mushrooms back at Castello Tiburtina and all sorts of fruits of the soil. It was a time of vacuum, and we were vacuous, in the nicest possible manner.

In fact, it was Caro's manners which made it so much the better. Sex is always pleasant when it's courteous. Noblesse oblige and all that.

The Baroness cured me. My addiction could never survive pleasantry, especially in a cute little hat, under an umbrella. I have never been back to Italia, and now it's too late, but I sometimes sit in my mind's eye in that square in Trastevere and recapture the ambience, careless days, Caro's courtesy – and the conundrum, of what happened to our gold.

PEACE

SOLIDARITY

It was that time in the morning. I lay there and I dreamt, on and off, the dream rewinding, repeating familiar scenes – or were they just fantasies, memories revisited time and again in that other world, or perhaps a different reality in the half-light between sleeping and waking, semi-conscious daydreams, woven into the real world?

They seemed real enough, the grasses waving as I ran through them, away from the Seret towards the mountains, where the wild birds sailed on the summer winds and the shadows of Rosalia's horses rippled silently...

For some Poles back from the war, like Eduard, the reality was Hodgemoor Camp. The huts in the Buckinghamshire beechwoods were concrete, and damp with green slime in the dark corners, hangovers from wartime need, good only for housing DPs – displaced persons, who should have gone home, now the war was over.

These were the same Poles who had fought at Anzio, in the Battle of Britain, at Arnhem, for Monte Cassino and with SOE. Remnants from havoc, holocaust, ghetto and gulag, they were denied their homeland by its Communist masters.

Some Poles caught the eye of a local reporter, and their plight became a scandal, and the scandal a cause, and soon council houses were offered to those who qualified.

Eduard decided to qualify, to become an Englishman. With his small skills, he reasoned, if he worked hard, he could make a living, for already he was 'that Pole who can fix your radio'. Demobbed, he asked Teichmann for help and Teichmann did his best, but the process was painfully slow. He also enquired at the Red Cross for Audrey, and eventually he found her.

They married – Audrey Richardson to Edward Tudor, who plucked his new name from schoolboy memories of English history; just the right side of grand, a label of respect. Soon there were two children – and a council house. That might have been that, but for Eduard there were still restless echoes of home. He missed Cjortkow, he missed his family and, most of all, he missed his small mother, Rosalia.

He tracked her down – to Mombasa, to an Anglo-Indian family whose cousins had cared for her in the foothills of the Himalayas, which she had somehow reached from Afghanistan, a cottonseed blown on the currents of war. He scoured his savings, borrowed from the bank, took Audrey's insurance, shipped to the big toe of Empire, and brought her back. Three generations lived in the neat semi in a leafy road on the flank of a Chiltern hill, and Edward worked for a local tradesman.

He was well rewarded by the customers, many of them women, for they all loved Edward Tudor, and he loved them. The children grew and were gone, the marriage diminished and died, and so did Rosalia; Edward moved out. He yearned for Poland, but the nearest he could get to his beloved Cjortkow was a British memorial to lost comrades, where he stood with Johnnie, gazing through the mortal stone at their infinite memories.

He befriended a German, a Jewish entrepreneur, interned for the duration and, like Edward, now naturalised, with a prosperous pencil factory. They went gambling together, yet they made an odd couple – the German Jew who seemed to revel in his losses and the Catholic Pole who had nothing much to lose. Edward would stand and wave when the German's golden Rolls slid into the night, and silently wonder what happened to *his* gold?.

He tried to reach Teichmann again, but all he got was 'Teichmann? Never heard of him' or dark warnings and 'Remember you signed the Official Secrets Act'.

He was talking to the wrong people. Britain had sped the gold on its way and that was that – just another tiny rivet in the war machine. Now the war was long over there were more serious concerns than some long-lost consignment that might never have been, and a crazy Polishman, who should understand how lucky he was.

Johnnie had made a new life in London and, from time to time, they met in the West End, to share what passed for vodka, which they both agreed was 'crap potato juice'. Sitting in the bar of a Soho drinking club, Edward contemplated the slim little thing at the table next to them. He wondered if she might be worth the effort, and if that really was auburn hair, and would he find it elsewhere and if he did, should he kiss it or simply ignore it and plough the furrow notwithstanding, when Johnnie suddenly said, 'I wonder what happened to Colonel Harry?'

Edward looked sharply at him, drained his glass, and closed his eyes, his mind wired to Fivizzano, and Cotto, and the Casa del Monaco, and the poverty and peasantry under the shadow of its copper dome and dissonant tower, as he too wondered for the millionth time what had happened to the false priest and his commission from Kolanski. And that set him to wondering what had happened to Kolanski, which started him off yet again to wondering about what had really happened to the gold, and this time he told himself 'I really must find out'. Aloud, he said, 'We must find out.'

The trail was cold, overgrown beyond recognition, newly surfaced with successive priests and completely untraceable paymasters. Where to start? There was only one live thread in the rotten tapestry of deceit and error. Colonel Harry was paid through a Swiss bank account. It must therefore follow that Kolanski had used the same medium to convert his bullion.

It was unlikely that his name would rise like some renewed Dracula from the long-dead records, or that Flinders would still be Flinders. Swiss bank accounts were virtually impenetrable but, and it was a potentially useful but, Edward had a faint if fortuitous link.

Dog Haagen and Jools Bosch had joined forces; their combined skills, honed in and out of combat, had taken them into Wall Street where, to their surprise, they went entirely above board and together built a fortune.

It was an American friend of Audrey who had observed 'Met a man the other day who said he knew some Poles in the war. Small world ain't it?' at which Edward had laughed and said 'I think a lot of you Yanks met a lot of us Pollacks in the bloody war' and was about to offer him another scotch when he added 'Funny name – Jewels, or something like that' and suddenly Edward believed in destiny.

When they met, Johnnie was there too. 'Where's Wolski?' was Dog's first question and, since no-one knew, the next was 'And whatever happened to that sonnuvabitch Harry Flinders?' They could only shake their heads. Jools exploded. 'Well yoh must know where Kolanski's at? After all, he gaht the gold.' So Edward said about the Swiss bank and Jools looked at Dog and Dog looked at Jools, and they ordered another bottle, and Jools smiled, tapping his nose. 'Member what ah tole yoh? Ain't nuttin' cain't be done, if yoh knows wheah ter look.'

It took several months, by which time Edward had consigned it to the dustbin of old friends' kindness, wanting to help, other things intervene, 'ah meant ter do that; gee, cain't do everthin'', when the 'phone rang. It was Dog.

'Found yer man. Least, think we hev. They's this CollinsCorp. Big deal. Very big deal. Global. Mines, steel, shipping, lottsa third world stuff. Pretty tight op-er-ray-shun.' Edward asked, 'Can we prove anything?' and Dog said, 'I guess if yer seed him, yer might rekkernise him, 'cept ain't nobody seed him, no photos, nuthin', but the foundin' feyther wuz a guy called Kolanski, and it all begun in fowty-six – with Swiss bucks.'

And there it rested – until Edward went to Cracow.

At last, his visa had come through and Johnnie and he decided to drive across Europe – to Cracow, for Cjortkow was too far, the wrong side of the 'new' border, and he had no wish to risk his memories. Brother Frank was in Cracow, where father Jozef once drilled the decencies into his policemen.

They met in the cathedral, by the tomb of King Kazimierz. There for a moment they stood in silence. Frank looked old, Edward's senior by several years, and scaled further into age by the hard waters of occupation, oppression and despair. He looked as Jozef had looked, that day they brought him back from prison.

They moved into one another's arms, merged the Cjaikowskis past and present. Johnnie watched them for an instant, then turned away. Then together they walked out of the building to the market square and made for the Redolfi, with its apt Swiss connotations, and ordered a really Polish coffee.

They talked of family and of Edward's return and, as they did, Edward for the first time realised what the deaths and the captivity, love's links broken and all the warring, had achieved. After so many years of wanting, of craving, of seeking, he was no longer part of his own dream. He was truly displaced, neither of Poland nor yet of England, nor ever would be of either, except in longing, in memory, in everyday survival. He told Frank he would like to buy somewhere, a small space on Polish soil, so he could attempt a recreation of his Polish persona in his own time, apart and alone.

Edward bought a summer cabin, a wood-walled forest home in the hills, not far from the ancient city, and then he and Johnnie went back to Britain.

Before they left, Frank introduced them to the cousins, and they produced tickets for the Szymanowski Philharmonic Hall, where the Cracow State Orchestra was in concert. Edward saw her immediately, young, far younger than him, with that Slav bone structure, that high-cheeked, high-browed look, softened by the blur of youth, long before cousin Tadeusz pointed her out with understandable pride – his daughter, poised to play.

As the music soared, Edward held his breath for what he knew would be her solo, the sweet song of the Sara of his dreams. Afterwards they were introduced and, as she took his hand, she knew too. He took her back to England.

He took something else back too – a poster for Polish resistance to the Communist state, for Solidarity, and its bright red and gold and black badge.

Johnnie had just left Edward when the 'phone rang. Jools was in Geneva at one of those conventions where money meets money and people change hands; rumour had it that the founder of CollinsCorp was dead or dying. There was talk of change, developments, opportunity, money to be made. Edward should find the means, buy shares, attend the annual meeting.

Edward protested. He had no means. Jools laughed, reminded him that he might not have the means, but he knew the goddamn way, and wired him a thousand dollars. The meeting was in London in Park Lane, at the Dorchester.

There Edward met a man whom, in another place, he might have killed.

465

'My name's Collins, Chris Collins.'

He had stepped down off the platform, to mingle with the shareholders. Edward watched as the man brushed through jostling groups. He stopped in front of him, smiled, held out his hand. Edward felt nothing, his mind barren except for the second-hand thought that one read about moments like this.

'Your name's Kolanski. You're your father's son.'

Collins still smiled.

'Cjaikowski – I read your name on the list. I've heard that name on and off all my life. Let's start again.'

He gripped Edward's arm, ushered him through the babbling crowd, smiling left and right, until they were alone, in a small side room.

'Let's start again. My name's Kolanski, Krzysztof Kolanski, and I am not entirely my father's son.' He looked directly at Edward and added, 'I am his heir, apparently.'

He sat and motioned Edward to join him, dragged a bottle across the small table, poured two slugs of vodka, and started to tell a story – of bad birth, damaged youth, appalling deprivation, gradual rebirth: ruthless, unforgiving, disciplined, utterly without warmth or affection or caring, other than for survival. It was his father's story.

'And now he is neither dead nor exactly alive, and most important, not here. You are here, Eduard Cjaikowski, and there is a debt to be paid.'

He picked up the bottle, staring at its label, then suddenly at Edward.

'No. It can never be paid, not really, can it?'

He set the bottle down, carefully.

'Let's say, it should be honoured, perhaps in the breach.'

He pushed the bottle away, closed his eyes, rubbed his forehead; his hand dropped and he looked at Edward and Edward felt mortally cold, as he remembered that day, long past, in the house on Border Street, when those same eyes, or so it seemed, bored into his. Then Kolanski smiled, and there crept into them a warmth entirely lacking that other time.

'One million pounds, adjusted for inflation, with interest. What shall we do with it?'

There was no hesitation, no discussion, no point. They both knew. Edward said nothing. Kolanski answered his own question.

'It is Poland's money, and we shall give it back to Poland, you and I.'

He raised his glass. Automatically Edward raised his. They touched.

'To Solidarity.'

EPILOGUE – *As it Strikes Me*

In the silence of the skull, there is no war.

I am struck by the smallness of it all. Sweet Sara would have found the words, the borrowed words, how some are great, born to it, have it thrust upon them, or simply find greatness seeks them out. For us, it was not greatness, but the extraordinary smallness of it all that strikes me now, as I lie struck, left with the fading warmth of those close companionships, which superseded fear and cauterised the pain, so that we came through it all, scathed yet scantly hurt, full of wonder and love and lives lived far, far beyond all reasonable expectation. We were not great as some are great. We were, as you English say, a mere bagatelle. We were but infinitesimal jots in war's dusty, sombre, smoke-scattered sunlight, but we were a little part of others' greatness.

As I sit here, watching her, loving her, wanting her and no other, and owing to her my striking survival, I gradually wake to the small memories which we became, for each man and every woman is only remembered in the minds of those who knew them, especially those who knew them well. We, or our events, our doings, may perhaps be chronicled, and read by generations not yet found, but we will not then be us, but third persons past tense, arms'-length recorded and, when those who knew us, well or not so well, or even thought badly of us – for our enemies are also part of our past and remember us too – when those remaining selves are also struck by death, our reality will die with them. Each man's immortality is only as eternal as the remembrance of him by others. Once they too are gone, he is gone. Only ill-writ echoes remain, and they lack credence, dimension and feeling.

Yet, and in this I find myself strangely moved, I remember them and, while I shall take them with me when I too go, yet will I also leave a little of them behind, for they are so worthy of remembrance, that I have told my wifelet, and she will tell my Anna, and thus all our thin infinities will shimmer in reducing memory unto the next generation and, like those waves of sound loosed by key and by code, they will never entirely disappear.

I hear myself think thus, and scorn my hid desire to leave something behind. For God's sake, I have left enough scattered about the place – my seed, my careless acts, the detritus of my dark days and wasted weeks. I really should go.

Begone! And somewhat gone am I, in the mind at least, even if the body continues to function in parts, mainly private, while the crucial ligaments of tongue and lip and glottal start are rigid, paralysed as if in thrall to vodka. Come on, pass the bottle, let's have another one, for tomorrow... no, not a good idea. I am not yet ready to die. I still have some loving to do.

Acknowledgements

To list all those who have helped would be difficult. Most of them know and all have my thanks. However, some should be named.

Christopher Leaver kept faith; Rick Hobson and David Thomas lent enthusiasm – and the keys to the marketplace. I am grateful to Bryan Colley and Tom Keneally for their public support.

Gary Hall was a generous facilitator, while Mark Ralph (1) in particular and Mark Radley helped to shape the product. Mark Ralph (2) discovered and deleted most of my mistakes.

Carolyn listened with patience and understanding, James was supportive, Katie was confident and Chris egged me on. It could not have been done without Ted.

For certain facts I am indebted to Steven Badsey's *D-Day the Illustrated History*, N.N. Baransky's *Economic Geography of the USSR* and Georges Jorre's *The Soviet Union*. Charles Messenger's *Second World War in the West* was invaluable and Churchill's monumental history of *The Second World War* was indispensable.

Arnold Hague clarified *The Allied Convoy System 1939–1945*, Helene Mousset explained the *Canton de Vimoutiers Orne,* and Richard Whittington-Egan guided me through *The Great Liverpool Blitz.* *Cracow* was described by Teresa Czerniewicz-Umer and Barry Davies explained *SAS Self Defence.* Jeffrey Bines's *Operation Freston* was helpful and our conversations illuminating.

Air Historical Banch, RAF Bentley Priory and the USAAF archive service were most co-operative, as were the Bank of England and the Goldsmiths' Company. I consulted numerous sources on London clubs, the Rubens Hotel, Audley End and other locations, and visited the Hotel de Ville, Vimoutiers, several times. Military and other service personnel have advised, and I have had helpful discussions with Continental friends, and with Eduard's family.

The process of reconstruction and infilling factual gaps decrees some poetic licence. If errors there be – and some are inevitable after sixty years, given the secret nature of deportation, prison and clandestine war – they are mine alone.

Historical Note

The 1939 dual invasion of Poland is well documented, the deportation of Polish families less so. Camps like Tara existed, as did places like Fort Kermener. The trains there and back are burnt into the memories of those who rode them, but they are a dying generation.

The movement of Anglo-Polish forces across the Middle East and North Africa and their dispersal throughout Allied military and intelligence services is not widely recorded or remembered.

Polish SOE trained in Scotland, Kent, Italy and Audley End. Operatives were dropped behind German lines, to seek out high-ranking individuals for disposal, to assist the resistance, to pursue, expose and target the Luftwaffe's last European gasps and to spirit millions in gold to Poland in several tranches – with varied success.

Rommel and the Hitler Jugend were in and around Vimoutiers post-D-Day; Vimoutiers was blanketed with USAAF bombs on an intelligence tip that an unnamed, high-ranking German would be there on a specific June day. Rommel was strafed near Vimoutiers.

Eduard Cjaikowski over many years disclosed fragments of his odyssey. Detailed descriptions, events, names, characters and dialogue are imagined or reconstructed. The narrative is a fiction, based on available facts.

Eduard returned to England, married (twice) and had children, eventually revisiting Poland. He lived in Bucks for some fifty years, until his death after a series of strokes.

This book is his story and that of other brave Poles like him, who fought for freedom. They should not be forgotten – ever.

Clive Birch mbe is a man of Bucks born in London with a home in France. Editor at 24, he has since run local and national media, including the *Illustrated London News*, his own publishing company, founded a charity and made a museum. He is a Freeman of the City of London, Past Master of its transport guild, and a visiting tutor at the Royal College of Art.

He writes about the past, and about transport futures; this is his 24th book and first novel. He is married, with an extensive family.

Other books by
Medavia Publishing

FICTION

Married to Albert by Annie Waller
A turbulent tale of marriage, mayhem and the military

'A real page turner, this book appeals to all'
Cheryl Stonehouse, Daily Express

Kate is a straight-talking Yorkshire girl, who longs to meet the right man. She falls for Guy, an RAF pilot, but he's in love with Albert – an aeroplane, the RAF's mainstay, first into Kabul and Basra. This is a story of marriage to the military, its dangers and its rewards and an insight into what happens to the people who defend us, here and in harm's way.

NON-FICTION

No Big Deal about Becky Measures, with Simon Towers
'My breasts or my life' – beating cancer before it happens

'A testament to the human spirit'
Tessa Cunningham, Daily Mail

Becky Measures' forbear died in 1834 – of breast cancer. Her mother, Wendy, found the family tree blighted from generation to generation – and was the first to choose a preventative double mastectomy. Now Becky, 24, vivacious, blonde, a radio presenter, has done exactly the same and claims: 'It's no big deal'. This is Becky's story – from childhood, through her mother's trauma, her teenage years and her decision to take the battle to the big C.

Kirsty – Angel of Courage by Susie Mathis
The little girl who touched everyone's hearts

'Her attitude is amazing and her courage is extraordinary'
Chris Tarrant

Kirsty Howard was born in 1995 – and given six weeks to live. She is the only UK child born with her heart back to front. After nine major operations, she is still here, her future grimly uncertain. She has met Royalty, pop stars, sporting heroes and movie actors. She has the support of the Prime Minister and across the nation. Kirsty's Appeal for Manchester's children's hospice has raised £5 million.

Medavia Publishing
an imprint of Boltneck Publications of Bristol

Medavia is a major media agency and Medavia Publishing brings people in the present and facts about the past into print.